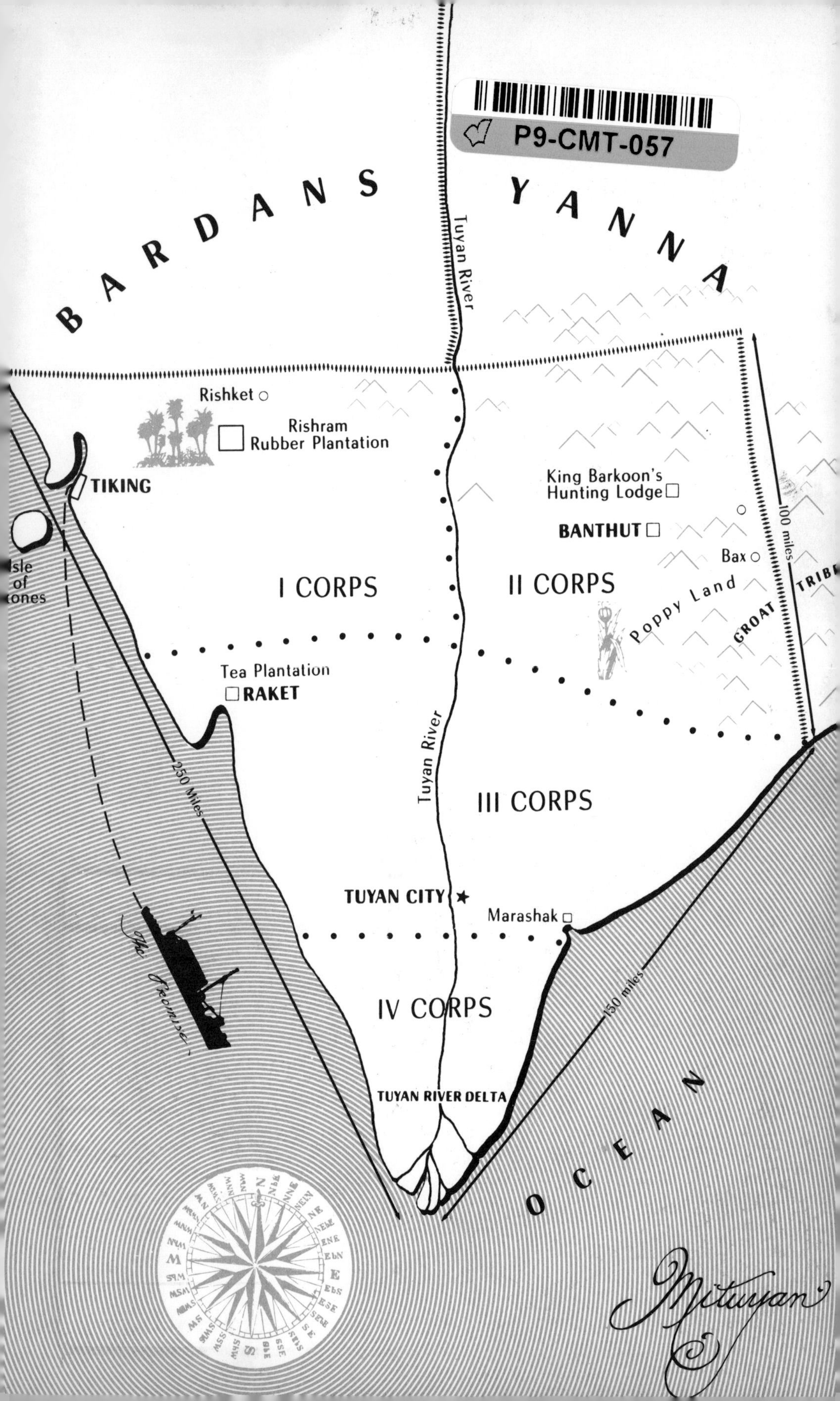
P9-CMT-057
BARDANS
YANNA
Tuyan River
Rishket
Rishram
Rubber Plantation
TIKING
Isle
of
tones
King Barkoon's
Hunting Lodge
BANTHUT
Bax
100 miles
I CORPS
II CORPS
Poppy Land
GROAT
TRIB
Tea Plantation
RAKET
250 Miles
Tuyan River
III CORPS
TUYAN CITY
Marashak
The Promise
150 miles
IV CORPS
TUYAN RIVER DELTA
OCEAN
Mituyan

THE COUNTRY TEAM

To Jon
From Rosaleen

This Book I give to you as a
Token of gratatude in all the
ways you have helped me.

May God Bless
you Always, Rosaleen

Books by Robin Moore

THE COUNTRY TEAM
THE GREEN BERETS
PITCHMAN
THE DEVIL TO PAY (WITH JACK YOUNGBLOOD)

THE COUNTRY TEAM

A NOVEL

BY ROBIN MOORE

CROWN PUBLISHERS, INC. NEW YORK

Library of Congress Catalog Card Number: 66–26198
Printed in the United States of America

I find that many people think a novel springs forth in its entirety from the author's imagination and efforts. This is not true. There is a man called an editor at the publisher's office who takes the author's raw work—no matter how refined the writer may consider it—and goes through the agonizing task of editing it, making it readable. To my editor, Arthur Fields, this book is affectionately dedicated.

INTRODUCTION

As was proved by the furor over my earlier book, *The Green Berets,* truth can frequently be more dramatically and completely told through the medium of fiction than through that of nonfiction. The Republic of Mituyan that I created and peopled in this book gave me the latitude to explore the tangled affairs of human beings engaged in protecting a typical independent Asian nation from outside Communist subversion.

Mituyan actually could be any one of the many underdeveloped countries around the world today. The problems dramatized in THE COUNTRY TEAM are basically the same as those we encounter in Iran and Peru and as those we knew in Vietnam before the advent of American combat troops, and as they are in Thailand today. Mituyan, then, is a microcosm that makes it possible for me to tell what is going on in underdeveloped nations without having to expose the shortcomings of actual individual Americans helping backward nations to achieve a higher standard of living for their peoples and thus to resist insidious Communist aggression.

In underdeveloped countries around the world—and this I have observed in Latin America, the Middle East, and Africa, as well as in Asiatic countries—customs and morals are diametrically opposed to those of our highly industrialized society.

Nepotism and corruption are the way of life in many of these countries. Sadistic torture of political enemies is taken as a matter of course. I at first resisted portraying the horrors so common to any experienced Asian hand. However, this would have been to paint only a partial picture of what we go through in trying to bring a better way of life to backward nations. Though I have tried to be judicious in describing the more sensational mores of the people of Mituyan, what I have written tells the way things are, every day and night in the week in the "Republics-of-Mituyan" around the world; and not to face the issue squarely would only detract from the basic truth of this work.

The people of this book are entirely fictional, and were invented to illustrate the points raised in THE COUNTRY TEAM. Probably because the events and individuals created are so typical of situations occurring all over the world, some readers will try to draw a parallel between actual persons and the characters in the book. While this is always a fascinating game, I assure everyone that I have lifted no individual from real life to place him in THE COUNTRY TEAM.

BLUE LAGOON
JAMAICA, WEST INDIES
February 1, 1967

ROBIN MOORE

PART I

THE INSURGENCY

Mituyan

The Republic of Mituyan is an Asiatic country close to India, which explains its traditional association with the British Empire until the British pulled out in the early 1950's leaving Mituyan to rule itself. Since Mituyan had been under British protection and economic domination for close to two hundred years, the language barrier usually found in Asia is negligible. Everyone, from top diplomats and government officials down to the village and hamlet chiefs, uses English for transactions of an official nature, and commerce. To westerners the Mituyan language is almost incomprehensible, and unreadable, with its strange, long horizontal scrawls of squiggles and loops.

The country is shaped somewhat like an equilateral triangle. It spreads across the bottom half of a peninsula also occupied by the republics of Yanna and Bardans. Its northern border, the base of the triangle, is two hundred miles long. Mituyan has two hundred and fifty miles of seacoast running from its northwest border point, where it touches Bardans, down the western leg of the triangle to the tip of the peninsula, the termination point of the five thousand or more square miles of the Tuyan River Delta. Only the Mekong River Delta in South Vietnam has a higher annual yield of rice and other agricultural products. The third leg of the triangle runs from the Tuyan Delta back up to the northeast point of the country—over a hundred miles of seacoast and another hundred miles of mountainous jungle bordering on Yanna. The capital of Mituyan is Tuyan City, which straddles the Tuyan River sixty miles north of its mouth in the delta.

Mituyan should be a self-contained, wealthy, happy country, but unrest and violence are growing. Agitators are infiltrating from Bardans and Yanna, nominally "neutral" countries. "Neutrality" in this part of the world generally means pro-Communist. Mituyan's rubber plantations run across the top of the country in a fifty-mile-wide belt parallel to the northern boundary, and the rubber workers are becoming especially susceptible to anti-government propaganda.

The twenty thousand American soldiers and civilians involved in the U.S. military and economic aid mission in Mituyan are captivated by Tuyan City—its winding streets lined with colorful arts and crafts shops, the restaurants and bars, the temples and pagodas painted in bright reds and yellows, gold-leaf trimming everywhere, and the tailors who can duplicate any Western garment for about one-fifth its stateside price. The city is slashed by canals and rivers all leading to and from the mother Tuyan River. The floating market, hundreds of sampans selling merchandise and food of all sorts, is one of Asia's most colorful attractions. Many of the most popular native bars are afloat—complete with enchanting almond-eyed bar girls who willingly entertain American customers in private enclosed sampans tied to the big bar boat.

The government of Mituyan, though a ruthless family dictatorship directed by Premier KaritKi, gives the appearance of stability. Westerners, Americans in particular, are much admired by the Mituyans, by the beautiful, delicate-featured, all too hospitable Mituyan women in particular. The United States Information Service in Mituyan spends over a million dollars a year trying to convince the fifteen million Mituyans that their well-being is due to American aid dispensed by Premier KaritKi's compassionate and strong central government in Tuyan City. The corps of U.S. military advisers plus the thousands of soldiers constantly on leave in Mituyan from the wars in Southeast Asia shower the women and children with money and rations and, by and large, treat the men with respect.

In the mountains a hundred and fifty miles to the northeast of Tuyan City is the plateau town of Banthut. It has the most salubrious climate in all of Asia, a fairly constant seventy-four degrees. The administration of the many mountain tribes is handled from Banthut, which is also the capital of the country's opium-smuggling operations. Growing opium poppies is the chief source of income to the tribesmen, of which the Groat tribe is the largest. Banthut also boasts the finest and most varied big-game hunting in Asia.

Mituyan's most important seaport is Tiking on the northwest coast, just twenty-five miles south of the Bardans border. Tiking is the capital of the sea trade with India and the Middle East, and the rubber plantations send their product out to the world by way of this seaport.

Mituyan is one of the world's truly beautiful and delightful countries. But today the Mituyans and Americans who dominate Tuyan City decisions seem to be deliberately ignoring the increasing dissidence among the impoverished and landless people of the countryside. A social revolution against the injustices of Mituyan's ancient mandarin system is in the making, and management of the revolution is in violent contention.

The sudden inflation in the price of rice shows that the wily Chinese rice speculators, whose formidable intelligence networks make the operations of the United States Central Intelligence Agency station chief in Tuyan City seem a childlike game, have information that is causing them to hoard their stores against future profiteering. Only mass conscription of the peasantry by both government and revolutionary forces would seriously reduce the rice crop in the coming year, driving prices skyward.

In the major cities of Mituyan the price of American currency on the black market has soared from 90 to 120 metas to the dollar. This means that wealthy and informed Mituyans are converting their savings into dollars and sending them to Hong Kong or Switzerland for safekeeping.

A few experienced Americans recognize what is coming and talk about taking the "r" out of the revolution. But an orderly evolution in standards of living for the vast majority of the Mituyan people involves such serious political considerations as land-reform legislation and free elections of the people's representatives and administrators. The highest ranking American and Mituyan policymakers in the little republic's capital city find it prudent and politic to get through each day and hope, like the unmarried pregnant girl, that if the distressing situation is just ignored it will go away.

CHAPTER ONE

THE SOFT, FRAGRANT scent of tea leaves drying in lofts momentarily dispelled the sense of anxiety that had gripped him all day. The modest plantation, overlooking the southern sea smashing itself against the rocky coast five miles from the cool plateau property, always had a soothing effect on him. Still, he knew inwardly that the inevitable was indeed becoming reality in Mituyan. This deceptively lethargic Asian country first had been his refuge and then a financially rewarding haven, when all the misfortunes that can befall a man had crashed down on him.

Even though the violence that had been raging in Vietnam had not yet reached sizable proportions in this part of Mituyan, Mike Forrester was worried. In the rice-rich Tuyan River Delta to the south, small-scale battles were fought every week with the Mitcoms, as the insurgent guerrillas were known here. Yet Mike thought his plantation workers appeared to be content, and the rice farmers of the northern areas of Mituyan were going about their business as usual.

He drove the Land Rover past the tea lofts and a mile up the road shaded by trees that kept direct sun off the growing tea leaves; ahead stretched the low white house he and Luna had built a year before on the profits of their tea, rubber, and various commercial enterprises in Tuyan City, one hundred and sixty miles to the south. This house and the plantation house on Rishram, his rubber property in the North, were perhaps his most valued possessions after the luxurious, hundred-foot, reconverted minesweeper he'd salvaged from his creditors in the United States, who naturally found it impossible to realize that if he was to recoup and make good his personal guarantees, he needed the spiritual uplift that living aboard the *Promise* gave him.

Luna was waiting for him in the main hall of their home. In the distance behind her he could see the blue ocean. She came to him, her ebony hair pulled tightly, framing her honey-tan face and almond-shaped eyes, and from below the silver clasp holding it behind her head spilled loose black tresses. As always at home, she was wearing a Western-style dress, a frock with a low, square-cut neck.

"Good evening, darling," he said.

She kissed him, but her back was stiff. Luna usually melted to him. "What's the matter, dear?"

"Bunghole is waiting in your study."

Mike chuckled. That had been the closest he could at first come to pronouncing the name of the Mituyan manager of his rubber estate. The accommodating Mituyans all began calling him Bunghole, so that by the time Mike became fluent in Mituyan is was too late to go back to the proper pronunciation.

"What's he doing down here?"

"You had better go ask him yourself," Luna replied.

"Let's go." Mike strode down the hall and turned left into the corner study overlooking the sea. It was a sparse room devoted to work, a room undisturbed by trophies, souvenirs, pictures, or framed documents from his past. Only books, all he could buy here plus those he had brought with him—these filled the built-in bookshelves.

Bunghole was standing nervously in the middle of the room. His unlined, brown face and jet black hair gave him a youthful appearance, although Mike knew from the references he had first presented three years ago that he was at least fifty. He stood about five foot five inches tall, which made him taller than average; he towered above the other rubber workers. As befitted an estate manager calling on the owner, Bunghole wore a spotless white suit, white socks and white shoes, and a yellow tie with matching handkerchief flowing from his breast pocket.

Even though both knew they could talk perfectly together in Bunghole's native tongue, Mike knew his manager would have felt demeaned if they conversed in anything but the language befitting his position. So they spoke in English.

"What happened, Bunghole?" Mike asked, coming to the point a little too quickly. Luna had worried him.

"You are looking very well, sir," Bunghole replied.

"Thank you." Mike took the cue. "You appear youthful and resplendent."

There was a short pause, and then Bunghole, apparently feeling the amenities had been observed, broke out: "Those ungrateful peasant dogs working at Rishram! The rubber tappers are asking for more money."

"But we pay higher wages than any other plantation. The other owners are very angry with me because of it."

"Yes, sir. I tell them that thing. But they say Yankees take all the money from the poor people and should pay more."

"Who is their leader? Who talks for the workers? Is it a man from the North?"

Bunghole nodded dejectedly. "They are coming across the border from Bardans and Yanna, even all the way from North Vietnam. They are making much trouble." It was predictable, Mike thought; the rubber workers were especially susceptible to agitators from across the border. The second largest university in the country was located in the northern seacoast city of Tiking, only twenty-five miles south of the Bardans border, where the *Promise* lay in port. Tiking University was a natural target of the revolutionary intellectuals and theoreticians.

Rishram, Forrester's rubber plantation, was a scant ten miles from the Bardans border. A mere four years ago this border country had been peaceful. Mike, after marrying Luna in Tuyan City, had brought his new bride up to the rubber country to look for a plantation. The decision to invest in a rubber property had been made in New York City almost a year earlier. Luna Hargraves, a lovely Eurasian, had been studying at Columbia when she was impressed by a lecture given by Mike Forrester. At the time he had been a successful international financier. But less than a year later the deteriorating political situation in Cuba, where he had invested his money and that of clients, caused bankers to demand payment on personal guarantees he had made. He realized that only by withdrawing such cash assets as were left him and finding a new country in which to invest and recoup his losses could he pay his creditors back one hundred cents on the dollar. By then Luna was ready to sail aboard the *Promise* with him halfway around the world to her homeland.

The former owner of Rishram, a Britisher who had been through the ten years of guerrilla terror in Malaya and had seen his plantation destroyed by the terrorists, had sold out to Mike at a very good price. Perhaps he had sensed what Mike now was facing and for that reason had disposed of his very profitable estate.

"What have you done about these demands?" Mike snapped.

"I refused, of course, sir, to consider a raise in pay. As you said, we are already in trouble with the other owners for paying as much as we do."

"Why don't these labor leaders or whatever they are go to the other owners?"

"You are the only American owner. They are trying to stir up hatred of the American imperialists."

"What happened when you refused?"

"That Vietnamese, Nguyen Van Can, told me that twenty trees would be destroyed every night until the wages were doubled. The last two nights twenty trees were hacked."

"What about the police and the army garrison? Aren't they giving protection?"

"They come by once a night in armored cars. But Can is many years a guerrilla and avoids them."

"Won't our workers inform on Can, where he can be captured?"

Bunghole shook his head sadly. "They are afraid. One of my headmen was murdered, his head cut off, after he talked to the police a week ago about this new trouble. As a result of what he told them, the army captured two of the men who have been spreading discontent; but my headman is still dead, leaving a wife and five children with no support."

Mike looked at his watch. Only an hour to darkness. The ninety-mile drive to Rishram took a good three hours, since the last thirty miles was over rough dirt roads. Besides, he preferred not to drive at night, if possible, particularly with the new signs of impending violence.

"Bunghole, you stay here tonight, and tomorrow we'll drive to Tiking and see General Dandig. Then we'll drive to Rishram and see what can be done."

"Twenty more trees will be gone tomorrow," Bunghole reminded.

"That's still better than taking a chance on being ambushed tonight." He frowned deeply. "It almost seems impossible. The Mituyans of the North consider rubber trees minor gods. To kill a god is a serious thing in their religion."

Bunghole, who had adopted the Church of England as part of the trappings of being an estate manager, said, "That is true, sir. This heathen worship of trees has always been one of our great safeguards. Only the hard-core terrorists would destroy a rubber tree. That is why I worry so much and come down here to see you instead of trying to take care of the problem myself."

"You did the right thing, Bunghole. And tomorrow I'll see what can be done."

"I will go with you, Mike." A determined Luna was standing in the doorway. While he would have liked to argue with her, he knew better. Also the rubber estate, while in his name, was really a joint venture, and if Premier KaritKi decided to pass his new law severely curtailing the value and acreage of property owned by foreigners, the estate would have to go entirely into Luna's name.

"All right, my dear. We'll leave when the sun casts its first shadow in the morning." Then, to cover his apprehension, he said, "Let's have cocktails on the patio and watch the sun set."

✠✠✠

The coast road between Tiking and the port city of Raket, nearest the Forrester tea plantation, was an excellent highway sixty miles long that afforded spectacular views of the ocean from high cliffs. Usually when they made this drive they stopped at one of the many beautiful powder-white beaches for a swim in the surf and a few tall, cold, rum punches. That day, however, Mike wanted to be in General Dandig's office as early as possible. Dandig was the commanding general of Mituyan's I Corps, which was charged with maintaining order and preventing an invasion or infiltration in the northwest quarter of Mituyan.

The town of Tiking was spread out around a colorful waterfront alive with red and black fishing junks, all with two big eyes painted on either side of the prow. Several minesweeper-size ships of the Mituyan Navy were tied up to the main dock, and crowds of urchins stared at them and shouted at the sailors. Mike caught sight of an American naval officer adviser on the bridge of one of the ships and waved; the officer waved back.

The headquarters of I Corps was set on a slight rise above the seaport. The long, low buildings, a drab yellowish color, looked like army installations everywhere. One building, freshly painted, with the flag of Mituyan proudly flying in front, was immediately recognizable as the commander's headquarters. Mike pulled up his Land Rover, while Bunghole, driving his own car, parked behind. Mike helped Luna out, and they walked past the two guards, who were posted on either side of the main entrance.

"Mr. Forrester from Rishram Estate to see General Dandig," he said to the Mituyan sergeant-at-arms seated at a desk inside. After a few moments conversation in rapid Mituyan, the sergeant briskly put down the phone, stood up, and ushered Luna, Mike, and Bunghole into Dandig's office. It was just nine o'clock.

The general greeted them most cordially, elaborately kissing Luna's hand and exchanging pleasantries with Bunghole. He looked even younger than his thirty-five years and stood about five feet four inches tall. Except for his yellowish brown complexion, he was the picture of a British brigadier. Even the Mituyan uniform was a copy of the British tropical uniform—shorts, swagger stick, and all. The American advisers, who had completely taken over military assistance to Mituyan, were trying to change the uniform to the more practical jungle-combat fatigues, but tradition gave way slowly. The general indicated chairs.

After another few minutes of pleasantries, during which a batman brought them cups of green tea, General Dandig, as befitted his position, brought the talk around to the point of the meeting.

"I'm glad you called in, Forrester," he said. "What's all this about trouble at Rishram?"

Mike gestured toward Bunghole. "My manager tells me he reported the destruction of our rubber trees."

"Yes, yes." Dandig nodded wisely. "I have ordered a company of the Third Battalion of the First Regiment to patrol your property nightly. They have not reported any unusual activity."

"By now sixty trees will have been destroyed," Mike answered. "Bunghole tells me a North Vietnamese named Nguyen Van Can is the ringleader." He paused. "It sounds to me as though Mituyan is well into Phase Two of the blueprint for a Communist takeover."

"Oh, I cannot believe that," Dandig answered. "These are just some bandits trying to frighten you into paying them off."

"Look, General, my plantation is small as rubber properties go. Just a bit over six miles square. One full company of your soldiers, properly deployed, should be able to capture whoever is actually destroying my trees. If you can catch the culprits, you should be able to extract much valuable information from them. What did you find out from the men you captured as a result of information supplied by my headman?"

Dandig glanced down at his fingers, as though inspecting his nails for dirt. "The two men both died while being questioned," he remarked casually. "I'm sorry about that."

Having had some experience with police and military interrogation in such Asiatic countries as Mituyan, Mike wasn't too surprised. "Well, what do we do now, General?"

"I'll order the company from the Third Battalion to continue surveillance of your estate, Forrester. If one company isn't enough, we will throw in another." Turning to Luna, he said, "For the daughter of my friend, Colonel Hargraves, and his wife, the beautiful former Miss Sarakit, nothing can be too much."

Luna smiled. "Thank you, General Dandig. I'll tell Daddy and Mommy when next I see them."

"Please express my fondest wishes," Dandig said, shifting slightly in his seat to indicate that the interview was over. Mike stood up, followed by Luna and Bunghole. Just then there was a knock at the door.

"Come in," Dandig called. An American colonel pushed upon the door and walked in. He looked too young to be wearing an eagle on his collar, but a row of ribbons and paratrooper wings attested to his military experience.

"Ah, Colonel Lawton," Dandig said pleasantly to the American dwarfing him. "Meet a countryman of yours, Mr. Mike Forrester, and his wife, our lovely Luna."

"Glad to meet you, Mr. Forrester." Lawton took Luna's hand and held it a moment. "A pleasure, Mrs. Forrester."

Mike introduced Bunghole, and then Dandig briefly explained the purpose of their visit. Lawton was immediately interested. "General Dandig, I've been wanting to see some of your men on an operation. How would you feel if I went out to observe this company you have assigned to guard Mr. Forrester's plantation?"

"I wouldn't call it an operation, Colonel Lawton," Dandig answered cautiously. "A very uninteresting business really, except of course to Mr. Forrester, whose trees are threatened."

"Colonel Lawton," Mike said, "my wife and I will be up here only a few days. We would like you to come to dinner; Rishram is a long way out, you probably should plan to spend the night."

A slow smile spread over Lawton's face. "Thanks, I'd very much like to see your place."

"Good," Luna said. "We'll expect you, Colonel Lawton. Tonight?"
"Tonight will be fine."
Dandig seemed slightly taken aback, but he quickly composed himself. "Well," he boomed cheerfully, "good thing for you Americans to get to know each other."
"Any time at all that you are out our way, you will always be most welcome, General," Luna said graciously. Mike smiled inwardly. To his knowledge Dandig had never been in the field with his troops. He never even left Tiking except for trips to the capital, where he periodically went to court the favor of Premier KaritKi and the Premier's brother and political counselor, Tarot.
"I'll be expecting that company before dark, General," Mike said.
"Orders will go out immediately," Dandig answered, perhaps a bit testily.
Colonel Lawton followed them out and thanked Mike for the opportunity to observe the Mituyan troops.
Mike helped Luna into the Land Rover and they drove out of I Corps headquarters compound. "Think we should just have a look at her before we head out to Rishram?" he asked with a wink.
"I'd take the wheel away if we didn't," Luna replied. Mike turned the Land Rover toward the waterfront and a few minutes later parked on the dock he leased. Looming above the dock was the *Promise,* its teak decking shining in the sun, its mahogany railings highly polished, the steel hull and superstructure freshly painted a glistening white. Converting the *Promise* from a drab navy minesweeper to its present sleek state had been an expensive but exhilarating two-year project for Mike. Her fuel tanks gave her a range of well over four thousand miles at a steady twelve knots. She had been redesigned for heavy seas and long-distance traveling with a minimum crew and maximum amount of comfort. It was almost as though Mike had foreseen the troubles that were to assail him when he had purchased the ship and had it rebuilt. The *Promise* had been his escape hatch and had performed nobly when her time arrived.
Captain Batki, the Mituyan skipper, let down the gangplank for them, warmly welcoming them aboard.
"Morning, Skipper," Mike said heartily. He patted the brightwork lovingly, always happy to board the *Promise*. "We'd like to make a quick inspection, have a cold drink, and then we'll be on our way out to Rishram."
Mike, followed by Luna, went up to the bridge of the sturdy ship, looked over the automatic pilot, the radio equipment and radar, and ran his hand over the spoked wheel.
"Darling," he said, "we should take another cruise down the coast, around the delta and up the Tuyan River to Tuyan City."
"Oh, Mike, when? Remember the last time? Everyone from the palace was aboard and Dhuna didn't want to leave."

"And so KaritKi tried to buy it from me for his wedding present to her. The old bastard. What does that beautiful Dhuna see in him other than that he's the Premier?"

"I think she really loves him, Mike."

"Hard to see. Well—" He led the way from the bridge down through the forward salon, then back to the master stateroom at the stern. It had an enormous double bed, a skylight, and large portholes looking out to both port and starboard and also astern over the ship's wake when she was at sea. Luna sighed, remembering the beautiful times they'd had aboard.

"We'll do it again," Mike promised. They inspected the two other luxurious cabins below decks, the midships tavern, as Mike called the cozy little lower salon he had decorated to look like a captain's cabin on an old British man-of-war, and then climbed back up on deck where their long, cold, rum punches were waiting. After finishing the drinks they regretfully bade the *Promise* goodbye, promising Captain Batki to return as soon as possible. Then they shopped for an hour and set off on the difficult drive from Tiking to Rishram. The dusty, twisting road climbed and dipped, providing a hundred natural ambush points per mile. Mike couldn't help thinking that if the insurgency situation in this part of Mituyan really became serious it would be impossible to supply Rishram by road—or to get the rubber out. He'd either have to do what the French plantation owners in Vietnam did, pay off the Communists, or give up the place. He made a mental note to improve the old airstrip on the property.

It took an hour and a half to cover the thirty miles, but finally they came to the long, straight road, flanked on both sides by lines of rubber trees. The perfectly aligned trees, changing from rows perpendicular to the road to diagonal and then back to perpendicular again, almost made him dizzy. There were over one hundred thousand trees, and each tree represented about a dollar's yearly profit. They drove for two miles before reaching the end of the trees.

The main house at Rishram was considerably simpler than that of the tea property; but it was comfortable and well equipped. There was no telephone, and their Mituyan chef, who greeted them happily at the door, had never been able to master the use of the radio transmitter and receiver, so he'd had no idea they were coming. He seized the packages of goods Luna had bought in the Tiking market and carried them into the kitchen.

After a quick lunch, Bunghole and Mike went out to look at the destroyed trees. It was an ugly sight. Twenty trees had been unmercifully hacked up with machetes only a few hundred yards from the house. Then they drove a mile and a half and walked a hundred yards from the road to where a second group of twenty trees had been similarly destroyed. They picked up a headman, who showed them the twenty trees that had been hacked the previous night in yet another part of the plantation. Anger welled up in Mike. It had been a long, hard struggle to make this plantation earn every possible meta. He cherished every tree and would have thought nothing of shooting anyone he caught damaging one.

"I'm going to be out with the soldiers tonight," Mike bit out. "I just hope I'm in the right place."

Bunghole shrugged hopelessly. It was a large property, and the ring of a machete on a rubber tree would not carry far.

Just at sunset, about seven o'clock, Colonel Lawton drove up in a jeep. At the wheel was an American sergeant. Mike shook hands with Lawton, who introduced Sergeant Jennesen.

"I brought Jennesen along just in case we ran into trouble. He's the American instructor at the Mituyan Ranger school. An old jungle fighter," Lawton said proudly. "We saw a lot of action together in Vietnam." Jennesen touched the sweatband of the green beret he was wearing.

"Always glad to meet a Special Forces man, Sergeant," Mike said, and shook a hard, strong clamp of a hand. "You can leave the jeep here. Come on in. I guess you both feel like a shower after that dusty drive."

Half an hour later on the patio, Luna offered Lawton and Jennesen cocktails. Jennesen settled for a soft drink, saying he was on duty.

"It was mighty decent of you to invite us over, Mr. Forrester," the colonel said.

"Call mc Mikc."

"OK, Mike. I'm Fritz. Fritz Lawton."

"Right, Fritz, what'll it be?"

"Scotch is fine. See you have an in with the embassy."

Mike glanced at the bottle of Chivas Regal. "Ambassador Whittelsie fixed me up," he acknowledged.

They were just settling back when they heard a rumble of trucks, headlights flashing, coming up the road. Lawton and Sergeant Jennesen were immediately on their feet.

"It's enough to make you real discouraged, sir," Jennesen said. "Here I teach them to leave their trucks camouflaged at least a couple of miles from their objective and move in quietly on foot—and what do they do? Roar in here, lights blazing, letting everyone know they're coming!"

"Just like Vietnam," Lawton muttered. "I guess it'll always be the same." He walked down the road to meet the lead truck, Sergeant Jennesen and Mike behind him. The truck stopped and a Mituyan captain stepped down into the road. Seeing the eagle on the collar of Lawton's khaki shirt shining in the headlights, he saluted listlessly. Lawton returned it.

Lawton and the captain conversed for a few minutes, the colonel advising the Mituyan officer to tell his men to be quiet and spread out around the plantation. The Mituyan troops climbed out of the vehicles, and the company commander began to give orders in stern tones. Lawton, Jennesen, and Mike returned to the patio. It was dark now. They finished their drinks, and Luna called for dinner.

"It's going to be a long night," Lawton said when they'd finished eating. "I'm going to get a couple of hours sleep. You'd better do the same, Jennesen. We'll start patrolling about midnight."

"I'll join you, Fritz," Mike said. "I'd like to talk to whoever's butchering my trees."

At eleven thirty, after two hours' sleep, Mike awoke. Luna was sleeping, and he waited until he was outside the room before putting on his boots. Jennesen and Lawton were in the kitchen drinking the hot coffee the chef had made for them. Mike sipped a cup; then they started out into the plantation.

Lawton and the Mituyan captain had agreed on "seven" as the password. If challenged by a soldier saying "three," the counternumber was "four." They walked through the trees about twenty rows in from and parallel to the road. Far out on the edges of the rubber trees there appeared to be fireflies winking; Mike knew they were nothing of the kind.

"Some discipline that Mit captain's got," Jennesen growled softly. "Every one of them dickheads has got himself a lighted cigarette to smoke the night away. Do them good if they got zapped. Then maybe they'd learn."

As they walked along in the chilly night they even heard snatches of conversation. Then, to Lawton's audible disgust, they saw a campfire burning half a mile down the road bisecting the rubber trees. They walked up to it and were not even challenged. Beside the fire, smoking and toasting a piece of meat on a stick, sat the Mit captain. As they drew near they could hear music; the officer had a transistor radio on the ground beside him.

"Captain!" Colonel Lawton snapped. "What kind of light and noise discipline do you call this? Put out that fire and turn off that radio and get out on the perimeter—and make your men stop smoking."

"Yes, thank you for your advice, Colonel," the captain said, standing up slowly. "But you do not know this country as I do. It is better we let anyone know we are here. Then they will not come and start trouble."

"But we want to capture the people who are destroying these trees."

"If they come we will capture them." There was no mistaking the insolence in the captain's tone.

"Either you put out that fire before it's too late, and tell your men to stop smoking and talking, or I'll report you to General Dandig for incompetence."

"Minister Branot is my father's best friend. He knows I am a competent officer." Branot was Minister of the Interior, and directly in charge of the army serving under Premier KaritKi. Branot's niece, Dhuna, was Premier KaritKi's new young wife. This Mituyan captain standing loosely before them was indeed a competent captain, Mike thought wryly.

"What's your name, Captain?" Lawton asked sharply.

"Nooram," the captain answered. "Captain Nooram, A Company, Third Battalion, First Regiment, Second Division."

"Well, Captain Nooram, I suggest you tighten up discipline in A Company, beginning this moment." Lawton walked to the fire and began kicking and stamping it out. Sergeant Jennesen picked up the radio, turned it off, and handed it to a sullen Captain Nooram.

Some time later, Mike checked the luminous dial of his watch. It was two thirty. Just then a loud, sharp explosion shattered the air. White flames lit up the darkness. Instantly, Lawton and Jennesen began to run toward the point of detonation, Mike a step behind them. Jennesen unslung his automatic carbine as he ran, Lawton drew his pistol. Mike wished he were armed. They heard the grating noise of trees falling ahead of them. In a few minutes they arrived at a knot of chattering soldiers standing in the newly made clearing. Both Lawton and Jennesen had flashlights focused on the destruction. Even, white tree stumps shone at them. The trees lay next to the stumps, as neatly as if they had been sawed through.

"They used det cord, sir," Jennesen said after a moment's examination. "This was no amateur bandit job."

"Detonation cord—that's high explosive," Lawton explained. "Convenient for blowing trees, among other things."

"That's eighty rubber trees I've lost," Mike cried angrily. "There must be some way to stop this."

"You saw the effectiveness of the army," Lawton replied. "We've got ten thousand Americans trying to teach the Mituyan Army to defend its country," he went on bitterly. "But damned near every Mit officer is related to or has friends in the palace. That means they don't have to train or inconvenience themselves. I'd swear I was back in Vietnam under President Diem."

After a few brooding moments of staring at the fallen trees, Mike turned back toward the house. "Let's go back and have a drink and talk this over," he said, suppressing his frustration and anger.

"Not much else we can do," Lawton agreed. Then he said to Jennesen, "See if you can find Nooram and get him to fan out and try to find the Mitcoms who did this. Ask him to meet me at the main house when he has deployed his men. I want to talk to him."

"Yes, sir," Jennesen said, touching the sweatband of his beret in a salute.

Vainly, Jennesen shouted at the squad of Mituyan soldiers standing around the blown trees to go out and try to make contact with the enemy. A lieutenant merely shrugged helplessly and said he had to await orders from Captain Nooram.

Back at the main house, Mike and Lawton poured drinks and listened to the crackling of the two-way radio, tuned into the police and army band, which occasionally gave way to Mituyan conversation.

"Aren't you going to report this immediately to the police?" Lawton asked, glancing at the transceiver.

"Nothing they can do now. They're not much better than the army. There's supposed to be a man from our Agency for International Development up here training the cops, but I guess the cops have trained him instead. Last time I saw him he was sipping green tea with a local police chief while a line of people waited outside for a chance to complain or inform on someone."

They worked the drinks slowly, and finally Lawton asked, "What kind of people do you think are behind your trouble?"

"Dissident Mituyans trained in North Vietnam, Peking, and most recently our so-called neutral bordering republics of Bardans and Yanna."

"Any ideas what you're going to do?"

"Sure. The same thing the French owners did in Vietnam. Negotiate a settlement."

"In other words, you'll be helping the insurgents financially."

"It's that or get wiped out. I've got a lot at stake here. They know it. And now it's too damned late to sell out. Nobody would buy a rubber plantation for even half its value with this going on. The bankers who hold my mortgages aren't going to let me off because of a Communist insurgency."

When Jennesen appeared with Captain Nooram, Mike waved at two chairs and the captain and sergeant sat down. Nooram turned to Jennesen. "In your army, Sergeant, is it customary for enlisted men to socialize with officers?"

In the Mituyan tongue, Mike shot at Nooram, "The sergeant is my guest, just as you are. Rudeness to my guests is rudeness to me and will not be tolerated." Nooram understood this perfectly. There were only two serious offenses in Mituyan government and army circles: political instability and rudeness to a superior or a highly placed civilian. By speaking in Nooram's own tongue, Mike not only caught the captain off guard but reminded him that both Mike and his wife enjoyed the highest esteem in Premier KaritKi's court.

To Sergeant Jennesen, Nooram said in English, "It's been a damned trying day, Sergeant. One gets irritated easily."

Jennesen nodded but did not answer. Fritz Lawton was taking in the whole situation carefully, saying nothing as Mike offered drinks. Finally Lawton spoke. "Captain Nooram, what, in your opinion, is the function of the Mituyan Army up here on the border?"

"Our function is to follow orders from the Palace," Nooram answered.

What else did Lawton expect him to say, Mike thought. Like most Asiatic officers his ambition was to live as well as possible and take every possible opportunity to pocket as much money as possible through graft or bribes. This was the time-honored custom of all Oriental armies, and no amount of westernization was going to change it.

The radio suddenly emitted loud Mituyan words uttered in obviously urgent tones. Mike paused to listen and then glanced at Nooram, shocked. The captain too seemed shaken at what he was hearing. "Fritz, that's the radio operator at district headquarters ten miles west of here . . . he says the police station is being attacked by bandits and is calling for help."

Instantly, Lawton was on his feet. "Talk to them, Nooram. Tell them to hold out. You have a company that can relieve them."

Reluctantly, Nooram went to the transceiver and picked up the microphone. There followed several minutes of two-way talk. "The headquarters is surrounded by perhaps fifty men," Mike translated for Lawton. "The bandits are calling on the police and troops inside to surrender all their weapons and open the arsenal and they won't be killed. Nooram is telling them they must put up a brave resistance and not give in. But there are only ten men there now," he added.

"Tell them you are on the way, Captain Nooram," Lawton commanded.

Nooram looked at the colonel and shook his head. "I will not lose my company to an ambush. You should know the old game, Colonel. These bandits, or whatever they are, attack a small outpost for the purpose of luring a relief column into an ambush. Better they get only ten men and a small supply of weapons and ammunition than let them decimate my company."

"You can put out sufficient flank security to locate any ambushes," Lawton snapped.

Luna, who had entered the room, was listening intently to the radio conversation. Suddenly the transceiver went dead, emitting only empty crackling sounds. "You must save those men," she cried vehemently. "All their families live here in this district. What will they think if the commander of a company of soldiers refuses to help their husbands and fathers?"

"I could not take the responsibility of going without orders," Nooram snapped back. "My orders are to remain here until morning."

"Why don't you radio back to headquarters in Tiking and tell them what's happening?" Lawton suggested.

"I will go out and try to locate my radioman and call Tiking."

"Use mine," Mike offered.

Nooram shook his head. "You do not have the headquarters band."

"I have the emergency band. Someone will be monitoring it."

"For communicating with General Dandig, I must use only the corps headquarters band. That is orders."

They all looked at each other in frustration as Nooram left the room. "I will try to contact General Dandig," he muttered over his shoulder.

"What's going to happen to those men?" Luna asked.

"If the old pattern holds," Mike answered, "the men will surrender.

Then the guerrillas will execute the district chief, who represents central authority, take all the weapons and ammunition, and tell the rest of the police and troopers to quit the government while they're still alive."

"Can't we do something?" Luna cried.

Mike put his arm around her and led her from the room. "Darling, go back to bed. I'll be with you very soon. There just isn't anything we can do. Should Lawton, Jennesen, and I try to relieve the headquarters alone?"

"Oh, no, Mike! Please. I didn't mean anything like that. Promise me —come just as soon as possible." He watched Luna's graceful body move under the sheer nightgown as she climbed the stairs; then he returned to the sitting room. Sergeant Jennesen was gone, but Lawton was morosely sipping a drink. Mike poured himself a fresh one and sat down.

"I guess we're in for real trouble," Mike said bitterly. "Vietnam, Mituyan—one damned 'war of liberation,' as Mao calls them, after another. And no end in sight!"

Lawton looked up, interested. "Do you mean what you're saying?"

"Damn right, I do," Mike said heatedly.

"How would you like to do something about ending it before it gets started here, Mike?"

"What do *you* think?" Then, cautiously—"What do you have in mind?"

Lawton drew a pack of cigarettes from the breast pocket of his khaki shirt. "Actually, you are in a position to do quite a lot."

CHAPTER TWO

MIKE FORRESTER wondered if he had trapped himself. It had been his policy to keep himself and his activities removed as far as possible from the United States mission to Mituyan. He shook his head when the colonel offered him a cigarette, and waited. Lawton took out a silver lighter decorated in relief with temple dancers and slowly lit his cigarette. After a long, deliberate inhalation he said casually, "Have you ever heard of JRB?"

Mike smiled. "Joint Research Board? Of course. Fritz, are you some kind of a spook?"

Lawton shook his head. "There's much more to JRB than covert intelligence operations. I work on specialized research projects. I think you could be of tremendous help to us."

"In what way?"

"More than any other American in this country you know what's going on out here in the boondocks. Regular reports to JRB from you could help us tremendously."

"If it's merely information you want, I'll be glad to oblige."

"There was some thought that you might be of operational assistance," Lawton continued.

"You mean you want me to be some sort of unofficial hood for the Agency?"

Lawton chuckled. "I suppose you might say that. A friend of yours is head of JRB in Mituyan now. He's convinced JRB is way behind on gathering information and recruiting reliable agents."

Mike nodded. "I know Jack Cardinez—from two countries ago. Tell him he can have all the information in my head anytime, but I don't want to be an agent for the JRB or its parent, the CIA."

Lawton ignored the statement. "You have the perfect cover, Mike. No other American could get around this country the way you can without compromising himself." Mike remained silent and Lawton went on. "This has gone right up to the Country Team level. You know the term?"

"I think so," Mike replied wearily. "Five men in charge of our operations here, tragically insulated from reality in air-conditioned offices in Tuyan City." He reached for his drink, took a long sip and put it down. "Let's see. There's my old friend ignore-it-and-it'll-go-away Whittelsie, the ambassador. Then you've got Cardinez or whoever his CIA station chief boss is. And General we-are-winning Macker, who's never lost a statistic yet, is head of Military Assistance. I don't know the new propaganda chief who's just come in from the Information Agency in Washington—and the fifth is that labor leader who never leaves Tuyan City but is supposed to decide how half a million dollars a day should be spent out in the countryside." Mike pulled a cigar from a mug beside him, bit off the end viciously and spat it onto the floor. "Yes, I know the Country Team, Colonel." He fired up the cigar and puffed in agitation.

Lawton stood up, began pacing the room, and then turned to Mike, apparently taking another tack. "Do you understand the importance of the coming elections to us?"

"The elections are a farce," Mike answered shortly. "My friends in the palace tell me they've been forced on them by this Country Team you want me to work for as part of the CIA."

"I didn't exactly put it that way," Lawton said quietly. "But the elections are damned important, not only to gain world opinion but to win over Americans so that they'll favor using U.S. money and men to keep the Communists from taking over this country."

"I know the argument, Fritz," Mike said. "Since we have to back a government, let's make sure it's one elected by the people. Then it's OK for us to send in three hundred thousand American combat troops when our present do-nothing, see-nothing, say-nothing policy makes it necessary to save the Mituyan government."

"Well, I wouldn't state it that way—"

"So first each province of Mituyan elects representatives to a congress in Tuyan City which will review and make changes in the Republic of

Mituyan's constitution and work out the ground rules for a general election of a representative assembly and a president of Mituyan." Mike shook his head. "It will never work."

"Of course it will work." Lawton continued to pace. "Someone's got to get elected from each province. Once the representatives of the thirty-eight provinces are in session in Tuyan City, the folks back home who pay the bills will see that things over here are being done in a way they can understand, and we can hang in here and keep this insurgency from becoming another Vietnam."

"There won't be one man elected who truly represents the people of his province. Either KaritKi will control the election or the Communists will wreck it. Probably it'll be a bit of both."

"What's your suggestion on how to make this election work?"

"Don't have one at all."

"We have to have one. Our government wants an election here, and it's the job of the Country Team to see that one is held."

Mike shrugged, stood up, walked to the sideboard. "Fix you another Chivas, Colonel?"

Lawton walked over to Mike and put his glass down. "Not too strong, we still have something to talk about."

Mike made Lawton another highball. Handing it to him, he said, "Besides, I don't see how I can be of any help."

"You understand the people and speak their language. Among other things you could help set up machinery to make sure that the polling is handled fairly."

"That, as I just said, is impossible. Since every delegate elected to this congress must agree upon ground rules that can only keep KaritKi in power, the world will say America was party to a fraudulent election. Why not leave things the way they are? KaritKi does an effective job of running the country."

"Your friendship with the Palace has been very profitable for you, hasn't it?"

"To do business in a country like Mituyan, you have to work directly with the people on top." Mike smiled blandly, trying not to let Lawton irritate him.

Lawton was silent a few moments. Finally he said, "There are many —too many—problems for us to solve in Mituyan. But we have to try. We need you working actively with us."

Mike concealed his anxiety by shooting a question: "Fritz, what was your primary reason for coming out here tonight? To observe a Mituyan Army operation?"

Lawton smiled and shook his head. "No. I was hoping for a chance to talk to you. And you provided it." Lawton paused a moment, then went on. "You know, Mike, you of all people, certainly of all Americans in this country, should be especially concerned about the Communist conspiracy here."

"Why do you say that?"

Lawton looked at him before answering. "According to my information, twice before you've suffered financially and personally when Communists have subverted a country in which you had sizable investments. Guatemala in 1953 and Cuba in 1960."

The expression on Mike's face acknowledged that the colonel had hit home. When Mike made no answer for some moments, Lawton, as if consulting a dossier, continued to probe. "You were a respected international businessman until late 1960. You had everything. A society beauty for a wife, the best financial connections. And then the Communists made you run. Not just out of Cuba, but away from your own country, the United States."

In Guatemala most of his personal fortune had been wiped out overnight by the Arbenz Communist government. Adrian, the social and extravagant wife Mike once had been so in love with and thought so fortunate to marry, had openly mocked him in front of friends and their two daughters for his inability to maintain their standard of living. She never let him forget it was her family that kept up the heavy mortgage payments on the house and paid the servants so that he could continue to appear the successful international financier. Finally, after more than six years of recouping his fortune in other overseas transactions, Mike had again lost heavily in 1960 when Castro's Communist government wiped out his investments in Cuba.

"I can't deny it," Mike finally replied. "I had to leave. We all thought, the United States government was convinced, that under Castro business would go on as usual back in those days. Sure, I had to run. When Castro nationalized the sugar plantations and industrial plants I had financed, would the bankers in New York give me a break? They called their loans. All of a sudden real property in Cuba was no longer a hard asset. It was just by luck I found out they were going to attach everything I had. What would you have done? Go broke in New York or grab every asset you could get your hands on and try to start up somewhere else?"

"So you decided to give Mituyan a whirl," Lawton said. "Interesting place to pick. Back in late 1960 only a few scholars and obscure State Department officers had ever heard of Mituyan."

Mike thought back to the lecture on foreign investing he had given at the International Student's League at Columbia University. That was 1959; financially, things were going well for him. Afterward, the Eurasian girl from a country he had barely heard of had come up to the lectern to ask questions. He had been immediately captivated by the grace, exotic beauty, and complete seriousness of Luna Hargraves. It had been an early-evening lecture and he invited her to dinner: from then on they were together frequently.

Adrian's face had become as hard as her outlook on life. She lived only for exorbitant spending and a perpetual round of parties. She and their two daughters constituted a solid anti-Mike Forrester front; small wonder, then, that Luna's soft beauty and the pleasure she took in simple things completely delighted Mike.

"Well, Fritz," Mike said, "I first met Luna in New York, as you probably know. I'm sure you have my life history on file. She started me on one hell of a research project; you're right, it wasn't easy to find people who knew much about Mituyan."

Luna's simplicity, straightforward manner of talking and thinking, and her tolerance about having dates with an older, married man were so appealing that he lived for their times together. When, in the early spring of 1960, she had a two-week vacation from college, Mike invited her to fly down to Miami with him and cruise aboard the *Promise*. She readily accepted.

On the cruise he had not in any way rushed her—the sun and sea had been his allies. At a small island in the Exumas on the way to Havana he ordered the *Promise* anchored, and they took a small boat and spent the day alone together on a sand spit surrounded by clear blue-green water and fish-laden reefs. After an hour or two on the island, and a number of rum punches, they looked at each other, laughed, pulled off their bathing suits and spent the rest of the day frolicking in the nude together.

"I'm surprised you didn't recognize that Castro was a Communist in time to save your investments in Cuba," Lawton broke into Mike's thought.

The gibe made him wonder whether he had been so delighted with his beautiful cruising companion that he had failed to realize the full significance of Castro's takeover. The Castro government had encouraged tourism and American investments. Castro had given lavish parties for American travel agents who were having a convention in Havana, and the farms and ranches and cigar factories seemed to be running at full efficiency.

Still, as Mike had berated himself many times since, had he taken the time to look a little deeper into things, talk to a few more people instead of spending a delicious week in Havana with Luna, he knew he would have sensed the danger signs and perhaps been able to pull out of Cuba financially whole. At least he could have battened down for the onslaught of creditors and bankers who were to jump him when it suddenly became apparent during Castro's visit to the United Nations in the fall of 1960 that the government of Cuba was Communist, anti-business, and anti-American.

"As I said, Fritz," Mike replied wearily after a long pause, "even the U.S. government figured we could live with Castro."

"Not my part of the government," Lawton shot back.

"If I'd thought, I would have asked Jack Cardinez's advice—if I could have found him," Mike added.

The day came when Mike had been called upon to meet his notes and personal guarantees. Luna's solution had been what he hoped for:

"Let's take the boat and the money you've liberated and go to Mituyan."

That year-long cruise to Mituyan had been the most exhilarating of his life. When crews were hard to find, Mike and Luna, alone with the loyal skipper who had been with him since the old minesweeper had been converted, sailed *Promise* over vast distances. Mike thanked himself a hundred times for all the modifications he had put into *Promise*—the extra fuel tanks, the new heavy-duty automatic pilot, the special radio equipment. They had used everything before finally sailing up the Tuyan River into Tuyan City. And by then Luna had drilled into her husband a good grounding of the Mituyan language—which blossomed into fluency over the succeeding years.

Again Lawton's voice broke into his thoughts. "How about it? Will you join us, Mike?"

When he made no reply, Colonel Lawton hammered in again. "What will you do if the Communists take over here? Desert another wife? Run for another underdeveloped country?"

"I didn't exactly desert Adrian." Mike tried to keep his tone level. "The marriage was finished long before I left the States. What does your dossier say about how I left my wife and daughters fixed financially?"

"Oh, I know all about the trust funds. You handled that very well. Of course there's the small matter of bigamy. You're a bigamist in the United States, no matter how legal your friends in the palace made it here."

"That's not true!" Mike could feel his temper running all but out of control. "Adrian is divorced from me and remarried."

"Yes," Lawton went on relentlessly, "her divorce was granted more than a year after you married your present wife in Mituyan. But no matter"—Lawton's gaze shifted to the cigarette—"that can be taken care of by a grateful government." Lawton suddenly stood up. "Even such things as absconding with funds owed to creditors . . . the boat you took was also collateral on a personal guarantee you knew you couldn't meet—"

"I finally paid off all my debts in the States in full, and at damned near ruinous interest rates," Mike interrupted heatedly.

"Yes, yes. However, your case is still in the criminal-action files at home—but, as I said"—the colonel's voice trailed off—"a grateful government . . ."

"So, it takes a form of federal blackmail to recruit your agents?"

"Most Americans in this sort of work do it out of dedication to the best interests of their nation," Lawton replied blandly.

A dozen retorts flashed through Mike's mind—*what has my country done for me beyond encouraging investments in underdeveloped countries, which broke me, and supplying the legal machinery for bankers to rub my face in it*. But prudently he said, "We can talk more about it later. I'll have to discuss it with Luna. . . . You'll have to stay here for what's left of the night anyway. Those so-called bandits probably have the roads ambushed."

"Thanks for your hospitality, Mike. And incidentally, I don't blame you one damn bit for your reaction. That was my job. But I'm aware of how hard the going was for you. All of us who know of your background admire what you've done out here."

Mike grunted an acknowledgment. Then, as an afterthought, he said suddenly, "Besides, I'm not qualified to be a member of such an intricate and highly trained group as yours."

Lawton smiled. "Let's see. Combat infantry officer in Italy, fought across France after D-Day. I presume your Bronze Star, Purple Heart, and Silver Star were deserved. You speak Mituyan like a native." Lawton nodded. "Yes, I'd say you are not only qualified but are probably the best qualified man in this country to be part of JRB."

Lawton saw the unhappy look on Mike's face. "Look, if we didn't need you, I wouldn't be here. You know that. The people like you and trust you. They'll give you intelligence. They know you stand for their best interests. You gave them decent wages and a sense of security for the first time in the history of this country. You are the first big employer to build clinics for the people and pay doctors and nurses to staff them. You revised the school system so that all the families in your districts can educate their children free. No plantation owner before has bothered to teach sanitation. Your people no longer take a life-long case of dysentery for granted."

Mike stared silently into his empty glass without replying. After a few moments Lawton said, "You know how to win the hearts and minds of the people here. This is the biggest single job ahead of us."

"They must really love me to let me lose twenty trees a night," Mike replied bitterly.

"That is entirely the work of the Communist guerrillas, and nobody knows it better than you. But with your help we can stop them." Lawton sensed that Mike had listened to enough for one night. He stood up. "Guess I'll go see what Captain Nooram is up to. Talk to you in the morning, and we can finish this chat."

Lawton left and Mike went over to the sideboard and poured himself another drink. The colonel had torn open his life. Since his arrival in Mituyan he had tried not to let himself think about his life before the day he and Luna started out on *Promise*.

Now so many old memories rushed in upon him. His ordinary western-Pennsylvania upbringing. His parents, who disparaged the way he constantly thought and talked about travel to far-off places. His older brother and sister had gone to preparatory schools, but the money had run out when his turn came. He studied hard at high school; and at the fringe Ivy League college he had worked his way through, he made up his mind he wanted a military career to see the world. He had enrolled in Army ROTC and had enthusiastically attended every vacation and weekend encampment—anything rather than go home.

In June of 1943 he graduated, his high ROTC standing having protected him from the draft. Lawton was right. Mike nodded in satisfaction. His military career had been exciting, distinguished—and short. After the war his battalion commander headed back to the family investment-banking firm and brought Mike into the company with him with the promise of extensive foreign travel.

And the Wall Street firm had not disappointed him. In the three years before he met Adrian at twenty-six, he had become his firm's Latin America expert. And after the marriage, with the host of new social and financial contacts Adrian and her family had given him (though that was *not* why had had married her, he always had to remind envious associates), his foreign financial transactions multiplied and he began to build a personal fortune.

Of course, he thought wryly, as fast as he made money Adrian spent it. That house on Long Island that rivaled his father-in-law's, her clothes. Finally, in desperation, he had taken a private safe-deposit box and began putting in cash, even jewels he bought on his travels. The small hoard gave him some feeling of security.

But one thing was undeniable: Adrian had been beautiful, probably still was in her brittle, hard way. And he had been in love with her from the first moment he had seen her. He had been asked to go out and brief her father, Ernest J. Martin, on a large investment he was considering making through the firm. He would never forget it. Adrian had been wearing a bathing suit, sunning by the pool—

"Mike? Aren't you going to come get some sleep?"

He turned from the sideboard, drink in his hand.

Luna had walked down the stairs and was standing in the doorway, the breeze from the terrace blowing her negligee out behind her.

"Yes, of course. I was just thinking. I knew I couldn't sleep just yet."

She looked at him hopelessly. "They never tried to help the men at the district headquarters," she half asked, half stated.

Mike placed an arm around his wife's shoulders. There was no answer he could make. He thought he loved her more right then than ever before. Luna lived with an almost personal sense of obligation to the people of the district in which their rubber was the chief source of the economy.

"What are we going to do, Mike?"

"I'm afraid it's too late to do anything about the men in the station." He sighed. "Looks like Mituyan sure is in Phase Two of its so-called war of national liberation."

Luna shook her head. "I never thought it could happen here."

"That's what they think in every country until it hits. Premier KaritKi has been a friend to us, but he lives in a dream world with his young wife and all the court intrigue."

Luna turned to her husband, pouting impudently. "Your wife isn't exactly middle-aged."

Mike leaned over and kissed her in the hollow of her neck. "I'm only eighteen years older than my bride, and for a dirty old man of forty-five I think I do all right by her."

Luna agreed emphatically.

"Now KaritKi, he's fifty-eight. How old's Dhuna?"

"Twenty-five."

Mike's tone hardened. "A young wife requiring extra attention is still no excuse for a premier not seeing an insurgency developing in his country. If we don't stop this thing before it goes any further, we'll be in a full-scale Vietnam-type war."

"What about our trees? The army isn't going to be any help."

Mike nodded. His jaw tightened. "We've got too much invested here to lose. As it turns out, that old Britisher who sold us the place on such attractive terms wasn't doing us any favor."

Luna looked at him quickly but said nothing.

"The French faced this problem in Vietnam right up to a few years ago when they finally had to get out. Much as I hate to do it, I guess we'll have to adopt the Gallic solution. I'll have to negotiate, and then we'll try to get every meta we can out of this plantation, bleed the trees out of five years' life for immediate gain, and try and sell cheap."

"Oh, Mike." Luna looked stricken. She loved their property; she believed in conserving all its resources.

"The way KaritKi runs his country these days we have no choice, darling. You've just seen his army's idea of protection. The sort of social reforms that might keep the Mituyan people from sympathizing with Mituyan Freedom Front propaganda are way overdue. How much longer can you expect them to believe the lies our energetic United States Information Service is telling them about Premier KaritKi's great interest in their welfare? They want action, not words. The MFF at least offers them relief from their frustrations through violent action against the tyrant, KaritKi."

"KaritKi and Dhuna made everything you and I have gained in my country possible," Luna chided gently.

"Yes. What a damned ironic twist. The same force that made me potentially rich again is responsible for our problems now."

He walked across the room to one of the large windows and looked out at the rubber trees. "Premier KaritKi and your friends at the palace helped us in so many ways to get started, gave us valuable tax concessions, ordered the province chiefs to be helpful to us. . . . And yet"—Mike shook his head slowly—"KaritKi and his ancient and outmoded system of giving all to the family and members of the mandarin class is driving the small farmers, eighty percent of the population, right into the arms of the insurgents."

Luna followed Mike across the room and leaned against him. The proximity to his beautiful Eurasian wife began to calm him down. He put his arm around her shoulders. "Don't worry, darling. I've been caught and cleaned out through a misdirected social revolution once too often. I won't let it happen again here."

They embraced—their tender kisses became passionate. "Let's go upstairs, dearest," he whispered. "I think I'll be able to sleep now."

CHAPTER THREE

AFTER AN EARLY BREAKFAST Mike and Colonel Lawton returned to the site of the previous night's destruction. Sergeant Jennesen was waiting there for them. Captain Nooram's company was still bivouacked in the trees, cooking their morning meal.

"Efficient work," Lawton muttered, examining the neatly cut tree stumps. "No noise until the detonation, and by then the guerrillas could be a quarter of a mile away or more."

Jennesen glared at the soldiers around him. "These Mits sure as hell aren't ever going to stop the pros who did this job."

Captain Nooram sauntered across the blasted clearing. "Good morning, Colonel," he said pleasantly enough. "I have just received orders to relieve the district headquarters. We will be moving out as soon as my men finish breakfast."

"You're going to be a little late, don't you think, Captain?"

Nooram frowned. "Colonel, I follow my orders."

"All right, Captain. Sergeant Jennesen and I will follow you in my jeep."

"As you wish, Colonel." Nooram turned on a heel and returned to his campfire, where a bat man was ready to serve breakfast. The transistor radio was blaring out American rock 'n' roll.

Sergeant Jennesen looked after him, shaking his head. "I'd sure hate to be an adviser to any unit that dipshit commanded."

"Guess we'll have to go back to your place and get our kits," Lawton said to Mike. "I want to get to district headquarters even before Nooram does."

"I'll go along too," Mike said. "This is my district. If anything needs to be done—like funeral arrangements," he said grimly, "I should be there."

"You can ride with us," Lawton offered. "Give us a chance to talk a little more."

Mike nodded. "OK, Fritz, you're on."

Luna was waiting for them when they got back, and Lawton thanked her for her hospitality. "Come again, Colonel," she said, "we'd love to see you any time." But when she heard that Mike was going to district headquarters, she asked to be taken along.

Mike shook his head, but she persisted. "The wives of those men may need me."

"If they do, I'll call you on the radio." Mike himself dreaded the scene awaiting them; certainly he did not want Luna exposed to it.

"I can take it, Mike."

"Mr. Forrester is right, Ma'am," Lawton interjected. "If you're needed, I'll send Sergeant Jennesen to escort you back."

Reluctantly, Luna waved goodbye as the men drove off.

"Have you put your mind to what we were discussing last night, Mike?" Lawton asked after they had driven a while in silence, passing and taking a comfortable lead on Nooram's convoy.

"Sure I have. Of course I've got a few other problems on my mind, like saving all I've worked for in this country over the last four years."

"Sure. But when you get things back on the track, will you come and see me in Tuyan City—say, next week?"

"I wish I was that optimistic about getting my rubber problem squared away."

"On the Country Team level you can help us do something permanent about this insurgency."

"Luna and I will be in town for KaritKi's Decade of Progress celebration in a week. Is that soon enough?"

"I guess it will have to be. In the meantime—"

"In the meantime, Fritz, I'll be collecting a dossier of information for you on the MFF. It looks like I'm going to have to do some talking with the Front's leaders in these parts."

The jeep rumbled along the rough dirt roads, and a long silence ensued. Finally Lawton said, "If you were working for JRB, we'd pay you of course. Say an amount equal to what you're going to pay off to the Mitcoms to leave your rubber alone?"

Mike thought about the Chinese bankers in Tuyan City and Hong Kong. Once the mortgages and loans were paid off, he and Luna would be in fine shape financially, but as it was, every three months it was a strain to make all the payments—and it would be worse now.

Mike said, "You make the arrangements sound a hell of a lot more attractive than you did last night."

Lawton smiled. "If you can get into town before the flaps start to generate around KaritKi's celebration, we'll have more chance to talk. There are a few people I'd like to have you meet."

"Like Jack Cardinez? We're old adversaries from other countries. Actually, I admire your top spook."

Lawton shook his head and tried to suppress a smile. "Just for your information, Mike, Jack Cardinez may be top man in JRB, but that doesn't make him the CIA station chief in Mituyan. Our"—Lawton paused, a wry grin on his lips—"head spook, as you call him, the chief of the Agency's mission in Mituyan and member of the U.S. Country Team here, is someone else. I don't know who he is. Of course I have some pretty well-founded ideas. Jack Cardinez is more or less overtly in charge of JRB operations which, we don't deny, comes under the administrative control of the Agency."

"Our ponderous U.S. apparatus to advise and give aid to the Mituyan government never ceases to amaze me," Mike said, watching the twisting road ahead as Sergeant Jennesen expertly guided the jeep through the bumps and turns.

"We can expect you in Tuyan City before the Decade of Progress?" Lawton asked, ignoring Mike's comment.

"We'll be there—and I'll be glad to meet everyone."

Lawton nodded. "Good." He turned in his seat and checked the position of Captain Nooram's troop trucks. Nooram's lead truck was sufficiently behind so that the driver wouldn't have to breathe in the dust from the jeep.

"We're almost there," Mike said. "Around the next turn." Mike braced himself; he had too much experience with Communist terrorism to expect anything but a horror show.

As the jeep swung around the last bend and into the village, the three men in the jeep stiffened unconsciously. The combined police station and district-headquarters building was black from fire. Smoke still rose from the ruins. The barbed wire around the building was torn and blown apart. And on a pole in front of the building, they saw the head of the district chief impaled; the headless body hung upside down from the second floor. Two bodies, torn up by bullets from head to feet, lay in front of the remains of the headquarters.

Across the street, women and children were crying and moaning. Jennesen halted the jeep in front of the headquarters and swung out onto the ground, closely followed by Lawton and Forrester.

"What does that sign say?" Lawton asked.

Pinned to the headless body was a sign written in Mituyan squiggles. Mike stared at it. "Same old Communist line," he said. " 'The district chief was a pawn of the tyrant, KaritKi, and his United States-dominated puppet government. Any other KaritKi district chiefs can expect similar treatment.' "

Mike turned from the grisly sight and walked across the street to the weeping women. A younger woman, stoically dry-eyed, approached the American planter. She and Mike talked for several moments, and then the army convoy drove into the street and came to a halt. Captain Nooram and a small detail gingerly inspected the carnage while Mike reported his conversation to Colonel Lawton.

The men in the headquarters, the young woman had told him, held out most of the night; but just before dawn they were overpowered. Of the ten men who had been in the headquarters four had been killed, including the decapitated district chief, three men were wounded, and after the terrorists left with all the weapons and supplies, the wounded men had been taken to the clinic Mike had helped the district chief build two years before. Three unwounded men had been taken off with the terrorists, presumably to be drafted into the guerrilla band.

"That was the district chief's wife I was talking to," Mike reported. Lawton glanced at the handsome young woman desperately trying to keep her eyes averted from her husband's mutilated body. "She said if help had come anytime up to the first light of dawn her husband would be alive."

Colonel Lawton turned to see Captain Nooram ordering a detail to cut down the body of the district chief and remove the head from the pole. "I wouldn't blame the people for collaborating with the MFF if this is all the protection they're getting from their government." He looked at the weeping women and children. "The families of the men killed?"

Mike nodded. "Things are going to be even worse for the wife of the district chief. They believe that if a man dies by beheading, his soul wanders the earth to eternity. His wife will never have a peaceful moment so long as she clings to her religious beliefs."

"Is there anything we can do for them?"

Mike shook his head. "Give the dead a funeral this afternoon, and I'll see what kind of pension plans the men had. If they worked even part time in my rubber, the wives are covered for accidents and death. The government has no protection for families of men killed in line of duty." Mike sighed. "One of the points I've been trying to make with Interior Minister Branot is that the families of all government employees should be protected."

"Are you making any progress?"

"They don't even understand what I'm talking about, Fritz," Mike said. Then, changing the subject: "I'd appreciate it if you'd ask Sergeant Jennesen to go back for Luna—after we've tidied up here. She should be present for the funerals and to help with the women."

Jennesen, who had overheard Mike's words, said, "Any time you say, sir. It might be good to ask Captain Nooram to send a security guard behind me in one of those trucks."

Mike nodded bitterly. After the years he had traveled in complete safety all over the country and in the jungles of Mituyan, after all the good will he thought he had built up, it had come to this: A security guard was now necessary in this district.

By the time Jennesen had returned with Luna, the bodies had been placed in caskets that Mike bought from the local undertaker. As he helped the four new widows make their arrangements, he had little time to wonder how the plain wooden boxes had been so readily available.

Red ox-drawn carts, followed by the families of the deceased, made their way to the outskirts of the village where the burial ground was located. A Buddhist bonze, or priest, summoned hastily by the undertaker, conducted the services. Luna had brought an extra supply of red candles for the widows to burn; but the young widow of the district chief did not even bother to light the candles, convinced, as she was, that her husband's spirit would now never rest. Luna particularly concentrated on trying to console her and her three children. The district chief had been a friend of Luna's, and he had put into operation several of the welfare programs financed by the rubber property.

On the way back to the village after the burial, the undertaker slipped up to Mike, who was silently striding along at the end of the procession of mourners. After a few perfunctory remarks he said, in Mituyan, "Mr. Nowat asks if you want to talk to him."

"Nowat?" Mike asked. "The Nowat who was once my headman in the eastern sector of Rishram?"

"The same."

"He disappeared over a year ago. I was sorry to lose him."

"He is back."

"He was always very clever, too clever. Is he a member of the Mituyan Freedom Front?"

The undertaker shrugged. "He said I must tell you that he can help you right now."

So the undertaker is part of the MFF organization, Mike thought. How appropriate! "How do I make contact with Nowat?"

"If you will stay here after the soldiers leave, he will come to you. But he said you must be alone—no other person must even bc in town when he comes to you."

Mike wondered how safe he would be alone in what was now obviously a MFF controlled town. But, he reasoned, since the MFF hoped to get financing from him, they couldn't afford to harm him. He tried to remember all he could about Nowat. His former headman, he recalled, had a fetish about education. Indeed, it was Nowat who had convinced him to improve the educational facilities for the district's children, and who had worked on his own time, after hours, to put up school buildings and bring in books and teachers. Only Luna's friendship with KaritKi's wife had kept Mike from being censured for interfering with the archaic Mituyan school system that ignored children of the country peasant class. He recalled now that Nowat had got into trouble with the government when he tried to join the local school board. He could not remember all the details, but he seemed to recall that Nowat had violently protested the government's decision and had to flee before the province chief imprisoned him.

To the undertaker, Mike said: "I will stay. Bring Nowat to me as soon as you can. I must be back at Rishram by dark."

"This will be done," the undertaker assured him.

Back at the district headquarters Captain Nooram said his orders were to proceed back to Rishram and bivouac one more night in the trees before returning to battalion headquarters at Tiking. The captain led his company out of the village in a storm of rising dust, and when the Mituyan soldiers had all left, Mike asked Luna to drive back to Rishram with Colonel Lawton.

"Send the Land Rover for me just before dark," he instructed.

"It isn't safe for you here alone, Mike," Lawton protested.

"I wouldn't stay if I didn't think it was necessary. I also think it's safe for me. Now the sooner the rest of you get going the quicker I'll get my business over with. So go," he urged smiling.

Jennesen touched the sweatband of his green beret. Lawton shrugged. "I guess you know what you're doing. You've been around long enough. Let's go, Sergeant."

The jeep drove off in the wake of the convoy's dust, Luna looking back anxiously at Mike. He waved encouragement to her, and, when the vehicle had disappeared, turned back to the charred district headquarters to await word from Nowat. The wait was a short one. The undertaker approached him and led the way out of the village and into heavy bush. They walked along a narrow trail for a few hundred yards and stopped. After a few minutes, a Mituyan man wearing a floppy cloth hat, black pajamas, rubber sandals cut out of an old automobile tire, and carrying an M-1 carbine, the type American military advisers were supplying to the Mituyan Army, materialized from the jungle.

Wordlessly, the undertaker and Mike followed the armed man along the path and then off and into a well-concealed camp beside a stream. There were a number of men in black pajamas sitting around the camp, and several were lying on crude litters, bandages on their legs, arms, bodies, and faces. Under a thatched roof, neatly stacked in cases with yokes for easy carrying, Mike saw two dozen assorted rifles, machine guns, shotguns, and ammunition boxes.

"Mr. Forrester. Thank you for coming." Mike looked around and recognized Nowat. Dressed in khaki slacks and shirt, the former headman wore U.S. Army jungle boots and an officer's billed cap without insignia.

Before speaking, Mike deliberately eyed the weapons and wounded men. Then he turned a direct gaze on Nowat. "So this is the way you return to your home district, Nowat?"

"We must free our people," Nowat answered. "Premier KaritKi's American-backed puppet government must be destroyed and a true people's rule established. In this district it is my assignment to teach the people to make their lives better by throwing off the KaritKi tyranny."

Although Nowat had always spoken well, Mike was amazed at the man's improved command of English. "So, Nowat, you begin your lessons by murder and torture."

"The district chief was a corrupt tool of the corrupt province chief appointed by the corrupt despot KaritKi. First we tried to reason with the district chief; then we had to make an example of him."

"And three other men of the district who happened to be at the headquarters?"

"They were protecting the KaritKi officials."

"Where are the three men you kidnapped?"

"We did not kidnap any men. The three who were unwounded volunteered to come with us to be trained to fight for their freedom."

"May I see them? Talk to them?"

"They have already gone to the North to start their indoctrination."

"Up to 'neutral' Bardans, eh?"

Nowat ignored the thrust. "What we want to talk to you about is the wages you pay the oppressed people who work your rubber."

"Oppressed?" Mike cried. "My people are the best paid and cared for in Mituyan. You should know, Nowat. You were treated in the Rishram free clinic. You helped me put in the free school system at Rishram and down at the tea property."

"The schools taught loyalty to KaritKi," Nowat answered doggedly.

"Loyalty to the central government," Mike corrected. "And the clinics had nothing to do with politics."

"The medicine came wrapped in government propaganda leaflets."

"The government supplied most of the medicine," Mike countered.

Brushing aside all arguments, Nowat said: "We expect that a percentage of the profits of Rishram shall now go directly to the people."

"How big a wage increase do you expect?"

"Twenty percent," Nowat replied flatly.

"But that's impossible. You know it. You were a headman at Rishram."

"You have become rich out of the people of Mituyan, Mr. Forrester. You can afford it."

Mike fought down anger and, trying to keep his voice level, said: "You people always think we're rich. Don't you know about mortgages, bank loans, Chinese merchants, money lenders?"

"We'll kill all of those people for you, Mr. Forrester," Nowat answered blandly.

"I'm already paying ten percent above the wages at most of the other plantations in this country. Why don't you go to them?"

"We will, Mr. Forrester, we will. But you are an American. You can give more."

Hopelessly, Mike looked around the guerrilla camp. Once again the Communists had moved in on him. His only answer was to gain time to either sell or get maximum value in minimum time from his property. "I cannot afford more than another five percent increase. Any more and Rishram can make no profit."

"All right, Mr. Forrester, since I believe you do have the best interests of the people at heart, I will advise my political superior to accept a ten percent pay increase."

"Impossible!"

"No, it is not imposssible," said Nowat. "But every morning you wake up with twenty less rubber trees it makes it more difficult."

Mike knew he had no choice. "I'll advise the accountants to give my workers a ten percent raise beginning next Saturday."

"Oh, we will make it easier for you, Mr. Forrester. A man from our organization will collect the amount of ten percent of total wages paid each week, and we will use it to benefit the people as we deem best."

Desperately suppressing his rage, knowing he had no recourse, Mike replied, "Send your man in next Friday. I'll still be at Rishram."

"I knew you were a reasonable man, Mr. Forrester. But remember, should you change your mind, your trees will be destroyed retroactive to tonight."

"My word will be kept."

"I'm sure it will." Nowat's manner relaxed and the other men in the camp, seeing their leader had accomplished his business successfully, seemed to adopt an easier air.

"You must realize, Nowat," Mike said when he had gained some measure of equanimity, "that this MFF movement of yours will ruin the country economically and only wind up in a lower standard of living for your people. For more than two years in Vietnam the soldiers from the North have been defecting as they see how much better—in spite of the war—the people in the South are living."

"Do you know how well the people in Mituyan are living?" Nowat asked. "Do you really know? I don't mean the people of your private little welfare state that KaritKi lets you run for propaganda reasons. I mean the people all over the country."

"Certainly there are reforms that should and will be made," Mike conceded.

"That's what your American propaganda experts say. But we see no improvement." Nowat turned from Mike to the group of perhaps thirty guerrillas in the camp. "You see these people, Mr. Forrester? Every one of them made a big effort to find and join the MFF. They were all ordinary citizens until driven to the Front, hoping to find an answer to their miseries."

Nowat switched his gaze back to Mike. "You are probably the only Caucasian in Mituyan who can talk to these people and judge for yourself what's going on in this country." He pointed to a one-eyed, one-eared, young-looking guerrilla. "Be my guest. Talk to Mung over there."

Mike's first reaction was to refuse to have anything more to do with Nowat and his band of Communist guerrillas. Then he thought of Lawson, the fact that JRB would help him pay off the MFF, and realized it was his duty to learn as much as possible about the MFF and how the organization was set up.

In Mituyan, Nowat instructed Mung to talk with the American frankly and honestly, answering all questions that might be put to him. To Mike, Nowat added, "None of us have any military information. We do not know from one day to the next where our camp will be or what our orders from the MFF will direct us to do."

Mike nodded and squatted on his haunches opposite the squatting Mung. Mung was at first surprised and a little frightened to hear his language spoken with such fluency by an American, but Mike skillfully put him at ease with talk about rice paddies in Mung's home area of Tiking Province.

As Mung and Mike talked, the rest of the guerrillas and Nowat went about their chores, cleaning and stacking weapons, getting ready to break camp, tending to the wounded.

"How did you join the MFF?" Mike finally asked.

"When I was released from the province prison in Tiking, a man I knew slightly from the village in which I was born was waiting to see me. He brought me to a cool tea shop and gave me tea and we talked all day and into the night about politics and what had happened to me. He let me sleep in his shop and we talked more. Soon I was asking him what I could do to help the MFF. I was passed on to a recruiter and then taken to the North for training."

"In Bardans?" Mike asked.

Mung looked hesitantly over Mike's shoulder at Nowat. Mike heard Nowat say, "You may answer all of the American's questions. But tell him why you were in the province jail and what happened to you and other prisoners you knew."

"Yes, I trained in Bardans with many other MFF recruits," Mung replied. "We are all very well trained," he added proudly. "I hope that soon, when the Front is ready, I will have command of a MFF platoon here in my own province." His eye flashed. "I want to execute first the chief of my home district and then the province chief and finally Poramat, the brother of the tyrant KaritKi, who is the boss of all the provinces in the north of Mituyan. But they will not get off so easily as the district chief here. He died easily, of wounds, before we cut his head off. The next time we will hang up the district chief, open up his belly while he is alive and healthy and let his entrails spill out. Then we will put hot coals in his gut. We will make his wife and children watch before we kill them." His voice rose. "And then we will do the same to Poramat and the province chief of Tiking."

"Did you learn these methods in the North?" Mike asked, fully expecting Nowat to cut Mung off.

"No, I and other prisoners made them up while we were in the province prison in Tiking."

"Why were you in prison?"

"I could not afford to pay the back rent on my land. I could pay the regular rent I had been paying since I married. But then five years ago Premier KaritKi pardoned many landholders and politicians who had been in exile abroad. One landholder came back to my district. He had been away four years, and he told me I'd have to pay him my rent for the last four years he was away. The district chief who had been taking the rent from me would not help. The landlord was back in good grace with KaritKi. I must pay the rent all over again or be turned off the land I had been working. My wife and three children and I would have nowhere to go because the district chief said he would tell other landowners not to rent to me."

Mike, listening intently, remembered rumors of retroactive rent charges by returning landlords, but this was the first time he had talked to a Mituyan who had actually suffered such an injustice. Mung continued in low tones.

"I could not pay double. It seemed unjust to make me pay double. I did not believe that the district chief would make me leave the land. When he came around with two men to make me and my wife and children go, I refused. Then they took me to the district jail and next the province prison for making trouble against the government of Premier KaritKi. My wife was not allowed to see me, but prisoners who came in after me said that the landlord had used her for himself, then made her do the lowest work, and my children were sold. When the province chief was satisfied that the landlord had been paid back through the use of my wife and the sale of my children, I was released. I did not know where my children were; I could not have bought them back even if I knew. My wife was wasted and dying. In the prison were many men like me from all over the province. Some had not paid the high taxes on land they owned, and it was taken from them by the province chief. The landlords divided with the province chief the money he extorted for them from us."

Mung sighed deeply. There was misery on his face as he paused before going on. "The prison was so bad I would not tell an American about it because he wouldn't believe me. The worst was when they brought women in. First the province chief and his staff had them, then the jailers. Every man and woman in the prison was there for the same reason—defying the rule of Premier KaritKi. Not half the people who went into the prisons lived out a year."

Mung stared at the ground. "My wife was happy when I joined the MFF. She said she would die happily alone and untended if I was fighting against KaritKi with the MFF."

"Tell him what happened to your eye, Mung. And your ear," Nowat urged.

"My left eye was destroyed when a jailer pushed his rifle barrel into it when I and other prisoners tried to stop the torture of one of the women who had bitten and scratched one of Poramat's special police officers while he was raping her. They cut my ear off for trying to keep the other prisoners' spirits up by telling them how we would overthrow KaritKi and Poramat. I was lucky that they did not cut out my tongue as they did to others." With that Mung lapsed into silence.

"You have suffered, Mung, it is true," Mike said. "But does that make it right for you to go out and kill others?"

"We only kill those who maintain the evil KaritKi regime."

"There is a nonviolent, legal way to win the reforms you seek," Mike told the ragged group as he rose from his squatting position.

Nowat laughed derisively. "Reforms?" He looked at the men around him. "We want more than reforms. We want our own government. A people's government."

The guerrillas growled in affirmation. "We will destroy KaritKi," Nowat cried. "We will kill his brothers and their supporters. They will not allow changes or," he sneered, "those reforms you talk of. Things are good for them the way they are. The province chiefs have absolute power over every man and every woman in their province. They take everything they can from the people and pass it up to KaritKi and his government, which is his family. Only a violent revolution and the death of KaritKi and his family can make things better for the people."

"You think violence and killing is really going to help?" Mike asked. "You are an educated man, Nowat. There are other ways."

"Tell me about them, Mr. Forrester. I'm listening with interest."

Mike thought a few moments. The futility of the people's plight was undeniable. KaritKi had indeed executed or imprisoned all those who offered real political opposition to his regime. Now that his American advisers had persuaded him to hold elections, he allowed a figurehead opposition to operate—but it had no power.

"There are legal ways," Mike said lamely. "The coming elections. Without killing and extortion you could form a political party that could demand recognition."

"The elections!" Nowat mocked. "KaritKi and his American-equipped army and national police would quickly find and execute the leaders of a peaceful, unarmed political party." Nowat gave Mike a sardonic look. "You Americans are so naive. All the time you help men like KaritKi in Mituyan, and before him Diem in Vietnam, all the time you are sending money and goods to help the governments of tyrants, you merely waste the money of your American taxpayers, using it to grind the poor people of a country into the dirt. Why don't you Americans who give so much to KaritKi come out in the countryside and see what really goes on. Nothing you do to help the economy of Mituyan gets to the people. It's turned into money which goes into the pockets of corrupt army officers, corrupt government officials from district chiefs on up, and into KaritKi's banks in Hong Kong and Switzerland."

"That was quite a speech, Nowat," Mike said sarcastically. "It sounds to me as though you've been thoroughly trained by the terrorists from the North."

Nowat scowled. "It is the backing you Americans give to despots and ruthless oppressors of the people like KaritKi that makes me see that your capitalism is designed to squeeze everything out of the working people and give it to the rich few."

Mike searched his mind for rebuttals, but it was getting close to dark now and he knew that even if he stayed and argued all night Nowat had become, in fact probably always was, a hard-core Communist dedicated to violent revolution. There was no way of arguing with him. Yet he felt a vague sense of guilt at not trying.

He fired a weak volley as he nodded at the undertaker who would take him back to the district headquarters. "You are an educated, intelligent man, Nowat," he said in English. "You could have become part of the government and worked for reforms from within, instead of being a leader of guerrillas dedicated to bloodshed and terrorism."

Nowat laughed drily. "As I said, Mr. Forrester, you Americans are very naive." He gestured impatiently at the undertaker. "Goodbye, Mr. Forrester. One of my agents will call on your paymaster every Friday."

"You know, Nowat, I could sympathize with what you are trying to do if it wasn't that the MFF seems to be run by North Vietnamese Communists like Nguyen Van Can."

"We run our own war to liberate the people of Mituyan from KaritKi's tyranny," he cried.

Seeing Nowat on the defensive Mike pushed him further, this time speaking loudly in clear Mituyan for the benefit of the other members of the guerrilla band. "If you were running your own movement for social reforms, perhaps Americans would help you, but when you can't even handle your own affairs without the help of foreign terrorists like Can who have been killing their own people for the past ten years, you and all the members of the Mituyan Freedom Front can only be considered murderers and terrorists no better than your Vietnamese Communist leaders."

Nowat burst into a tirade of rage and invective against the Americans and KaritKi. But Forrester clearly saw he had made a point with some of the guerrillas who considered themselves true freedom fighters. Several of them looked questioningly at the furious Nowat.

Nowat pulled a U.S. .45-caliber pistol from his belt and waved it at Mike. "I will kill you the next time I see you, maybe even now." He leveled the weapon at Mike's chest, shrieking in Mituyan. "*You* are the foreigner who comes to our country and lets your puppet KaritKi rape the people!"

The guerrillas watched their leader. Mike stood firm, staring into Nowat's burning eyes, fighting his compulsion to glance down at the pistol. Slowly Nowat regained his composure. "You may go, Mr. Forrester. We will not kill you—now."

Without another word, Mike turned his back on the group and followed the undertaker out of the camp and into the bush. The walk back to the district headquarters took half an hour, and it was dusk when they reached the burned-out building. Bunghole, dressed in his khaki working clothes and bush hat, was sitting behind the driver's seat of the Land Rover, waiting with considerable agitation. Forrester stepped into the front seat and Bunghole threw the running motor into gear. The Land Rover leaped forward and out of the village.

Luna was waiting for him at the plantation house, her face betraying her anxiety. "I was so afraid for you, Mike, darling."

"They won't bother us for a while now." The lines around the corner of his mouth deepened. "I'm worth too much to them alive and running a going rubber property."

"What happened?"

"Let's have a drink on the veranda. I'll tell you everything."

"You go out. I'll get the drinks."

Mike nodded and wearily made his way to the veranda overlooking the mathematically perfect rows of trees. He sagged into the high-backed wicker armchair and waited for Luna. He was absorbed in the technicalities of doubling the year's yield of the trees when Luna placed the highball in his hand.

CHAPTER FOUR

AMBASSADOR NORMAN ASHLEY WHITTELSIE, waiting for the Country Team to assemble, walked over to the plate-glass windows that constituted two sides of his large, air-conditioned sixth-floor office. Tuyan City was fascinating, he thought. After a year as ambassador he still found it possible to get excited about Tuyan and the surrounding countryside. From this, one of the city's tallest buildings, he could see the crisscrossing canals and rivers choked with sampans, houseboats, cargo ships, and the floating markets. Metropolitan Tuyan City spread out over several square miles and was one of the largest capitals in Asia. Many people—Connie, his wife, for one—had found it too hot. God knows it smelled bad, most of it. Yet he still found it fascinating. Whittelsie returned to the conference table as the members of the United States Country Team in Mituyan filed in.

The ambassador called two regular meetings a month. To keep the sessions short, he scheduled them for four o'clock on Friday afternoons, which had the added advantage of cutting down much of the customary invective and strife, since frequently the members had already left for weekends on the seacoast and sent deputies in their place.

But today it looked as if he had drawn most of the top brass, thought Whittelsie, a lean, suntanned, athletic-looking man in his early fifties, as he smiled at the four men seated around the glossy-topped round conference table. Whittelsie's iron-gray hair was close cropped, and his seersucker suits, button-down blue shirts, and white buck shoes all attested to his Ivy League background.

General Willet Macker, commander of the U.S. Military Assistance Command Mituyan, was seated on the ambassador's right. Jowly and heavy-featured, he looked even more heavyset beside Whittelsie. Whenever he became piqued at the general, Whittelsie would suggest that Macker get out and play some tennis. Macker had never been much of a tennis player, and in his first match with the ambassador he had lost two love sets in a row—and never played again.

The general, at fifty-nine, was eligible for retirement in less than a year at the convenience of the government, so Whittelsie treated him with indulgence. Actually, in spite of his contentiousness—Macker had little use for civilians, particularly those who helped form the policies that affected his command—the general measured up to the ambassador's standards very nicely. No waves. According to all the military reports that went across the general's desk prior to being forwarded to Washington, things were going well in Mituyan. The U.S.-advised, -equipped, and -paid Mituyan Army was developing on schedule and effectively fighting off the Communist insurgents trying to gain a foothold in the country.

"Gentlemen," Whittelsie opened the meeting, "I'm glad you could come." He turned to his left. "This is the first Country Team meeting for our newest member, Mr. Theodore Baum, new Public Affairs Chief. We're glad to have you with us, Ted."

"Thank you, sir. I'm looking forward to this assignment."

"Mr. Baum, in case any of you are unfamiliar with his background," Whittelsie continued, "left a distinguished career in journalism to enter government service. Mr. Baum is breaking in, so to speak, with us." He turned back to Baum. "We will try to help you learn what the foreign service and the Country Team are all about."

Baum silently resented the condescension in Whittelsie's tone. He had spent twenty years rising from police reporter on a small city daily paper to bureau chief for the world's most important wire service in the leading capitals of the world. He felt, therefore, eminently qualified for his new job as chief of the United States Information Service in Mituyan; at the same time he knew his journalistic background made him suspect to most top foreign service officers and to this Country Team—long at war with the press—in particular.

As much or more for the benefit of the other members of the team, Baum felt, Whittelsie made one emphatic point. "Each member of the Country Team quite understandably finds he must communicate often with his agency or department in Washington. I realize that many little crises arise every day and the tendency is to bung off a cable home." Whittelsie looked at Baum sternly.

"However, I do not like the petty grievances of members of my team being sneaked back to Washington. We should be able to settle most problems right here."

Whittelsie glanced at Grady Rourke sitting stolidly across the table from him. "I would not appreciate it at all if, for instance, the head of the Agency for International Development and the chief of the United States Information Agency had to personally battle out a question in Washington that our USOM and USIS representatives, Mr. Rourke and Mr. Baum, should have brought to me to decide."

Whittelsie smiled to lighten the atmosphere. "In other words, Ted, there has been a bit of a 'my old man can lick yours' attitude among members of some country teams around the world. I do not condone this in the U.S. mission here in Mituyan."

Ted Baum knew perfectly well that every member of Whittelsie's team communicated secretly with his own instrumentality in Washington. The amount of unilateral traffic to Washington from Tuyan City was a joke during the three months of lectures and briefings he had received before taking over his post.

"In conclusion then, Ted," Whittelsie said brightly, "the members of my team will continue to clear all their traffic to Washington through my office." The ambassador looked at each member of the team individually, and each nodded solemnly.

General Macker gruffly broke a moment of silence. "You'd better get the press corps around here under control, and damned fast, Mr. Baum. They're making it look like the place is falling apart."

"Is it?" Baum snapped back without thinking, and then cursed himself inwardly for his lack of restraint. He was, after all, the new man.

Macker looked startled. Then from the opposite side of the circular table a calm voice said, "Yes, I'd say so."

Gratefully, Baum met the snapping blue eyes set in the swarthy face of Jack Cardinez. General Macker turned sharply on the Central Intelligence Agency representative; and Whittelsie, sensing the meeting was already getting out of hand, quickly tried to assert his authority. "Gentlemen, we have an agenda to follow. Today Mr. Cardinez is once again the—able"—nobody missed the pause—"representative of the deputy assistant ambassador, Mr. Filmore Dickerson."

The lengths to which foreign-service men went to avoid any mention of the CIA had never ceased to amuse Ted Baum in his days as newsman. Even in a meeting of the Country Team itself, the ambassador apparently only used the cover role of the CIA station chief in referring to him.

Whittelsie's voice took on an edge of annoyance as he continued. "And it is a pleasure to have Mr. Grady Rourke at a Country Team meeting," he said, his eyes resting on the pugnacious, burly man sitting to the left of Ted Baum.

"Glad I could make it, Mr. Ambassador," Rourke replied in a grating voice. "I've been pretty busy with this new AID program we've got to handle at USOM."

"Everything is progressing satisfactorily, Mr. Rourke?" Whittelsie inquired of the labor leader who, like Baum, had turned temporary foreign-service man and member of the U.S. mission in Mituyan.

"Going full blast." Rourke's rough speech was in decided contrast to the patrician ambassador. "I get a meeting every day with that Branot at the palace, you know? Minister of the Interior around here."

"I know Minister Branot, of course," Whittelsie replied coldly.

Once again Rourke experienced the sense of inadequacy that had haunted him since he first arrived in Mituyan three months earlier. He had been a successful labor organizer and administrator back in the States. Tough jobs were the only kind he knew. But now there was no way he could muscle these Mits into doing what he advised. He lived in a permanent if well-disguised state of frustration. He longed for the docks of the big eastern cities of the United States which he knew, understood, and could ruthlessly dominate.

A labor-union mission to Southeast Asia was responsible for his being offered this foreign-service job. He had led a delegation of labor experts who managed to solve many of the problems of getting supplies off the Saigon docks and into warehouses. Next Rourke had come to Mituyan and accomplished the same job in the principal ports of this country.

Rourke returned to the United States a hero and an international figure among labor leaders. The President of the United States was having serious problems with national labor leadership at this time, and it seemed politic to offer a prominent union man an important government post. So Grady Rourke had been appointed, with much fanfare, to head the AID team in Mituyan, known as USOM—United States Operations Mission. Grady Rourke was responsible for seeing to it that close to a quarter of a million dollars a day in U.S. goods were moved from ships and planes to where they were needed to bolster the national economy—the cities, hamlets, and fields of Mituyan. But he had long since resigned himself to the fact that he would never learn to understand the Mituyan people beyond the fact that for the most part they were damned crooks. There was nothing he could do about it; he couldn't even fathom the exact manner in which the stealing took place from the warehouses. And as for the docks, the security police were so ineffective that the big crates with the clasped hands of friendship were broken into and looted whenever they had to stand overnight. One of these days, he had resolved, he'd take a field trip, but he always had to be careful not to offend his Mituyan counterparts by directly challenging them and perhaps causing them to lose face. The hell with it. If he could just last through this tour, he would win great prestige and probably become the president of his union, the biggest shipping union on the eastern seaboard.

"Now, gentlemen," Whittelsie said in a business-like tone, "there is only one item on our agenda today. The elections."

General Macker cleared his throat loudly. "If the damned jackals that call themselves journalists hadn't written so many irresponsible, sensational stories about the government's so-called harsh, repressive measures against students and Buddhists; if the press corps, getting drunk every day at the St. George Hotel, hadn't made it look like an incompetent dictatorship under Premier KaritKi was losing the war against the guerrillas and throwing all his opposition in prison"—Macker's florid jowls quivered as he drew in a deep breath—"if it wasn't for these hack yellow journalists trying to make a name for themselves, we wouldn't have this problem of elections to worry about and we could go ahead and win a military victory over here."

Ignoring the outburst, Ambassador Whittelsie said, "As usual, Miss Crossfield will take notes and prepare our talking papers to go up to our IRG in Washington."

Whittelsie leaned toward the new member of the team. "IRG," he explained, "stands for Interdepartmental Regional Group, Ted." Baum knew all about it but submitted to a second lecture. "Our IRG, as we call it, is a sort of country team in Washington that specializes in the problems of Asia. There are a number of IRG's in Washington, of course, each with a different region of the world to worry about."

Baum nodded. Didn't Whittelsie know he had spent three months in schools and briefings for his job here?

"The notes of our Country Team meetings, our talking papers we call them, go to our IRG. The IRG, after digesting our problems, makes up its own talking papers, which go on up to SIG, the Senior Interdepartmental Group. SIG is the master country team made up of top men from State, Defense, USIA, AID and"—unconsciously Whittelsie's tone hushed—"the Agency. SIG goes over the problems and recommendations of all the country teams around the world and makes final recommendations to the President of the United States and the National Security Council. So"—Whittelsie's voice rose cheerfully—"it behooves us to be accurate in these meetings. Our words are studied by many experts. Of course all of us will have an opportunity to make final changes in our individual talking papers before they're sent to our IRG."

Whittelsie nodded to Miss Crossfield sitting primly beside him, shorthand pad balanced on her knee, pen poised.

"We are on the record now, gentlemen. First I want to say that the new attitude at the palace is most gratifying. Premier KaritKi and his brother, Counselor Tarot, are being most cooperative in getting the machinery for the election of delegates to the Constitutional Congress in good working order. I think we can report that in six months the American public and the world will see an orderly, impartial, and wholly fair election. This should do much to justify the United States mission in Mituyan and our wholehearted support of the legal government of Premier KaritKi and, after his government, the next legally elected government, which world opinion can never deny will be one representative of the people's wishes."

General Macker unconsciously reached into his pocket for a pack of cigarettes and then realized what he was doing and folded his hands on the table. Whittelsie did not smoke and did not like smoking in his office. While he never forbade anyone to smoke, there were no ashtrays or any kind of receptacle like potted plants that could be used to dispose of ashes and cigarette butts. The embarrassment of having to drop ashes on either the polished table top or the carpeted floor was sufficient deterrent. These meetings, so dull and usually meaningless, drove Macker, and he suspected most of the others, into a frenzied craving for tobacco.

As Ambassador Whittelsie explained all the reasons why he was optimistic about the success of the elections and the cooperation he felt the U.S. mission was receiving from the Palace, Grady Rourke twisted and shuffled his feet. He was used to dominating meetings, not sitting around listening to a Harvard professor-type talk theory. Finally he pulled a package of cigarettes from his pocket. As the rest of the team watched in hypnotic fascination and Whittelsie, seeing what

Rourke was doing, began losing his train of thought, the USOM chief calmly lit up and inhaled deeply.

Whittelsie ceased talking altogether and stared at the unconcerned former labor leader. Finally, to break the silence, Whittelsie said, "Mr. Cardinez, perhaps you would report any late intelligence developments on the elections."

"It's too early to come up with much dope now, sir. There were no overt indications this week of Premier KaritKi suppressing opposition candidates. But he's probably quietly doing it in one way or another."

"I think you're jumping to unfair conclusions, Mr. Cardinez," Whittelsie snapped. "I just finished my analysis of the attitude at the palace toward the elections. It couldn't be more cooperative." Whittelsie paused and stared in horror at the growing length of ash on Rourke's cigarette.

"From all I've observed in over a year here in Mituyan," Cardinez replied imperturbably, "I don't believe there is a chance that Premier KaritKi will peaceably let go of his hold on this country."

Only Miss Crossfield seemed to be hearing Cardinez; the others were totally absorbed in a long, curved ash that could hardly adhere to Rourke's cigarette more than a few more moments. Rourke turned the cigarette straight up to gain another second or two. Then he pulled his right leg out from under the table, lifted it, and carefully carried the cigarette toward his trouser cuff, spreading it with one finger just as the ash fell safely into the fold.

An almost audible sigh escaped from General Macker; Whittelsie watched the performance in disbelief. Rourke appeared completely unaware that anything out of the ordinary had occurred.

"You must remember, Mr. Ambassador," Cardinez continued, "that Premier KaritKi did not willingly agree to any sort of election procedure. He was forced into it when we suspended part of his U.S. aid program."

"I believe he's with the program now," Whittelsie retorted, his eyes still riveted to the smoking cigarette in Rourke's fingers.

"Sir," Cardinez argued, "we have intelligence of at least three separate coup plans against the KaritKi regime. His own generals don't believe he intends to allow a free election. They talk of overthrowing KaritKi, bringing in a military junta to run the country, and properly policing the elections. Then when a government is elected, they'll turn over their power."

"This is the first I have heard of any coup plots. What generals are plotting against the regime?" Whittelsie demanded.

"Well, sir," Cardinez answered, a trace of a smile at the corner of his mouth, "a Mituyan general or colonel without a coup plot up his sleeve is about as common as a wealthy Frenchman without a mistress."

Ted Baum laughed aloud and drew a cool look from the ambassador, whose glance then flickered to Rourke, dumping another ash into his pants' cuff.

"You indicated a specific plot," Whittelsie persisted.

"Yes. Of course this must be regarded as very secret information." Cardinez met the eye of each member of the team, even Grady Rourke, who was looking up with new interest.

"General Dandig, I Corps commander, doesn't like the way the military operations are being run in this country. Of course he has the disadvantage of being military commander in the corps area run as the personal fief of Premier KaritKi's brother Poramat, whom Dandig detests. The general and one of my men are very close. Already Dandig has made discreet inquiries as to what the U.S. position would be if the army overthrew KaritKi."

"I hope your man told him that the United States mission's attitude is to live or die with KaritKi," Whittelsie said jocularly.

"He said he didn't know," Cardinez replied. "And you must realize that Dandig isn't the only dissident military leader in this country. It seems that KaritKi's entire huge circle of family connections try to influence the army for their own gain. All we have to do to get rid of KaritKi is let the generals know we will support their man as interim premier until the elections decide who will lead the government."

"And who do you think is competent enough to be this interim premier?" Macker demanded.

"I don't know, General," Cardinez answered, "but I'd begin by looking for an impotent only child." The dry remark brought understanding smiles around the table.

"Are there any candidates for the election that are known to be anti-KaritKi as well as anti-Communist?" Ted Baum asked.

"Not many." Cardinez glanced at Grady Rourke, whose cigarette was burning dangerously close to his fingers. "KaritKi and Tarot hustle opposition leaders off to the Isle of Stones as fast as they surface. This election may well be a blessing in disguise for them. They'll know exactly where to find their opposition and so destroy it quickly. Our whole concept of a free election here is a delusion."

"For the money we pour into Mituyan, the United States government and the American people are entitled to this election, and they'll get it," Whittelsie declared. "Surely, Mr. Cardinez, there are some impartial candidates who could be publicized to make the world see that we are supporting a fair election here."

"I guess Professor LakaLit at Tiking University best answers your requirement, sir," Cardinez replied. "He has an international reputation as an expert on government and economics. Also, he is a Buddhist—a reincarnationist—and is popular with the people in Tiking Province as well as at the University."

"Very good." Whittelsie was pleased. But his face fell as he watched Grady Rourke carefully pinch out the stub of cigarette in his fingers and drop it into his cuff. Not a sign of cigarette ash marred the floor. Macker's eyes had never left the USOM director's cigarette during the entire operation. There was silence for several moments and then Whittelsie, groping for his line of thought, turned to Ted Baum.

"I think we have your first assignment, Ted. Get a newsman, the most widely read man reporting from Mituyan, and have him sent to Tiking to do a story on Professor LakaLit. You know what we need —the man who opposes KaritKi yet whom the government encourages in order to give the people the widest possible choice of delegates to decide on Mituyan's future constitution and election procedures."

"A damned good idea," Macker agreed. "You take Krakhaur up there, Baum. He's done us enough harm in the States, so he owes us a constructive story about now."

"Right," Whittelsie chimed in. "Krakhaur's just the man."

"I'll try, sir."

"Try?" Macker bellowed. "Your job is to control these young hacks."

It didn't take much conjecture on Ted Baum's part to envision how relations between the Tuyan City press corps and the Country Team had degenerated into constant bitter skirmishing. "I've known Roger Krakhaur since long before he became the Star Syndicate's leading writer on foreign affairs," Baum said. "I'm pretty sure I can get him up to do the LakaLit interview."

"Fine, Ted. That's what we need." Whittelsie smiled. It looked as if he'd soon be able to adjourn the meeting. His mind was already wandering to the red phone in his desk, a private line to the woman who both frightened and excited him at the mere thought of her. He hoped tonight would be opportune for him to visit her.

"Sir"—the urgency in Cardinez' voice brought Whittelsie's thoughts back to the table—"you must realize that a story on Professor LakaLit could really backfire if KaritKi decided to let his brother Poramat, shall we say 'talk' the professor out of running."

"Nonsense, Mr. Cardinez." Whittelsie did not bother to keep the irritation from his voice. "The Premier has told me personally that he is one hundred percent behind these elections. He feels as strongly as we do that Mituyan should have a government truly representative of the wishes of the people."

"That's right, sir. Just as long as that government is run by KaritKi and family," Cardinez commented drily.

Whittelsie regarded the CIA representative distastefully and made no reply. He dropped his eyes to the agenda sheet on the table before him. "The next point is Premier KaritKi's Decade of Progress celebration. This should be another opportunity for our new Public Affairs chief to marshal the press corps behind the government and get some stories published at home on KaritKi's ten years of progress and stability. If the people of this country vote to keep KaritKi as their Premier, which I personally think is likely, we want the Premier to know that we were behind him all the way."

The four other members listened stonily to Whittelsie's speech, obviously designed for the talking papers in Washington. Cardinez wondered if the ambassador was really so misinformed about the real feeling toward the KaritKi regime in the countryside. Did this career diplomat honestly believe that KaritKi would give up his power to a popularly elected leader? Did Whittelsie honestly think that even if KaritKi himself was willing to make such a Western-style democratic gesture, the Ki family and its political dependents would allow him to step down? Either of the brothers, Poramat or Tarot, was perfectly capable of taking over the family leadership, divesting Karit of the Ki at the end of his name, denoting his status as family head. Mituyan would then end up with TarotKi or PoramatKi as Premier.

Whittelsie went on a few more minutes for the record. Then he turned to General Macker. "Willet, what is the status of the war this week? The press says the government is losing real estate and support every day. I've had two cables from State expressing concern."

"Guerrilla incidents are up all over the country," Macker admitted. "But we're winning, not losing. I have been informed by the Palace, Minister of Defense Xuat, that government casualties are light and we're taking a heavy toll of the enemy."

"Is that what you hear from the advisers in the field?" Whittelsie asked. "The newsmen who write that we're losing say their sources are men involved in the actions."

"Disgruntled officers who don't understand their Mituyan counterparts will tell newsmen anything they want to hear about how bad the situation is," Macker replied angrily. "I've collected all the news stories from the States. Next week we conduct security investigations. We'll see who is leaking to reporters."

"You've got to tell them *some* of the truth when things go bad," Ted Baum protested.

"Don't tell 'em anything," Macker retorted. "Those are my orders to my men."

Baum shrugged and decided to keep his own counsel until he had more experience with the situation here.

"We're winning, dammit." Macker's face reddened. "The damned press should get with the program, see the big winning picture, not report isolated little setbacks."

Whittelsie stared coolly at the USOM chief and said: "Mr. Rourke, you have been unusually silent today. What do you find out in the countryside that might give us some insight into this election?"

"When were you last in the field, Mr. Rourke?" Macker asked gratingly.

Rourke looked from the ambassador to Macker and back again. "Like I said, I'm working eighteen hours a day right here in Tuyan City on the new aid programs. Right here is where you get things done. I came into this job and found USOM spread all over this place. It's like this Minister Branot says, if we'd just give the Mituyans the stuff here in Tuyan City, they'd see it gets where it's supposed to be going."

General Macker had a stricken look on his face. Cardinez was openly hostile and Ted Baum was trying to hide his contempt. "I'm trying to call in all these USOM people spread all over the map. They got something here called Provincial Operations that came from Vietnam. We don't need these guys wandering around the villages, sometimes getting themselves killed or kidnapped. It's wild out there." For a moment there was a plaintive note in his voice. "Best thing we can do is to let the Mituyans handle getting the stuff to the people. I'm checking on all the stuff we sent out and reading the reports from the Mituyan province chiefs who get the stuff out there. We're in good shape. The Mits are only stealing about ten percent of everything we send in from the U.S. That's better than it was," he added defensively.

"You mean, Mr. Rourke"—Macker fixed him with a piercing stare, as though the USOM director were an enlisted man caught lying at his court martial—"only ten percent is stolen between Tuyan City and the province chiefs, am I right?"

"That's right, General."

"What about between the province chiefs and the people for whom it is intended?"

"Once it gets to the province chiefs, that's where our responsibility ends. The stuff's out there. Minister Branot feels very strong on this."

"For your information, Rourke," Macker growled, "half the supplies that have been getting down to the peasants, eighty percent of the country's population, reach them through my officers and men in the field. And my men report every day it's getting more difficult to locate the material intended by our government to improve their lives."

"Maybe your men report 'isolated little setbacks,' to use your own words," Rourke returned. "I've been told to work with Minister Branot and I'm doing what I'm told." He appealed to the ambassador, who nodded judiciously.

"It is true that Mr. Rourke has been instructed by me to work closely with the Palace."

"Well, if Mr. Rourke gives a damn about what happens to a quarter of a million dollars a day worth of American taxpayers' money, to say nothing of the people we are supposed to be helping, he'll get out of his air-conditioned office, put a pair of boots on his feet, and go out to the boondocks, Branot or no Branot."

"I do my job as I see it, General, and I figure you do yours the same way. If you want military advice from me, I'll give it to you when you ask. Otherwise I keep my mouth shut. Let's just make this a two-way street, if you know what I mean."

Macker purpled, but said nothing.

"You have no comments on the elections, then?" Whittelsie asked.

Rourke thought for a moment, his forehead wrinkling, and then said gravely: "I think they're a good thing."

"Well," said Whittelsie, "this has been a constructive, if short, meeting. But I think we've covered everything. All in all the election situation is coming along in orderly fashion." The ambassador sensed that both Macker and Cardinez had more to say but he was anxious to terminate the discussion. "We can take up individual problems next week, so unless there are any other points with direct bearing on the elections I'd suggest we adjourn."

"There is one other point on the elections, sir," Cardinez interjected.

"Go ahead, Mr. Cardinez," Whittelsie said. "I assume this is a point Phil Dickerson would have brought up had he been able to attend our meeting."

"What's being done to give the Groat tribesmen a voice in this election? Our people working with the Groats report increasing interference from the Mituyans. We were supposed to be working with the tribesmen without Mituyan counterparts, but the Mituyan province chiefs are trying to take over our camps in the mountain country."

"Mr. Cardinez, we try to keep away from sensitive political problems. The feelings between the mountain people and the Mituyans is a touchy subject, and I prefer to leave it alone."

"The Groat tribesmen live in those mountains that make up almost one quarter of Mituyan, and they are all that stand in the way of wholesale infiltration by the Communists from Bardans." Cardinez leaned over the table toward Whittelsie. "We've got to keep them loyal to the government. The Mituyans hate them, and the Groats hate the Mituyans. Only our Special Forces detachments keep the Groats from going Communist. Premier KaritKi has got to make the Groats feel they have a voice in the new government or we'll lose them; and then from the mountains divisions of Communist troops can easily overrun the rest of the country."

Whittelsie thought a few moments. "Yes, it is a serious problem, Mr. Cardinez. Next week I'll have a private talk with Mr. Dickerson and we'll see what can be done." He turned to the rest of his team. "Now, if there is nothing more, this meeting stands adjourned. You can make changes on your talking papers on Monday afternoon; they'll get out to our IRG on Tuesday morning."

Uneasily, Whittelsie recognized that General Macker was determined to resolve his unfinished business. The general held back as Cardinez, Baum, and Rourke filed out of the office after wishing the ambassador a good weekend.

"What's on your mind, Willet?"

"Damn it, Whit! I damn well can't get appointments at the palace when I want them. And I know, and my intelligence staff knows, that Phil Dickerson gets in and sees KaritKi or anyone else over there whenever he damn well wants to."

Whittelsie decided to try the light approach. He laughed. "Trouble is, Will, you don't have the proper liaison with the women. It's those delicate little lovelies with the hidden fangs who run things at the palace."

Macker cleared his throat. He knew, as did a few other people around the U.S. mission, that Whittelsie was consumed with interest in young, exotic women. There was no better place in the world than Tuyan City to indulge such a taste, and even though Whittelsie thought he was being discreet, intrigue and gossip were the way of life in Mituyan.

"I guess crusty old soldiers like me have to leave the boudoir diplomacy to more experienced hands." Macker guffawed, giving Whittelsie a sly, infuriating smile. When Whittelsie made no answer, he took on a conciliatory tone. "Seriously, Whit, I have a hell of a time getting to see Premier KaritKi. I get shunted off to Xuat. And the Minister of Defense doesn't make the decisions."

"What do you need to see him about, Willet?"

"KaritKi and his dope-fiend brother are playing around with the TO and E of the army."

At Whittelsie's questioning glance Macker added, "They're making suspicious little changes in the Table of Organization and Equipment of the Mituyan Army."

"What does that mean?" Whittelsie strove to keep impatience from his tone.

"I'm not sure, Whit. There are rumors that Tarot is trying to organize some new elite military unit. If so, I should be consulted. The point is, KaritKi should see me any time I ask for an appointment. Instead he puts me off." Macker's tone became sharp. "Our assistant deputy ambassador sees KaritKi any time he wants to. I'll bet he's pulling off some cozy deal to bring this new unit under his authority and deliberately not keeping the Country Team advised."

"I know nothing of a new Mituyan military unit," Whittelsie replied firmly.

"Well then, why won't KaritKi see me?"

Probably, Whittelsie thought to himself, because you bore him out of his mind. "I'll call you next Monday, Willet," the ambassador promised. "I'll get you an appointment with the Premier as soon as possible."

"Thanks, Whit. Have a good weekend."

Once General Macker was out of his office, Whittelsie returned to his desk and sat down, leaning back and relaxing a moment. Sometimes he thought of himself as a lion tamer, always trying to keep the cats, the members of the team, from tearing him or themselves apart. It was up to him to make them perform, put on a smooth act for the audience—the readers of the talking papers. Another audience was the American public, which watched Whittelsie's team in action through the medium of the press.

After a few moments he unlocked a special drawer in his desk and pulled out the red telephone. Before all his misgivings and fears could assault him, he lifted the receiver, picturing the apartment at the palace where his instrument's counterpart reposed in an ivory-inlaid mahogany chest. He waited a few moments and then heard the high-pitched voice on the other end say, "Whit, did you finally finish that boring meeting?"

"It's over, Mayna." He paused. Here was the justification for his liaison with Mayna. "Look dear, I've got to set up an appointment with the Premier for General Macker and myself. Through official channels your brother-in-law can put off seeing me, if I insist on bringing Macker along, for ten days or more. Can you fix up a short meeting for next week?"

"It will be done, Whit. When will you be landing at Marashak—tonight?"

"We do have a date, then?" Whittelsie asked, his heart pounding.

"Of course, darling."

"I thought perhaps Counselor Tarot might be planning—"

"I have not invited my husband," Mayna interrupted haughtily. "Besides, he's going up to Banthut. I'm sure he plans to spend the weekend plotting political strategy and smoking Groat opium. But General Xuat will be in Marashak at his villa this weekend. You should be able to get in some good tennis with him"—she giggled—"if I leave you any strength."

"My plane will get me to Marashak airstrip at eight tonight," Whittelsie said.

"My limousine will be waiting for you." There was a pause and then, her voice dropping a register, "It's been eight days, Whit. We have all that time to make up for. I can hardly wait until tonight." Mayna hung up and the ambassador slowly replaced the receiver and slid his desk drawer closed.

Whittelsie looked down at the unopened letter from his wife; it had been there since morning. He was tired, discouraged—in spite of the official attitude of optimism he must always display—and had no desire to read the recitation of parties in Washington, Maryland, Virginia, and New York that took up Connie's time and seemed more and more to be her only purpose in life.

I needed you, Connie, he thought. *Even though you get more undersexed every year and,* he smiled wryly, *by some damned biological quirk of fate the opposite is happening to me. So I couldn't control myself when Mayna deliberately seduced me. This is no place for a high-ranking, politically vulnerable diplomat to be without a wife. If you'd stayed, Connie, I might have discreetly arranged to have one of these exquisite half-Caucasian half-Mituyan girls for a mistress, but most emphatically I wouldn't be having this damnable affair with the wife of the Premier's brother and political counselor.*

The ambassador opened another drawer and pulled out a bottle of the special Chivas Regal Scotch he had arranged for the exclusive embassy commissary to stock. He poured a measure of the light-gold liquid into a glass, put the bottle down without recapping it, and thoughtfully sipped the pungent Scotch straight. Mayna's husband was impotent anyway, from years of smoking opium, or so she and everyone else said. Whittelsie was sure Tarot knew that the American ambassador was exploring the full inventory of Madam Mayna's extraordinary sexual repertoire, and the counselor probably encouraged the affair. After all, it was one way to keep the U.S. Embassy in line. Well, to hell with intrigue. He would enjoy the weekend to the fullest.

CHAPTER FIVE

TIKING UNIVERSITY, far more than the University of Mituyan, had been the traditional seat of culture, learning, and liberalism in the Republic of Mituyan. Until the arrival of the American military advisers and their airplanes, Port Tiking was remote from Tuyan City, difficult to reach, and the primitive communications system was so frustrating that even Premier KaritKi seldom tried to call his northernmost city on the sea. For that reason Tiking Province had always been run with a minimum of government supervision.

Ruling supreme over Tiking Province as well as the other provinces that comprised I Corps or the northern quarter of the Republic of Mituyan, was Poramat, KaritKi's brother. Though the province chiefs governed their respective provinces, the spectre of Poramat's authority and power always hung over their heads. Officially he was counselor to his brother on civil affairs in I Corps, but he had extended his authority into all business and military matters as well as the civil government. He even had his own private police force, which moved throughout the provinces enforcing his edicts and spying on the province chiefs.

Poramat made his headquarters in Port Tiking, and while he had appointed Lieutenant Colonel Yunakit as province chief, he personally ruled the daily affairs of this, the richest and most important northern province.

The University dated back to before the British made Mituyan a protectorate at the request of the King of Mituyan, Barkoon II, in the late eighteenth century. Except for the Oriental faces and frail forms of the students, Tiking looked much like a medium-size American or British university. It was coeducational, with a student body of about four thousand undergraduate and graduate students. The girls wore Western dresses with a suggestion of the Chinese chongsam. The hip-high split in the side of their dresses had been blamed by the college authorities for most of the student troubles, but all efforts to persuade the young women to wear more concealing skirts were rejected by male and female students alike.

Professor LakaLit, who taught humanities and classics, was certainly the most venerated member of the college faculty; indeed, he was far more influential than the chancellor, who spent most of his time on University politics and fund-raising in Tuyan City.

Professor LakaLit's classes were the most popular among the student body; and he sometimes gave as many as five lectures a day, necessitating a number of junior professors and several instructors to provide his vast number of students with individual guidance. Fearlessly, he told the students what they wanted to hear—that they were the only hope of a free and democratic Mituyan. While it was imperative for them to understand the history, religious problems, and culture of Mituyan and all Asiatic countries, LakaLit also insisted they must learn all they could about the workings of Western governments.

Before Luna Forrester had traveled to the United States to take postgraduate work in government at Columbia University, she had been deeply influenced by Professor LakaLit. After her return to Mituyan, she visited him whenever the opportunity arose and had been deeply gratified to see the mutual admiration and trust that had developed between her husband and her old professor. Mike and Luna never went to Rishram without planning a visit with Professor LakaLit. But this time, before seeing the professor Mike had business to attend to—he wanted to supervise the first payoff to the MFF.

Precisely on schedule, the MFF representative presented himself at the Rishram accounting office just as it opened on Friday morning. Frakit, as he identified himself, wore a small black goatee beard that brought his gaunt face to a point. His black hair was slicked back from his forehead, and he wore the Western suit favored by the Mituyan professional class. Frakit asked to examine the books to determine that the bundle of cash Mike had ready for him was the correct amount. As he went over the records of the rubber plantation, peering through thick glasses and using the inch-long nail of his right little finger to index the figures as he asked questions, Mike realized he was an accomplished accountant, and again he wondered and worried about the high quality of some members of the MFF. After the examination, Mike, with great distaste, personally handed Frakit ten percent of Rishram's payroll for the week.

Even as he did so, it was all he could do not to become physically sick with disgust and anger. He recalled only too well the way he and other Americans had reviled the French plantation owners in Vietnam for paying off the Viet Cong. "Why don't they stand up to the Commie bastards?" the Americans had asked. "We'll give them protection." But what kind of protection could an owner expect, Mike knew now, from a reluctant native army led by inept commanders?

Mike and Luna arrived aboard the *Promise* early in the afternoon after the first MFF payoff. It took all his self-control—and a few healthy jolts of Scotch—to get himself in hand. He was seated on the afterdeck smoking a long cigar when he heard himself hailed from the dock. A long, lanky young man with a thick shock of black hair and wearing a business suit was standing on the dock below. He carried a typewriter in one hand, an overnight bag in the other, and a camera slung over his shoulder.

"Request permission to come aboard, Mr. Forrester," he called out.

"Permission granted." Mike watched the man walk up the gangplank. He knew he was familiar but was uncertain of the name until they met at the top of the gangplank and then, from the portable typewriter, remembered who the young man was. "By God, Krakhaur, what brings you all the way up to Tiking?" He led the way to the afterdeck and motioned to a cushioned wicker chair. "How about a drink?"

Roger Krakhaur put down his typewriter and bag and sat back gratefully. "I'd love a gin and tonic."

Mike pressed a button and a white-jacketed steward appeared, took the order, and went off to fill it.

Mike had vaguely known Krakhaur in Tuyan City and before that in Latin America. He respected the newsman and admired the way his dispatches cut directly to the core of a situation. Tough, embarrassing, uncompromising—but scrupulously fair—stories were his specialty.

"The Public Affairs chief asked me to come up here," the reporter explained. "He's an old friend, Ted Baum, and I'm really doing him a favor. It seems the ambassador wants some stories to come out on the opposition candidates in this election, and Professor LakaLit at the University is a logical choice. So, for the good of the U.S. mission, I'm doing a story on how Premier KaritKi is determined to have a fair election and encouraging non-Communist opposition candidates to run for the first constitutional assembly in the history of the Republic of Mituyan."

"Interesting," said Mike. "I didn't realize the professor is actually a candidate. But then I keep out of politics here."

"He's running all right. Giving his first political speech tonight as a matter of fact."

"He asked Luna and me to come, but we thought it was a lecture, not a political speech."

The steward returned with Krakhaur's drink, which he accepted gratefully. "It could be quite a story."

Mike looked at him. "Afterward, the professor is having dinner aboard the *Promise* with us. You're welcome to join us if you want."

"Hey, I'd really appreciate that."

"As a matter of fact"—Mike smiled—"I think the old professor might be very pleased to have you in the party. He asked if he could bring along a young Mituyan lady who studied journalism in the graduate school. He was going to ask me about opportunities for her in your field, but now you can do the talking."

"Be happy to tell them everything I can," Krakhaur replied.

The sound of automobile brakes came from the dock. Mike glanced at his watch. "Luna's a little late getting back. She's planning a special Mituyan dinner for us tonight. Fresh crabs. You're in luck, Roger."

At five-thirty, Luna, Mike, and Krakhaur entered the auditorium of the Student Union, an imposing new building built with funds from the United States AID mission and carrying the name KaritKi Hall. It was an outstanding example of the nationwide efforts of the United States Country Team to build an awareness of the strong central government in Tuyan City. But when mild criticism of the building's name had led to a demonstration by campus liberals, it was quelled efficiently and brutally by the province police with the approval of the chancellor.

Professor LakaLit was waiting in the backstage anteroom and warmly greeted his ex-student. With him was a charming girl, a younger edition of Luna, whom he introduced as Alana, his prize student in journalism and government.

Krakhaur appeared stunned by her beauty. She was part Caucasian, giving her small, chiseled features a less fragile look than that of full-blooded Mituyan girls. Her figure was full; through the long slit skirt he could see beautifully proportioned legs with slim ankles and one perfectly turned firm thigh. It was several moments before he realized that everyone was looking at him with amused smiles.

"Roger has promised to answer all of Alana's questions about becoming a journalist," said Luna.

"I'm sure they will have much to discuss," the professor said cheerfully. "So if you will find your seats, I'll start my lecture promptly."

Krakhaur, suddenly the newsman again, asked, "Is this to be a lecture, or a speech in support of your candidacy?"

"A little of both," LakaLit replied. "You can report it in whatever way it strikes you. Incidentally, this is the first time the American press has covered one of my talks. I confess myself flattered."

"What's the talk to be about, Professor?" Luna asked.

Professor LakaLit had small, black, twinkling eyes, gray hair combed straight back, the wispy beard of a revered elder. Had he been wearing Oriental dress instead of a Western-style white linen suit and brilliantly colored patterned tie, like a masterpiece of some child's finger-painting, he could have passed for North Vietnam's Ho Chi Minh. "There is much trouble in Tiking Province, and more to come," he warned. "In fact all over the country there is trouble. Be careful. I receive warnings each day, from all sides, that what I tell the students must be what they dictate to me." The old professor cackled. "I am too old, too much of my life is behind me, to be afraid. So I will continue telling what I believe to be the truth until one side or the other carries out its threats."

"The government realizes you want the best for Mituyan," Luna protested. "And Dhuna loves you. She would never let KaritKi harm you."

The professor smiled sadly. "Things I thought could never occur in my country are happening." He placed a skin-and-bones hand on Luna's shoulder. "Now lead everyone out front. We will meet here after the lecture."

Mike and Luna, followed by Krakhaur and Alana, left and came out to find the auditorium almost full. Mike, looking around, suddenly clutched Luna by the arm. "Nowat's here," he said. "He seems to have a whole row of people with him. Frakit, who was at Rishram to extort the money today, is sitting beside him. At least two of the men are not Mituyan. I'll bet the North Vietnamese, Can, is there too. I wonder what kind of trouble they're getting ready to stir up."

Krakhaur was so absorbed in guiding Alana down the aisle that he failed to notice Mike's consternation.

Luna and Mike found four seats on the aisle a few rows behind Nowat's group. She shuddered slightly. "I remember him. I didn't like him when he worked for us."

When LakaLit finally stepped out from the curtains and stood behind the podium, a long, enthusiastic applause broke out from the thousand or more students in KaritKi Hall. The atmosphere vibrated with excitement; the professor, it was rumored, was going to talk some hard politics. Professor LakaLit stood facing his audience, an indulgent smile on his lips. He waited for the applause to die down, then began talking in English, the language of the University.

Mike divided his attention between the slight but emphatic professor and Nowat's group, who were listening intently. To Mike, who had heard Professor LakaLit before, the lecture at first sounded like an orderly summing up of his prior positions.

"Our history must always be kept in mind in these changing and difficult times," LakaLit was saying. "Mituyan has one of the oldest cultures in Asia; even before the Chinese to the north, we had centers of learning, a written language, a benevolent form of government, and we traded our silks and goods with many other nations.

"Then more than two thousand years ago the Chinese invaded us and occupied Mituyan. They set up their mandarin system here, much like our present and sometimes equally harsh province-chief system, and ruled Mituyan with an iron fist. All Mituyans were responsible to the mandarin in their territory. The mandarins in turn were responsible for turning over half the tax money to the Chinese prince in what is now Tuyan City. We resented this system, but the Chinese had an army of barbarians to keep us in bondage. Sometimes in one territory or another a Mituyan leader would gather men together, and in what we would call a guerrilla war the Chinese would be defeated.

"A great Mituyan guerrilla leader became King Barkoon the First when he defeated the Chinese in Tuyan City and for ten years ruled our capital city on the Tuyan River. But the Chinese were all over our country, and to prevent the complete destruction of Tuyan City, which had become one of the most important and beautiful in Asia, he made a treaty with the Chinese. Their mandarin system would govern Mituyan, but Barkoon would remain king and be the final authority on all things affecting his people."

The professor smiled sadly. "In modern-day terms this would be called a conflict of interest. The Chinese were content to bleed us economically and let Barkoon think he was running his own country. A war lord does not a good administrator make."

Professor LakaLit appeared to note a slight restlessness among the students in his large audience. "I know most of you are well aware of all I am saying, but I repeat it for a reason. Soon I will draw the present-day, the present-hour parallels."

LakaLit paused and his eyes roamed about the audience for ten seconds of silence that crystallized the attention of the room. "The first traders from England arrived here late in the seventeenth century and through cunning and force caused the mandarins to let them trade in Mituyan. All through the eighteenth century British traders and the British fleet were a continuing annoyance to the Chinese mandarins. In the meantime the Mituyan people were crushed in the quest for our rice, our raw materials, yes, and our meager buying power, by the mandarins and British competing with each other. And then the two things happened simultaneously that changed our entire history."

Again silence. Even though the students had studied the facts on which LakaLit's lecture was based, they now listened carefully to hear the parallels that their professor promised to make. Already he had made a dangerous accusation against KaritKi by intimating that the present system of government, the province-chief system, was as evil as the hated Chinese occupation that had made Mituyan and China traditional enemies.

"The British adventurer who became Lord Trowbridge went up to the mountains in the east and discovered the truth of a rumor he had heard among some of the hardy Mituyan traders. The mountain tribesmen, especially the largest tribe, the Groats, grew the finest opium poppies in the world. The dried tears of their poppies were of a quality never before known. Trowbridge immediately brought teams of adventurers up to the mountains to live with the Groats and encourage them to develop their poppy fields and trade exclusively with British interests. The British had to have the opium to save their China trade. In the nineteenth century the Chinese emperor decreed that China would trade with the British merchants only if they paid in silver and gold bullion. Soon China had most of the world's available supply. But when the British started introducing opium in quantities, half of China became"—Professor LakaLit found Mike and smiled impudently at him—"as the Americans say, hooked on the habit."

There was a rustle of laughter throughout the auditorium. The students worked hard to learn American colloquialisms and appreciated them. "So," LakaLit went on when the laughter subsided, "the Chinese merchants of Canton defied the Emperor's edict and traded tea and their precious bullion for opium. The Chinese merchants could sell every grain of opium they could get, and soon the silver and gold bullion began to come back to Britain. The Chinese did everything in their power to prevent the opium from reaching the British ships. The mandarins in Mituyan were ordered to force the British out, and many battles were waged in our mountains and along the routes to the ports.

"Just at this time Barkoon the Second had organized a guerrilla force, and while the Chinese were losing an army fighting the British and the fierce Groat tribesmen in the mountains, Barkoon's guerrillas attacked Chinese garrisons all around Tuyan City. It was about an even stand until Barkoon requested of London that Mituyan become a British protectorate. To protect their opium supply and thus their China trade and the vital balance of silver and gold bullion, the British were only too happy to send in their warships and Marines. The Chinese mandarins left Mituyan with their brutish army, and Barkoon became ruler under a British royal governor.

"Until World War II the country of Mituyan was actually run by the British, long after opium was no longer a factor, and rubber, tin, tea, and rice from our abundant paddies in the South became England's chief trading items. But it was during World War II that we in Mituyan realized that we did not need England, that Mituyan should be an independent country with its own government. Our awe of Caucasian troops and power was destroyed when we saw how quickly and easily the Japanese conquered the British. We saw Caucasians penned up in filthy cages like animals, degraded and humiliated by their Oriental masters, the Japanese. The Caucasians lost face that they will never regain in Asia. We know that a determined army of Asiatics can destroy a European army on our soil. Most of you in this room remember how successfully Mituyan guerrilla bands, yes, and the Groats, under British and American leadership sometimes, and just as often under the leadership of Mituyans, harassed the Japanese, forcing them to tie up large numbers of troops which otherwise could have been used to fight the Americans in the Pacific.

"Then, after the war, many of our trained and armed guerrillas, under such Mituyan leaders as KaritKi, his brothers Tarot and Poramat, and many others, went back up to the hills or into the jungles and canals of the Tuyan River Delta and waged guerrilla war against the British, until in 1950 the royal governor left and—for the first time since the dawn of our history—Mituyan was truly a country ruled by Mituyans. First King Barkoon the Sixth tried to rule us, but the council of elders and the army sent him off to exile where, as I read in the papers today"—the audience tittered—"he has just annexed another cinema actress and taken her off on a yacht for a demonstration of Mituyan prowess."

The audience laughed and applauded, though Nowat and his group sat impassive. When the reaction died down, LakaLit continued. "In the next seven years we had many premiers and military strongmen trying to form a government. As you are all aware, on several occasions the Communist party in Mituyan tried to gain power here but never succeeded, although it took the help of American military advisers and the training and equipment they gave our army, which each successive premier or military governor asked to be continued, to put down Communist guerrilla groups. Our country, unfortunately, is all too hospitable to guerrilla armies. Thousands of armed men can train and hide in the mountains where the Groats still grow and sell opium. Thousands more could live in the rich rice bowl of the Tuyan River Delta and never be detected. And in the jungles just a few miles from where we are now sitting large guerrilla bands can easily hide, hitting at will, as happened a few days ago at the district headquarters near Rishram.

"But I digress. At last, in 1957, with the help of General Xuat, KaritKi took over the government of Mituyan, and we have now a strong central government, backed by the economic and military strength of America. Next week Premier KaritKi celebrates a Decade of Progress, a decade of strong, continuous leadership. For the first time in the recorded history of our country, Mituyan has had ten years of self-rule. This in itself is an accomplishment."

A hint of agitation rippled through the audience. Mike noticed that Nowat and his people were looking around, carefully studying the reaction to what sounded like a tribute being paid to Premier KaritKi. Some of the students seemed on the verge of sharply questioning Professor LakaLit. But the professor calmly stared down the unrest until the auditorium was once again silent. He waited a few more moments and then continued.

"So much, temporarily, for our history. Now, let me review for a moment the words of a powerful, the most powerful, leader in Asia, Mao Tse-tung. It is his avowed purpose to make the entire world a Communist state through violent revolution. His first target is the entire continent of Asia, and he has been all too successful in some of our neighboring countries. However, Mao has been good enough to put his entire pattern of conquest down in black and white for us to read. I am reminded of the evil Western leader, Adolf Hitler, who also put in a book his entire and detailed plan for world conquest. Just as I believed Hitler meant every word he put in *Mein Kampf*, I believe that Mao and his political apparatus mean every word they say." Again LakaLit paused for effect, his audience intent on his every word.

"Mao put forth the three stages of how what he calls a 'war of national liberation' should be fought. Let's take a brief look at these three stages and ask ourselves whether we are observing the second stage now taking place right here in Mituyan, in this very province.

"His first stage is a war of propaganda. A Communist organization is formed. But this organization does not call itself Communist. The members of the Communist front group, many of them, do not even know it is Communist-dominated and dedicated to the destruction of a free society. During this first stage, as Mao points out, the climate for the second and more violent stage must be created. Stage One is characterized by setting minority groups against the majority of the people. Dissident people are marshaled together, their grievances magnified in their eyes by Communist leaders. And of course we find student riots and student dissidence stirred up."

The professor stopped for another dramatic pause. Some of the students twisted uncomfortably in their seats. "The demonstrations last week among the Buddhist students here against Anglican Church dominance of the government might well have been ignited by mischievous outsiders trying to cause trouble. And the same may also be true of the counter-demonstrations by the Anglican students."

Again there was a short pause as Professor LakaLit stared directly at Nowat. "I see in the audience several non-University people whom I saw involved in the anti-American demonstrations last week. There is nothing more dangerous at a large university like Tiking than for students to allow outsiders to incite them to demonstrate or riot.

"This spreading of discontent all over the country falls precisely into the Communist timetable of subversion. When Stage One is considered to be successfully underway with the political and terrorist cadres organized on a nationwide scale, Stage Two begins. Police stations and underprotected government officials are attacked, arms stolen, and a climate of fear as well as discontent sown. Stage Two is guerrilla actions, starting on a small scale but stepping up to larger encounters, ambushes of government convoys, attacks on government garrisons, terrorist activities in the cities, the systematic assassinations of province chiefs, district chiefs, village chiefs, and particularly the leaders of the academic community. Mao's strategy is to bring about a state of anarchy where no man dares represent the central government out in the countryside. Teachers, professors such as myself, are prime targets of the Communist assassins. That is one reason why I wanted to deliver this lecture to you this evening. I am gratified that such a large percentage of the student body is present to hear what could be one of my last talks."

In the silence that followed a buzz of excited whispering rustled through the hall. "Stage Two of the war of liberation lasts until the government forces are worn down by the guerrillas and the people in the countryside are sympathetic with the movement, or too terrified to oppose it. Then the Communist insurgency goes into its third stage, large-scale battles against the tired government until it falls and the insurgents take over. We saw the successful termination of Stage Three in a Communist war of liberation in 1953 when the Viet Minh drove the French out of North Vietnam after their remarkable achievement at the Battle of Dien Bien Phu. We also are still seeing Phase Three being waged in South Vietnam, and only because of three hundred thousand American combat troops there have the Communists failed to terminate successfully their 'war of liberation.'"

After a pause, Professor LakaLit smiled and said in bantering tones: "Now the Americans have another apt phrase—'It takes two to tango,' or dance.

"For a successful war of national liberation to be waged, the Communists must have a cause. There must be a focus of discontent. Where, in Mituyan, do we discover the cause of discontent? We find it in the Palace in Tuyan City!"

A gasp of surprise burst from the audience. There was the scraping of chairs as the students sat up straight. Open criticism of the government was rare. No student or professor could prove that anyone had been punished for political opposition, yet the fact remained that many people known to be overly anti-KaritKi had simply disappeared.

But Professor LakaLit continued imperturbably. "The Palace and Premier KaritKi manipulate the people of this country in precisely the same way the Chinese did during their long rule of Mituyan. Instead of mandarins we have province chiefs. The chief of this province, Yunakit and his superior, the overlord of the entire North of Mituyan, Poramat, have virtually life or death power over all of us. Poramat, through the province chiefs, exercises his power, taxing people at his discretion, working with landlords to help them collect increasingly higher rents, and he passes on the largest amount of American aid goods to the province and district chiefs who please him.

"If Poramat or the district chiefs wish to sell the American food, farm implements, brickmaking machines, building materials, cement, and the many other things sent to us by the American people to strengthen our economy, they may do so at will, and no one can criticize them without fear of reprisal. The people of Mituyan are no better off under KaritKi than they were under the mandarins and not as well off as they were when the British civil servants ruled Mituyan. We see no signs of such needed reforms as control on rentals and taxes, fair court trials, and a limitation on the personal power of the province chief to take what he will from a man or a family, whether it be tribute in the form of money, goods, or—and this is one of our country's most evil customs—slaves."

There was dead silence in the room. Many in the audience, especially the nonstudents who enjoyed no immunity whatsoever from the province chief, were terrified to be sitting and hearing what the venerable professor was so unexpectedly saying.

"Young men who must go into the military service, well-educated university men, know they have no chance of real advancement unless they have Palace connections. Our university graduates experience the same problems in the civil service. The good jobs and pay raises are given out through KaritKi's long outmoded mandarin system. How does a student who has studied the humanities, ethics, comparative religion here at Tiking, reconcile himself to what it takes to achieve advancement in the present government of Mituyan?"

During LakaLit's next pause, Mike watched Nowat nod and smile with those around him. Then the professor continued. "These things I have said to you, my students, the wrongs of the KaritKi regime, are what the Communists will repeat to the people to win them over to what they call the Mituyan Freedom Front or MFF. But what does the MFF really offer you, should it succeed in taking power in Mituyan? Look at what happened in North Vietnam and Communist China. Ruthless thought-control, so-called land reforms that have robbed every farmer in these Communist countries of the pride of developing his own land. Therefore his produce drops and he is punished, and his crops fall off further and he is shot. As I have taught you, the regulation by the Communist state of personal freedom completely destroys the concept of individual self-determination to which this university has been dedicated for hundreds of years, ever since it was merely an informal center of learning."

Now Nowat and his MFF members shook their heads darkly. Professor LakaLit's gaze fell serenely on them a moment before he went on. "What you students here must understand, if you are to save Mituyan from destruction as an independent country, is the way you must talk to the people everywhere and explain to them that although there is much corruption in high places in the Tuyan City government, it is the duty of citizens to resist the propaganda of Stage One and Stage Two of the Communist schedule of subversion. This is the duty you owe your country as educated men and women. With the help of the American programs to assist our country, the educated, intellectual people of Mituyan can peacefully succeed in stamping out the cruelty and dishonesty in our government without succumbing to the violent revolution preached by the Communists. You must never lie to the people. Admit the wrongs being done by their present government. But never fail to make the people realize that in the next few years with courage and work they can achieve our most important national objectives: a strong central government that truly means to make their lives better, education for their children, hospitals to care for the sick. An end to the oppressive province-chief system, substituting free elections in its place, is in sight!"

Professor LakaLit smiled benignly at his huge audience. "The truth is never popular with those about whom the truth is told. What I have said is factual. You must determine for yourself how you will react. But the time for apathy is over. The Communists or MFF are trying to force a violent revolution against our central government. That central government, which is still Mituyan's most cherished possession today, has become corrupt and disinterested in the people. The task of deep-thinking, patriotic Mituyans is to preserve a strong, but honest central government against the Communists, from whom the individual will never achieve individual freedom to think and live as he pleases. At the same time we resist the Communists, we must work for better government on all levels, from the lowest district-chief level to the high councils in Tuyan City. That is our job."

A stunned silence followed these words, and LakaLit allowed it to last for ten or fifteen seconds. Then he continued. "The hope of the people of Mituyan lies in an honest election of delegates to the constitutional assembly in Tiking. If this assembly can draft a constitution that will make the Mituyan government truly representative, we Mituyans will have achieved the goal our freedom-loving leaders have dreamed of for more than two millenniums."

After his pause for effect, LakaLit said calmly, "I am a candidate to represent the people of Tiking Province at the assembly. The man who will run against me, as yet unnamed by Poramat, seeks to preserve the corrupt government of Premier KaritKi; I seek to find the means to install a government whose only purpose is to serve the people. My opponent and I do have one thing in common. We both know that without a strong central government, all individuality and self-determination will be lost to every man and woman in Mituyan. I forthrightly ask everyone in this hall who believes in a Mituyan government dedicated to the betterment of all Mituyans to use his influence to send me as the delegate of this province to the constitutional assembly."

Professor LakaLit inclined his head slightly to his audience. "Thank you for your attention."

After a stunned few moments of silence, the students began applauding and shouting and stamping their feet. Then they stood up and continued clapping. They realized perfectly that their professor had told them the truth at the risk of his life. His words had been enough to mark him both for Communist assassination and arrest by Yunakit's Province Police or Poramat's Special Secret Police.

Mike and Luna looked at each other hopelessly. Then Mike shot a look at Nowat, who was stalking out of the auditorium followed by a grim-faced entourage. Luna followed his glance. The students were still clapping in a standing ovation.

Luna's face reflected the deep concern she felt for the professor she admired and loved. "Oh, Mike, what will happen to him now?"

Mike shook his head. "Let's go back and find him."

Pushing against the main stream of the crowd trying to get out of KaritKi Hall, Mike led Luna, Alana, and Krakhaur to the stage entrance. They walked up the steps and found LakaLit alone, waiting for them. The other members of the faculty and the chancellor, who had been with him before he started to talk, had disappeared.

"I'm afraid Professor LakaLit is not going to be a popular man to be seen with for a while," Mike remarked softly. Then, to Krakhaur: "If an honest election is permitted in this province, the professor will win—if he is around." The reporter nodded.

"I expect I'll be hearing from the chancellor tomorrow," said the professor. "His nemesis is controversy."

"Well, sir, you were certainly controversial," Mike replied.

"Oh, Professor, you were so brave," Alana cried. She went to him, put her hands on his frail shoulders, and kissed him on the cheek.

"For that I'll cheerfully go back and deliver another one," quipped LakaLit.

CHAPTER SIX

As he drove in the tiny Austin toward the photographic shop that was the cover of the Tiking headquarters of the MFF, Nowat had thc uneasy feeling that perhaps he was not really the chief political officer of Tiking Province. Beside him in the front sat the Chinese, Tzung, and in the back seat the Vietnamese, Nguyen Van Can, and Nowat's deputy, the Mituyan accountant Frakit.

There had been some truth in Mike Forrester's words that the MFF was dominated by foreigners. Certainly Tzung and Can had the power to give and countermand orders. But then they supplied weapons and technical knowledge that none of the Mituyan members of the Front possessed. The drive to the photo shop was a short one, and they all went upstairs to Nowat's office for a conference.

Li Tin was waiting for them. She had hot green tea ready and was preparing soup on the iron firepot as they entered. Nowat smiled at her. She was the one pleasure he allowed himself in his austere life as number-one MFF leader in the most important province north of Tuyan City. Both Tzung and Can eyed her with contempt. They got along without women. The movement was too important for any diversion of energy or interest, they told Nowat, but he refused to give up his half-Mituyan, half-Chinese mistress.

The MFF leaders sat down around Nowat's flimsy desk and over the tea began discussing Professor LakaLit's lecture. There was no language barrier; the Communist leaders in Peking and Hanoi chose their emissaries well. Both Can and Tzung spoke fluent English and Mituyan.

"What will you do about the professor, Nowat?" Tzung asked. In the northern provinces of Mituyan, Tzung, it seemed to Nowat, was the chief and Can his deputy, although it might be the other way around. There was no telling.

"Poramat will take care of him for us after tonight," Nowat replied with much self-assurance. "When he hears what LakaLit said about the province-chief system, he'll have him arrested." He grinned. "And that is the last that will ever be seen of Professor LakaLit."

The four men sipped the green tea thoughtfully. Then Can said, "The professor's words at the University were more damaging to our cause than they were to the Palace. What do you think, Frakit? You are in charge of student affairs."

"I will discuss it with my student agents tomorrow," the accountant replied. "It is true that the professor is very, very influential. He could have won many students from our movement tonight. He told the truth about the government and yet made his students start thinking it was better to support it than the MFF. When we hold our student discussion and criticism groups, it is much easier to deal with KaritKi's lies than with LakaLit's hard truth."

"We are fortunate, nevertheless," Nowat interjected. "Poramat only thinks in the present. Professor LakaLit has made serious accusations, and Poramat will take him and torture him to death before it occurs to him that the professor does the MFF more harm than the Palace."

"Now you make the mistake we try hard to teach you not to make," Can cut in irritably.

"Can is right. You make the worst error of all. You assume too much," Tzung took up. "From reading your dossiers I see that Premier KaritKi's pretty new wife was a student of Professor LakaLit. Poramat knows this. He would not hurt the professor without asking Palace permission. And, at the palace, Tarot would be consulted. Tarot is a devil at plots and counterplots. He would think many things out. It is impossible to make a guess, much less an assumption on what the Palace would do."

Nowat, properly chastised, glanced at Li Tin to see if she had heard, but if so she gave no sign, and kept concentrating on her cooking.

Having made his point, Tzung patiently began a series of questions, aided by Can, designed to make Nowat see the solution for himself and thus be the first in the group to express it. Nowat would become a fine party leader in Mituyan one day, Tzung realized.

"And what would the student reaction be if Poramat were to arrest Professor LakaLit tomorrow?" Can asked.

"They could easily be incited to an anti-KaritKi and anti-Poramat riot," Frakit answered automatically.

Tzung smiled, and he and Can sucked into their mouths the soup Li Tin had put before them. Like a sudden clap of thunder, the indicated course of action hit Nowat and Frakit simultaneously.

Nowat outlined to the admiring and enthusiastic Tzung and Can his solution to the problem, stressing the need for immediate MFF action. Even tonight, Nowat's guerrilla forces, expanded and better armed now thanks to the successful siege of the district headquarters, were ready to carry out an operation long planned and trained for.

Tzung and Can complimented Nowat on his strategic thinking. This time Li Tin heard her man being praised and smiled to him proudly.

Ten miles out of the port city stood the most distant Tiking Province Police station. It was a large, well-guarded, square stone building surrounded by two perimeters of barbed wire. The windows were small and the stones thick. A detachment of about twenty-five police officers operated the station. Eight men were always out on patrol. It was the responsibility of the Mituyan Army to patrol and keep order in the area beyond this station. The police station, as Nowat knew, was stocked with American weapons, including riot guns and tear-gas grenades.

In the several days since the last successful raid, Nowat's guerrillas had staked themselves out in the thick jungle surrounding the police station, watching it carefully, making note of all the guard positions and the two .30-caliber machine guns mounted in the second-floor windows. Mung, Nowat's deputy for guerrilla fighting, had checked the machine-gun positions contemptuously. Part of his training in the North had been to infiltrate South Vietnam and participate in guerrilla attacks there. Obviously no American advisers had been invited to inspect this station; they would have made the chief of this police station place the machine guns in slits a foot above the ground for grazing fire. This was the hardest to fight through in an attack. The first wave was invariably wiped out.

At one o'clock in the morning following Professor LakaLit's speech Nowat ordered Mung to begin the attack. The four .60-mm. mortars that Tzung had given them opened up first, not with white phosphorus as was customary but regular high-explosive rounds. Each mortarman put three shells in the air and then ran with his tube, his ammunition men following, to set up a new location before the first round burst inside the station. At the sound of the rounds bursting from the tubes, the machine guns opened up blindly. Twelve mortar rounds exploded against the station and all the men inside began firing into the darkness.

Twelve more mortar rounds crashed into the station, and this time one of the machine guns was silenced. Mung waited until his mortar-men had poured in four more salvos and then led a squad of black-clad guerrillas through the bush close to the front of the station.

At an order, three men with long bamboo poles filled with plastic explosive began inching them one behind the other along the ground toward the barbed wire. Other guerrillas were keeping the riflemen inside occupied on the opposite side of the square station. One pole was attached to the next, and soon a long unbroken tube of explosive-filled bamboo had been pushed under both barbed-wire perimeters and was fingering its way to the heavy iron main doors.

Mung, watching the progress, grunted in satisfaction. He gave an order and the improvised bangalore torpedo let go with a shattering explosion, blowing a lane through the barbed wire directly to the door. Instantly, a squad of guerrillas were up and rushing through the lane, machine guns and mortars covering them. Three of the shadowy figures were cut down, but the rest reached the door. While five guerrillas pegged grenades through the windows, two others placed a satchel charge of TNT against the door and darted away, hugging the wall of the building. Policemen leaned out the windows to get a direct shot down on the guerrillas. But they were picked off and fell outside to the ground below.

Nowat was not expected to be a combat leader, so he stayed close beside Mung. The concussion of a sudden ripping blast almost knocked Nowat over. He looked and saw the iron doors of the police station hanging open on their hinges. Mung screamed an order and, followed by the rest of his guerrilla band, rushed into the police station, all firing submachine guns from the hip as they came.

Nowat watched from a safe distance until all firing inside the station had ceased. He heard shouts of victory from Mung and the other guerrillas and ran from his position through the blasted path in the barbed wire and through the broken main portals. Dead policemen in white uniforms splotched with blood were everywhere. Two policemen, one, from his insignia, apparently the station chief, were cowering under the guns of the guerrillas.

"Let's hurry," Nowat urged. To the slightly wounded police chief, he shouted an order to open up the arms room. Fearfully the chief obeyed, leading Nowat, Mung, and four of the guerrillas to another iron door. The chief hesitated a moment at the imposing, barred-iron slab.

"Open it or we will blow it open and you with it!" Mung commanded. Quickly the chief pulled keys from his pocket and did as he was told. It required another key to open a padlock locking three crossbars across the door. The police chief said his deputy had the other key, which, in the fight, had been lost.

"He's hoping to delay us until reinforcements arrive," Mung cried. "We blow it open and kill you very slowly," he said to the police chief. Shaking with fear, the chief produced another key and released the crossbars. With a burst of automatic fire Mung blew the chief in half through the stomach at close range and, pulling the door open, led his men inside.

Nowat, behind him, flashed on a powerful flashlight. "You should not have killed him until he released the locks on the rifle racks," he chided.

Mung raced outside again, brutally ripped the key chain through the red pudding that was the midsection of the police chief, and returned to the arms room. Nowat took the sticky keys from Mung and, after several tense minutes of experimentation, managed to unlock the gun racks. Then the guerrillas quickly carried all the weapons out to the road. Already ox carts were arriving and other guerrillas were piling the weapons into them.

Nowat was searching for something more important to his immediate plans than weapons, and finally found what he was looking for—the supply room. With the help of several men he began cleaning out all the uniforms: boots; the shiny, yellow and red painted helmets of the Province Police; belts; insignia—enough equipment to outfit a detachment of men in the spit and polish uniforms of the Province Police. With the supply room empty, Nowat yelled orders to fire the station and return to the rally point two miles away in the jungle. Guerrillas instantly gunned down the surviving policemen.

It took the small demolition squad only a few moments, using thermite grenades and white phosphorus, to turn the station into a white-hot inferno and rush from the fiery destruction into the jungle.

A short while later, down the road toward Tiking, three sharp blasts rumbled through the night. Mung stopped a moment to grin at his superior. "Our mines knocked out the reinforcements. We could have killed the other policemen more slowly."

"Save it for Poramat," Nowat cried harshly. "We have very little time, and the hardest part of the job lies ahead of us."

CHAPTER SEVEN

"It's beautiful out here on the deck late at night when the city has finally gone to sleep," Luna said. "You two stay and enjoy yourselves, but Mike and I are exhausted."

"Thanks, Luna." Krakhaur laid his hand lightly on Alana's shoulder. "I'll see she gets home safely."

"You have the keys to the Land Rover?" Roger held them up. "Good. Don't forget to drive on the left." Luna waved and disappeared down the companionway to the master stateroom below.

"Let's walk up to the top deck," Krakhaur suggested. "We should be able to see clear out over Tiking." He was getting to be an old *Promise* hand. Mike had asked him to sleep aboard, and had even offered the use of the ship's single side-band radio in case Krakhaur wanted to file a story to Tuyan City.

"Hold onto me, Roger," Alana said, laughing lightly. "I'm not used to climbing steps like these." Roger gladly held her thighs with both hands as she climbed above him into the wheelhouse. They stepped out on the bridge and walked behind the wheelhouse to a high, small afterdeck, where they could look across Port Tiking.

They leaned on the rail, stared out silently for a few moments, and then Krakhaur said, "You really must come down to Tuyan City if you're seriously interested in becoming a writer. Sometimes you girls can get information out of a tough officer or sergeant that a man can never extract."

"I'd like to, Roger," Alana said softly. "But my mother needs me. All the time I've been in college I have worked as an interpreter and part-time secretary. My step-father would be very angry with my mother if I stopped bringing in money every week."

"That's a hell of a note. What kind of man is he?"

"He saved my mother and me from disgrace many years ago when my real father, an English officer, was killed by the Mituyan nationalist guerrillas. He died before he was able to marry my mother," Alana said matter-of-factly.

"That still doesn't give your step-father the right to dictate your life."

Alana turned to Krakhaur earnestly. "He let me have a good education. He was perfectly within his rights when he married my mother and gave her face once again to take all the money my father left to me."

"The Englishman really wanted to marry your mother?" Krakhaur asked, bewildered as always with Oriental logic.

"Oh, yes! He was waiting for his divorce when he was killed. He had a special insurance policy for me and drew all his money from England and put it into a Tuyan City bank. That way, if he were killed his English wife would only get his pension, and the rest would go to me."

"Then how does your step-father figure you owe him anything?" Krakhaur asked angrily.

"He gave my mother and me face when we had none," Alana said again.

Krakhaur thought a moment, then said, "If you could make even more money in Tuyan City, I should think your step-father would want you to go."

Alana considered the statement. "Yes," she said at last. "I think you are right. Even mother, I think, feels it would be good for me to leave the house, but she doesn't dare tell me. Do you really think I could make money in Tuyan City?"

"I know it," Krakhaur said. "I need a girl Friday. A leg girl."

When she looked at him questioningly, Krakhaur laughed and explained. "That's an Americanism for assistant, a girl who runs around researching news stories."

She too laughed. "A sort of junior journalist?"

"Yes. Exactly. How about tomorrow night? Can we go out then?"

She was about to answer when she gripped his arm and with her other hand pointed out over the darkened port city. "Look, Roger, way out there. A fire. A big one."

Krakhaur saw the bright glow off in the distance. "What's out there?" he asked.

"Nothing, just the road to the North. There's a police outpost about ten miles up the road."

"Must have been a guerrilla attack on the police station then," Krakhaur surmised. "I'd better borrow the Land Rover and go see what happened."

"Oh, no, Roger. It's too dangerous at night. They'll surely ambush you. The Mitcoms are getting worse every day."

"It's a story, and I'm the only reporter on the scene."

Alana put both arms around him compulsively, holding him with all her strength. "You don't think I should go?" He tried to keep the smile from his eyes and tone.

"Please, why do you want to take such a chance?"

Krakhaur looked into her alarmed eyes and then bent down and kissed her lips. She drew away, but slowly. He tried to kiss her again, but she turned her head aside.

"All right, Alana. I'll wait until dawn. But by daylight the guerrillas will be a long way from the scene."

"Maybe not. They get bolder every day." Alana appeared to realize suddenly she was holding Krakhaur, and let her arms fall. "Roger, I must go now. Please take me home."

Krakhaur preceded her down the iron steps and at the bottom reached up to help her gain the wheelhouse deck. She giggled merrily as his hands caught in the slit of her skirt. As her feet touched the deck he held her and kissed her again. This time she did not resist.

Krakhaur had set out for the police station on the route north as dawn was breaking. He returned to the *Promise* at nine A.M., and gave a complete report to Luna and Mike as he wrote his story.

"A complete massacre," he said, tearing a sheet from his typewriter. "Mike, you mentioned you could raise Tuyan City from here. Could I file this story?"

By the time Krakhaur had dictated his story over the ship's radio it was almost eleven—the time he was due at Professor LakaLit's house for an interview. "Besides," he told Luna with a smile, "Alana promised to be there." He asked the Forresters if they cared to sit in.

"I thought we had a pretty good talk with him at dinner," Mike said, "but Luna and I were both a little worried about his fatalism last night."

"What was that business about astrology and his life line and all that?" Krakhaur asked Luna. "I've seen Mituyan generals whose chief advisers are their astrologist and palmist, but I think of LakaLit as a Western man, even though he looks like a Mituyan venerable, God knows."

"He is a Buddhist—a reincarnationist, in fact," Luna replied. "We all tend to forget that, he's so Anglicized in every other way."

Professor LakaLit's quarters on the University grounds were at the end of the newest dormitory, built in traditional British institutional style. Since red bricks were unobtainable, the dormitories were constructed of white concrete block. Krakhaur, Mike, and Luna were surprised and slightly concerned to see a large crowd of students clustered near the professor's quarters. Studying the crowd intently, Mike could pick out two older men who seemed to be going around talking to the fast growing group of students.

"I wonder what's going on," Mike mused. "They seem peaceable enough; yet there are obviously agitators among them."

Professor LakaLit answered their ring and let them in.

"What's going on outside?" Mike asked.

LakaLit looked worried. "Some of the students are keeping a vigil over me. They are afraid I'll be arrested for what I said last night. I've begged them to go away or at least promise not to cause trouble if the police arrive with a request for me to accompany them to see Poramat. For some reason they are not doing my bidding. Very strange." He frowned. "Very unusual."

Alana was standing by the window and Krakhaur went over and put an arm around her waist. She turned slightly and smiled, though she appeared as worried as the professor.

"You worried me last night talking about what was written for you in your charts and palm," Luna was saying to LakaLit.

He smiled gently. "What is written is inexorable."

"But Professor," Mike said, "yesterday you were looking way into the future. You talked about running for election and all the ideas and reforms you hoped to incorporate into the new constitution."

LakaLit, wearing a Western sport shirt and slacks, and thong sandals, said, "I needed very badly to say to the students all that I did last night. Someone else will run on the principles I expounded. But I can't expect to get away with it." He shrugged. "I built up much good karma last night. I am happy. It will stand me in good stead along my way. You understand, Mike? We build up good and bad karma from one life to the next. A sort of celestial accounting system. Our evil deeds build up bad karma, which we pay for with much pain; good karma makes our future lives useful and pleasant."

There was a knock on the door and LakaLit went to open it. One of his graduate students entered, breathless. "Professor," he blurted out, "another police station was attacked last night. All the defenders were killed, and when a rescue column went out it was severely damaged and several men killed by mines!"

"That's right," Krakhaur confirmed. "I was there early this morning."

LakaLit shook his head and gave Mike and Luna a despairing look. "So quickly, the second stage of Mao's subversion proceeds. Now is the time the Americans must help us. Otherwise, they must either abandon us later, in spite of your President's assurances, or fight another large-scale war with much killing. There is still time if you work fast. Force KaritKi to make the reforms that will give the lie to Communist propaganda. The people are not lost yet in Mituyan, but they will go fast. You will see. We must hold the students. But they are young and impatient and want a better chance for their future without political favoritism. Only immediate changes can keep the people. Talk to your ambassador, Whittelsie, and see what he can do. Explain things to him."

"We'll try, Professor. We're going down to Tuyan City for the Decade of Progress celebration," Luna replied. "Mike and I will do our best."

"And I'll put the message in my stories," Krakhaur promised.

"Do it," LakaLit urged intently. "Luna, try again with Dhuna. She used to understand."

"I will see Dhuna and tell her."

"Tell her that time is running out."

The graduate student, Hahn, who had been looking out the window, cried, "Professor! The Province Police are here. I thought they were all out chasing the guerrillas."

Luna gasped. "Poramat wouldn't dare molest you. He knows you are one of our country's venerated scholars. He also knows you are beloved and respected by Dhuna."

"I do not believe Poramat would intervene directly on the campus of

Tiking University," LakaLit acknowledged. He went to the window and looked out. A twelve-man squad of Province Police in shining red and yellow helmets, white uniforms with red and yellow sashes, were drawn up outside. A bemedaled officer stood in front of his men. The students began jeering at the policemen.

"They're really armed to the teeth," Krakhaur exclaimed. "Riot guns, tear-gas grenades on their belts, two submachine guns, carbines. Looks like they're expecting trouble."

The agitators among the students were plainly discernable now. They were circulating through the ever increasing ranks. Even through the closed windows the shouts of the students could be heard. "This is what I was afraid of," LakaLit moaned. "It is incredible that Poramat would have sent his police on campus without permission of the chancellor, who would have called me." He listened to the mounting cries of the student mob, misery etched on his haggard face. "There will be a riot. I must try and stop it."

He strode toward the door, but Mike cut him off before he could open it. "Don't go out, Professor. Let me talk to the police and see why they are here."

"They are here, obviously, to arrest me. The quicker I go with them, the less chance of a riot and bloodshed." Before he could be restrained, LakaLit threw open his front door and at a leisurely gait sauntered toward the squad of policemen waiting at the end of his walkway.

Immediately a shout went up from the students, several hundred of whom were now gathered across the road from the policemen drawn up on the edge of LakaLit's lawn in two ranks of six, like a firing squad, facing the youthful mob. Krakhaur, unslinging his camera, and Mike followed behind the professor as did Hahn, Luna, and Alana. It was obvious that the students were being whipped up by experienced agitators. And every minute new students swelled the ranks.

Cries of "Leave our campus!" went up, but the white-uniformed police stood fast.

LakaLit went up to the officer in charge. "If you are here to take me with you, let us go before these youngsters get out of hand," he urged. "I'll go peacefully. I'll try to calm the students." He cupped his mouth with both hands and shouted, "Peace! I will go with them for a time, but I will be back before classes on Monday."

But the officer in charge seemed in no hurry to arrest Professor LakaLit, Mike noted. In fact, he deliberately ignored the professor's words, letting the student mob grow louder and uglier.

Cries of "Hit the Province Police!" and "Down with Poramat!" rang out.

Mike clearly saw a weathered agitator pick up a rock and throw it at the ranks of the police. It landed at the feet of the front rank, which stood impassively. Another agitator threw a stone—and then the students began throwing clods of dirt, stones, books, whatever they had.

"Will you go? Take me with you, but go!" LakaLit implored.

Krakhaur snapped pictures, expecting to have to fight the police to keep his camera; he was amazed to see the police pose for him, aiming their weapons into the mob of students. The shouts of the students increased and then the mob, swelled to hundreds now, began moving menacingly toward the twelve white-uniformed men.

Mike wondered why more Province Police hadn't arrived to break up the riot. Of course, most of them would be pursuing the guerrillas who had wiped out the police post, but still there should be enough men on duty to keep order throughout the city of Tiking.

"Mike, Mike!" Professor LakaLit suddenly shouted over the cry. "Something is wrong. These are not—"

The professor sagged under a backhanded blow by the officer in charge. This was the signal for a full-scale charge on the police by the students. The police, at their leader's command, brought their weapons to bear on the students. The leader glanced at Krakhaur, turned to give him a better camera shot, and aimed a pistol at the students. The mob surged forward, screaming epithets against KaritKi and Poramat and the government. Suddenly, the riot guns blasted out a dose of light buckshot. Blood began pouring out of the faces of the front rank of students, red spots appeared on their light shirts. But the mob was uncontrollable now. Next, the men in white opened up with their carbines, killing and wounding more of the rioters. Professor LakaLit, holding his hand up, was trying to shout something at the students pushing toward him.

"No," he cried feebly. "Stop! . . . all a terrible mistake. . . ."

Mike tried to rush to the professor's side but was clubbed to the ground with a pistol barrel by the leader of these men in Province Police uniforms. He tried to pull himself to a sitting and then a standing position, vaguely aware of Luna's frantic cries. Now the men in white had a sagging Professor LakaLit between them and were leading him away from the campus. The students, realizing that real bullets were being fired and that comrades were dead and dying, fell back.

Mike's head pained him intensely and blood flowed into his eyes, but he tried to follow the police squad.

The agitators among the students continued their harangues. "Do not let the Poramat police take the professor!" they shouted. "We will die if we must, but resist the tyrant's police!"

Led by the professional inciters, the emotionally charged mob of students, many hundred strong, rushed the police. The professor, bleeding from his mouth, half dragged and half stumbling along weakly, tried to motion the students back. He was totally ineffectual. The mob was now under the control of the highly trained riot manipulators. As the screaming students surged close to the left flank of white-uniformed men, riot guns were leveled at them. As Mike watched, the agitators seemed to melt away, and when the front row of youths were within five yards the command was given. The guns cracked and a dozen students fell to the ground. Another row of frenzied young Mituyan students stepped over their comrades and closed in on the twelve supremely confident, unhurried men in police uniforms and their disdainful officer in charge.

Deliberately, it seemed, the men also allowed them to come within a few feet, so that the students were reaching out, almost clawing the white uniforms, when the two ranks quickstepped ahead, releasing Professor LakaLit, who staggered into the arms of the advancing mob. Shouts of "Hit the police!" rang out from the rear of the students, and the crowd pushed on.

Suddenly, on sharp command, the two ranks turned; the front rank dropped to one knee, the second aimed over their heads. Eleven rifles and a submachine gun loosed a splitting volley. Then the men of the rear rank smartly pulled tear-gas grenades from their belts, bit out the pins, lobbed them into the crowd, turned into the wind and double-timed, still in two perfect ranks, to a covered two-and-a-half-ton truck. In seconds the last white uniform disappeared and the truck had sped off.

Krakhaur, snapping pictures as fast as he could, was astonished at how over and over as he was about to take a picture and the stability of his camera was threatened, someone in the swirling mob—at times it looked like a flying squad—knocked students to the ground before they could jostle his arm. His film was loaded with pictures of bloody students, Province Police firing into the crowd; then, unbelievably, just as the Province Police fired their final volley a pathway opened for him and he found himself shooting pictures of the fallen Professor LakaLit.

Mike tried to rush to the scene of the final volley but was sickened, his eyes streaming, from the tear gas. Uncontrollably he ran from the clouds of gas back toward Luna at the professor's quarters. He could hardly see where he was going and Luna rushed to him and led him behind the building. The only cure for tear gas is to fight from rubbing the eyes and try to stare into the wind, he knew, letting it blow the gas out of the nostrils and eyes. Mike turned his red, fiercely irritated eyes to the wind and waited.

"Mike, Mike," Luna wept. "Even for Poramat, it was so unbelievably monstrous. How could he have ordered his men to do such a thing?"

Finally, Mike's eyes cleared. "Water, Luna!" he gasped.

Luna rushed back to LakaLit's quarters and brought him a glass of water. He drank some, dashed the rest in his face, shook his head, and again made for the spot where he had last seen the professor.

The carnage was appalling. Students, bloody and vomiting from the gas, were lying on the street. Others, hit by rifle and machine-gun bullets, were dead or dying. The unwounded students stumbled in shock from the bloody scene.

Then a new detachment of Province Police arrived. At the sight of them, the wounded who could dragged themselves away, bleeding. Others groaned and, holding up supplicating hands, begged to be spared.

In the center of this slaughter Mike found Krakhaur, untouched by the violence and still snapping pictures. Professor LakaLit was lying among dead students who had been in the van of the mob. His shirt was plastered in vermilion to his chest.

"How did you get here?" Mike cried.

"I don't know," Krakhaur replied in bewilderment. "I don't know how I ended up here, out of the tear gas, perfect camera angles of everything."

Both of them looked down at Professor LakaLit. His eyes were open, staring up, a look of utter shock on his face. Death vastly magnified his frailty. A Province Police officer strode toward them.

"What happened?" The dumfounded, white-uniformed, bemedaled officer asked. "Who did this?"

"We need doctors and ambulances more than police," Mike snapped. "See what you can do. And I wouldn't go walking around here in that murderers' uniform, if I were you."

"Oh, my God!" the officer cried. He turned and double-timed back to his men. In the distance the wailing of sirens was a welcome sound. There were many wounded to care for, some who would not live without immediate attention. Mike, with no bandages, could do little but try to comfort the more seriously wounded as Krakhaur continued photographing the scene. A handkerchief in Mike's pocket served for a tourniquet to stop the bleeding in one boy's badly torn forearm. Most of the youths, Mike grimly noted, had been shot in the chest or stomach. Deliberate aim by the firing squad.

Ambulances began to arrive, and faculty members looked on sadly as the dead and wounded students were taken away. The chancellor of Tiking University, his face ashen, head bowed, stood silently watching the tragic sight. It was beyond understanding! Mike turned to Krakhaur. "You'll want to file this story right away, I guess."

Krakhaur didn't answer at first. Then, slowly, "I'm not sure what I saw. I've covered riots all over the world. This is the first time a wild-eyed mob actually made it easy for me to take pictures. And the police, it was as though they staged the thing for me. Something's wrong."

"That's what the professor was trying to call out," Mike mused. "My God! In the middle of that horror I wasn't thinking but—"

"Got you!" Krakhaur replied. "I'm going to Province Police headquarters and check this thing out."

"It had to be the Mitcoms wearing the Province Police uniforms they seized in last night's raid." Mike looked at the torn bodies around him.

"I'll meet you back at the *Promise*." Krakhaur held out a roll of film. "Keep this for me," he said, putting a new roll in his camera. "I'll let them confiscate a blank roll. For once when I write the truth it's going to save KaritKi's ass, but his cops wouldn't understand. Ask Luna to take care of Alana." With a determined set to his jaw he added, "I'm taking her back to Tuyan City with me."

PART II

LIVE OR DIE WITH KARITKI

CHAPTER EIGHT

PREMIER KARITKI's Decade of Progress celebration had drawn to Tuyan City a broad section of the Far East-based journalists of the Western world. Bureau chiefs and reporters from Hong Kong and Tokyo swelled the ranks of the permanent Mituyan press corps, promising wide coverage of KaritKi's tenth anniversary as Premier. The headlines generated all over the world by Roger Krakhaur's exclusive eye-witness report of the Tiking University massacre had added hard news value to Premier KaritKi's celebration. What kind of progress had been achieved when eleven students and a prominent professor running for political office could be shot dead on a university campus—apparently by the local police?

Krakhaur was the acknowledged dean of the youthful Tuyan City press corps, and as befitted his status he gave a party at his villa in honor of the visiting members of the press. His villa had a wide front lawn, and a high wall protected it from the street. The main room had been thrown open and the guests moved from the lawn into the living room, where Krakhaur's major domo supervised several lesser servants who served Mituyan delicacies and drinks.

"Good living here in Tuyan City, right, Roger?" Ben Morris observed. He was a good-natured bear of a man who had just arrived in Tuyan City as manager of the United Press office.

"You'll learn to like it, Ben," Roger replied. "When do you get the new direct Teletype?"

"We should be sending to New York via Tokyo in a few weeks. Why don't you get Star Syndicate to become a UPI client? I'll have six hours a day to send out copy. It would be a hell of a lot easier for you to file with me than through the Tuyan City Cable office."

"Damned right, Ben," Krakhaur agreed. "Mayna and the rest of the Palace gang read everything that goes through the cable office and sometimes hold up copy forty-eight hours."

Mike Forrester walked over to his host, and Krakhaur introduced him to Ben Morris. Morris looked at him with interest when he heard the name. "I've been wanting to meet you, Mr. Forrester. My predecessor suggested I do a story on you."

Mike shook his head and smiled. "Sorry. I'm not good copy."

Ben Morris shrugged, and then Alana caught his eye. The beautiful Eurasian girl was causing a mild sensation; she was gracefully making her way toward them through the throng of reporters, many of whom tried to stop and engage her in conversation. "There's nothing more lovely in the world than these half-Mituyan, half-Caucasian girls," Morris commented.

"Mike," Alana said, holding out her hand, "I'm so glad you could come. Where's Luna?"

"After the long, hot drive from the tea property, she's holed up in the air-conditioned bedroom of our apartment."

"Oh, I'm sorry. I wanted to tell her all about my quick trip from Tiking."

"Come over and see her tomorrow. As a matter of fact, we thought you'd be living at the apartment, so we made plans to stay with Luna's mother and father."

Alana smiled shyly. "It's so convenient here at Roger's villa. I have a lovely little two-room apartment all to myself. This way I'm always ready when Roger needs me—to cover a story. But if you don't mind," she added hastily, "I've been going over to get my mail at your place. My mother and friends in Tiking think I'm staying there."

"Your secret's safe with us."

After talking for a few minutes with Ben Morris, who assured her that if Krakhaur or the Star Syndicate was not treating her properly he'd give her a job at his office, Alana excused herself to see to the other visiting correspondents.

As Mike happened to glance toward the gate leading from the street to Krakhaur's lawn, he was jolted. The girl who was entering wore her blonde hair long; her regular, chiseled features might have given her an air of aloofness were it not for a certain *joie de vivre* that seemed to radiate from her. Suddenly Mike was transported from the party to a Sunday afternoon during the summer of 1947. He was waiting to discuss an investment with a client, Ernest J. Martin, and had been shown out to the pool terrace. There he found a beautiful girl with obvious breeding, sunning by the pool.

The long fairway of the Martin's par-five one-hole golf course stretched out behind her, the red brick ell of the elegant Georgian home enclosed one side of the flagstone pool terrace. The girl came toward him, smiling warmly, and held her hand out, introducing herself as Adrian Martin. Before the day was out Mike knew he wanted to marry her more than anything else in the world. And she had expressed delight and keen interest in knowing a man who "really did things"—such a change from the men she met at the society balls.

That Adrian had changed after they were married did nothing to alter the fact that for a time they had loved as only youth can love. Though his love for Luna was happy, contented, spiritual, the pure physical and emotional force of first love comes only once.

As the blonde girl slowly walked among the guests at Krakhaur's party, Mike was surprised that anyone could have revived that scene so remote from his present life and thoughts.

"You're lucky to have a leg girl like Alana," Morris was saying to Krakhaur with undisguised envy.

"Hey, Roger, you've been holding out on us," Mike said. "Who's that blonde?"

Krakhaur followed Mike's stare. "Oh, Marlene Straltz. German girl. Newcomer to the press corps."

"She's stunning." Mike's eyes followed the girl as she came toward them.

"She's all right," Ben Morris allowed. "But give me one of these half-and-halfs any time."

"Depends on what you see every day," Mike retorted. "That girl's a *reporter?*"

"Sort of." Krakhaur chuckled. "She writes for some German and Swiss magazines. The tall, white-haired Hun with the dueling scars across his cheek is her father, Herr Straltz. He's head of the West German trade mission in Mituyan, which makes him a hell of a lot more important than the German ambassador. Straltz got the Mituyan government to go Volkswagen for its entire bus-transportation service."

Now the magnificently proportioned girl with long blonde hair hanging in coils just above her shoulders was standing in front of them. She wore her dress in Mituyan style, and the rustling silk skirt slit all the way to the upper thigh revealed the most beautifully turned leg Mike had ever seen, bare of stocking and satin smooth up to the knee. Above, he noticed exciting white peach fuzz barely visible against her rich tan.

"Mr. Krakhaur," she said holding out her hand, "I hope you do not mind that I bring my father."

"We are honored," Roger replied, holding Marlene's hand and bowing to Herr Straltz. Then he introduced Marlene to Mike, Ben Morris, and Ted Baum, who had appeared from nowhere.

"Mr. Baum," Marlene said, "yes, it is you I must see."

"Any time," Baum said agreeably.

"I have much trouble with your office. Oh, the men, and those nice officers are very gallant, but they do not help."

"What is the trouble, Fraulein Straltz?"

"The American Information Office does not give me"—she paused—"what you call? Credentials? I must have them to go out and cover the guerrilla war."

Baum turned to Herr Straltz. "You would allow her to go out into the countryside where the war is going on?"

"Marlene Straltz is well-known journalist in Germany," Herr Straltz said, looking proudly at his daughter. "The reason she comes to visit me is to write about what happens here. I am happy she comes. But she will stay only if she can write for her magazines and newspapers."

"So far I write about the politics and the diplomats. Last week I interview Madam Mayna and send beautiful story to Germany. But I must go to see what you call the boondocks. I must write about the fighting." She looked enviously at Krakhaur. "You write magnificent story on the massacre. That is the kind of story I must write."

"All thanks to Mike Forrester," Krakhaur replied. "If you want to write about the boondocks, talk to Mike."

Marlene turned the full force of her personality and beauty on Mike. "I love to talk to you, Mr. Forrester. When you have time, I will be happy if you tell me everything about the boondocks. I want to know the people, the country, and the Americans who work and fight here to keep Mituyan free."

Mike couldn't help himself. The sight of her golden hair and chiseled features—that might have given anyone else an air of coldness—reawakened old excitements in him.

"It will be a pleasure to tell you, and for that matter show you, everything I know about Mituyan," he replied, completely under her spell.

Ben Morris guffawed. "Bet he never offered to do that for any other newsman in this country."

"Do you have a United States Department of Defense clearance, Fraulein Straltz?" Baum asked.

"No, sir. I come direct to Mituyan from Germany. Frankfurt I live." She looked at Baum, her sparkling blue eyes sad now. "I don't even get into the five o'clock briefing the Public Affairs Officer gives every day."

"You're lucky, dear," Ben Morris said. "All they do is confuse you." He grinned at Ted Baum. "How does it feel to an old bureau chief to be in charge of the local Liar's Academy?"

"We're making changes." Then to Marlene, Baum said, "Tomorrow is Sunday, but come in and see me in the morning anyway. I'll try to get you accreditation papers."

"Come on up to the veranda now, all of you," Krakhaur said. "I promised to answer a few questions for the tourists."

Marlene, already questioning Mike, followed with the others. While a white-jacketed waiter served them drinks, Krakhaur took his place in front of the map of the Republic of Mituyan. "OK, fire away," he invited.

The questions came fast. "Any chance these elections won't be rigged?" a reporter called. "What was the reaction at the embassy to the massacre story?" a bureau chief asked. "Is this Communist insurgency real? If so, is it under control the way KaritKi and the embassy claim?"

Krakhaur held up a hand. "I'll try to answer those three questions first." He smiled broadly. "Official reactions? Let's see. In the first place, by official request of Ambassador Whittelsie relayed to me through Ted Baum I went up to Tiking to write a constructive story about the coming elections, showing that the government here wanted them to be fair and representative. Since Professor LakaLit seemed to be anti-KaritKi, the fact he was being allowed to run, proved, to the embassy anyway, that the elections would be honest."

Krakhaur looked around the crowd of visiting journalists and smiled again. "Well, yesterday Ted Baum and I went back to the embassy. Needless to say, Whittelsie and General Macker forgot that they had asked me to go to Tiking. I believe Macker has chewed out poor old Ted most severely for sending me right into a controversial story.

"Whittelsie asked me why I didn't get with the program and told me I was damaging his efforts to work with KaritKi for peace in Mituyan. And as for Macker, America's answer to Chamberlain's black umbrella, he said that the sensationalism and yellow journalism of my stories, and those of the whole press corps here, was giving the world the wrong impression of that George Washington of Mituyan, that lover of the common people, that pillar of integrity, Premier KaritKi. He ended by bleating that the Tuyan City press corps is making it look as though we're in a big war in Mituyan—and worse, that KaritKi and his American advisers are losing it! There was some talk that the Premier might expel me for the story, but my answer was that if KaritKi wanted to hold up the three quarters of a million dollars a day he's getting in U.S. aid, pending a full investigation of his regime, kicking me out is a hell of a good way to accomplish it. And you know the pompous answer I got from Macker?"

Krakhaur paused, enjoying his role as dean of the press corps. "Macker said, and I quote, 'the regime of Premier KaritKi will bear any amount of impartial investigation.' Whittelsie agreed emphatically."

Krakhaur smiled wanly. "So to sum up official reaction to my story on the so-called Tiking massacre, my sources tell me—and only our liaison with the U.S. Country Team, who is here tonight, can confirm it—that Ambassador Whittelsie has requested Ted Baum to request USIA to request the White House to request the Star Syndicate to find another place of exile for me—Mituyan is too sensitive these days." There was raucous laughter.

"Do you figure on any more trouble in Tiking during the celebrations in Tuyan City?" Krakhaur was asked.

"I'll give that one to my leg girl, Alana," Krakhaur replied. There were some appreciative whistles. "For the past week, posing as a student, she has attended meetings at the University in Tuyan City and listened to the speeches. Tell them what you think, Alana."

"I think we will see trouble. There is a Buddhist bonze we call the Mad Monk of Tiking. Han—that means Reverend—Li Phang is preaching that the Anglican KaritKi regime is keeping young Buddhists from advancing in the government and military and even in industry. The Communists are always trying to make trouble at the University and cause the students to riot. Sometimes I think that the Communists and Buddhists are working together."

"Are you a Buddhist?" someone asked.

"I am an Anglican."

"Maybe the Buddhists *are* being discriminated against," a voice called out.

"I don't think so," Alana replied. "It is a matter of education, and the ratio today of Buddhists to Anglicans in the University is the same as in the entire country—about seventy-five percent Buddhist, fifteen percent Anglican and the rest Catholics and others. It is true that when this was a British protectorate the Anglicans were favored, but not any more."

"What's with this broad, Mayna?" a visiting reporter asked. The question must have been on almost everyone's mind, for there was a chorus of speculative comments about the Premier's sister-in-law.

"What do you mean, what's with her?" Krakhaur replied. "Do you mean, does she really run the country? Well, she has a great deal of power. Her husband, Tarot—or Political Counselor to Premier KaritKi, to give him his full title—controls the secret police. Mayna is supersensitive about what appears on Mituyan in the U.S. press, and she gets her husband and KaritKi upset over stories they might otherwise ignore. All of us regulars here have been threatened obliquely and sometimes pretty directly when we file a story Mayna doesn't like. She makes the cable office send her a copy of every story we file, and while the Palace doesn't exactly censor the stories, they can hold them up for a couple of days. That's one reason why UPI is putting in its own Teletype to Tokyo."

"The rumor is she's having an affair with a certain high American official here," someone called out.

"Oh-oh, the party's getting rough," Krakhaur said, beginning to walk away from the map.

But the reporters wouldn't let him go and questioned him for another twenty minutes on everything from corruption in the government to the opium trade and the status of the U.S. military in Mituyan.

Finally, in answer to several questions about the high-ranking members of the U.S. mission in Mituyan, Krakhaur said, "OK, to sum up the Country Team—and needless to say this is off the record—you bureau chiefs had better start figuring who's going to cover the war here for you next year, because we're sure as hell going to have one. Talk to a man like Mike Forrester, who's here tonight. He knows what we're up against trying to keep Mituyan from going Communist. It's interesting how much and how fast you learn about a country when you have all your money invested there."

Krakhaur looked at the people gathered around him, spotted Ted Baum, and then addressing his guests, said, "One last thing and then I'm going to stop talking. Ted Baum, as we all know, is basically one of us. He's doing his best to help improve the information system here in Mituyan. May I suggest we give him all the cooperation possible. He has a lot of press releases that his fellow members of the U.S. mission here in Tuyan City expect him to get placed in the newspapers at home. If each of us would take one of these little gems of optimistic observation and get it printed, at least in part, it will help our old colleague one hell of a lot and make his job of helping us a little easier." Krakhaur waved at the Public Affairs Officer. "Right, Ted?"

"Right. And thanks, Roger. We start passing out the gems at the five o'clock briefing tomorrow. We work seven days a week here."

The crowd began thinning out. As Ben Morris left he stopped beside Marlene, who was still talking to Mike. "Honey," he said, "if you come across any stories of immediate importance, I'll buy them and send them over the Teletype direct to New York. I'll even give you a by-line."

"Oh thank you, Mr. Morris. I come see you if I get a scoop."

"There you go," he patted her shoulder.

"When the mob clears out," Krakhaur said, coming up to Mike and Marlene, "why don't the four of us go to Frenchie's for supper?"

Mike gave Marlene a questioning look. "I love to," she said without hesitation.

CHAPTER NINE

"I THOUGHT ALL the foreign correspondents go to the roof bar at the St. George Hotel," Marlene said to Krakhaur as Mike started up the Land Rover.

"Sure, if they're interested in hashing over old stuff with the competition," Krakhaur said. "But for fresh news, the only place is Frenchie's, the Knave of Spades. It's a bar and restaurant inhabited almost entirely by Special Forces, our green berets. You know who they are, Marlene?"

"Of course I know," she replied.

"It's also a hangout for the spooks and hoods that work for JRB and CIA," said Krakhaur. "As a matter of fact, this is the only bar in town Jack Cardinez will go into."

"I know him," Marlene said. "He is friend of my father."

"He's also number-two spook in the country," Krakhaur said.

"Who is spook number one?" Marlene asked.

"Sorry, Marlene, that's officially classified. Although it's no secret that some of us favor Filmore Dickerson, who's officially assistant deputy ambassador. One reason is that he doesn't seem to do anything much."

Mike parked and they all got out. "I assume Frenchie knows you, Roger."

"Damn right she does," he said, taking Alana's arm. "Y'know she doesn't let every reporter in. But I get a lot of stories out of this place."

"I never know about here," Marlene said excitedly. "Maybe I get exclusive story for my German papers."

"The big thing is to know when *not* to file a story you may pick up here," Krakhaur said. "That's why they let me in."

The Knave of Spades was presided over by a shockingly pink-haired, busty, overweight, middle-aged English woman of indeterminate origin, who, for reasons known to few, was called Frenchie. The pretty hostesses arrayed along the bar and the blowzy proprietress well understood their responsibility to the elite and specialized clientele they served. They knew that many of the men who came here were probably on covert missions in Mituyan and other parts of Asia.

Frenchie greeted Krakhaur warmly, shook hands with Mike whom she knew slightly, and then eyed the two girls. The blonde would cause a sensation and take everyone's eyes from her own girls, she thought irritably. Frenchie did not like her customers bringing their own girls to her establishment; she made a large part of her profit from the sale of the girls' favors. But Krakhaur was a good customer and Mr. Forrester a prominent citizen.

She led the way past the bar, at which some thirty Americans in civilian clothes were buying drinks for the hostesses consisting of thimbles full of cold tea at fifty cents each and talking to or holding hands with the enticing, almond-eyed bar girls. As Frenchie feared, every man in the place turned and stared at Marlene, forgetting her girls. Sometimes after seeing a beautiful Caucasian girl, a man would not talk to a bar girl for a whole evening.

Krakhaur enjoyed the scene thoroughly. "There're a few officers that still won't talk to me because I'm a writer," Krakhaur said to Mike. "But tonight there isn't a guy in this joint who doesn't wish I'd invite him over." He waved at the occupants of a corner table. "I told you the top spooks hang out here. There's Jack Cardinez, Colonel Fritz Lawton . . . and damned if old Charging Charlie Prescott isn't with them."

Mike nodded at a surprised Lawton.

"I'll bet there's some fancy plotting going on over there," Krakhaur said.

Mike turned to Jack Cardinez, whom he hadn't seen for five or six years, maybe longer. He must be about fifty now, Mike mused. But his hair was still black, his face lean without a sign of jowl or double chin. And those bright blue eyes were still startling in that swarthy face.

"Remember Cardinez from your operations in Domania, Mike?" Krakhaur asked.

"Yes. And Whittelsie too."

"It looks like everybody knows everybody else from somewhere before in American foreign service," Marlene observed. "Do you two know each other from another country?"

"We were in South America, Republic of Domania . . . about eight years ago, wasn't it, Mike?"

"That's right. Whittelsie was acting ambassador, Jack Cardinez was the CIA station chief, you were covering the country for one of the wire services, and I had a land-development deal going. Whittelsie as usual was making a mess of things by doing nothing. The Commies were about to take over, and, of course I was late spotting them and desperately trying to save what I could for my investors." Mike paused and glanced again over at the corner table. He guessed that Cardinez and Lawton were talking about him.

"Fortunately," Mike went on, "Cardinez had guts and experience. They say he arranged for the assassination of that colonel who almost made himself a Communist dictator. Then he helped the president, who was strictly pro-American, get a big AID program going, and Domania became the strong, self-sufficient democracy it is today. And incidentally, I came out very healthy financially."

Mike looked at Krakhaur thoughtfully. "Cardinez saved the situation, but Whittelsie got all the credit. I've always meant to ask why you gave all the play to Whittelsie? He should love you to this day. Your reporting advanced his career." Mike smiled mischievously. "Did it ever occur to you, Roger, that you may be personally responsible for Whittelsie's being given this important post?"

Krakhaur made a grimace. "Too damned often: I get sick thinking about it. But we're boring the girls."

"No, no, please!" Marlene said emphatically. "What *did* happen? I am very interested."

One of the bar girls arrived, and Krakhaur ordered drinks all around.

"I've never told anyone that story," Krakhaur said when the girl left with the order. "I guess there's no reason why I shouldn't, except it shows what a naive young reporter I was in those days. It's really a Jack Cardinez story."

"Seems I'm collecting Jack Cardinez stories these days," Mike said wryly.

Krakhaur gave him a quick, searching glance. "That sounds like a story in itself." But when Mike made no response, he went on. "I had some good connections in Domania. It didn't take me long to find out that the cultural attaché, one Jack Cardinez, was the CIA station chief. The day those bandits held up, robbed, and killed Colonel Arbenz—he was no relation to the Communist dictator of Guatemala, by the way, although I always thought he was a brother or cousin or something—I had the story and went to Cardinez for more information. I thought I might get a sidebar to the story from him."

Krakhaur smiled ruefully and shook his head. "Remember, I was young and brash and filled with the power of the press. Naturally, Cardinez said he didn't know anything about coups and Commies. He said he was only interested in an exchange of students between Domania and the United States. So then I told him what I knew about the assassination of Arbenz. No bandits had the machine guns or the kind of high-performance car it took to go after the colonel's high-powered new staff car, overhaul it, and blast him.

"I pushed Cardinez pretty hard, and finally he stood up from his desk. I'll never forget it. He stared down at me. I stood up too, and of course I'm taller, but that didn't make me feel any better when he said his piece." Krakhaur winced at the memory. "Those ice-blue eyes in that Latin face. Look at him." Both girls stared across at Cardinez.

" 'Mr. Krakhaur,' Cardinez bit out at me, 'you're kind of new at this foreign-correspondent business. Now let me give you a quick word of advice. We are in a dangerously sensitive position in Domania today. If I was what you say I am—which I'm not—and I had been behind what you intimate I was behind, namely the death of Colonel Arbenz—which I was not—and I thought you were going to file a story about it—which I know you are not—then in the best interests of my country I would arrange an unfortunate accident to happen to you before you could get from this office to the cable office, which happens to be six blocks away through a bad district of town.'

"Cardinez wasn't kidding me," Krakhaur said, awe still in his voice. "I could feel it between my shoulder blades. And then suddenly he changed and became very genial again, just like that—which scared me even more.

" 'So everything is going to be just fine in Domania,' he said cheerfully. 'Just fine. And if you want to do something worthwhile and file a story that will be in the best interests of your country, you just go over and have a long talk with Acting Ambassador Whittelsie. He's the boss of all the Americans in this country.' So I was a good patriotic American reporter—and I was scared in my guts of Cardinez—and I filed several stories on Acting Ambassador Norman Whittelsie and how he was captaining the American mission in Domania . . . the usual stuff, how he was steering the republic away from the shoals of communism toward a bright, economically sound, anti-Communist future. That answer your question, Mike?"

"Ach, that *is* some story," Marlene said.

"Our friends in the corner seem to want words with me," Mike said casually. "Here comes Fritz."

"Hello, Mike," said Colonel Lawton, coming over. "Glad to see you in town. Roger, what kind of a sensational story are you trying to mine out of this place tonight?"

"I'm open to suggestions." Krakhaur introduced Lawton to Alana and Marlene.

"Do you ladies mind if I take Mr. Forrester from you for a few minutes? I'll send over Major Prescott to keep you company." Lawton feigned a stern expression as he turned to Krakhaur. "And I don't want you pumping Charlie for information. He's just in from the mountains and he's tired."

"The mountains?" Marlene repeated. "Banthut, where those wild tribes live?"

"That's right," Lawton confirmed, his eyes twinkling at the gorgeous blonde's obvious interest.

Lawton beckoned to Prescott. He was tall, with a gaunt face, close-cropped hair, and deep-set and weary eyes. He was wearing slacks and a sport shirt. A smile replaced the hollow look of fatigue when he saw the empty seat next to Marlene. Krakhaur greeted Prescott warmly and introduced him to the girls as "Charging Charlie," the hero of many battles in Vietnam who had volunteered to bring his skill with mountain tribesmen to Mituyan.

Cardinez shook Mike's hand when Lawton brought him back. "It's been a long time."

"Eight years and four countries ago."

"I didn't know you were a habitué of the Tuyan City bars."

"I never pegged you as a bar fly either," Mike retorted.

Cardinez turned to Lawton. "Frenchie's has become a sort of colorful club for us, right?"

"Yes, sir," Lawton said. Cardinez' civilian rank was equal to that of a one-star general, and Lawton always showed him the respect due a general officer. "Mike," Lawton said, "Mr. Cardinez and I were just talking about you."

"Right, Mike. Ordinarily we'd spend a month fencing, but we've got too many troubles to waste time. What about the proposition Fritz made to you? We need you badly."

"It's an awfully ambiguous proposition," Mike countered. "I'm not at all sure I understand all that's involved. And there's Luna to consider."

"It's pretty simple, as I see it." Cardinez' blue eyes snapped. "You go on about your business, but your first priority is to us. Even here in Tuyan City there are things only you can do, but it's out in the countryside that you can really help us."

"What's the trouble in Tuyan City?" Mike asked.

"This Decade of Progress spells trouble," Lawton replied. "The Mitcoms will figure some way to sabotage it."

"Decade of Decadence, it should be called," Cardinez growled. "I've been in Mituyan exactly four months, and I'm appalled, outraged, at what our Country Team has been allowing to go on in this country since we supported KaritKi's coup ten years ago. My God! King Barkoon would be an improvement."

Lawton chuckled. "I see by the vernacular papers that Barkoon has got himself a new movie starlet to play with on the Riviera and in Hong Kong."

One of the greatest mistakes of the KaritKi government, Mike knew, was the way it misjudged the feelings of the Mituyan people toward their exiled King. "For your information," he said, "those stories that KaritKi and Tarot keep planting about Barkoon just prove they don't understand their people. The more the people read and hear about their ex-King's exploits with women, race horses, sport cars, yachts, the more popular he becomes. These poor people do all their high living vicariously through Barkoon's adventures."

"Barkoon must be the richest exiled monarch in the world, judging by the way he lives," Lawton commented.

"King Barkoon's father probably put half a billion dollars away in Hong Kong and Swiss banks before the Japs took over during the war," Mike said. "All his life he cooperated with British and German industrialists. He personally controlled the opium business—and the Mituyan hill tribesmen grow the finest poppies in the world."

Cardinez and Lawton exchanged significant glances. "That's another thing we want you to look into for us, later," Cardinez said.

"I'll be in Tuyan City for a few days. Here's the address and phone number of both my office and apartment."

Cardinez leaned across the table. "You will work with us, Mike?"

"Let's say my sympathies are with the job you're trying to do."

Colonel Lawton's tone became hard. "Look, Mike, back at your place we talked all about this."

Mike held up a hand. "I remember what you said." He locked eyes with Cardinez a moment. "If I go with you it will only be because I believe it is what I should do. Raking up my past problems will have very little effect on my decisions."

"OK, Mike. We'll call you tomorrow."

Cardinez raised his hand palm outward. "Live or die with KaritKi," he intoned.

"What?" Mike looked at him unbelievingly.

"That's practically become the salute at the embassy," Cardinez said with a tight smile.

"I've been fortunate enough to enjoy the protection of the Palace in the past few years," Mike said as though it were a confession. "But from personal observation in the countryside I would say there's a hell of a lot more likelihood of the U.S. mission *dying* with KaritKi than living with him."

"As I said, Mike, we need you."

They walked over to the other table, and while Cardinez and Lawton said good night Mike drew up a chair on the other side of Marlene.

The JRB men started past the crowded bar, but had to back up to let a tall, rugged, young man, huge biceps swelling the short sleeves of his sport shirt, bulldoze his way inside.

"Oh, oh, here comes Barton—better known as The Animal," Prescott said ominously. The big man, his blonde hair cropped to his skull, recognized Colonel Lawton and apologized for blundering into him.

"Who is The Animal?" Marlene asked, delighted.

Just then one of the street boys boldly pushed open the door to the bar and, brushing past a protesting Frenchie, walked up to the men drinking. He carried a bird cage with a small multicolored bird inside. The little peddler approached several of the drinkers to buy the bird for a pet, but all declined. Finally the boy reached The Animal, who stared at him unblinkingly.

"He'll do some damned crazy thing," Prescott warned. "He hates the street boys. One of them left a time bomb gift-wrapped in a bar last Christmas which killed two of Barton's buddies on liberty."

"Frenchie should keep them out," Alana observed.

"She can't, really," Krakhaur replied. "The police won't do anything about them."

The street boy placed his bird cage on the bar next to The Animal. The boy, sensing interest, opened the cage and poked in his forefinger.

The bird perched on the finger, and the boy withdrew it and held it up for The Animal to see. Everyone at the bar turned to watch.

The Animal put out his finger, and the bird fluttered to perch on it. The boy pressed in close, intently talking money, when suddenly, with a fierce look, The Animal stuck the bird's head in his mouth and bit it in half. The boy's eyes popped wide in fear as The Animal, staring wildly at him, proceeded to munch away. With a shriek, the boy turned and ran for the door, leaving the bird cage on the bar; he was still screaming as he gained the street. As The Animal spat out the mangled mess, the bar girls shrank from him. Calmly he wiped off his mouth on the shoulder of his shirt and threw back a glassful of beer. His comrades-in-arms stared—then began laughing lustily, turning back to their drinks and women. Frenchie shook her head and shrugged.

"The *Beast* you should be calling him," Marlene said.

"That's the goddamnedest way of getting rid of a street urchin I ever saw," Krakhaur said in wonderment.

Then, all at once, The Animal seemed to freeze. He bowled his way past three men and came to a dead stop at the bird cage. One of the men started to reach for it, but The Animal intercepted him, pushing his arm away. He glared at the cage intently, moving around to get a better view of it, pulling himself to his full height to look down on it.

Suddenly he let out a yell, "Bomb! Down!" and with a powerful swipe of his arm sent the bird cage hurtling against the door. Men vaulted over the bar, crashing to the floor behind. Bar girls threw themselves to the ground. Even as Prescott kicked the table over and pulled Marlene behind its top, a tremendous flash and deafening explosion rocked the room. Pieces of furniture, broken glass, and chunks of the cement bar scythed through the air. The shrill screams of wounded girls mixed with the shouts of American patrons.

"Anybody hurt here?" Prescott cried. He stood up, hauling Marlene to her feet and brushing her off. Marlene looked at the badly chewed top edge of the overturned table and blanched, swaying against Prescott.

"*Mein Gott,* Charlie." One hand explored the table edge. "If we were sitting up, we get it."

Prescott nodded soberly. Alana and Krakhaur had also taken refuge behind the table and were unhurt. Mike was bleeding from superficial cuts on the back of his head, neck, and arms. He had fallen in front of the table, but he had been low and far enough from the blast so that only a few flying fragments had scratched him. From behind the bar the soldiers in civilian clothes emerged cautiously. The girls, jabbering, some weeping, clustered together. None of them seemed badly hurt.

"Jesus!" Krakhaur breathed, "look at Frenchie!" The proprietress had been blown in two; an arm was missing.

Prescott tore off his sport shirt and made for an American, bleeding profusely from a neck wound. He set to work bandaging the wound, trying to staunch the blood. The unwounded bar girls shrank from the carnage; some of them ran shrieking out the back door.

Marlene reached up under her dress and tore her slip off, moving toward another seriously wounded man to begin binding his head wounds with her sheer silk undergarment. Alana followed Marlene's example, and stuffed a handful of her slip against a bloody, burbling chest wound. Mike tore his shirt in half and ministered to one girl whose arm had been shredded.

Sirens wailed outside as U.S. Military Police and an ambulance squad arrived on the scene. Soon, civilian doctors and military medics were working on the wounded and carrying out bloody corpses. Three Americans had been killed. Krakhaur, ever the professional reporter, went over to The Animal and asked how he knew the bird cage was a bomb.

"First place, I never trust them little dipshit street boys," Barton growled. "When the little bastard left the cage on the bar, I began to wonder. Any time them little mothers leave something in a bar I get suspicious. But a bird cage? I see that it has a thick bottom and I figure if it is a bomb there must be some kind of detonating device. So I don't touch it. Then I see a little watch worked into the handle at the top. And I see it has only one hand. I see the hand is about a second or two from making contact with a brass point at twelve o'clock. I know it's too late to stop the contact. So—"

Sergeant Barton shrugged. "Only one thing to do, save as many people as I can. Sorry about Frenchie, but there was nobody but her at the door. Hadda save as many as I could . . . ."

"You did the right thing, Barton," Prescott said, clapping a hand on the sergeant's shoulder.

"This is some beginning to the Decade of Progress," Krakhaur remarked. He turned to Mike, "Take me to the cable office in your Land Rover, will you? I've got to get this story out now."

"Me too," Marlene said. "Then I go home and stop shaking."

"Will I see you again?" Prescott asked Marlene.

"Of course, Charlie," she replied warmly.

He smiled. "I'd take you home, but I'd better stick here and help out. Mr. Forrester, hope I'll see you again."

"You will, Major," Mike said quietly. "As of tonight we both have the same boss."

CHAPTER TEN

ON MONDAY, the day before the formal military review and the opening of the industrial exposition, Premier KaritKi decreed a reception day at the palace. Tarot was in charge of protocol and arranging all the appointments.

The palace stretched between the two main streets of Tuyan City, Disraeli Boulevard and Bismarck Avenue. The parallel avenues symbolized the equal help England and Germany had provided in the nineteenth century to make Mituyan one of the first modern states in Southeast Asia.

Tarot had worked out a elaborate traffic-control system—with Bismarck Avenue a one-way street running north to south, Disraeli Boulevard one way running south to north. All the lesser streets running into either Bismarck or Disraeli were one way, so that automobiles authorized to enter the east wing of the palace were kept a mile apart from those destined for the west. Since the oval audience room was in the center of the palace, and the waiting rooms stretched to the east and west, it was thus possible for Tarot to control precisely which visitors would meet and which would be kept unaware of others' appointments with the Premier.

The palace stood in the middle of thirty acres of lawn and shade trees, surrounded by a formidable iron-spike paling fence that opened the grounds to public view. The main office and reception area was the large, square, glistening white, three-story central stone building. The two wings, stretching east to Disraeli Boulevard and west to Bismarck Avenue respectively, constituted the residential sections of the palace. Premier KaritKi's apartment was in the east wing, Tarot's in the west.

Ambassador Whittelsie and General Macker arrived at the east-wing entrance in accordance with the invitation delivered the evening before. The ambassador handed the gold-bordered white card to the captain of the east-wing guard, resplendent in a white uniform hung with multicolored medals, a scarlet sash about the waist of his long tunic. Inspecting the card, the guards' officer snapped a hand to the gleaming gold helmet, with its purple plumes rising from the crown, in a brisk salute and promptly ushered Whittelsie and Macker to Tarot, who was waiting for them in an anteroom richly decorated in white and gold.

Tarot was a thin man with a gaunt face. His teeth were bad, and he rarely smiled. The small black pupils of his eyes gleamed fanatically. A pencil-line mustache emphasized petulant lips and a short, straight nose. He wore a Western-style white suit and a thin black necktie.

He looks like a dope fiend, Macker thought to himself. And Whittelsie always felt uncomfortable in Tarot's presence. Even though Mayna had told him that her husband was now nearly incapable of any sort of normal sexual activity, and had no objections to her discreetly satisfying her own strong sexual appetite, Whittelsie could not help wonder how Tarot felt about the affair. Surely he must suspect it was going on. Miserably, Whittelsie knew it was wrong, damn near treasonable—these trysts with Mayna.

"The Premier is waiting for you and General Macker, Mr. Ambassador," Tarot said. "Before I take you to him, may I express my sympathies to the families of the Americans killed in the unfortunate terror bombing Saturday night."

"Thank you, Counselor," Whittelsie said. "I will convey your sentiments."

Whittelsie and Macker followed Tarot from the white and gold room directly into Premier KaritKi's oval reception room. The Premier sat in a large hand-carved chair behind a highly polished oval-shaped wooden table that was completely bare of papers. There was only a red leather-bound folder in front of him. Behind KaritKi in the curving wall were four full-length red-draped windows, through which could be seen the lush, meticulously kept gardens where only KaritKi and his guests were permitted.

It was always a surprise to Whittelsie when he entered KaritKi's office. The austerity of the white room, with its carpetless parquet floor, was in sharp contrast with the rest of the opulently appointed palace. The Premier, like his brother, always dressed in Western suits or sports clothes.

KaritKi stood up as Whittelsie and Macker approached. Unlike his brother, the Premier was rotund and clean-shaven. His black hair, only slightly flecked with gray, was brushed straight back from his unlined face. With all the intrigue and battling he's been through in his life, Whittelsie thought, it was incredible that his face should remain so unrevealing.

"Mr. Ambassador," the Premier greeted him, coming from behind his table. "And General Macker." They all shook hands. "Before we begin our talk, may I express the Republic's deepest regret over the unfortunate terrorist incident that took the lives of three Americans and wounded so many. We have doubled the surveillance on all—ah—establishments catering to Americans."

"Thank you, Mr. Premier," Whittelsie replied. Macker and Whittelsie sat down opposite KaritKi, as Tarot took a seat at the end of the desk.

"Mayna told me you had wanted an appointment earlier in the week," KaritKi began. "We're sorry indeed, and please forgive us, but the press of business preparing for Mituyan's Decade of Progress has kept us most occupied." KaritKi's eyes flicked back and forth between Whittelsie and Macker. "Perhaps now we could discuss the points you and General Macker were so anxious to bring up with us." He nodded slightly at Tarot, thus making him an official member of the group.

"Perhaps I should let General Macker begin this discussion, Your Excellency," Whittelsie said.

"Yes, Your Excellency. At Military Assistance Command Mituyan—MAC-M, as we call ourselves—we are, as you well know, dedicated to helping your government build up a strong, well-trained, well-equipped army. The United States government and our President have vested in me the ultimate responsibility for establishing your army as a potent force in Southeast Asia. No other agency of the U.S. mission here in Mituyan has either the right or the means of giving you military assistance."

KaritKi nodded, giving Macker his full attention.

"I have heard, Your Excellency," Macker went on, "that you are contemplating adding a new unit to the Mituyan Armed Forces. I was anxious to discuss with you the formation of this new unit, how far you have gone in your thinking, and what role MAC-M and MAAG will be expected to play."

KaritKi looked questioningly at his brother. "Are we trying to add a new unit to the army?"

Tarot shook his head. "I have no knowledge of it. Perhaps the Defense Minister has some idea that he has not yet taken up with us."

"What we have heard at MAC-M," Macker prodded, "is that the Ministry of Defense is in the process of organizing a Mituyan Special Forces unit patterned after United States Army Special Forces. Is this true, Your Excellency?"

KaritKi gave the question some thought before answering. Then, looking Macker straight in the eyes, he smiled. "Ah, I see now where the confusion lies. There is no new army organization considered at this time, but there has been some thought among my ministers of establishing a Mituyan Special Forces unit entirely separate from the army. It would be more of a paramilitary unit, and its ultimate commander would not be a military man but a civilian. My brother Tarot, as a matter of fact, first broached the idea and, should this unit be organized, *he* would be its commander. So you see, General Macker"—again KaritKi smiled blandly—"we aren't talking about an army unit at all."

"But it will be an armed force, will it not?"

"Over here your own Special Forces are not under your command," KaritKi sidestepped.

"They are part of the United States Army," Macker insisted.

"In Mituyan they work for one of your civilian agencies," KaritKi reminded the general gently.

"That is a mistake I hope soon to correct," Macker snapped.

Whittelsie smiled inwardly as Macker became more enmeshed in KaritKi's Oriental ploys. After a long pause, KaritKi patronizingly said: "If we decide it is wise to go ahead and create a Mituyan Special Forces unit, we will certainly discuss it further with you, General."

So, thought Macker bitterly, the damned spooks had reached KaritKi! A paramilitary palace guard, or terrorist police force, was well on the way to being formed, under the control of this dope fiend, Tarot, and backed by Dickerson and Cardinez, using the limitless funds at CIA disposal which never had to be accounted for.

Macker bridled to see that Whittelsie was giving him no real support at all, and he resolved that as soon as the meeting was over he would unilaterally report back to the Secretary of Defense that the CIA was deliberately undercutting the authority and prerogatives of the U.S. military in Mituyan. There was obviously little more he could do directly with KaritKi.

"Were there any other specific items you wished to discuss?" KaritKi looked at Macker a long moment and then at Whittelsie.

"Not at the moment, Your Excellency," Whittelsie replied. "All reports indicate that the election campaigns are progressing well."

"They are," KaritKi agreed. He sat back in his chair, turned to gaze out at his garden a moment, then abruptly turned back and leaned forward, his eyes fixing Whittelsie's. It was a device the ambassador had come to know well, yet it always startled him, made him unprepared for the unpleasant business that inevitably followed.

"Mr. Ambassador," KaritKi began, his voice no longer bland, "we have been most distressed to hear from our ambassador in Washington that all over the United States, indeed the world, our so-called Tiking massacre has received so much publicity. One man, the American journalist Krakhaur, is responsible for this highly embarrassing story. I am requesting, therefore, that you inform your President to instruct the American press not to print any more such inflammatory articles about my country."

"Your Excellency, I wish, believe me, every member of the American mission in every troubled country of the world wishes . . ."

"Mr. Ambassador," KaritKi broke in, "Mituyan may be in a war with communism, but it is not a 'troubled' country, in spite of the lies men like your Krakhaur print."

"Excuse me, Your Excellency," Whittelsie apologized. "What I mean to say is that the American country teams all over the world, like ours here, desperately wish we could control the American press. We feel it frequently abuses its power, *but* it is a fact of life in our country that we *have* a free press, and there is nothing we can do about it except try to make the reporters see our problems from our side."

KaritKi stared at Whittelsie, unconvinced. "Every strong government controls its press." KaritKi placed a hand on the red folder. "I have given orders to close down two of the vernacular papers and the English-language *Mituyan Daily News* for carrying false and misleading information about this 'massacre.' "

"Your Excellency, I will pass on to the State Department your displeasure with the way reporting is being conducted here in Mituyan. But I must try and make you understand that even the President of the United States cannot force the American press to print or not to print what it likes."

KaritKi smiled cunningly. "But Mr. Ambassador, this Krakhaur who caused this trouble, was he not, at the request of your government, taken from Vietnam and *exiled* to my quiet little country by his news syndicate?"

Always KaritKi took an obscure fact and used it to prove an overwhelming generalization—such as the CIA's control of the small U.S. Special Forces detachment in the mountains, and now this business of Krakhaur being rusticated here in Mituyan, of all damned inconvenient places.

Whittelsie shifted in his seat. "There may have been a little horse trading between the Star Syndicate and the State Department," the ambassador allowed. "But I must reiterate, we do not have a controlled press in America."

"There's one thing I can do," KaritKi said. "I can deport Krakhaur as an example to the other journalists in Mituyan. I have heard that he is now planning a series of articles on the alleged miseries of the people and the harsh treatment they receive from my province chiefs, which he says causes them to sympathize with the MFF. I want him out of my country."

"You have every right to expel him, Your Excellency. My only concern, however, would be the peculiar nature of American public opinion. Congressmen will hear from their constituents. An investigation into the economic and military aid the United States sends to Mituyan might follow. Powerful voices, uninformed voices I might add, even now are calling for a complete abandonment of our commitments in Southeast Asia. An incident such as the expulsion of a prominent newsman from a country to which we send massive aid gives the bloc urging withdrawal from this part of the world great force."

Whittelsie had tried to keep his words neutral and his tone emotionless. KaritKi's bland expression slowly disappeared; his eyes narrowed and glinted at the American ambassador.

"It is incredible, it is unbelievable, that one man, a journalist, can be so powerful," KaritKi said at last. "Maybe you are right, Mr. Ambassador. Perhaps I cannot expel Krakhaur now."

"There are other courses of action open." Tarot's high-pitched voice cut across the table.

Whittelsie and Macker both glanced at him uneasily. There could be no doubt as to what courses of action were snaking through his mind.

"Your Excellency," Ambassador Whittelsie said in his most diplomatic manner, "the understandable hostility toward Krakhaur on the part of the Palace is well known to the press. It would be most awkward if Krakhaur, even through his own clumsiness, were to have an *accident* that, ah, incapacitated him. In spite of all that the American mission here, and the State Department in Washington, could do, the vituperation of the press of the world would fall on you. The journalists would believe the accident was arranged. Such an incident could cause the fall of your government."

KaritKi jumped to his feet. "By God, Whittelsie, are you threatening me?"

Sweat running down his back, Whittelsie stood up also. "I have as much to lose, every member of the U.S. Country Team here has as much to lose, as you, sir. Our careers could be terminated if we allowed the situation here in Mituyan to disintegrate into another Vietnam mess. Mr. Premier, we are on *your* side! You must realize that. You know what we say at the embassy: Live or die with KaritKi! But if you cannot accept certain facts of American life, there is really nothing I or my team can do to help you."

Whittelsie stared across the table at KaritKi. Slowly the Premier sat down. "Are there any other matters we need to discuss this morning, Mr. Ambassador?" His voice was flat again.

"No, Your Excellency. I have already had a long talk with Krakhaur. I think we will find him cooperative in the future."

KaritKi, his composure recovered, managed his bland smile. "As a matter of fact, I myself shall be talking to Mr. Krakhaur, and the rest of the press, later this morning. I do appreciate your advice, and as much as I can I will act on it."

Tarot stood up, the signal that the appointment was finished. Whittelsie and Macker took their leave, following Tarot from the reception room.

CHAPTER ELEVEN

TAROT WALKED BRISKLY down the hall from the east wing after seeing Whittelsie and Macker out of the palace. If only they had known who was waiting in the west wing, he thought with satisfaction; he hurried to the anteroom where Filmore Dickerson and Jack Cardinez were waiting for their appointment with the Premier.

Dickerson was and looked to be a desk man. Even in his younger days in the OSS during World War II he had held down a desk. He appeared soft and tired in his light-gray suit stretched over a bulky form. His pudgy hands were not what one would expect of a cloak-and-dagger operator. Actually, Dickerson left most operations to JRB, concentrating on analyzing the daily activities of the members of KaritKi's government, the diplomatic community, the business community, and, of course, the military operations. But he did have his own special group of American and Mituyan hoods and spooks whose identities were unknown even to Cardinez.

"Mr. Dickerson," Tarot began affably, "my wife asked if she might be permitted to talk to you a few minutes before the Premier is ready to receive you."

"It is always a delight to meet the beautiful Mayna."

As if on schedule, Mayna came into the room. She was wearing a sleek silk sheath with the traditional slit showing her famous leg, which news photographers were so fond of shooting. Tarot excused himself, saying he would be back when the Premier was ready, and Mayna sat down on an overstuffed chair facing Dickerson and Cardinez. As always she was self-possessed, smiling slightly, her long black hair hanging straight down to her shoulders.

"Hello, Phil. Mr. Cardinez, it is good to see you again. Why don't either of you ever call me?"

"The deputy ambassador has been away," Dickerson said, "and as his assistant I've had to perform all his duties as well as my own."

Mayna's laugh was a merry tinkle. "Please, Phil. You don't have to keep up your cover with me. What do you say to dinner tomorrow evening?" She gave him an intimate, sidewise glance. "You look as if your nerves are frayed, Phil. You must let me relax you." Now her smile was bold. "Let's have dinner at my beach villa in Marashak—far away from this hot city. There are many things I would like to tell you." Jack Cardinez studiously avoided Dickerson's eye.

"You have a date, Mayna," Dickerson said.

"Good. Now I have something I need you two gentlemen to help me with."

Dickerson smiled encouragingly.

"For two years, Phil, I have been active in building and running rehabilitation camps for girls who get in trouble," she began. "Many of the girls were prostitutes or from the homes of politically unreliable families we have had to detain. Other girls broke laws in black-market operations, some were outright thieves. I have personally picked a cadre of two hundred of my best girls, girls who are completely reliable. I can trust every one of them. With ancient rifles and the few modern weapons I could acquire, I have created a crude paramilitary women's unit. But I need rifles, machine guns, instructors, equipment, jeeps and trucks. My girls could be one of the best disciplined secret-fighting forces in Mituyan. The MFF is stepping up its campaign of violence every day; my girls could be a potent weapon to oppose them. Suppose the MFF attacked what they thought was a defenseless village with most of the men gone. A hundred of my girls could wipe out the enemy attackers. But I need help. Would the CIA take over training and equipping my unit?"

"Have you talked to the Premier about it?" Dickerson asked.

Mayna laughed derisively. "My poor brother-in-law becomes more separated from reality every day. He says an army of women is useless. He seems to forget that Mituyan women are aggressive and combative. In business, politics, and the military we women have a much more important part in making the decisions than you American advisers over here realize. What do you say, Phil?"

The appeal in her eyes, the way she held out her hands, and the white thigh exposed through the slit in her dress seemed to have a powerful effect on Dickerson. "Perhaps the idea isn't so outrageous as it sounds," he answered. "Let me think about it a little, Mayna."

"You can give me your answer at my villa tomorrow night, Phil," she said, just as Tarot entered the waiting room and announced that the Premier was ready to receive them.

Tarot led the way to the oval reception room, standing aside as he ushered Dickerson and Cardinez into the Premier's presence. KaritKi's bland smile was firmly in place as he shook hands with the two Americans.

There followed several minutes of devious talk all around the subject of the elections before Tarot finally brought the discussion to the point. "Mr. Dickerson, what do your sources tell you about the conditions in the mountains to the northeast, on the Yanna border? Your American Special Forces are working with those dirty, incorrigible savages up there. Just what is being accomplished beyond arming and training them to a point where they might successfully attack our large town of Banthut and perhaps move on the lowland cities?"

"Mr. Minister," Dickerson began, "you must be aware of the increasingly large-scale infiltration of Communist-trained guerrillas through the mountains from neutral Yanna. The Groat tribesmen, under the direction of our experienced men, men who have fought in the jungles of Laos and Vietnam, are successfully interdicting the Communist infiltration routes. They are also separating the Groats from the Communists by getting them on our side, *your* side, I should say. Our men are building clinics, setting up avenues of trade for Groat handicrafts and crops all through the Groat country, and organizing fortified camps, safe from direct attack by the guerrillas. We have even given the tribespeople, through our AID mission here, fine goats and pigs to improve the strain of their animals. The mountain tribesmen, except for those villages and tribes reached by the Communists before we set up the mountain program, are loyal to the Tuyan City government—to you, Mr. Premier."

To emphasize the point, Dickerson kept shifting his gaze from Tarot to KaritKi. "Were it not for this program, most of the mountain country of northeast Mituyan already would be controlled by the Communists, and they could attack and destroy Banthut and every other town on the edge of the hill country. That means that one-fifth of the republic of Mituyan would be under absolute Communist control right now—all your tin and, for what it's worth"—he stole a sly glance at Tarot—"all the opium crop would benefit the Mituyan Freedom Front movement."

The Premier listened without comment and then directed the discussion to his main topic of concern. "Mr. Dickerson, you and I have discussed organizing a Mituyan Special Forces unit to be advised and equipped by your agency of the United States government. Your General Macker, of course, is much against this. In fact, he told me that U.S. Special Forces in Mituyan would soon be brought under his direct command and out from under Mr. Cardinez and his JRB."

Cardinez managed not to show the stab of anxiety the statement caused.

"It is our thinking here," KaritKi went on, "that your American Special Forces teams in the mountain country should have Mituyan counterparts with them. We do not want any more arming and training of the tribesmen without its coming under our direct supervision."

Cardinez groaned inwardly; this was what they had all feared. "We would have to train your proposed Special Forces units to get along with the mountain people, Your Excellency," he said carefully. "They would have to respect them and help them if we are to keep the tribesmen on the government side."

"The Groats and the other tribes interpret kindness as weakness," Tarot stated. "The province chiefs are worried that the barbarous aborigines are already becoming *too* independent, with all the training and equipment you Americans are giving them."

"But we're winning them over," Cardinez protested.

Premier KaritKi's voice rose in pitch and his hands moved agitatedly. "I know General Macker would be perfectly happy to take over the Special Forces program, both U.S. and Mituyan, with my officers in command."

"Now, Your Excellency," Dickerson said soothingly, "I have no objection to Mituyan Special Forces, once they are properly trained, being in charge of the camps—as long as they take the advice of our experienced Americans."

"It won't work here," Cardinez appealed to his superior. Then to the Premier: "Your Excellency, leave the mountain program the way it is for another year. We'll train your Mituyan Special Forces. Then, when they're ready, but not before, they can work with the tribesmen."

"We have many good officers, known to us at the palace personally, who can be trained in a matter of weeks," Tarot stated flatly.

"Your Excellency," Dickerson said decisively, "I'll request a training detachment of U.S. Special Forces be assigned to JRB. We should be able to turn out Mituyan detachments within a few months."

A broad grin split the yellowish moon face of Premier KaritKi. "Now, Dickerson, we are talking realities. I can promise you that we will not discuss Mituyan Special Forces again with any other member of the American mission in this country."

"Oh, Macker and the ambassador will find out soon enough," Dickerson said. "But we'll get a head start. Perhaps we should train them right out in the mountains. On-the-job training so to speak. Stand-up, shoot-back targets. Men learn fast that way."

Tarot and KaritKi laughed exultantly. "We knew you were the correct person to discuss this matter with." Tarot's eyes glistened with cunning. "I think perhaps we should have two training centers. One should be close to Tuyan City."

With victory in hand, Tarot stood.

Cardinez felt the need of a closing shot. "Incidentally, Your Excellency, what, if anything, do you want to do about the opium trade in the mountains? We get reports that it is thriving, and as much as five hundred kilos a week during the harvest is coming out of the tribal areas."

KaritKi and Tarot stared thoughtfully in front of them and said nothing. "You know," Cardinez prodded, "the United States belongs to the Geneva Narcotics Conference. It is our duty to do our best all over the world to see that opium goes only to legitimate medical-processing laboratories. Perhaps we should try to curtail the poppy traffic."

There was another brief silence, and then KaritKi opened his red folder and addressed himself to Dickerson. "I have here, Mr. Dickerson, a report on the guerrilla incidents in Mituyan in the past thirty days. The average is fifty a week. Some have been unbelievably savage, especially in the North, although in our Tuyan River Delta rice bowl guerrilla units are trying to capture food to sustain their campaigns. We are not releasing these figures to the press. We wish they would not be reported at all. It makes it look to the Americans and the world as though this is not a stable country, although we know it is the most stable in Asia. Ten years—a Decade of Progress under one strong and dedicated government. However, this dirty little Communist insurgency persists. It is the primary job of this government and its armed forces to rid Mituyan completely of the Communist MFF. We must capture and execute every Communist agitator and sympathizer in Mituyan. We have no time for the hypocritical little headline-gathering, so-called vice raids so dear to the hearts of the American enforcement agencies in America, especially at the time of your local elections. Our job is to kill Communists until there are no more. If you would concern yourself and your agency to this end, you would be acting in the best interests of Mituyan and the United States."

Dickerson flashed an annoyed glare at Cardinez.

Tarot started toward the door. "This has been an excellent meeting, gentlemen." To Dickerson he said: "I will be in communication with you personally next week."

Cardinez and Dickerson did not speak a word to each other until they were out of the palace.

"Damn it, Jack, I wish you wouldn't be so difficult. We do have to work with them, after all."

"Why?" asked Cardinez.

"Well," Dickerson began, "our policy. Live or die with—"

"I know our policy," Cardinez replied, irritated. An idea that until this moment had only been a fleeting thought suddenly exploded full-blown in his mind. He turned with a grin to Dickerson. "Why not, 'avoid our doom with King Barkoon'?"

"What the hell are you saying, Jack?" There was a note of fear in Dickerson's voice. He knew the reputation his second in command had for drastic action when he thought it was warranted. "Don't forget who's running things here and go off half-cocked trying to pull off some crazy coup. That's an order."

"Right, sir," Cardinez said, climbing into his staff car.

CHAPTER TWELVE

THE REVIEWING STANDS for the Decade of Progress parade had been set up in the center of Tuyan City on Bismarck Avenue in the tree-lined park that ran through to Disraeli Boulevard. One stand, covered with colorful bunting, was reserved for the Palace and official guests. Next to the Palace stand was the press section, complete with a tower for television cameras. Ted Baum had worked closely with his counterpart, KaritKi's Minister of Information, to provide extra amenities for the press, including a bar.

Mayna's position in the Palace reviewing stand was strategically planned. Self-possessed, delicately beautiful, her right knee bent slightly so that her leg and thigh showed white through the scarlet dress that she had instinctively chosen when informed that the Americans were taking colored film for television, she was the object of all attention; the camera zoomed in to project her full screen on the television sets of Mituyan and the world. Dhuna, the actual first lady of the land, had somehow been placed in a spot less convenient for the photographers.

Even though the Mituyan Army had recalled all its troops for the occasion, thus suspending the war against the Communists temporarily, it had neither the manpower nor the equipment to put on a particularly formidable show as military processions went. Beyond the fact that every weapon, vehicle, and tank were U.S.-manufactured, there was little for the reporters to note in their dispatches. Only the anticipated unexpected—the potential riots—had turned out the press.

The Mituyan Air Force, with considerable reinforcement by American pilots, staged a flying show of fighter planes, helicopters, and light bombers—some cynical reporters remarking that they were probably seeing the same planes making several passes. Again, most of the photographers planned their pictures to include Mayna reviewing the meagre military "might" of her country.

Following the military procession was a float parade depicting Mituyan industrial progress. Sewing machines, models of new factories, government buildings, the dam and the bridge over the Tuyan River—all were driven by the reviewing stand. A tableau depicting Mituyan farmers casting their ballots in the coming election drifted by; and then, one by one, on floats symbolizing the various regions of Mituyan, each candidate for the constituent assembly that would draft the new constitution of Mituyan drove past.

It was then that the anticipated incident the press had been waiting for occurred. From out of a side street, a mammoth flat-bed truck transporting a huge veiled tableau pushed its way into the parade of candidates. When it was in full sight of the reviewing stands, and as photographers instinctively trained their cameras on it, the float was unveiled.

The Palace group stared with unconcealed horror at the papier-mâché scene slowly moving past. It depicted a bleak island of stone peaks. Four gaunt men and two women in rags, chains hanging from their wrists and legs, glared defiantly at the reviewing stands. In big block letters a sign running the length of the float said in English, KARITKI OPPOSITION SENT TO ISLE OF STONES.

Mike and Luna, guests of Dhuna, held their breath, furtively glancing at KaritKi and Tarot. The Palace guards nervously switched the air with their rifle barrels. The brothers looked at each other, then both stared over at the press stand, indecision and rage on their faces.

In the press section, correspondents not assigned to Mituyan were excitedly turning to the old hands for clarification. Krakhaur supplied the information that the Isle of Stones was an infamous prison camp near Tiking, to which chiefly political prisoners were sent.

All eyes turned to the Palace enclosure, as KaritKi and Tarot tried to make up their minds what to do. Their natural inclination would be to gun down the people on the float and the driver, but they knew that would make them appear ruthless, repressive, and undemocratic in front of the press of the world.

For once KaritKi was not master in his own country. Even he had learned to fear adverse outside opinion. "Those terrible people!" Dhuna exclaimed. "My husband does everything for the people, gives them a chance to express themselves in a free election, and they spoil his day this way."

Slowly the float pulled away from the reviewing stands, and then, in full sight of the press, an open jeep sped alongside, and the six protesters and the driver of the truck jumped into it and were sped down the street. This was too much for the volatile Mituyan police. Although both KaritKi and Tarot still were too stunned to give the orders, several of the "rabbits," as the white-uniformed police were known, opened fire on the escaping vehicle. As though this were a signal, members of the Palace guard also opened fire, and the crowds threw themselves onto the sidewalk.

Crouched low, the driver of the jeep spun it around a corner off Bismarck the wrong way down a one-way street, but even as he made the turn some of the bullets found their mark. A man and a woman fell twisting to the street. Momentum carried their bodies bouncing over the curb and hard against the wall of a house.

Already cameramen were bolting from the reviewing stand and scrambling for the bodies. But before they could reach them, a squad of police formed a human wall around the corpses and roughly fended off the newsmen.

Mike pushed his way toward Tarot. "Counselor, if you don't want an absolute fiasco here, call the police off the press."

Tarot yelled orders at his personal bodyguard, who charged out of the Palace reviewing stand just as a policeman knocked a camera from the hands of one reporter. In anger and dismay, KaritKi, Tarot, and Mayna watched the melee. And then, as suddenly as it had started, it broke up. The alert police, who had managed to get the two bodies into a police car, sped from the scene. Sharp orders shouted by Tarot's bodyguard dispersed the police and troops, and in an instant the reporters found themselves alone with no action or bodies to photograph.

Ted Baum and the Mituyan Minister of Information reached the scene together and pleaded in vain for the press to return to the reviewing stand, see the rest of the parade, and enjoy drinks and a buffet at the Palace afterward. The reporters instead began to make for their offices and hotel rooms to write their versions of the scene they had just witnessed, while the wire-service photographers rushed to get their film developed and radioed around the world. The TV cameramen in the tower were already unreeling the film from their cameras and tossing it to legmen, who would rush it to the airport where it would be sent by Pan American or BOAC to the Western world.

"Well, that blew the ball game," Mike remarked to Luna. "Let's get out of here."

"Please stay," Dhuna begged Luna. "I'm so worried and confused."

Luna looked questioningly at Mike, who shrugged and said, "All right, Dhuna, if we can be of any help to you of course we'll stay."

Three hours later, Mike and Luna finally were excused from the palace, after promising Tarot they would do everything they could to make the press realize that this was a typical Mitcom terrorist incident, not a true political protest.

CHAPTER THIRTEEN

MIKE DROVE LUNA to her parents' home and then went to see Jack Cardinez at his office. The JRB chief welcomed him and, after extracting an eye-witness story of the incident, called in Colonel Lawton.

"Well, Mike, have you made a decision yet?" Lawton asked.

Mike turned to Cardinez and grinned. "Yes, Boss."

A slow, triumphant smile spread across the faces of Cardinez and Lawton. "I guess that bombing at Frenchie's had something to do with it," Mike went on. "And incidentally, I'm not convinced that the Mitcoms are our only enemies. Our biggest problem is the whole outlook at the palace."

"Now you *are* thinking our way," Lawton said.

"That shooting today was inexcusable," Mike declared. "Even though KaritKi didn't order his men to fire, it shows how the Palace guards think. And their thinking comes right from Tarot."

"When can you go to work for us, Mike?" Lawton asked.

"Today. Now."

"Let's see—this is Tuesday," Cardinez said. "We have a job for you beginning next week. Meanwhile, take it easy and see a lot of your wife. You won't see much of her when you get started with us."

"What's the assignment?" Mike asked.

"Ever been into the Groat country?" Cardinez asked.

"I've been up to Banthut a few times. The climate is the best in this part of the world and so is the hunting."

Cardinez walked across the office to a map of Mituyan and pointed at Banthut. "Up here lies the answer to licking the worst of the Communist infiltration from the North. One quarter of the entire land area of Mituyan is dominated by the various mountain tribesmen.

Through terror and persuasion the Communists are getting them on their side. We're trying to win the Groats—the biggest tribe—and the others back to the central government. At the same time our job is to win a better central government for Mituyan. In fact—he gave Mike a significant look—"it may take a new government to achieve honest elections. When you read my agents' reports, you'll see there is little doubt that KaritKi and Tarot are trying to eliminate all political opposition."

"Are you suggesting we engineer a coup against KaritKi?" Mike asked.

"We will do whatever has to be done to keep Mituyan a free country," Cardinez answered.

"What do you want me to do up in Banthut?"

"As a well-known American trader in Mituyan there is no reason why you can't investigate getting into the opium traffic. We know that both the Communists and certain Palace favorites are in it together. Your first mission is to provide a complete report on all aspects of the opium business."

Mike whistled softly. "That's going to be a tough one, Jack."

"Right. And you are the only person who can do it without raising Tarot's suspicions that the U.S. mission here is interested in knowing more about the poppy business."

"You'll get all the help you need from our people," Lawton said. "After we've had a chance to assess the full significance of this shooting at the Decade of Progress parade we'll give you a complete briefing on the situation up in the Groat country. You'll find that Charlie Prescott will be your chief ally."

"I wonder how he's doing with Marlene."

"He deserves a little fun with a beautiful round-eyed girl—after what he goes through up there in the mountains. You'll see," Lawton said. Then: "She's a fine girl."

"She sure is," Mike agreed. "The way she pitched in and helped the wounded right after the bombing was wonderful."

"You sound interested," said Cardinez, laughing.

"Of course I'm interested in her," Mike answered. 'But not in the way you think. My wife and I are very happy."

Cardinez stood up, closed and locked his files, and led Mike and Lawton from the office. "Well, Friday or Saturday we'll have the final briefing. Meanwhile"—he held his hand up solemnly, palm out—"Live or die with KaritKi."

Mike and Lawton laughed.

CHAPTER FOURTEEN

THE U.S. ARMY twin-engine Beechcraft Bonanza streaked eastward from Tuyan City toward the coastal resort city of Marashak. It was growing dark, this Friday evening, but the maze of canals, rivers, and rice paddies of the Upper Tuyan Delta still made a hypnotic pattern of brown water, green plains of reeds, and square diked-in rice paddies, dry at this time of year.

But the rainy season will soon be on us, Ambassador Whittelsie thought grimly. And with it full-scale guerrilla activities. The problems of Mituyan overwhelmed him, particularly the press reports that had made front-page reading all over the United States and, for that matter, the world. Whittelsie had been required to answer no less than three cables from the State Department. Congress was incensed that a government supported by the United States condoned shooting non-Communist political opponents.

Ted Baum had done his best, but the reporters wrote what they saw, and since with only a few exceptions they were against KaritKi he had emerged as a tyrant. Already an investigating committee was being organized by the administration to determine whether or not the coming elections would be run fairly.

After the shooting incident, the Decade of Progress celebrations had been quietly boycotted by the people of Tuyan City. As a result, the press, led by Krakhaur, observed that in an honest election KaritKi candidates would lose. To Whittelsie's intense annoyance, they said further that a KaritKi victory would prove the elections had been rigged.

Whittelsie chuckled to himself at the one bright spot of the Decade of Progress. Hardly a newspaper around the world had not run pictures of the seductive second lady of Mituyan who reputedly ran the country from behind the scenes. And the television cameras, in living color, had captured her beautifully, catapulting her into world fame.

The ocean appeared in front of the plane, and Whittelsie's mind turned from the problems of the moment. Soon Mayna's limousine would be picking him up at the airstrip and whisking him to her villa.

Twenty minutes later the courier plane made a smooth landing just as darkness fell, and rolled to a stop at the administrative building. Whittelsie stepped out onto the wing and then to the ramp as a black Rolls-Royce drove up. A chauffeur jumped from behind the wheel, Whittelsie stepped into the limousine, and in moments he was being sped from the airfield.

Mayna's villa, which even her husband Tarot did not visit without making an appointment, was surrounded by a high wall, topped with broken glass and barbed wire. The walls plunged to the ocean on either side of the villa, and sentries were posted on the walls at the beach to keep swimmers or strollers at a distance.

One of Mayna's girls, a submachine gun slung over her back, opened the front gate when the limousine drew up. She silently ushered him to the villa's main entrance. Two more girls, in camouflage fatigues cut skin-tight, giving them a very feminine appearance in spite of the carbine each had slung on her shoulder, opened the double doors, and he entered the long paneled hallway that led through the house to the beach. Floodlights gave the lapping surf a phosphorescent quality. A totally charming young girl in Mituyan skirt came down the stairway at the end of the hall. She bowed. "Madam Mayna waiting for you, sir."

Whittelsie followed the girl up the stairs, his eyes on the twinkle of white thigh and small round buttocks. The entire front of the villa, facing the sea, comprised Mayna's apartment. To the right as he walked into the foyer was the parlor, floor-to-ceiling windows catching the sea breeze. To the left was the bedroom. The girl, seeing Whittelsie into her mistress's rooms, discreetly closed the door behind him. Mayna was waiting.

Long ebony hair, instead of being piled on her head, hung straight down around her shoulders. Tonight she was wearing a shimmering aquamarine gown, with gold embroidered dragons across the bodice and waist acting as clasps to keep the raiment tightly about her. He noticed that this costume, which was almost floor-length, had not one but two slits from hip to hem. He had planned to tell her immediately that this would be the last night he would be able to spend with her, but as she came toward him he forgot his resolutions.

"Whit?" she asked with a smile, "where or what is Seventh Avenue?"

"*What?*"

"Seventh Avenue. I received a lovely letter from a Mr. Grubman telling me how beautifully dressed I always am. He said he and everyone in his company fell in love with me on television."

"Seventh Avenue in New York City is the center of the garment, the dress business of the United States."

"Well, Mr. Grubman was very gallant, and he says he is one of the biggest manufacturers on Seventh Avenue. He wants to pay a lot of money, good American dollars, Whit, if I'll put my name on"—she paused and wrinkled her nose—"his new line. He wants to call it Empress Mayna Originals." She smiled mischievously. "Wouldn't it be gorgeous public relations, Whit?"

"In a word, no. You shouldn't be endorsing a product like some movie actress."

"But I've already written the letter," Mayna protested.

"Did you mail it?"

Mayna looked up at him, then said, "No. I wanted you to advise me on how much money I can get from Mr. Grubman."

"Oh, my God! You aren't serious, Mayna."

"Why not? With your policy of never letting us get our hands on actual dollars, just the things the dollars buy, how can I have a numbered Swiss bank account?"

Whittelsie saw that she was becoming serious. "Mayna, why are you talking about numbered Swiss accounts?"

"Every day a coup d'état is being planned against KaritKi and Tarot. How do I know you'll always support us?"

"You know damned good and well I'll always support you as long as I'm the ambassador."

Mayna allowed a significant few moments of silence. Then she put her cool fingers on his forehead, worked the wrinkles, and led him to the comfortable, low sofa opposite a coffee table on which stood a bottle of his Chivas Regal Scotch.

"Alright, Whit," Mayna said, as they sat down. "Don't worry. I will not demean the dignity of my position by endorsing dresses. Poor Mr. Grubman. I guess I'll just have to keep buying dollars on the black market."

"Mayna, there is not going to be an overthrow of the KaritKi government. The elections will decide the future of this country. Even if I leave, the next man will be committed to our policy here. You know what I say every day at the embassy—"

"Yes, Whit. Live or die with KaritKi. We all know and appreciate it." The way she said it, Whit knew she doubted whether that would remain U.S. policy in six months, or less. As usual she had completely taken the initiative from him.

Slowly Mayna took her fingers from Whittelsie's forehead and the nape of his neck. "Shall I make you a Scotch and soda?"

"Please."

She poured the drink and Whit took it gratefully.

Mayna watched him silently a few moments and then leaned toward him. "Very seriously, Whit"—her dark eyes were mournful—"KaritKi's regime is in danger. We don't know which generals are completely loyal. That's why we must have our own Mituyan Special Forces under the command of Tarot. It's the only way we can have a force we're sure of."

Mayna saw the tension lines creep across the ambassador's face, and placed her hand behind his neck and began stroking it, loosening his tie with the other hand. "You Americans wear such tight, hot clothing. And first the British and now you have forced the poor men of Mituyan to dress your way if they want a share of your money and power."

Whittelsie lolled back as Mayna pulled off his tie, opened his shirt and playfully twisted the hair on his chest. He had never been to an Asiatic country before this tour, and it still amused him that Mituyan women were so fascinated with the hair on the bodies of many Caucasians. As she massaged his forehead and neck, he began to relax. There were things he wanted to discuss with her, about Tarot, about KaritKi, but they could wait.

"You will give us what we need, Whit?"

He didn't feel like talking business at the moment. "Yes, Mayna," he sighed. "You shall have your own Special Forces. At the next meeting of the Country Team I will recommend immediate activation of the unit."

"Under Phil Dickerson's jurisdiction?"

Whittelsie felt pushed, and Mayna's talk of numbered Swiss accounts had distressed him. Was she really so afraid that the United States would withdraw its support from KaritKi's regime?

"Is that what you want, what you feel will be best for stability in the Palace?"

"Oh yes, Whit. We can work so much more easily with Mr. Dickerson's agency than with General Macker."

"That's the way I'll recommend, then. I'll be in the middle of a hell of a row, but I guess Washington will support me. Always has."

Mayna's fingers vibrated slightly over his forehead and Whit's pulse quickened.

"And, Whit," Mayna wheedled, "you must agree to KaritKi's demand that all operations in the country be commanded by Mituyan officers. We are happy to have, we need, American advisers; but we must have control."

Whittelsie sat straight up in the sofa and looked squarely at Mayna. He wanted her so much it took enormous self-control to be firm with her. "You know perfectly well that we have never been other than advisers to the Mituyan Army. And most of the time your officers fail to take American advice and let the guerrillas get away rather than face a fire fight and take casualties."

"But Whit, you have operations all over the Groat country completely run by the Americans."

"That's a different sort of operation, Mayna. You know that the Mituyans and Groats can't work together. If Mituyan soldiers go up into the mountains, you'll have a rebellion of tribesmen that could lose this whole country to the Communists."

"Give us a chance, Whit. It's our country after all. Let our best Mituyan Special Forces teams work with the Groats and other tribes advised by your men. The Groats have always wanted to attack the lowlanders, and the way you are arming and training them they'll be able to do it pretty soon, unless they are under the supervision of loyal Mituyan officers."

Mayna saw tension and irritation in his face and in the set of his shoulders. Again she let the fingers of one hand vibrate over his forehead and with the other hand reached through his open shirt collar and stroked the back or his neck in gentle, circular motions.

As the ambassador eased off under her ministrations, Mayna whispered gently, "You will give it careful consideration? We do know our own country better than foreigners."

Though Whittelsie seriously doubted her statement, he couldn't refute one point: it was still her country and not his. The gentle movements of her fingers began to relax him once again. He settled back and met Mayna's anxious smile with a strong, steady one of his own. "Of course Mituyan is your country, Mayna. I'll recommend a new study aimed toward giving command of the tribesmen projects to qualified Mituyan officers. It's Phil Dickerson's baby, but he usually goes along with me."

He noticed Mayna's inscrutable smile. "I know, Whit dear, that Mr. Dickerson will accept your recommendations," she said, reaching to the table and handing Whit the highball she had made for him.

"I do wish there were something that could be done about Mr. Krakhaur," Mayna pouted. "He was so unfair describing that Mitcom incident at the parade. We don't put our non-Communist political opponents in prison, and his articles on the reforms we are going to make are most unfair. You know we have to drive the Communists out before we can make changes."

"Some feel that the sooner you make the reforms the sooner you'll get the people on the government's side against the MFF," Whittelsie answered gently. "And now, before the elections, is the best time."

"Oh, Whit." She pouted prettily, though he was sorry she had so abruptly stopped her exciting finger movements. "You know we can't fight the Communists if we suddenly alter the whole province-chief system."

Whittelsie had had his fill of Mituyan politics. "Mayna, my dear, the elections will decide all these things."

Mayna realized she had pushed him far enough. Having won most of her points, she now smiled suggestively. "You are very nervous, dear."

"Yes, yes I am."

"Come on with me then. We won't enjoy dinner until I completely relax my Whit."

His heart pounded, a smile spread across his face.

"See, just thinking of Empress Mayna's nerve massage relaxes my favorite ambassador. A pity Western women never learned what we know. A lot less men in America would have nervous disorders, tension headaches—and they'd stop tiring themselves out pursuing other women if their wives knew how to take care of them."

She stood up, reaching out a hand. Whit sprang to his feet and followed Mayna from her salon to her boudoir. Her bed was very wide and high off the floor, a bit hard by Western standards, but most Mituyans slept on a board bed covered with a thin matting. Mayna said that hard beds made for straight backs, and it was true that in spite of the many diseases to which Mituyans were heir, backaches were not one of them.

"Now, Mr. Ambassador, let me undress you."

Whit stood beside the bed as Mayna took off his shirt and undershirt. She gave him a playful shove and he sat down on the side of the bed. First she untied his white shoes and pulled them off, then his white socks; and finally she came to his trousers. Surreptitiously, he had unbuckled his belt and disposed of two key buttons.

"You are impatient tonight, Whit," Mayna whispered. "Let the empress do it all for you."

She captured his trousers finally, and leaving Whit sitting only in his undershorts she carefully hung up the white pants. Back at his side she gently pushed him down on the hard bed. He closed his eyes a moment and then opened them to drink in her delicate loveliness.

Mayna unbuttoned his undershorts and pulled them off, leaving him lying naked on her bed. Then, with just the tips of her fingers and thumbs, she began caressing his face and forehead. There was no pressure on him, just the soft finger tips that vibrated now on his closed eyelids, then on his lips and cheeks and at the back of his neck. He felt her lips gently touch his, as her fingers found all the nerve endings around his neck and shoulders. Years, troubles, extraneous thoughts drained away. Then he felt only one set of finger tips on his chest, vibrating over his nipple. He marveled at the exquisite muscular control it took her to massage him in this way.

Opening his eyes, he saw Mayna's other hand deftly unhooking the gold dragons that held her gown so tightly about her. It fell apart revealing her bare breasts. They were small and as hard as those of a young girl. The Oriental sheath slithered from her to the floor, leaving her nude but for her sheer black lace panties.

The second phase of this nerve-treatment game that she had taught him now unfolded. Her tongue darted over and around his other nipple as both hands were still vibrating on him. Her whole body, which she now pressed to him, vibrated. Every part of her quivered. His part in the game was to resist, until he could no longer, before finally pulling off her panties and taking her. He and Mayna were at one and the same time making love to each other and in combat, she trying to drive him to rape her, he fighting the desire that surged through him, making her continue the exquisite undulations of her body on his.

Mayna's finger tips, lips, and darting tongue found and stimulated every nerve, every sensitive and ticklish part of his body and finally—he lost track of time, was it seconds? an hour?—he could stand it no more. He ripped the flimsy undergarment from her. Mayna laughed and then cried in passion as she felt every nerve in his body, all the tension, every particle of his desire and longing erupt within her. Her tongue vibrated inside the mouth crushed to hers.

Later, when Whittelsie became conscious, his mind resumed functioning with a clarity that was painful. He *must* tell Mayna that he would have to end this aspect of their liaison.

Mayna felt him stir and reached her tapering fingers for him. "Oh . . ." she whispered, a note of disappointment in her voice, "we really are all gone."

"Yes," Whit sighed.

"Shall we take a bath and have dinner? I have that special turtle soup you like."

"In a few minutes, my dear."

Mayna lay beside him as Whit reviewed the problems of the U.S. mission in Mituyan. If only he could always think as clearly and dispassionately as he did just after Mayna's nerve treatment. He turned to look at her, and he knew he hadn't the strength to do without her.

PART III

LAND OF THE GROATS

CHAPTER FIFTEEN

Mike Forrester watched the foothills rise out of the rice field far ahead of the Air Mituyan DC-3 bound for Banthut, the chief city of the mountain country of Mituyan. He was a hood now, he thought grimly. In all his experience in foreign countries this was the one thing he had always avoided. He was a businessman, not an intelligence agent, and had maintained his status despite many attractive and sometimes threatening offers to use his natural cover as international promoter to work under cover for his own and even other governments.

At least, he thought ruefully, the show was all his. Take over the opium trade, keep it from the Mitcoms, work with Major Prescott in dealing with the tribesmen, and come up with a report on government officials rumored to be in league with the Communist opium operation. The briefing had been short because JRB was short on information.

"Use your own contacts, Mike," Cardinez had told him. "Recruit your own agents. Just one rule: nothing you do must be attributable to the U.S. mission here. When you need money, let us know and you'll get it."

So far Mike had enlisted the aid of one man in Tuyan City. Jimmy Gems, as he was known, sold jewelry at a fair price and enjoyed a reputation with Americans all over Asia as the man to see when you wanted a bargain in precious stones. How he acquired the stones, gold, and curios he sold was another story. One of Jimmy's biggest sources of revenue was arranging the sale of smuggled artifacts considered national treasures to museums and wealthy private collectors.

Jimmy had three wives, each with her own luxurious establishment, and countless mistresses. He loved to live in opulence, so he had to keep making a great deal of money.

Opium? He'd give it a try. Mike had opened up with Jimmy to the extent that he was not getting into this business strictly for the money. Jimmy, to Mike's immense satisfaction, was even more enthusiastic when he discovered he would be working for the Americans, and gave him the name of a man to see in Banthut, Charlie Tiger.

The plane tossed about as it hit the turbulence rising from the edge of the hill country. Banthut was on a high plateau noted for its year-round cool climate and magnificent big-game hunting in the mountainous jungles; and many of the wealthy Mituyans and foreigners had villas in the mountain resort city. King Barkoon's villa had been the most magnificent of all; but because it was outside the area patrolled by the Province Police and the army, no one dared occupy it until JRB leased it for Major Prescott's headquarters.

Mike Forrester had only visited Banthut once before, when Luna had come down with a mysterious fever that the doctors said could be cured only by a long visit to a cool climate. As the plane circled over the city he tried to pick out familiar landmarks. The hotel, once known as the King Barkoon and now called the National, was a large, white, square structure rising four stories. Tennis courts, a nine-hole golf course, bungalows for rent by the fortnight, and a large swimming pool surrounded it. There was no more enjoyable resort in Asia, and Mike wished he had dared bring Luna along; but, being new to the agent business, he was afraid he'd make a mistake that would compromise him, or even endanger Luna, since Communist agents must abound in Banthut.

The plane landed and taxied up to the terminal, a neat, white, concrete block and glass building. There seemed to be a large crowd of Mituyans waiting, many of them saffron-robed bonzes. Then he remembered that three Buddhist monks had boarded the plane in Tuyan City. They must be pretty important to stir up all this fuss. The plane cut its engines and Mike watched the bonzes debark. One of the three, who seemed to be the number-two man in the group, looked vaguely familiar. Perhaps he was the bonze they called the Mad Monk of Tiking. Mike had seen Han Li Phang twice in Tiking. He thought this was the same monk.

The Buddhist priests were greeted with great respect by the crowd and led through the VIP entrance to the street beyond. Mike and the rest of the passengers went through the regular entrance to claim their suitcases. The cool air, a fairly constant seventy-four degrees, was refreshing after the heat of Tuyan City. If I have to fight Communists, at least this is the right climate to fight them in, he said to himself. He claimed his suitcases and took a waiting taxi to the hotel.

Once established in his bungalow, Mike took a cab down to the main business area of Banthut. Most of the shops specialized in curios, skins, elephant tusks, and Groat handicrafts. There were a number of stores, mostly in disrepair now, which advertised that they arranged hunting trips. With the rise of Mitcom activity in the mountain country, there were few safari customers. Occasionally, mountain tribesmen in loincloths and black pajama shirts walked in their funny birdlike strides down the street and stopped to peer into the windows of tinsmiths; pots and pans were always in short supply with the poverty-stricken mountain people.

Finally Mike found the store he was seeking—Charlie Tiger's—and walked in. A bold decorative scheme at the back of the shop dominated the entire room. Facing each other were two huge curving elephant tusks, their points almost touching. Beneath the tusks hung the ancient flag of the Barkoon kings of Mituyan. The only difference between it and the modern flag—three thick vertical stripes, two yellow, the center red—was the inclusion of the facing tusks. This was a dangerous display of pro-Barkoon sentiment, Mike thought. The device of the tusks, symbolizing Barkoon I's victory over the Chinese by the use of war elephants three hundred years earlier, had been outlawed by KaritKi. Mike was inspecting the flag when the proprietor approached.

"You want real imperial flag of Mituyan for souvenir?" The shop's owner, Charlie Tiger, was a tall, well set up Chinese with several gold teeth gleaming from his mouth. "Very old." His voice lowered. "Very rare."

"I thought it was against the law to display imperial flag," Mike said.

Charlie Tiger shrugged. "Maybe so in Tuyan City. Here"—he grinned knowingly at Mike—"no sweat." He ran his hand over the flag lovingly. "You want to buy?"

Mike shook his head. "I live in Mituyan, Port Raket, and Tiking. I have big friends in Palace. I have to be careful."

Charlie Tiger burst out laughing. "Minister Branot give out imperial flag to his American friends as rare souvenir. I know; I make for him. But this one"—he clucked his tongue—"very old."

Mike smiled back at the Chinese and stuck out his hand. "I'm Mike Forrester. Jimmy Gems sent me to you."

"Aie yee!" Charlie Tiger's grin was wide. "Come back to my office." He led Mike toward a door and shouted something in Chinese. Immediately a pretty Chinese girl appeared in a chongsam with the Mituyan slit up to her hip.

"This is Peone," Charlie explained. "My number-three daughter. Aie yah. Three daughters, no sons." He proudly introduced her. "Peone, this is the man we have been expecting, Mr. Mike Forrester."

Peone smiled and held out her hand. "It is a pleasure and honor to meet you, sir. We have heard of the famous American businessman, Mr. Forrester. Now at last we are privileged to meet him."

"Peone went English school since little girl. Aie yah! Expensive."

"I will earn it all back for you, Father, plus"—she winked at Mike—"a bloody healthy piece of interest."

"We will be in my office," Charlie Tiger said. "Later at Tat time we have eat."

Mike followed Charlie Tiger into his office, the den of an exceptionally well-to-do Chinese merchant. A trader himself, Mike's eyes roamed over a hundred thousand dollars worth of jade carvings, ivory inlaid furniture, and a fluorescent-lighted showcase of blue and black sapphires, rubies, black and white strands of pearls that made his fingers twitch to touch them. Delightedly, Charlie Tiger watched Mike's open admiration, then seated himself behind his desk and gestured to the richly upholstered mahogany chair opposite. "Two days ago Jimmy Gems send telegram. Say you come. Not say more."

Mike pulled a sweat-proof oilskin folder from a pocket sewed into the inside of his sport shirt, opened it, and drew out a folded piece of parchment that he handed to Charlie Tiger.

"Read this. It will explain everything. Jimmy Gems is old friend. I buy my own wife's jewelry from Jimmy. We do much business together. Many years."

Charlie Tiger studied the Chinese characters carefully. Then he breathed deeply and put the sheet down. "Aie yee! Aie yah! Very, very dangerous!"

"Very much money," Mike said.

"You very big trader—big rubber, big tea. But this very big, even for you."

"I can handle it," Mike replied with confidence he hardly felt. "I have many friends out with the Groats now."

Charlie Tiger shook his head. "There only one time when KaritKi government men and Communists work together, use guns together against outsider. That in poppy business. I know. I try. I almost dead."

"It's not the guns I'm worried about. I have more, better guns. I need the machine to move and sell a hundred, maybe two hundred kilo heroin a month." Mike stared into the shocked eyes of Charlie Tiger. "Jimmy Gems wants to be part of the machine. How about you?"

"Maybe Jimmy Gems don't know this poppy," Charlie Tiger evaded him. "Province Police, Mituyan Freedom Front, Mituyan Army—they got strong machine, too strong."

"Their machine is useless if they have no poppy," Mike stated. "I have an air service available. I have an army of Groats trained and armed and led by Americans. I can get the poppy at its source as well as they can. I can even sell half of it legitimately, maybe one hundred kilos a month. But I want to take it all, all the poppy in the Groat country."

"Mr. Forrester," Charlie said quietly, his eyes shrewd, "you are big trader, but this poppy business—not money you really after. Tell Charlie Tiger what you look after, for true."

"Charlie, you tell me first. What do you know about the poppy? Then I'll tell you what I want."

Charlie Tiger nodded. "OK. My business mostly gold, gems. My people smuggle sapphires, emeralds, jade, mostly gold to me here. I send out—to Jimmy Gems, to others. They sell. My people know poppy business. It change much in last few years. The poppy sold here in Banthut by the Communists. TrangTi the province chief get very rich. Mitcoms take the food, the medicine, the machinery, even jeeps sometimes that come from United States in boxes with hands shaking in friendship. You know?"

"Sure, our economic aid distributed through USOM here."

"Yes, USOM. Communists take poppy from Groats very cheap and get everything they need to make strong army. They trade poppy for supplies which TrangTi given free by Americans to pass out to people in this province."

"I will be seeing TrangTi," Mike said. "At the Palace in Tuyan City my wife and I have friends. They send word to Colonel TrangTi that I am a friend."

"Are you friend of Palace?" Charlie Tiger asked.

"I am a friend of Mituyan. It's good business at the moment to have Palace and high-government connections."

"Good business for me too," Charlie Tiger admitted. "TrangTi get paid in many different money. I discount TrangTi's money fifty, sometimes sixty percent and give him gold. Of course, if American dollars, can only discount ten percent. He happy, money come free to him, I send money with my people to Hong Kong. My bank give me U.S. dollars or gold for maybe only twenty-five, thirty-percent discount on Mituyan metas, Bardans pesetas, Yanna dollars, Vietnam piastres. Gold come back to me here and start all over again." Charlie Tiger shrugged. "Big business now in Mituyan selling American dollars and gold to people who think their country collapse and they have no money left. Even big government people."

After a long silence Mike sighed, feeling himself backed into a corner and realizing Cardinez had asked a far more complicated, dangerous, and near-impossible job of him than he had realized. "Well, Charlie Tiger, I guess there's not much I can do for you. You're getting yours as it is."

"Jimmy Gems know all this when he send you to me," Charlie Tiger answered inscrutably. "But he send anyway."

"What does that mean?"

"So far I tell you about half the poppy. You know where half, maybe more go?" When Mike shook his head, Charlie Tiger smiled and continued. "OK, I tell you. Communists take half poppy to Yanna border. Yanna neutral." Charlie Tiger grinned. "That mean Chinese, Vietnamese Communists have plenty big camps there. Mituyan Communists trade much poppy to Chinese and Vietnamese for Chinese, even Russian guns and bullet."

Charlie Tiger smiled wryly. "So you see, poppy make Mituyan Communist strong. And you know what else? Chinese Communists take poppy they get for weapons, and you know where it goes?"

"Where?"

"It go to New York Maybe to Cuba first. It become dollars, dollars come back, give Communist China balance of trade with Western world. Americans become—what you call?—junkies?"

Mike almost felt sorry for the men of the American mission having to make sense out of their jobs. Some of the men, he amended, not all. Not Grady Rourke, for example. If the fat, lazy slob would just once get off his tail and see that U.S. taxpayers were supporting the narcotics trade and Communist infiltration, then perhaps something could be done to stem this self-perpetuating drain on American men and money.

Charlie Tiger chuckled softly at the bleak expression on Mike Forrester's face. "OK, I tell you. Now you tell me. Why you really here? You here make more money in poppy? I hear about Mike Forrester. I hear he never go into business he not understand first."

Mike smiled sheepishly. "I guess you got me, Charlie Tiger. I don't know anything about poppy. I never want to know. And the more I know the less I like it." He let his eyes feast on the gems in the case. "Believe it or not, Charlie, certain high-ranking Americans in Tuyan City think I can slow up the Communists, hurt them bad by taking over the poppy business. What you say proves they are right. I must build up an organization out here and in Tuyan City to monopolize the trade. My contacts can sell more than half of it to legal drug-processing plants around the world. The rest I figured would keep my machine well oiled. My contacts feel that the people who yell the loudest would be those closest to the Communists."

"Loud yell sure to come from Palace," Charlie Tiger said, grinning.

Mike nodded dourly. "You're right. So why bother?"

"Maybe if some people bother, not too late to save this country."

"Would you, a Chinese, bother?"

"This is my country. The Communists take China because nobody bother, everybody steal everything. I like Mituyan. No place else in the world for me but Banthut. Nice air here, best in Asia."

"Are you saying you'd be interested in helping me keep the Groat's poppy from the Communists?"

"We talk later. Now, Tat time. Number-three daughter make us tea, good eat."

When, late in the afternoon, Mike left Charlie Tiger's establishment, he could no longer think of it as a shop; for the first time he felt there might be a chance of successfully controlling the poppy trade, at least long enough to force everyone working with the Communists to expose themselves.

Back at the hotel Mike showered, changed, and at six o'clock told a driver to take him to The House of Jasmine. The large reconverted mansion belonged to one of Barkoon's uncles who was also in exile and served as one of Banthut's most popular meeting places for men. Its downstairs was a series of private dining rooms, a bar, and a restaurant. Ten girls, sometimes more, sometimes less, depending on the season, had private rooms on the two upper floors. The scent of the jasmine bushes growing thickly around the place gave the house its name. This was Mike's first visit, and he looked around uncertainly. A Mituyan girl immediately invited him to buy her a drink, but he politely declined. He walked through three rooms before he saw Major

Prescott in slacks and a sport shirt sitting on a sofa in the crowded bar. "Mind if I sit down?"

"Help yourself," Prescott answered.

A girl appeared and took a drink order. Casually, Prescott asked: "Make your contact OK?"

"Under control," Mike replied.

"You'll make it as planned to my headquarters at Barkoon's old lodge in two days?"

"Right. My man is Charlie Tiger. He has a cousin, Johnny Elephant, who's taking me there on a hunting safari. We leave the day after tomorrow."

"Fine. I'll have the sacrifice set up for the next day, and you'll be made an honorary member of the Groat tribe."

"Tomorrow I'll pay a courtesy call on TrangTi and get that out of the way."

"Sorry about that," Prescott said. "I hate that bastard, burns my ass to have to be polite to the murdering, thieving sonofabitch."

"Got to be done." The drink arrived and Mike held it up. "Luck to our side." Prescott nodded somberly as Mike sipped the drink.

Finally the question that had been on Prescott's lips slipped out. "How's Marlene? Have you seen her?"

"As a matter of fact my wife and I saw her yesterday. When I mentioned I was coming to Banthut she asked me to give you her fondest wishes."

"She's the most beautiful girl I've ever known."

"Of course living in the Orient for any length of time makes any blonde round-eye look good," Mike said, talking as much to himself as to Prescott.

"Maybe. But my memory of Caucasian girls hasn't faded yet. Marlene beats any I ever saw."

Mike looked around the room. "This is quite a place," he said, changing the subject.

"We do alright."

"We?"

"The House of Jasmine was started by JRB."

"No one told me. It was just given as a contact point."

"My predecessor out here was a civilian hood. Before he joined the Agency he used to run a bar in Maryland, a few miles from D.C. He became such a powerful source of information in Washington, his waitresses were all spies and the booths were bugged, that they finally took him into the big spookery at Langley. Naturally, when he was assigned to Banthut, he started a bar and whorehouse." Prescott chuckled. "Sure, we get some of our hottest information out of this place. If you ever need to make contact with any of us, see Madam Susie. I'll introduce you to her."

Mike shook his head wonderingly. "I guess I wasn't cut out for this business. I get a feeling that I'm dreaming it all, that it isn't real."

"It's not bad duty when you get used to it. Biggest question here at The House of Jasmine is what to do with all the profits. Fortunately there's this missionary, the Reverend Maynard, who's got a lot of things going. He gets most of the money for the leprosarium, the orphanage, and a couple of clinics he's started. We don't tell him where the money comes from, and I don't think he cares as long as he can keep all his projects going. He's with us, one of our best sources, so if you need information, go to him."

A handsome, middle-aged Eurasian woman walked across the room toward them. "That's Susie. She's your number-one asset here. She can always raise me or one of my men on the single side-band we have up in the roof of this place."

Prescott introduced Susie to Mike and said, "He's with us, Susie."

"You come here any time, Mike," she said. "Anything you want to know now?"

"If you can find out why the Mad Monk of Tiking is in town, it might be interesting."

"I'll put my girls on it," she promised.

A huge blond American in civilian clothes barged through the room and pulled up beside Susie. "Sir, the U-10 pilot wants to make it to the lodge before dark. Are you ready to go?"

"Sergeant Barton, you met Mr. Forrester, didn't you?"

The Animal nodded. "Yes, sir. The night Frenchie's was bombed." He reached a hand across the table and Mike shook it.

"We'll be seeing Mr. Forrester around for a while, Barton."

"That's good with me. He's almost as good a medic as Cavanaugh. I remember he worked on some of the guys with just his shirt for a bandage."

Prescott stood up. "See you day after tomorrow. Can we drop you off anywhere in the jeep?"

"How about the Reverend Maynard's mission."

"No sweat, sir." The Animal grinned. "We're over there all the time."

"Check with me tomorrow, Mr. Forrester," Susie reminded him. "I'll have something for you on the shavehead."

"Tomorrow," Mike said and followed the big sergeant and Prescott out of The House of Jasmine.

CHAPTER SIXTEEN

The first thing the following morning Reverend Maynard called for Mike in the Evangelical Mission's pickup truck. As he had promised the night before, he set out to show Mike as many of the mission's projects as they could safely visit. The Mitcoms were constantly pushing their attacks, kidnapings, and murders closer and closer to the large cities.

The Reverend Maynard wore a pith helmet, a khaki shirt tucked into the waist of his khaki pants, and laced boots. He seemed to be in his fifties and was as lean as a combat colonel. The entire Evangelical Mission was under his supervision. Three medical missionaries were spread about the Groat country, and a number of "jungle beachheads" —as he called his churches—had been built out in the villages.

Their first stop was the leprosarium. It was five miles from Banthut on the mountain road up to the Yanna border. A barbed-wire fence enclosed its approximately twenty acres, which were given to the mission by the government. "Major Prescott got us the barbed wire," Maynard said, "and had one of his engineers and a team of Groat tribesmen build the fence."

He drove the pickup through a gate and up a long dirt road to a clean, white, concrete-block main building with two long wings projecting from either side.

"The wings are the ladies' and men's wards. Already we're running out of room. But we are successful in getting the lepers to come in. Have you ever been in a leprosarium?"

Mike shook his head. "We have none in my part of the country, and the lepers have nowhere to go. I should get one built."

"What we try to do is catch it in its early stages, when it can still be cured. Our medical missionaries test every person for the disease who comes to them, and any doubtfuls are persuaded to come here." Maynard led the way into the main hall of the leprosarium. Both Mituyans and Groats were seated on benches, fearful expressions on their faces. Maynard entered an office where a Mituyan nurse and a medical missionary were conferring over a young Groat woman. She wore a black wraparound skirt and a blanket loosely over her shoulders. Her bare breasts were large and firm. The nurse had a feather in her hand, and while the missionary in a white jacket held the Groat woman's attention, talking to her in her language, the nurse switched the feather over the woman's ankles, insteps, and bottoms of the feet. Reverend Maynard watched anxiously. Not once did the Groat woman evidence any sensation of tickling or feeling.

"She's got it," Maynard said. "No sensation in her feet or ankles. Fortunately I think she was brought to us in time for medication to have some effect."

Maynard nodded to the nurse and medic and led Mike into the men's ward. "It isn't really contagious under controlled conditions," he said reassuringly. "If it was, I'd have contracted it long ago."

"I'm worried," Mike said with a smile.

"Every man in here has the disease under some control through medication," Maynard said. "If we had about ten more of these clinics spread throughout the mountain country, where leprosy seems to be most prevalent, we could perhaps lick the disease." Soulful eyes stared out of sagging, leonine faces, some with ears and noses partially eaten away.

"What do you do with the hopeless cases?" Mike asked.

"There's a colony further out where they are taken care of. We support that one too. It's one place the Communists never go near," Maynard added grimly.

They left the ward and went back out through the waiting room, where the eyes of the patients waiting for testing and medication rolled at them half hopefully, half fearfully. "I just wanted you to see what we are doing out here," Maynard said as they left the leprosarium. "Now let me take you to our orphanage where the children learn their own language and English, so that when they leave us they are ready for high school."

By lunchtime Mike had inspected the orphanage, two churches, a clinic for non-lepers, and a school. He was deeply impressed and told Reverend Maynard as much. "It's too bad more people don't understand what missionaries in countries like Mituyan really do."

"It takes a great deal of money to finance these works," Maynard replied. "Before we talk further and get to what I know is on your mind, I wanted you to see for yourself how we put your money to good use. Of course my people and I know the risks we take as part-time intelligence agents for your agency; but our finest converts among the Groats, those who finally do find Jesus Christ and bring Him to their people, are murdered and kidnaped by the Communists, so we realize that we must be activists in the fight against them."

"I'm very new at this business, Reverend Maynard," Mike said. "Like you, I was recruited because of special qualifications and capabilities. This is my first experience fighting the Communists. I was wondering if you knew of any USOM program that is being successfully carried out that we could visit?"

"My friend, Mr. Alvarro—he's a native of the Philippines on contract to USOM—is in charge of the government-protected villages for the mountain tribesmen. We'll try to find him."

They drove to three temporary mountain tribesmen's villages until they located Alvarro, a small, dark-skinned, intense Filipino in his mid-forties.

Mike and Reverend Maynard followed Alvarro around a Groat tribe village. The women were industriously grinding manioc and working on shacks, but the men seemed inert, incapacitated. Alvarro, seeing Mike's eyes move from one lethargic Groat tribesman to the next, explained. "The men are hunters," he said. "When we take them away from their hunting grounds and give them their food, they become idle and drunken. We try to encourage them to join fighting units armed, trained, and led by Major Prescott's teams, but they don't want to go without their wives. We are coordinating with the JRB projects, and as new Groat families come into this camp, others, after screening and medical attention, go out and join the fortified camps that patrol against Communist infiltrators."

"Sounds as though the program is working," Mike remarked.

"Yes, but I see the American mission in Tuyan City making all the same old errors. Just yesterday I was talking to TrangTi, begging him to release USOM supplies for this village. You know," Alvarro digressed, "Mr. Grady Rourke, our chief in Tuyan City, forbids USOM materials to come directly to the USOM representatives at province level. He has never been up here personally to see our problems."

"That's what I wanted to ask you about," Mike said.

"Mr. Rourke gives all supplies to the Mituyan authorities in Tuyan City, and we have to beg and sometimes buy them back from the province chief. At any rate, what I was saying—TrangTi, after much pleading on my part, finally sold me enough rice to keep this village alive another week. I paid him in USOM funds.

Alvarro sighed deeply. "All the same old mistakes from the days in Vietnam when perhaps we could have avoided the big war are being made here. And now TrangTi is already talking about putting Mituyan soldiers and commanders over our Americans in the mountains with the tribesmen. This is what happened when I was in the Central Highlands of Vietnam just as we were gaining control of the entire area. Our Country Team there in 1962 and '63 went ahead and let Diem and Nhu have their way. We lost more than half the tribesmen to the Communists, and the rest hated the Vietnamese. I can say that the heavy casualties Americans suffered fighting in the Central Highlands of Vietnam can be directly blamed on the apathetic American officials in Saigon for letting the Ngo Dinh family hand over the entire mountain country to the Communists."

Alvarro returned them to the pickup truck, and on the way back to the hotel Mike asked Maynard if he knew whether anything was happening in Banthut with the monks. "Three of them came up on the plane with me; one of them I think was our big agitator in Tiking. Are we going to have religious problems on top of everything else?"

"That's one I can't answer."

"If the Buddhist leaders are anything like the ones in Vietnam, and I see no reason to believe that we don't have a Trich Tri Quang running around loose in Mituyan, he's probably in town for some kind of political meeting. We ought to know everything we can about them."

"I'll put the Buddhist section of my organization on the case," Maynard chuckled as he let Mike off at the hotel.

In his box Mike found a note to call the province chief's headquarters as soon as convenient. He had done so routinely on his arrival in hopes of seeing Colonel TrangTi; now, even though it was Tat time, he called TrangTi's office again, and to his surprise Mike found himself put directly through to the province chief. TrangTi invited Mike to come over right away and have lunch; from his inflection, the invitation sounded more like a command, and Mike lost no time calling for a car and driver.

The province chief's headquarters was a large villa confiscated from a member of the imperial family—down to the last chair, Mike surmised. TrangTi certainly had the most luxurious establishment of any province headquarters Mike had visited. A guard led him through a courtyard to a wing of the villa that served as TrangTi's living quarters. The province chief was waiting in his well-appointed parlor and greeted Mike warmly. He was a small man with a large mustache for a Mituyan and beady, protruding eyes under a beetle brow. His thick black hair was combed straight back from his forehead.

"It is an honor to be asked to share Tat time with you," Mike said. "The Premier told me you were one of his most important chiefs when I was at the palace last week."

TrangTi beamed at the praise. "The Palace sent word that I could expect you. I hope I will be able to assist you in what you are here to accomplish."

Mike thanked him, but said there was little he could do right now. "This trip is more in the nature of an exploration."

TrangTi gestured at a chair across a coffee table. "Exploration?"

"I believe there must be potential business opportunities in these mountain provinces. If I can find something the Groat people can make and sell, perhaps we can improve their economic opportunities. Obviously it will then make it much harder for the Communists to subvert them."

"The Groats are dirty, savage, lazy animals," TrangTi spat out, not bothering to hide his traditional Mituyan contempt of the tribespeople. "They are beyond help. We can only try to control them with the army."

"But you don't want them fighting for the Mitcoms," Mike argued.

"We are trying to keep them apart from the Communists. Have you visited the hamlets we are building?"

"Yes, I saw one this morning. The Groats don't like to be cooped up in hamlets like that, from what I could gather."

"The Groats will do what they're told. The plan is to give them all a chance to come into our hamlets. At the end of six months all Groats not in government-protected hamlets will be considered Mitcom sympathizers, and we will treat them accordingly. The air force will bomb their villages and army patrols will find and destroy them."

Mike knew that arguing was fruitless, but he felt a sinking sensation in his stomach hearing this "solution" to the Groat question. It was not so much its cruel ruthlessness as its utter ineffectiveness, and the fact that TrangTi thereby would surely lose the entire mountain country to the Communists.

"Now, Mr. Forrester," TrangTi probed. "What sort of business do you think you can do with these savages?"

"I don't know yet, Colonel. I'm taking an eight-day safari into the Groat country to see. There are many tourists in Tuyan City, and the number of American officers and men grows. Perhaps elephant tusks, tiger skins, Groat crossbows, and the like could be sold in the city for a profit. At any rate, I was asked by members of the American mission and Minister Branot to look at the situation with the eyes of a trader."

"You set yourself a dangerous mission. There are many Mitcom bands working with the Groats."

"I have a good guide, Charlie Tiger's younger brother, Johnny Elephant. He knows the Groats. Also, we will try to reach a Special Forces camp before dark each night. I don't think we'll be in much danger." Mike smiled to himself; throughout his stay in the Groat country he would be with well-armed Special Forces-led Groat tribesmen.

TrangTi rang a bell and a pretty, young Mituyan woman appeared with a pot of tea and two cups that she placed on the table. TrangTi introduced his wife and then dismissed her.

"I could lend you a squad of soldiers," TrangTi suggested, picking up his cup and sipping the green tea.

"I appreciate your concern, Colonel, but I'll be all right. Going into a Groat village with soldiers would give the people the wrong impression. It is important that they trust me from the beginning.

"They're savages—filthy," TrangTi said venomously. "I strongly oppose this so-called"—he paused, disbelief shining from his pop eyes and in the twisted smile under the thick mustache—"exploration trip of yours. However, since the Palace asked me to help you, I can only advise you that you are taking a heavy risk. I will put my feelings in a letter which will be delivered to you this afternoon. If anything should happen to you, I must be on record as having advised you against this expedition."

"I appreciate your concern, Colonel," Mike repeated.

The cunning look never left TrangTi's eyes. "Other than these skins and tusks is there no other Groat-country"—he paused as though choosing the words carefully—"*produce* you are interested in?"

"I am interested in anything I can sell for the Groats"—it was Mike's turn to pause—"legally."

TrangTi stared at Mike a few moments and then smiled and relaxed slightly. "All right, Mr. Forrester, enjoy your trip and when—perhaps I should say, *if*—you return, I will be most interested to hear what you have discovered. The Groats are my charges, and savages though they are it is still my job to help them."

TrangTi's wife returned to tell them lunch was ready, and the province chief led Mike into the ornate dining room. A crystal chandelier hung suspended above the long mahogany table. Cool mountain air circulated through the large windows. Mike and TrangTi sat at opposite ends of the table.

"Do you like beer with lunch?" TrangTi asked. "It is an American custom I have come to enjoy."

"Good thought."

TrangTi rang his bell and a man servant brought in two frosty bottles of beer and chilled glasses. "To a good trip," TrangTi said pleasantly, raising his glass.

They ate in Oriental style, holding a bowl of rice in the left hand

and mixing bits of meat and fish sauce into it with chopsticks held in the right hand. Mike put down his rice bowl and chopsticks, took a few swallows of beer, and asked: "Does our American aid program help you up here? I suppose that my work comes under USOM now."

"I can safely say that this province gets its share of your aid program. USOM is doing a fine job maintaining the Groat hamlet we have built." TrangTi concentrated on his rice, taking occasional swallows of beer. He had no more to say on the subject of U.S. aid.

Mike decided to try him on one more subject before giving up. "I noticed three bonzes on my plane yesterday. Do you have some sort of Buddhist convocations here from time to time?"

"I am an Anglican myself, Mr. Forrester. However, if you are interested, Banthut and Tiking are the two centers of Buddhism in this country, as you probably know. This would be a likely place for a meeting of the upper-level bonzes. My man at the airport did tell me that Han Li Phang, I believe some call him the Mad Monk of Tiking, came in yesterday. We are keeping an eye on him. He has a record for subversive activities. However, until recently he has been quite passive, I believe."

"None of the Groats are Buddhist, are they?"

TrangTi grinned. "You don't know your Groats, Mr. Forrester. They are strictly animists. They worship rocks, certain trees, rivers, and such. Also blood. You may see some of their practices—although for your sake I hope you don't. But Buddhists?" He laughed. "They have no religion whatsoever. These Groats are dirty savages, as you will find out."

"I talked to an American missionary who said he was converting some of the Groats to Christianity."

"Many missionaries have tried. I don't know of many Groats who stayed converted. It would probably be a good thing if they could be converted to some faith. But they are among the world's most primitive people. They are filthy walking-disease factories. I opposed the first Groat hamlet being built so close to Banthut, but the USOM people said they have to be close enough so the army can protect them."

Mike and the province chief finished eating in silence. TrangTi belched and stood up. "Mr. Forrester, I am very happy you could join me for lunch."

"I appreciate your inviting me, Colonel. It has been most interesting to hear your views on the Groats. When I come back from my trip, perhaps I'll be able to give you some new ideas."

"I will be expecting to see you as soon as you return." The province chief led the way from the dining room. "Well, I have much business waiting for me, I'm sorry to say. I'd like to sit and talk with you at length, but I am too pressed to take a decent Tat time. Of course we don't really need it in this cool climate. As a matter of fact, I notice that even in Tuyan City the Americans manage without Tat time."

TrangTi sent Mike back to the National Hotel in his staff car. At the desk Mike found a note from Reverend Maynard asking him to call as soon as possible at the Evangelical Mission.

"I've managed to acquire quite a bit of information in the last couple of hours on the bonzes," Maynard said when Mike arrived. "My Buddhist section is very efficient." He grinned. "Have to keep tabs on the competition, you know."

"Do the Buddhists go out and actively try to convert the heathen?" Mike asked.

"Never to my knowledge. They take a passive view, fortunately for us Christian missionaries. 'Come to us and we will tell you of the wisdom of The Buddha, or the Wisdom of Confucius,' they say if they're Confucian, but they never go out after converts. That's why Groats only get converted to Christianity."

"What have you learned?"

"It seems that this bonze who was on your plane, Han Li Phang, has come to Banthut to try to effect some alliance with the leading bonze in this area. Phang actually represents a very small number of Buddhists. His is a militant and political sect, and he has been active in bringing down governments since the last days of King Barkoon. He is a master at turning out demonstrations. Even though Barkoon was a Buddhist, Phang was against him. The various civil servants and ministers who succeeded Barkoon after he was exiled all suffered from Phang's political maneuvering."

"What is the Mad Monk really after?" Forrester asked. "Could he be a Mitcom sympathizer?"

"Basically he's an anarchist. He wants no government and no authority except his interpretation of Buddhism. I'm told, however, that Counselor Tarot made a deal with Phang just before his brother KaritKi staged his coup. Now it seems that whatever Tarot and KaritKi were doing for Phang has stopped. Phang is apparently trying to solidify his position as top spokesman for all the leading bonzes in Mituyan. My guess is he'll succeed because most of the true Buddhist leaders dislike politics and agitation."

"So, they'll allow a madman, and that's what I've heard he is, to manipulate the Buddhists rather than leave the serenity of their pagodas?"

"That's about the size of it, Mike. I hope my information will be of some use to the Agency."

"I'll see it gets into the right hands," Mike promised. "And now I'm afraid I have to leave you. There are many arrangements still to be made."

"Good luck. God go with you," the missionary said as Mike left to meet Charlie Tiger and Johnny Elephant and make final plans for the safari that would start out early the next morning.

CHAPTER SEVENTEEN

MIKE FORRESTER MET Charlie Tiger and Johnny Elephant at Charlie's store. It was seven in the morning, and Peone served them hot tea as last-minute plans were reviewed. Johnny Elephant, so named because before the guerrilla fighting became serious he was one of the finest elephant hunters in the mountains, was in high spirits at the prospect of a safari, even though hunting was not the main purpose of the expedition.

"It will take us no more than six hours to reach King Barkoon's old lodge," Johnny Elephant was saying. "I know the lodge well. Many time I hunt with the King." He frowned. "We all be much better here if King Barkoon back."

"That could happen too, Johnny," Mike said. "Now don't worry about Mitcoms or Communist Groats ambushing us. From the time we get into dangerous country there'll be friendly flank security along the route. If any shooting starts, we'll blast right back with these elephant guns. Help always will be only a few minutes away."

Johnny Elephant caressed the 40-mm. grenade launcher that looked like a giant-size single-barrel shotgun. The M-79, or elephant gun, as it was affectionately known among troops who had used it in combat, was the best answer to an ambush yet devised. It could aim grenades accurately at a point target, and anyone within a radius of twenty-five yards of impact was surely dead.

"Your men are all pretty good with weapons, I take it," Mike asked needlessly. "They may have to use them. In my suitcase are two M-16 automatic rifles and one thousand rounds of ammunition."

"Very good," Johnny said. "Don't know where you get this arsenal, but very good."

"OK, Charlie," Mike said, "We'll be back in eight or nine days with a couple of hundred kilos of poppy to sell."

"Main thing Mitcoms no get."

Mike nodded. "Right, Charlie. That *is* the important thing. No poppy, no trading. We'll put the squeeze on all of them."

They finished their tea, and then Mike and Johnny Elephant went out to the Land Rover. "JOHNNY ELEPHANT FAMOUS HUNTING" was painted on the sides, and two elephant tusks were mounted on the engine hood, giving the car a raffish appearance. Johnny and Mike got in the rear, and Johnny's two assistants sat up front to take turns driving along the rough jungle roads.

The town of Banthut was just coming awake as they headed into the mountainous jungle that surrounded the province capital. Five miles out of Banthut the roads became pitted dirt trails, and their vehicle bumped along at a slow pace. Five-gallon gas cans were strapped into holders all around the Land Rover, and every few miles they had to stop and tighten the straps that had worked loose.

Two hours out of Banthut, Johnny nudged Mike as they came to a small clearing in which stood a dozen bamboo and thatched houses on stilts. "This is new village. Hope friendly."

"Don't worry. There are friendlies around."

The inhabitants stared at the Land Rover with great curiosity. The men wore loincloths so tight that from the rear they looked naked. The women wore black skirts; blue and red beads hung from their necks, partially covering their bare breasts. Many of the women had babies strapped to boards on their backs. Some of the men carried crossbows and others the traditional tribesman's ax, blade cross-tied into one end of a bow-shaped wooden handle.

"They seem peaceable enough," Mike remarked.

"Groats peaceful except when Communists come to them and make them fight and hate the government."

Mike followed Johnny Elephant's example and waved and smiled to the people as the Land Rover jogged through the village. A few minutes later the jungle was as thick as ever, with no signs of human habitation anywhere. Slowly Mike relaxed his grip on the automatic rifle and slumped back against the bucking seat.

Every hour the Land Rover stopped and the two drivers changed places. "Plenty jaguar here," Johnny said. "Soon we get to tiger country. Maybe we see one in the road." He was carrying his high-powered sports rifle across his lap, ready for immediate use in case a wild animal appeared in their path. "Tiger, many wild animal like to walk in road; easier than jungle," Johnny explained.

"Looks like we're really deep in the mountains now," Mike said a little later, looking around. "I sure hope these friendlies *are* keeping an eye on us."

"Plenty Mitcoms and Groatcoms around here," said Johnny. He exchanged the sports rifle for the elephant gun, covering his side of the trail with it. Mike was doing the same on the other side of the Land Rover. The man in the front seat beside the driver had the lightweight automatic rifle pointed under the raised windshield straight down the trail.

"How much further do you figure we've got to go?" Mike asked.

"Taking longer than last time I come, two years ago. Road very bad." He looked at his watch. "Maybe another two hours."

Mike groaned and silently cursed Cardinez, Colonel Lawton, and the whole CIA and JRB, as the Land Rover battered his buttocks, liver, and kidneys. He firmly resolved to resign from the whole program as soon as this impossible caper was finished. He just wanted to be back with Luna on the tea property or on a sunny beach.

The hourly ten-minute breaks seemed longer and longer in coming. At noon they stopped for twenty minutes to eat sandwiches, and then pushed on through the jungle, up and down hills, sometimes having to stop and pull fallen branches out of the road. One man cleared the trail while the other three covered him with their weapons.

"We soon there," Johnny Elephant said cheerfully.

"How the hell did Barkoon make it out here?" Mike asked.

"Road much better ten years ago. Also, sometime King Barkoon fly. He have two airplane, build nice landingfield."

Mike would have liked to have come by plane, but that would have shown how closely he was working with the U.S. government, now the sole supplier of airplanes in Mituyan. After this little outing, he resolved, he'd never again make the trip by land vehicle.

Finally the pitted jungle trail widened and became a gravel and stone road. "Almost there," Johnny announced. The Land Rover stopped pitching and bucking and crunched along the ever improving road smoothly. Suddenly they burst out of the jungle into a huge cleared area in the center of which was a rambling two-story building set eight feet off the ground on concrete blocks. It was a series of three Swiss chalet A-frame structures surrounded by verandas. To the rear of the imposing hunting lodge, built in brown, rough-hewn planks and trimmed in white, stretched out a long, wide, grass airstrip. Two airplanes stood under a camouflaged roof at one end of the runway. One was a twin-engine ship, the other a single-engine plane with an abnormally high vertical stabilizer and high cantilevered wings. Mike recognized the single-engine plane as the ubiquitous U-10, or Heliocourier.

As they approached the lodge, Mike saw that all along the verandas facing out toward the jungle were armed men, as many as two dozen, on guard duty. They all wore the tiger-stripe jungle fatigues that were a trademark of Special Forces civilian irregulars. Wide-brim and camouflage fatigue hats shaded their faces, and on their feet were the canvas and rubber bata boots, highly prized by jungle fighters all over Southeast Asia.

From the center A-frame structure, two tall Americans in dungarees, boots, and green T-shirts stepped out on the veranda and walked down the steps to greet the Land Rover. Mike immediately recognized Major Prescott and waved.

As he and the three Chinese hunters piled out, Mike pressed both hands to the small of his back and tried to straighten it, grimacing as muscles pulled and sore spots began to work themselves out. Prescott introduced him to Captain Jenkins.

"If I'd known what kind of a ride it was going to be, you'd never have got me here by land," Mike declared.

Prescott grinned broadly. "I know what you mean, Mike. We all have to do it once, just to appreciate the air ride next time."

"How about a cold beer?" Captain Jenkins suggested.

"Cold beer damned good right now," said Johnny Elephant, looking around the lodge admiringly. "Say, this place look as good as when I hunt with King. Too bad King can't see it now."

"Come on in and see our TOC," Prescott said. Mike and the three

Chinese followed him up the steps and into the main hall, which had been made into a large Tactical Operations Center. The walls were covered with charts and maps, and the desks were neatly marked "G-2," "Air Operations," "G-3," "Personnel," and all the other designations found at the headquarters of a regimental-size operation. Americans, a few Mituyans, and several Groat tribesmen neatly and proudly dressed in combat fatigues, sat at the desks or were studying the maps on the wall. From the rear of the TOC came the steady crackling of radios.

"We run the whole mountain-tribesmen program out of here," Prescott said proudly. "One more year, the way we're going, and we'll get all the Communists out of the Groat country and have most of the tribes on our side."

"Aren't you afraid of an attack?" Mike asked.

"We always have a minimum of two companies of well-trained Groats patrolling in the jungle around here and setting up ambushes. We've been following your progress for the last four hours by radio, ever since you came through that village; it's our last outpost toward Banthut."

"Do you make much contact with Communist patrols?" Mike asked.

"They're out there. Sometimes we catch one in an ambush. But our biggest job is working with the Groats in their own villages. We've got the number-one poppy village in the mountains under surveillance now. We have a team of six Americans trying to win the people over with civic-action projects. You'll be spending the next week in there. By God, if you can win over that chief and a couple more like him to trade with you, you'll be the biggest dope peddler in Asia."

"Thanks," Mike said drily. "That is indeed a distinction worth fighting for."

"I'm afraid you'll get in enough fighting to satisfy you," Captain Jenkins said. "We're getting agent reports that Mitcoms and their Groatcoms are on their way down from the Yanna border to collect their poppy. We're going to have to work fast to get set up before they come."

An American of indeterminate rank and outfit passed around bottles of beer, as Mike asked how they reached this poppy-peddlers' paradise.

"It's a day's march through the jungle. We're already building an airstrip for the U-10. Couple more days and we'll be able to fly."

"I never seem to hit it right to fly," Mike complained good-naturedly. "But if I'm going to get so rich, I guess a little hiking won't hurt me. I'd rather walk than get my insides racked up again."

"Sure, it's a nice walk. We might even get some action," Prescott added. "There's a couple of Communist platoons wandering out there somewhere."

"How's the hunting?" Mike asked.

"Good. One of our sergeants shot a tiger last week. But the sonofabitch, three tours in Vietnam behind him, got so scared of the tiger he riddled him with his M-16. Blew the tiger so apart there wasn't any skin to hang up."

Mike turned to Johnny Elephant. "Your job is to go hunting around here every day so that when we go back I'll have some trophies to explain what the hell I was doing in this jungle."

"OK, good duty." Johnny asked Major Prescott: "You have movies here?"

"Every night, Johnny."

"Westerns?"

"We've got a big one in color tonight," Captain Jenkins answered. "Every off-duty Groat will be knocking the doors down to get in."

"Let me show you your room for tonight, Mike," Prescott said, and, as The Animal appeared, added: "Sergeant Barton will show Johnny Elephant and his boys where they can stay."

Mike followed Charlie Prescott out of the main building and into one of the side chalets. "Say, this place is damned luxurious," Mike exclaimed. Tapestries, paintings, rugs, ivory-inlaid furniture, and glass-covered bookcases containing books in many languages adorned the living room. The windows looked out over the jungle and the valleys below the lodge's mountaintop location.

"These were Barkoon's quarters. On orders from the top we have a bunch of Mituyan craftsmen restoring it to the way it used to be. Don't ask me why. You might as well have the master bedroom tonight, Mike," he continued. "It's got two bathrooms. One's a woman's bathroom, complete with bidet."

The master bedroom had a breathtaking view of the mountains and valleys. Mike stared out of the windows for some moments, then he turned and gazed about the room. The floor was covered with priceless Persian rugs; two overstuffed sofas faced the mountains. The bedside tables were ivory covered, and royal-blue draperies hung on the wall above the bed.

"This is a little too rich for my blood," Mike said finally. "You need a first-class, beautiful mistress to sleep in this room."

Prescott nodded. "I know just the girl I'd like to bring out here for a week. A dirty old soldier like me never runs into class like this woman has."

Mike smiled. "I share your views on Fraulein Straltz. . . . Let's get out of the King's suite and find me a cot some place. I don't like the vibrations in this room. Too goddamned sumptuous for one man going out in the jungle the next morning."

"OK, Mike, there's an extra sack in my room. I guess I'm in the servants' quarters, but in this joint they're not bad either."

At six o'clock the next morning, just as the sun was rising above the jungles, Major Prescott, Sergeant Barton, Mike, and a strong platoon of fifty Groats disappeared into the jungle, heading for the village that was the poppy-growing center for this part of the mountain country. Although the security around the hunting lodge was excellent, it was always possible that Mitcoms could have the area under observation by telescope from a mountaintop miles away, and Prescott made sure his men were under the green canopy before daylight to keep the Mitcoms from observing the size of his patrol and the direction they were taking. Once in the jungle, they were safe unless they walked dead into a Mitcom ambush.

Beside Prescott walked a bright-eyed Groat tribesman who was the platoon leader. The Groat and Major Prescott were able to talk in a language they had evolved based on English.

"Flank, flank, Goween," Prescott said, pointing ahead of them on the trail to the right and the left. Goween jabbered out orders, and a dozen men detached themselves from the main column and went on ahead, half of them disappearing into the jungle on the right, the other half on the left.

"If the Mitcoms do have an ambush set out, our boys will hit it and give us warning," Prescott explained.

"Must be tough for the guys, fighting through the bush," Mike commented.

"They change every hour during the ten-minute break."

Sergeant Barton had been walking behind Mike and Major Prescott, watching the way Mike held his rifle. "Excuse me, sir, I see you're left-handed."

"That's right, Sergeant."

"A number of the Groat tribes take it as an insult if you reach for something with your left hand. To them it shows disrespect or contempt for what they're giving you. Also, if you give them a present, make sure you hand it to them with your right hand. I don't know what superstitions these Groats we're going to visit believe, but until we find out we might as well play safe."

"Thanks, Sergeant. I got a pretty good briefing from Reverend Maynard, but he forgot to mention that. I'll remember."

"Lieutenant Panton has been in there with a split A detachment, six men in all, for ten days. He and Sergeant Cavanaugh, the medic, should be pretty hip to the ways of this village by now," Prescott said. "Main thing we've got to remember is to walk in very slowly, not touch anything; you never know what tree or what stone or what post is sacred. Cavanaugh will tell us how to proceed."

"I'll watch you, Charlie," Mike promised.

"Right. They should treat you as a big celebrity. One of Red Cavanaugh's main missions was to build you up to the chief as the big white trader from beyond the mountains."

"I'll try not to disappoint anyone," Mike said wryly.

Each fifty-minute march was followed by a ten-minute break. Because of the height, the air was not uncomfortably hot, and the heavy green jungle canopy shaded them from direct sun. The walk was more comfortable and less taxing than the Land Rover jog the previous day. Still, Mike would have far preferred to be striding around his own tea or rubber properties than walking through the Groat country wondering each moment if he was going to be ambushed.

The fourth break lasted an hour while the Groats prepared themselves a meal, ate, and took a rest. "These people are damned good in the mountains," Barton said as the three Americans sat in the shade, waiting for the tribesmen to build up their strength during the rest period. "If they'd eaten right all their lives, they'd probably be able to take it as well as we do. But they just don't have our stamina. Of course the Mituyans—Jesus! they're as bad as the Vietnamese. They want three hours rest in the middle of the day, and they knock off and make camp at five. I'd hate to be on a Mit patrol with Groatcoms after us."

After the hour break a new team moved ahead on flank security, and the patrol pushed on through the jungle. From time to time Major Prescott pulled the radio transceiver from the pack of the stubby tribesman walking ahead of him and tried to call Lieutenant Panton in the village they were approaching. In the middle of the afternoon, he finally raised him.

"We're less than five miles out," Prescott announced after the conversation. "All's under control, Panton says."

Less than two hours later the patrol broke out of the jungle and made contact with the village. It was a large one, built along the bank of a fast-flowing mountain stream. There were perhaps fifty longhouses, thatched bamboo structures built on stilts, every one oriented in the same direction, the end facing into the setting sun. There was a bamboo fence built around the entire village, and the main gate also faced the setting sun. As they approached, Mike, peering ahead, asked what was going on up at the gate.

A young man not much more than a boy, wearing a loincloth, was propped in front of the left gatepost. His hands were tied behind his back, and a rope around his neck hung taut from the top of the post. It seemed that if he were to sag at the knees he would hang himself. A young woman wearing a black skirt and bodice was similarly attached to the other gatepost. The hot sun beat upon them and their lips were dry and splitting, their eyes barely open, as they obviously struggled not to collapse and strangle themselves.

Prescott, leading the column, halted about fifteen yards from the gate and waited to be invited into the village. He looked compassionately at the boy and girl, pain and misery carved in their faces. "This is one of the old traditional tribe groups," he said. "They must be brother and sister, or cousins—anyway part of the same family. She must have been caught letting him hack her." Prescott shook his head. "The Groats believe that incest offends the spirits of the rivers and the trees worse than anything they can do, and bad luck will fall on the whole village. The boy probably had to stab a goat to death beside the river as a sacrifice. Then they take all the possessions of the boy's and girl's parents and divide them up among all the inhabitants of the village to make up for the bad yang, or spirit, these two kids have brought down on everyone."

"I hope we aren't mistaken for the bad yang," Mike said.

"That's the chance you take with these people. If the chief's wife dreamed of a red blanket last night, for instance, we're in trouble. Red-blanket dreams mean trouble from foreigners. You just can't tell. We've got to be damned careful."

After a five-minute wait, during which Mike tried to avert his eyes from the suffering boy and girl, an American in tiger camouflage fatigues walked out the gate with a barrel-chested, squat man wearing a loincloth and perhaps a dozen strands of blue beads around his neck.

"That's Lieutenant Panton," Prescott said. "I guess he's got the chief of the tribe with him." As they walked out the gate, the chief hawked up and spat at the feet of the girl. He carried himself erect, drawn up to his full five-and-a-half feet. Both ear lobes were drastically stretched by ivory disks that had been inserted in slits cut when the chief was a boy, with larger and larger disks added as he grew older.

As they approached, Lieutenant Panton and the chief both held up their right hands. Mike, Major Prescott, Barton, and the leader of the Groat platoon, Goween, also held up their right hands. When Panton and the chief were directly facing Prescott, they lowered their hands; Prescott and his party followed the chief's lead.

"Major Prescott, this is Chief Beemeer, near as I can pronounce his name," Panton said. "He runs this village they call Ba To. They use the regular Groat handshake, sir." The chief smiled, showing black rotting stumps of upper front teeth. His bottom teeth were mostly intact.

Prescott bowed to the chief and then, grasping his right wrist with his left hand, he stuck his right out. The chief did the same and they shook hands.

The Groat platoon leader and the chief exchanged words and a handshake. Then the chief and Mike shook hands. Panton saying a few words to the chief that caused him to hold Mike's hand longer than he had Prescott's. He looked Mike up and down curiously. Mike's height—he was a couple of inches taller than Prescott—seemed to impress Chief Beemeer, who then said a few words to Prescott and Mike that Panton translated as meaning they were invited to come into the village. The chief turned and led the newcomers into the compound, pausing at the gate to spit at the feet of the agonized boy.

"They're not usually this tough on the kids," Prescott said. "I guess this just isn't a reformed village. That means that when we have the sacrifice it'll be a hairy one. Notice the chief's teeth? Wait'll you see what they do to the kids here in the name of puberty rites."

"Sacrifice?" Mike asked.

"Damned right. You've got to become a blood brother of this tribe if you want to get a monopoly on their poppy."

"My God, what we do for the U.S. mission! I wonder if Whittelsie and his team in Tuyan City have any idea what happens in the boondocks."

Prescott laughed mirthlessly. "They don't know what the boondocks are, except for Mr. Cardinez. They think they're daring if they stay a couple of days at the National Hotel in Banthut." He raised his voice slightly. "Hey, Panton, where's Cavanaugh?"

"He's kind of busy, sir, at the dispensary."

"Let's see what he's doing," Prescott said. "I like to have that redheaded mick around me when I'm with Groats, particularly wild Groats like these."

"I'll ask the chief, sir." After a few guttural words and hand signals, he pointed toward what looked to be a new small bamboo house and provoked a toothless smile and a nod from Beemeer. "OK, sir. I'll take you over to Massachusetts General Hospital. That's what Cav calls it, sir. He's got these Groats saying 'Mass Genul' when they get sick."

"Cavanaugh comes from Boston," Prescott explained. "And out here I'd rather have him than any doctor Harvard Medical School ever turned out."

As they approached the dispensary, which was the only building not on stilts, a wizened old Groat in loincloth, richly adorned with red and blue strands of beads, popped out the door carrying a white rooster whose throat had been cut. He was squirting blood all over the tribesman, the building, and the ground. The old Groat held the rooster upside down so the blood splashed on the ground, and walked around the dispensary making a ring of blood in the dirt. When the ring reached the front door, the tribesman splashed the blood still left in the rooster around the entrance, and holding the drained fowl reentered the dispensary.

Major Prescott and Mike followed the old man to the door. Prescott explained that the old man was undoubtedly the village sorcerer helping Cavanaugh tend a sick person. As they approached they heard the wail of a baby. "Sonofabitch," Prescott chuckled. "Cav can't keep away from delivering babies. Show him a pregnant woman, and he'll follow her until she drops foal."

Prescott and Mike poked their heads inside the dispensary in time to see a redheaded American in a green T-shirt and khaki pants bending over a naked woman. A frightened, anxious Groat in a loincloth was looking on. There was a big daub of congealing blood on the woman's forehead and blood covering the floor. The medicine man took a sharp knife from his belt and cut one of the legs off the cock, and the father, mother, sorcerer, and even Cavanaugh studied the way the reflex muscles made the claws close together.

The sorcerer let out a triumphant shout, and Cavanaugh said something to him, patting him affectionately on the shoulder. Nevertheless, there was a worried look on the medic's face. Then he caught sight of Prescott.

"Hello, sir. Got a problem here. This woman is having twins. Second one is about to come out. But the Groats think twins are a bad sign. The father here says he's got to kill one of them. That's what all the blood is about. The sorcerer here has just protected the rest of the village from the evil spirits of the twins. Now he's helping the father decide which one to kill."

"Can't you talk them out of it?" Prescott asked, shocked.

"Maybe, sir. That cock's claw just indicated that the first kid, a boy, is going to be a mighty hunter. Oh, oh, here comes the second one. It's going to be a bitch, head's turned bad."

"Sir," Panton said from outside the dispensary, "the chief wants to talk to you."

"Will we be able to figure out what he's saying?" Prescott asked as he followed the lieutenant.

"I know a few words, and we can use Goween, who speaks enough English to tell us what the chief says."

"Do you think we can get him to cut down that boy and girl before they hang themselves?" Prescott asked. "Tell him we'll take them both to live with another Groat tribe at headquarters."

"We can try, sir," Panton replied doubtfully. "But you know how they feel about incest. At this village a daughter-in-law can't eat out of the same bowl as her father-in-law, and the same is true of a mother and son-in-law. Maybe you can talk to him."

"I guess now is the time we give the chief the presents," Prescott said to Mike, who had swung up his heavy pack and was following Prescott, Panton, and Sergeant Barton to the chief's longhouse.

The chief's wealth was evidenced by the treasures on the veranda in front of the door facing the east or rising sun, whose spirit was very potent: several large colored jars, four brass gongs—each a foot across—an old iron spear, and four sets of cymbals hanging on fiber strings from a bamboo crosstree.

The chief invited them to climb up the notched log that served as a ladder to his porch. Then he presented his wife—his senior wife as it turned out. He had two more much younger wives who were little more than concubines to him and slaves to the first wife. The senior wife still had firm breasts, which thrust through the glass beads she wore. Unmarried girls in the tribe were required to wear some form of blouse or bodice, but the moment they were married they could go bare-breasted.

Mike bowed to the senior wife and then opened his pack, hoping that the Reverend Maynard had advised him correctly. He pulled out a packet and, as the senior wife and the chief watched, opened it. The wife gasped with pleasure when she saw what it was. With his right hand, Mike held up to her a heavy necklace made out of three rows of polished silver, gold, and brass coins. The chief approached the necklace, his eyes wide, hands trembling. Coins were money to use when the Groats traded with foreigners, and to fashion such a display of sheer wealth into a neck adornment for his wife gave the already rich chief much additional prestige.

"Well, you picked that one right on the nose," Prescott said admiringly. The senior wife called one of the lesser wives from the house, who came out, and removed her old glass bead necklace. The senior wife immediately draped the new chain of coins around her own neck, holding her chin high so the curious men and women of the tribe gathered below could see and be properly impressed.

Once again Mike reached into his pack and pulled out the chief's present. The Reverend Maynard had told him it got very cold at night, and one of the reasons so many Groat tribesmen suffered from tuberculosis was that they lacked warm clothing. They slept close to the hearths in their longhouses, but even so there was never enough heat to keep everyone warm.

Mike handed Chief Beemeer a heavy, multicolored wool blanket, which he accepted with great show of gratitude, caressing the rough wool and smiling his toothless smile. The senior wife also felt the heavy blanket, nodding in satisfaction. "OK, Mr. Poppy Man," Prescott said with a grin. "You're in, I'd say."

Chief Beemeer, after admiring the blanket, had a short exchange of words with Lieutenant Panton, who turned to Goween for help and finally managed to understand the thrust of the chief's conversation. Panton turned to Mike and said, "Sir, Chief Beemeer is pleased, very happy with the presents. He wants to know what he can give you in return. He wants you to have a gift from him. He knows you want to talk business, and my guess is he doesn't want to feel obligated."

"Wasn't the idea of the presents to make him feel obligated?" Prescott asked Panton.

"Maybe, sir. But I think Mr. Forrester will win more concessions from Beemeer later if he takes something from him now."

"I agree, Panton," Mike said. "I don't suppose Beemeer understands any Mituyan?"

"I don't think so, sir. But he *has* had contact, as we know, with the Mitcoms. You can try a few words."

Mike addressed the chief in Mituyan, and Beemeer suddenly stiffened and looked at the white man in surprise. Seeing that perhaps Beemeer did indeed speak Mituyan, Mike went on complimenting the chief on the village and the wealth he displayed on his porch. The thoughts were undeniably getting across to Beemeer, Mike could see; but this both encouraged and worried him. Beemeer would have to have had lengthy contact with Mituyans, whether Communist or not, to be able to understand the language.

In Mituyan, Mike finally said to Beemeer, "You are gracious to offer me whatever you have as a present." He thought back to what the Reverend Maynard had told him about Groat customs. "I want two slaves, a man slave and a woman slave, to work for me in my home in the lowlands. Do you understand me?"

Beemeer nodded and repeated in Mituyan, "You ask for two slaves, a man and a woman. I will give you anything you ask that I have, but my slaves cannot leave the village. I promised when they were given to me."

"Two slaves, a man slave and a woman slave, is what I want," Mike repeated. He could see that Beemeer wanted to please him but was troubled. Even though the Groats owned slaves, they treated them well, and it would be considered excessively cruel to send them out of the Groat mountain country. Mike let the chief worry for a few moments and then said, "I will take the man and woman at the gate."

Beemeer looked up, surprised. Then he thought a few moments and finally said, "Since they will die before tomorrow morning anyway, the village will not be angry. If you take them, the angry spirit of the river will be soothed." He nodded and smiled as though just having solved a difficult problem. "I give you that man and that woman as your slaves."

Beemeer walked to the edge of the platform and shouted out orders, and immediately several village men started running for the front gate. The chief's porch commanded a clear view of the gate, and Mike watched as the Groats held up the fainting, strangling girl and cut the rope. She collapsed into the dirt. Then they cut down the young man, who also fell to the ground. Their hands still tied behind their backs, Mike's two newly acquired slaves were dragged into the compound and deposited on the village square. There they lay as Beemeer bellowed orders, and a man with a bucket began ladling water into their mouths.

Prescott looked at Mike in surprise. "What the hell happened?"

"I'm the proud owner of two slaves."

"Well I'll be damned. What are you going to do with them?"

"I don't know. At least they're spared a horrible death." Mike gave Prescott a serious look. "The chief speaks Mituyan fairly well. He must have spent plenty of time with the Mits."

"I guess that means that the Mitcoms will be this way again soon. We've got a lot of groundwork to accomplish in the next week."

Chief Beemeer and Panton were engaged in a painful exchange of words for several minutes, and then Panton announced: "The chief will have you shown to a longhouse where you can sleep while you are here. He invites everyone to take part in a sacrifice tomorrow." To Prescott, Panton said, "That's the sacrifice we contributed money to the chief for. It's going to be an extra big one. We're all going to be taken into the tribe. Mr. Forrester has made a big impression on the chief, by the way, sir. Beemeer knows what Mr. Forrester wants, of course. I think he may get it."

As they left the chief's house Prescott suggested that they look in on "Mass General" and see how Cavanaugh was doing with the second twin. Panton relayed this request on to the guide, who led them to the dispensary. The lusty wailing told them before they entered that the second baby had been born successfully. Inside, Cavanaugh was having an earnest conversation with the father across the prostrate body of the new mother. The sorcerer was standing by noncommittally. Cavanaugh was holding his right arm up, right fist clenched, his left hand slapping the bulging muscle of his right upper arm as he drove his right fist up into the air.

The father was nodding and grinning his toothless smile, while the mother clutched two tiny red babies to her bosom. Cavanaugh then turned to the old sorcerer, repeating the gesture. The sorcerer grinned foolishly and nodded vigorously.

"Looks like you've got them all with you, Cav," Prescott said. "What happened?"

Cavanaugh chuckled. "Well, sir, I managed to get this second boy delivered. It was a tough one, but the boy's OK now. Then the father wanted to kill it. He says twins bring the evil spirit from the mountain down on him. He also says his wife can only nurse one baby at a time. I told him I could keep the second one alive with my special medicine. The mother wants to keep both of them."

The Groat father was happily repeating Cavanaugh's arm gesture to the sorcerer, who grinned back. "I finally convinced the father that twins are a sign of extreme virility in a man. An ordinary man can't put two babies in his woman at the same time. This began to interest him. Then I said that twins would be a living symbol of his big sexual prowess—" Cavanaugh smiled sheepishly. "I used short Groat words and some sign language, as you saw, sir. He liked that idea; the whole village would always be reminded of how strong he was with his woman. Luckily the sorcerer bought it too. So both twins are going to live."

"Good work, Cav," Prescott complimented him. "Are you getting a lot of business?"

"Yes, sir. I treated almost one hundred people today. Everything from worms and skin ulcers and infected eyes to leprosy. I told the sorcerer the leper would have to leave the village, and he took care of it. They have a place they send them."

"Isn't this witch doctor making it tough for you to treat the people?" Mike asked. "I should think he'd feel sort of upstaged."

Cavanaugh shook his head. "I've been with these tribesmen types for the last five years, off and on. I was in Laos, then Vietnam, and now here. The witch doctors can be a big help if you use them. When a patient comes in, the witch doctor here draws a cross on his head, rubs his belly with a silver coin or whatever the cure is. Then I go ahead with my treatment. It doesn't take the people long to figure out whose cure is working, but the sorcerer is right there in the act too, and his face is saved."

Cavanaugh said a few words in Groat to the old sorcerer, who beamed back. "Now this one," Cav went on, "tells the people just what I want him to tell them. Gives them a good psychological feeling when they come in here sick, and old skin-and-bones magician and I have a consultation over them."

"There's one more chore you could do for me, Sergeant," Mike said. "I'd appreciate it if you'd look my slaves over and see if they need treatment."

"Sir?"

"The chief just gave Mr. Forrester those two kids that were hanging out on the gate."

Cavanaugh broke into a wide grin. "That's great, sir. How'd you manage it? I tried to do what I could, but we're here to do a job with these people, not convert them. There's a lot of little customs they have I wish we could change."

Prescott agreed. "We can only do our best, but we have to be damned careful not to alienate these people. The boy and girl are lying inside the gate. I'm going to have a look at what Brandt and Teeter are doing, and I'll check with you later."

Prescott and Mike followed Lieutenant Panton past the two crumpled forms of Mike's new slaves, outside the gate and around behind the village to a clearing, where they found an American sergeant with two dozen or more squatting young Groat tribesmen. A well-trained Groat in tiger-stripe jungle fatigues and soft canvas-and-rubber bata boots stood beside the American, acting as interpreter and assistant instructor. He was holding a .30-caliber carbine, half assembled. The tribesmen were working on assembling the carbine, three men to a weapon. The American, watching the Groats progress, would walk among them to correct a mistake or help them when they were stuck.

"These boys learn fast," Panton said. "This is the first day of the second platoon's weapon training. We had the first group one week, and they were just learning to fire aimed shots from prone and standing position when they had to go back to the rice fields or tend the poppies. The chief is tickled pink that we're training a little army for him. He doesn't know who we have in mind for them to fight yet."

"I suppose he thinks he'll take his men out and attack Banthut," Prescott chuckled. "Well, between these kids we're training and Goween's platoon we'll be able to give the Mitcoms one hell of a big surprise next time they come around for their opium."

"Would you like to see the airstrip, sir?" Panton asked.

"Right. How's Brandt doing?"

"Pretty good, sir. He can't get as much help as he'd like, because they're harvesting the poppy." Panton led the way to the airstrip, which ran parallel to the river a few hundred yards past the rear of the camp. A tall, thin American in a green T-shirt and dungarees was supervising a group of Groats slashing at the bush growing at the end of the strip. Others were filling pot holes and shoveling out hillocks.

"How you coming, Brandt?" Prescott asked when he reached the gaunt sergeant. "We want to start landing here as soon as we can."

"You can bring in the U-10 tomorrow, sir," Brandt replied. "We've got four hundred feet of smooth dirt strip. It'll be a while before you can get anything else in except the choppers."

"We can operate just fine out here with the U-10," Prescott replied. "Looks like our project is shaping up on schedule. All we need now to get into phase two of this operation is to become members of this tribe. That we'll take care of tomorrow."

The boy and girl were no longer on the ground when they returned to the village. Panton led Prescott and Mike to the longhouse the chief had given them. Barton was standing outside talking to a thin, young-looking American who was introduced as Sergeant Minelli, the communications expert of the team.

"Where's Cav?" Prescott asked The Animal.

"He got a couple of his Groat friends to carry those kids down to the river and cool them off. They both had sun stroke—not too bad though. A rough way to lynch a couple of kids." He guffawed. "Back where I come from, up in the hills, we always say the family that lays together stays together."

"Sergeant Minelli, can you get headquarters on the single side-band?" Prescott asked.

"Usually can, sir," replied the communications man. "What do you need?"

"Get through to air operations and tell them to send in the U-10 tomorrow with the movie projector, a couple of Technicolor wild Westerns, and the generator."

"Yes, sir," Minelli said happily. "I hope they got some new ones we haven't all seen."

"Doesn't matter, the Groats sure haven't seen them." Prescott turned to Mike. "Let's go have another talk with Chief Beemeer. Since you can talk to him direct it makes things a hell of a lot easier."

The chief was squatting on his porch, admiring his new multicolored blanket spread out in front of him. The sun was setting, and already the night chill was descending on the mountaintop. The chief motioned them to climb up the notched log to his porch and gestured for them to squat around the blanket. Squatting was a difficult, even painful, position to maintain for long without a great deal of practice. But Prescott had been working with tribesmen for several years and had perfected the art, and Mike too had learned that squatting for long periods of time was essential in conversing with many Asiatic groups.

The three men were silent a few moments, and then Prescott reached into his breast pocket and pulled out a pack of cigarettes, offering them to the chief. Beemeer took one. Although he rarely smoked, Mike also took one and with Prescott's lighter lit the chief's cigarette, then Prescott's, and finally his own. Instead of putting the pack away again Prescott handed it to Beemeer, who took it gratefully and tucked it into his loincloth.

After a minute of puffing on the cigarette the chief said in Mituyan, "You are first foreigners who help Ba To. The others sometimes very bad."

"What do the others do?" Mike asked.

"They come into village, sometimes point guns at us. They say they kill me, the chief, if we do not sell them all the poppy tears we harvest.

The Chinese traders pay more for poppy, but they do not come now."

Mike translated for Prescott. "Tell him he does not have to be afraid of the people who come for his poppy. He will have armed young men, and our Americans will stay and help him fight any people who bother the village."

Mike put Prescott's thoughts into simple Mituyan. A look of hope blossomed on the chief's face. "That is why you ask to let my men learn your weapons?"

"Of course, Chief," Mike replied. "We want you to be strong and trade with whatever people you want to trade with."

"Suppose I do not trade with you?" the chief asked shrewdly.

"We will go away and take our people and guns with us if you ask us to," Mike replied. "And then the other people will be free to be disrespectful to you, the chief, and threaten your life."

The chief shook his head. "You are good foreigners. You stay."

"We will stay as long as you want us, Chief. And we will fight the bad foreigners for you. Kill many for you."

The chief's eyes sparkled. "We will have sacrifice, burn the bad foreigners alive. This will scare bad spirits of the mountain away."

Mike realized he had gone a little too far in stirring up the chief's bloodlust. He changed the subject by asking when the sacrifice would start the next day.

The chief pointed directly above him. "When the sun there, we start." Mike again translated for Prescott.

"Tell the chief that during the sacrifice some of his men must stand guard with my platoon of Groats. We don't really need them," Prescott said, "but this tribe and Chief Beemeer had better get used to security measures right now if we're going to make them open enemies of the Mitcoms."

Mike translated, and the chief agreed. "One more thing," Prescott said, "beginning tomorrow, sacrifice or no sacrifice, we're going to have to build some fortifications around this village. The men on guard duty can do that. I just want the chief to know what we're doing and realize that Ba To must be ready for the Mitcoms."

Again Mike put Prescott's words into simple Mituyan. The chief listened carefully, and then answered curtly.

"Chief Beemeer has decided we should talk business first," Mike told Prescott. "I'll make a deal with him on his poppy if you'll just wait a few minutes. Then we can discuss fighting the Mitcoms."

"You handle it, Mike." Prescott sat down on the floor and watched Mike and Chief Beemeer square off, bouncing and rocking in squatting positions.

"A fair price for their poppy would be about twenty dollars a kilo tops; that would be about two thousand metas. In Turkey the poppy growers get fifty dollars a kilo and the buyers do all the transporting, but our Groat friends are a little more inaccessible."

"Go to it," Prescott encouraged.

"The Mitcoms only give you beads, a few tin pans, and maybe hundred metas a kilo for your poppy tears," Mike began the negotiations. "What do you want from me?"

"One jug, two gongs, ten cooking pots, one thousand metas," Beemeer replied.

"I have no way to bring you jugs," Mike said.

"OK. No jugs. Two thousand metas."

"But that's twenty times what the Mitcoms give you," Mike protested. He knew Beemeer would be both disappointed and suspicious if the bargaining came to an end so soon.

"Mitcoms shoot us, destroy village if we don't sell."

"But now we have armed your young men and taught them to fight the Mitcoms. You sell me poppy for five hundred metas a kilo."

"I sell for fifteen hundred metas—no jugs, no gongs. If we sell Mitcoms we don't need young men to fight; they stay out, grow plenty poppy, we sell half to Mitcoms take other half into Banthut ourselves and sell to Chinese for two thousand metas."

"One thousand metas. You have plenty money to buy jugs, gongs, pots yourself," Mike bargained. "Too dangerous for you to take poppy into Banthut yourself. Lowland province chief take away from you, keep all for himself."

Beemeer rocked back and forth on his haunches thoughtfully. Mike called down to Sergeant Barton who was standing over his pack below the chief's porch. "Hey, Barton, there's a canvas shotgun case in there. Would you bring it up to me, please?"

Mike and Beemeer both rocked back and forth in their squatting position, studying each other. The Animal bounded up the notched log ladder and handed the case to Mike.

"Here, Chief Beemeer," Mike said, "we seal the bargain." He opened the case and took out an automatic shotgun with much silver scroll work about the breach. "One thousand metas a kilo. And I give you this fine shotgun."

Beemeer stared longingly at the shotgun. "Twelve hundred metas a kilo—no gong, no jug, no pot."

There was indecision in the chief's voice and manner as he eyed the shotgun, and Mike knew Beemeer would make the deal at the thousand metas a kilo. Mike took on an air of suffering for a few moments and then, abruptly, thrust the shotgun into the exuberant chief's hand. "Twelve hundred metas. OK."

The chief jumped to his feet and let out a victory whoop. He pushed the shotgun into the hands of one of his sons and turned back to Mike. They exchanged a vigorous Groat handshake.

Mike explained to Prescott what had happened. "Twelve hundred metas a kilo. Unbelievable price! Say, Charlie, since things seem to be settled maybe we could skip the sacrifice tomorrow." He looked at the major hopefully.

Prescott shook his head. "Anything that's important to the Groats starts with a sacrifice. Don't think I wouldn't be damned happy to skip it, but it's part of their religion, such as they have, to commemorate any important new transaction with a sacrifice. Also, it'll be easier to deal with them if we've been made members of the tribe."

"So be it," Mike said in resignation.

The chief shouted over his shoulder into the longhouse and two young men emerged. He let out a torrent of Groat, pointing at the ground near the bottom of the notched log. Both boys took crude hoes from the porch, scampered down the ladder, and began attacking a point in the ground specified by the chief. After a few minutes they put the sharp hoes aside and began scraping with their hands. The chief let out a pleased bellow as the two young tribesmen unearthed a large jar. Removed from the ground, it seemed about three feet tall. The dirt was brushed away from the jar's side and plugged top, and the two young Groats came back up the ladder, bowed to the chief and disappeared back inside.

Beemeer said a few words to Mike, who turned to translate to Prescott. "I know," the major said before Mike had said a word. "The two boys are his sons, and the jar of rice wine has ben buried to ferment and get strong until a big occasion came along. Now we're going to have to drink the stuff—God help us."

The chief stood up and went into his house, returning in a few moments with a small jar full of long, thin bamboo reeds. To Prescott and Mike he said a few words in Groat.

"I know what that means," Prescott said again. "He's inviting us to have a drink with him. What kind of shape is your stomach in?"

"I'll be all right," Mike said with more assurance than he felt.

The chief led the way down the notched log to the jar, carrying his reeds. He put the jug of reeds on the ground beside the large earthen jar and went to work on the plug, which was made of leaves thickly wrapped around a wood disk. Soon he had the top off and a yeasty smell filled the air. The chief sniffed happily, his nose twitching. He handed a drinking reed to Prescott and one to Forrester and took one himself. The chief stuck his straw into the jar of liquor, took a long draw, and spat a mouthful onto the ground in front of him.

"Do the same thing," Prescott advised. "This is the poison test. If they want to poison someone, they invite them for a drink and put the poison in the reed. By cleaning the reed this way you assure that your straw isn't poisoned." Prescott drew a long draught of the liquor and spat it in front of him on the ground; Mike did the same.

"Now we get down to a little serious drinking," Prescott said grimly. "It's considered impolite for you to take your mouth off the straw until the chief does."

Chief Beemeer fastened his lips to his hollow bamboo shoot and began sucking up his aged-in-the-ground fermented rice wine. His eyes went from Prescott to Mike as he sucked on his bamboo straw. Mike gingerly drew on his straw and sipped the rice wine as it filled his mouth.

It was strong with the flavor of fermentation, but, while this was hardly what he would have chosen for the cocktail hour, it wasn't as bad as he had expected. He kept slowly sucking and swallowing, watching the chief lustily sucking the liquid into his mouth, some of it spilling out the corners and running down his chin. Prescott pulled steadily on his tube, and the level of the liquor in the jar could be seen dropping. Finally, after perhaps two full minutes, the chief took his mouth from the straw and Prescott and Mike immediately followed his example.

"Would it be polite for me to try and get us out of drinking any more of this stuff?" Mike asked.

"Go ahead," Prescott answered. "We've shown him we're happy to drink with him. Tell him anything you want. Tomorrow we won't get off so easily."

In Mituyan, Mike told the chief that he and Major Prescott would like to get back to their men, who are not having the pleasure of enjoying such fine liquor. He assured the chief that they were all looking forward to the sacrifice tomorrow. The chief nodded in understanding and excused his two American guests.

At their longhouse, Mike noted that the two young Groats seemed partially recovered from their ordeal, and the young girl, bathed and dressed in a clean black skirt and blouse that Cavanaugh had found for her, looked quite pretty. The boy, in a loincloth, stoically squatted under the raised floor of the guest house, uncertain of his fate but thankful not to be hanging by his neck from the front gate.

"What are you going to do with these two, sir?" Cavanaugh asked Mike. "We got to get them out of this village pretty quick. The people will blame anything at all bad that happens in Ba To on bad spirits if we keep these two kids in the camp."

"We can put them on the U-10 coming in tomorrow," Prescott answered. "Headquarters can take care of them until Mr. Forrester gets back and figures what *he's* going to do with them."

"The Reverend Maynard tells me he has a jungle beachhead close to your headquarters," Forrester said.

"That's right. We've got a damned good missionary couple near us working with the Groats. The Reverend Starrett speaks their language, and he's mighty useful to us besides."

"We'll give these two to him and his wife. They should be good candidates for Christianity after what their own religion almost did to them."

"Good idea," Prescott agreed. "The Starretts will teach them English, and someday they'll be ready to spread the good word to their people."

"You sound like a missionary yourself, sir," Sergeant Barton laughed.

"I've seen a lot of good they've done. And I'm not just talking about the help they give us in translating and intelligence."

"Sir, Lieutenant Panton said, "we'd better decide right now who goes to the sacrifice and who stays sober with the guard detail."

Prescott agreed. "OK. Mr. Forrester, myself, Panton, The Animal here—he can outdrink anything—and Teeter will attend this sacrifice. Cavanaugh is already so popular with them that he can afford to skip it, and we may need a good medic around before the sacrifice is over. Sergeant Brandt will be in command of the Americans if Panton and I are temporarily disabled."

There was much rough laughter. Barton said, "Right, sir. I'll drink them back into their jugs."

"OK, men," Prescott called. "Let's cook some chow and then get ourselves bedded down."

Mike looked at him in astonishment. After what he had just heard, he'd be lucky if he slept a wink.

CHAPTER EIGHTEEN

Although the beds they made for themselves were hard, Mike slept well through the cold night. The Americans took turns on guard, two hours each; it was the guard's job to stoke the hearth and keep the longhouse warm.

As the sun rose, the Groats, hugging themselves against the cold, walked about doing their morning chores. The women were returning from the river with pots of water for the morning meal. There seemed to be an air of jubilation in the village, Mike noticed. Large jars, like the one the chief had ordered dug up the evening before, were set out; and in the middle of the square a water buffalo already had been tied to a mast by a long length of crude hemp rope. The beast was pawing the ground uneasily. And well he might, Mike thought.

This would be a good day to have behind him, Mike knew. He was getting too old for living out with the tribesmen, and he missed Luna acutely. As he walked by a longhouse, he heard the wails of a youngster. In the next house he heard similar noises; there was genuine terror in the cries.

"Unlike the buffalo, those kids know exactly what's waiting for them," Prescott said, falling into stride beside Mike. "It's damned hard not to try and change these people. I asked one of the missionaries about it once, and he repeated a prayer he's been living with since he came up here. It's something like: 'Give me the strength to change for the better that which I can, the courage to live with what I can't change, and the wisdom to know the difference.' It's a good one to remember in our line of work."

Back at their longhouse, Prescott advised Mike to eat a good breakfast. "The Animal is fixing up some chow. Cavanaugh got us some eggs from the sorcerer. Said they'd be good for us."

Mike ate as much as he could and drank a glass of powdered milk and water. The others who were participating in the sacrifice did the same. Already some of the Groat tribesmen were sipping from the jars.

Prescott made sure that the guard detachment, including those who had received the most training, were set out around the walls and that a patrol went out to guard the jungle trail into Ba To from the North.

"Well, we've done everything we can. Time to become members of the tribe," Prescott said cheerfully to his men. "Everyone get his stuff from Cavanaugh?"

The redheaded medic had dispensed a small bottle of chalky, thick, pink liquid to be swallowed regularly during the sacrifice.

Prescott and his men, all dressed identically in green T-shirts and khaki pants, set out for the chief's hut. It was mid-morning; Beemeer was impatiently waiting for them. He, the sorcerer, and other tribal elders immediately led the way to the jar of rice liquor. After the chief solemnly made prayers to the spirits of the hills, rivers, trees, air, and stones, inviting them to join in the drinking, the ceremony with the reeds was observed.

"The chief thinks that the spirits will get just as happy as he does, as we're all supposed to," Prescott said to Mike. "Even if you can fake drinking the stuff, you've got to act happy. If you'll take my advice though, drink a few good slugs. You'll need to feel happy before this day is over."

The five Americans and four Groat notables dipped their reeds into the jar and began to sip. The level dropped rapidly. Then the chief stopped, and the others removed the straws from their mouths. The chief dumped a jug full of water into the diminishing rice wine, and again they started sucking on their reeds.

Although Mike was sipping slowly, it was not long before he felt the effects of the wine. He had a rather pleasant, light-headed hope that the mixture in the jar would grow steadily weaker as the level sank. Groat men and women in their best dress, wearing their finest glass beads, were drinking steadily at the jars arranged in a large semicircle around the square. The young boys and girls of the village were now teasing the buffalo, hitting the bull with bamboo poles, poking at the animal's large, exposed sexual organs. A direct hit brought a bellow from the buffalo, which jumped away, putting himself in range of another small tribesman, who scored with a thrust of his pole. All the while other children whacked the beast on the nose and eyes.

The buffalo's anguished bellows became louder and more frequent, and the drinking continued. As the sun approached its zenith, three tribesmen appeared from a longhouse dragging a kicking, screaming twelve-year-old girl into the middle of the semicircle of Groats slurping from their jars.

Events seemed to move in slow motion and in a completely directionless manner, as tribesmen and women drank, ran to poke at the buffalo, and then drifted to their longhouses, returning with another twelve- to thirteen-year-old child.

The first girl was thrown down on her back and held by two men. A third sat on her chest and thrust a filthy rag in her mouth under her upper front teeth. In his right hand was a crude file. The drunken tribesman began to saw at the girl's front teeth at the gum line, bearing down hard, trying to file through. The jarring crunch of the instrument against the child's teeth could be heard above her screams muffled by the bloody handkerchief.

Mike and the other Americans pulled heavily on the wine. The crude file evidently wasn't doing the job, for the tribesman stood up from the girl's chest, her mouth gushing blood, and in disgust threw the instrument down. He wandered to one of the liquor jars and began to suck for some moments as though thinking what to do. Finally he walked to the edge of the circle, picked up a rock the size of his fist and another smaller stone. Drunkenly, he lurched back to the girl, still being held on the ground and pulled the rag, thick with blood from her mouth. As her screams burbled forth, the Americans, horrified but helpless, drank from the jars along with the chief and the elders, watching the cruel ceremonies.

Now the tribesman once more sat on the girl's chest and forced the small stone into her mouth behind the upper front teeth. Then with the large stone he began to smash her teeth off at the gum line. The process was mercifully short, and when the job was done the men released the little girl, who vomited blood and broken teeth. She raised herself on hands and knees, still spitting out the mess in her mouth, and then, suddenly realizing she was free, fled from the village square, out the front gate toward the jungle—like a wounded animal running from hunters.

Three more drunken Groat tribesmen repeated the process on a young boy, first trying to cut or file out his teeth and then smashing them out with a stone forced into his red, pulpy mouth, another pulverizing the teeth. As the children, one by one, were subjected to this "ceremony of passage," as the Groats call the passing from childhood to adulthood, Mike, Major Prescott, and the other Americans heard the sound of a plane flying overhead. Everybody looked up as the U-10 circled the camp. The chief had seen airplanes before and had been warned that planes would be coming in, so he waved to it and told the other elders that this was a good omen, a good spirit brought in by the foreigners to help the tribesmen.

Prescott and the Americans temporarily excused themselves from the proceedings and, followed by a column of drunken, curious Groats, walked none too steadily out to the airstrip.

Sergeant Brandt had already led Mike Forrester's young Groat slaves to the airstrip. Long before Prescott arrived, followed by a procession of Groats, laughing, falling, picking themselves up and in general delighted at this new feature of a sacrifice—a spirit visibly coming from out of the sky—the U-10 had been unloaded, Mike's two slaves shoved aboard, and the plane sent airborne again over the heads of the waving, yelling villagers.

Chief Beemeer—face flushed, eyes wild—nudged Mike excitedly and babbled forth in Groat and Mituyan. From what Mike could gather, the chief was saying that this was the greatest sacrifice yet—and it was only getting started. The mob, when they realized that the mysterious spirit was not returning, headed back for the village and the wine jugs, partially sobered by the excursion.

Behind them came Sergeant Brandt and the other on-duty Americans who, helped by some of their trained Groats, lugged back the plane's cargo and stored the movie projector, generator, film cans, and food supplies in the guest house.

The first thing Beemeer did on returning to the village was to order another jar of his old and mellow fermented rice wine dug up, washed off with water, and placed in a prominent position in the square. The glazed earthenware jar was of many colors—a prominent sign of the owner's vast wealth; it gleamed like porcelain in the sun. Beemeer wasted no time in getting the plug out of the mouth of the jar and then repeated the reed ceremony with new hollow bamboo tubes. The ground around the jar quickly became wet as the notables and the Americans spit out mouthfuls of the liquor and began assaulting the powerful brew. Beemeer watched the Americans with bright eyes to make sure they were sucking strongly from the jar.

Only two more youngsters had to endure the "passage ceremony"—both boys. It was considered a point of pride to be able to open one's mouth and thus prove one had gone through the excruciating pain of the ceremony. A child, a boy in particular, who had not been through the ceremony was considered a coward and not fit to be married. The last two boys put up with the painful disfigurement of their mouths with a minimum of crying, and were given bowls of liquor to wash out their mouths.

The torment of the buffalo went on unabated throughout, the beast howling piteously as its badly bruised genitals were again and again the target of the children's pokes and slashes. The sun was beginning its descent into the west when a drunken Groat tribesman suddenly plunged a sharpened stake into the buffalo's side. The animal shrieked, and blood began pouring from the wound.

"Now Mike, old boy," Prescott muttered, "you're gonna see a big strong animal die slower and bloodier than you ever figured. The more blood, the more the buffalo suffers, the better the spirits like it; and these kids who've just become half-toothless adults will be strong men and women, the girls bearing many boys, the boys becoming brave hunters."

Suddenly the sorcerer scuttled out of the crowd, brandishing a shining machete. With one clean blow he lopped off the buffalo's left foreleg at the knee joint. The beast toppled and tried to stand up again and face his tormentors. Though the missing leg kept throwing him off balance, the animal managed to stand on three legs. The tribesmen shouted and sucked on their reeds. Once again the sorcerer approached and slashed off the other foreleg—and again the buffalo fell to the ground. Somehow the strong beast managed to get up, standing on the bloody stumps of forelegs, its hindquarters grotesquely in the air.

"Those buffalos have more strength and guts than any animal I know," Panton was saying. "I've seen these sacrifices in three different countries. I swear to Christ I don't know how they stay alive and defiant so goddamned long."

While everyone was watching the buffalo, the Americans slacked off on their drinking. Just when they had thought they would get by on diluted wine, the chief had dug up another jar. In the excitement, the new jar had already dropped to a point where a jug of water had to be poured in to raise the level.

The sorcerer crept around behind the struggling beast and lopped off first one and then the other hind leg. Now the buffalo was standing, bellowing in pain at his tormentors, on four stumps. The animal tottered, moving a stump out in one direction or another to keep his balance and stay upright.

Chief Beemeer grabbed a spear that had been thrust into the ground beside him and ran toward the buffalo, skewering it in the side once again. A second gaping wound began pouring blood down the black flank of the animal.

"They'll keep stabbing it in the side for a while before they go for the heart and lungs," Prescott advised. "If we have to stab the poor beast, be damned sure not to hit it in a vital place. The chief does that."

Hardly had the major said these words when Beemeer shoved the bamboo spear at Mike.

"Go get 'em, tiger," Prescott encouraged. "Don't forget the mission. We gotta be members of this dipshit organization."

Mike hefted the spear and approached the suffering buffalo. He would have liked to drive it into the beast's heart and end its suffering, but remembering Prescott's advice he came up from behind and with a sharp lunge drove the spear into the buffalo's flank close to the bleeding wound the chief had inflicted.

The chief shouted in approval, took the spear from Mike and passed it to Major Prescott. Each of the Americans drew blood as the buffalo tottered on its stumps, desperately trying not to fall to the ground in final defeat.

Other members of the tribe dazedly wandered toward the buffalo, wounded it, and shambled back to their drinking position. It was clear that the buffalo could not remain standing much longer. The chief now hefted his spear again, and from in front of the beast drove the spear into the buffalo's lung. Blood wheezed and burbled from this wound, and the buffalo abruptly fell on its side, still alive, snorting, and groaning.

Once again the sorcerer came forward and with his sharp knife swiftly and skillfully split open the buffalo's stomach. The entrails fell out on the ground. The children rushed to the sprouting innards and began to gnaw on them. Some, with crude bamboo knives, tried to cut off pieces of intestine.

"Like a drink, old man?" Prescott invited Mike. They both sucked vigorously on a drinking reed. Mike recalled what the chief had said about using human beings who were enemies for a sacrifice, and he shuddered.

As the children fought for pieces of the dying buffalo, the chief drove his spear into the animal's chest. Blood spurted through the wound.

"Finally got it through the heart," Prescott said. "Thank God!"

For the next two hours the Groats cut the buffalo apart and cooked every part over individual fires—drinking, falling asleep, staggering, eating and drinking again.

As it became evening, tribal drummers started beating their drums and the Groats began to dance. "Now, if these Groats are like the last bunch I got tied up with, you'll see the goddamndest sobriety test ever invented for a drinking party," Major Prescott said. "And I know the way to spook them on it."

"You be careful, sir," Panton mumbled.

"Don't worry about me," Prescott said in a strong but slightly garbled voice. "They make us members of this tribe next."

Two sturdy young women of the tribe, each carrying a bamboo pole about six feet long, appeared in front of the chief's fire.

"Now watch," Panton cried. "Watch the way these crazy bastards do it."

Sharp slivers were thrust through bored holes in the bamboo poles until one side of each pole became a vicious row of sharp, inch-long bamboo spikes. The girls squatted, facing each other, on the ground, holding the end of a pole in each hand. Then, in time with the rhythm of the drums, they clapped the poles together and pulled them apart. The Groat women had turned the poles so that the sharp slivers were turned up at a forty-five-degree angle; the teeth on one pole fitted neatly between those on the other as the poles were snapped together. The slap of bamboo poles became syncopated with the drums, and the Groats watching began to clap their hands in the clap-apart-clap-apart beat, chanting all the while.

As the beat became more and more infectious, the tribesmen jumped to their feet, dancing to the clapping of the poles and the booming of the drums. The old chief regarded the two girls and the poles intently; by now there was barely a second between each cruel meeting of the tiny bamboo stilettos.

Suddenly a tribesman danced forward and jumped up and down alongside the poles, putting first one foot and then the other in and out as the poles moved apart and together.

"Those bastards would really tear your leg up," Panton said. "I hope to hell we're not supposed to dance through there to become a member of this tribe. I sure don't need that."

"Let the beat really get to you," Prescott advised. "Get so every move you make works with the beat. You'll be able to do it."

"Do we really have to?" Panton asked.

"No. But Mike and I do."

Mike looked at Prescott in surprise. "Good God, what a man has to go through to get into a new line of business."

"Do – it – with – the – beat – beat," Prescott chanted. "If the Groats can do it, we sure as hell can. Oh, Christ!"

One Groat had misjudged the beat, and the slivers slashed into his leg. The girls kept going without missing a beat as the tribesman pulled his clawed leg, bleeding profusely, out of the trap. A shout went up and another Groat tribesman danced over to the clapping poles.

About a dozen tribesmen danced through the poles before another one was rewarded with a shredded ankle. The sight of the blood pouring from the wounded leg slowed up the dancers, and the poles clapped together without anyone trying his luck for a minute or two. Finally Prescott called out, "Let's go, before the chief has to tell us!" He jumped to his feet amid howls of encouragement, and dancing up to the poles he nimbly leaped in and out of them, forward and backward, to tumultuous cheers.

"Nothing to it, Mike," Prescott said, returning to the jar and squatting. "Just stick with the beat."

Reluctantly, Mike got to his feet. He wished Luna could see him now. Dancing to the beat, which he allowed to play through his mind and body, possessing him, he did a jump step toward the two girls. To his surprise the beat of the drums, the clapping of hundreds of primitive hands, the chants, literally carried him through ten steps between the slashing poles. Neatly he bounced back out of the springing-upspringing trap and danced back to the jar of wine, taking a straw and sipping mightily. The chief was afire with elation and pounded Mike on the back.

Not to be outdone by their white guests, more of the tribesmen danced up to the pole, but these were Groats who had consumed a tremendous amount of their liquor and could hardly keep a beat. Almost every other one was mercilessly slashed. One drunken tribesman slipped in the gathering pool of blood and actually fell, getting the full register of bamboo knives a second time through both sides of his thighs. The girls, long since hypnotized by the beat, the blood, and the savage atmosphere, kept their poles clapping and raked the tribesman before he could drag himself free. Again there was a fall-off in enthusiasm. The girls went on slapping the poles together, their glazed eyes staring at each other, until Panton finally stood up. "Oh hell, Cav can fix me up if those two harpies get me."

"The beat, the beat, Panton. Stick with it and you'll be OK," Prescott cried. Panton danced toward the clapping poles and then was in and out of them a dozen times before leaping agilely backward and turning toward the rest of the Americans. The whole village let out a shout and again Groats were shamed into trying their own game. It was a bloody sight, the drunken Groats missing their footing and dragging torn legs away from the relentlessly slashing, cracking poles.

"Well, sir," Barton cried, "the old lady always told me I couldn't dance worth a damn. Said I had no kind of ear for music. I hope these drums get through to me and make me do it right."

"Just a couple of steps, Barton," Prescott called, worried. The Animal was a number-one fighting man, but as he lumbered to the poles he scarcely seemed agile enough for this. By now the row of little spears on each pole had dulled themselves somewhat, but they were still dangerous.

"Kick some dirt over the blood first," Prescott yelled. The sergeant did a shambling dance and succeeded in kicking dirt under the poles. Then The Animal jumped in and out successfully once, and tried it again. The second time his timing was off, and the spears bit through his long pants. He yelled, pulled his foot out, and hobbled back to the Americans, blood staining his trouser leg, while the Groats yelled gleefully. The invincible Americans could be hurt too.

"Pain bad, Barton?" Prescott asked anxiously. "We'll get you to Cavanaugh."

"I'm all right, sir," Barton answered sheepishly. "I guess the old lady was right. Shit! Hey, don't move me now, sir. We'll lose face. It looks like it's OK to get stabbed so long as you don't let that spoil the party."

Cavanaugh materialized from the shadows beyond the fires with a tin box in one hand. "Hey, Teeter," he called, "get up there and do it right while I take care of Barton. Wouldn't be good to have them see an American getting special attention!"

"Shit, I can't dance," Teeter protested.

"Well, someone's got to get their attention," Cavanaugh cried.

Prescott stood up. "I'll show these dipshits how to really play their game."

All eyes followed the major, making his second trip to the clacking, flaying poles. Cavanaugh immediately set to work on Barton, slitting his pants, disinfecting and bandaging the wounds, and then cutting a slash in the seat of his pants and giving The Animal a shot of penicillin.

Prescott danced around the poles, kicking dirt under them until he had completely covered the blood. To be safe he kicked still more dirt, while keeping up continuous gyrations to the beat of the drums and the slapping of the poles. Every Groat in the camp was watching and shouting. Suddenly, as if from a single throat a mighty gasp of surprise went up. For Prescott had fallen on outstretched arms between the poles and heaved himself in a mighty pushup, clapping his hands together above the poles as they came together and falling on his wrists again as the poles opened. With a prodigious heave his wrists cleared the poles a second time just as they clawed together, and again he clapped his hands and then fell on them between the poles. The shouts of the Groats rang violently through the village. Their excitement, their now stupendous reaction, deafened the Americans gaping at Major Prescott. Six times he executed the Herculean snapups and then neatly recovered on his haunches. Before he could stand up straight Chief Beemeer was upon him, both arms around his shoulders, pounding him in a frenzy of excitement and joy.

"Old Prescott could take over this tribe right now," Cavanaugh cried above the din. "We got no sweat here anymore."

Slowly the Groats settled down after Prescott's great feat, and now the chief decided it was time to take the Americans formally into the tribe. He held his hands up for silence, or at least a lull in the rumbling talk and laughter. The drums stopped, the girls ceased their rhythmic clacking, and the chief began spouting words in Groat. His speech lasted a minute or two, and then without more ado he called for one of his sons, who came up to him with a handful of brass bracelets. He placed a bracelet on the right wrist of each American, laughing as Barton hobbled up for his badge of tribal membership.

"Well, we're Groats of the Ba To village now," Prescott said happily. "Let's hope it pays off."

With the presentation of the bracelets, the chief and the rest of the tribesmen went back to their liquor jars for a night of serious drinking. "I think we can fake it from now on," Panton said.

"I'm gonna hit the sack," Barton said thickly. "A few more pulls of that wine and I'll sleep without feeling my cut-up ankle!" He put his mouth to a reed, sucked on it a few moments, and then limped heavily off to the American longhouse.

One by one the Americans slipped off until only Mike and Prescott were left, laughing with the chief and tribal notables and pretending to drink from the jar.

"I figure we ought to wait until the chief passes out before we leave," Prescott said.

"I jus' might go out first," Mike replied, his lips and tongue numb.

"Remember the mission," Prescott urged. "It may seem like nothing but a drinking party to you, but what we did tonight and do tomorrow could save hundreds of GI lives." He looked up at the chief.

"I don't think our friend has much longer to go."

The chief was draped across the mouth of his liquor jar, his head almost inside, as though checking the liquid level. Grunting unintelligible Groat words, he slowly slipped from the jar onto the ground, snoring in long, tearing blasts.

CHAPTER NINETEEN

THE GROAT TRIBESMEN who had celebrated the sacrifice were in no condition to do anything the following morning but moan and hold their heads. But thanks to Cavanaugh's potions none of the Americans were suffering anything like the hangovers of their hosts. Barton rested his wounded leg. Prescott and Panton spent the day studying and mapping the terrain around Ba To. By the end of the day they had a section of the longhouse partitioned off as a command post, with maps and charts on the wall.

"This is a naturally defensible position, Panton," Prescott said late in the afternoon. "You'll have to live here for the next few months and try to create a sanctuary at Ba To so that all the Groats in the area can come here to escape Mitcom terror. We'll get you a second medic and set up a good dispensary. We'll start a school to teach these Groats to speak and write Mituyan and English and do simple arithmetic; I'll talk to the missionaries about taking over that project. From Ba To we should be able to control a radius of twenty-five miles. Now if we can set up about eight or ten more villages, we can control the entire mountain region of Mituyan along the border with Yanna."

Panton looked dubiously at the map. "Damned rough country, sir. And an area that size is going to be rough to patrol."

"But we can do it, once we get these Groats trained and really with us. We've got all the support we need right now from the Agency and plenty of men with heavy Vietnam experience coming in all the time." He turned from his maps. "I'll outline our program to the chief as soon as he feels better. I think he'll go along."

One Groat who was feeling better than most was Chief Beemeer's eldest son, Radam, who had not drunk heavily the night before and was now leading one of the newest members of the tribe through the jungle to a Groat poppy field. The locations of these fields were kept secret from all but members of the Ba To village. Not even with threat, persuasion, or bribery had the Mitcom terrorists been able to get Beemeer to show them any but some of the poorer fields around the village.

As he stuck close to Radam, Mike marveled how climate, altitude, soil conditions, and the skills handed down from one generation of Groats to the next had blended in exactly the right proportions to produce opium poppies here that so far surpassed any in all of Asia. Wars had been fought and would continue to be fought over the produce of this small area; for out of the millions of square miles under cultivation in Asia this triangular area running one hundred miles on a side grew poppies twice the quality of any other. This opium, and subsequently heroin, Mike knew, had the highest dilution potential in the world.

Beemeer's son led him along obscure paths for two hours before they suddenly broke out of the jungle onto an open field of several acres red with poppy blossoms . . . empty of harvesters because of the sacrifice. Radam showed Mike the delicate cuts made in the bulb below the poppy blossom; each tiny slit produced a brown-black tear of dried liquid. The men and women from Ba To produced several harvests a year, meticulously capturing each tear in special earthen jars made for the purpose. The chief was the keeper of the crop and bargained with the traders who came through. Most of the opium had gone to the Communist guerrillas, although occasionally a delegation from the village would make the long trip to Banthut where they would barter their poppy tears for pots and pans and cloth.

Mike gathered from the words he and the chief's son were able to exchange that there were many more fields like this one. The Groats had learned that a field was good only for two years, and then new fields had to be cleared and the old ones abandoned. Every two years, therefore, the tribesmen had to venture further from the village to tend their crops; and sometimes even freshly cleared fields would not, for some mysterious reason, produce poppies that gave tears properly. It was hard work producing opium poppies, Mike discovered that day; and on the long walk back to the village he decided the Groats were certainly vastly underpaid.

Just before sunset, Mike, Prescott, and Chief Beemeer squatted on the chief's porch. The chief's brown eyes were more bloodshot than normal—because of vitamin deficiencies in their diet most Groats had perpetually bloodshot eyes. The chief listened to Prescott's plan to make the village a powerful fortress against the Communist terrorists. At first he was reluctant to have other Groat tribes join his village, but Prescott persuaded him that the more trained and armed men there were at Ba To the more powerful a chief he would be. Mike went into the economics. They would now sell all their opium to him for twelve hundred metas a kilo—ten times the price at which the Communists were forcing the Groats to sell. When Beemeer understood that his wealth would more than double in a year and would continue to increase—now he could easily afford the young new wife he coveted—he invited the two Americans to partake of a new jar he had opened to combat the effects of his hangover.

Prescott demurred and through Mike invited the chief and all his tribesmen to come to a show the Americans would put on that night.

"Another sacrifice?" the chief asked, new light coming to his eye. Rather than try to explain what a motion picture was, Mike merely repeated the invitation, and the chief eagerly accepted.

"Well, looks like we've got this village right where we want it," Prescott said jubilantly as they left.

"I hope so," Mike said. "After all these years, I'm not only working as an agent for the CIA, but I'm up to my ears in the narcotics business."

"All in a good cause," Prescott said brightly. "There's Minelli, getting things ready."

The communications sergeant had tacked a large white sheet up against the bamboo fence that ran around the village. The sound projector stood on its portable stand; the generator was mounted, ready to be started. Minelli waved.

"All set up and ready to go, sir. I thought I'd start with a color cartoon. That'll bring 'em in. Then we'll show the Western. It's Technicolor, Cinemascope, and believe it or not they sent the Cinemascope lens for the projector, so for once we won't have to look at long, thin cowboys and Indians."

Prescott told Minelli they'd start right after supper. But by the time the Americans returned from eating, a number of Groats were already squatting expectantly in the village square, some facing the screen, others facing the projector and its big reel of film. Minelli waited for the generator to heat up, then flicked on the projector. Music blared forth and a Donald Duck cartoon began. The tribesmen howled with glee, and the longhouses emptied in a rush. Entire families squatted, transfixed by the music and the bright-colored moving pictures.

"Well, we've got this village hooked," Panton said happily above the roar of laughter. The Groats rubbed their eyes in disbelief; even Chief Beemeer and his entourage of wives, sons, and daughters, watched in wonder.

After the cartoon came the feature film. Before the credits began to roll, there was a spirited cavalry charge. The Groats cried out, startled. The chief rocked back from the screen and jumped to his feet in fear as the horses charged at the screen. Finally, realizing it was all an illusion, he and the other tribesmen in the front row sat down again.

It was unnecessary to understand the words—and the tribesmen quickly identified with the white soldiers and families traveling across the plains. Halfway through the picture, the Indians massed for an attack; the Groats could see what was coming and shouted warnings.

The attack of howling, shooting Indians hurled itself at the screen, showering lances and arrows, firing rifles, wielding tomahawks.

The Groats screamed back at the Indians—and then suddenly the sheet disintegrated in a mass of tears as the tribesmen, their crossbows ever close by, began firing arrows at the onrushing Indians. Not until the picture disappeared from the shredded sheet did the Groats calm down. And then, led by Chief Beemeer, they cried out in disappointment.

"What the hell do we do now?" Panton exclaimed.

"I've got a couple more sheets, sir," Minelli answered calmly. "But if they keep shooting them up, we aren't going to be able to show any more movies."

Prescott ordered Minelli to rig another sheet on the double and asked Mike to please explain the situation to the chief and ask him to tell his people not to shoot up the screen. "Make 'em understand it's just a picture."

While Minelli rigged up a second sheet, Mike squatted beside the chief, who finally stood up and shouted at the villagers squatting around him. After much murmuring, the chief squatted back down on his haunches and stared at the new screen impatiently.

The Indian battle resumed, this time unhampered by a counterattack of Groats, who nevertheless shouted their excitement and pounded each other, never taking their eyes from the screen. "Put a dozen white sheets on the next requisition form," Prescott said to Panton. "And we'd better make them leave their crossbows home next time."

When the movie was over, the Groats sat staring for some minutes at the white screen. Mike went over to the chief.

"Tomorrow night we show a new picture," he said in Mituyan.

"OK," the chief said in the first English he had learned. Then in Mituyan, "Tomorrow night everybody here."

The following day, and in the days ensuing, training schedules and poppy harvesting returned to normal. Prescott, however, was worried by an intelligence report he received from headquarters that Communists had been spotted by aerial reconnaissance coming over the border from neutral Yanna, headed in the direction of Ba To. The detachment of Groats who had come in with Prescott were out on patrol every day trying to locate any enemy forces in the area, and, with Beemeer's approval, the training of the Ba To tribesmen was stepped up. At the end of five days Brandt, Teeter, and a steadily improving Barton proclaimed that they had one platoon of Groats sufficiently trained to fight a defensive action. Prescott ordered four 60-mm. mortars flown in from headquarters and had mortar positions dug in and sandbagged.

As the poppy tears were harvested, the tribesmen brought their jugs to the chief, who, as keeper of the poppy, poured them into a large, ornate jar he kept in his house. To show Beemeer how much better off he was financially, Mike carefully translated into Mituyan metas the value of the items the Groats had bought in town using opium for trade. The chief began to realize that he had wanted a well-honed knife so much that he had traded many times its values in poppy for it. With all transactions in metas now, the chief and his people could order whatever items they wanted at a fair price and Mike would have them flown in.

Mike had proposed a new opium-packaging idea to the Groats, which they enthusiastically adopted. One of the many items that USOM had introduced into Mituyan was the portable brickmaking machine. Instead of mud and cement, Mike showed the Groats how to pack the black tarlike congealed poppy tears into the brick-shaped mold and then with the long lever exert tremendous pressure, creating neat bricks of opium, so that the value of a stack could be quickly determined.

On the evening of their seventh day in Ba To, Prescott, Mike, and Sergeant Barton made preparations to return to the lodge. Counting the opium bricks stacked in Beemeer's special storeroom under his longhouse, Mike determined that one hundred and fifty kilos of opium had been harvested, and he paid Beemeer one hundred and eighty thousand metas from the heavy bankroll he had brought with him—equivalent to eighteen hundred dollars.

"Not much point in waiting for them to bring in more from the fields," Mike said, showing Prescott the stacked black bricks that gave off a strong musky odor. "A hundred and fifty kilos is a hell of a good load. Damn near a quarter of a year's crop out here."

"I agree," Prescott said. "No telling what could happen to it if we get into a fight with the Communists. I'll order a U-10 in first thing in the morning. Do you want to go out with it?"

"No. Just the poppy. But ask your air operations to bring in my man Johnny Elephant tomorrow morning. By now he should have bagged enough game as a cover, and I want him to meet Chief Beemeer. Johnny Elephant and his brother Charlie Tiger are going to be key personnel in Mituyan's new opium machine."

"No sweat, Mike. But I advise you to get out as soon as possible. We're sure as hell going to have trouble when the Communists show up to collect their opium, and that could be like tomorrow. I'm surprised none of our patrols have made contact yet. The Communists know when poppy time is here. Also, we've had intelligence reports that your friend TrangTi is building up a hell of a supply of USOM goods. That dipshit Grady Rourke has a new giveaway going for the province chiefs: USOM is installing radio transmitters and receivers at all district headquarters and police stations. The radio equipment goes to the province chief, of course, and he makes the distribution. As you know, the Mitcoms' biggest problem is communications. I figure the number-one trading item for poppy next week in Banthut is going to be USOM transceivers."

"Well, when there isn't any poppy to trade with, some of those radios just might get where they're supposed to go if USOM puts on some pressure," Mike grinned. "By God, I *am* developing a sense of mission."

The U-10 plopped into the short airstrip at Ba To in the middle of the following morning. A grinning Johnny Elephant stepped out, cradling his sports rifle in his arms. Mike and Sergeant Barton hefted the four burlap bags of opium bricks into the plane. "Over one hundred fifty kilos of the best in here, Johnny."

"Ah, numbah one," Johnny replied. "Shot tiger, plenty big game. No elephant yet."

"Maybe you get some shooting here," Mike said. "Maybe you like stuffed head of Mitcom?"

"Like to kill Mitcom any time."

"You speak any Groat?" Mike asked as they walked from the airstrip after they had watched the U-10 take off with its valuable load.

"Sure speak Groat. Must speak Groat if hunt in Groat land."

"Good. From now on you are number-one man in our poppy business. You buy from Chief Beemeer, take to Charlie Tiger. Charlie will send it to Jimmy Gems in Tuyan City, and Jimmy and I sell it. OK?"

"Numbah one," Johnny Elephant agreed. "Make big money."

"Big money, but plenty dangerous. Mitcoms need this poppy bad."

"Johnny Elephant not afraid of Mitcoms."

After Mike took him to meet Beemeer, Johnny Elephant and the

Groat chief quickly became friends. Johnny accepted a drinking reed and, talking in Groat, they sipped on a jar that the chief had dug up for the occasion and discussed the best times for Johnny Elephant to visit the village and buy the poppy crop. Feeling he had already more than done his duty in the drinking line, Mike left them together and went back to the American longhouse.

A worried Major Prescott was waiting for him. "You should have gone out when you had a chance, Mike. We just got a call from Teeter out with a patrol. He had to let a full platoon of heavily armed Mitcoms go by his ambush. Too many of them for his Groats to take on, he reported. He had mostly the new men we've been training."

"When will they hit this camp?" Mike asked.

"Hard to say. Teeter was twelve clicks out of here when he spotted them. They could be here before dark."

"Sir," Panton volunteered, "I could take a couple of squads of Goween's men into the jungle. Most of them have grease guns. We could ambush the Mitcoms before they get here."

Prescott shook his head. "There must be no Mitcom survivors. In any ambush a few will get away, you can't help it. Every Mitcom must be dead or captured. We'd better tell the chief to warn his people to be ready to pop into the fox holes we made them dig under their houses."

By mid-afternoon the village of Ba To was ready for the Mitcoms. Goween staked out three twelve-man squads in the jungle side of the village. A fourth squad, out on patrol, had been radioed orders to return to camp cautiously and be ready to hit an attacking enemy. Lightly trained and armed tribesmen from Ba To were crouched behind the village's bamboo fence, which had been reinforced with chest-high walls and four sandbagged and concealed machine-gun positions on each corner. Since the river ran along one side of the village, making a difficult angle from which to attack, most of the defenders were on the wall facing the jungle.

The Groats were excited and looking forward to testing their new weapons and skills on an enemy. As tension built, Beemeer conducted himself every inch the war chief. Prescott manned the command post, standing on the tower that had been built to command a view of the entire surrounding area. The four American sergeants were ready to run for whichever of the mortar positions would prove most advantageous, two men to a position. Mike manned the corner machine-gun bunker at the main-gate end of the camp, Panton the bunker at the other side of the gate. Johnny Elephant crouched exultantly with an automatic rifle just inside the gate.

Three clicks on Prescott's radio from a Groat radioman signaled that the Mitcoms had walked by one of Goween's squads. The three clicks indicated that the squad on the trail leading from the north to the main gate had sighted the Communists. This probably meant, Prescott reasoned, that the Communists did not know that their source of poppy had been interdicted. If it was at all possible, Prescott wanted to capture the leaders for interrogation. He hoped that the leaders would leave their troops outside the village and come in alone to talk to Beemeer. But this was unlikely even if the Communists were unsuspecting.

Minutes after the warning clicks, the van of the Communist platoon broke out of the jungle one hundred and fifty yards from the front gate. They were wearing black pajamas, the typical Communist-guerrilla rubber-tire sandals, and conical straw hats. All were armed with rifles, and some had submachine guns. It was still impossible to tell who the leader was. By the time the entire platoon had emerged from the jungle, the front ranks were less than one hundred yards from the village and still coming. Two men now seemed to be the leaders. Both were dressed in khaki and wore the bata boots issued to friendly Asiatic troops by the United States.

Prescott kept waiting for the two leaders to disengage themselves from their men and enter the village, but it looked as though the Communists were planning to march forcefully into the village and take it over. That would be the Communist way of doing it, terrorizing the village and intimidating the chief and the tribal leaders.

The American sergeants were at their mortar positions, zeroing the tubes in behind the rearmost of the Communists to give them minimum chance of escaping back into the jungle. Prescott allowed the Communists to come within fifty yards of the camp, still hoping that the leaders would proceed the final distance alone, as would regular traders or friendly troops. Now he could allow them to come no closer. They still appeared to be completely ignorant of the trap set for them; the submachine guns were slung on shoulders and the rifles carried awkwardly, as though by men tired from a long march.

Prescott signaled the mortarmen, and they plopped their first rounds into the tubes. At that instant Mike, Johnny Elephant, and Panton opened up with their guns, and with screams of joy the Groats, who had stalked to the front of the camp upon seeing the Communists massing there, pressed the triggers of their carbines as fast as they could. The withering grazing fire from the machine guns blasted the legs out from under the front ranks of the Mitcoms. They collapsed into the low flying hail of bullets and were stitched apart.

Goween's squad began to cut the Mitcoms down from the jungle. The surviving Communists, when they recovered from their shock, turned to retreat back into the jungle but only ran squarely into the mortar rounds, which blew them apart. Single Mitcom survivors of the initial onslaught who tried desperately to run for the jungle cover were picked off one by one. Chief Beemeer, wielding his new sports rifle, banged away, shouting happily at the carnage in front of the camp. Mike, Johnny Elephant, and Panton all had been told to try to avoid killing the leaders, and they missed several guerrillas who succeeded in finally making it into the jungle. But there they were met by new bursts of fire from Goween's tribesmen.

One of the men in khaki lying blood-soaked in front of the camp managed to raise his arm in surrender. The other had been shot a dozen times trying to run for cover, not by the machine guns but by the Groat tribesmen's indiscriminate heavy fusillade of bullets.

The whole slaughter had taken less than two minutes, and the tribesmen stood stunned and then disappointed when there were suddenly no more targets left. Only a few rounds had been returned by the enemy, and no casualties were suffered by the village. Except for a few moans there was silence from the field of frayed, crumpled bodies.

"Cavanaugh," Prescott yelled, "get your tools and get out there. See if you can save their honcho in khaki. He's still alive."

Cavanaugh, followed by the entire village, started out toward the remains of the Communist platoon. Prescott estimated it at fifty men. From the jungle, Goween's men came proudly marching in. They held ranks at first and then broke and headed for the corpses, pulling their knives as they ran.

Prescott watched them and shook his head. "Goddamn it, Panton, how do they know there isn't another Communist platoon out there ready to give us a surprise? We've got to get better discipline out of these Groats. Orders were that they'd hold their positions until after dark and then quietly move back into the camp."

"Yes, sir," Lieutenant Panton agreed. "I've told them; we all have. I guess until they get themselves hit disobeying orders they'll always run out to look at the damage the minute the shooting stops."

"What in God's name are they doing?" Mike cried as they reached the dead Communists.

"After we lost our third American killed in a Communist ambush," Prescott said, "one of my predecessors here, Major Talltree, decided to give these Groats an incentive to track down and kill Mitcoms. Talltree is three-quarters American Indian, and he taught Goween and his men the fine art of scalping. They get ten dollars a scalp; that's a month's pay."

The Americans reached the bodies about the same time as Goween's men did. Cavanaugh knelt by the khaki-clad leader and went to work on him. "He's pretty bad, sir," the redheaded medic said to Prescott.

"Try and save him, Cav."

"I think I can, sir. He won't ever be much good to anybody, but he'll be able to talk."

"That's all we need."

Mike grimaced with disgust as the Groats descended on the Communist corpses. "Scalping scared the hell out of the Viet Cong when we taught the montagnards how to do it," Prescott observed. "Never forget the first time I saw it done. The day before we'd found two buddies from our Special Forces camp who'd been captured alive by the Cong. They'd been hung up and given the standard treatment: stomachs slit open and hot coals shoveled in, hands cut off at the wrists and their privates cut off and shoved in their mouths. Next time we hit the

Cong our medic, he was no Indian either, scalped a few and the 'yards have been doing it ever since. I guess they still are."

Screams of delight came from the Ba To Groats as they saw what Goween's tribesmen were doing. Savage as they were, this was new to them.

"Things never seem to change," Mike sighed.

Prescott nodded. "These Groats have had a taste of blood now. I'm sorry, actually, they didn't take a couple of casualties. They're going to think all their battles will be like this until a few of them get killed and wounded. And I'm afraid that day isn't far off. The Commies will find out about this and try another attack on Ba To."

Although the Groats were reluctant, Prescott made Goween and Beemeer order their men to dig pits and bury the bodies. It was impossible to explain that dead bodies constituted a serious health hazard. Then Johnny Elephant, who had lifted a scalp for his trophy collection, told Beemeer that the bodies would attract many tigers; and the Groats, who were terrified of tigers, got to work at once. Supervising the burial detail, Prescott noted that about ten of the guerrillas had been Groat tribesmen. The heads of the Groatcoms had not been scalped.

Once the field had been tidied up and the Groats had returned to the village, it was difficult for Prescott and Panton to explain that they must continue being alert and post many guards. They had killed all the terrorists, they reasoned; now they must celebrate. Guards were finally posted, and Beemeer was persuaded that the village's fighting men must not drink liquor but be ready in case of another attack. The thought of more slaughter appealed to Beemeer, and Prescott found it impossible to suggest that next time it might be the Communists mutilating the bodies of the Groats.

"Well, Mike," Prescott said that night after the movie—the excitement of wiping out a Communist platoon had not lessened the Groats' appetites for the movies, even the same one repeated for the third time—"I figure it's about time we went back to the lodge. We've performed our mission. Panton can handle the Ba To operation from here on in, and Johnny Elephant is in with the chief. Gave him his .30-.30 rifle. What do you say?"

"Get that U-10 in for us," Mike answered. "You know, I keep thinking how different it could have been today if the Mitcoms had been up to their usual high standards as intelligence gatherers."

"I'll tell you one thing that I learned in Vietnam," said Prescott. "If you really want to keep an operation secret from the Communists, keep it a secret from your Asiatic allies. If I'd had a Mit counterpart at the lodge, he would have had to brief his superior, and his superior would have had to brief the province chief, and we would have been hit with mortars, recoil-less rifles, and a couple of companies just when we weren't looking for them—and that would have been the end of Ba To and all of us."

Prescott's voice became bitter. "If those dipshits in Tuyan City do to us what those fuckin' Saigon experts did to us in Vietnam—saddle us with counterparts and that whole mandarin system the Viets used to have—I'm quitting the army. Because even if the ambassadors and generals figure it's good politics, that's what kills Americans. . . . Well, good night."

Mike lay down on his sleeping mat and gazed reflectively at the thatched roof of the bamboo longhouse that he would be leaving the next morning.

CHAPTER TWENTY

MIKE FORRESTER breathed a sigh of relief as Johnny Elephant's Land Rover rolled through the Groat village that served as Prescott's nearest listening post to Banthut. His muscles ached and he was sure he'd pass blood the next time he urinated. The Land Rover was filled with Groat artifacts he had purchased from Beemeer: a liquor jug, crossbows, brass gongs, several sets of cymbals dangling from the sides of the vehicle. The skin of the tiger that Johnny Elephant had bagged was secured to the roof of the jeep. They certainly looked like hunters coming back from a successful safari.

Under his feet, in metal boxes, were packed the bricks of raw opium. Charlie Prescott had been unable to fly Mike into Banthut, where the airport was always under surveillance, because that would have violated the cardinal rule Cardinez had laid down: no one, correspondent, American congressional investigator, or Mituyan government official, must ever be able to trace Mike's opium trade to the JRB operation in the Groat country.

At least it had been comforting to know that all the way from the lodge to this outpost a plane had been watching from the air to make sure they were not molested by Mitcoms; and they were never more than a few miles from a patrol that kept radio contact with the plane, which was equipped with .30-caliber machine guns for strafing.

After everything he had been through to wrest the opium trade away from the Mitcoms and TrangTi, it would have been tragic to lose the fruit of the poppy to Mitcoms along the way—to say nothing of his own life. Again, so there could be no connection to JRB, Mike had purchased the opium with his own funds, drawn from his account in his Tuyan City bank. A great deal of his money was tied up in the four boxes at his feet—money he could not afford to lose.

Charlie Tiger was waiting for them with a broad grin as the heavily laden Land Rover, which had made the desired spectacle driving through the crowded streets of Banthut, lurched to a stop in front of his store. The vehicle was quickly unloaded, passersby stopping to gape at the strange cargo. The four metal boxes, covered with jaguar skins, were carried by Mike and Johnny in two trips to the vault in Charlie

Tiger's back room. With the unloading finished, Charlie, his brother, and Mike sat down and sipped tea brought to them by the number-three daughter.

"Plenty more American goods come to province headquarters," Charlie said. "Seems big trading planned."

"And we have the stuff right here," Mike nodded toward the vault. "That poppy would have brought TrangTi more than ten thousand dollars worth of metas from the Tuyan City opium traders. Looks like you may not be doing much money-changing for TrangTi."

"Very sorry about that," Charlie answered.

It was almost five o'clock when they finished, and Mike asked for a ride to the hotel. He picked up his messages and went to his bungalow, where he drew a deep tub of hot water, flopped into it, and read as he soaked.

He smiled at the Reverend Maynard's note thanking him for two potential young Groat converts, already studiously learning English at the Starretts' mission. A message from province headquarters asked him to report to the province chief as soon as he returned; TrangTi obviously would know he was back, so he'd have to drop by his office. Another message dated that morning said, "Meet me at House of Jasmine tonight." It was signed "Jack."

So Cardinez was in Banthut! Well, there was a lot to tell that spook.

Bathed and dressed in clean clothes, Mike went to the lobby to use the hotel's one telephone and call province headquarters. It was almost seven; he hoped TrangTi would not want to see him until the next day. But he quickly got through to the province chief, who politely but unmistakably ordered him to come over forthwith.

Fifteen minutes later, Mike was sitting across from the province chief's desk being interrogated about his safari.

"You were never bothered by Mitcoms?" TrangTi asked, unbelieving.

"I never was," Mike replied. "Maybe they decided to go away?"

"Did you see any men dressed differently from the Groats—perhaps headed along the road toward Banthut?"

"No, Colonel, I didn't."

"Strange." The province chief thought a few moments. "What conclusions did you reach about putting the Groats in business?"

"They really haven't much to sell, although"—Mike paused—"I heard rumors that some of the tribes grow opium poppies. Have you any idea how they sell the stuff?"

"What did you hear? And from whom? Your Special Forces?"

"Oh, I guess everyone out there figures there's a lot of trading going on in poppy," Mike hedged.

"Mr. Forrester!" TrangTi betrayed annoyance. "If you think that I, the province chief, am deluded into thinking that a businessman of your reputation would waste his time trying to market Groat crossbows and gongs, you are being insulting."

"Well, I can't deny that getting into the opium trade might be lucrative for me, especially since the Mitcoms are slowly ruining the investments I've made in this country," Mike drawled blandly. "But I've come to the conclusion that it would be difficult to make the proper Groat contacts. Also, I'm sure that if opium is coming out of the Groat country, it's being transported by a well-armed and protected organization and that one man alone, like myself, would be ill-advised to attempt securing a piece of that trade for himself."

TrangTi regarded Mike with undisguised suspicion. He started twice to ask him a question, appeared to think better of it, and remained silent. Mike did not break the silence. Finally TrangTi asked: "How are the American Special Forces teams progressing with their plans to isolate the Groats from the Communists?"

"They seem to be doing well," Mike replied cautiously. "The medical program in particular seems to be successful. Every Groat who comes to a government-controlled village and gets cured of even a few of his many ailments is an advertisement for the Mituyan government."

TrangTi shook his head. "No. It merely makes them think the Americans are on their side against the Mituyan people."

The logic of this was lost to Mike, but he didn't want to antagonize TrangTi so he did not answer. The province chief stared at Mike a few moments. "Soon there will be a change of policy in the mountains. Mituyan officers will take charge of those Groat camps. The Americans' only job will be to supply them."

"I hope you use only Mituyans who are sympathetic to Groat problems and treat them as people, not dirty savages."

"They will be treated as they deserve to be treated," TrangTi replied. "As province chief I will be the final authority on how the Groat camps are administered."

There goes my opium trade, Mike thought to himself. What was worse, of course, there it goes to the Communists.

"In the meantime, Mr. Forrester," TrangTi said as a parting thought, "do not forget that I am the province chief here. If you have any ideas of going into business in this province it would be well for you to discuss the proposition fully with me."

"I quite agree, Colonel."

"How much longer do you intend to remain in Banthut?"

"I like the climate. I was even thinking of bringing my wife up here for a few days."

"Yes, you should do that." TrangTi turned from inquisitor to affable host. "I would like to meet her. In the meantime, perhaps I will have some ideas on how you can establish business relations here worthy of your great financial talent. When I have tightened my personal control throughout the Groat country, which should be in the next two or three months, there may be matters we can discuss."

Now I'm back in the opium business, with a new partner, Mike thought wryly. "Thank you, Colonel," he said.

Mike had himself driven directly to The House of Jasmine. In the bar he looked for Jack Cardinez, and not seeing him headed for one of the recessed booths that provided maximum privacy. A Mituyan waitress seated him and he ordered a drink.

Casually, Susie strolled over to the table. "Hello, Mike." She placed a scrap of paper in front of him. "Anything you want? Maybe go upstairs?" she gave him a suggestive wink.

"Nothing at the moment, Susie." He reached for the piece of paper and glanced at it. It read, "General Dandig, I Corps, had meeting in Banthut last night with Li Phang and other bonzes." He smiled at the proprietress. "Thanks, Susie." She nodded and walked away.

Cardinez and Colonel Lawton, in civilian clothes, walked in just as his drink arrived and sat down with him.

"Had a profitable week?" Cardinez asked.

"We were lucky. Things worked out well. I've got the machinery set up now. And there seems to be no lack of poppy to keep it oiled. We can talk at this table, I assume," he added.

"Every table, every bed, even the bar is bugged and taped," Cardinez said cheerfully. "But keep talking; they're our bugs."

"Have something on everybody in our business, I always say," Mike laughed mirthlessly. "I'm glad I didn't go upstairs."

"OK," Cardinez said, after ordering a round of drinks. "Let's have your analysis of the situation."

"My analysis is that I'm out of business before really getting started."

"Why?" Lawton shot back.

"I had a meeting with TrangTi. He said that every U.S. Special Forces camp in the Groat country will have a Mituyan team directly in command."

Cardinez nodded somberly. "That's what they're trying to do. It will wreck our whole operation. I'm fighting it, but KaritKi and Tarot insist. Our own people, the ambassador, our station chief, have agreed."

"Well, it was a good business while it lasted—one week." Mike waited until the waitress left, then went on. "Looks like the Communists and TrangTi, get it back again. By the way, I have a souvenir for you. Charlie Prescott thought it might be useful in our private guerrilla war with the Palace and the Country Team." Mike reached into his pocket and pulled out a roll of currency, placing the bills on the table.

"We got these, and a lot of other papers that G-2 out at the lodge is examining, from the bodies of the Communists. Can you read the Mit language?"

Cardinez nodded, studying the bills. "A little, but I can't completely translate what's on this Mitcom money."

"Each one of those Mitcom one-thousand-meta bills says it is redeemable for one hundred grams of opium," Mike said. "That's about three and one-half ounces. That currency is backed by opium. And it's damned accurate. Fifty dollars a pound is just about the trading price in Tuyan City. That's a little over three dollars an ounce, ten dollars or one thousand metas to one hundred grams of raw opium."

Cardinez studied the Communist money. "I've heard about these, but this is the first time I've ever seen opium certificates." He shrugged. "Well, if Whittelsie and his team want to play politics to the point where we're helping the enemy back his money . . ."

"I suppose your sources have informed you about the bonzes meeting here, and Lawton's friend, General Dandig, talking with them."

Cardinez smiled. "That's under control. As a matter of fact, Fritz is going to be in Tiking in a few days. You planning to be there?"

"I'd like to check on my rubber—if, of course, the Agency can spare me."

"We can't. It would be helpful to us for you to be in Tiking."

"Can I know why?"

"No reason to burden you with overinformation now. Let's just say that Fritz has a new operation we want to try out in Tiking, and we might need your help."

"OK. I'll pick up my wife in Tuyan City."

"Fine. Now let's finish this round and we'll go upstairs to a private room for dinner and your complete analysis of the Groat situation."

"While it's on my mind, Jack, when I get to Tuyan City have you any objection to me having a discussion with Grady Rourke?"

"What about?"

"As a private citizen, I'd just like to know why the hell he allows so much USOM stuff to be diverted—*stolen* is the word I'm looking for. If he'd just get out in the boondocks . . ."

Cardincz snorted. "You be careful what you say to him. If you let him know what we know about TrangTi, he'll tell Branot, and then our entire Groat operation will be called off. They're all in on the take, you know."

Grimly, Mike looked down at the opium certificates, and put them back in his pocket.

"I don't want you to talk to any member of the American mission, or anyone else for that matter, including your wife, about anything you've seen, heard, or suspect. Clear?"

Mike nodded, "Let's go eat. I haven't had a real dinner in eight days."

PART IV

ISLE OF STONES

CHAPTER TWENTY-ONE

ROGER KRAKHAUR and Alana waved goodbye to Luna Forrester as her car drove down the dimly lit street. "It sure was thoughtful of her to invite you to stay aboard *Promise* while you're in Tiking and Mike's up with the tribesmen," said Roger as he led the girl back through the gate to his villa.

"And I promise to check in over the ship's radio twice a day," said Alana, as though this were a compromise wrung from her after much discussion.

"You also promised to take no chances. No scoops," he added sternly. "Poramat could be very nasty if he thought you were digging up material for an exposé on the way he runs his feudal state up North."

"I'll be careful, Roger."

"Well, you've got to take an early plane, so it's about bed time. Right?" She nodded and they went upstairs. Alana's bedroom was to the right and Krakhaur's to the left; in the three weeks she had been living at the villa they had kissed goodnight tenderly and Alana had always gone on to her bedroom. Now she stepped into her room but did not close the door right away.

"I'll be lonely tomorrow without you."

"Don't stay long in Tiking," he said. "I need you here." He entered her room and held her tightly, his kisses becoming more passionate.

"Roger, you promised." She pulled away from the demanding caresses.

"I know, darling. It's just I love you so damned much."

"I love you too. But it isn't right." She arched back from him and looked up at him impudently. "I know; everybody thinks we are, but you and I know better."

"Yeah, I sure do," he replied ruefully. "I'm ready to marry you tomorrow."

"As soon as we can, darling." He released her and she stepped back. "I've got to make it right with mother and my step-father."

"The old bastard still figures you should be sending him money?"

Alana placed her fingers on his mouth. "I'll see them just before I leave Tiking. When I come back I'll have something definite, I promise you, darling."

Reluctantly Roger retreated from her bedroom. "See you early in the morning."

"You understand, Roger?" Alana's eyes were anxious and compassionate. "I want everything to be right when we're married. I've seen what it's like when things aren't right." Her voice lowered. "My mother . . ."

Roger was ashamed of himself for pressing her. "Of course I understand, my dearest. Forgive me."

"There is nothing to forgive. Good night, my love."

When Alana stepped off the airplane at Tiking Airport the next morning she did not notice the two men in sport shirts, slacks, and wearing dark glasses who watched her intently. Nor did she see the jeep follow her cab to where the *Promise* was docked and Captain Batki was waiting.

Alana went directly to the radio room, where she easily contacted Krakhaur. Then, after a cup of coffee, she took a cab out to the University, called on several of her old friends, and began compiling notes. She finished her work at the University late in the afternoon and took another cab back to *Promise*. It was then that she noticed the jeep following her. The two men watched her board *Promise*.

Batki saw them also. "Those two are part of Poramat's special police," he said. "You should tell Mr. Krakhaur when you make radio contact."

"I will," Alana promised. But she didn't want to alarm Roger, and made no mention of being under surveillance when she talked to him that evening.

Leaving the main gate of the University at noon the next day after a morning of interviews, she looked up and down the street for one of the minicabs that cruised the streets of Tiking. A black sedan pulled up beside her and a man in sunglasses stepped out and took her by the arm. "We will take you to where you are going," he said. She tried to resist but was forced into the car, crying for help. A number of students saw what was happening but none dared interfere. Only Poramat's police drove black American sedans.

Sitting in the back seat between her two abductors, Alana cried: "Where are you taking me?" In answer, one of the men cupped her breasts and the other ran a hand up under her dress. They giggled at her struggles. "Leave me alone. I am chaste," she cried.

Angrily and then weeping she protested her innocence as the two continued their intimate exploration of her body. The staff car pulled up in front of the headquarters of the province chief and immediately her two captors released her. They led her into the building, up a flight of stairs, and down the hall to a comfortable office, complete with a wide sofa and air-conditioning.

A squint-eyed man with a pencil-line mustache, wearing the rank of Lieutenant Colonel on his uniform, entered and introduced himself as Colonel Yunakit, the province chief. At once he began to interrogate her about her purpose for being in Tiking. She was staying aboard the boat of her friends, the Forresters, she said, and she was visiting Tiking University with a view to taking post-graduate courses. She never mentioned that she worked for Krakhaur.

"Then, why," Yunakit asked, "were you asking a certain faculty member of political science yesterday afternoon, and a student leader this morning, how many arrests a week could be attributed to Counselor Poramat?"

"I was curious," Alana answered. "We hear such rumors." Then, heatedly: "You have no right to detain me like this. I am a Mituyan citizen. I demand to telephone my friend, Mrs. Forrester, in Tuyan City."

"Would you like to telephone the journalist Krakhaur?" Yunakit moved closer to her now and Alana could see he was eyeing her hungrily. Stark fear almost paralyzed her, but she kept control. "You were here to provide more filth for his stories," Yunakit stated.

"I know Mr. Krakhaur," Alana admitted. "I know all the members of the American press. I studied journalism at the University."

"You will tell us everything in time," Yunakit said. "You will write out for us a complete denunciation of Krakhaur and his reason for telling sensational lies in the American press."

"I know nothing of this," Alana cried.

Yunakit took the girl by both shoulders and stared down the bosom of her dress. Then he dismissed the two police officers, one of whom came over to the province chief and said loud enough for Alana to hear: "She claims to be a virgin. If this is true, Counselor Poramat should be notified." He grinned lewdly.

Yunakit nodded and backed away from the girl. "You are right," he said reluctantly.

"We will all receive credit if this is so," the officer said.

"Wait, then," Yunakit said to Alana's abductors. He took the girl by the arm. "Come with me. We will go to the counselor. Perhaps you can convince him that you have nothing to do with the damaging lies Mr. Krakhaur writes."

Alana breathed a sigh of relief. Poramat was, after all, the Premier's brother. He *had to be* a partially responsible man. She prayed that he was.

Willingly she went with Yunakit and the two secret policemen back to the staff car. During the drive to Poramat's headquarters, Yunakit questioned her further on her relationship with the press corps in Tuyan City; always he came back to her being not only an employee but the mistress of Krakhaur. She denied both accusations hotly and again repeated that she had never had any man.

"We will soon discover whether you are telling the truth," Yunakit said, and led her past the guards into Poramat's headquarters and upstairs to his office. The guards opened the double doors and Alana was pushed through first, Yunakit and the two secret policemen following. Alana instinctively sensed that he and the plainclothesmen mistrusted and to some extent feared each other—which was, she had learned, not uncommon in Poramat's thralldom.

"Sir," Yunakit said to the waiting Poramat. "This young lady, hardly more than a girl"—he smiled significantly—"was detained by two of our most alert agents." The two men drew themselves up proudly.

"This Alana has been asking questions at the University about the way you administer the provinces under your control. She is known to have close connections with the American press, particularly the notorious liar, Krakhaur."

Poramat nodded in interest, his small eyes running up and down her body. Alana shuddered, knowing at once that she could expect little mercy from the Premier's brother.

"Have you interrogated her yet?"

"I thought . . . we thought, Counselor, that you should question her first. She is very young and, she claims, unwise in the ways of men. I feel that perhaps, in your own delicate manner, you would be able to learn more than we could. Later perhaps . . ."

"Excellent thinking, Colonel." Poramat nodded to the two policemen. "I will call you as soon as the young lady and I have talked."

Yunakit shepherded the two agents from the office, closing the double doors behind him. As soon as they were alone, Poramat came from around his desk. His bland round face and small boring eyes, the coarse expression on his heavy lips, terrified her—but she tried to remain cool.

"So, you are here to spy on me for Krakhaur?" he began, without venom. "But I am not so interesting."

"I came here to spy on nobody," Alana insisted.

"We will have to find out the truth, you know," Poramat said, his eyes never ceasing their constant search of her face and body. "You are far too young and delicate to be interrogated by Colonel Yunakit's people. Why don't you just tell me everything, sign a harmless little confession which will make you a heroine of our government. Give us the opportunity to expel this Krakhaur. Oh, we know you work for him."

"I have done free-lance work for many American journalists," Alana replied. "And I am a personal friend of Madame Mayna," she added. Saying this was taking a terrible chance, she knew. She had been friendly with Mayna and had even written a favorable article about her that was published in the English-language paper. But Mayna also knew how close she really was to Roger now. Perhaps, thought Alana, Mayna, as a reputedly gracious woman, would not allow her brother-in-law . . .

Poramat regarded her silently for some moments.

Alana's voice was clear and steady. "You had better call Madame

Mayna before you subject me to your inquisition." She wondered how she managed to conceal her alarm.

Poramat nodded and reached for the phone on his desk. "I have a direct line to the palace which the American communications experts put in for me only a few weeks ago."

Alana watched, trying to push back rising panic. She forced herself to hope that Mayna would issue the reprieve that would save her. The palace switchboard took the call and transferred it to Mayna's wing. "Now, I push this little button on this little black box and you will hear for yourself what Mayna says."

A purring of static and a phone ringing on the other end of the line came loudly from the amplifier. "The Americans are children about our politics, but they are indeed geniuses with their devices."

The familiar, high-pitched, mincing voice of Mayna suddenly came from the small speaker, startling Alana. Poramat chuckled.

After a few casual inquiries, Poramat, continually staring at Alana, came to the point. "We have detained a young woman named Alana who says she is your friend. She appears to be on an assignment for the American newsman, Krakhaur. From the information we have gathered she is collecting damaging and irresponsible gossip for Krakhaur to put in his articles. What do you know of her?"

"She does work for Krakhaur. It is true," Mayna replied.

"Is she important to you? What shall I do with her?"

"What do you want to do?" The question was followed by a knowing chuckle.

"I want her to confess that Krakhaur seduced her and pays her money, as only the Americans can, to be his mistress. She will also say that she made up sensational lies to please him and because he paid her well." Poramat paused. "However, if you want her released as she is, of course I will."

"Counselor Tarot will be pleased with his brother's thinking. But let us draw up an accusation against Krakhaur for her to sign. That will be stronger. Tarot will send it up by a trusted political aide tonight. I'll request a special airplane from the Americans."

"Then your only interest in the girl is to have her sign the papers?" Poramat asked pointedly.

"That is right. . . . Give Mr. Krakhaur's girl my regards."

"Oh, no!" Alana cried. "No. Please!"

"Is that the girl I hear?" Mayna asked.

"Yes. She is in my office."

"Since she went to Tiking for information, I'm sure you're the person who can give it to her first-hand," Mayna tittered. "Goodbye, brother."

Poramat hung up the phone and came around the desk to Alana, trembling in her chair.

"It doesn't have to be so bad," he said, stroking her cheek. "When you sign your accusation against Krakhaur, you will be free." He bent closer to her and she could see the Adam's apple working in his fat neck. Then his hands were on her, all over her. He pulled her to her feet and forced her to accompany him through a side door into another room. Suddenly she tripped over an enormous mattress-like affair and fell sprawling.

"Everything will be much easier if you do not fight," Poramat whispered hoarsely. She fought with all her strength, pounding and tearing at him. But he fell heavily on top of her, pulled off his own loose garments easily, and then ripped her dress from her body, muttering, snorting, struggling to violate her prostrate form. The discovery that she was indeed a virgin inflamed his lust. He was driven to an intense pitch of violence, and she screamed in excruciating pain. For an instant a new valve of strength opened in her frail body. Twisting violently, she found his ear and, barely aware of what she was doing, bit almost through the lobe just as Poramat expended himself into her.

At first he seemed unconscious of what she had done in the intensity of his passion. But the pain suddenly stabbed through. Pulling a bloody hand away from his ear, he backhanded her sharply. Then, holding his ear with one hand, he pulled the silk loose fitting slacks over his obese stomach with the other. Leaving the naked, bleeding girl on the mattress, he waddled into his main office, picked up the phone, and called for a physician.

That evening Alana, in a state of semishock, was raped by Yunakit and then by the two plainclothesmen who had arrested her. Only then was she finally sent down for "interrogation."

Alana's mind was alternately clear and dim during the ordeal. Each of the interrogators raped her. She fainted, came to, and found herself lying naked and semiconscious on a bench. Next to her was a guard, busily cranking a large two-handled generator. He reached forward with two electrodes; suddenly shock hit her brain and her whole body convulsed. She heard herself scream. One electrode had been touched to one of her nipples, the other arching a blue electrical flame to the other.

One of Yunakit's torturers again began asking questions. Desperately she wanted to say the right things, to end the agony. "Please, let me sign the papers," she moaned.

"Did the American Krakhaur force you to spy on the government? Did he write lies for the American press and force you to say they were true?"

"No!" Alana cried. Then, but too late, "Yes, he made me lie."

Again the electrode. She screamed and bucked against the restraining straps.

The door to the room opened and Yunakit appeared. "The accusation against Krakhaur has arrived. Are you ready to sign it?"

"I will sign it," Alana choked.

"I will read it to you."

"I will sign it," Alana whispered. She tried to move her shackled hands toward the paper.

"Let her up," Yunakit commanded.

When she was freed of her bonds, Yunakit pulled her to a sitting position. He handed her the accusation, neatly typed in English and held securely to a clipboard. She reached out for the pen but it clattered to the floor, her fingers powerless to hold it.

Holding the clipboard in one hand, Yunakit grabbed Alana by the upper arm and led her from the chamber, yanking her up as her knees buckled to a small air-conditioned room with several cots and a basin—the guards' rest room. Yunakit shoved her down on one of the cots, told her to sleep, and pulled a dirty sheet over her. Immediately Alana lost consciousness.

How much later she was awakened she did not know. She was offered a bowl of hot rice soup that a guard, greedily staring at her body, helped her to drink. Her hands had steadied when Yunakit returned.

"You can sign this now," he commanded.

"Then will you let me go?"

"You can go as far as I'm concerned," he replied. "But I must get Counselor Poramat's permission."

Without bothering to read it, Alana signed the document, her hands and fingers just strong enough to scrawl her name legibly. When all the copies had been signed, Yunakit nodded in satisfaction and started from the room.

"Please, can I go?" Alana begged.

"I will go to the counselor with these papers. In the meantime you will be moved to another detention chamber."

"I want to go!" Alana cried. As Yunakit smiled wanly and left the room, she collapsed back on the cot.

Alana had no idea how much time had elapsed when a man wearing sunglasses, even in this dank dungeon, walked into the cell and said: "You have committed a criminal act. You have assaulted and wounded Counselor Poramat. His orders are that you will be subjected to further interrogation and then sent to the Isle of Stones."

Even in her weakened and almost mindless state the words registered. Interrogation. Isle of Stones. What dread words!

"We know there is much you have refused to tell us," Poramat's agent said harshly.

"I signed!" Alana cried.

Two guards came in, pulled the girl to her feet, and dragged her across the dark hallway into another room.

The stench in the cell made her retch. Then she saw that two guards and an interrogator were working on another girl who, by the condition of her dress, apparently had not yet been long under questioning.

"Do you know this girl?" Alana was asked by the special police agent. Alana shook her head. "We strongly believe she is part of the Mitcom movement at the University. We will find out for certain."

The girl had been strapped to a bench. She glared up defiantly at her captors, saying nothing. The interrogator, a man dressed in a spotless white suit, leaned over and questioned her. Alana heard her answer in Mituyan that she worked in Tiking and only attended a few lectures at the University. If she had taken part in a student demonstration, it was only to give herself a feeling of identification with the student body.

Abruptly, one of the men picked up a bucket of filth and poured some of its contents in her face. The girl gagged. A thick gauze rag was pressed tightly to her face and more from the bucket was poured over her. Desperately she tried to breathe. Just as she was losing consciousness the rag was removed. The girl gasped wildly for air. Again the man in the well-pressed white suit asked her questions, and again the near-drowning treatment was applied.

"You will be next," the torturer harshly assured the shuddering Alana. Finally the girl was no longer able to talk, and the guards dragged her semiconscious form from the room. Then the inquisitor approached Alana, who screamed and shrank back. Roughly he and one of the guards grabbed her and threw her down on the bench. But at that moment an immaculately uniformed army officer entered the room, holding a scented handkerchief against his nose. "Clean the girl up well," he commanded. "Dress her. Poramat has men who have just come from the mountains and need a woman." The officer peered at Alana. "What a waste of so beautiful a young girl," he said regretfully. Then, "Hurry. You have your orders."

"You are very lucky," the man in the white suit said.

For a day, perhaps three—she had no consciousness of time—Alana was imprisoned in a villa north of Port Tiking. Over and over she was used sexually—first by officers of diminishing rank and then by the sergeants of Poramat's special army group.

No longer aware of faces or events she was finally taken from the villa in a special-police sedan and driven to a Tiking dock. There, with dozens of other wailing men and women, she was loaded aboard an open ferry. Vaguely she knew the destination of this boat: the Isle of Stones.

CHAPTER TWENTY-TWO

AMBASSADOR WHITTELSIE and General Macker regarded Roger Krakhaur with ill-concealed hostility. "Why don't you and the other reporters give Premier KaritKi and his family the benefit of the doubt sometimes?" Whittelsie said petulantly. "You always make him out to be a feudal dictator."

"Sir, as I told you, my female Mituyan employee, Alana, is missing. I can't help being worried sick about her. The captain of Mr. Forrester's yacht, where she was staying, hasn't seen her for two days. He reported that Poramat's secret police were following her the last time he saw her. All I ask is that you make an official inquiry and demand an answer."

"You come running to us for help quick enough," Macker said. "But *you* put this young lady in danger. You admit you sent her to Tiking to spy—"

"Not to spy," Krakhaur corrected Macker for the fourth or fifth time. "To ascertain facts for a story I am writing."

"Another anti-KaritKi story." Macker shook his head. "You seem to feel it's your mission in life to damage relations between the Country Team and the legal government of Mituyan. Dammit, Krakhaur, why don't you get with the program?"

Ignoring Macker, Krakhaur said to Whittelsie, "Sir, they don't dare touch me, so they've kidnaped my employee. If you made an official request for information they'd have to give you some answer."

"Krakhaur"—the ambassador made no attempt to conceal his annoyance—"I can't be running to the palace with official inquiries every time some American's native girl *employee*"—he underscored the word with heavy irony—"can't be found."

Krakhaur could see he was defeated. "OK, forget it then. But if anything has happened to her, you're going to read some stories that will really shake up KaritKi and the American mission, shake it up so bad that you may all go the way of Ngo Dinh Diem in Vietnam." He tried to fight down his emotion, but could not. "And you can look for a congressional investigation that's never going to get off your back."

Redfaced, General Macker leapt to his feet. "Are you threatening the American ambassador? Are you trying to blackmail him for your personal benefit?"

"If requesting him to try and save the life of an intelligent, patriotic, educated young Mituyan girl is blackmail, I guess the answer is yes, *sir*."

"Now, now, Mr. Krakhaur," Whittelsie said. "You're upset, of course, but there's no proof that anything has happened at all, much less that KaritKi or Poramat have done anything to her."

"I'm sure your little Mituyan girlfriend will turn up," Macker added.

Krakhaur was suddenly too weary to get angry. "Thank you for your time, Mr. Ambassador, General Macker."

"You're quite welcome, Mr. Krakhaur," Whittelsie said airily. "Any time you want to see me, I will try to make myself available." But after Macker left his office, Whittelsie opened the drawer with the red telephone in it and in a few moments he heard Mayna's voice.

"Why, Whit, a lovely surprise!"

"Mayna, Krakhaur's threatened even more damaging stories than he's produced to date if I don't find out what happened to some girl named Alana who works for him. Of course he blames Poramat and the Palace for using her to get at him."

"I'll try to find out what I can," Mayna promised. "And I'm so sorry if that sensation-monger is being difficult with my Whit."

Roger Krakhaur grabbed a taxicab in front of the Embassy and gave the driver the address of Major Hargraves, Luna Forrester's father. Luna's connections, he knew, were strong both at the Palace and with Poramat.

Hargraves himself came to the gate and let him in. A retired British officer, he had an enormous belly, a complexion ruddy from many years of heavy drinking, a walrus mustache, even a black eye patch over his glass eye.

"Ah, Krakhaur, come in, old boy. You have been giving them the devil of a time around here, what?"

"Is Luna here?" Krakhaur asked.

"She's around somewhere." He clapped his hands and a Mituyan servant appeared. "Find Mrs. Forrester," he commanded.

Luna came downstairs and rescued Krakhaur from a long dissertation on the role of military police in a protectorate or colonial state. Seeing he seemed distraught, she asked her father to get him a drink.

Instantly old Hargraves was on his feet. Both his daughter and wife conspired to keep him from liquor, and when an opportunity came he seized on it.

"I think Poramat has picked up Alana," Krakhaur said to Luna. "Whittelsie won't do a damned thing. You know what's probably happening to her if she's in one of Poramat's lockups."

Luna looked stricken. "What can I do?"

"Maybe you could get someone at the palace to intercede?"

"I'll call right now."

Hargraves was on his third Scotch when Luna returned. "Dhuna has arranged for Mike and me to come to the palace at six-thirty this evening for an informal chat," she said to Krakhaur. "Mike sent me a wire from Banthut that he'd be back this afternoon. She promised to get Premier KaritKi to talk to us. We'll be going back to our apartment this evening. Why don't you drop in around eight thirty and I'll give you a full report."

"I'll be there," Krakhaur said, "and Luna, thank you. There was nobody else I could go to."

"We'll find her," Luna replied with a brightness she scarcely felt.

At nine o'clock that evening at the Forresters' apartment, where Luna only stayed when her husband was in Tuyan City with her, Krakhaur listened intently to Mike's account of the meeting.

"As you can imagine, the name Roger Krakhaur isn't very popular at the palace," Mike began.

Krakhaur nodded and sipped his drink.

"At first the Premier denied knowing anything about Alana," Luna said. "And he kept saying that you are giving the impression in your stories that his brothers, Tarot and Poramat are suppressing all opposition in the coming elections."

"Well, they are," Krakhaur declared.

"Now look here, Roger," Mike snapped, "if you ever want to see Alana alive just forget you're a reporter for a while and concentrate on trying to save her. God knows Luna and I went on the line for you and Alana this evening and put ourselves in a damned bad spot doing it."

"I'm sorry," Krakhaur was genuinely contrite. "I'll do what you say."

"Right," Mike acknowledged. "KaritKi kept Luna and me for two hours, most of that time listening to his harangue on Americans who meddle in Mituyan affairs. And he kept coming back to one point. Roger Krakhaur is contributing to American support of a coup against the present government."

Krakhaur shrugged silently, letting Mike and Luna do the talking. "Finally," Mike went on, "the Premier, after scolding me for trying to help you, told Dhuna, his wife, that if she wanted to help us she could call Poramat herself and ask what had happened, but he would have nothing to do with the situation himself."

"Dhuna promised to call me first thing in the morning," Luna said. "She will try to help, Roger, as a personal favor to me. But I think Mike and I will have to go to Tiking if we're really going to find out what happened."

"I'll go with you," Krakhaur said eagerly.

"You'll follow my advice—strictly," Mike cut in. "You're a fine reporter, Roger," he said more softly, "but you are so far over your head in this country you'll only get yourself in trouble and Alana killed if you start trying to do things on your own."

"Sorry, Mike. It's just I'm worried sick about Alana. I don't know what the hell I'm doing."

"Leave it to us, Roger. If anything can be done we'll do it," Luna said gently. She took his glass to the sideboard. "How about another Scotch?"

"Thanks, I need it. And just tell me what you want me to do. Anything that will help Alana."

"Don't worry, we will," Luna said.

CHAPTER TWENTY-THREE

LUNA ENTERED Poramat's palatial headquarters villa, more frightened than her cool exterior indicated. Mike had been torn between sending his wife alone into the lair of the man he considered chief villain and monster of Mituyan and his sense of urgency to rescue Alana before it was too late.

Premier KaritKi's brother occupied a powerful if ambiguous position in Mituyan's political hierarchy. He was not a province chief, yet the chiefs of the five northern provinces, including that of Banthut, were subservient to him and followed his orders. Though he carried no military title, few generals would have dared to disobey any command he gave.

Business leaders, particularly those operating near Tiking, where Poramat's influence was strongest, consulted him on all transactions and awarded him a share in all profits. Businessmen who failed to pay him a percentage had been known to disappear entirely and their businesses expropriated by a large holding company he owned. Because no one could be sure the next person either was not working for Poramat or one of his legion of paid informers, there was little intrigue in Tiking. Only the Communists, ironically, could safely conspire against him, since they were intimately known to each other and sworn to a cause even more terrifying to its defectors than Poramat's despotism. Besides, Poramat was more interested in hunting down anti-KaritKi Mituyans than Communists.

Poramat's Tiking residence and his enormous estate and country headquarters, which was the largest rubber-producing property in the country, were guarded by his personal police. Trained and supplied by USOM and paid from U.S. government funds, they were the most effective police force in northern Mituyan.

An officer met Luna at the reception desk and escorted her up a flight of wide, carpeted stairs to Poramat's second-floor office, which faced out over the well-guarded patio of his headquarters complex. Guards in the distinctive white uniforms with red and yellow sashes about their waists were posted everywhere. Two guards with Thompson submachine guns stood at the big double door to Poramat's office. They presented arms as the officer knocked and then pushed open the doors.

Poramat was standing in front of his desk. As always he wore the traditional garb of the Mituyan elders, baggy white silk pantaloons and a black, long-sleeved loose-fitting tunic with high collar, which hung halfway from waist to knees.

Seated in a chair was a thin Mituyan army officer with a pencil-line mustache who stood up as Luna entered. Poramat eyed her silently as she crossed the room. Speaking in Mituyan he gave her a perfunctory salutation and introduced her to Colonel Yunakit, chief of Tiking Province.

"The colonel and I have known each other since my husband and I purchased the Rishram rubber plantation," Luna answered, graciously smiling at the province chief.

"My sister-in-law, Dhuna, called me very emotionally three days ago about your problem, Mrs. Forrester," Poramat began. "Since all detentions in the province are the concern of Colonel Yunakit, I have asked him to be here."

Luna thanked him in Mituyan. "Since Dhuna has explained the situation, it will not be necessary for me to go over it again."

Poramat regarded her coldly. "On the contrary, there are many aspects of this case to be discussed."

"I told Premier KaritKi and Dhuna all I know about Alana," Luna protested. "She is one of our most educated and patriotic young women. She is very anti-Communist."

"But is she pro-KaritKi government?" Poramat snapped.

"Of course," Luna answered. "We all are."

"Then why does she work for this anti-government journalist, Krakhaur?"

"Krakhaur is not against anything," Luna replied. "As a journalist from America, used to reporting what he sees, he writes the stories he thinks will interest his readers."

"Did my brother tell you why this *loyal* young woman came to Tiking?"

"He may have. I don't remember now."

"This patriotic girl was trying to find damaging information about me—using me to attack my brother's government."

Before Luna could decide what to say next, Poramat went into a tirade against the American press, then Americans, and finally a pointed outburst against Mituyan women who allied themselves with Americans. This old-fashioned mandarin was more dangerous to Mituyan than the Communists, she realized, but she made no defense, nodding, appearing to agree with him. Finally, when he paused, she asked, "But what of the girl? The wife of the Premier is most worried about her."

Poramat turned to the province chief. "What about the girl, Colonel?"

"She has confessed to working for the overthrow of the government," Yunakit replied off-handedly. "Therefore, as always, we hold her pending disposition on her case."

Poramat's eyes bored into Luna's. "You are Mituyan. You are well aware of the penalty for disloyalty to the government, particularly in time of war."

"She did not mean to be disloyal," Luna pleaded. "She was merely doing the work she was trained to do right here at Tiking University where she studied journalism. Let the American suffer, not one of our Mituyan girls."

"I would like to make the American suffer." Poramat's eyes blazed. "My brothers tell me I cannot. At least he will see what happens to Mituyans he seduces into anti-government ways!"

"Let me have the girl," Luna begged. "I will be responsible for her rehabilitation. The wife of the Premier and I, whose loyalty to the Palace has never been questioned, will guarantee her reform."

"So you admit she has done wrong! She deserves then to be punished."

"I don't know what she has done, but I promise that she will never again be disloyal to Premier KaritKi—if ever she was."

"She confessed," Colonel Yunakit said.

"So you say. But what did you do to her?"

Poramat gave her an injured look. "Mrs. Forrester, the Premier and his government are working against great odds to keep this country stable. We want to do what's best for everyone. One person working against the government injures every loyal citizen of Mituyan. In spite of the fact that this woman Alana actively was working for the overthrow of the government of Mituyan and should be executed or imprisoned for life, I will ask Colonel Yunakit to release her in your custody. You will be personally responsible for any future treasonable activities on her part."

"Oh, thank you, Counselor Poramat," Luna said. "I promise that she will always be loyal to the Premier."

"Colonel Yunakit will conduct you personally to where she is being detained. Since this Alana was a confessed traitor to her country, you will understand why she has been subjected to certain—hardships."

Luna's heart sank; she fought to hold in her hatred. "When can I see her?"

"Oh, soon," said Poramat. "Colonel Yunakit will take you to her. But there is one thing you must understand. We will be watching this loyal young woman, and if she shows any signs of resuming anti-government activities she will be picked up and returned to the condition in which you will find her. Do you understand?"

"Of course. I told you; I guarantee her conduct."

"In that case, should there be a relapse on her part or, of course, on the part of her employer, the journalist Krakhaur, you will also be detained."

Oh no, now they hold us *responsible for what Roger writes!* Her face betrayed her emotions.

"Indeed, Mrs. Forrester, I hold you and your husband, as well as her, entirely responsible. You will soon see to what lengths Colonel Yunakit is forced to go to discourage anti-government activity."

"Just take me to the girl." In his notorious Machiavellian style, Poramat had cruelly trapped Mike and herself—as well as Alana and Roger Krakhaur.

Luna followed Colonel Yunakit out of Poramat's office. Her car was waiting below, but Yunakit pushed her into his own and motioned her driver to follow.

The iron gates of the province chief's headquarters swung open, Yunakit's driver pulled in, and the gates closed behind them—leaving Luna's car and driver waiting outside. At a grimy, stucco-faced cement-block building the car stopped. Inside, Yunakit's paratrooper boots clacked along the cement floor until he came to a guard at a reception desk, who sprang to his feet and saluted. Wordlessly, the province chief took a ring of keys from the desk and led Luna down a flight of stone steps to a dank cavernous room underground. An official sat at a table at one end of the grotto, a naked light bulb dangling above him. Luna heard a low, mournful hum of voices, and as her eyes became used to the dim light she saw men and women of all ages and in every sort of dress seated on benches; others squatted on the stone floor because the benches were full. To her horror she saw many young women, eyes red from weeping, who looked to be from well-to-do families. Guards armed with rifles and long billy clubs walked among them; their faces and postures reflected hopelessness and bleak misery.

"Those people are waiting to be interrogated," Yunakit told Luna. "All of them have demonstrated anti-government feelings. Sometimes they sit there as long as three days and nights before their turn comes. You would not enjoy the wait, but it saves time in the interrogation rooms."

"Please, take me to Alana." The stench was making her sick and faint.

"Stay close to me." Yunakit unlocked an iron door to the right of the turnkey's desk, pushing it inward. A pulsating scream echoed from the dank corridor beyond. The stench was worse than it had been in the waiting room. Yunakit continued down the corridor and stopped in front of a numbered door. Inserting a key in the lock, he kicked it open.

Luna gasped at the sight before her. Mercilessly illuminated by high-intensity lights, naked men and women were sitting and lying in rank pools of body waste. A man opened his eyes and, shielding them, saw the province chief's uniform and billed cap. He let out a scream and threw himself face down into the reeking mess on the floor.

"They have developed an insane terror of uniforms," Yunakit explained off-handedly. "Do you see your friend?" He held his handkerchief, heavily scented against the stench, next to his nose.

Before Luna could look further she heard the sound of booted feet running down the hall. The turnkey reached the door of the cell and cried out, "Colonel, the girl you seek is not here, she was taken to the Isle of Stones."

"Well, Mrs. Forrester," Yunakit said, taking her arm, pulling her from the cell, and closing the heavy door on the miserable political prisoners, "we won't waste more time here." He led her back down the corridor toward the waiting room. "But then Counselor Poramat did want you to see with your own eyes where we put those disloyal to the regime."

The bright daylight made her squint as they emerged from the province prison and walked to the staff car. "The Isle of Stones never has visitors," Yunakit remarked as he hurried Luna into the car. "This perhaps is further proof that Counselor Poramat wishes to grant you every opportunity to know what happens to those who work against his brother the Premier."

As the staff car headed toward the Tiking docks, Luna's apprehension grew. She wished Mike could be with her. The car pulled into a warehouse-like covered dock, and Yunakit led Luna to a small cabin cruiser tied up to the pier. He stepped in first and helped Luna to climb down onto the boat's deck.

"Hardly in the class of your husband's ship, but I assure you far more comfortable than the boat we put the prisoners in."

Two armed guards rode with them. The small craft's skipper, in the uniform of an officer of the Mituyan Navy, cast off the lines and headed out into the harbor.

It was a fifteen-minute high-speed run from the dock to the end of the harbor. Straight out, Luna could see the sun glinting off the solid stone island for which they were headed. Whenever the *Promise* went to sea it always gave the Isle of Stones a wide berth. It was forbidden to sail within three miles of the infamous penal colony. Armed patrol boats enforced this rule.

Twenty minutes later Luna had her first close view of the Isle of Stones. Conical rock pinnacles rose from the island like stalagmites, and the look of death and desolation hung over it.

"We require very few guards," Yunakit said. "Sharks patrol the island thoroughly. No man has ever escaped from the Isle of Stones and reached the mainland alive." Luna shuddered. "Yes, Mrs. Forrester, this is not a pleasant place. But since you guarantee that the girl Alana and her American master, Krakhaur, will no longer indulge in treasonable activities, there is no reason for you to fear becoming a resident here."

The boat pulled up to a wooden dock jutting out from a stone promontory, and two guards, rifles slung listlessly over their shoulders, came out to meet them. At the end of the dock there was a large rectangular building from which came the loud chuffing of a powerful diesel engine.

"That is something new, Mrs. Forrester," Yunakit said. "It is our distiller, the only source of fresh water on this rock. Before, we had to ship water out here. Only the hardiest prisoners lived. In ancient times, prisoners were given one jug of water and left here to die slowly."

"Where is Alana?" Luna asked in a quavering voice.

"This island is two square miles in size. She could be anywhere."

"You don't have cells?"

"Some. For solitary confinement. But I'm sure *she* would not have been put in one of them. Only *rebellious* prisoners are put in the"—he glanced at her—"the roasters."

"Please," Luna was on the verge of tears, "help me find her?"

Yunakit walked ahead of her from the dock to a white cement-block administration building. He kicked open the door and walked in. A cross-eyed Mituyan in open khaki shirt and shorts, his hair unkempt, a scraggle beard hanging from sallow cheeks and weak chin, looked up. "This is Lieutenant Leet," Yunakit said in obvious disgust. Slowly

Leet pulled himself to his feet, regarding the intruders with bloodshot eyes. The smell of stale liquor hung heavily about him.

"I have come to take back a woman prisoner who was sent out here a week ago. Her name is—or was"—he smirked—"Alana."

"She is here somewhere," Leet acknowledged with a shrug.

"Find her."

Leet looked at him hopelessly. "Find her? It would take all day. I don't keep track of what shelter each prisoner finds for himself."

"Well, pull the water horn," Yunakit demanded.

Leet shambled to the door and looked up at the sun beating down out of a cloudless sky. "Not time yet," he replied.

"You idiot," Yunakit shouted, roughly shoving Leet out of the way and walking outside the building, "do you think I want to be here all day?" He grabbed an iron ring at the end of a chain that hung down from the tower outside the building and gave it a sharp pull. A mournful honking noise came from the horn. Yunakit kept jerking the rope viciously, and before long a procession of half-dead prisoners, bones showing through tight skin, began to appear from the rocks and stone pinnacles. Each held a bowl or gourd as, dragging one foot after the other, they headed for the salt-water distiller.

"Find out where she is!" Yunakit demanded. Leet walked over to the tank of fresh water. As each prisoner, many barefoot or with pieces of cloth wrapped around their feet to protect them from the blistering heat of the stones, dipped his bowl into the water, Leet asked if he knew where the new woman prisoner was. Each time he was given a hollow-eyed, feeble headshake. Luna noticed that some of the prisoners carried two bowls.

"When a woman comes to the island the men fight for her," Yunakit sneered, "and the winner gets her water and food and brings it to her. Those with two bowls have women."

"May I talk to them?" Luna asked.

"Go ahead. Whichever man owns Alana probably won't tell you, if he thinks she's going to be taken from the island."

Luna went up to the line of men; several with single bowls broke the line and came toward her. Instantly a guard rushed to them, swinging his rifle barrel at their faces. Two sank to the ground, blood running from their mouths.

"Now they know *you* are not for claiming," Yunakit laughed. Luna began asking the men, in soft tones, if they knew where Alana, the new girl, was. Although several of the single men shifted their eyes, they did not talk. They looked fearfully at the men with two bowls.

"We never had the problem of taking a lone woman off before," Yunakit said. "Occasionally, in their humanity, Premier KaritKi or Counselor Poramat have pardoned a whole family sent out here, but I don't remember coming after a single girl. If one of these men betrays the man with Alana, all the men with women will kill him."

"Please," Luna begged, "please find her."

Yunakit nodded. "Leet, you piece of buffalo dung," he shouted, "get the bull horn. Tell the guards to hold the men here while we look for the girl."

Leet cried out orders, and the guards held those who had filled their bowls from returning to their craggy nests. He sauntered into the administration building and returned with a bull horn.

"Follow me, Mrs. Forrester." Yunakit helped her over a rock. "I'm afraid we shall have to see more of the Isle of Stones than I had hoped. You can call out to Alana through this horn."

They walked into the interior of the island, Luna picking her way over the stones, trying to avoid tripping and falling onto the rock, which burned through the thin soles of her lightweight shoes. Shockingly emaciated men and women, too weak to go for their own water, sat in the meager shade offered by the stone pinnacles. But there was no escaping the heat that radiated from the rocky formation of the island. The bull horn to her mouth, Luna cried out for Alana to come out, that she was to be freed. A woman who was probably as young or younger than she, Luna realized with a shock of horror, painfully hobbled over on heavily calloused bare feet.

"Take *me,* take *me,*" she begged. "Please. There's money in Tiking if you will take me."

Luna, fighting back tears, pressed on, calling for Alana. As they walked around a rock pinnacle they surprised a swarm of redheaded buzzards, which took to the air flapping their wings. Luna started to scream, but the cry froze in her throat as she saw where they had been feasting. "The carrion keep the island clean, and the sun soon purifies the bones," Yunakit commented. Sun-bleached human bones and skulls were everywhere.

Yunakit regarded the surroundings with distaste. "I have never been back in here before," he said. "If we do not find her soon we shall leave, and I must write a report presuming her dead."

"Oh no!" Luna wept. "You promised. Counselor Poramat promised."

"If she's dead, there is nothing we can do," Yunakit replied.

"Just a little longer?" Luna begged. Again she cried through the amplifier for Alana. Roughly taking Luna by the arm, Yunakit turned her around and began to half drag her back. The two guards behind them grinned in relief at getting out of the inferno.

Then, as Luna looked wildly around, she saw a man, rags hanging from him, walking toward her. Somehow he seemed less emaciated than the others. He beckoned to her to approach. She tried to twist from Yunakit's grasp, but he held her.

"That man is trying to tell me something!" she cried. "Maybe he knows where Alana is?"

Yunakit peered across the stones at the man, who again beckoned directly at Luna. "Please let me talk to him," she pleaded. "Maybe—"

"You may talk to him," Yunakit agreed, "but if he has no news of the girl, we leave immediately." Luna walked from Yunakit toward the man. "Do you know where Alana, the new girl is?"

The man nodded. "Yes. I took her to my hut." The misery in his sun-blackened face cut her. "I was afraid someone had come for Alana. When the water horn sounded, I did not go. I was selfish."

"Please, sir," Luna wept, "take me to her. Is she alright?"

"I do not know. I believe so. She has said only her name since I claimed her. I was able to give her extra water and rice. Follow me."

The man hobbled toward one of the stone corner pinnacles, Luna beside him. Yunakit and the two guards trailed behind. "Who are you, sir?" Luna asked.

"I am Baliwit, a nephew of King Barkoon the Sixth, now in exile. I stayed in Mituyan after he left since I had experience in engineering that the country needed. But Tarot thought I was plotting and sent me here. I have been here three years. Now, just the other side of this rock."

Under an overhanging ledge Luna saw a relatively comfortable looking lean-to. There were some cooking pots in front of it and rotted wooded planks covering the rock floor.

Luna's eyes passed over the string-haired stick of a miserable creature as she looked in vain for Alana. "Where is she?"

Sadly Baliwit pointed at the female staring vacantly from sunken eyes. "Oh no!" She scurried down. It was indeed Alana. Putting her arms around the bony shoulders, Luna rocked the wasted girl, crying to her softly: "Alana, it's Luna. I've come to take you away. We're going back. Roger is waiting." The odor that hung about the girl sickened Luna.

Alana looked at her dreamily for a few moments. Slowly she seemed to float back from some faraway inner world.

"Alana!" Luna cried. "Do you understand? We're leaving here!"

"No!" Alana moaned faintly. "Please. Not Roger. Never again."

"Come with me," Luna said, gently pulling the girl to her feet. Baliwit watched morosely as Alana, helped by Luna, stumbled from the lean-to.

"Thank you, sir," Luna said to him. "And please, don't lose faith. Things will change soon."

"Is that true?" Baliwit grasped at the slight message of hope. "Will the Americans help? I worked with the Americans when I was arrested. For a year I prayed they would help me. But finally I gave up hope," he said almost to himself. Baliwit helped Luna to steady Alana as they made their way through the stony rubble of the island.

"It will *not* be much longer," Luna said with conviction she didn't feel.

"I do not have much longer."

Yunakit strode toward them, cutting off further conversation. "So you found her," he said, ignoring the ragged Baliwit. "Hurry." He took one of Alana's thin arms and propelled her, stumbling, toward the administration building. The wretches still assembled with their gourds by the water distiller watched them bleakly.

In minutes they were on the boat, and Yunakit wasted no time ordering it to head for the mainland at full speed.

Looking back at the island of death, Luna shuddered uncontrollably, holding the all but weightless girl to her. The heat waves shimmered visibly from the solid blistering rock, the pinnacles pointing hopelessly to the blue sky. Yunakit, watching Luna, chuckled.

"Please, Luna, don't take me to Roger," Alana kept whimpering. "I can't see him. Not now."

"Roger loves you," Luna repeated, holding tight to her.

Once on shore, Yunakit allowed the two women to enter Luna's car, which had been waiting. He held the door open for them and said with quiet intensity: "At the risk of repeating myself, Mrs. Forrester, may I remind you that we would not hesitate to put *you* in the cell you visited this morning, or out on the Isle of Stones, if the American journalist Krakhaur publishes anything further against the government." He slammed the door shut and turned on his heel as Luna's driver sped from the covered dock.

CHAPTER TWENTY-FOUR

IT WAS A SOBER Mike Forrester who turned up for his prearranged appointment at Colonel Lawton's new Tiking headquarters villa. He had heard all of Alana's horrifying experiences. In spite of the girl's pleas that she could never face Roger Krakhaur again, that she had betrayed him by signing Poramat's paper, Mike had radioed the reporter and told him what had happened and that Luna was devoting all her energies to restoring Alana's health.

"I made this happen to her," Krakhaur had said miserably over the sideband. "I've got to come up there and be with her."

"She's not ready to see you now, Roger," Luna had said. "We'll take Alana out to Rishram, and in a few days she may be in a healthier state of mind."

"Please let me come," Krakhaur pleaded. "I have to do a story on this Han Li Phang, the Mad Monk of Tiking. I'll stay away from Alana as long as you say."

"Come ahead then," Luna agreed. "You can stay on *Promise*. But you be careful what you write."

"The Mad Monk story is strictly one requested by KaritKi's Minister of Information." Krakhaur reassured her. "The Palace should appreciate it."

Two guards in the jungle fatigues of the civilian irregulars being trained by JRB stopped Mike at the entrance to Colonel Lawton's villa. He produced a special identification card that permitted him to drive in through the gate of the villa. The colonel was waiting for him upstairs; with him was a lean, dark-haired young man of medium height, regular features, with either a deep tan or naturally swarthy skin.

"I don't think you've officially set Scott MacWhorter," Lawton said, introducing the men. "Mike spent ten days with Charlie Prescott up in the Groat country recently."

"Oh?" MacWhorter's face lit up. "How is the old dipshit?"

"Fine, last I saw him," Mike replied. He looked around the room. "What kind of a spookery is this place?"

"I'm going to tell you." Mike and MacWhorter sat down opposite Lawton's desk. "Scott MacWhorter here has been in-country about three months. He's out of USIS in Saigon. His nominal boss here is Ted Baum. But Ted and Jack Cardinez worked out a friendly temporary loan of Scott to us."

An Information Service type mixed up with Lawton's operations provoked Mike's curiosity. "Scott's an unusual USIS man," Fritz said. "He's a perfect example of how the broad spectrum of one country-team agency overlaps that of another. Scott here has stolen from the Communists their most potent weapon, 'people's war.' He used it effectively against the Viet Cong in Vietnam, and now we hope to get permission from the Country Team in Tuyan City to try it here."

This was a revelation to Mike. "People's war? The Mao, Ho, Giap theories?"

"They're not theories any longer," MacWhorter protested. "The Communists took over all of China, North Vietnam, and most of South Vietnam using the people's war concept, and they're on their way to doing the same here."

"Scott built up agit-prop cadres in Vietnam to beat the Communist agitation and propaganda teams at their own game," Lawton explained. "He and his men, a platoon-size group of highly trained and motivated Vietnamese soldiers, would go out into hamlets in Viet Cong territory and live with the villagers, buying food from them, helping them to build houses and reap crops, becoming intimately acquainted with everyone in the village. They would conduct discussion groups and let the people of a village come to their own conclusion that although the Saigon government was not ideal, still they must support it until the Communists were driven out. Then they must work to change the government and make it truly representative of the people."

"That sounds like the way the Mitcoms here are operating."

"It is, Mike," MacWhorter said earnestly. "My cadre in Vietnam followed Mao's principles to the letter. We held self-criticism sessions with the villagers and talked about the four principles and eight rules that we, as representatives of the true Saigon government, followed. Of course, these were the exact same principles and rules put forth by Mao and used so successfully by him in subverting China. Each member of my cadre carried a card in Vietnamese with the four principles and eight rules on one side and the emblem of the government of Vietnam on the other."

He reached into his pocket and pulled out a laminated card and handed it to Mike. On one side were the red and yellow colors of the Mituyan flag, with KaritKi's colorful symbolic crest, a dragon rampant over a kneeling elephant. On the other side were the four principles taken from Mao and used by the famous North Vietnamese guerrilla fighter, turned Minister of Defense of Ho Chi Minh's government, Vo Nguyen Giap. The principles and rules were written in both the Mituyan squiggles and in English.

"When a man is accepted into my cadre he is given one of these pledge cards and becomes a member of what we call the Special Government Commandos. With the help of another American—a Special Forces captain on temporary duty to USIS—and an Australian, an expert on this country, we've built up two cadres. One is in the Tuyan River Delta with my green-beret friends, the other is now assembling here in Tiking. All we need now is permission from the Country Team to go ahead and operate."

Mike studied the pledge card. "I don't see how anyone can quarrel with this," he said. He read the card aloud: "The four principles: One, Respect the people; two, Help the people; three, Protect the people; four, Follow orders." Mike looked up. "Sounds like a Boy Scout manual."

Mike continued to read aloud. " 'The eight rules: One, Speak politely and truthfully; two, Pay fairly for what you buy; three, Return everything you borrow; four, Pay for anything you damage; five, Don't mistreat the people; six, Don't damage crops; seven, Don't rape women; eight, Treat captives well.' "

Mike handed the card back to MacWhorter. "If the Communists really acted that way, I could live with them quite happily."

"They do follow these rules with the people," Lawton cut in. "At least until they find that the people are completely committed to the other side. Then they use selective terrorism. Scott's cadre does the same. That's where we're having trouble with the Country Team. The ambassador is terrified that the American people will hear we are backing cadres trained in assassination and all the dirty guerrilla tricks."

"Well," MacWhorter replied, "my people are ready to go. I have about twenty-five men quartered here in Tiking. The rest are on their way up with my Mituyan counterpart, Major Song."

"We've still got to get permission from the ambassador," Lawton pointed out, "and the Country Team is still fighting it out whether to employ this concept."

"Every day we waste could mean innocent lives and whole villages lost," MacWhorter persisted. "Wherever I go my trouble is always with the top officials," he added bitterly. "They'll never understand the boondocks as long as they live; the only thing they worry about is 'world opinion' and 'what the people at home will say.' Well, if the people at home knew what we're facing out here trying to keep the Communists from creeping right into their backyard—"

"Scott MacWhorter may be one of the greatest American experts on people's war," Lawton declared quietly. "To wage people's war effectively you must know how to deal with a dedicated and unswayable enemy. Scott and his men are probably the most skilled killers operating in Mituyan on either side. That's why he's working with the spooks, as you call us."

MacWhorter pulled another card out of his pocket. It was black with a hideous white eye in the center. "That's a creepy little item," Mike commented.

"USIS printed up twenty thousand for us in Vietnam," MacWhorter said. "When we discovered who the Communist agents in a village or city were, we assassinated them and put this eye on the body. It made people afraid to become Communist agents. Suspected Communist sympathizers would find one of these cards on their door and know they were being watched. They at once became very ineffectual."

Mike nodded seriously and then turned to Lawton. "This is all well and good, Colonel, but how does Scott's work affect me?"

"Tell him, Scott."

"Right," MacWhorter said. "In the first place you know the people and the villages around here. I'd like to take my cadre into a village that's in Mitcom territory. We'd operate just the way I've described. We quickly become an integral part of their day-to-day life, and by buying everything we need from the people for a fair price we help the local economy. At night we go out on patrols, set up ambushes against Mitcom guerrillas, and in general give the people good protection. We build up within the village a cadre of the young men who we train both in anti-Communist propaganda and in self-defense."

"Rishket!" Mike exclaimed. "That's a hamlet of about six hundred or more people five miles from my rubber estate, Rishram. I know there are Mitcom guerrilla bands around Rishket. Maybe Scott would like to visit there," Mike said to Lawton, "and get the feel of the place until he gets the go ahead and his cadre can meet him."

"Very good plan," Lawton agreed. "But there's another mission we want Scott and Major Song to perform first. We'd like to cripple the Mitcom political apparatus right here in Tiking. We'd like to get rid of as many leaders of the so-called Mituyan Freedom Front as we can."

"Do you know who they are?" Mike asked.

"What we'd like to do," Scott said, "is put some of my cadre into your plantation, let them get to know the place a bit. Then when the Mitcoms come to your plantation to collect their payoff next Friday, we'll grab them and interrogate them, find out who the Tiking underground leaders are . . . and then assassinate them. This is the sort of operation we can pull off, Mike. Nobody will know who disposed of the Mitcoms, and we won't have to bother to get permission from the Country Team."

Mike threw a questioning glance at Lawton, who shrugged and said, "Jack Cardinez gave us the go-ahead. The CIA station chief has cleared it both with the Palace and the ambassador. The trouble with the Rishket project is that all hamlets are under USOM, and Grady Rourke thinks he'll get himself and AID involved in a big controversy if the Country Team officially endorses putting Scott's cadre in a hamlet. Actually, Rourke is trying to get rid of all his people working below the level of the province chief and leave all aid in the village to the Mituyans."

"Why doesn't he go home and give the countryside away altogether?" Mike asked wryly.

"What about it, Mike?" MacWhorter asked. "I'd like to go ahead with the plan right away."

"That will get me about fifty trees destroyed a night and a bomb laid under my house for sure," Mike replied bitterly.

"No it won't," Lawton interjected. "We'll see that you have a crack platoon of well-trained counterterrorists around your house and grounds. I'm not saying you may not lose some trees, but we'll get the Mitcoms. And once the Communists see they're up against something one hell of a lot more effective than the Mituyan Army, they'll get discouraged, particularly when we kill off their leaders as fast as they come up."

"I'm game to kill Mitcoms," Mike said. "But my wife and I have promised to take Alana to Rishram this afternoon, with your permission of course, Colonel—and I'd be putting the girls in real danger."

"Perhaps. But we'll provide good protection. Scott's counterpart in this operation, Major Song, is one of Tarot's top secret-police officers."

Mike shook his head. "We really go to bed with some savory characters. This Song probably helped Yunakit set up his prison operation."

"Likely," Lawton agreed. "But he's a good man for what we're trying to accomplish, right, Scott?"

"The best," MacWhorter agreed. "Dedicated to his work. What do you say, Mike?"

Forrester looked from one to the other, then threw up his hands.

"All right. Sure, I'll go along. Reluctantly."

"Fine," Scott said. "How would it be if I drove out to Rishram this afternoon and met you there?"

"That's all right with me," Mike said morosely. "If I'm going to lose everything to the Commies again, it might as well be now as later."

"Come on, Mike," Lawton said. "You haven't a thing to worry about. I'll guarantee personally that you have the protection you need."

"Thanks," Mike replied, unconvinced.

He wished he had never become involved with spooking. But he was more convinced than ever that it was necessary.

PART V

SELECTIVE TERRORISM

CHAPTER TWENTY-FIVE

NOWAT'S EXCUSE for bringing his lovely part-Chinese part-Mituyan mistress to the meetings at the Golden Dragon had long been accepted by Tzung, who used the restaurant as a front for his Communist organizational activities all over northern Mituyan. In the Communist shadow government that exactly paralleled the government of Premier KaritKi, Tzung, though Chinese, was equivalent in power and influence to Poramat, his duties taking him all over the large I Corps area of Mituyan.

Nowat, as the Communist chief of Tiking Province, was equivalent to Colonel Yunakit. The North Vietnamese, Nguyen Van Can, headed all military operations in I Corps and thus was the counterpart of General Dandig. The one-eared Mung, now leader of the largest and best-armed guerrilla band in the area and camped in the hills above the rich hamlet of Rishket, was a Communist parallel to the district chief.

While Nowat was responsible both for military and organizational affairs in Tiking Province, reporting to Tzung and Can, his greatest interest lay in building the Communist underground in the port city. His camera shop was MFF province headquarters.

Whenever a meeting had to be held of province and corps leaders, Nowat went to the Golden Dragon for dinner and later to the back room where, under the cover of a permanent game of mah-jongg at which huge sums of metas changed hands nightly, the MFF authorities could meet and plan strategy. So far neither Colonel Yunakit's secret police nor Poramat's special agents had discovered any trace of the Mituyan Freedom Front Organization in I Corps. However, the leaders of the MFF government were always extremely cautious, and it was natural for Nowat to bring his mistress along to dine with him and later watch him gamble; it helped allay suspicion. Even so, Tzung and Can never allowed him to leave a meeting without their making some remark that for a true leader the Communist party and the MFF were the only necessary companions.

Nowat and Li Tin finished their meal and went through the kitchen to the room in which the sharp clicking of the mah-jongg tiles could be heard. A bare light bulb hung suspended over a round table crowded with players, spectators watching over their shoulders. Nowat caught Tzung's eye and followed him to yet another room. Since Li Tin had proved her worth as organizer of a woman's auxiliary group in Tiking—her women had been particularly effective in stealing supplies of such drugs as penicillin and morphine, which were cached in various MFF "safe" houses in Tiking—she was permitted to sit in on certain meetings.

Tzung, Nguyen Van Can, and the guerrilla leader Zgret sat around a table, and Nowat and Li Tin took the two empty spindle-legged chairs. Tzung quickly came to the point of the meeting.

"Zgret has come to report a failure," the Communist leader said. "It has been impossible to gain friends for the Front at the village of Rishket. The Americans have done their work well. The village chief, the two school teachers, the head bonzes at the pagoda, and especially the American missionary and the Mituyan leader of their Christian church, have such a powerful hold on the people that we get no intelligence and no food from the people. Zgret reports that Mung's group, which now numbers one hundred fighting men willing to die for the Front, are on the verge of starving. We must take control of the hamlet of Rishket."

Zgret, a wily Mituyan, taller than average, nodded vigorously. "We need more weapons, too," he added forcefully. "Now we have but one gun to every three men."

"When Rishket is under your control," Tzung said, "I will notify General Phat in the North and he will arrange for your group to be completely supplied with new rifles and machine guns directly from our leaders in mother China."

"Naturally, I have been watching the situation in Rishket closely," Nowat pointed out. "As a matter of fact, my agents tell me that a defense cadre will soon be created."

"All the more reason we must take control first," Can declared. "I will personally direct the operation."

"It is in my province and I should be in charge," Nowat protested. "It would be wrong for a non-Mituyan to enter Rishket in charge of our men."

"You will lead. I will direct," the North Vietnamese stated. "But this action should have been initiated sooner. I was the one who had to request permission from Commander Tzung to take control before the defenses of Rishket became stronger."

"Today I received orders from General Phat that we could take Rishket," Tzung said. "It will be the first target in this corps area for our new campaign of selective terror. We must be very skillful, and for that reason Can will direct. He has had much experience in these matters."

"What is the condition of our treasury?" Can asked. "I have made contact with a certain sergeant who can arrange for us to find an open door at a police armory just beyond the east end of the city."

Tzung gave Zgret a hard look. "Your group is responsible for making the collections at Rishram and bringing all the money to me."

"We do that, Commander. But sometimes it is dangerous to try to bring the money all the way from our camp to your headquarters here in the city."

"From now on," Tzung decreed, "our accountant, Frakit, Mung, and you will be personally responsible for all the money collected, and I want proof that we are getting a full ten percent of Rishram's payroll. The money comes in very irregularly. The amounts are not consistent."

"The payroll changes each week, Commander," Zgret replied. "But I will see that from now on our highest leaders make the collections. It is perfectly safe to go to Rishram. The American does not want his estate destroyed."

Tzung turned to Can. "How much does it take to bribe this sergeant?"

"He asks five thousand metas. It is reasonable."

"Next Monday, when we have the money from Rishram, we will bribe the sergeant," Tzung said. "But we will not wait until then before beginning our takeover of the village." The Chinese Communist nodded at Zgret. "We will expect the money over the weekend without fail."

"Mung and I will personally supervise the collection this week."

"I will send Frakit to count the money," Nowat said. "He is a valuable man when it comes to finance. And he will also be most important to us in wrecking the coming elections."

Nowat sipped at the cup of green tea that had been put before him and said with satisfaction, "We will be lucky to duplicate our last victory, the assassination of Professor LakaLit, but we will keep trying."

"That was a great coup," Tzung agreed. "This must be even better. We go into the hamlet tomorrow night and begin consolidation by dawn."

"We have guests, Mike," Luna said as they drove up to their plantation house at Rishram and saw the two jeeps.

"Looks like Scott MacWhorter beat us out here," Mike observed, parking his Land Rover next to one of the jeeps, which was badly battered. "And this one's Jerry Otis' jeep. It looks worse every time I see it. He's a USOM civilian, the provincial operations chief in Tiking Province," he explained to Alana. "He knows more about what goes on in the hamlets than anyone I know."

"I hope you won't mind if I don't see anyone," Alana said. Although she had been resting aboard *Promise* for two days and was beginning to eat solid food again, she still looked pitifully frail and the haunted look persisted in her eyes.

"There's a nice cool bedroom at the back of the house that will be all yours, dear," Luna said.

Two houseboys came for the luggage, and Luna led Alana directly upstairs. Mike walked out to the terrace and greeted Scott MacWhorter and Jerry Otis, a leathery-complexioned young man, very lean, wearing a sport shirt and slacks and rubber thong sandals.

"Hope you don't mind a couple of tired wayfarers taking advantage of your hospitality." The provincial operations chief for Tiking smiled.

"Glad to see you Jerry." Mike grinned ruefully. "Where've you been—Rishket?"

"Right. Taking pictures and working up a report to present to Mr. Rourke. He doesn't believe in us, and we're trying to save the program. Rishket is one of my most successful projects."

"I must get over there again some day," Mike said. "Most of my workers come from that village or have families there."

"Come with me tomorrow. My job there is as good as done," Otis said proudly. "Every family has a concrete pig pen, and I brought in the Great Whites to improve the local breed. All the farmers are using my fertilizer and getting fifty percent better yields. I've built a new school and found two new teachers. USOM is paying them extra to work at Rishket. I've even helped the Anglican pastor build a new church and the Buddhists put up a new pagoda. It's a happy, tight village with an excellent village chief, completely loyal to the Tuyan City government. And now with elections coming up, the people feel they have some say in their government; the Communists don't stand a chance of getting a foothold around here."

"How did you work with Yunakit?" Mike asked.

"Like most province chiefs he's a damned crook, of course. Rourke won't allow reports to be written on the subject, but for every bag of cement, every pig, every pound of fertilizer, every load of building materials that went into Rishket, Colonel Yunakit took the same amount of stuff for himself to sell. I had to look the other way." Jerry took a big gulp of the drink Mike offered him. "Anyway," he said, "the project has been a success, and the people are healthy, prosperous, happy and loyal . . . and ripe for a Mitcom attack."

"Damn, but I'd like to get my cadre into Rishket before it's too late," MacWhorter said. "But at least the hamlet can call for help if there's trouble."

Otis frowned. "The damned district chief hasn't given out any of the radios, because Colonel Yunakit says if anything happens to one the district chief has to pay for a new radio. So all the radios are locked up in district headquarters."

"I'll visit the village tomorrow, Jerry, and then drive over and speak to the district chief about those radios." MacWhorter's eyes glinted with anger.

"Say hello to Captain Cunningham for me," Otis said. "He's the adviser to the Mituyan battalion. A number-one man with a lot of problems."

"You won't be able to go with me?" MacWhorter asked.

"I've got to drive back to Tiking tomorrow and grab the milk run into Tuyan City with my report. Rourke is trying to put me out of business."

"Anyone who doesn't believe in your program has never seen what goes on in the provinces," said Mike.

"Watch yourself on the roads, alone," MacWhorter cautioned. "If I know my Communists, you're a number-one target."

"What about you?"

"In the first place, I haven't shown what I can do, so they won't be after me yet. In the second place, I carry a Swedish K submachine gun and a box of grenades."

Luna came out onto the terrace and the men rose. Mike made a cocktail for his wife, then noticed the empty glasses. "Let me make you two a couple more. Never know how long it's going to be to the next time."

Before dark the following day the MFF team from Tiking had gathered on the hill above the large and rich village of Rishket. A lush green pattern of fertilized square rice paddies surrounded the hamlet of over two hundred homes. Mung and Zgret laughed at the frail barbed-wire fence around the village. Can and Nowat held a last planning conference, the details of which were so barbarous that Frakit not only could not listen but begged to be released from going into the village.

"All right, Mr. Accountant," the North Vietnamese said agreeably, "since you serve the Front so well with your figures and statistics, we will give you a job to do up here. You will not have to watch our selective terrorism."

Frakit thanked the North Vietnamese. "Now, Frakit," Can said, "you are familiar with radio operations?"

"Yes. I have knowledge of many different radios."

Good. Up here we have a powerful transmitter that one of our Front auxiliary workers was able to buy from Colonel Yunakit's selling agent. We broadcast on a standard band that any transistor or home radio can receive. You will be the voice of the Mituyan Freedom Front and tell the people all over this part of the country about the success of our Rishket operation. We will report to you with our field radios, and you will relay our messages to the people."

"I will do it, Commander," Frakit agreed happily.

"Where is the American?" Can growled. Jerry Otis, a noose around his neck held by a guerrilla, both hands tightly bound behind his back, was led forward.

"Unless you try to escape, we will not kill you," Nowat said, matter-of-factly. "You American enslavers of the people have no right to be in our country, supporting that bloody tyrant KaritKi and his family, deceiving our people into believing that KaritKi is good for Mituyan."

"You have an election—" Jerry's voice was cut off by a vicious jerk on the rope. His face purpled and his eyes bulged. Can stepped forward and with a back-handed slap sent Jerry's captor reeling. He quickly loosened the noose. The young USOM representative gulped in air.

"You cursed pile of buffalo dung," Can hissed in Mituyan at the stunned guerrilla. "We want the American alive and in good health. That is the only way he is of use to us." To Mung the North Vietnamese said, "Choose another, wiser keeper for the American."

Then turning to the guerrilla band, he said, "It was good alert work capturing this American on the road to Tiking. Where is his jeep?"

"None of us knew how to drive it, so we left it burned on the road," Zgret replied.

"You should have hidden it somehow," Can said. "When it is discovered, the Americans will force General Dandig to assign soldiers to look for this prisoner. Still"—Can smiled wickedly—"perhaps that will be just the trick to make the Mituyan Army accomplish for us what we have been unable to achieve in Rishket ourselves."

After dark, the poorly armed though highly motivated guerrillas of the Mituyan Freedom Front snaked down from their hilltop camp across the valley toward the village. All were thin and weak from a month on a meager diet. The prospect of taking the hamlet and its rice stores, pigs, and fowls gave them new fortitude.

At the gate to the hamlet, two young men, carrying the big American Garand rifles they had been given to protect the village from stray bandits, challenged the three men who seemed to materialize out of the darkness in front of them.

"We are friends of the people," Nowat answered. "We want to come into your village and discuss the problems of the people."

"We have no problems," one of the young guards answered.

Mung took a step toward him. A knife flashed and was driven into the young man's belly. A gurgling grunt of agony came from the guard. "You have no problems *now*," Mung rasped, pulling the knife from the youth's guts with a twist, and leaving him dying on the ground.

The other guard dropped his rifle and put his hands up, his eyes glazed with terror. "That's better," Zgret said.

"Don't kill any more of the young ones than necessary," Can cautioned. "We will take them with us and send them North to be politically retrained."

The guerrillas entered the sleeping village, surrounding it. Armed men took up strategic posts around the low mud walls. The few sentries on duty were silently disarmed and tied up, their weapons and ammunition appropriated by unarmed guerrillas. When the entire village was secured, Can ordered the fires in the center meeting square stoked up and then a fusillade fired to awaken the population. Nowat,

Zgret, Mung and some of the other guerrillas, who had previously visited the village in unsuccessful efforts to stir up dissent, took positions outside the new cement-block houses of the village chief, the school teachers, the missionary, and the village security chief, who was also in charge of the few weapons his self-defense corps possessed. The church was staked out, and also the Buddhist pagoda, although due to twenty years' effort by various Protestant missionaries the village was predominantly Christian.

The village leaders were taken to the square, and the rest of the villagers sleepily left their houses and walked fearfully to the center of the town to see what was happening. As soon as the village chief saw Nowat and his men, he began to rail at them, crying out that he and his people never would become Communists or members of the MFF. For the benefit of the people more than the chief, Nowat reminded him that the Premier and his brother did not care for the people and stole their land and overtaxed them. The MFF only wanted to help them gain their rights and rid the countryside of the monster, Poramat.

The chief brought up the point that had been drilled into him by both American and Mituyan political officers—that the people would settle their problems with the coming election.

"But Poramat will kill or send to the Isle of Stones anybody who is an anti-KaritKi candidate," Nowat insisted. "Look at what he did to Professor LakaLit."

There was murmuring among the people who flocked around the square, but the village chief stood up to the Communists. "We know that the Mitcoms killed the professor and made it look as though it was the police," he said.

"That's what the Americans say, but they are only trying to take over Mituyan for themselves. Here's an American. He'll tell you."

Jerry Otis was dragged up to the fire where everyone could see him. "Tell these people that even the Americans know what a corrupt and vicious government KaritKi and his brother Poramat are running," Nowat demanded.

Jerry looked around the sea of faces that had become so familiar to him. "Perhaps Poramat and KaritKi *are* corrupt," he said. Nowat nodded in satisfaction. "Perhaps they steal much of the material the American people send for the people of villages like this one." A murmuring rustled through the crowd. They had never heard an American even hint that there was anything bad about the government in Tuyan City before. "But the people of Rishket and all of Mituyan are about to have a chance to change the government if they want to."

Nowat frowned and nodded to one of his men. "Make changes peacefully through the elections," Otis shouted, "not with these murderers who call themselves—"

A guerrilla stepped up to Otis and plastered his face with fresh water-buffalo dung.

"See your American now," Nowat cried out. "He is bad. He knows you will be enslaved by the American puppet government of KaritKi, yet he keeps lying to you."

There were shouts of "No!" from the people. "The American is good! He helped us build our homes; He brought us big pigs from the government in Tuyan City!"

A blow behind the knees with a pole brought Jerry to the ground, and more dung was heaped on him. "There is your American imperialist who wants to make colonial slaves of the people! Remember the Americans this way! On their knees, covered with buffalo dung."

Then Otis was hauled away, and Nowat harangued the crowd for twenty minutes on why the village should help the MFF. Before he was finished, the village chief turned his back and started to walk to his house. The other village leaders started to do the same, and the people followed their example.

"Enough of your speechmaking," Nguyen Van Can growled. "Get on with the object lesson!"

"Bring back the chief," Nowat ordered. Immediately, two guerrillas grabbed the chief by his arms, spun him around, and led him to the village square.

"Your chief will be executed by the Mituyan people's Freedom Front for betraying the people to the American colonialists who support the monster KaritKi's cruel and oppressive government."

A tall, gaunt white-haired American strode from the crowd directly up to Nowat. In the language of the people, so that no one in the village would miss his words, he said, "I am Reverend Athol. The people of this village, whether Christian or Buddhist, are happy. They do not need you. They do not want you. They will resist you in every way. They have their religion, and they are not afraid of you." He turned to the people, "Is that true?"

"It is true, Reverend Athol!" the crowd cried out.

The Mituyan pastor and a head-shaved Buddhist bonze detached themselves from the crowd and walked up to the Reverend Athol and stood beside him, defying a suddenly deflated Nowat. Can, seeing Nowat had lost his grasp of the situation, shouldered past him toward the tall missionary.

"You are the religious leader here?" he asked insolently.

"I am, with the Reverend Hakalut here, and Han Letit of the pagoda."

"Your God is all powerful?" Can mocked. "He can do anything?"

"He can make His people go their way without fear," Reverend Athol answered in ringing tones; a loud answering response came from the people.

At a gesture from Can a guerrilla hit the reverend in the face with a flat board piled with more buffalo feces.

"This God doesn't seem to mind seeing the reverend humiliated," Can laughed. "Let us see what this powerful God of the American imperialists can do for his disciple in Rishket village."

Two guerrillas gave the Reverend Athol sharp jabs behind the knees with pointed stakes. He collapsed with a stifled cry.

"Mung," Can ordered sharply. "Let us see what you learned about religious cases in my country."

The one-eyed, one-eared guerrilla came forward. Zgret handed Mung a thin, sharpened bamboo stake. A collar of slivers had been sliced into the bamboo shaft around the base of the point. As the reverend tried to regain his feet in spite of wounded tendons and muscles behind his knees, Mung made a small circle with the thumb and forefinger of his left hand and holding both hands high slid the pointed stake through the circle. When it was all the way through, he pulled back on the stake and the slivers became barbs, catching on Mung's fingers, tearing at them as he tried to pull the stake back through the looped fingers.

The people, suspecting what was to come, groaned in horror. Zgret and two other guerrillas dragged the bloody pants and underpants off the missionary, who prayed aloud, alone. His people now were too terrified of the consequences to join in.

The Reverend Athol's buttocks were turned up, and suddenly his prayers turned to involuntary high-pitched screams as Mung forced the bamboo stake into the missionary. The villagers tried to turn away from the brutal spectacle—an ancient torture used throughout Southeast Asia—but were roughly forced back by the MFF guerrillas.

As the missionary writhed and moaned, Can shouted, "Let's see his God remove that stake from the American. We'll see. We'll be here a day or two."

The schoolteachers and the hamlet chief were tied, wrists to ankles behind their backs, and left out in the square. The villagers were ordered to prepare a large meal for the guerrillas, which they hastily did.

When all the guerrillas had eaten their fill and prepared bundles of the village rice stores to carry off, the inhabitants were again herded to the village square for a political lecture by Nowat. Over the low moans of the missionary, beside whom Jerry Otis knelt, Nowat declared that the MFF would take over Mituyan and restore it to the people. He blasted the elections as a device to make the outside world think the people wanted the tyrant and murderer of Professor LakaLit, Premier KaritKi, as their dictator. He threatened the village with extinction and the inhabitants with death if any of them went to the voting booths.

The village of Rishket must contribute to the people's effort to rid Mituyan of its present oppressive government, Nowat proclaimed, and the MFF would take ten of the strongest young men with them when they left, to be trained to fight the army of KaritKi and Poramat and liberate the people. Wails went up from the women of the village.

But the barbarity was not yet over. Looking down at the trussed-up hamlet chief, Nowat cried out, "This man is a traitor to the people of Mituyan and this village. He tells you to allow KaritKi to go on oppressing you. Any leader of the people who supports KaritKi against the Freedom Front is a traitor and will receive a traitor's death. In the name of the people of Mituyan this man is condemned to be executed by the ancient punishment dealt to traitors—bleeding to death."

Those who cried out against this further cruelty were clubbed with rifle butts. All quickly became silent. "Always remember," Nowat shouted, "that the Freedom Front's fighters can come into this village and any village in Mituyan and punish those who do not support us."

The terrified and miserable people dared not utter a sound as the ugly, one-eared, one-eyed guerrilla chief began the horrible execution which could take as long as two days and nights. With a razor-keen knife Mung cut long needle-sharp slivers from a bamboo. He walked toward the moaning hamlet chief who now had been stretched between two posts some eight feet apart. Deftly he stabbed a sliver into the chief's ear. A screech came from the victim as blood trickled from the punctured eardrum. Mung repeated the process with the other ear. Jerry Otis, still kneeling beside the agonized missionary, watched helplessly, unable to comprehend how such inhuman cruelty was possible.

Mung slowly inserted long bamboo splinters into every orifice of the hamlet chief's body, even into the penis, so that when the shrieking hamlet chief moved to relieve one agonizing splinter of pain, two others took its place. Blood trickled continuously, its flow increasing as the victim writhed, changing positions.

Leaving the chief to slowly bleed to death, Can told the Communist leaders they would tend to the teachers later. "Order one squad to take all the food and pigs they can carry up to the new camp; another squad can take the ten strongest young men. One squad will remain on guard in camp, the other will return as soon as possible to Rishket. We will need every armed man we have on the walls of this village by tomorrow morning, so you must make a forced march both ways."

As Mung relayed Can's orders, the North Vietnamese, Nowat, and Zgret walked around the crowd of villagers looking over the young men. Each time they spotted a likely candidate they tapped his head and guerrillas locked his arms behind his back and forced him to the square. When ten youths had been so picked, and the burlap bags of rice assembled and two pigs killed, the two squads of guerrillas left the village for the campsite back in the hills above Rishket.

"Get your men ready to hold this village against government troops," Can ordered Mung. The guerrilla leader took his men to the walls and positioned them strategically. He ordered each man to build up dirt walls directly behind his position or dig himself a fire hole directly into the wall, so that exploding shells could not wound them from behind.

All day Mung and his guerrillas improved the fortifications of the hamlet and placed homemade claymore mines out in front of their positions, which could be electrically detonated and spew a deadly shower of metal fragments, cutting down a frontal assault. By nightfall

Mung proudly announced that his men could hold the village at least twenty-four hours, longer if they could capture more ammunition, against a battalion of regular Mituyan Army soldiers.

The village chief and the American missionary, covered with flies, suffered hideously in the hot sun. Jerry Otis was not allowed to give the hamlet chief any succor, although he had screamed for water all day. The chief grew weaker and weaker from loss of blood and the excruciating agony, as the slivers were driven deeper each time he moved.

Before dawn of the second day of the occupation of Rishket, one guerrilla squad returned. They brought intelligence that indeed two companies and perhaps a full battalion of troops from district headquarters were out searching for Jerry Otis and probably would arrive at Rishket at any time. Can and Nowat nodded in satisfaction.

"There will not be a village in Tiking Province that will feel safe from us," Nowat grinned. "Now our agit-prop teams will be listened to with respect when they go to the villages and tell the people not to vote in these elections."

"The people of Rishket will never trust their government again," Can agreed, "especially when they see the way the troops that are supposed to protect them fight today. We only tortured the traitor and gave the religious man a chance to prove his God is real. But the troops from Tiking will kill the innocent people, not us."

As the sun rose and the guerrillas alertly manned their positions, the sound of trucks could be heard coming up the dirt road to the hamlet. The trail of dust was visible two miles away. The road leading to the front gate was covered by Mung's prized weapon, a 57-mm. recoil-less rifle.

Mung, at the gate, watched the rising dust come closer to the hamlet, smiling in satisfaction at the thought of the coming action. The first truck roared into sight, heading direct for the main gate. Behind it were several more. Mung patted his well-trained gunner as the trucks approached without slackening their speed. The gunner stared through the sights of his 57-mm., and when the first truck was only fifty yards from the gate and the second right behind he squeezed the trigger. With a swoosh the projectile rocketed from the hamlet and slammed into the first truck with a thunderous explosion, blowing up both troop trucks, turning them into a fiery pyre. The screams of the wounded and burning soldiers could be clearly heard inside the hamlet walls.

CHAPTER TWENTY-SIX

THE COLUMN OF TRUCKS abruptly halted. Government soldiers jumped from their vehicles and dug into positions behind the dikes of the rice paddies facing the front and long east side of the village, careful to stay out of the effective range of the guerrillas' rifles.

Major Nooram, newly promoted commander of the battalion, established his command post fifty yards to the rear of the company opposite the front gate of the village. His American battalion adviser, Captain Ralph Cunningham, stood beside him as the Mituyan officer sized up the situation.

Scott MacWhorter, greatly concerned for his friend and fellow civilian worker, Jerry Otis, had accompanied Major Nooram's battalion, hoping to find some trace of the young USOM provincial operations man. "They may have Jerry in there," he speculated. "It's an old Viet Cong trick that the Mitcoms have picked up, to capture an American and parade and degrade him to show the people Americans are weak."

"It's possible," Cunningham conceded. "This whole operation reminds me of Vietnam."

"If the village chief had only had his radio, he might have been able to call for help sooner," MacWhorter lamented. Jerry tried several times to get Rourke to personally order the province chiefs to make their district chiefs distribute USOM transceivers. God knows we've brought enough into this country."

"Maybe we should mortar them," Nooram said thoughtfully.

"We're apt to kill a lot of civilians," Cunningham said.

"We will mortar the walls."

"We've got to drive them out in man-to-man combat," Cunningham advised.

The battalion signal operator appeared at Nooram's jeep. "Sir, the Mitcoms are broadcasting messages from Rishket to their big transmitter. They are boasting over their regular AM frequency, which reaches sets all over the country, that they will hold Rishket for two days against the inferior Mituyan Army."

Scowling at this loss of face, Nooram turned to Cunningham. "We must drive them out today."

Cunningham concurred. "Let's fix bayonets, move up the rice paddies, and when we're close, charge the walls. There's no barbed wire, no mines that we know of. My guess is we outnumber them three or four to one."

"All the houses have reinforced pits where the people can escape small-arms fire," MacWhorter added.

"Sir," the radioman went on, "the Mitcoms say they have executed the hamlet chief as a traitor to the people of the village and the country."

MacWhorter cursed loudly. "He was a damned good man. Always the good ones get it. They'll probably kill the teachers, the security chief, and the pastor of the church. Christ, I hope old Reverend Athol is all right. If he just keeps his mouth shut, they'll probably leave him alone."

"Let's hit 'em, Major," Cunningham exhorted.

Nooram gave the order to his three company commanders by radio. "Mortar barrage on the walls."

"Don't do it, Major. You'll kill too many civilians," Cunningham vainly pleaded. But already the pops of projectiles being fired from the tubes could be heard all around the government positions. They were followed by crunching explosions on and behind the walls.

MacWhorter and Cunningham watched in despair as the mortar barrage continued for five minutes. Cunningham shook his head sadly. "Same old story. Whoever wins, the civilians always lose heavily."

After the heavy pounding of the village ceased, Nooram ordered two companies to move up through the paddies and hit the walls. The third he held in reserve.

"Maybe I should go up with them," Cunningham suggested.

"Too dangerous," Nooram replied.

They watched as the two companies slithered toward the village walls, using the dikes for cover. Just as the government troops reached effective firing range, the guerrillas on the walls opened fire on them. One of the claymore mines went off, filling the air with a deadly spray of metal. The soldiers were still crawling, so the shrapnel and bullets went over their heads.

"Go get 'em!" Cunningham yelled.

The soldiers stopped moving forward, and in the delay the guerrillas pinned them down with heavy fire. The claymore mines had had a devastating psychological effect as the lethal shards of metal tore through the air. The troops immediately began a retreat from the walls, and the guerrilla fire diminished.

"They're conserving their ammo," Cunningham cried. "Hit 'em now." He turned to the major. "This is no time to retreat. We could take the walls."

"Too many Mitcoms," Nooram answered. He called for his radioman. "Send a message to bring up the artillery. Tell them it's urgent. I want to get the Mitcoms out today."

"You can't hit Rishkct with the 105's!" Cunningham cried, shocked. "The mortars were bad enough, but the howitzers will chew up the whole village. Let's hit the walls again. I'll lead the attack."

Nooram smiled condescendingly. "Too dangerous."

"We'll never have a victory without taking some casualties," Cunningham insisted. "Let me lead the men over the walls."

"It would be very bad to have you a casualty. General Dandig does not want casualties."

"Well, goddamn, Major, how the hell do you expect to win this war?"

Silently, Nooram watched the two companies pull back to their former positions, and then the major climbed into the back seat of his jeep, put his feet up on the front seat, and lolled comfortably. "When the artillery comes, we hit," he yawned.

"Major!" Cunningham cried. "This is an old Communist trick. I saw it dozens of times in Vietnam. They want you to shell the village and kill civilians and destroy their property. This turns the people against the government and makes it easier for the Communists to gain control of the village. Let's hit the walls. We can take Rishket and drive out the Mitcoms."

Nooram did not bother to answer. Cunningham turned to MacWhorter.

"If Jerry is in there, we might be able to save him if Nooram would attack now. The Mitcoms would have to use every man they had to defend. Actually, if I know my Communists, they would probably put up only a token defense and then exfiltrate. But the way it is they know damned well that the Mituyan Army isn't interested in taking casualties."

MacWhorter gave the major a look of disgust and shrugged hopelessly.

All morning and well into the afternoon Nooram's battalion drowsed in position around the hamlet of Rishket. There was no fire from either side, and it was hard to realize that two opposing enemy forces were facing each other a couple of hundred yards apart. Finally, late in the afternoon, the distant rumbling of heavy trucks could be heard.

The radioman came to the jeep. "Sir, I am in contact with the artillery company."

Nooram pulled a map from a case on his belt and studied it a few moments, then handed it to Cunningham. "Give the artillery the coordinates," he ordered. "Tell them to hit the walls."

"Look, Major, you know there is no way the 105's can register without dropping rounds in the middle of the village."

"We do not go in there until the artillery has hit the Mitcoms on the walls. Deliver the coordinates!" Nooram demanded.

Reluctantly, Cunningham went to the radio and picked up the transceiver. The American artillery adviser and Cunningham discussed the target, and though the artilleryman was sympathetic with the problems of the villagers he could only obey orders, which were to shell the village according to directions of the forward observer. A Mituyan officer from Nooram's staff went up to the forward positions, from where he would direct the barrage of the 105-mm. howitzers.

Cunningham watched the spotter from the command post and then turned to his counterpart.

"Major, that spotter isn't close enough to the walls to call in accurate fire."

"We'll see what happens," Nooram said noncommittally.

"At least let's call for medics now so they can save some of the wounded when we get into Rishket."

Nooram shrugged. "Do as you like."

"There's a USOM medical detachment at district headquarters," MacWhorter said, "Why don't you radio the district chief?"

"Thanks. Will do."

It was almost dark when the 105's were set up and ready to start registering for a thorough battering of the walls. Morosely, Cunningham watched as the shells landed, one by one, straddling the village and then narrowing in range. Cunningham and MacWhorter shuddered as heavy rounds landed in the middle of the village. The guerrillas in Rishket answered the fire with occasional rounds from the 57-mm. recoil-less rifle. One round landed dangerously close to the jeep, and Nooram leapt from the vehicle into a hole he had ordered dug.

"Those rounds are landing in the village, not on the walls, Major!" Cunningham shouted above the barrage. "The forward observer should get a damn sight closer to the walls."

Nooram did not answer. A string of shells crashed into Rishket. Cunningham turned to MacWhorter. "This is just what we're supposed to be preventing!" he cried out. "I'm going up and relieve that so-called forward observer. General Macker will have my ass for not letting the village die rather than tell this dipshit Nooram to fuck off. . . . But I'm going!"

Cunningham started to crawl forward when Nooram grabbed him by the arm. "Where are you going?"

"To call in some accurate fire!"

"You are my adviser. You stay here. The lieutenant is a trained artillery spotter."

"He's wiping out Rishket and everything we've worked a year to build up," MacWhorter shouted. "Go to it, Ralph!"

Cunningham shook himself loose from the major's grasp and started running, crouched low, toward the forward positions. Nooram shouted threats after him. The American officer soon reached the forward positions, causing dismay from the Mituyan company commander because he had attracted guerrilla fire from the walls. The 57-mm. let out a whoosh and stream of flame, and the rocket plowed into the ground near the company commander. The forward observer was crouched in a hole near the command position, sticking his head up for a look now and then, and radioing back corrections to the artillery company. To the surprise of the Mituyan company commander and the lieutenant, Cunningham jumped into the hole with the spotter, snatched the radio from him, climbed out of the hole and began inching his way across the paddies toward the walls of the village. It was dark, but the guerrillas, perhaps sensing what his mission was, kept up a harassing small-arms fire in his direction. He kept moving across the paddies, stopping behind dikes to call back corrections to the artillery. He finally stopped behind a dike only yards from the walls.

Now Cunningham was able to call in artillery with pinpoint accuracy, and the walls began to crumble. He could clearly hear the screams of the wounded as the rounds scored.

With the artillery perfectly registered on the walls, Cunningham changed the frequency to that of Major Nooram's CP. "Tell the major I'm almost on the walls and there's damned little signs of enemy resistance. Tell him to call an assault. I'm up here. I'll lead."

The radioman acknowledged the call, but there was no reply. Suddenly, ahead of him, Cunningham saw figures of men in peasant garb and black pajamas crawl over the wall and start toward him. He brought his light M-16 automatic rifle to bear on the exfiltrators—but then held his fire. This could be another favorite Viet Cong trick taught to the Mitcoms.

When the Viet Cong terrorists took a village like Rishket, they executed the village chief and marked certain of the other village officials and teachers for execution later. Then, when government troops attacked, those of the village who knew they would be dead anyway would escape in the confusion of the battle, jump the walls, and try to join the attackers. Invariably, the ill-trained, trigger-happy government soldiers would be the ones to kill the escaping villagers, thus greatly increasing the resentment of those villagers who survived the attack.

As Cunningham strained his eyes in the darkness, focusing on a point a few yards to the right of the figures so that he would see them out of the corners of his eyes—a method that gave better night vision—the flash of a shell gave him a moment's clear look. Sure enough, the figures were unarmed. Instantly, firing broke out from behind him at the villagers desperately trying to dash away from the walls. The guerrillas still withheld fire.

"Don't shoot!" Cunningham called into the radio. "Tell them to hold fire. Those are escaping friendlies."

But the target was too tempting to the soldiers, who laid in volleys of rifle fire at the exfiltrators.

Cunningham jumped to his feet and screamed back at the government troops to hold fire, exposing himself to a hail of bullets from both the government and Communist positions. Fiery pain seared first his right shoulder, then his right arm. An excruciating stab through his side collapsed him back behind the dike.

MacWhorter had heard Cunningham's radioed appeal, and uncontrollable anger seized him as Nooram ignored his adviser's plea from the front. "Tell your company commanders to let up," he cried at the immobile major.

"My adviser will be relieved as soon as this is over," Nooram said stonily. "Soon we drive the Mitcoms out."

"Haven't you shelled the village enough?" MacWhorter shouted. "Don't you want any of the people to live?"

"You are not even an adviser. You're a civilian. But I will see that the Minister of the Interior contacts your director and relieves you of *your* job."

Frustration and rage overwhelmed MacWhorter. It took all his will to keep from grabbing the little Mit major and throttling him on the spot.

The barrage continued another hour. With the artillery being directed by the lieutenant, now safely in the company CP, the rounds strayed inaccurately about the village.

A shouting from the walls of the village and a white sheet waved on the end of a pole finally convinced Major Nooram to stop the artillery and order his troops to move toward the walls, alert to fire if it were a trick.

By the first light of day, Nooram's batallion, having suffered minimal casualties marched triumphantly into the smoking village of Rishket. Dead and wounded were everywhere.

MacWhorter found Captain Cunningham lying in a paddy close to the gate. He was alive and had managed to press the bandage from his first-aid kit into his wounded side. The USOM medical team and two green-bereted Special Forces medics from a camp fifteen miles away arrived on the scene shortly after Nooram's men entered Rishket. The government troops had not found a single Mitcom, dead or alive, in the village. If any had been killed, their bodies had been carried away. As the Communists had planned, the teachers, village officials, and the American had gone over the walls when they saw that the guerrillas were getting ready to break off their engagement. They had been promised death before the Communists would leave the village, and each had met death. Not one man was shot in the back from the walls by the Communists—which the villagers clearly noted. MacWhorter found Jerry Otis, stitched up and down by government automatic rifle fire. Sorrowfully, he stood over his friend as the medics came by, looked, and kept going into the village.

Cunningham was evacuated by helicopter to the hospital in Tiking, and MacWhorter promised he'd visit him the next day.

"You'd better hurry," Cunningham groaned. "Because they're sure going to ship my ass back to Clark Field and court-martial me as soon as I can stand up."

"If they do, no matter how much my country needs me, I'll never work for the United States government again," MacWhorter declared vehemently.

"Start looking for an outside job, then."

MacWhorter watched the helicopter ascend, then slowly walked back into the suffering village.

In the center of town he found the bodies of the village chief and the American missionary. His face twisted at the sight. He had seen both methods of torture before, but, like all Vietnam veterans in Mituyan, he had hoped these things would never get here. One good thing about the shelling—the only good thing, he thought—was that both the chief and the missionary had died of shrapnel wounds, cutting short their agony, which could have lasted another day or more.

Wandering down the main street of the town, MacWhorter stopped at one of the better houses which, miraculously, had escaped destruction. He expected to find it put to use as a hospital but instead found a jubilant Major Nooram, surrounded by his three smiling company commanders, in the act of taking it over as battalion headquarters. Nooram was reporting by radio to his superiors in Tiking. They had scored a major victory, driven the Mitcoms out of Rishket and taken no casualties of any consequence. Nooram said he was dispatching a courier to headquarters with a request that Captain Cunningham be disciplined by the American authorities. Particulars would follow, Nooram concluded, seeing MacWhorter standing in the door.

"I have not forgotten your conduct, either," Nooram said ominously. "My advice to you is to go away from here right now. Perhaps I will forget to request your transfer from my country."

MacWhorter turned on his heel and walked down the street, his nose wrinkling at the smell of burned flesh, his eyes welling with compassion at the suffering all around him. As he neared the end of the tragic main thoroughfare, his black depression lifted somewhat: he saw Mike and Luna Forrester, both with large, white first-aid boxes slung over their shoulders. Hurrying into the village with them was a tall, thin, bespectacled man in army combat fatigues; he had a shock of thick black hair protruding from under a baseball cap.

Mike and Luna began working on wounded children, Mike talking to everyone he could and translating for his companion, who was busy noting everything and taking photographs. When Mike had done all he could for one girl, he put a candy ball in her mouth, which the hurt child sucked cheerfully.

"Scott, meet Roger Krakhaur," Mike said as he continued to clean and dress the wounds of people who came to the temporary aid station he and Luna had set up. "Roger writes for a large number of big papers in the States through the Star Syndicate."

"You just missed a hell of a story," Scott said.

"How about a recap?"

"Later I'll tell you a story that will make you wonder what the hell we're all doing here." He stopped abruptly. "Abort that last comment. We goddamned well have to be here in Mituyan. . . ."

It was a somber drive from the ruined hamlet to the rubber plantation. MacWhorter had answered all of Krakhaur's questions as frankly as he could. Just how Jerry Otis had been captured was impossible to say. He had taken Krakhaur on an inspection trip of the village, and even suggested he interview Major Nooram, to get an idea of what American advisers were up against.

About his own job, he didn't go into details, explaining only the less sensational aspects of "counter agit-prop."

It was mid-afternoon when they drove up to the Rishram house. Krakhaur excused himself. "I want to go up and see Alana. Then I'll have to dash on to Tiking and file this story somehow."

"You know what's likely to happen to Alana if you do send out a story so unfavorable to the Mituyan Army," Luna cautioned him.

"It's too important a story not to file," Krakhaur replied. "Besides, I just filed a story the Palace will love—about the Mad Monk of Tiking. Shows the readers at home what the government here is really up against."

"It's taking a big chance," Luna insisted. "Well, go up to Alana."

Roger nodded and ran up the stairs to Alana's room. He knocked gently at the door.

"Come in, Roger," she said hesitantly.

Alana was standing at the window, looking out over the rubber trees toward the hills that rose above the recently embattled hamlet of Rishket. Though still wan and thin, her beauty was beginning to return. She had a red flower in her hair and was wearing one of Luna's Mituyan slit dresses. He walked over and tried to take her in his arms; gracefully she moved away from him.

"Was it very bad at Rishket?" she asked.

Krakhaur nodded. "I'm going to have to get to Tiking as soon as possible and figure some way to file this story."

"It will show how bad things are in our army, in our whole government?"

"I'm afraid so. But it's important news."

"Then file it," she said with sudden determination. "No one else will have the story, will they?"

"The Public Affairs Office in Tuyan City will announce a great Mituyan Army victory over the Mitcoms, and that's the story everyone else will file."

"Be careful at the cable office," she cautioned. "Do you think you can find a pigeon?"

"There's not enough time. I may fly to Bangkok and file from there and get back to Tuyan City before my story hits." Krakhaur stepped toward her again. "I love you, Alana. You know that, don't you?"

"You're very sweet, Roger." The haunted look returned to her eyes.

With gentle force he took her shoulders, holding her facing him. "Darling, I know what you've been through. But that only makes me love you more. I want to marry you."

Alana closed her eyes. She shook her head slowly. "No. You can't know, not really, Roger. . . . I will never be able to have a husband. Never, now."

"But I love you, darling. I need you." He tried to kiss her, but she turned her face from him slightly.

Again he turned her to him and again she avoided his kiss. He breathed deeply and said: "I'll be back as soon as I get the story out."

Luna met Krakhaur at the foot of the stairs. "I'm sorry, Roger."

"She'll get over it, won't she?" he said anxiously.

"I don't know. I hope so."

"I leave for Tiking shortly." He turned to MacWhorter. "When will you know if Cunningham is going to be in trouble?"

"The Mituyan Army doesn't waste time in harassing an American counterpart. I guess by now the complaint has reached MAC-M and gone up to General Macker. He'll be making the decision."

"Can I interview Cunningham at the hospital?"

MacWhorter shook his head. "You do that and Macker is bound to hear. You know he orders a security check whenever a story comes out that he or the Mits don't like. Better for Cunningham that he never sees you. I'll visit him this evening and let you know what happened. . . . How are you going to get out?"

"I don't know. Maybe Air Mituyan. I think they have a flight from Tiking. Otherwise I'll have to grab the milk run to Tuyan City and get out that way. I don't dare go near the cable office with this story."

"If you'd seen what I have, what Alana has been through, you wouldn't dare come back to Mituyan at all after you send *this* story," Luna stated tonelessly.

"They can't really hold you responsible for my stories," Krakhaur said with conviction.

"Who's going to stop them? The fearless American ambassador?" Luna asked sarcastically.

Krakhaur's resolution collapsed as he thought back to his meeting with Whittelsie and Macker. "You're right, of course." He clasped and unclasped his hands pondering the situation. "Maybe I'd better forget the story. It's just—I feel the record should be set straight about what's really happening over here." He grimaced. "Rishket: A big government victory!"

"Did you tell Alana you wanted to file the story?"

"She said to go ahead but—" He shrugged. "I don't know."

"You do what you have to do," Luna said.

Krakhaur looked at MacWhorter. "Will the truth help the program here?" he asked.

"The way things are going in Tuyan City, nothing can hurt us more than the Country Team does now. *Anything* that can force a hard look at the situation here by competent people in Washington can only help."

"I think I should file," Krakhaur declared.

CHAPTER TWENTY-SEVEN

THOUGH CONVINCED he was doing the right thing cooperating with Fritz Lawton's crazy scheme, Mike couldn't help feel angry at himself. The risk to his property was bad enough, but there was Luna's and now Alana's safety to be considered. If anyone suspected he had any part in the operations MacWhorter, Major Song, and their government commandos were planning, the Communists would destroy everything he and Luna had built up and even hunt them down and kill them. But as his term with the CIA stretched out, Mike was surprised to discover he was developing a strong sense of mission. He still longed for the day when he and Luna could go back to their peaceful lives, but this would have to wait until the Communists were eradicated from Mituyan. Just as well, then, that he make himself into the implacable Communist-killer until peace returned to the country.

Early Friday morning breakfast was served on the terrace at Rishram to MacWhorter and the leaders of his cadre who had arrived from Tiking with Mike the night before. Besides MacWhorter, there were two Mituyan officers, Major Song and Lieutenant Drit—and a Sergeant Zap.

Both Mituyan officers were dressed in the civilian garb of estate headmen, with pistols concealed under loose shirts. Major Song seemed suspicious of Mike and kept throwing him sidewise glances from behind his dark glasses. Mike blamed the apparent hostility on Luna's rescue of Alana—since this first mission of the USIS cadre had to be coordinated with Tarot in Tuyan City and Poramat and Yunakit in Tiking. For his part, Mike instinctively disliked Song, and only the fact that they were both fighting a common enemy enabled him to make plans for the coming operation with the Mituyan officer. But he had insisted that Luna and Alana stay upstairs for the entire length of the cadre's visit.

"We have a dozen men in peasant clothes, posing as plantation workers, watching this house and the pay office," MacWhorter, also in black-pajama peasant garb, assured Mike. "Once we grab this Communist tax collector, we'll interrogate him on the spot and get out of here; but you'll have a full platoon of specially trained men to protect your property."

"If Frakit or whoever comes to collect this morning ever gets away and tells what happened, no amount of protection will save my wife and me," Mike replied dourly.

"I assure you, Mr. Forrester," Major Song said, "that no Communist who visits this plantation today will ever see his fellow guerrillas again."

"What time does the Communist usually come for his money?" MacWhorter asked.

"For a long time it varied—sometimes early in the morning when the office opened, sometimes just before it closed. Since there has never been any trouble, my manager now tells me they have been coming regularly at eight in the morning. Frakit himself usually comes, checks the books to see how many men are being paid for the week, then takes his cut. He generally arrives with at least two bodyguards."

After breakfast Mike drove the three Mituyans and MacWhorter to the plantation office half a mile from the house. If they were being watched, the procedure would have appeared normal for a Friday payday, when the various headmen came in to supervise paying their workers. Bunghole, the estate manager and paymaster, looked questioningly at the strangers, but since they were with Mr. Forrester no comment was made. Patiently, Song and Drit waited, squatting on the floor of the office, conversing in low tones. Sergeant Zap watched outside. The headman who had been talking to Bunghole when they arrived started to leave the office, but Song, in authoritative tones, told him to stay. The headman looked at his boss, and Mike nodded and pointed to a corner of the office. MacWhorter and Mike sat behind the paymaster's wicket, waiting silently. Surveying the scene, Bunghole could ill conceal his fear at the strange behavior of Mr. Forrester, who seldom came to the office on payday. He tried to keep his fingers from quivering as he counted out metas into neat piles and put them in the pay envelopes.

At exactly eight, Frakit arrived carrying a neat attaché case. Behind him, armed with U.S.-made automatic carbines, walked the one-eared guerrilla Mung and another equally fierce-looking man in black pajamas. They looked around the room, their eyes not even pausing on the two squatting men, and stood behind Frakit as he went up to the paymaster's cage and opened his attaché case. It was then that with surprise he saw Forrester. Mike grinned at him and stood up.

"Well, Frakit, I am pleased at the fine protection you are giving my plantation. It is expensive, but necessary."

Seeing the one-eared, one-eyed guerrilla, Mike addressed him in Mituyan: "Ah, Mung, glad to see you again."

Taken aback, the guerrilla fingered his rifle, lifting the barrel slightly. The three Communists, still surprised, were all turned toward Mike behind the cage. Behind them Mike saw Major Song and Lieutenant Drit rise catlike to their feet, pistols held ready, and creep toward their intended victims.

"Tell me, Mung," Mike said conversationally, "when do you expect to take your revenge on Poramat. He killed my friend Professor LakaLit, you know."

Mung opened his mouth to answer. Two sickening thuds resounded as pistol barrels viciously chopped into the heads of the guerrillas. Both bodyguards sagged to the floor.

Frakit whirled and, seeing what had happened, started to reach for his own pistol. He stared into the black holes of two .45's and slowly raised his hands.

"What's happening, Mr. Forrester?" the accountant asked. "It is hard to believe that you could be so foolish to think that by capturing me you can cease paying off the Freedom Front. I assure you that if you and your headmen here don't let me go this minute your whole plantation will be destroyed and you will die. Even if you kill me now, you will die and your wife will *pray* for death."

A sharp chop across the jaw with a pistol by Lieutenant Drit staggered Frakit.

"Be careful," Song cautioned the lieutenant. "This man has much talking to do."

"I have nothing to say to you," Frakit said thickly.

"You will," Song replied confidently. "Drit, tell Sergeant Zap outside to make sure there are no more of these guerrilla dogs around here. Then come back with our truck."

While MacWhorter helped Song disarm the prostrate guerrillas, Mike, after cautioning Bunghole to remain in the building, went outside, where he found Drit talking to Zap and two other men in peasant black. They started for the rubber trees, and Drit and Mike drove the Land Rover back to the plantation house, where they picked up the personnel carrier belonging to the Mituyans and drove it back to the paymaster's office.

Inside the office, Song and Drit kicked the guerrillas to their feet. Mung's one eye burned hatred at Mike, but none of the Communists said a word. Frakit's mouth was still bleeding, and he spat blood on the floor frequently. The three Communists were clubbed and prodded into the back of the canvas-covered truck and made to lie in a heap on the floor. Drit and two of Zap's men now carried the rifles taken from the guerrillas as they climbed in back to guard them.

"OK, Mike, lead the way," MacWhorter called out.

Mike in his Land Rover led the way to a deserted section of the plantation, one of the patches where twenty of his trees had been destroyed. Since it was possible that there might be Mitcom spies among the ordinary workers, they had agreed to deal with the captured Communists far from sight. Mike finally brought his Land Rover to a halt beside a workers' outhouse. A rain barrel full of water stood under the overhang of the roof; Mike always instructed his workers in sanitation and insisted they wash after leaving the building.

Song pulled up behind him and looked the place over with satisfaction. "Bring out the money man," he commanded.

Frakit was roughly jerked out of the truck and hauled over to the Mituyan major.

"If you would like not to die, you will tell us what we want to know," Song said quietly. "We know the MFF leader in Tiking Province is Nowat. We also know he has the assistance of foreigners, the North Vietnamese Nguyen Van Can and a Chinese Communist. We are anxious to talk to them. We want you to tell us where we can find them."

Frakit said nothing; he turned on Mike. "You will die, your plantation will be destroyed, your wife—"

A vicious jab of Song's pistol into Frakit's solar plexus dropped him gasping to the ground.

"Bring out One-Ear," Song commanded.

Mung also refused to talk, but the Mituyan major never lost his patience. MacWhorter, watching, said to Mike, "That Major Song is a real pro. An amateur would get mad and butcher the job."

Song said a word to his lieutenant, who handcuffed Mung's wrists, then tied a rope from the chain of the handcuffs to the rear bumper of the truck. Mung understood what was going to happen to him, but stared back defiantly as Song continued to ask him questions. Major Song shrugged, regretfully, it seemed. "Get the generator out of the truck."

Two men carried the green radio generator and tripod from the truck and put it down next to the rain barrel. Frakit was jerked to his feet, still in shock, and placed in the back of the truck. He looked down at Mung, attached to the bumper, and a shudder convulsed his body.

"Does anyone want to help me with some information?" Major Song asked plaintively.

There was no answer. "Very well. Watch carefully, Frakit. Your turn will come next."

Mike and MacWhorter watched the truck start slowly and jerk Mung to his feet. The guerrilla walked to keep from falling and then trotted as the truck gathered speed. Finally, he tripped and fell on his face and twisted onto his back. He could not get to his feet now. The truck zigzagged through the trees.

"Song's a rough little sonofabitch," MacWhorter commented. "But he'll get answers."

Mike watched the truck stop. Song strolled back to the battered figure lying at the end of the rope. He prodded the heap with the toe of his boot, then squatted beside Mung. The guerrilla tried to rise up but could not. The major appeared to be talking to him.

Finally Song stood and returned to the back of the truck, where he apparently had a conversation with Frakit. The major climbed back into the rear of the truck, and it started up again. Mike and MacWhorter watched as Mung attempted to get to his feet before collapsing again. The truck gained speed.

Five minutes later the truck returned to the outhouse and Major Song hopped out. Frakit was unceremoniously dumped beside the battered body of Mung.

Frakit stared down at the mangled guerrilla in terror. Mike could not help feeling momentary compassion for the man who had turned Communist guerrilla because of Poramat's inhuman treatment of the peasants.

"No, Frakit," Major Song said, "your friend is not dead. Will you enjoy being in such condition and still alive?" He paused a moment. "Now—where do we find Nowat?"

"He is in Tiking City," Frakit answered hoarsely, still staring at the barely living remains of the man.

"Where exactly in the city?"

"I don't know."

"Where do you deliver the money?"

"To Nowat."

"Fine. Where do you meet Nowat?"

Suddenly, Frakit seemed to stiffen and he turned from Mung. "I don't know." He shook his head. "Someone finds me and leads me to him."

"That sort of evasiveness just won't do. You are an important man in the MFF. You know where Nowat's headquarters are."

After two full minutes of silence Song commanded, "Strip him and put him in the rain barrel."

Song's men did as they were told, handcuffing Frakit's wrists behind him so that he was helpless to climb out of the barrel. Lieutenant Drit motioned to one of his men, who started grinding current out of the generator. He took the electrodes, dropped them into the barrel of water, and Frakit screamed as the electric charge, magnified by the water, danced through his body.

Song gestured, and one of the electrodes was removed from the barrel. "Please, where in town?" he asked.

"The camera shop," Frakit sobbed. He gave the address of MFF headquarters in Tiking.

"What is the name of the Chinese? Where do we find him?"

Hesitantly, Frakit told his tormentors about the Golden Dragon, the Chinese restaurant used by Tzung as a front.

"There must be many more Communist sympathizers and active helpers," Song probed. "I want the names and addresses of all of them."

"I don't know them," Frakit cried.

Song came over to where MacWhorter was standing with Mike. "This is our chance to completely destroy the MFF apparatus in Tiking. If we can get all the names from him and where they sleep, where the guerrilla camp is, everything, we save the lives of hundreds of government officials and schoolteachers, the chief targets of Communist terror."

"That's our mission," MacWhorter answered, tight-lipped. "Always in my experience the accountant of an organized guerrilla band—in the earlier stages of an insurgency, particularly—has the names, functions, and addresses of every member of the group. He knows the identity of the underground operators in the city, the auxiliaries, down to the actual guerrilla fighters encamped in the countryside, like One-Ear here."

"There's only one way to find out," said Song, walking back to the prisoner.

"For God's sake, Scott—" Mike turned away from the proceedings in disgust.

"I know, Mike," MacWhorter said sympathetically. "I'm not even going to say they'd do the same to us—worse, even—if the tables were turned. I'm not going to remind you what happened to Jerry Otis or the Reverend Athol." Scott scrubbed a hand over his face. "I'm not even going to tell you this is Asia, a different culture, where barbarity and butchery and atrocity are accepted as part of everyday life. Christ, how do you think I feel, seeing this day in, day out? Seeing it happen to our own people—*much* worse, let me tell you—if they're unlucky enough to get caught . . . No, all I can think of—all I *let* myself think of—is that this is war, a ruthless, primitive war, and as long as the roots of the organization are intact, as long as the guerrillas are an organized band, another leader can and will quickly appear to carry on. Communist terrorism will continue to spread and get worse. . . . Do you realize how many lives we can save if right now we can extract the complete breakdown of the Mitcom organization in this part of Mituyan?"

Mike nodded wearily.

"Frakit can betray the boss, but he knows the organization is still there to carry on. That's why he has to spill everything right now."

A high-pitched shrill scream came from the rain barrel.

"Now, accountant, are you ready to account for the whereabouts of every member of the MFF of your region?" asked Song.

"I told you what I know," Frakit gasped.

Song took the free electrode and moved it toward Frakit's eyes. The accountant's face contorted in horror. He whispered, "My briefcase."

"We have searched your case," Song said, advancing the electrode.

"Under the leather lining of the lid!" Frakit screamed.

Song strode for the truck and jerked open the attaché case. With a pocket knife he explored the underside of the lid, found a place to insert the small blade under the lining and peeled it back.

Song let out a grunt of satisfaction as he withdrew several sheets of tissue-thin paper covered with names and addresses. Scott and Mike bent over his shoulder. Leading the list were the names Nowat, Tzung, Nguyen Van Can. Song studied the paper for several minutes, then carefully folded it and put it in his pocket. He walked back to the rain barrel.

"You are to be congratulated, Frakit, for being so helpful. Now there is one more thing."

"I don't know the location of the guerrilla camp," Frakit shrieked. "Mung knew. The other one in the truck knows. I do not."

Song nodded. "I believe you, Frakit." The Mituyan officer gave orders, and the accountant was pulled from the barrel.

"Bring the other one out," Song commanded.

Mike turned to MacWhorter. "I don't see where I'm much help here. When you're ready to go back to Tiking, let me know. I want to get back to my wife."

MacWhorter nodded. "I don't blame you. This must seem pretty nasty stuff to you. It does to me too. But remember, I've been seeing this as a steady diet for damned near fifteen years. They do it to us. We do it to them. Korea, Laos, Vietnam, Mituyan, and a few other places I'm not allowed to talk about. Hundreds, thousands of American guys killed. This sort of brutality going on all over this part of the world every day as the Communists try to expand and we try to stop them."

MacWhorter's face mirrored his disillusionment and bitterness. "Do you know there are hardly any combat soldiers in the United States Army today who have ever seen us win a war? I was too young for World War Two, but I fought in Korea and saw what happened in Laos. We damn near had it licked when we negotiated out. Our government won't let us go all out for the big win in Vietnam, they wouldn't in Korea, so we 'professionals' go on fighting a delaying action as best we can in the back alleys, these dirty little wars the people back home never hear of."

Mike put an affectionate hand on MacWhorter's shoulder for a moment, and then quickly headed for the Land Rover.

CHAPTER TWENTY-EIGHT

COLONEL LAWTON'S OFFICE headquarters seemed mighty relaxed, Mike thought on Saturday morning, considering the nature of the work the assembled members of MacWhorter's special government commandos were to perform in the next twenty-four hours. MacWhorter himself appeared calm as the cadre gathered around a large street map of the city of Tiking—covered all over with multicolored pins.

"Ordinarily, this would be a job for Yunakit's secret police," Lawton conceded after Mike had studied the plan of action. "But we want the job done right. Tarot himself agreed to this caper, although if he knew how many Mitcom sympathizers we've turned up I'm sure he'd take this part of the project away from us—and botch it up for sure."

"Neat. Very concise," MacWhorter said approvingly to Major Song. The Mituyan leader of the special government commandos smiled back. They understood each other, these two men; they had a professional respect for each other, although on many doctrinal points they might disagree, particularly on reform measures that would give the people a better life. Song was from a wealthy mandarin family and as committed to the old ways as the KaritKi government he supported. In vain MacWhorter argued the need for a new way of life for the people embodied in the spirit of the elections, if the Republic of Mituyan was to resist effectively a Communist revolution.

Song and MacWhorter studied the map intently. The pins with red heads marked the dwelling places of those to be assassinated. One pin was stuck in the address of Nowat's camera shop, another marked the location of the Golden Dragon restaurant. There were two more red pins in the chart. One indicated the home of Nowat's chief underground agent in Tiking, the other Nowat's chief organizer of auxiliaries, people who sympathized with the MFF and would help in ways that did not involve overt fighting. Truck drivers, men and women with access to medical supplies, farmers willing to provide a pig or rice to feed guerrillas, people who worked in the local telephone and telegraph offices and could move messages for the Front or gather intelligence by listening in to calls and reading cables and telegrams from the capital and abroad—all these made up the web of auxiliary workers indispensable to the successful operation of guerrillas in the field.

The other pins, over a dozen, marked the homes of sympathizers who perhaps could be terrorized or persuaded to stop aiding the Mitcoms. Very politely today, each family would be called, and skilled cadremen would talk with the residents. When they left, the black card with the white eye would be tacked to the door. These same cards would be conspicuously attached to the bodies of those assassinated.

The first of the special government commando teams left JRB Tiking headquarters and set out on foot toward the center of town. Sergeant Zap and Lieutenant Drit were dressed in pressed slacks and clean sport shirts. Both carried cameras slung over their shoulders, looking like any two young Mituyan sports out for an afternoon stroll. It was just after Tat time, and many Tiking girls, thighs flashing through their skirts, were also strolling around the ancient port city. Saturday afternoon was the time in Tiking for young men and women to become acquainted.

Sergeant Zap and Lieutenant Drit reached their target just after four o'clock. The day was beginning to cool. Drit caught the eye of one of his men drinking fruit juice at an outdoor refreshment stand. The man nodded and held up two fingers: both targets were inside. Casually, Drit and Zap strolled into Nowat's camera shop. The girl Li Tin was alone behind the counter as they entered, and both men made complimentary remarks about her appearance. When she asked what they wanted, Zap asked if there was someone in the shop who could take a look at his camera—the shutter refused to open. The owner was very busy at the moment, she said; he was developing films in the darkroom. Drit nodded. Most camera shops did their developing after the heat of the day, he realized, but even so he would greatly appreciate it if his camera could be fixed now. He laid a hundred-meta note on the counter. The girl looked at it disdainfully and informed him there were other camera shops nearby. Taking out his wallet, he brought forth the MFF identification card taken from Frakit and laid it on the counter. Li Tin looked at it and asked Drit to wait a moment.

"We would like to meet upstairs," Drit said. "The matter concerns the accountant Frakit."

Li Tin's eyes opened wide. She glanced at the card again. Drit wanted to surprise Nowat—if possible. He certainly did not want to be standing with Nowat in front of the shop, exposed to the street, when the Mitcom province chief's suspicions were aroused, as they were bound to be. There might be Mitcom sympathizers watching the shop, ready to give the alarm if anything unusual happened.

"This is a most urgent matter," Drit said, insistently. "Frakit had trouble with the money from the Rishram plantation. He has asked us to tell Nowat before Tzung finds out. Please take us to him immediately."

Li Tin nodded, looking worried, and led Drit and Zap behind the counter into the back of the shop and up a flight of steps. She knocked at a door, then walked in. Nowat was seated behind his desk studying a map of Tiking Province and making notes. He frowned at the interruption, but Li Tin, in a flurry of words, explained why she had brought up these two members of the Front. Drit could see that Nowat was suspicious already.

"Frakit would never send anyone to me here," he said. He started to stand, one hand reaching into a drawer. Quickly, Drit flashed the Front card, which for a moment stayed Nowat. "What has happened?"

Drit moved closer to the desk. With his head he gestured questioningly at the girl.

"It is all right to talk in front of Li Tin. She is active in the Front," Nowat said.

"I have a letter from Frakit written this morning."

"Where is the money? He was supposed to take it to Corps Commander Tzung by noon today."

"This letter will explain everything," Drit said, "and we'll help recover the money."

"Recover?" Excitedly Nowat reached for the envelope. Just as he did so, Drit grabbed the outstretched hand and jerked Nowat over his desk, twisting the arm so he hit the floor on his back. Drit thrust the instep of his foot into Nowat's throat so he could not utter a sound. Zap threw an arm lock around Li Tin's throat and held her immobile.

"Now, we want all your records on the MFF. Where are they? Point to them."

Nowat said nothing, staring up defiantly.

Drit ground his foot into Nowat's throat, producing a muffled gurgle. Then, with a nimble backstep Drit danced off Nowat's throat, shifted his weight and slammed the metal toe of his shoe into the man's temple. The MFF province chief lay as though dead, as Drit approached Li Tin. "Where are the records?" He pulled a switch blade open. "If you make any noise, your throat will be cut."

Zap released his hold as the girl gasped, "I know nothing." Deftly, Drit ran the knife lightly over her throat. Li Tin tried to shrink away from him. Hate burned from her eyes, but she remained silent.

"I could make her talk, but we haven't much time," Drit said. "However, I hear she's supposed to be in love with this Mitcom province chief. Let's see how much she cares . . .

"All we want are the records of your man's political activities," he said to her. "The secret police will search this place until they find them anyway. This little war will soon be over—and it's up to you what happens to Nowat." He moved the knife toward the figure on the floor. "You wouldn't want him sexually incapacitated, would you? What would he say if he could talk?"

Although clearly frightened now, Li Tin remained silent. The problem, as Lieutenant Drit well knew, was that Li Tin realized she was going to die whether she cooperated or not.

"You are both young people," Drit argued. "We do not want to kill you. We would not even separate you. But together you could be sent to a comfortable training home in the country, where at leisure you and your man will reexamine philosophies, ours and those you presently hold."

Drit could see he was making progress now. The girl's eyes betrayed the hope that was beginning to stir within her.

At a gesture, Zap approached the unconscious form of Nowat, naked knife blade probing the Communist's groin. "In a year," Drit went on hypnotically, "everyone will have forgotten whether you did or did not help us this afternoon." The blade snicked a rent in the front of Nowat's pants. "But he will *never* forget. Do you want to be responsible for your man going through life without his manhood?"

Li Tin shook her head. "The photo enlarger is the file. In the darkroom." She motioned with her head toward the rear of the office. Drit disappeared through the door, returning moments later, a sheaf of papers and manila envelopes in his hand.

"She told us the truth. Looks like we've got the whole Mitcom apparatus described here."

He looked at the girl sadly. "OK. Let's get it over with and take these papers back."

"We still have a little time," Zap said suggestively.

"Sergeant!" Drit bit out.

Before Li Tin knew what was happening, Zap had pulled out the .38 revolver with the long silencer on the barrel; quickly he shot her through the temple. She collapsed beside her lover. Zap bent over and quickly dispatched Nowat just as he was regaining consciousness. Drit pinned the black card with the white eye to both bodies.

Then, nonchalantly, the two men walked down the stairs, carrying the MFF files under their arms. Drit unobtrusively pinned another card to the door of the shop and hailed a miniature taxi that putted down the street, streaming noxious fumes of cheap gasoline. The mission was complete.

Major Song, wearing the rough clothes of a peasant and guerrilla, his face and hands dirtied to look as though he had just come out of the jungle, was driven to within a few blocks of his target. It was early evening as he stepped out of the nondescript civilian car the cadre had acquired in Tiking. He carried Frakit's attaché case with the tiny black star, identifying it to the initiated as belonging to the Front.

Song arrived at the alleyway that ran alongside the Golden Dragon restaurant to the back room where the mah-jongg game clicked on endlessly. In his left hand he held the attaché case and in his right the Front card—red and yellow with a black star in the center; it was the card Mung had been carrying. In the folds of his shapeless black pajamas was a machine pistol he hoped he wouldn't have to use.

One man looked up from the mah-jongg game as he entered. The major immediately recognized him as Vietnamese and concluded it was Nguyen Van Can.

He pushed into the crowd of players. "Who are you?" He'd been challenged by a Chinese.

"I come from Frakit." Song held out the card. "I have orders to deliver this case to Tzung and Can. Are they here?"

There was no answer, but another Chinese came up to him. "Who are you?" he asked roughly.

Song showed his card. "I come from Mung and Frakit. The accountant sent me to you with this case. He said he would come as soon as possible with the keys."

"Why did he not come here himself?"

"Are you Tzung?"

"Yes. Give me the case," he demanded.

"I have shown you my card. Now let me see yours. Frakit and Mung said they would have me bled to death if I gave this to the wrong man."

"You are right." Tzung took out his card and showed it to the filthy guerrilla.

"Frakit also said I must have the Vietnamese, Can, present when I give over this case."

"What's the matter with them?" Tzung growled.

"My leaders in the hills tell me that this money was promised for the use of procuring more guns for our men. That is why they insist I show Can, the fighting man, this money."

Tzung laughed and gestured to the Vietnamese, who left the game and came over. Tzung explained the situation, and Can laughed too. "They deserve the guns. Of course, we will kill the government sergeant after he leads us to the guns—and get our money back."

"What happened to Frakit?" Tzung asked suspiciously.

"We ran into a government roadblock on our way in. Frakit gave me this locked case and told me to deliver it to you. He said he would be able to talk his way out of the roadblock and bring the keys with him to open it for you."

"Since our attack on Rishket, the government troops have been more active than they were all last year," Can said. "But the success of our attack was worth it." He laughed derisively. "And the Americans and Mituyans announce they won a victory, drove us out in less than a day." He reached for the attaché case. "Here, I'll break it open."

"Frakit begs that you will not destroy his case. He will be here as soon as he can." Song tried hard to be convincing. "Please, give Frakit one hour more."

Tzung and Can both looked at him skeptically. Finally Tzung said, "You wait until Frakit comes. If he isn't here soon, we'll break open the case, and I want you here when we see what is . . . or what isn't, inside."

"If I wanted to steal from the Freedom Front, would I do it this way?" Song asked, feigning deep hurt.

"You wait here." Can reinforced Tzung's order.

"May I have some food? I haven't eaten all day."

Tzung nodded. "If what you say is true, you've done an outstanding job for the Front. Go and eat all you desire." Tzung shouted an order to one of his men at the mah-jongg table. "Stay next to this man. See that he gets all he wants to eat, but don't let him out of your sight."

Song and his new companion, ostentatiously displaying a pistol butt poking from under his loose sport shirt, walked out to the alley and up to the Golden Dragon. Inside, Song requested they sit close to the front door where it was cool. He had to call on all his professional composure as they waited for the meal. It was impossible to avoid anticipating the explosion he expected would rock the whole restaurant at any moment.

As he sipped the hot soup he tried to plan his actions. He was sure that Can and Tzung would not wait for Frakit. His nerves tautening, he ordered a number of courses and ate as slowly as he could.

His guard fidgeted, eager to get back into the mah-jongg game. Surely, Song thought, Tzung and Can wouldn't wait much longer to examine the collection from Rishram, unless they suspected something. The cold metal of the machine pistol pressed his side reassuringly.

Suddenly, a violent explosion blew Song through the air. His eardrums felt as though they would burst, and he found himself lying in the street. Unhurt, he picked himself up and peered into the smoking rubble of the shattered restaurant. His guard had been hurled against the wall, pieces of plaster filtering down on him. He gave Song a surprised look, shook his head, and started to reach for the pistol butt, but Song, who had drawn his machine pistol and was holding it behind his back, turned the weapon on the guard and pressed the trigger. A short burst of three rounds knocked the watchdog back into the rubble, where he lay still, his chest spurting blood.

Holding the machine pistol before him, Song stalked down the alley to the back room, climbing over debris. Ahead of him was a tangled mess of walls and furniture—and broken bodies. It seemed impossible that anyone could still be alive. Four pounds of C-4 plastic explosive encased in hundreds of metal splinters and shot, set to explode when the attaché case was forced open, would have wiped out twice the area of the Golden Dragon's back room. There was not a sign of life. All the bodies were mutilated beyond recognition. Song dropped the black card with the white eye on top of the rubble and hurried back out of the alley, mingling with the gathering throng of shocked spectators.

Back at headquarters, Lawton, Mike, and MacWhorter heard the distant rumble of the explosion. Drit and Zap had already returned with their invaluable prize.

"Chalk up a second hit," MacWhorter said. "I hope Major Song was able to get away before that one went off."

Lawton and a Mituyan intelligence officer who had been sifting through the records Drit and Zap had brought back kept exclaiming over their find.

"By God, Scott, with these records we'll set the Mitcoms back years. I hate to do it, but I guess we've got to turn the case over to Poramat now. It will take his entire secret-police force to track down everyone listed here."

"Then I can get my cadre out in the boonies where we belong," MacWhorter replied, pleased.

Lawton turned to the city map. "I guess about now is the right time for your discussion groups to pay their visits."

MacWhorter grinned. "I may not be the highest ranking Information Service civilian around, but I think I'm one of the most persuasive."

Lawton nodded. "Amen to that, Scott."

PART VI

ESCAPE ROUTE

CHAPTER TWENTY-NINE

As WAS ALWAYS the case whenever he was on his way to visit Mayna, Ambassador Whittelsie was stimulated and disgusted with himself at the same time. But this time he was concerned as well. Just before leaving the embassy for Mayna's apartment at the palace, Ted Baum had showed him the latest Krakhaur story. It gave the full report of the attack on Rishket, prominently featuring the actions of Captain Cunningham and his Mituyan counterpart, Major Nooram. After the initial shock of reading it, worry set in about the Palace reaction. He had wanted to cancel his luncheon appointment with Mayna, but when Baum assured him that the Palace would not receive the playback until early afternoon he decided to keep the date. If he'd cancelled, Mayna would later realize he'd been afraid to face her—and that would make things worse. Also, Mayna might have information on this whole distasteful business of Krakhaur and his girlfriend, assistant, or whatever she was.

On top of everything else, one or more members of his team had apparently committed the one unpardonable disloyalty and communicated unilaterally with Washington. Exactly what had been said, and by whom, was impossible for him to discover. But this morning he had received word from his immediate boss, Undersecretary of State for Far Eastern Affairs Robert Hartland, that a fact-finding delegation had been appointed by the President to go to Mituyan and check on recent disturbing reports that had filtered out of Tuyan City. And, Hartland had made clear, it wasn't merely the newspaper stories he was referring to.

A short drive took him to the palace, and he was rapidly conducted to Mayna's quarters. Try as he would, he could not dispel a sense of impending doom. He berated himself for recommending the huge expenditure for a direct Teletype service between the palace and the Mituyan Embassy in Washington. That had been the first of many concessions Mayna had wrung out of him in return for her delights.

"Tarot is having lunch with the Premier," Mayna said, leading him to the sofa in her sitting room, "so you can have my Tat time all to yourself."

She sat down beside him. "I found out all about Mr. Krakhaur's—"
Whittelsie started.

"—problem with his little girlfriend. I'll tell you about it after you've had a drink."

Mayna knew exactly how to relax a man, Whittelsie thought, relieved it wasn't Krakhaur's latest news story she was about to mention. She expertly poured him a highball and seated herself close beside him; her bare leg pressing against him shone ivory under the open slit in her deep-red dress. Hastily, he gulped the drink, resolving once again not to chance indulging himself with his host country's number-two lady—number one in actual influence.

"I've had such a terrible morning," Mayna said, a feline look of contentment on her face. "Everybody is plotting against us. I had to go to the police station and personally talk to several young women who belong to a new reincarnationist group uncovered by Tarot's secret police." Carelessly, her hand rested high on his thigh as she turned to talk to him about the necessity of harsh measures against plotters. He had to force his mind to rise from his desire for that slim, delicate hand to reach higher—knowing so well what those tapering fingers could do to him—and concentrate on what she was telling him. "Whit," her voice came out, suddenly rich and throaty, unlike the high-pitched dainty public tone, "you haven't called or seen me for days. Why not? I've missed you, sweet man. Haven't you missed Mayna a little too?"

Of course he'd missed her and those exquisite techniques of hers. How could he explain that he tried to fight off coming to her and was always defeated by desire and a need he could not conquer. He pleaded his busy schedule, to which she laughed merrily, her fingers sliding up his thigh.

"Would you like me to tell you about Krakhaur and his pretty little toy, Alana, now . . . or later?" she asked, leaning to him, her lips close. He thrust his mouth to hers. One of her hands went to the back of his neck, the other moved directly to the swelling in his lightweight white trousers. Her tiny, pointed tongue darted around the inside of his lips; fingers played at the nape of his neck, inducing pleasurable shudders all through his back and shoulders.

After a few moments, Mayna's lips parted from his, and she whispered, "All right, Whit. Affairs of state later."

As she began her delightful preliminaries, gently unknotting his tie and opening his shirt, the ambassador kept wondering when a palace messenger would arrive at the door with the playback. Pulling the shirt apart, she bowed her head to his chest and ran her tongue around first one, then the other of his nipples. He groaned in pleasure as one of her hands returned to his trousers and expertly began unbuttoning them.

"Oh, Whit," Mayna whispered, "you *have* missed me. Don't let it ever be so long again." Quickly she freed him completely and then fell on her knees on the floor in front of him. Her high pile of swirling black hair bobbled before him as he looked down at her and then, unable to restrain himself, he dug both hands into the raven tresses and forced her face tightly against him.

Mayna wriggled free and laughed. "Oh, no, Whit. You do not go anywhere without me, darling."

Tantalizingly, she took off his shoes, helped him undress and then led him to the bed opposite the sofa. Whittelsie lay on his back and then Mayna, releasing one snap on her dress, stood naked before him. She stepped out of the rich red heap of silk at her feet and laid herself on top of his body.

"Today is mine, darling," she murmured. "I need everything. I want you to make me hurt. Hurt little Mayna, you great big long nose!" she cried. She lifted herself up slightly, and reaching down expertly guided him into her.

Now she sat upon him, her thighs flanking his, meeting his quickening undulations with her own. He looked up into her slanting eyes, staring down hotly at him, her face contorting in passion, her mouth open, teeth working, biting her lower lip as the words of erotic exhortation she first whispered, then cried and now shrieked at him poured from her. He suddenly believed all he had heard about her libidinous delight in witnessing the tortures of political prisoners.

Mayna's scream stabbed at him just as his own ejaculation seared her. Savagely, she fell forward and viciously sank her teeth into his shoulder. Whittelsie yelled in pain. Her head lolled from the shoulder, her glazed and hooded eyes seeming to stare through his.

All at once Whittelsie knew terror. He had never seen Mayna this way. Before, her own pleasure always seemed to derive from giving ecstatic pleasure to him. This time she had indulged herself in such passion that he knew instinctively she could literally kill in its throes. He lay silent, not daring to disturb her. For he also knew that in some savage way he had derived intense gratification from Mayna's primitive display of pure sensuality. And this realization frightened him all over again.

In tones still guttural, Mayna finally said, "Oh, God, you large long nose! You did hurt me. We Mituyan women are small, you know."

"How about my shoulder?"

"Um?"

"Look."

Mayna shifted her gaze. "Oh, Whit," she cried. "Did I do that? I'm sorry."

She sat up and smiled down at him. "I'm afraid for a few minutes I was somebody else. It's all right now. I'm your Mayna again. Oh, I feel so badly about your shoulder. Can I put something on it?"

Whittelsie sat up on the side of the bed. "Don't worry, it's just a bruise. But it's a good thing my wife is out of the country. I'd hate to have to explain it to *her*."

"From what you tell me, it's likely she wouldn't be seeing your bare shoulder or any other part of you bare," Mayna replied tartly.

Later, after they had both bathed and were sitting in Mayna's private parlor waiting for luncheon to be served, Whittelsie reminded her that she had some information for him about Krakhaur.

"The girl Alana has made a formal accusation against Krakhaur. I have a copy of it here, which I'll give you. He not only forced her to become his mistress to keep her job, which the poor girl valued highly, but he also intimidated her into collecting imagined grievances against Poramat for the attack he was planning to write on the Premier and his brothers."

"In my opinion, Mayna," Whittelsie said drily, "what you are telling me is a gross misstatement of the actual facts. But since they cannot be ascertained, and since Krakhaur has been a thorn in the side of the entire United States mission, if the Premier can expel him in a way that embarrasses neither your government nor my mission, I will only make a token protest. He is responsible for many of the embarrassing cables I receive from the State Department."

Mayna smiled with self-satisfaction. "I thought you'd look at it that way, Whit. Do you want to read the accusation the poor girl made?"

Whittelsie shook his head. He knew that the wily Poramat would have extorted documentation from the girl that could blight Krakhaur's professional career. Ordinarily, as an ambassador and an honorable human being, Whittelsie would have insisted on getting all the facts. But the latest cable from Washington had so upset him that he didn't care what happened to the newsman so long as the Country Team and the government came out clean.

"Mayna, I'm not fooled by this accusation. Don't think I am. But partly as a result of the irresponsible and sensational reporting coming out of Mituyan, and probably an irresponsible report by a member of our Country Team, I am receiving a delegation from Washington in ten days."

"What!" Mayna looked up at him in sudden alarm.

"It hasn't been announced yet, but the Secretary of Defense, the Chairman of the Joint Chiefs of Staff, the Assistant Secretary of Defense for Public Affairs, and the Undersecretary of State for Southeast Asia, plus a few more VIP's, are all coming to Tuyan City."

Mayna was clearly worried. "What's wrong?"

"I don't know, but the Tuyan City press corps hasn't helped us any."

"Well, we aren't planning to expel Mr. Krakhaur," Mayna said quickly. "As a matter of fact, since we released his girlfriend he has become a good boy. I just read his latest story."

"His latest?" Whittelsie looked at her, amazed at the calm reaction.

"I'll get it for you." She went over to her rosewood secretary, returning with two long sheets of Teletype paper.

"It's a good story. I like it," Mayna said, handing them to Whittelsie.

"He calls it 'The Mad Monk of Tiking' and shows how dangerous Han Li Phang really is. The Buddhists are all anarchists and subverted by the Communists."

"He said that?" Whittelsie asked, skimming the story. It hadn't been brought to his attention before, but then only the bad stories ever were.

"He hints at it. While I was at the police station," she added, "some Buddhists were brought in for questioning. They finally confessed organizing to bring down the government."

Whittelsie looked up to see the same frightening fanatic gleam in her black eyes and did not press for any further details on the interrogation of the hapless Buddhists.

"This is a sound story," Whittelsie agreed. "If these bonzes start trouble again, as my intelligence sources say they will, stories like this will help prepare the American public for the suppressive measures the Premier may have to take."

"That's the way we felt," Mayna said smugly.

"Where is Krakhaur's girl now?" Whittelsie asked.

"Probably with the Forresters. Poramat arranged for her to be released in Luna's custody. I begin to have doubts about Mike and Luna. They used to be good friends of the Palace, but I wonder, even after all we've done for them, if they are still loyal to us. Mike is doing a lot of strange things. He was up with the Groats, you know. Tarot thinks he's trying to get into the illegal opium trade."

Whittelsie, who by now had been briefed on the use of Forrester as a JRB agent, laughed aside the suggestion. "That's nonsense, Mayna. I've known Forrester for ten years in three countries. He may not be the most savory character, but at least he's always kept within the law of the country in which he was operating."

Just then Mayna's phone gave a discreet buzz. She picked it up and listened, said merely, "Yes, right now," and hung up.

The ambassador looked up at her questioningly.

"That was the Teletype operator," she said. Whittelsie's stomach reacted violently. "Apparently another story by Mr. Krakhaur is just coming through. We will get the carbon copy. The operator is taking the original to the Premier. . . . He sounded quite upset."

Mayna stood in the middle of the room pensively. "I can't think what it could be," she mused. "The cable office has standing orders to submit all news stories either to Counselor Tarot or to me before sending them out. We always let them go, of course, but at least we can delay them a day or two sometimes."

Mayna walked over and sat down beside Whittelsie. "Krakhaur must have found what the journalists call a 'pigeon' to take his story out. Well, we'll soon see. Don't look so worried, Whit," she laughed. "Whatever happens, you can always come to Mayna to forget for a while."

She moved closer to him, stroking the back of his neck. A gentle rap sounded at the door, and she went over and returned with the two long Teletype sheets. She sat down to read them beside the ambassador who, afraid of what he was about to see, peered over her shoulder.

Each sentence wrung a sharp cry from Mayna. She flung the papers aside. "This is a cruel insult to the army and the government of Mituyan! This last sentence—an atrocity against our people. Listen, Whit, listen to what your Mr. Krakhaur leaves the American people believing at the end of his story."

She fumbled for the spot and read aloud, her voice rising in pitch: " 'The tragic incident at Rishket is repeated frequently all over the country of Mituyan. Villages and hamlets, built up at great expense to American taxpayers, are rendered anti-government and sometimes pro-Communist by cowardice and ineptness on the part of the Mituyan government. So this is the way dedicated Americans are dying out here, the advice and aid they traveled halfway around the world to impart to a backward and underdeveloped nation, ignored.' "

Mayna slapped the sheet of paper in anger. "What are you going to do about this?"

"Do you suppose it's true?"

"What difference does that make? He says we are cowardly and corrupt. Oh!" her eyes blazed, "I would personally like to get Krakhaur into our secret-police headquarters. I would make them keep him alive for a week, while he prayed and begged for death!"

"This is very serious, very," Whittelsie agreed, wanting to get away from Mayna and the palace immediately.

He stood up. "I think I'd better go right now and find Macker. I'll have Ted Baum find Krakhaur and bring him to my office. Please express my deepest regrets to the Premier."

"He probably has the police out looking for Krakhaur right now." Mayna's voice trembled.

"Tell Counselor Tarot or Premier KaritKi I would appreciate it if they would let me check out all the facts before they make any hasty moves. With the Washington delegation coming so soon, we should avoid creating an incident."

"Incident!" Mayna screamed. "What do you call this story? We'll take Alana and Luna Forrester back to Poramat's jail for this."

"Please, Mayna, don't talk so irrationally. Let me talk to Krakhaur before anything is done. He has the power, whether dead at your hands or alive and given sufficient provocation, to cause the government of the United States to seriously consider cutting off all aid to your country. Please, don't forget that."

"How can you Americans have such a decadent, water-blooded government?" Mayna cried. "We torture to death anyone who tries to overthrow our government. You treat a man like Krakhaur, trying to bring about our downfall, like a hero!"

Mayna's railing echoed through her chambers as Whittelsie beat a hasty retreat.

CHAPTER THIRTY

ROGER KRAKHAUR GRIPPED his battered but serviceable Olivetti portable typewriter, thankful that he'd been able to book a seat on the early-morning Air Force C-123 milk run that lumbered around the country daily with freight and personnel. He had packed his most cherished possessions in his B-4 bag and briefcase, since he expected not to see Tuyan City again so long as KaritKi was Premier.

A U.S. Army truck in the military section of the Tiking Airport transported him into downtown Tiking, and a minicab delivered him to Mike Forrester's private dock on the Tiking waterfront. He quickly entered the main salon of the *Promise,* where to his surprise he found Mike just finishing breakfast.

"Well, welcome aboard, Roger. What took you so long?" Mike asked, grinning. "Your breakfast's been ready for half an hour."

"The milk run was late—" Krakhaur began to say. Then: "How did you know I was coming?"

"A lot of people have been doing one hell of a lot of talking about you since last night," Mike answered, as a white-jacketed messboy deposited a cup of coffee in front of Krakhaur.

"I thought only Ted Baum knew where I was heading," Krakhaur said, sipping his coffee gratefully.

"Ted Baum had the good judgment to call Jack Cardinez as soon as you left him last night. They work together on certain projects. Cardinez called Lawton, who sent a heavy security patrol out to Rishram about midnight to bring me into Tiking. As I said, a lot of us have lost a lot of sleep over you.

Krakhaur apologized sincerely.

"Well, you'll have a chance to make it up to us. We've got big ideas for you."

"I doubt if I'm apt to be around here much longer."

"That seems to be the consensus of opinion. About six more hours."

"Hell, they always give you twenty-four hours to get out of the country," Krakhaur protested. "Besides, I've got to see Alana. That's why I came up here."

"She's waiting for you at Rishram. We'll drive over together, complete with security patrol."

Krakhaur looked relieved. "I'm not worried about the Mitcoms as much as the secret police."

"That's what our security is for—to protect us from any ambitious plan Poramat or Yunakit might have to pull you in. However, we don't anticipate that the Palace will receive the playbacks before afternoon. That should give us time."

Krakhaur decided not to ask the obvious question: Plenty of time for what? He had been moving fast since leaving Tiking two days ago—three, now. It seemed incredible he had covered so much ground in that time. He'd let Mike carry the ball from here.

After breakfast Mike and Krakhaur bid Captain Batki goodbye and started off for Rishram in the Land Rover. On the outskirts of the port city, an open two-and-a-half-ton truck with twenty red-bereted Mituyan irregulars swung into the road behind them. Ahead, a jeep driven by a Mituyan irregular and with an American sergeant and a Mituyan officer in the back seat led the way for the entire hour-and-a-half drive to Rishram.

"We're in pretty good hands now. That's Sergeant Jennesen up ahead with one of the new Mituyan Special Forces officers. We have what the U.S. Special Forces call a split-A detachment camped in Rishram under the direction of Colonel Lawton. A hard charging young lieutenant and five sergeants make up the American complement, and there are about a hundred Mituyan civilian irregulars and six Mit Special Forces men."

Krakhaur was interested to know how the American and Mit Special Forces got along. "I remember some pretty dire predictions."

"I don't know how it is at other camps, but here Lawton went all out to find a good Mituyan officer—the fellow you see in the jeep ahead. When you meet him, you'll notice he seems to be about thirty-five and is still a first lieutenant. That's a very good sign—means he has no political connections. After all, General Dandig is thirty-five. And one young general, a special favorite of Mayna's, is twenty-eight. Worthless, of course."

As they drove along the road to Rishram, Krakhaur kept wondering whether he had done the right thing in filing the story. Yes, he knew; somehow the real truth had to start coming out. But Alana? Surely the regime wouldn't dare pick her up again. He had to leave it to Ted Baum to negotiate with the Palace on his behalf: he would refrain from writing a truly damaging series if they promised not to molest Alana. Of course, his story of Rishket would set off a chain reaction. . . .

"Ted Baum had a copy of your story hand-delivered to each member of the Country Team at eight this morning," Mike said. "But instead of thanking him for forewarning them, they now blame *him* for the story, on the theory that if he hadn't helped you get your information you wouldn't have given him an advance copy."

Krakhaur shook his head. "Baum is the squarest shooter in the whole mission. . . . Is that why you were sent to Tiking?"

With one hand Mike pulled a long, thin cigar out of his breast pocket and stuck it in his mouth.

Krakhaur lit it with a Zippo.

Mike puffed a few times and said, "Next business I'm going to get into is tobacco. They ought to be able to produce better cigars than this in Mituyan."

He took a deep drag on the cheroot. "You once told me you could take over the Hong Kong bureau if you ever had to get out of here. That still goes?"

Krakhaur nodded. "Confirmed yesterday morning in Bangkok."

"Good. Because what I'm going to tell you now has got to be treated as very secret information. Not even Whittelsie knows. You can stop me if you like. You may not want to be burdened with knowledge you have to keep absolutely secret until the right time."

"Are you asking me to spook it on the side?" Krakhaur chuckled.

Mike grinned back. "This is a role I detest, but I'm in this thing pretty far. It's like being a vampire. One of them comes along and gets his fangs into your throat, and the next thing you know you're looking out for fresh blood to bring into the unholy fold."

Mike pulled on his cigar. "And of course the reason *I'm* talking to you is so that anyone in an official capacity can always honestly claim they never saw you, talked to you, or had any contact with you."

"Understood," said the journalist, his senses alerted. "If it's anything at all that will help get the KaritKi regime out of this country, I'm for it all the way. What do you want me to do?"

"OK. Here's what's happening. General Dandig in Tiking, along with your friend the Mad Monk and a number of Buddhist leaders and army generals, both Anglican and Buddhist, have been plotting a coup to bring down KaritKi." Krakhaur seemed scarcely surprised. OK. But they're missing one major ingredient: a popular national figure whom all the people will rally around and support. This leader has got to be in favor of the elections and assert authority pro tem. The leader has been found. He's living in Hong Kong."

"Barkoon!" Krakhaur exclaimed.

"Right. He has been discreetly sounded out by certain Mituyan civilian and military leaders of the coup. Barkoon would apparently love to come back as King, acting as the symbol of stability, while the people went about their elections to decide on a government that would have the real power."

"Now that makes what I call sense!" Krakhaur seemed genuinely enthused. "The people need the pageantry of a king, particularly out in the boonies where they have no symbol of central government. What do you want me to do?"

"Well, you're on your way to Hong Kong. When you get there, no reason why you wouldn't interview Barkoon for a story, right?"

"I'm sure I would have thought of it."

"So, you write a series of articles on what a masterful, potentially wise and fair statesman Barkoon is. He is intensely interested in what is happening in Mituyan and very concerned for the welfare of his people. But Barkoon is very much afraid that between KaritKi and the Mitcoms there isn't a chance for a fair election. You get the drift?"

"Perfectly. I use my name and the syndicate to make a reasonably prestigious figure out of ex-King Barkoon. Barkoon for King!" Krakhaur intoned sarcastically. "Have you been keeping score on his escapades? In Banthut they still talk about how much he paid families for fifteen-year-old girls."

"You don't like the idea?" Mike looked at him sharply. "OK. All I ask then is that you forget everything I've told you."

"I don't usually like the idea of writing anything I don't believe in personally. But in this case I will go along—enthusiastically. Anything to get KaritKi out before it's too late."

"Good," Mike said, relieved. "Now there's another little assignment you can do, and this one you *will* believe in wholeheartedly. Tell the whole truth as you know it about the KaritKi regime, even what they did to Alana. We must make people realize what a menace he is to the security of Mituyan, Southeast Asia, in fact all of free Asia, because the Communists will take over for certain if he remains the dictator here."

"Amen! That's what I've been trying to say, and look how the Country Team abuses me. I wonder why, instead of automatically calling every pessimistic story we reporters file a sensation-mongering pack of lies, the U.S. mission doesn't make an impartial study of our charges to see if perhaps we may be right in saying we're losing this country fast."

"I can't answer that one for you. I know as well as you that the Country Team tries to give their bosses in Washington what they think the administration wants—fairy tales with happy endings. But from what I hear there may be some changes in the Country Team before long. You can't quote me, and I don't know this for a fact, but Cardinez knew something when he talked to me this morning. He has personal lines to certain very important people in Washington."

"Pardon me for being indiscreet, but how high in American government circles does this interest in a coup go?" Krakhaur watched Mike intently, waiting for the answer.

"I don't have that information in any detail," Mike replied. "On the Country Team level, my hunch is the preliminary planning has never gone above the chief of JRB, Jack Cardinez. However, I have the distinct impression that in Washington very highly placed members of the administration are pushing the plan directly with the President." He looked at the journalist. "I'm quite certain, however, that Ambassador Whittelsie has absolutely no idea that such a course is being considered."

"OK, Mike. That's good enough for me. I'll do my best to help."

"Welcome aboard."

"There's just one problem—Alana. In the first place, if I write exposé pieces they'll surely grab her. Then they have that statement signed by her, saying how I seduced her and made her say untrue things about the government." A smile spread across his face, and he glanced at his watch. "There's only one way I can really successfully flay KaritKi's regime."

Mike laughed. "We spooks are ahead of you already. Alana doesn't know it, but she's packed, ready to go. She even has a U.S. passport. A light twin-engine plane belonging to Global Air Charter Company will be landing at Rishram about one o'clock this afternoon to pick up two passengers for a trip to Hong Kong. The pilot is prepared to accept your personal check for the trip. In Hong Kong you'll be contacted and reimbursed for your expenses in cash."

"Mike!" Krakhaur exclaimed happily. Then his face clouded. "But will Alana go for this? After all, I can't kidnap her, much as I'd like to."

Mike nodded. "That's the real problem. They've made an emotional cripple out of her. Luna and I hope it's only temporary, but, quite frankly, Roger, we're worried—although I personally think this adventure might make her whole again, if anything can."

The security column entered the stately symmetrical rows of rubber trees. A short while later Mike pulled the Land Rover up to his doorway; the jeep stopped beside him and Sergeant Jennesen jumped out, touching his green beret.

"Colonel Lawton told us to be real alert, Mr. Forrester. There'll always be one American with the Mits on guard detail." He watched the truck halt twenty yards back from the house.

"That's good to know, Sergeant." The Mituyan officer strolled up, and Jennesen introduced Lieutenant Pakitlat to Mike and Krakhaur. If the Mituyan officer recognized the journalist's name, he made no acknowledgment. He excused himself to take charge of the men climbing out of the truck.

"He's as good a Mit officer as I've run into in this country," Jennesen said. "Knows his business. Wish all the Mit Special Forces officers were like him." Then he too went to see after his men.

"Roger, time is short and Alana is alone on the terrace. You'd better talk to her now," Mike suggested.

Krakhaur nodded and walked through the spacious living room to the flagstone terrace. He found Alana seated in a high-backed wicker chair that framed her gaunt face.

"I filed the story," he said, trying to sound cheerful.

"I'm glad," she replied and continued to stare out vacantly over the rubber trees at the distant mountains.

There was a long silence. Finally Krakhaur said: "I'm certain to be expelled, but I have the job of Hong Kong bureau chief of the syndicate waiting for me."

"I'm glad."

Roger pulled up a footstool and sat down in front of her, looking up into her deep-set eyes. "I want you to come with me."

She looked at him a little startled. "Why ever for?"

"I need you. I love you, Alana."

She shook her head slowly. "I'm no good to you or any man, now."

"Don't say that, darling." He moved upward to kiss her, but she turned her head slightly, emphatically. "I *do* love you, I want us to be married when you're ready. I need you with me when I really start to write about the KaritKi government. If you were in Hong Kong I could blast the whole Palace gang right out of Mituyan. And you can help me."

"How?" She looked at him questioningly. "How can I help?"

"I couldn't write about Mituyan unless I knew you were safe. And of course there's that confession, accusation, or whatever it was they made you sign. If you were in Hong Kong with me it would never stand up."

"Oh, Roger. I'm so ashamed I signed it—"

Krakhaur reached up and gently pressed his fingers to her lips to stop her, but she would not be silenced. "I'd be no good for you anyway." The stricken look on her face made his throat lump. "I'll never be able to have any man. It was all so disgusting and degrading. I'll never look at another man without thinking what he could do. . . ."

"Darling, let me try to help you."

"Maybe if we'd had each other when you wanted . . . if those beasts hadn't . . . Oh! I can't talk about it!" She put her hands to her face and began sobbing.

Krakhaur stood and put his arms around her shoulders.

"No!" she sobbed. "Don't touch me!"

Shaken, Roger saw with relief that Luna had come out on the terrace. She went to Alana and gently took her by the arms. Slowly, the girl stopped sobbing.

"Alana, dear," Luna began, "Roger loves you. He needs you with him in Hong Kong. Go with him."

"I can't, Luna. Not now. Don't you see?"

"But dear, now is the time you can do the most to help Roger and our country. He'll never need you more than he does right now. A week from now, perhaps even tomorrow, will be too late."

She seemed on the verge of tears again. Krakhaur stood by helplessly.

"I'm sorry, dear, but I have to speak frankly." Alana felt the compelling new edge to Luna's tone. "We all think you're enough of a woman to fight back against KaritKi now that you have the chance. If you are, you're woman enough to get over this thing. Roger loves you and needs you in Hong Kong."

"It's so unfair!" Alana cried. "To Roger too. Suppose those animals made me pregnant?"

"We'll have it taken care of immediately in Hong Kong, darling," said Krakhaur.

"Oh, Luna, I can't go through with it!"

Luna shrugged. "Suit yourself. You cripple Roger's chances of doing something that could really help bring about the change our country needs."

"Roger doesn't need me. He can find all the women he needs in Hong Kong."

"All right, Alana," Luna said crisply. "You might as well go upstairs if you're going to have a fit of self-pity. Go on." Then to Krakhaur: "I'm sorry, Roger. I see I misjudged her."

"Drink, Roger?" It was Mike, who had quietly joined them on the terrace.

The reporter didn't move at first. Then he turned slightly, glancing anxiously at Alana. She was sitting up straight now. She closed her eyes tightly for a moment; then, suddenly opening them, she stood up and walked toward the bar, where she stopped and turned.

"Roger . . . I'm sorry. I've been so thoughtless. Can you forgive me?"

"Forgive? After all you've been through?"

"If you really need me"—she paused—"if I can really help by being with you, of course I'll go."

Roger took two long strides and held the frail form in his arms. Luna sought her husband's eyes, smiling triumphantly.

"I don't know how you're going to arrange it," Alana went on, "and I haven't anything to wear—"

"Everything is taken care of, darling," Krakhaur interrupted. "We'll get you what you need in Hong Kong."

"Luna, what about you?" Alana asked anxiously. "They said they'd hold you responsible for me."

"You do your part by going. I'll do mine by staying." Luna looked out over the rubber trees. "We've got a lot to fight for, Mike and I." As Mike put his arm around her, they heard the sound of an airplane flying low.

"Here comes your flight," Mike said. "The sooner you're both out of the country, the better we'll feel."

"Just let Alana and me go upstairs a minute. I want to put a few things together for her," Luna said.

"OK, but make it quick. I don't like leaving that pilot out on the landingstrip alone too long."

"Is it secured?" Krakhaur asked.

"Jennesen has a few men guarding it. It's the secret police I'm thinking about."

"Already?"

"Once KaritKi makes up his mind, they won't waste any time." Mike looked at his watch. "One o'clock. We can expect action damned soon."

Ten minutes later Roger and Alana were boarding the speedy little Cessna 310. Mike and Luna watched the plane taxi down the runway, turn into the wind, heard the engines roar as the propellers bit into the air, and waved a last time as the ship streaked ahead and quickly lifted into the sky, its landing gear immediately retracting.

"It's like seeing the bride and groom off," Luna whispered.

"I'm afraid they have a lot of hard times ahead of them in that department," Mike replied. "Anyway, Jack Cardinez' mob will be much relieved. You did a fine job, Mrs. Michael Benning Forrester, Jr. Now we can get set for the inevitable visitation from the secret police."

They drove back to the plantation house in silence. To their astonishment—and chagrin—MacWhorter and Major Song were both waiting for them. The American cadre leader looked worried. Mike asked how things were at Rishket. "I suppose the people are still pretty bitter."

"To be expected," MacWhorter replied. "But Jerry did his work well before he got it. The people still have faith in the Americans, thank God; Major Song and the whole cadre have been helping rebuild houses."

Mike motioned them to the terrace. "Any more deaths from wounds?" he asked.

"Not in the village," MacWhorter answered. "I understand a couple more children died in the district hospital. You and Luna and all the other medical people saved a lot of lives, for which the people are grateful."

"What's the trouble then, Scott?"

"I'm afraid I've got some bad news for you, Mike."

Mike glanced at Luna, who stood resolute. "Go ahead," he said.

"Well, one of the first things we do when we move in with a cadre is to set up an intelligence net in the area. Those guerrillas are still in the Rishket hills, of course."

"We expected that," Mike replied.

"But what I came to tell you is this. Last night one of Major Song's agents reported that a guerrilla agit-prop squad was coming into a hamlet north of Rishket. So he went out with a patrol and brought back two prisoners. He interrogated them separately, and they both told him the same thing."

"Yes?"

"Both prisoners said that their leader was North Vietnamese."

Song looked down at his feet ashamed. "I do not make mistakes often," he said. "But some way, the Vietnamese Communist escaped death at the Golden Dragon. I do not understand it. He must have left before the explosion. But why? I can only think he must have gone to look for Frakit."

"The point is, Mike, Can has surely figured out what happened, and I'm afraid he'll really start harassing you and Rishram."

Mike's hand tightened on Luna's shoulder. "I was afraid of this."

"How's your security here?" Scott asked.

"I will gladly assign half my cadre to help protect your house, Mr. Forrester," Song offered.

Mike shook his head. "I've got half of a U.S. Special Forces A detachment and a hundred or so irregulars camped around the place. I just hope the army doesn't waste any time hitting the Mitcoms."

"Major Song has been able to keep their location pretty well plotted," MacWhorter replied. "It looks like my own cadre will be in on the operation. I don't know what's holding up the attack."

"Well, I appreciate your coming here and telling me. We'll be doubly prepared. I'll pass the word to the detachment commander. We'll try to tighten up the plantation's security." Mike smiled wanly at his visitors who—quickly, it seemed—took their leave.

Mike sent for Sergeant Jennesen and told him about Can's escape.

"We'll have to maintain a fifty-percent alert every night," the sergeant said. "I'd also like to secure the house better."

"I guess I'd better send my wife to a safer place," Mike said quietly.

"I'm staying with you," Luna said with determination. The high-backed wicker chair rose above her head, framing her oval face, her wide luminous eyes and thick black hair.

Mike mixed her a cocktail. "Well, I *had* hoped to have a few days of peace to see how our rubber is doing, before going back to my nefarious duties with Colonel Lawton and company."

The two men heard the sound of light vehicles coming down the road.

Mike calmly looked at his watch. "Yes, just about the time I would have expected them. Sergeant, are you armed?"

"Got an AR-15 automatic rifle in my jeep in front of the house."

"Maybe you'd better have it handy."

"Right." Catlike, he went quickly to his jeep and returned just as the first of three staff cars pulled up in front of the house.

"You won't see me, Mr. Forrester, but I'll be there if you need me."

"Thanks, Sergeant. I hope this will be a peaceful confrontation. But Poramat's boys have a tendency to do rash things."

There was a loud, insistent rapping at the front door. Mike went to answer it and found two Mituyan secret-police officers, easily identifiable from their dark glasses. Behind them, Mike saw three men in two of the staff cars, only a driver in the third.

"Mr. Forrester?"

"I'm Michael Forrester. And you are?"

"We are from Colonel Yunakit's province headquarters," one of the plainclothesmen said. Both wore white shirts, khaki pants, and .45-caliber automatic pistols in shoulder holsters. "We would like to ask you some questions."

"Come in and let's talk." Mike did not lead them to the terrace but stopped in the living room and gestured toward two chairs. They did not sit down.

"How can I help you?" Mike asked pleasantly.

"We have an official communication for Mr. Roger Krakhaur, the American journalist."

"Oh, I'm sorry you didn't come earlier," Mike said. "Mr. Krakhaur was here but he left about one-thirty or two o'clock."

"That's impossible. We have had the road from Rishram blocked since two o'clock."

"He left by airplane," Mike explained. "Too bad you missed him."

"We have written permission from Colonel Yunakit to search your house." The secret policeman pulled a piece of paper from a pocket and handed it to Mike. It was indeed a letter addressed to Mr. Forrester or to whom it might concern, demanding the right, in the name of Premier KaritKi, to search the premises of said Mr. Forrester. Angered though he was, Mike stuffed the paper into his pocket and offered to give the officers a tour of his house.

The one who had been doing all the talking asked for the letter back, but Mike insisted on keeping it as a receipt, signifying that he had complied with the province chief's demands. After a short argument, during which Mike insisted he would be glad to submit to a search of his premises but would not return the paper, the secret-police leader waived his request. He then demanded that two more of his agents accompany them on the search.

"I will not permit four of you to tramp through my house," Mike said, really enraged now. They finally settled for *one* more man, who was hastily summoned, and Mike took the three agents through the entire first floor and then upstairs. They looked under beds, in closets, pulled draperies aside, pounded walls—to no avail.

"If you would tell me what you are looking for, I might be able to help," Mike offered.

"Our orders are if we do not find Mr. Krakhaur we must bring in the journalist's woman, Alana, who is your guest."

"Ah. If you'd told me that in the first place, I could have saved us all a great deal of time. She went away with Mr. Krakhaur."

"Where did they go?"

"I believe I heard Krakhaur mention Hong Kong," Mike replied.

"Was this an American Air Force plane?"

"No, it was civilian," Mike replied, further infuriating the police leader by his patronizing tone. "A red, twin-engine aircraft, as I recall."

One of the secret policemen had wandered out to the terrace, and he let out a shout. The other two hurried to join him and found Luna sitting serenely, reading a magazine and sipping a cocktail. Mike, right behind them, said: "Gentlemen, allow me to introduce my wife, Mrs. Forrester. Darling," he continued, "these three gentlemen are from Colonel Yunakit's headquarters. They didn't believe me when I told them that Roger had left by plane with Alana earlier today."

The leader approached Luna. "Ah, yes—Mrs. Forrester. We have orders to bring *her* back to district headquarters with us if we can find neither the American journalist nor his woman."

He turned to Mike with a sneer. "I regret that we must take your wife with us for questioning. She pledged her word to the province chief and Counselor Poramat that she would be responsible for the conduct of the journalist and his female companion."

Mike's eyes narrowed and hardened. "That I will not permit."

Ignoring the protest, the secret-police leader moved toward Luna, taking a pair of handcuffs from his belt. Instantly Mike was upon him, chopping him in the back of the neck with the sharp edge of his palm. The police agent sagged to his knees, dropping the handcuffs, which clanked to the terrace. By the time he regained consciousness Mike had disarmed him.

Furiously he screamed at his two companions to shoot the American, only to see his men, stiff with fright, hands held high, staring into the snub muzzle of Sergeant Jennesen's AR-15.

"You will regret this, Mr. Forrester. I am acting on the highest orders, from Counselor Poramat himself."

"You won't live to tell him if you and your men don't leave here immediately," Mike replied in tight tones. He stooped, picked up the handcuffs, and locked the secret-police agent's hands behind his back. Then prodding him in the back with his own .45, Mike searched his pockets until he found a key chain.

"I'll see you in the province prison," the agent hissed. Mike swung a punch to the ear with his left fist full of keys, and the agent pitched forward on his face. As the officer again lay semiconscious, Mike went through the keys until he found the one for the handcuffs. This he slipped into his own pocket, returning the rest of the keys to the man's pocket. Then he kicked the agent into consciousness. This time he struggled to his feet in silence and made no comment.

"Now listen to me," Mike said. "This road is ambushed and mined by my people. If you do not go directly back to Tiking, you and your men will find yourselves in a fire fight against a much larger force than you can handle. If you try to turn around and return, you will be ambushed and killed. Is that understood?"

The leader nodded, hate glimmering in his eyes. Mike relieved the other two agents of their .45 automatics and tossed them onto the lawn beyond the terrace.

"Jennesen," he said, "just so there is no misunderstanding, let's have a few of your men surround the cars and give these boys a proper sendoff."

"Good idea, sir," Jennesen whistled softly, and forms in black pajamas seemed to materialize from the darkness, holding their rifles at the ready. The secret-police leader, his hands locked behind his back, seemed visibly shaken at what he had walked into.

"You know, Jennesen," Mike drawled. "Perhaps we should kill them all right now. In Tiking they'd think the Mitcoms did it."

"Good idea." The Sergeant sighted down the barrel of his rifle and immediately all three agents fell to their knees, begging for their lives.

Mike and Jennesen pretended to consider. Then Mike said, "They cry so eloquently and promise not to tell so convincingly, perhaps we should let them go. If we change our minds, we can always radio ahead and have them ambushed."

Mike glared down at the police leader, whose face was now white with fear. "All right, we'll let you go. But remember, there are ambushes set out all along the road from here to Tiking. If even one of your cars so much as looks like it might slow down to turn back, all three cars will be blasted. Now go!"

Mike followed the three secret policemen out to their cars and watched them start up. The American-supplied staff cars gunned out of the drive and through the rubber trees back toward town.

Jennesen watched the tail lights twinkle through the trees. "Sir, what do you reckon the repercussions will be?"

"I don't know. First thing, I'm going to get Lawton on the radio and tell him what happened. You know, maybe we really should have killed them all."

"I was being straight when I said it." Jennesen's face became hard. "I've been around a lot of these countries, and I learned one damned thing good. You're always better with a dead enemy."

"I guess you're right, Jennesen. Well, too late now. I'll get on the sideband to Lawton."

"Mind if I come along, sir? I'd like to talk to the colonel too."

"Come on." He turned to Luna, who was still shaken but trying to retain her composure, and asked if she wanted to stay on the terrace.

"I'll stay close to *you*," she replied tremulously. "Oh, Mike, they really would have taken me to that horrible place, wouldn't they? My country isn't a good place any more. I think I never faced that fact before."

"The trouble is, neither of us ever had to face it before. You know these things, but until they hit you where you live you ignore them as long as things are going well for you personally. You and I, darling, are now at war. Never forget that! We now have two enemies—the Mitcoms *and* KaritKi."

"You've also got some good friends, sir," Jennesen said.

"Right. I'm sure glad you were here, Sergeant."

"So am I. And I'm damned glad my counterpart wasn't. He just might have gone along with that slopehead slant-eye goon squad." He caught Luna's eye and flushed in embarrassment. "Excuse me, Ma'am. No offense meant to the Mituyan people."

"Of course not, Sergeant. Not *all* Mituyans belong to Poramat's secret police."

Luna and Jennesen followed Mike upstairs to the radio room, where he turned to the frequency he and Lawton used. It was a special band which, with foresight, American radio advisers had kept from receiving and transmitting equipment provided to the Mituyan Army and government. Mike soon was in contact with the colonel and explained what had happened.

"You did the only thing a man could do in your spot, Mike." Lawton's voice was reassuring. "*I'd* sure have done the same thing. But you and Luna are in real trouble now. What do you want me to do?"

"I think we'd better get into Tuyan City and try to talk to KaritKi or Dhuna," Mike replied. "I don't think the Premier would have ordered my wife arrested; I'm not even sure Poramat did. But I damned sure wasn't going to let the secret police take her. Now they'll probably go after me for interfering with special-police agents in the performance of their duty."

"By tomorrow they'll have roadblocks out. I'll have a civilian plane pick you up at dawn tomorrow morning. When you get to Tuyan City, go see Jack Cardinez."

"Will do, Fritz. By the way, it might be just as well if Sergeant Jennesen got out of here with us. They won't be back tonight, but they'll probably come back in battalion strength tomorrow."

"Good idea. We'll leave the rest of the contingent to guard the property."

"Good, Fritz. Well it looks like Luna and I are in for it from both directions now."

"Don't worry about KaritKi, at least not for a while. A jetload of VIP's arrives from Washington in a week. You can be damned sure Tarot isn't going to let an incident involving an American citizen crop up just now."

"That's good to know," Mike signed off. "We'll be looking for the plane at sunrise."

CHAPTER THIRTY-ONE

Both by memos and last-minute telephone calls, Ambassador Whittelsie had summoned each member of the Country Team to the special meeting; he had made it clear that no excuses for nonattendance would be accepted. Between returning from his visit to Mayna's apartment and the beginning of the meeting, he had talked at length to Ted Baum and General Macker. Now, with even Phil Dickerson present, he must prepare a solid, integrated U.S. and Mituyan front to face the delegation from Washington.

"Gentlemen," the ambassador began, "this is a most important session. Even though I know you all have special problems and complaints, I would appreciate it if you would help me stick to the agenda I have prepared and make only constructive comments apropos the points under discussion. Later in the week we can go over individual problems. Is that understood?"

Each member looked at Whittelsie in uneasy anticipation, wondering what had happened to make waves now.

"I have been advised," Whittelsie went on dramatically, "by the Secretary of State, that at the request of the President a delegation from the Departments of State and Defense will be arriving for an inspection trip in about ten days."

Grady Rourke's expression didn't change, but his heart thumped. *He* would come out clean. It must have been his unilateral report to the director of the Agency for International Development in Washington that had precipitated this visit. Things were obviously coming apart at the seams in Mituyan, and he had been the first to go on record to his boss that the ambassador and other members of the Country Team were undermining his efforts to distribute to best advantage the huge quantities of goods coming in from the United States.

"Detailed travel plans will arrive later," Whittelsie continued. "The cable indicated that the Secretary of Defense himself would head up the delegation."

A smug smile tinged the corners of General Macker's lips. So they had taken notice of his secret cable at Defense, he thought. Well, it was about time the military thinkers cracked down on this raunchy squad of civilians. At least nobody could blame *him* for the mess here. He'd gone on record, the first to do so, that it was rout step all over Mituyan. The ambassador didn't support him, the damned spook was trying to undermine him, the Public Affairs chief was blowing security every day, and the USOM head was letting the Mits steal more than half of everything sent into the country.

Whittelsie gave Baum a meaningful look. "The Secretary will be accompanied by the Undersecretary for Public Affairs." Baum was surprised. He had heard nothing from the Information Agency presaging such a visit. Uneasily, he conjectured on the reasons for this inspection. The unfavorable stories in the press were obviously partially to blame. He knew that the entire Country Team and most of the Washington bureaucracy expected information officers to keep bad reports out of the papers and get good stories published. The fact that blunders and untoward events—not the information officers—were responsible for stories being published never entered the minds of officialdom.

Whittelsie leaned over the table, looking from face to face. "The Undersecretary of State for Southeast Asian affairs will represent the Secretary. I will soon receive a complete list of the members of the party."

Filmore Dickerson tugged at an ear. Robert Hartland was an old friend of Jack Cardinez, he knew. Could Jack have been doing a little unofficial direct communicating?

"Undersecretary of State Hartland has had occasion to be critical of our work over here, as you all know," Whittelsie went on. "We must try to convince him we are on the right track, doing our best, and that the situation in Mituyan is not nearly as critical as the journalists of the Tuyan City press corps would have the public believe."

General Macker glowered at Ted Baum. "If our Public Affairs chief could control the press a little better, we wouldn't have this big flap from Washington." Macker pulled out a pack of cigarettes before remembering that even Grady Rourke now suppressed his urge for tobacco in the ambassador's office. He jammed the cigarettes back into his pocket. The other members of the team shot brief looks of annoyance at Ted Baum.

"Let's try to stick to the agenda," Whittelsie said drily. "The purpose of this impending visit is twofold: The first is to make a study of progress on the elections. I understand they are bringing a professor in government from some university with them."

"My God," Macker roared, "don't we have enough professors and researchers, living better than they ever did before or ever will again, crawling all over this mission? I know of four separate research projects costing the taxpayers over two hundred thousand dollars, and we've had all the answers ourselves for a year. Doesn't the administration believe what its own full-time government employees tell it? Seems like information has to cost a lot of money before anyone believes it."

The men around the table nodded in agreement. The high cost and unrealistic—to government officials at least—academicians were a constant source of irritation.

"I sympathize with your views, Willet. But right now, can we stick to the point?" Whittelsie looked around his circle again. "The second purpose of the visit is, and I use the language from the cable: 'A routine study of the problems we are facing in helping the Mituyan government combat the insurgency threatening it.' "

Whittelsie paused a moment. "I think the most important thing they're interested in is being satisfied that the elections will be run with absolute impartiality. One suggestion I have is to arrange for the delegation, or as much of it as is interested, to meet some of the anti-Communist opposition leaders who will be running for seats in the constitutional congress."

Keep this a "constructive" meeting, Dickerson told himself, thinking of recent agent reports that three respected and patriotic leaders of anti-KaritKi groups had been arrested and sent to the Isle of Stones before they could get their campaigns under way.

"This is our chance," Whittelsie continued, "to show Washington that things are not so bad as the press corps makes out. Both Defense and State want to make optimistic evaluations of the Mituyan situation to the American public. After all, we're right up against an election year in the United States too."

The ambassador turned to General Macker. "Willet, you arrange visits to some crack Mituyan outfits with high morale, whose officers and their American advisers work smoothly together. Get your dissidents out of town. You know how to do it. Just a few men can give a false overall impression."

"I'll handle my end," snapped Macker.

"Mr. Rourke, you can expect some scrutiny of your operation," Whittelsie warned. "The Undersecretary for Southeast Asia will want to see what's being done for the people in the villages and hamlets."

"I'll introduce him to Minister Branot," Rourke replied. "Branot can call any of the province chiefs the undersecretary wants to meet into Tuyan City. Like you said, my job is to work with the Palace—keep 'em all happy."

"The press has been pretty hard on you lately, Mr. Rourke," the ambassador said. "I hope you will be able to display some model hamlets out in the countryside."

The ambassador turned to the CIA station chief. "Phil, the cable indicated that some of our visitors would like to talk to a representative group of Buddhist leaders. Can you fix that?"

"I'll try, sir," Dickerson said. "We should be able to set up a meeting with the top monks of the Lodung and Dicut sects. The Lodung Buddhists believe in reincarnation, the theory of karmic debt; they're at odds with the Dicuts, who believe in ancestor worship. It'll be confusing, but perhaps we can help our visitors understand a little better what happens."

"Which is this Mad Monk?" Whittelsie asked.

"He's nothing but a political opportunist. He represents the smallest number of the faithful, but he's the most militant," Dickerson answered. "I will say Krakhaur did a damned good story on him. I understand even the Palace was pleased."

"We'll get to the subject of Krakhaur in a minute," Whittelsie said quietly. "What we must show this group from State and Defense is stability over here. All of us must work toward that theme in our briefings."

"Then I'll give you a list of a few Mituyan generals to keep them away from," Dickerson said quickly. "If they go to someone like Dandig, he's apt to ask if the U.S. would support him if he mounted a coup against KaritKi in order to ensure free elections."

Whittelsie nodded. "Yes, we must be careful."

"Another trouble spot is the Groat country," Dickerson went on. "The Mituyans are forcing counterparts on us who antagonize the tribesmen."

"That's a very sensitive political question. I'd like to keep away from the Groat problem entirely. . . . Next—the biggest problem we seem to be facing. Mr. Baum and I had a discussion before this meeting. I'll let him take over."

"By now everybody has read Krakhaur's latest piece in the Star Syndicate," Ted Baum began. "I just received a cable that it has caused a real furor, coming as it did the day after we announced—at the urging of the Mituyan Minister of Information—a big government victory at Rishket. The Public Affairs Office, along with the MAC-M Information Office, is known as the Liar's Academy as it is."

"Why don't you control these sensation-seekers, Baum?" Macker growled.

"If we'd give them some true information once in a while, I might be able to influence them, General. This story of Krakhaur's is true. I tracked it down. You, General, are bringing charges against Cunningham. What seems a little thing to you could end up in a full-scale investigation."

"As soon as I saw that story we checked Cunningham's record. He was passed over for major because he couldn't get along with a counterpart in Vietnam. Matter of fact, we just issued a statement that the captain was suffering from battle fatigue. He must be psycho to give out a story like that."

"Cunningham didn't give it out, General, someone else did. And you made a serious mistake, issuing statements without checking with the Public Affairs Office."

"Are you trying to tell me how to run my command?" Macker demanded angrily.

"Please, Willet, calm down," Whittelsie pleaded. "This is a serious situation. Ted Baum is as professional in his line as you are in yours."

"Well, I control my men a hell of a lot better than he controls the press."

"No man controls the American press, General," Baum snapped. "Not even the President of the United States. So let's quit using that phrase."

"Krakhaur should be expelled," the general muttered.

"In spite of our efforts to dissuade KaritKi this past hour," Whittelsie answered, "he has given the order for Krakhaur's expulsion. The journalist was in Bangkok, but unfortunately he returned. The secret police should have found him by now and given him twenty-four hours to leave Mituyan."

"Good!" Macker boomed. "Now maybe we can fight a war in peace!"

"There are plenty more journalists here, General," Baum reminded him. "Some of them are *truly* irresponsible, which Krakhaur is not."

"Well dammit all, Baum, what do we do?"

"May I suggest, General, that we stop reacting publicly to unfavorable stories? We only build up the ego of the reporter involved, especially if he really is a sensation-seeker." Baum stared intently at Macker. "My advice to you, sir, and to the rest of the mission, is the same that Abraham Lincoln gave to one of his cabinet members who was being bombarded by a particularly vitriolic critic: 'Don't get into a pissing contest with a skunk!' "

"Yes. . . . Well gentlemen," Whittelsie said hastily, "I think we've covered the problems for today. This meeting is adjourned."

PART VII

MISSION FROM WASHINGTON

CHAPTER THIRTY-TWO

THE RITUAL OF VIP's arriving from Washington to examine the situation in a country receiving U.S. economic and military assistance varies little from year to year and capital to capital. The size of the press contingent depends upon the importance of the country receiving the visitation and its value in the current world-news market.

The entire Tuyan City press corps turned out for the Secretary of Defense and his party, and was reinforced by Far East bureau chiefs from Hong Kong and Tokyo, who chose the occasion to take a sampling of the winds of discontent blowing across the country. Krakhaur's expulsion, the attempts by Mituyan officials to discredit him and the stories he was writing, combined with the worldwide interest in his rescue of the Mituyan girl, Alana, from Premier KaritKi's secret police, had bellowed up the fires of global curiosity in what had been an obscure little Asian republic on the U.S. dole. The final chapter of the Krakhaur saga had been written even as Washington officialdom was cramming the mission to Mituyan with last-minute instructions.

The Republic of Mituyan was putting enormous pressure on the United States and British governments to extradite Alana from Hong Kong, on the grounds that she had left without an exit visa. Moreover, as KaritKi pointed out, to Washington's embarrassment, Alana had somehow acquired a U.S. passport. And then, at a ceremony widely attended by the world press, Krakhaur and Alana were married just before the British governor general of the Colony of Hong Kong would have been forced to accede to Mituyan demands for the girl's return. Married to an American, she could not be extradited. World sentiment was now heavily anti-KaritKi, which acutely dismayed Whittelsie's Country Team.

It was eleven o'clock in the morning and Whittelsie and his team were arrayed in front of the new international airport, which had been recently constructed with USOM funds. A long flat-bed truck crowded with photographers had been driven out parallel to the red carpet stretched from the terminal along the concrete ramp. The mayor of

Tuyan City was present, and the Palace was officially represented by Minister of Interior Branot. Vainly, Whittelsie had urged Premier KaritKi and Counselor Tarot to be present at the airport, but this did not meet with Tarot's ideas of face. The visiting dignitaries should come to the palace to see the Premier and his brother.

A colorful company of palace guards was on hand, and the USOM-trained and -equipped Mituyan National Band was lined up blasting out martial music, as the United States government blue-and-white Boeing 707 screamed up to the ramp. Whittelsie and General Macker walked halfway down the red carpet to the steps being placed in front of the jet's door.

The mission from Washington deplaned in order of importance. Whittelsie shook hands with the Secretary of Defense and somewhat warily greeted Undersecretary of State Robert Hartland. Strictly speaking, Hartland was Whittelsie's immediate superior. The ambassador walked with them back to the air-conditioned VIP lounge, where a press conference was scheduled. Macker accompanied the Chairman of the Joint Chiefs and the Chief of Staff of the Army past the cameras and into the lounge, where the press was assembled. Ted Baum joined the Undersecretary of Defense for Public Affairs, while Grady Rourke greeted two AID officials.

The press conference lasted half an hour. The reporters discreetly avoided referring to some of the more sensational press stories of the past few days and asked, rather, whether the purpose of this visit was to study methods of escalating American involvement in the war against the Communist insurgents.

At a signal from Whittelsie, Ted Baum terminated the press conference with the announcement that the Undersecretary for Public Affairs would hold another news conference at five o'clock in the USIS auditorium. Whittelsie escorted the Secretary of Defense and the Undersecretary of State to the ambassador's residence, and the other members of the Country Team took care of those members of the mission specializing in their areas of concern. A cavalcade of automobiles whirled into town from the airport.

"Well, Mr. Secretary," Whittelsie said heartily, when they reached their destination, "I'm afraid we have a strenuous few days ahead for you. It's the hottest time of the year in Tuyan City too, but we have two air-conditioned limousines which will help keep exhaustion down."

He led the Secretary of Defense and Undersecretary of State Hartland to the large, cool living room and indicated the well-stocked sideboard. The Secretary of Defense demurred, but Hartland walked over to the array of bottles and picked up the round bottle of whisky approvingly. "I see you carry my brand in this saloon, Whit."

Whittelsie smiled. "Chivas is one of the few luxuries we allow ourselves out here."

Hartland made himself a Scotch and soda, carried it to a chair with a footstool, and sat down, putting his right foot up.

"Still bothering you after all these years?" Whittelsie asked solicitously. "I had a bolster put at the foot of your bed, just in case."

"Thanks, Whit," Hartland replied. "I appreciate your thoughtfulness, but I won't be staying at the residence this trip."

The ambassador looked startled. "But on all the lists we have you here. Surely you don't want to stay in a hotel."

Hartland shook his head. "Hell no, Whit. I'm not staying at a hotel; although for twenty-two years, since we got the Japs out of here, I've always liked the St. George. No, I'm staying with an old OSS buddy, one of your top men, matter of fact—Jack Cardinez."

"I didn't know you knew Jack," Whittelsie said weakly. Then to the Secretary of Defense he explained, "Cardinez is chief of JRB and Dickerson's deputy."

"I know Cardinez," the Secretary answered.

Whittelsie suspected this would not be an easy time for him, but he hadn't expected things to deteriorate so quickly. He and Phil Dickerson had both agreed that Cardinez, an outspoken activist, would be left out of the briefings. Delicately, the ambassador asked, "Jack is expecting you then? Surprised he didn't say anything to me."

"We thought it would be better to wait until I got here before announcing where I would be." Hartland took a long pull on his drink and stared meditatively at his right foot cocked up on the stool. "Jack was with me when I messed up my career in his line of work, as a matter of fact. Damned fool thing, stepping on a Jap mine after they'd surrendered. We were out with our hill-tribesmen guerrillas, policing the Japs up. Hadn't been for Jack, I probably wouldn't have a leg now."

In the years he had known Hartland, Whittelsie had never heard just what had happened to his foot, merely that it was a wartime accident. "I don't know whether Cardinez has a car, but I have put one at your disposal, Bob. Driver's a good, reliable man, well checked out by the Mituyan secret police."

"Thanks for the information, Whit. I'll be careful of him."

Whittelsie looked at Hartland in puzzlement. He had never been able to understand him and, moreover, it had shocked him and many other top foreign-service professionals when Hartland had been jumped over all of them, by the President personally, it was said, and made top man on Southeast Asian policy.

"I arranged for lunch here as soon as the others get settled into their rooms," the ambassador said, "and then we can go over the latest schedules. Premier KaritKi will receive us at four."

"Does he still talk as much as he used to?" Hartland asked. "When he was a guerrilla leader, he used to talk to the Jap prisoners for a day or two straight. We always thought it must have been a relief to them when he finally shot them."

"I sent a communiqué to the Premier telling him how tight our schedules were," Whittelsie replied. "But, after all, he is the Premier. As we say out here, 'Live or die with KaritKi.'" Whittelsie guffawed.

"After a four-hour session with him, I guess I sometimes feel like the latter."

"Whit, if you and the Secretary don't mind, I'm going to skip this lunch." The Secretary of Defense nodded in acquiescence. To Whittelsie, Hartland said, "Don't worry, I'll be back in time for the appointments. I'm sure you can brief me in a few minutes on what I have to do here and what I can avoid."

"You have plans other than what we have on the agenda?" Whittelsie asked.

"Nothing definite. I'll just poke around here and there. If you'll call that driver you mentioned, I'll leave you now for a while."

"How about security arrangements?" Whittelsie asked.

"I'll be all right, Whit. Why? Is terrorism in the cities getting worse?"

"KaritKi's secret police are doing a fine job trying to curb it. There are a few incidents a week. The most recent one was the bombing of a Chinese restaurant in Tiking—no Americans involved. But the Mitcoms may try something again with all of you in town."

"I'll be careful, and you'll always be able to find me," Hartland promised, standing up and walking with a slight limp toward the door.

Whittelsie accompanied him outside the residence and introduced him to his driver, who flashed a gold-tooth smile as Hartland stepped into the car and gave him the address of Cardinez' house.

Jack Cardinez greeted Hartland with all the warmth a man feels for an old wartime friend. Betty Cardinez welcomed Hartland fondly, and then the two men sat down in the air-conditioned study.

"This room is bug-proof, Bob. I check it every evening when I come home. Can I make you a drink?"

"A light Scotch and soda." Hartland sat down and cocked his foot up on the footstool that had been placed in front of the big easy chair.

Cardinez made a highball for each of them and took a seat opposite the Undersecretary. "What was Whittelsie's reaction when you told him you planned to stay with me?"

"He seemed dismayed." Hartland sipped his highball. "We're going to have to work fast, Jack."

"I'm ready. Phil Dickerson may be a bit of a problem, but we'll get the job done. I've enlisted the aid of a very knowledgeable American resident of this country to accompany you. For one thing he speaks Mituyan fluently and will give you the true shades of meaning when he translates for you."

"Excellent. I never stayed here long enough to learn more than the necessary words."

"I have one of the new turbo-prop Heliocouriers at your disposal. All I need now is a schedule of your availabilities."

"I'll know that this evening. Just have the plane and this chap standing by. What's his name?"

"Mike Forrester. He's in the other room now if you'd care to meet him. Incidentally, he's on the JRB staff. Very covertly. All the non-attributable negotiating we are doing goes through Mike."

"A very sensitive position for Mr. Forrester."

"It is. His biggest problem is that his wife is Mituyan. Half Mituyan, half English," he amended. "He's afraid that both the Mitcoms and the Palace will take it out on her if they find he's working so closely with us."

"Something like that Krakhaur situation. That was a messy one. It's amazing how a boy-girl thing like that captures the attention of the world. I guess her ordeal, as he wrote it, did more to turn opinion against KaritKi than anything that's happened so far. And as for Whittelsie—" Hartland shook his head. "We've known for some time he wasn't heavy enough to handle this assignment. The question was how to get rid of him nicely. His wife's family have powerful connections on The Hill, and she's back there touting what a fine job he's doing and how close he is to the Palace."

Cardinez couldn't restrain a grin. Hartland noticed it but only said, "Let's have Mr. Forrester in."

Cardinez left the den and returned a few moments later preceded by Mike.

"May I say, Mr. Secretary," Mike began, "how gratified I am, as an American with a big stake in this country, that someone high up in the administration has some interest in the true facts of what's happening in Mituyan."

"I am long on interest, too damn short on facts," Hartland replied. "I expect that between you and Jack I will return to Washington far better armed for the conferences that will follow this visit than the other members of our mission."

"Have you given Mr. Hartland a rundown on the situations we propose for him to see?" Mike asked.

Cardinez walked to a bare paneled wall and pulled down a large map of Mituyan from the ceiling. "The first situation he should be apprised of is the Groat-tribesmen problem." He smiled warmly at his old friend. "Both Bob and I have had experience at first hand with hill tribesmen in Asia."

"They're fine people if handled properly," Hartland observed. "During World War Two I found them to be excellent guerrillas, intensely loyal to those of us who worked with them. We hear very little about the hill people of Mituyan now."

Cardinez scowled. "If Whittelsie had his way, you wouldn't hear the name 'Groat tribesmen' mentioned. Yet"—he laid a hand on the northeastern quarter of Mituyan—"the Groats are the key to one quarter of the country, the most important quarter in some ways, because the trained Communist cadres coming into Mituyan are infiltrating through Groat country. If the Groats become actively pro-Communist, the Mitcoms could build up strength in these hills and crush the country at will."

Hartland nodded. "That much we know. The question is, how effective is your Groat program?"

"I'll let you find out the answer to that question yourself, Bob," Cardinez answered. "The Mituyans are very sensitive about foreigners working with the Groats. They think we spoil them, and they're afraid that if we arm and train them to fight the Mitcoms, they'll turn on the Mituyans instead."

"In other words," Hartland summarized, "Americans working with the Groats are about as popular with the Mituyan authorities as, say in the United States, northern civil-rights workers are in our Deep South."

"Good analogy," Mike agreed.

"So, since Ambassador Whittelsie is committed to upholding the whims, prejudices, and policies of the Palace and its province chiefs, he's not about to mess with the Groat question."

The conversation went on for two hours, covering election problems, press-corps hostility to the U.S. mission, increasing Mitcom incidents, and Country Team insistence that everything was going well in Mituyan and at the palace.

The undersecretary became more and more agitated at the lack of understanding in official Washington of the Mituyan war. Finally Hartland glanced at his watch. "I'll have to go back now, but I consider my mission here is to see personally what is happening in the countryside in the next few days."

Hartland walked over to the map and studied it a few minutes. "All right, set up tomorrow for an all-day and if necessary all-night visit to the Groat country. I'll clear myself with our mission. I think General Macker has an all-day session set up on military briefings."

"Good," Cardinez said. "In that case all the officers who really are concerned with the military situation in this country will be out at their posts where they can't upset the Secretary of Defense with unpalatable and critical facts. You'll find Major Charles Prescott an interesting and able authority on our problems in the Groat country."

Cardinez saw Undersecretary Hartland out to his car and then returned to lay out strategy with Mike.

CHAPTER THIRTY-THREE

EARLY THE following morning Mike Forrester and Undersecretary Hartland boarded an unmarked U-10 headed for Banthut. Jack Cardinez and Hartland had agreed that the less official connection between the CIA and the undersecretary's extemporaneous survey trip, the more credible his findings would be considered by jealous and suspicious heads of departments and agencies at forthcoming conferences in Washington. Fortunately, Hartland was not known to any but the top-echelon ministers in the Palace, and it had been decided he would operate under the cover of an American businessman interested in making investments in Mituyan.

When they landed, Hartland was immediately delighted with the climate. "I always forget how refreshing it is up here. I wonder why the capital of the country isn't moved to Banthut."

"The Tuyan River," Mike answered succinctly.

They called upon TrangTi first. The province chief was at once interested when Mike introduced his potential business associate whose firm had earmarked a large sum of money for investment in Southeast Asia.

"Mr. Hartland and I were associated in other enterprises," Mike explained. "Now he suddenly finds himself with a large amount of capital that must be invested outside of the conventional Western markets." TrangTi returned Mike's wink. "Naturally, Mr. Hartland and I would want you to be part of any venture we might organize in this province."

TrangTi, seeing a new opportunity to acquire U.S. dollars in return for sanctioning a dubious operation, was polite and informative. Mike led him into the subject of the hill tribesmen, and TrangTi talked for an hour on the suppressive methods he had instituted to control the Groats, preventing them from organizing independent rule or participating in any meaningful way in the Tuyan City government or the coming elections.

Mike's small organization had apparently cut sharply into the opium business, for TrangTi insisted that if they had any ideas of doing business in the tribal territories they should realize he was increasing his personal control over all the villages.

"The Mituyan and American Air Force still regularly bomb unauthorized Groat centers at my orders," he said with satisfaction. "In another month I think you will find that I control every Groat village in the province. And, Mr. Forrester"—TrangTi's smirk was irritating—"if we are going to work together, I caution you to keep me well informed of your activities. Do we understand each other?"

"I think so," Mike replied evasively.

"To be specific, Mr. Forrester, for every American Special Forces team in my province out with the tribesmen, there is or soon will be a Mituyan Special Forces team in command of the camp, reporting directly to me and to Counselor Tarot in Tuyan City. Your friends at the lodge no longer control the Groat program. We are, however, grateful for their advice and generous supplies and equipment."

TrangTi turned to Hartland. "There is always room for another successful business operation—providing, of course, that all dealings are closely coordinated with me." His gaze shifted back to Mike. "You may find that one of your agents here is in serious trouble because he did not clear a recent buying trip with me."

Mike felt his heart sink, but concealing his concern he merely said, "I have no agents here yet. Just friends and potential associates."

"Colonel TrangTi, we appreciate your time," Hartland said, having satisfied himself about the province chief's attitude toward the Groat tribesmen. "If Mr. Forrester and I decide we would like to do business here, we will surely be in touch with you."

The next stop was Charlie Tiger's shop. "We're probably being followed by TrangTi's secret police, anyway," Mike said. "They'd be disappointed if we didn't head straight for Charlie's emporium. They know we work together."

Charlie's number-three daughter was in the shop when they arrived, and although she greeted Mike with her usual pert politeness, he sensed an unaccustomed coolness in her manner. Instead of leading them directly to her father, she asked them to wait.

A few minutes later she returned and led them into the ornate office. Charlie Tiger's smooth face betrayed no emotion, but Mike felt he, too, was somewhat withdrawn. This time, as they had agreed, Mike introduced Hartland to the Chinese entrepreneur as a representative of the highest levels of U.S. government.

"Things bad here," Charlie said to Mike. "These elections make things very bad. Aiee! Two good men want election. One Chinese fellow, one Mituyan missionary work with Groat. Both make speech against KaritKi. Say, 'vote for me.' Now both not around."

"Were they put in prison?"

Charlie shrugged. "They not around."

Hartland shook his head. "We had a four-hour briefing yesterday afternoon, first at the palace with Tarot, then back at the embassy, on the effort being made by the Palace to ensure free elections and encourage opposition candidates."

"No more opposition this province," Charlie declared. Then to Mike: "We in trouble. Johnny Elephant gone ten day. Suppose be back five, six day ago. Also, my people see many, many boxes your merchandise, hand shaking on outside box, carry out to jungle from province headquarters. You know what that mean?"

"The Mitcoms are getting the poppy again and trading it for USOM supplies." Mike turned to Hartland. "I explained to you the way this thing works."

Hartland nodded. "I wish I could see it for myself."

"There may be a way," Mike said.

"Hey, Mike. You can find Johnny?" Charlie asked.

"Where was he heading?"

"Same place. That chief have another load. You can find last brother mine?"

"I'll try, Charlie Tiger. We have to see a few more people; then we go out to the lodge. Maybe they will know."

"You try, OK, Mike?"

"I will try. Maybe see you tonight."

"Wait here for you," Charlie replied.

Next on the agenda was a visit with the Reverend Maynard, and then to the office of Al Alvarro, the USOM provincial operations supervisor; he had just received orders to close up his office and report back to Tuyan City—but not before the end of the week. Mike noticed that the undersecretary's visage was growing progressively grimmer. It was almost noontime when Mike suggested that if he'd seen enough of Banthut they would take the plane and see some of these problems at their roots.

Hartland was sitting heavily in the back seat of the car, his right leg up on the front seat.

"Your foot bothering you?" Mike asked.

"It's all right. Probably the altitude. Yes, by all means, let's keep pushing on."

"Good. It's just a short hop by plane, but hell on the ground. I can testify from personal experience."

The small plane soon had them on their way to King Barkoon's hunting lodge. Hartland munched a sandwich and stared out at the jungle below, deep in contemplation. Less than half an hour later the Heliocourier circled the lodge and then made its landing, using up no more than fifty feet of the runway from touchdown to dead stop. A jeep driven by a big American sergeant in a green beret drove up, and the Special Forces man jumped out. "Good to see you again, sir. We wondered who was landing. Major Prescott wasn't expecting anybody today."

Mike shook the sergeant's hand. "Mr. Hartland, this is Sergeant Minelli, a veteran of my last mission into the Groat country. Minelli, meet Mr. Hartland, Undersecretary of State for Southeast Asia."

Minelli stared and gulped, then touched the sweatband of his green beret. "Afternoon, sir. Sorry we didn't know you were coming. We aren't really prepared. Major Prescott will sure be surprised. He *sure* will."

Mike climbed into the back of the jeep and Hartland sat up front, his right leg cocked up on the fender.

When they got to the lodge, Hartland and Mike followed the sergeant up to the Tactical Operations Center. "This place certainly has changed," Mike observed as they walked inside. An equal number of Mituyans and Americans were seated at desks, studying the maps on the walls.

"Every one of us has got a damned counterpart now," Minelli said. He led the visitors to a lounge off the main room presided over by an attractive Mituyan girl. "This is Lan. She'll give you a drink—coffee, a coke, whatever you want. I'll go get the major and be right back."

"Something seems to be on the sergeant's mind," Hartland observed. "I suppose we should have sent word we were coming, but then Jack said he wanted me to see things as they are, with no preparation."

Major Charlie Prescott, looking slightly unsettled himself, soon arrived and shook hands with the undersecretary.

"Sir, if we seem a little shook up, it's just that I was ordered out of

Tuyan City two days ago so there'd be no chance I'd meet any of you. And now you come out here to us."

"That's why," Hartland replied. "I want to find out all those things they're trying to"—he thought about his phrasing—"protect us from."

Prescott nodded. "It sure makes us feel good out here in the boondocks to know someone's interested in the truth." An embarrassed half-smile crossed his face. "If this is a covert visit, we have one little problem, sir. There's a member of the Tuyan City press corps here doing a story on the smooth working relations between the U.S. and Mituyan Special Forces." He paused, then added, "She came here with a letter from the Public Affairs Office in Tuyan City requesting my full cooperation."

Mike flashed a broad, understanding grin at Prescott. "If this correspondent is who I think she is, I'm sure we'll have no trouble convincing her she must not mention the undersecretary's visit, at least for the present."

"No sweat with Marlene," Prescott agreed.

At the questioning look from Hartland, Mike explained about Marlene Straltz.

"It does liven things up to have a pretty Caucasian girl out in the wilds of this jungle, I suppose." Hartland smiled to show he saw nothing irregular. "But I can see why the sergeant thought we might misinterpret the young lady's visit. How about a quick trip around the place, Major? And if we should meet the visiting journalist, all I ask is that she keep my presence here out of her copy."

"Yes, sir!" Prescott led Hartland through the TOC and then around the lodge, explaining how the center coordinated the operations of the Special Forces camps spread all over the Groat country. Finally he conducted them into his office and closed the door. "Now, sir, what else would you like to know?"

"Is this program really bringing the Groats to the side of the government?"

"Not any more, sir," Prescott answered crisply.

"Why not?"

"Same old story, sir. I've sent in my reports to JRB, and I guess they've gone up to the Agency, predicting that the Groats will either join the Mitcoms or unilaterally rebel against the government. We were doing real well until we got the Mituyan Special Forces inflicted on us."

"Charlie," Mike said, "think we have time to take Mr. Hartland in for a look at Chief Beemeer's village?"

"If he wants to go in, I'm game."

"I'd like to see for myself how this program which had so much promise in the beginning is being mismanaged," Hartland said.

"Well, you'll be going to the right place." Prescott looked at his watch. "My counterpart is taking Tat time, so we can go into this village without telling him. He raises hell if anybody comes to his quarters during Tat time."

"I'm hoping I'll find some word about Johnny Elephant," Mike said to Prescott as they entered the Heliocourier. "He disappeared, and his brother is worried about him."

"The goddamned counterparts have taken over most of the poppy business out here as well as everything else. And we have orders direct from the top not to mess with them. So we have to sit back and watch quietly. Hell, you'll see."

The flight to Ba To took twenty-five minutes, and the pilot put down neatly in the small strip behind the village. "Lieutenant Panton or one of his men should be out here to pick us up in a minute," Prescott said. "Say, Mike, remember the first time we came in here on the ground?"

"I sure do. Incidentally, I talked to the Reverend Maynard today, and he said those kids are doing fine, becoming good Christians and learning to speak English and Mituyan."

"Glad to hear it." Prescott looked across toward the village. "Here comes a jeep now. Looks like Cavanaugh driving. He's our medic, sir," Prescott said to Hartland. "I'd say the only thing holding this whole Groat program together now is the medical treatment we give them. Now that they have it, they wouldn't want to lose it. They know the Mitcoms won't give them medical attention. I'm afraid they might give it up though, to start a revolutionary movement for Groat independence from the Tuyan City government."

The tall, redheaded medical sergeant was introduced to the undersecretary, and a broad grin of appreciation spread across his face. "Sir, you couldn't have come to a better place to see what we're up against." He turned to Prescott. "Would you like me to conduct this guided tour, sir? Lieutenant Panton's out on patrol."

"Go ahead. The briefing's all yours—and if General Macker or the Agency station chief finds out about it—hello, civilian life!"

"We're all taking a chance, Major," Hartland said pleasantly. "After all, I'll be exposing some of our cabinet secretaries and agency heads to the truth they don't want to hear. So full speed ahead and damn the torpedos!"

"Yes, sir!" said Cavanaugh. "You'll probably want to talk to Chief Beemeer first, Mr. Forrester. He's gotten pretty damned bitter lately. I don't blame him."

"You'll find this interesting, Mr. Secretary," Mike said, "since you've worked with tribesmen before."

"The chief first," Hartland agreed.

Groat men and women stared at them curiously as Cavanaugh drove the visitors to the center of the village; Hartland stared back with equal curiosity.

"I must say, the people look healthier than the last time I was here," Mike observed, as they walked toward the chief's longhouse. "That dull reddish color is out of their hair too."

"That's right, sir. But their red hair, unlike mine, was a sign of vitamin deficiency. I've got the women mixing vitamin diet supplement in their food, and of course the pig program has been the biggest help. These people never get enough meat."

"The babies look well too," Hartland said. "They all had legs like sticks and bloated stomachs when I was working with the tribesmen."

"I try and provide the best pediatric care, sir."

From below the stilted front porch Mike called up to the chief, and heard an acknowledging series of grunts. Then Beemeer, dressed in his loincloth and a black shirt, smoking a pipe, emerged and stared at the men below. He sure looks sad, thought Mike as he waved up at his old friend. Beemeer, squinting down, finally recognized Mike; with a shout he slid the notched log ladder to the ground, slapping Mike on the back, smiling toothlessly. Mike introduced Hartland as a number-one adviser to the chief of all the Americans in the United States. Impressed, Beemeer invited them to squat, but Mike explained that Hartland had been wounded in the foot during the war and that he was in pain if he could not sit with one foot elevated. Beemeer shouted, and soon a box and extra mats were brought out by one of his sons; gratefully, Hartland arranged himself. "Damned thing does get in the way sometimes."

Mike and Beemeer began to converse in Mituyan and in the limited Groat vocabulary Mike had learned on his previous visit. Mike stopped frequently to translate for Hartland, and he also translated Hartland's comments back to Beemeer.

Before long Mike asked how things were going.

Beemeer puffed sadly on his pipe. Then, looking directly into Hartland's face, he answered, surprisingly, in English. "I am sad. I don't know."

"We've been teaching him English, sir," Cavanaugh explained. "But that's about all he ever says. His son, Radam, speaks number-one good, though." Cavanaugh smiled at the young man squatting beside his father.

Mike, ascertaining that Beemeer meant exactly what he had said in English, pursued the point. "Why are you sad, Beemeer?"

"For the first time in our history the lowland people come to our villages as masters," Beemeer said, now in Mituyan. There was no mistaking the unhappiness in his dark, eroded countenance. "We take them in; my men fight for them because you Americans ask us to do so. But the men from the lowlands do not have respect for us and our customs. They laugh at us. They buy our women away from us with their beads and silver necklaces from the cities. And they give very cruel punishment to my men for small things. One of men has died in the pit already."

Mike translated and gave Cavanaugh a searching look.

"What the chief says is true," the medic confirmed. "They took a man we'd made corporal of a squad of irregulars and put him in the pit for two days and nights. He roasted in the day and froze at night. By the time they let him out, there wasn't anything I could do."

"What other things bother you?" Mike probed gently.

"They eat much of our food and pay us too little for it. We are often hungry. When my men go out into the jungle on patrol, the lowland officer makes my men hunt for animals instead of the enemy. Then, when my men bring back the animals they have shot, the lowland officer takes all the carcasses and skins and sends them to Banthut to be sold. He does not even give us one carcass to keep and eat ourselves.

"We love the Americans," Beemeer continued. "They give us pigs. They say the pigs are gift of the lowland government, but we know better. The Americans save many lives, many children." Beemeer smiled at Cavanaugh. "The red-hair sorcerer is good. So we keep doing what the Americans ask, but why do the lowlanders have much face and the Americans little?"

"Does anybody want to try and answer that?" Mike asked after translating the question.

"The answer to that lies in Tuyan City," growled Prescott. "Maybe the ambassador, or our fearless station chief, would like to come out here and talk to Chief Beemeer."

Hartland nodded somberly. "Forrester, ask the chief if he has heard about the election to send representatives to Tuyan City and make changes in the government."

Mike and Beemeer conversed for several minutes and then Mike gave Hartland the reply. "Beemeer says he has been told nothing of such elections. He also states that even if such a thing happened, there would be no chance for the Groats to have any voice in what the government does." Mike paused thoughtfully, then went on, his eyes holding Hartland's. "Beemeer also said that only the Americans are keeping the tribe here together. Many of the younger men want to join with the other villages and drive the lowlanders out of their mountains. His son Radam, sitting over there, is a leader in this movement. There is much talk, apparently, of an outright rebellion against the Mituyans. The young men discuss joining the Mitcoms, who promise that when the government is beaten the Groats can have their own country with their own laws and no lowlanders to interfere."

Hartland looked distressed. "A revolt of the hill tribes would be a disaster."

Chief Beemeer, now that he had started to catalogue his miseries, seemed unable to stop. Soon he reached a topic in which Mike was most interested.

"The lowlanders try to take our poppy from us and pay us only in cheap beads. You taught us the value of our poppy and paid us fairly, but they try to steal it." Beemeer grinned in rueful satisfaction. "We have much poppy hidden in the village, but the lowlanders cannot find it. Maybe we have to go back, do what other villages do—sell the poppy to your enemy. They pay us something at least. A man from the province chief in Banthut comes here to take the poppy which the lowland commander of the soldiers steals from us." Beemeer laughed. "This man was very mad when there was so little poppy. He was as rude to the lowland commander as the commander is to us."

"How much have you got here now, Beemeer?" Mike asked, forgetting the others for the moment.

"Maybe six bags."

"I'll buy it all from you right now at our old price," Mike offered.

"I sell," Beemeer replied promptly.

"Can your men put the bags in the little truck of the red-haired sorcerer?"

"They will do it," Beemeer agreed.

"Have them do it now while the lowland commander is still in his house."

Beemeer shouted orders to his sons, and they scampered down the ladder and ran off on their errand. Mike began to explain what was going on to the others. "Beemeer just told me that the Mituyan Special Forces steal their poppy and that a collector from the province chief comes to get it every couple of weeks. Now Beemeer's people are hiding the stuff and are planning to sell it to the Mitcoms, who at least pay something. So I just told Beemeer I'd buy the whole load right now."

"Christ!" Prescott exclaimed. "We're apt to get into a war with our counterparts over it."

"It's still best to get it out of here," Mike argued, "and the money will raise the morale of Beemeer's people."

"What are you going to do with it?" Hartland asked.

"JRB put me in the opium business in order to keep the poppy from the Communists. We sell it to legal medical refining laboratories at the legal rate. I make a little money on the transaction, about enough to cover my expenses on JRB missions." Mike reached into his pocket and pulled out a thick roll of meta notes.

Beemeer grinned as Mike counted out the money. "Six bags, Beemeer. This is about right."

"This is our first chance to sell for a fair price since you last here," the chief said happily. "The Chinese agent try to come, but the lowlanders catch him."

"What!" Mike exclaimed. "Why didn't you tell me that sooner?"

"I think you know," Beemeer replied. "I think that why you here."

"Is the Chinese here, in Ba To?"

"Yes. Lowlanders capture him on patrol."

"Cavanaugh, did you know the Mits have Johnny Elephant?"

"Hell no, sir. We thought it was just a few Mitcom suspects they'd picked up on patrols."

"You haven't interrogated them?"

"Our orders are to go along with our counterparts, sir. The Mits say they've got a couple of suspects, and someone's coming out from province headquarters to take them back for questioning."

"Cav's right, Mike," Major Prescott confirmed. "We have orders directly from the station chief that we're *advisers* now and can't cross our sensitive allies. . . ."

Mike appealed to Hartland. "Mr. Secretary, Johnny was on a JRB project. I've got to get him out."

"What do you want me to do?" Hartland asked.

"The plane that will fly you back can return for me. When I see it land, I'll get Johnny away from the Mits and we'll fly out of here together. That way there's no chance of your being compromised."

"If you don't mind my asking, how do you expect to pull this stunt?"

"We have very specific orders as to what we can and can't do, Mike," Prescott said. "Wouldn't it be better to leave poor old Johnny than get into some big flap at this time?"

"I've got to try. I got him into this."

"You and he were doing your duty," Prescott argued.

"Not Johnny Elephant. He thought he was strictly on a commercial adventure. I'll get him into the airplane myself."

"This I'd like to see," Hartland said. "My life has been so musty in State for so long I'm beginning to enjoy the change. I'll stay."

Prescott shrugged. "Whatever Mr. Hartland says."

"OK," Mike said. "First thing, Cavanaugh, will you drop my six bags of poppy into the back of the plane? Three hundred kilos extra weight should be no sweat for the turbo-prop."

"Will do, sir."

"And we'll need two jeeps."

"That's OK. We've got 'em. I'll get Sergeant Jones to drive the other one."

"Good. Have them ready in fifteen minutes in the town square. Now, I'll just have a chat with Beemeer here, and then we'll put this operation into action. All of you can be innocent and surprised observers."

Beemeer laughed heartily as Mike unfolded his plan. Then the chief brought out the double-barrel shotgun Mike had given him on the last trip. Mike checked to make sure it had been properly cleaned and loaded and handed it to the chief's oldest son, Radam, who was now a sergeant in the village irregulars and delighted to be part of a plan to humiliate the Mituyan Special Forces.

"You're crazy, Mike," Prescott said shaking his head.

"You don't think I can pull it off?"

"Of course you can. But what happens when you get back to Tuyan City. They'll deport you."

"No they won't." He turned to Radam, who was wearing camouflage fatigues, bata boots, and a wide-brimmed floppy jungle hat, the shotgun stuck under his right arm. "Let's go, Radam!"

Radam, holding the gun on Mike, prodded him toward the prisoner cage at the far end of the village, where the Mituyan Special Forces with the help of the Americans had built a fortified compound.

This was a desperate sort of thing to do, Mike realized, as he crossed the village. He had been told in no uncertain terms that he could expect nothing but repudiation from the JRB if he got caught in circumstances that proved embarrassing to the United States, even on an assigned mission. Perhaps he wasn't really a CIA type at heart then, because he knew he would be unable to live with himself if he did not at least try to spare Johnny Elephant the endless interrogation and torture he would receive in the province chief's prison.

At the barbed-wired Mituyan Special Forces perimeter, they were stopped by an MSF guard. Radam said this American had tried to buy poppy, and he was taking him to the detention cage to await the arrival of Captain Narit.

The MSF guard waved them through, and Radam marched Mike fifty feet or so beyond the guard post to the cage where two Groat tribesmen and a Chinese were exposed to the searing sun all day and the mountain cold by night. All three were too weak to look up.

"Johnny, Johnny Elephant," Mike called in low tones. Listlessly, Johnny Elephant, who because of the size and shape of the cage could neither sit up straight nor lie down, rolled his head and shoulders in the direction of the voice. The deep misery in his eyes only intensified as he saw Mike. "They take you too, Mike," Johnny groaned. "Very sorry about that."

"Not yet, Johnny. I'm going to try and get you out of here."

Hope flickered in the Chinese hunter's eyes. "You think can do?"

"Try and be very alert, Johnny. Can you walk?"

"To get out this place I can run." New strength surged through his voice.

Mike looked around to see if the MSF captain was coming; sure enough, Captain Narit and an MSF sergeant had arrived at the cage, surprised to see the tall American being watchfully covered by the small Groat with the shotgun.

Before the captain could say anything, Mike said to him, in harsh Mituyan so there could be no chance of misunderstanding: "You have imprisoned a very good friend of mine, and I want him out of here."

"Who are you?" Narit said.

"I am Michael Forrester, an American trading in Mituyan. This man works for me."

"You are the one who takes the poppy illegally," Narit exclaimed. "You won't take any more." To Radam, the captain said, "You are an alert soldier to capture this man." Then to Mike: "We will put you in the cage with your friend until Colonel TrangTi sends for both of you."

Mike stared at the captain, a sneer on his face, then said in perfect Mituyan—so loudly that all the captain's men could not help but hear: "I urinate on the grave of your grandmother and her mother. My feces are too good to spread on the graves of your ancestors."

The captain's face drained and his lips quivered in fury. To be thus insulted by an American prisoner cost the officer all face until he revenged himself.

"If the American moves, blast his body open with that shotgun," Narit shrieked in rage. He strode toward Mike, pulling a thin stiletto from a sheath on his belt as he came. As Mike had hoped, Captain Narit was of the Lodung or ancestor-worshipping sect of Mituyan Buddhists; the insult had made him lose his head completely. Just before Narit's knife point was in slashing range, Mike's right hand went smoothly to the end of the shotgun barrel that Radam, as instructed, was holding loosely. Mike slid his fingers down to the trigger guard, inside it, and around the stock; he jerked the gun from Radam's light grasp, his left hand guiding the barrel, and jabbed it into Narit's throat, momentarily paralyzing the knife-wielding Mituyan officer.

"Drop the knife or I'll blow your head off!" Mike rasped. For an instant the startled officer could only stare at the American. Then he slowly dropped the knife.

To the guards, Mike shouted, "If any of you get in my way, your captain will have his throat shot out."

Narit rasped at his men not to shoot.

"Tell one of your men to let the Chinese out of the cage," Mike commanded. Eyes wide with fear, Narit did as he was told, and the trap door on top of the cage was unbolted and opened. Johnny Elephant instantly leapt from the cage.

"Listen to me, Narit," Mike said. "You will not be hurt if you do exactly what I say. But if I even suspect you or any of your men are trying to get me, you will be dead—with no head."

"Do what he says," Narit screamed to his men. "Make no threatening moves." Obediently the men shrank back.

"Tell them not to leave their compound until you return here," Mike ordered. Narit gave the command, and then Mike told the MSF captain to walk very slowly beside him to the center of the village. Narit set out as bid, staring straight ahead, the muzzle of the shotgun in his throat. It was a slow procession through the village, and all the Groats watched, trying to hide the elation they felt at this abject humiliation of the hated government officer. The usual loud babble of Groat voices had subsided to a sudden silence, and the unusual stillness brought villagers from all the longhouses to see what was happening. In awe they watched the big American pick up the small Mituyan officer in one hand and roughly swing him into the back of the jeep—which at a command drove out of the village, followed by a second jeepload of Americans, toward the airstrip.

"Well, Cavanaugh," Mike said cheerfully when Hartland, Johnny Elephant, and the others were safe aboard the airplane, "I may have caused you a little trouble here, but don't worry too much. I'll be seeing TrangTi in under two hours and get this little operation accounted for."

Then, hard-eyed, Mike turned to Narit, "Perhaps, Captain, if you follow the advice of the Americans very closely you will not be relieved of your command. Just remember that Colonel TrangTi and I are partners in a business enterprise out here which you very nearly wrecked in your stupidity." As he saw Narit's confusion change to fear, he added, "I will not tell Colonel TrangTi how easily one unarmed man was able to overpower an entire Mituyan Special Forces detachment—and I advise you to do the same, that is, if you wish to preserve your army career."

Leaving the MSF captain staring shamefacedly at the ground, Mike entered the overloaded plane. The pilot lost no time in getting his ship airborne.

"Well, that was the goddamnedest performance I've ever seen in my life," Hartland said when they were aloft.

"No American in an official capacity could get away with pulling a thing like that off," Prescott said. "Are you serious about TrangTi being in business with you?"

"In a sense, yes. Because of the ham-handed handling of the Groats by the Mit troops, TrangTi can't get the poppy he wants, so he'll be glad to do business with me."

"And *I'm* supposed to be the fount of knowledge on this whole area." Hartland shook his head in bewilderment. "Out of curiosity, Mike, how much money would this load fetch in New York City?"

Mike gestured at the six bags in the baggage compartment. "There's about three hundred kilos of raw opium back there. A kilo can be sold to transporters for a minimum of $100, so say that's $30,000. Of course, both in Banthut and Tuyan City there are backroom laboratories that can extract the morphine base from the raw opium at the rate of one kilo of morphine base to ten kilos of raw stuff. Besides, one kilo of morphine base sells at more than double the price of ten kilos of raw poppy and is far more easily transported to Hong Kong or the Philippines."

"So, how much would this fetch in New York?"

Mike shrugged. "It's hard to say exactly, of course. The Oriental gangsters pass on the morphine base to the Mafia, who make it into heroin by a fairly sophisticated laboratory process; and they wind up with a pound of heroin per pound of morphine base. One pound of raw opium like we've got, after the heroin has been cut, recut and adulterated, at the retail pushers' price might produce $25,000 worth of fixes in New York City. So with about three hundred kilos—let's round that off at six hundred pounds—this load, if illegally sold, could eventually gross a cool $15 million."

Prescott whistled loudly. "I never thought it was possible to see $15 million worth of anything in so small a space."

"The point is, when TrangTi finds out what I've got he'll want to do business with me. So there shouldn't be too much repercussion about taking Johnny Elephant out of Captain Narit's cage."

The plane landed at the lodge, and Prescott invited everyone to his quarters.

"You still haven't taken over Barkoon's quarters for yourself?" Mike asked.

"We use his room as a guest house, although my Mituyan counterpart is making noises about wanting it for his quarters," Prescott explained. He added sheepishly, "Our visiting journalist, Fraulein Straltz, is using it at present."

"I would enjoy meeting Fraulein Straltz," Hartland said, after he and the others had washed and joined Prescott in his sitting room. Its wide, full-length windows attracted the cool mountain breezes and kept the room at a refreshingly low temperature. He was seated comfortably, his right foot up on a table.

"I've asked her to stay in her quarters while you were here," Prescott said, "but I know she'd be interested in meeting you, sir."

He returned with Marlene, and Hartland professed himself stunned to find such a beautiful blonde out in the jungle.

"According to my research," Marlene said, "I find that King Barkoon always had beautiful blondes at his lodge." She gave Mike a broad smile. "We meet everywhere, Mike. It is very nice. Makes me feel safe."

They talked for twenty minutes, and Marlene completely captivated Hartland. Mike, on the other hand, was unusually quiet—strangely affected by the presence of the blonde. He had heard of this happening to others married to non-Caucasians; much as he loved Luna—and he *was* happily married—every once in a while he would feel this strong yearning for a woman of his own kind. Perhaps Marlene sensed this. Even in the presence of Charlie Prescott, who Mike assumed was her lover, she seemed to be saying that she, too, felt an attraction—if only it were possible.

As if reading his thoughts, she asked after Luna and promised to see them in Tuyan City before her next trip north.

Major Prescott interrupted to say they had better be leaving if they wanted to make Banthut before five. Then to Hartland he said, "There's one thing I'd like to show you, sir, if you have one more minute. And you too, Mike. Marlene, you'll forgive us?"

"Of course, Major," Marlene replied in a particularly intimate tone. Mike and Hartland smiled broadly to see Prescott's ears turn red with embarrassment.

In his office Charlie went to the classified file, turned the combination, and extracted a memo and covering sheet with a red border around it marked SECRET.

"All commanding officers of detachments under MAC-M received this," he explained. "I just want you to know what kind of trouble I'll be in if what happened today reaches General Macker."

Hartland read the classified document and shook his head, then silently passed it to Mike. "The Country Team is really afraid you'll find out how bad things are over here, sir," Mike said. "What a hell of a note." He read aloud: " '. . . It is incumbent to use, therefore, not to say anything to visitors that could in any manner be construed to be criticism of our gallant allies, the Mituyan Army. It is further incumbent to us not to leave with any visitors, official or unofficial, the suggestion that the war being waged by the Mituyan Army against the Communist insurgents is anything but successful.' " Mike looked up, "Somebody at MAC-M not only is trying to deceive you but could use grammar lessons."

Hartland shook his head, "No, it's worse than that. The Country Team is honestly convinced that everything is going smoothly in Mituyan and the army is winning the war rapidly. Since the Country Team does not know what is happening in this country, it does not want me and other members of the Washington mission to hear what Whittelsie and Macker would term 'damaging statements' from hotheaded young dissidents that would give us the 'false' impression that the Republic of Mituyan is on the verge of collapse." Hartland breathed deeply. "*This* is what is so tragic about the United States involvement in Mituyan. I'll be sure that nobody in the U.S. mission finds out you helped me," Hartland said. "And thank you, Major Prescott. Thank you very much."

CHAPTER THIRTY-FOUR

After a day of pat and optimistic briefings in which every sensitive subject was ignored or delicately circumvented and declared irrelevant to the overall picture of KaritKi progress, Undersecretary Hartland felt liberated to be flying out to the countryside again to see for himself what was really happening. In the faithful unmarked Heliocourier winging he and Mike—already fast friends—north to Tiking, Hartland looked down on the fields and villages below. "You know, Mike, yesterday we heard that the people in the countryside, especially up here in the northern provinces where KaritKi's brother Poramat rules, are wholeheartedly behind the government and the Americans."

"Before the day is over we'll arrange for you to sample public opinion in Poramat's fiefdom in a way you'll never forget." Mike looked at the foot propped up on the front seat of the airplane. "How's it feel today?"

"That was the only good thing about yesterday's intolerably long and fatuous briefings—I had a chance to rest it."

Mike shook his head. "Seems to me, Bob, that if you manage in spite of constant pain to come see what happens where it's really happening, the Country Team and the other members of the mission should be able to, too."

"I guess I'm the only unorthodox foreign-service officer around these days. As a matter of fact, the President said to me just a few days ago—seems like a year—that he can only afford one like me at a time because it takes five more of ambassadorial rank to oil down the waves I make. One thing I can tell you: it's going to take a lot of oil to smooth things out after this trip."

As the plane began its descent into Tiking airport, Mike pointed out his ship, the *Promise,* tied up to the dock.

"Looks like a beauty. That's where we're meeting Jack tonight?"

"He wanted our talk to take place aboard. She's a comfortable ship," Mike said proudly.

The plane landed and taxied to the military section, where Colonel Lawton was waiting to drive them in a black staff car to General Dandig's headquarters.

"Dandig seems to be the chief plotter," Lawton explained, after ascertaining Hartland had been briefed on the generals' coup plans. "I think the reason he exercises so much influence on the other three commanders is that they know he does not want to become Premier, President, King, or whatever the new honcho of Mituyan wants to call himself." Lawton smiled wryly at the undersecretary. "At least he doesn't want the job *now.* He's been a serious Vietnam watcher and must have noted that it takes many changes of strong men before a real boss takes hold and lasts."

At the headquarters of Mituyan's I Corps the dapper little general greeted them affably.

"Do you believe, General," Hartland asked, after they had sparred verbally for a few minutes about the military and political situation in I Corps, "that the candidates in Tiking Province reflect opposing points of view? In other words is there a pro- *and* an anti-KaritKi candidate?"

Dandig laughed. "The so-called anti-KaritKi candidate has been a loyal Poramat retainer for the ten years the regime has been in power. His anti-KaritKi speeches are all written by Counselor Tarot himself."

"What is the feeling in the countryside about KaritKi?"

"The people have little or no concept of central government. Unfortunately, KaritKi does present the Communist agitators with the bones of dissension that they sow volubly in the villages and hamlets."

Hartland smiled at Dandig's oratory. The young general had been one of many aspiring officers from intellectual and wealthy Mituyan families who had been given a military education in England by the British. "I was told in Tuyan City yesterday that the people in this part of the country, your corps area, were loyal to KaritKi but that opposition candidates were being given every encouragement to seek election to the congress."

"The opposition *is* encouraged to discuss its aims—on the Isle of Stones," Dandig said wryly. "No, sir, whoever told you that was either a liar or a fool; if a Mituyan government official, the former; if the latter, a member of the permanent American mission."

Lawton gave Hartland a sidewise smile and received a sly wink back.

Now it was Dandig's turn to ask a question. "What would the reaction of the United States government be if KaritKi were replaced by a new ruler backed by the military?"

"This replacement to be in the nature of a military coup?" Hartland asked guilelessly.

"There is no other way, of course," Dandig said.

"It's difficult for me to sit here and tell you that the U.S. government would back a new regime immediately. However, there's a good chance we would. The news reports of KaritKi atrocities have provoked a great deal of sentiment against his regime. This reporter Krakhaur has done considerable service to any possible anti-KaritKi movement."

"The problem is to find a man who would capture the enthusiasm of the people," Dandig said. "The government-controlled press has never been permitted to praise any political or military figure out of fear he might become a rival to the Premier or his brothers. However, there *is* one man . . . who also belongs to the majority religion."

"Yes?" said Hartland, dead pan.

Dandig smiled. "Yes. As you have apparently been told, I and the other generals would all rally behind one person."

"And he is—?"

"You may be shocked by the suggestion but—" Dandig for a moment was unsure whether to continue, but Mike and Lawton encouraged him. "In spite of his questionable press notices, or perhaps because of them, King Barkoon is still popular all over the country. We feel the people would rally behind him if he were to return."

"And of course the religious factor is in his favor," Hartland said, giving no indication whether he had been informed of the Barkoon plan.

"You Americans insist on regarding Buddhists as uniform. Besides the two main sects, the Lodung and Dicut, there are many smaller ones who are no more similar than, say, the Catholics and the Protestants in the United States."

"But wouldn't the fact that Barkoon represents the Buddhist faith be a prime reason for supporting his return?"

Dandig's conspiratorial smile broadened. "There is in this city a Buddhist monk of no particular sect or persuasion—Han Li Phang, also known as the Mad Monk of Tiking. Although he probably represents fewer Buddhists than any other religious leader, his militancy and ability at political manipulation have made him the most important Buddhist in the country. He, more than any other Buddhist in the history of Mituyan, has been able to make the many sects think of themselves as Buddhists first, and reincarnationists or ancestor-worshipers second. Li Phang has been plotting for a year to pull together all the Buddhists in the country in frenzied demonstrations against KaritKi. . . . No, the religious issue is only a hook, a gimmick as you Americans would say, to embarrass KaritKi, make him look like a bigot who tortures those who do not share his religious beliefs."

"I would like to meet this Mad Monk," Hartland said.

"He speaks only Mituyan, although I am sure he does understand English."

Hartland nodded at Mike. "I have a very reliable interpreter here."

"But of course. Mr. Forrester is one of the very few Caucasians I know who does speak the language. Of course, he had a most devoted instructress."

"Luna has been a great help," Mike agreed with a smile.

"As a reincarnation-oriented Buddhist myself," Dandig said, "I must remind you that in many ways Li Phang has perverted the faith in order to manipulate the people. He has organized entire cadres of reincarnationists around the country who, on his orders and to protest the atrocities of KaritKi's regime, will commit suicide in dreadful ways. In Vietnam they merely burn themselves to death. Li Phang has his self-immolationists, but others are ready to kill themselves far more gruesomely. Li Phang feels he needs far more effective measures than such comparatively archaic methods as burning oneself alive."

Dandig's talk shocked Hartland, but he listened attentively.

"Li Phang tells his fanatically devoted reincarnationists that by sacrificing themselves they build up enormous quantities of good karma which will assure them in their next lives of attaining nirvana and eternal spiritual harmony. Very heartless of him. The evil karma he must be building for himself will torture him for his next hundred reincarnations. But that is neither here nor there. . . . As for us, Mr. Secretary, we are ready to make our move the moment we receive assurances that we will receive the full support of your government."

"General, I'm going to try to convince our President that the KaritKi regime must be ended. If I'm successful you will be notified, and we'll give you as much covert help as we can."

"Thank you, Mr. Secretary. I hope that time will not be too far off. Already KaritKi, Tarot, and Poramat suspect a generals' coup, and if they start arresting and questioning us the whole plan would be destroyed."

"I will hurry, never fear. The mission leaves tomorrow night to return to Washington."

Back in the staff car, the undersecretary scrubbed his forehead and eyes in fatigue. "Sometimes, when I haven't been over to this part of the world for a year or two, I find it hard to believe I'm really seeing and hearing what's being done and said. . . . OK, the Mad Monk is next on the agenda. Let's have at him."

"How's the foot, Bob?" Mike asked.

"If I had any guts I'd let the doctors do what they want—cut it off. Trouble is the foot doesn't *look* too bad; the docs fixed it on the outside just fine. But inside the bones are all scrambled up in the wrong places."

"How about a belt before we see the monk?"

Hartland shook his head. "One thing about pain. It keeps your mind sharp."

"Good, you'll *need* your wits about you," said Mike. "This pagoda is one of the most venerated and sacred in the country. It's on top of a small mountain. After we've talked to Li Phang, maybe I can get him to show you around a little, if your foot isn't bothering you too much."

"Anything that will help me understand the problem better, I want to see," Hartland said.

Twenty minutes later the black staff car snaked to the top of a twisting road and came to a stop before the entrance of the pagoda, an undistinguished, brown stucco structure, its roof—much of it covered with zinc sheets—in sad disrepair.

"These must be the most poverty-stricken Buddhists in the world. This is their number-one pagoda?" Hartland asked.

"It's run down in the past couple of centuries," said Mike. "During some of my past incarnations this was a beautiful place. . . ."

Lawton and Hartland looked at Mike. "Did you get converted while you were out here?" Lawton asked.

"No, but I learned a lot about what this place stands for, or did represent before Han Li Phang took over." Mike led his two companions past shaven-headed monks in brown and saffron robes into the musty interior. Outside the sun was shining, and it took their eyes a few moments to adjust to the gloom. Ahead of them, under a patched roof, stood a huge statue of the Buddha, seated cross-legged, the soles of both feet facing to the ceiling. Gold leaf covered less than half the statue, but all three could sense a feeling of majesty and serenity radiating from the altar. They stood a few minutes staring at the Buddha and the bare interior; monks were seated cross-legged or lying on their foreheads before the image.

A monk came up to them and asked in understandable English if they would like a tour of the pagoda. He carried a begging bowl into which Mike dropped one hundred metas. Then, in Mituyan, which startled the monk, Mike asked if he and his friends could be conducted to Han Li Phang.

The monk, without a word, gathered the folds of his robe about him and bade them follow him up a flight of crumbling masonry stairs to a gallery. Rooms without doors lined the gallery, and monks were seated within, presumably in meditation. Mike nudged Hartland as they walked by several rooms from which a steady clacking could be heard. The undersecretary looked in and saw a mimeograph machine, long sheets of paper spewing from it. In the next room a nun, her head covered in much the manner of a Catholic sister, was busy at a typewriter and two monks were operating a second mimeograph machine. They had counted three busy typewriters and four mimeographs before they reached the end of the gallery.

"They ought to send an adviser from this pagoda to the Public Affairs Office in Tuyan City," Lawton cracked.

At the end of the gallery they climbed another flight of crumbling stairs and reached a tower room that looked out in four directions. Sitting cross-legged on a mat, apparently in deep meditation, was Han Li Phang. His saffron robes were dirty and looked to be of the cheapest orange cloth. His shaved head, unlined face, and huge bulging forehead gave him an ageless appearance. Their guide sat down cross-legged beside other meditating monks, leaving Mike, Lawton, and Hartland standing uncomfortably in the Venerable's presence.

As Mike addressed the monk in Mituyan, small, black pupils glistened from Li Phang's almond-shaped eyes. He showed that he recognized Forrester, listening to him carefully. Then his eyes went to Lawton and to Hartland; he stared for some moments at the undersecretary. "I told him who you are, Bob. He seems to be impressed. You're the first American of any official importance who has called upon him."

Before Mike finished, the monk, his eyes glinting straight at Hartland, began to talk in high-pitched, almost eunuch-like tones. "He says that the Buddhists have particularly suffered under the KaritKi regime," Mike translated, "that all the promises KaritKi made when he took over as Premier have been broken. It is for all the people that he opposes KaritKi, who imprisons and tortures his political prisoners."

"Doesn't he feel the elections will help bring in a truly representative government?"

Mike phrased the question in Mituyan, and the monk merely gave the undersecretary a gold-toothed smile and shook his head. "I thought the United States was on our side even though the ambassador here is a fool," Mike translated, as Li Phang began talking after a pause. "Why else would so much anti-KaritKi propaganda be in the American newspapers, especially lately?"

"Tell him the government doesn't control the press," Hartland said.

"In that case," Li Phang replied, "the American press is doing much to save the image of the United States government and the President himself, because we will make the world realize what an evil dictator KaritKi is. There will be one hundred, two hundred self-sacrifices, if necessary, to expose KaritKi to the world as the enslaver and torturer of the Mituyan people. It will be bad for the President and his closest advisers to be associated with KaritKi."

Li Phang's eyes burned out of his massive head at Hartland as his statement was translated.

"Are you threatening the United States government?" Hartland asked heatedly.

"Certainly not," the monk replied. "But since you took the trouble to find me I feel it only right to tell you what is going to happen."

"I am impressed with your frankness," Hartland said. "Are you not worried that I may tell the people of America, the world, that you are really nothing more than a manipulator trying to pull down a government?"

"Nobody would believe you," Li Phang replied serenely, and Mike, after a moment's hesitation, translated. "When the government's soldiers and police attack us as we demonstrate for religious freedom and the right to own our land, when despair drives our faithful to public suicides of a sort the Americans have yet to see on their television screens and in their papers, people will only remember that KaritKi's oppression brought this all on."

"But won't all this confusion, the street riots, student demonstrations and the like, cause many needless deaths and injuries?" Hartland asked through Mike.

"It is good for some of us to die, brutalized by KaritKi's police." Li Phang's eyes shone fanatically like two beacons from beneath his domelike forehead and shaven skull.

Mike could not help but notice the thin-lipped, strained look on Hartland's face as they sat cross-legged opposite Li Phang. The pain in the undersecretary's foot must be growing more intense. And the hardest part of the day was still ahead of them.

"I am grateful to you for your time and your outspoken explanation of your aims and methods of achieving those aims," Hartland said, acknowledging the end of the discussion. "Perhaps we shall meet again when a new regime is in power in the Republic of Mituyan." It was the only time Hartland had given any hint he might condone a change in government. Once again, before he had translated, Mike saw Li Phang react to the words, nodding once and bowing his head a moment.

"Perhaps," the monk said to Mike, "the American visitors would like to visit the caves. It might make them understand better our complete lack of fear of death, pain, or violence. I will send Han Grang to guide you."

Mike thanked the monk but said that the American representative had a pain in his foot from the war and perhaps would find the walk through the caves difficult. But Hartland said, pain or no pain, he wanted to go.

The monk conducted them from Li Phang's bare tower room into a passage behind the statue of Buddha, and they descended inside the hill on which the pagoda was perched. They walked down the cavern, lit by oil lamps, passing monks in brown or saffron robes, peasants, well-to-do citizens, and young and old women alike.

They rounded a bend and found themselves in a cavernous room. Stalagmites rose from the floor all around them, stalactites hanging down from the ceiling, dripping calcium carbonate at an unusually fast rate.

All along the edges of the wall, so encrusted in dripping calcium carbonate that each had become a stalagmite itself, were grisly, well-preserved bodies.

A bright oil torch burned beside each human remain. The monk stopped in front of one body, the leathery skin and teeth intact under its coating of transparent calcium, even the eyebrows still in place over sunken, empty eye sockets. He pointed to the macabre shrine proudly and spoke to Mike.

"He says that was the body he occupied two hundred years ago when the entity that is now Han Grang first left the worldly life and entered the life of contemplation. Through four incarnations he has improved the spirituality of his entity, although he says he lost"—Mike shrugged —"it's hard to translate; what he's saying is he came back as a woman two lives ago, and before he could get her into a nunnery she lost a lot of points for the entity."

Hartland chuckled. "Now he's got several pure lives to go before he catches up, I suppose."

"No, as a matter of fact he intends to make it almost to nirvana in this life. That's because he's number one on the sacrifice list," Mike said grimly. "He spends much time contemplating the most hideous methods of sacrificing himself, in full sight of the television cameras, so the world will understand the plight of the Buddhists in Mituyan."

"Jesus Christ, Mike," Hartland exclaimed, "how the hell do I explain this to them in the National Security Council? They'll think I—oh, hell."

"Han Grang wonders if you would like to see some of the bodies inhabited by Han Li Phang?"

"Sure, why not? Maybe we'll learn some more about the Mad Monk —an apt sobriquet, I might add."

They followed Han Grang through the cavern and along a dank corridor into another large cavern lower down. "The lower we go the older and more venerable are the organic remains we see, as the entities which once animated them have gone on toward nirvana. Some, in fact, have reached that state where they never again have to experience human torment and are free to float about in some cosmic pool contemplating the universe."

"You sound like one of them," Hartland said. "How do they know which of these things was them?"

"Good question. I'll ask."

After several minutes of explanation, during which Han Grang led them to a stalagmite in which the body was barely visible, although torches burned on either side of it, Mike translated the answer: "It's very simple, really. Certain very devout monks have the power to see the entity hovering around and above the body of a living being. Although most monks develop the ability to see through a third eye, as they call it, only very few have developed this third-eye sensitivity to the point where they can recognize all the past physical manifestations of an entity and identify them. There is such a monk in this pagoda who visits all the reincarnationist or Dicut pagodas in Mituyan."

"OK, Mike. Who's this?"

"That's the earliest corpse around known to have housed the entity we now know as Han Li Phang."

Hartland peered closely at the deeply encrusted face and then looked up incredulously. "Obviously the bugger was crazy as a shithouse mouse even then. Mike, I'd be grateful if you'd thank the good entity and tell him we have to leave. This place is not having a salubrious effect on me."

Outside the pagoda, Hartland climbed into the back seat of the staff car, sagged against the cushions and using both hands hoisted his leg onto the front seat. "Now, Mike, I think a visit to your yacht would be an excellent idea."

A strangely silent Lawton drove down to the waterfront of Tiking and came to a halt beside the *Promise* lying at her pier.

"Wow," Hartland said later, settling back in a sofa in the air-conditioned main salon. "That's probably the most dangerous man in Mituyan today. That was an experience and a half. I need a long, cold one. What's on for this afternoon?"

Mike poured a strong shot of Chivas Regal into a tall glass of soda and ice and handed it to the undersecretary. "Your foot going to be all right? This will be rugged."

"My foot will get me through." Hartland took a long swallow and sighed. "That's more like it. No, you don't have to sweat me, Mike. I'll be OK. I'll be living off these experiences for the next six months, if I last that long at State."

"OK. Next stop, the hamlet of Rishket," Mike said. "You'll really see how accurate these briefings have been about how the people all love the Americans and won't have anything to do with the Communists."

Two hours later the Heliocourier landed on the newly completed strip cut out of the jungle twenty miles northeast of the village of Rishket. For a moment, as they stepped out, Hartland thought he'd been flown into a Mitcom trap. A fierce-looking group of about thirty men, wearing black pajamas, flat wicker helmets, and sandals cut from automobile tires, surrounded the plane. Their rifles were mostly old British Enfields or the French rifles captured in quantities by the Vietnamese Communists. The leader of the group carried a Swedish K submachine gun, a weapon prized highly by both sides. On close scrutiny, Hartland saw that there was one American, dressed like the others, in the band.

The American approached the plane, and Lawton said, "That's Scott MacWhorter. He's with USIS. He knows more about the problems out in the countryside than any American. This is a special cadre he works with in the field of counterpropaganda and countersubversion."

MacWhorter, who like the Mituyan leader carried a Swedish K, greeted Mike and shook hands with Hartland. "I understand you want to find out exactly how the people out here really feel about us Americans?"

"That's right."

"Can you walk a couple of miles, sir?"

Hartland nodded, lips pressed tightly.

"Good. Two miles from here is a fairly large village named Rishket. About once a week a patrol of government soldiers goes through the village and the people all claim to be pro-government. Actually, we suspect that the village now has very strong Mitcom sympathies. The village chief may be reasonably loyal to the Tuyan City government, but the Mitcoms have a political chief in the village also. We hope to find out who he is today. Are you set to go? This may be dangerous; and it won't be pleasant."

"Lead on," Hartland replied.

"Right." MacWhorter turned to Lawton. "You and Forrester wait by the plane; we'll be back in about three hours. I can pass as a Mitcom, but you two would stand out like cops at a pickpocket's convention."

"OK, but Mr. Hartland has a bad right foot, so anything you can do to make the walk easier for him. . . ."

"We'll rig a sitting litter for him on the way back," MacWhorter offered.

"I won't need that. Let's go."

Though his foot pained him, he tried to divert his mind by trying to keep pace with MacWhorter and Major Song, who briefed him as they walked.

"We're almost there," MacWhorter said in just under an hour. "I'm going to fit myself into the column to the rear. Major Song will take over now. He's going to have to be rough to be convincing. So do everything we told you."

"I will," Hartland answered quietly. Song and one of his sergeants took rope and tied a loop around Hartland's neck, then bound his hands behind his back and tied another leash to the foreign officer's wrists. They tore and dirtied his clothes. "This is how the Mitcoms lead their prisoners," Song explained. "Usually they take the prisoners' shoes and make them walk barefoot, but we look real enough without that. . . . Now we go," the Mituyan major said. "Please forgive me, sir."

The Mituyan platoon disguised as Mitcoms roughly headed their "prisoner" out of the jungle and into the cleared area at the outskirts of the village. As they walked across rice paddies and fields of corn, peasants working their crops stared at the ragged procession. Hartland did not have to fake pain. It was shooting up from his leg, and he allowed himself to show his agony clearly. They walked through the gates of the village, and the people inside began to cheer. Suddenly a mean-looking young man in peasant pajamas rushed up and threw a handful of buffalo dung at Hartland. Others came running up and beat him around the head and shoulders with sticks, screaming unmistakably anti-American slogans. Then an ascetic young man walked up to Song, and the two conversed. A heated argument sprang up between them. It was obvious to Hartland that he was the subject of the argument, since both Song and this gaunt villager kept gesturing at him as they talked. Finally Song put an end to the argument by unslinging his submachine gun. A crowd had gathered around the village leader, and all made menacing gestures at Hartland, who could barely stand. At a gesture from the leader a number of the younger villagers approached Hartland, carrying heavy clubs. Unquestionably they meant to club him to death. Village women and children stood around, some shouting, some impassive, perhaps even sympathetic—but afraid to show displeasure or fear.

With complete detachment, Song swung his submachine gun on the thin-faced agitator and cut him in half through the belly with a burst of fire. In neat, short bursts he gunned down every young man who carried a club. Meanwhile, other members of the cadre methodically shot the peasant who had thrown the dung at Hartland and each villager who had struck him with a stick.

Not one peasant who had remained impassive or had at least shown no overt hostility was harmed.

Appalled, Hartland stared at the sudden, savage, unemotional slaughter.

"We have been wanting to identify and kill the Communist leaders in this village for several weeks," Song said. "Most of the villagers here are Communist sympathizers. As you may have guessed, the Mitcom political chief lying here"—he gestured at the body—"wanted to make a public execution of you. He had several ideas of how to make your death slow and impressive. His followers, good Communists all, knew that a Mitcom detachment would not shoot them to save one prisoner. This village has been a big Mitcom food source and is typical of villages all over Mituyan. The men of the village are all potential guerrillas. They were going to take you by force. If we had been Mitcoms, we would surely have let them have you rather than jeopardize the flow of food and intelligence from this village."

"You said all the villages around here are equally subverted?" Hartland asked, still shaken by the violence and bloodshed. "Didn't Mike Forrester tell me this was once a strong pro-government stronghold?"

"It was better than that," said Scott MacWhorter. "It was a peaceful and prosperous and independent community. Didn't you read Krakhaur's article on the siege?"

"Yes I did," Hartland said quietly. "We all did."

"Every village that doesn't receive day and night protection from the government and a fair share of U.S. aid is a Communist bailiwick," MacWhorter said. Major Song nodded in assent.

The cadre returned from making a search of the village; they had collected over two dozen assorted rifles and a quantity of grenades. The rifles were placed in litters to be carried off, the grenades piled together in a rice paddy outside of town. After Song and his cadre made a short speech begging the people to expel the Communists among them, the grenades were exploded.

Hartland walked through the jungle back to the airstrip. The pain in his foot was almost forgotten in the more painful realization of how little they knew in Washington about the truth of what was going on out in the Mituyan countryside. He could hardly wait to get back to Washington and give the President a briefing of the sort he would never get from the other members of this most recent inspection tour. Hartland knew what had to be done, and he hoped he could make the top policymakers understand the significance of what he had seen and experienced. It was experience he would never forget as long as he lived.

CHAPTER THIRTY-FIVE

CHARGING CHARLIE PRESCOTT stirred languorously as the first rays of the sun, rising over the mountain, pried at his eyelids. He turned over, still half asleep, and suddenly came awake. She was there beside him, sleeping with her back to him. His fingers tenderly caressed her shoulders and then her breasts and the pink nipples he had kissed and loved during the night before. She came half awake and murmured something in German.

"*Ich liebe dich,*" he whispered. "I love you, Marlene." To himself he said, *I hope I get a chance to meet that old bastard Barkoon and thank him. His bedroom was what did it.* Marlene had been captivated and overwhelmed by the opulence of Barkoon's apartment. It had been completely restored in anticipation of the ex-monarch's return to his old hunting lodge, where he planned to await the moment to reappear in Tuyan City and take over the reins of government from KaritKi.

Marlene murmured sleepily as Charlie kissed the back of her neck under the golden tresses. He wanted her again with a longing that was painful now that it was morning and he was revitalized.

For almost two months since he had first met her, Prescott had wanted to make love to Marlene more than anything in the world. And now that he had at last succeeded, he knew his feelings went beyond what he had imagined. "I love you . . . I want to marry you, Marlene." Gently, he rolled her onto her back and buried his face in her neck.

"Charlie, what are you doing to me, darling?"

Without answering he tenderly forced one leg between hers. The soft, gold fuzz of her upper thighs inflamed his desire. She knew it would be impossible to deny him now. Once again she surrendered to the strength she had absorbed so often during the night. Once again she felt his tension and excitement build and then, in a torrent of endearments in English and poor German, expend itself deeply within her. She was amused, somewhat touched, that his long suppressed desire for her was so intense that not once had he been able to hold back his passion long enough to take her with him. But she was used to it; seldom indeed—and then only with an older, more experienced man—had she been able to achieve complete release. Actually, she could count the number of her lovers on one hand. Now she caressed his back with her fingers as he lay spent upon her, whispering that he loved her and was going to marry her.

Marlene liked and admired Charlie Prescott, though she was not in love with him. But the hunting lodge of the former King and the romance of being out in the jungle with the excitement of the guerrilla war going on all around them had heightened her sensuality, had made it seem natural to take Charles into the big bed in the luxurious master bedroom that had been assigned to her when she arrived to write her story.

It was just too luxurious to sleep in alone! She had not intended to make love to the big, rather brash American, even after several dates in Tuyan City. She didn't feel guilty about denying him after an expensive dinner and a pleasant evening, because she knew that right after leaving her at her father's villa he would go to one of his Mituyan girls. But here—well, there was nothing else she could do.

Reluctantly Charlie rolled away from the most beautiful girl he had ever known and faced up to the crises of the day.

The first one was not long in coming. Prescott had no sooner arrived at the communications center of the lodge, invariably his first move in the morning, than traffic began coming in from Sergeant Minelli, the radio operator who had returned to Ba To. Once Minelli knew he was in direct contact with Prescott he began his report.

"Sir, I made radio contact with Lieutenant Panton's patrol. I can't make voice contact, but their Morse signal over the Angry Nine has been coming in strong. Looks like we're in deep shit, sir." There was a note of excitement in Minelli's voice as he relayed the report from the patrol deep in the mountainous jungles of Groat territory.

"Go ahead, Minelli," Prescott said firmly, trying to steady the sergeant.

"Right, sir. Lieutenant Panton and Sergeant Barton took a company of tribesmen out to relieve Captain Holloway's men from the camp at Bax who've been holding the Forward Operating Base. They reported finding it deserted"—Minelli paused—"except for the bodies of Captain Holloway, Sergeant Matthews, and their two Mituyan Special Forces counterparts."

Prescott's face grew grim. "Does Panton know what happened?"

"He figures there's been a rebellion and the Bax Groats let the Mitcoms into the FOB. Lieutenant Panton said to watch for another rebellion here at Ba To, it may be spreading all through the Groat country. I think he's right, sir, because I haven't been able to raise the U.S. team at Bax on the radio."

"What's Panton doing now?" Prescott asked.

"He's returning to Ba To with the bodies. He said he'll report in every hour and should make it back here this afternoon. That's all the information I have now."

"Stay in communication with the lodge, Minelli," Prescott said. "I'll stand by for further reports."

"Right, sir. And for your information, my Mit counterpart has been in contact with Mit Special Forces radio at the lodge."

"Thanks, Minelli." Prescott turned to Marlene, who had entered while he was talking. "You may be getting a bigger story than you expected. I'm afraid we're in the middle of the full-scale tribal rebellion I've been looking for. If only they'd listen to us back in Tuyan City. . . ." He paused as Major Darat, his counterpart and the nominal commanding officer of the mountain-tribesmen program, strutted into the radio room.

"I figured he'd show up when he heard through his own channels what's happening," Prescott said to Marlene. Darat stopped abruptly, staring in surprise at Marlene.

"Good morning, Major," Prescott said pleasantly. "Since Fraulein Straltz is writing about the fine spirit of cooperation between American and Mituyan counterparts, I thought she should see our communications room. I'm sure you have no objections?"

Major Darat welcomed her politely. Then he said to Prescott, "My communications officer reports the crisis is getting worse." He looked questioningly at Marlene.

"You are quite right. It is," Prescott agreed. "And only in a crisis situation can Miss Straltz really see how we operate together."

Darat shrugged. "We hear nothing from Bax. There are twenty Mituyan officers and men in the camp besides the two men who were reported murdered with your Captain Holloway and Sergeant Matthews."

"There are also four more Americans in there, Major," Prescott said quietly.

"The only way to deal with the dirty savages is to kill them," Darat snarled. "I'll request a bombing mission on the village, and we'll drop in a battalion of paratroopers."

"That won't save the lives of our men, if they're still alive," Prescott pointed out. "And any chance of peacefully putting down this uprising will be destroyed."

"You Americans!" Darat snorted in disgust. "You spoil and coddle the savages until they think they are as good as we are. That's what brings about their uprisings!"

"The report said the Mitcoms were behind the killings," Prescott reminded his counterpart. "If we, you and I, would go out there together, promise these people some of the reforms they request, relieve your Captain Narit who is so unpopular—"

"I will not relieve a Mituyan officer who is doing his duty," Darat snapped.

"It might help to avert a rebellion at Ba To if you did."

Darat thought a minute. "I'll relieve my camp commander if you will relieve his American counterpart."

To Marlene, Prescott said, "This is what is known as saving face. The trouble is that when an American officer is relieved his career suffers. A Mituyan officer is merely sent somewhere else."

Minelli's urgent voice came over the single sideband radio. "This is Ba To calling lodge, Ba To calling lodge. Do you read?"

"Go ahead, Minelli," Prescott answered.

"It's happening," Minelli's voice crackled over the radio. "A squad of Bax Groats just came in. They're with Beemeer and his son Radam now."

"Are you still in contact with Panton?"

"Affirm. Just took another message. They're on the way in, but the Ba To Groats with them look like they might turn on them."

"Minelli," Prescott called, "how is the perimeter around the Mituyan Special Forces camp at the north end of Ba To?"

"Pretty secure, sir." Minelli's voice rose. "Beemeer and a bunch of them, armed, are heading for me now. They probably want to take over the sideband. They've got at least one Mitcom with them."

Prescott turned to Darat. "Shall I tell my men to go into the fortified camp with your Mituyan Special Forces?"

Darat thought a few moments. "Affirmative. If there is an attack, they can stand it off until we can move help in. We can napalm the rest of the village."

Prescott called into the transmitter. "Minelli, let them have your radio. Go get all Americans into the Mituyan fortified section. I don't think the Groats will attack you. Contact me through Mit channels; and try to get word to Lieutenant Panton to break into the fort with you instead of making a normal approach to the village."

"Roger, sir. I'll maintain contact with Panton and you on the Mit equipment. Here's Beemeer and Radam now."

"Tell Radam I want to talk to him. Then while we're talking you get the rest of the Americans into the fortified compound."

There was a tense pause, and then Prescott heard Radam's voice: "Major Prescott? Can talk?"

"Talk me," Prescott replied.

"Bad here. Sorry 'bout that. Maybe Mituyan go. Then good here."

"Mituyan stay, but good you."

"No good we!" Radam cried. "Groat need Groat, no Mituyan."

"Radam. Prescott me go you today. Talk. OK?"

"OK. Go me. Talk."

"No kill. Me you talk."

"No kill 'merican. Kill much Mit."

"Radam!" Prescott called desperately. "No kill no man. Me go you. OK, Radam?"

After a long pause, during which Radam seemed to be conversing with others, the guttural voice came back. "OK. No kill no man. You go me."

"Go now," Prescott closed off, sighing in relief. Then to Major Darat: "Would you like to come with me?"

"You make a big mistake to go into Ba To," Darat declared.

"Look, Major," Prescott said earnestly, "at this minute the Mitcoms and Bax Groats are surely moving through the jungles toward Ba To.

When they get there, your men and mine will be killed and the Groats and Mitcoms united in a solid front against the Tuyan City government. We've got to hold them off and try to keep Chief Beemeer and his son Radam on our side. I've got to go. And you should."

Darat shook his head. "As soon as your men and mine are in the fortified compound, we will destroy the rest of the village and bomb and strafe the Mitcoms if they try to attack the compound."

"I like the second part of the idea, but we'll lose every tribe in the mountains if we bomb a village because they want an end to the injustices of your officers. And if we lose the mountains, we give the enemy one quarter of Mituyan for a stronghold with every tribesman, almost a million men, women, and children up there, going to the side of the Communists. Is that what you want?"

"We do not need the dirty savages," Darat said with contempt.

"I'm going to get ready."

Marlene followed Prescott back to his private quarters.

"Honey," said Prescott, "you're seeing a lot of classified stuff you can't print. OK?"

"I promise I do not write anything you say is secret."

"Good. I've got a private little radio with a frequency we had the good sense not to give to the Mituyan government."

Marlene listened intently as Prescott contacted Jack Cardinez in Tuyan City and explained the entire problem.

"Go ahead as planned," she heard Cardinez say. "I'll contact the II Corps American senior adviser and try and get help out there to you in case you need it."

"Thanks, sir. And don't let them bomb those villages. Dropping bombs and napalm is only going to make new dedicated Communists out of them all."

"I'll do the best I can," Cardinez promised. "Goddamn, you predicted this—and I passed along your predictions. But no one else in the U.S. mission wanted to have a thing to do with the tribesmen because of KaritKi. Sorry about that, Prescott."

"I'll get all my Americans into the Ba To fort. We'll hold out if the Mitcoms attack. I'm sure none of the Groats of Ba To will help them against us. If we put on a show of strength and they see we can drive off a Mitcom attack, maybe we can get old Chief Beemeer and his son back on our side. And, by the way, if you see Mr. Hartland tell him it's all happening just the way he agreed with me it would if something wasn't done on the Country Team level."

"Hartland is in Tiking today but he'll be back tomorrow. I'll tell him," Cardinez promised. "Good luck!"

"We'll need it—and reinforcements if we get hit."

"Go to it, Prescott. Out."

"Lodge out."

Prescott next called the pilot of the single plane assigned to the headquarters, an old model U-10 Heliocourier. The pilot determined that it would take three trips to fly ten Americans with extra ammunition and weapons into Ba To.

"Get cranked up!" Prescott ordered. "I'm going out to get nine volunteers, and we'll be on our way."

"Charlie, do you have to go in there yourself?" Marlene asked.

"Of course I do. I'll leave you the key to my quarters and you can monitor all the radio traffic. This should give you a hell of a story."

"Won't it get you in trouble?"

"No, I don't think so, darling. As long as you don't mention things like me talking to Jack Cardinez."

Prescott put his hands on her shoulders and drew her toward him. "I do love you, Marlene. And I want to marry you. I should be on the lieutenant colonels' list in a couple of months when my temporary duty with JRB is terminated and I'm back under army command again. I love you, Marlene." He bent over and kissed her, and Marlene responded with all the warmth in her. She liked and admired him so much—perhaps that was as good as love. Maybe it could be better than love. It was a long kiss. Afterward, Prescott said huskily, "I wish we had time to go back to Barkoon's royal suite. But this won't be a long trip—I hope."

"I'll wait here for you, Charlie," Marlene promised.

"Do you love me too?"

"I think so."

"Well, when I get back, I'll make you know so, darling."

"I'll be here."

Major Prescott took the first U-10 trip into Ba To. While two of his heavily armed men stalked down the main street of the village and through the barbed wire to the Mituyan Special Forces camp, Prescott, unarmed, sought out Radam. He found him standing before his father's house.

They talked earnestly for almost an hour in the young tribesman's few, simple but adequate, words of English.

Radam and his father, Chief Beemeer, were sympathetic to the tribal rebellion and its aims, he explained. They wanted promises from the central government that when the Communists were defeated, the Groats could become an autonomous nation. In the meanwhile they wanted only Americans in their village. They wanted no Mituyan officers in charge of Groat fighting units.

The Communists had promised to give them everything they asked. The Mitcoms had been training Groats to be commanders of Groat fighting units for two and three years in the North, and these men would be their leaders in the fight against the government for freedom. The Mitcoms promised that the Groats would have their own country free of interference by lowland administrators, which was all they really wanted out of all this strife that had been imposed on them.

Radam pointed out that it was impossible to be neutral, because if they did not follow government orders they were bombed by government airplanes, and if they defied the Mitcoms their villages were terrorized and their young men kidnaped and taken North to be trained as guerrillas. At the moment, he said, most of the Groats wanted to join with the Mitcoms. Only the Americans had kept them from becoming anti-government guerrillas up to now. But the time for a decision had come. The Mitcom guerrillas were even now marching through the jungle to take Ba To. The Groat leaders of the rebellion at Bax had ordered Radam to arrest all the Americans and to kill the Mituyan soldiers.

"We Americans must fight this, Radam," Prescott said sternly. "We go fort, fight Mitcoms they come."

"Too much Mitcom," Radam replied.

"We fight them. Many, many soldiers come help us."

Prescott argued vainly with Radam to abandon the rebellion while there was still time and help him drive off the Mitcoms. As they talked, the U-10 came in twice with a group of three heavily armed American Special Forces men from the lodge. Radam was aware that the Americans were reinforcing the Mituyan fort but made no move to stop them.

Prescott kept talking to Radam, hoping that as long as they were conversing no move would be made against the fortifications which the Americans were working desperately to improve.

In the middle of the afternoon, a shout went up as Lieutenant Panton, Sergeant Barton, and the two Groat platoons appeared from the edge of the jungle. The tribesmen from Ba To separated from the others in an orderly maneuver and entered the front gate of the village, while the Americans and the platoon of tribesmen from headquarters headed for the outer wall of the Mituyan Special Forces compound.

Prescott breathed a sigh of relief. At least the Ba To Groats had not started a conflict with their American advisers and the loyal tribesmen. Panton's men were guided in through the barbed wire and the hastily laid mine field by Teeter, the demolition sergeant.

Radam made a last appeal to Prescott either to abandon the village or submit to being detained. Reluctantly, Prescott agreed to leave Ba To, but only if Captain Narit and his Mituyan unit were also permitted to leave.

"No," Radam answered. "Mit all stay. You go."

"No go." Prescott declared. Then he asked Radam to accompany him into the fortified compound to see what the Mitcoms do to Americans they capture. He wanted Radam to understand perfectly why they could not allow themselves to be detained. Even if Radam would have permitted him to take the Mituyans out safely with the Americans, Prescott knew it would have been a mistake to give up their gains. To abandon Ba To now was tantamount to giving over the Groat country to the enemy. The next step would be a Mitcom sweep of the entire highland region of Mituyan with the help of the fierce Groat fighting men. Prescott and every one of his men knew that they had to try to hold out until the policymakers worked out a means to save the tribesmen from going over to the Mitcoms.

Though suspicious, Radam followed Prescott to the fortified northern end; a barbed-wire barricade was swung out of the way to let them in. The four bodies from the FOB disaster were laid out on the ground under rubber ponchos. Prescott congratulated Panton on returning through the Mitcom-infested jungle, and Panton and Radam gave each other the Groat handshake. There was clearly respect between the young American officer and the son of the village chief.

"Radam asks us to allow ourselves to be detained by his men while the leaders of this rebellion confer and decide what to do," Prescott said. "I want him to see for himself what the Mitcoms do when they get us."

Panton nodded and motioned Radam toward the forms under the ponchos. Grimly he exposed the mutilated body of Captain Holloway. Radam looked on it impassively. Then Panton uncovered the equally butchered body of Sergeant Matthews. Radam showed no emotion. Panton redraped the bodies and asked the young Groat: "You want me like that?"

Radam did not answer. Prescott made it clear that the Americans weren't going to give themselves up while the Groat rebellion was partly run by the Mitcoms. Finally Radam said, "Mitcom come soon, Bax Groat come soon. They fight you."

"You fight Americans, Radam?"

"Radam sad. Not know. Go now." The chief's son left the compound, and the barbed wire was moved into place behind him.

"Well, we're in for a battle now," Prescott told his men. "Minelli, can you raise the lodge over the Mit radio here?"

"Yes, sir. And Colonel Gruen, II Corps senior adviser, is in touch with the lodge and will probably talk to us direct here when he's ready."

"Have you heard anything about reinforcements?" Prescott asked.

"Not yet, sir."

"Panton, let's have a meeting with that dipshit counterpart of yours."

They found Captain Narit in his quarters, seated in a chair, one of his men serving him tea. Narit was obviously a badly frightened Mituyan officer.

"Captain Narit, as commander of this camp, you will soon be inspecting the fortifications and making plans to fight off a battalion of Mitcoms and Groats. The attack could come at any time, so I'd advise you to get ready."

Narit made no answer. Prescott prodded him. "As senior officer, I could assume command if you want it that way. I have had much experience in these sorts of attacks in Laos and Vietnam."

Finally, Narit said, without emotion: "You Americans are advisers. I will command."

"Then I advise you to get with it!"

Slowly, as though in a trance, Narit stood up and wandered out into the compound.

"We'll have to run things," Prescott said, shaking his head.

"Right, sir," agreed Panton.

"Make sure all our men are positioned so they can't get shot by our Mituyan *allies*," Prescott advised. I've seen government troops panic and go over to the other side, shooting their American counterparts on the way."

"We'll be looking for something like that."

"Okay. Let's dig in and wait. I'm afraid we'll have to call a hundred-percent alert tonight—everybody awake all night."

"I'll pass the word."

Prescott went to the communications bunker. In spite of the deteriorating military situation in which he had placed himself, he thought of Marlene. They had arranged a few key code words to advise her of his situation. His heart lifted.

CHAPTER THIRTY-SIX

PREMIER KARITKI DISLIKED emergency meetings. Tarot, however, had persuaded him that this time it was necessary, and in the more intimate atmosphere of the living room of his apartment in the palace, KaritKi now conversed with Ambassador Whittelsie, General Macker, Filmore Dickerson, and his brother.

"We always kept the hillspeople under control until you Americans started spoiling them," KaritKi complained. "Your men give them ideas about a better life, and we end up with a revolt—the first we've ever had."

"Your Excellency will recall I opposed allowing the Americans to start their program in the mountains in the first place," Tarot said.

"My brother was right. I should have listened to him instead of your CIA." He glared at Dickerson.

"You must remember that I inherited the program," Dickerson countered.

"Yes, Mr. Dickerson," Tarot agreed. "But you allowed your man Cardinez to enlarge upon the program, give the tribesmen more training, medical treatment that they neither understood nor wanted, and your American political outlook—which is not healthy in our part of the world. And worst of all, you armed them so they could overcome my Mituyan Special Forces units which tried to undo the damage done by your so-called JRB with American Special Forces." He turned to Whittelsie. "Now we have a full-scale revolt. What do you intend to do, Mr. Ambassador?"

"What do you suggest?" Whittelsie asked warily. "We will do all we can. I understand we have reinforced the Mituyan garrison at Ba To with American Special Forces to help protect your soldiers."

"I think I can offer a solution," General Macker said. All eyes turned to him. "It is merely what I've been saying all along: Restore all these green-beret hoods to Military Assistance Command authority; that way I can control what goes on in the mountains. I will insure that they work in harmony with their Mituyan counterparts. There will be no running off to the hills to play capture-the-flag. Let Mr. Dickerson handle his spooks and hoods as he sees fit, but keep soldiers of the United States Army out of the CIA. I will continue to work closely with the chief of staff of the Mituyan Army, and if all military matters, both Mituyan and U.S., are handled by us without interference, we can put an end to this war before it gets worse." Macker glared at Tarot—the arch meddler in Mituyan military affairs as far as he was concerned—but Tarot made no reply.

"What do you say, Phil?" Whittelsie asked the CIA station chief.

"I agree with General Macker to a certain extent," Dickerson replied. "But the Premier should take into account that it was I who agreed to change the mountain-tribes' program, and against the judgment of both Mr. Cardinez and my predecessor here, who still wields a great deal of influence in Washington, I recommended and pushed through approval of giving Mituyan Special Forces teams command of the mountain camps and relegating our men to a strictly advisory capacity."

"That is true," KaritKi allowed. "We have no complaint at all about Mr. Dickerson's conduct. He has been most cooperative. But we are in trouble now. What do we do?"

"Let the military settle this Mitcom-Groat attack against the American and Mituyan garrison at Ba To," said Macker. "I will ask Colonel Gruen, my senior adviser in II Corps, to take over control from the CIA, and with General Thannit, commander of II Corps, quell this mutiny in any way they see fit."

Whittelsie looked at Dickerson. "Is that all right with you? I think a military solution is the only answer now."

"Just remember, for three years we have been struggling to win the loyalty of the tribes for Premier KaritKi's government," Dickerson said. "It may still be possible to do so if some responsible government officials listen to the grievances of the tribesmen and promise reforms and changes."

"We do not need the mountain tribesmen," Tarot said emphatically. "We have never needed them. The cursed savages are too spread out to destroy completely, but we are not going to give in to the demands of a horde of aborigines. Let the military see what it can do now. Later we will try to arrive at a political solution."

"Well, then," Whittelsie summed up. "this has been a most constructive meeting, I'd say. As I see it, American involvement in the

Groat program will be turned over from CIA to MAC-M. Fortunately that decision can be made on the spot, since the Secretary of Defense is still in the country. The II Corps commander will take over immediately. I hope *he* can end this thing at once. Very embarrassing to have it crop up the very day after we told the Secretary, the Chief of Staff of the Army, and the Undersecretary of State for South Asian Affairs that everything was under control in the mountain country."

"It will be again," Macker declared.

Whittelsie looked about the room cheerfully. "Well, Your Excellency, if there's nothing else, I'll report directly to the Secretary, who is waiting at my residence now."

KaritKi, too, was relieved the meeting was over. "Convey my respects to the Secretary," he said.

"This is a damned bad situation, Phil," Whittelsie said worriedly, as they drove back to the embassy through the unevenly lighted streets of Tuyan City. "It seems to me that Jack Cardinez predicted this would happen just a week or so ago, and we all said it was impossible."

Dickerson was tired. His self-confidence ebbed more every day. "We all have instructions to work with the Palace closely," he replied. "The Palace utterly rejected all my reports on the turmoil in the mountains. But quite frankly, I'm beginning to lose confidence in the Palace. I work under your political guidelines, which means, as you put it, I must live or die with KaritKi. But I feel that neither KaritKi nor his brother really understands their own people, and although I take orders as a member of the Country Team, I find it more and more difficult not to agree with Jack Cardinez that Mituyan will be lost if there is not a change of government very soon."

"The elections will solve all that, Phil," Whittelsie answered airily. "They can't come soon enough to suit me."

"Righto," said Dickerson listlessly. He felt desperately tired.

CHAPTER THIRTY-SEVEN

SINCE THE FIRST enemy white-phosphorous mortar round had fallen into their camp, Captain Narit had confined himself to the heavily armored and sandbagged command bunker from which he gave occasional orders on the field telephone to Mituyan positions. There were a total of ten Mituyan soldiers in the camp and fifteen Americans. In addition, thirty-odd loyal tribesmen were arrayed along the north, east, and west walls. The Mitcom attack had been carefully planned to spare the village of Ba To on the south side of the camp.

Prescott frequently went to the radio bunker, where he talked to Radam less than two hundred yards away in the village. Radam gave constant assurance that his two companies of well-armed Ba To Groats would remain neutral in the battle since they did not want to fight their American friends. But they would offer no help either, since the Americans were clearly opposing the tribal rebellion that Radam and his father were pledged to support.

Prescott tried to point out that the Bax Groats were controlled by the Mitcoms and therefore were more militant—they would neither negotiate nor permit the Ba To Groats to negotiate until the Americans and Mituyans were prisoners; but Radam and Beemeer refused to go against their fellow tribal leaders.

From their fortifications, the Mituyan and American Special Forces men fired a constant succession of mortar flares to keep the surrounding area well illuminated. The Mituyan barracks and other buildings soon burned down in the barrage of fire, but no casualties were sustained. The mortar shells had started coming in intermittently just after dark, and now that it was getting close to midnight Prescott expected an all-out attack at any moment. He kept up a constant flow of reports to Captain Jenkins back at the lodge. Jenkins was one of the few Americans proficient in Mituyan, Vietnamese, and some of the mountain-tribe dialects, and Prescott had disregarded his bitter protests and kept him behind to man the radio.

"Ba To, this is Lodge. Over," the radio crackled.

"Go ahead, Lodge," Prescott called back, pressing against the walls of the sandbagged commo bunk as mortar shells crunched into the camp.

"Two guerrilla leaders are talking in Vietnamese to each other," Jenkins reported. "We're getting a fix on the location now. One location is almost on your position, the other west of here in the mountains about halfway between the lodge and Tiking."

"Can you make out what they're saying?"

"The location in the west seems to be a Communist headquarters for the whole northern section of the country. The leader there, he identifies himself as Van Can, is telling the other guy out your way to hit hard, overrun your positions and kill every American."

"Thanks for the information," Prescott replied. "What about reinforcements?"

"Colonel Gruen at II Corps headquarters in Banthut is trying to lay on a helicopter lift. He's running into some trouble with General Bannort.

"Try to raise the boss and tell him if he doesn't want to find our heads on stakes around this village tomorrow morning he'd better get us help. But for God's sake, tell him and tell Gruen not to let the Mit Air Force or our own guys bomb Ba To. Even the Mitcoms are being damned accurate with their mortar fire."

"I'll pass that word along."

A string of mortar rounds crashed down. "Things are getting hot. Minelli will stay on the radio. I've got to go." Prescott paused a moment and then said, "*Auf wiedersehen, Liebchen.*" He switched frequencies back to the sideband in the village.

"Hello, Radam, Hello, Radam," he called on the American radio.

Radam replied immediately. In careful short words Prescott told him that the Americans had learned that the Communists from the North were behind this bloody stage of the Groat rebellion; foreigners all the way from North Vietnam were inciting the Groats to fight against their American friends.

Radam admitted that this was true, but once again he reiterated that this was the only way the tribesmen would ever be free of the low-landers who abused them so. Mortars continued to crash into the camp as Prescott again asked Radam and his two companies to fight with him against the foreigners, who would treat them even more cruelly than the government in Tuyan City. Radam made one concession. Worried at having taken the Americans' radio on orders from the rebellion leader at Bax, he offered to try and call in help for him. Prescott thanked him but said he could reach his headquarters from the camp.

Prescott made the rounds of the camp, diving for a ditch as the in-coming rounds thwacked the air above him. The accuracy of the Mit-com mortar fire—not a single round endangering the occupants of the village—proved that the guerrillas were no hastily mustered group of peasants but well-trained soldiers. In the medical bunker, Cavanaugh was ready to take care of casualties. He also manned the mortar posi-tion just outside the heavily sandbagged dispensary. So far there had been no serious wounds. It would have taken a direct hit to knock out any of the defenders dug in around the walls or crouched in the sand-bagged mortar pits. In an armored, sandbagged cockpit atop the com-mand bunker, the demolition expert, Sergeant Teeter, watched the terrain around the camp; the sickly pale yellow light of the flares prevented the enemy from creeping up to the walls unnoticed. At his fingertips were electric detonating switches that controlled various mines he had been putting out all day.

Sergeants Barton and Crenshaw manned the 81-mm. mortar, which was firing back methodically at the Mitcom mortars just inside the fringe of the jungle. The loyal tribesmen were ready for the attack on the walls, and the Mituyan Special Forces men were bunched together around the southwest bunker where, because it bordered the village, the fewest mortars were falling.

"Here they come!" Teeter shouted from his perch.

The initial attack was out of the west, and what appeared to be a full company of guerrillas, some dressed in black and some in khaki, came running across the terrain toward the camp. Prescott jumped up beside Teeter where he could give his mortarmen range and azimuth directions over the field telephone.

The small camp rained mortar rounds down on the advancing Com-munists. Black forms fell like sacks to the ground—but the guerrillas kept advancing at a trot. The machine guns opened up when the guer-rillas were at close range, ripping the advancing company but not stop-ping it. As the Groats and Americans picked off the guerrillas, Teeter watched the ragged line of attackers close on the fort. Prescott estimated that half the company—more than sixty men—reached the perimeter of mines Teeter had laid. Suddenly, with the walls of their objective in reach, the mines were detonated in terrific explosions, tearing apart the guerrillas as they stepped on them. The terrifying probability that the next step would blow their legs off slowed down the guerrillas, who fired their weapons into the ground in front of them, thus hoping to set off the mines with their bullets. The sharpshooting Americans on the west wall decimated the remaining guerrillas trapped in the mine field. In the light of the illuminating rounds, Prescott watched many of the men in black head into the village. The defenders had been ordered not to shoot into the village, so these survivors of the first attack were spared.

There was a lull in the battle now, and Prescott radioed what had happened into the lodge. "Sir," Jenkins said, "there's been a lot more traffic in Vietnamese. This Van Can has told the guerrilla leader hitting you that he must overrun your positions or their whole program to take over the Groat rebellion will fail. This Van Can must be a real sweetheart. He's given them loud and clear orders on what to do to the Americans when they take the camp."

"I can imagine," Prescott called back. "How about help?"

"Everyone's trying except General Bannort. He wants the Air Force to bomb out the whole village. So far Gruen, and I guess it goes right up to Macker, are resisting."

"Tell them we'd rather fight to the end alone than have them destroy Ba To and its people."

"Right, sir."

"Ba To out."

Then Prescott called Radam. In spite of himself the young Groat could not help sounding excited about the battle the Americans were putting up. "Many man from Bax stop fighting, come Ba To, stay Ba To," he reported. "Prescott you numbah one fight."

"Hey, Radam help Americans?" Prescott asked.

"No can," Radam replied.

Prescott looked at Minelli and shook his head. "He really thinks he can force the Mituyan government to stay out of the mountains and leave the tribal areas to Americans only. What a mess up here."

A lethal downpouring of mortar shells heralded the second wave of the attack. This time the camp was being attacked from both east and west. The Communists were not hitting from the north since that would have forced them to shoot across the walls and into the village, and they were still posing as the friends of the hill tribesmen.

So far the casualties had been light to the defenders. One mortar shell had landed in a Groat position on the wall, blowing a tribesman to pieces. Sergeant Barton reported a slight wound in the shoulder from the last blast, but miraculously, in spite of the accuracy of the Communist mortarman, light shell-fragment wounds had been Cavanaugh's only business, leaving him free to fire his mortar.

The two new waves of attackers moved steadily in on the camp, and, as the mortars continued to rock it, the guerrillas fired machine guns and American grenade-launchers. In the distance the ominous whoosh of a rocket gave Prescott sudden concern. They had 57-mm. recoil-less rifles! A blazing high-explosive missile tore at the machine-gun bunker in the outer northeast corner and stilled the chattering weapon. Prescott, crouched low, ran to the bunker and found a wounded American. Barton! He shouted to Cavanaugh, who came running over and carried the wounded man to the medical bunker. Prescott righted the .30-caliber machine gun and began firing it himself. More rockets from the recoil-less rifle slammed into the walls, the force of its hits tumbling men from their holes where they provided targets for grenades and small-arms fire until they could scramble back to cover.

Once again the Communists were on the outer perimeter of the camp, the mortars and recoil-less rifles having exploded the mines and cut through the barbed wire. Sergeant Teeter poked his head above the protective wall around his position and then, one by one, set off his claymore mines. Each claymore scythed a blast of shrapnel through the attackers, killing or badly wounding the front ranks of guerrillas, piling bodies in front of the walls. The defenders hurled grenades at those guerrillas still attacking, and the small-arms fire from the camp was accurate and intense. The momentum of the attack had been stopped, and once again the guerrillas began to pull back. Many forms limped for the village. More Groats deserting, Prescott thought triumphantly. He ran back to Teeter's post on top of the command bunker. "How many more claymores have we got?" he asked anxiously.

"I fired damned near all of them, sir," Teeter answered. "Maybe we have one or two left. Several of them didn't fire. I guess the mortars cut the electric lines to them."

Prescott made for the communications bunker and found Minelli in contact with Jenkins. The sergeant looked up as Prescott entered and shrugged hopelessly. "General Bannort won't release helicopters to airlift in troops. He wants to bomb and napalm the village and the area all around here."

Prescott picked up the transceiver microphone. "What's the matter with Gruen?" he asked. "Can't he pull weight with that damned Mit general?"

"Well, sir, from what the boss in Tuyan City says, Colonel Gruen thinks he might spoil his chances for making general if he gets into an all-out hassle with his counterpart. Bannort is famous for having a short fuse on his temper and hating mountain tribesmen. A tough combination for a colonel trying to make the general's list to face."

"We can't hold out very damn much longer," Prescott called. "We've killed a lot of them. There must be over a hundred bodies in front of our walls, but a couple more assaults and they'll have us."

"The boss said to tell you he's doing everything possible."

"Roger, Lodge. Ba To out." Prescott left the commo bunker just in time to hear a Mituyan voice, amplified by a bull horn, coming from the Mitcom position. He listened carefully, understanding a few words, and strode toward the Mituyan Special Forces men huddled terrified in the safest corner of the camp—against the wall dividing it from the village. The Mituyans stirred. Hope came to faces drawn with fear. One of them picked up the field telephone and called Captain Narit, safe in the command bunker.

Panton left his position, submachine gun in his arms, and ran toward Prescott, his weapon pointed at the Mituyans.

"Sir, do you know what they're saying?"

Prescott shook his head. "Something about surrendering and they won't die."

"The Mitcoms are telling the Mituyan Special Forces men that if they turn their guns on us and go into the village they will not be killed." Panton stared at the frightened Mituyans in disgust. "Wouldn't surprise me a bit if they did just that."

Captain Narit emerged from the bunker and started for his men. Prescott stopped him, fastening a clamp of a hand on the little Mituyan officer's arm. "Look, Narit, don't be crazy! If you pull out of this camp, the Groats will kill you no matter what the Mitcoms say. You should know how much the tribesmen love you."

Narit stared at him blankly, and when Prescott let go he went on to his men. Prescott watched them converse, as the bull horn continued its amplified words, then made for the commo bunker again and flipped the switch on the radio to the band Radam had been monitoring. It took almost two minutes before the chief's son was finally summoned and answered.

"Radam," Prescott called. "Mitcoms say Mituyan soldiers can come to you, can come Ba To and no kill. Mitcoms say they only kill Americans. You want kill Americans?"

For the first time Radam sounded shaken. His father had probably translated the Mituyan words for him, Prescott reasoned. "No want kill Americans. Just Mituyan."

"Mitcoms say no kill Mituyans, kill Americans. . . . Help us, Radam!" Prescott pleaded.

But still the fever of tribal independence and the goals of the rebellion burned fiercely. "Groats not fight Groats," Radam declared. "Fight Mituyans." There was a pause then. "Hey, Prescott, you fight numbah one. Kill plenty. Many Groat quit fight with Mitcom, come to Ba To. Mitcom chief talk me, talk Beemeer, talk we fight American now. Help them. Radam say no. Keep fight good. Mitcom soon stop fight."

"I hope you're right, Radam." Prescott went to find Teeter, who was examining his explosive devices on the wall.

"We've got one more secret weapon, sir. Then we've had it."

Teeter and Crenshaw were tugging at tight rolls of barbed wire they had put in a bunker to protect them from the mortar barrage. They dragged the rolls one by one, to the walls and lowered them over the sides in front of the mouths of barrels that pointed out toward the attackers of the walls like huge gun muzzles.

"We've still got plenty of claymores on the north side, but they aren't attacking from the north," Teeter explained. "These fire barrels will break up one more charge, but after that—" When a roll of barbed wire had been placed in front of each of the protruding barrels, Teeter checked his wiring again and return to his vantage point.

Prescott went into the dispensary and found several of his men being treated for wounds. Barton was bandaged about the head and shoulders, but his right arm seemed operative.

"I'm going back to my weapon, sir," the big sergeant rasped.

"Every American in here is still able to fight, sir," Cavanaugh announced proudly.

"Thanks, men," Prescott said, deeply moved. "I'm afraid this is it for all of us. Let's take as many of them with us as we can. I have a feeling that just by staying here and holding off and destroying a battalion of Mitcoms we're breaking up the entire Groat rebellion. The Mits are losing face right now with the Groats. Each time I talk to Radam on the sideband I can tell he's less and less favorable toward the rebellion. The Mitcoms will never regain the confidence of the Groats if we keep mauling them. And pass the word, watch out for our *allies*."

Prescott strode out of the medical bunker and made another tour of the fort, encouraging the loyal tribesmen on the walls, placing a hand on the shoulder of each of them. Then he walked over to the Mituyan Special Forces men talking with their captain. "Narit, your men could do a lot more good spread around the walls than right here against the village wall. The Mitcoms won't attack through the village or chance shooting up the Groats. They're trying to make Groatcoms out of Ba To. And they will, unless we beat them here and now."

"My radio operator says that General Bannort is being prevented from sending help by the Americans," Narit said accusingly.

"Not true!" Prescott barked. "We don't want them sending in the air force to smash the village and kill civilians. We're trying to get American high-accuracy strafing pilots to help us."

Narit looked at his counterpart with complete mistrust. "You Americans will get us all killed," he snapped. "What does it matter if we kill every Groat in the village as long as we defeat the enemy?"

Across the fields Prescott heard the pops of mortar shells. "Everybody in position!" he yelled. He made it to Teeter's observation bunker just as the first rounds fell into the camp. They were followed up by the fearsome whistle of the rockets, and then once again, in the illumination of flares, another wave of guerrillas attacked both east and west. The blaring of the bull horns calling to Narit and his men to turn on the Americans and be spared could be heard over the sound of the small-arms fire. Suddenly, from the Mituyan positions, with their backs to the Groat village, Narit's men began firing into the camp, spraying rounds at the Groat and American defenders on the walls. Teeter, a grenade in his hand, was able to pull the pin and lob it from his raised bunker into the Mituyan Special Forces group. He reached for another, but Prescott gripped his shoulder.

"No, Teeter!" he cried. "They're still our allies. They can't do us too much damage before they bug out."

A fusillade of rounds tore into the sides of their bunker, and both men ducked low behind the sandbags. The men on the walls also crouched down, taking fire from both front and rear. The shouting from the Mituyan Special Forces lessened, and Prescott cautiously poked his head up to see them crawling out over the walls and barbed wire into the village. From the walls a few men turned and sent rounds singing after the deserters, until Prescott shouted at them not to fire toward the village. The loyal Groat commander understood and relayed the orders to his men. Prescott watched the last of the Mits crawl into the village and disappear in the darkness.

By now the screaming black-clad guerrillas had for the third time reached the shredded outer perimeter and were lobbing grenades into the fireholes, killing or seriously wounding the occupants.

"Christ, where do they keep coming from?" Prescott cried. "They're all over the east and west perimeter."

Teeter kept poking his head up, snatching a glance at the situation and ducking again, as fire filled the air immediately above the observation bunker. "Here we go, sir!" he shouted and threw the knife switches.

One after another, the fire barrels, which had been filled with highly combustible heavy oil and gasoline, were detonated by one-pound charges of plastic explosive. Spurting out from the walls came a path of flaming fuel combined with a thousand particles of barbed wire, as the rolls placed in front of the fire barrels were minced and hurled into the enemy. Screams of guerrillas burning to death filled the air.

The defenders hurled grenades and pressed heavy fire volume on the shocked attackers, who had been convinced this time that they would breach the walls. Once again the tiny garrison had blunted and turned back a fierce stab from two directions and destroyed another company of Communists. The Americans and Groats inside cheered lustily.

"That's the end, sir," Teeter said. "From now on, it's man to man. I'll try to sneak out and change the positions of the claymores on the north side. That will give us a little help."

Prescott watched the survivors of the fire barrels struggle back from the walls under fire from his sharpshooters. "I don't know what else they've got, Teeter, but we've got to hang in here as long as one man's alive. I'm going to the radio room and report back to the lodge."

Major Ding of the People's Army of Vietnam stared aghast and dismayed at the fiery destruction of the third company of his battalion. His intelligence reports had been reassuring: A handful of Americans and poorly trained Mituyans were all that stood between his Mituyan guerrillas and their North Vietnamese advisers and the important Groat village of Ba To. He had quickly subdued the Americans at Bax and had taken over the tribesmen's rebellion that had been brewing for a long time, needing only a leader and reassurances of success to break into open warfare.

But now once again he had to face the gut-twisting obligation of reporting failure to Colonel Nguyen Van Can. He forced himself to walk to the temporary radio post and ask his aide to make contact with Colonel Can on the powerful American field radio his agents had purchased in return for the Groat opium.

A Mituyan guerrilla cranked the generator, and soon Ding was describing the failure of the last attack.

"I want the heads of the Americans on stakes around Ba To by morning," Can shouted over the radio. "If we do not show the tribesmen that we can kill every American who comes to the mountains, we will not maintain the confidence of the Groats. Their revolt will dissipate and we will lose our chance to create and control a whole new war against the government."

"But, sir, I have lost a battalion. I have barely one company of Mituyan guerrillas left."

"Use the Groats in Ba To to fight the Americans. You were successful in making the Mituyans desert. Now order the Groats to attack."

"They have refused," Ding replied.

"*Every* Croat in Ba To has refused to fight for their cause?" Can returned scathingly.

"Their leader, the son of their chief, refuses."

"You must make the Groats fight!" Can cried. "Take the American camp no matter what you have to do. That is an order! I go to Tuyan City in a week for meetings and a special mission. I must report success in the mountains. Report back when every American head is on display."

"Yes, Colonel." The sudden cessation of crackling static indicated that Can had broken contact. Wearily, Ding set to work mustering his guerrillas. His contingent of Groats had dwindled after each disastrous attack. But Ding knew that Colonel Can was right. If he failed to overrun the Americans before dawn, the years that the Mituyan Freedom Front and its parent group in Hanoi had spent training Mituyan tribal leaders to launch a full-scale rebellion would be lost.

Ding desperately wanted to talk to Colonel Can and ask him how far he could go in alienating the tribesmen of Ba To in order to overrun the Americans. If he could attack through the village he could almost surely take the fort, but many villagers would be killed in the return fire, and they would not blame the Americans, who were defending themselves, but the MFF. Can had assured him that the Mituyan Air Force and the Americans would kill many Groats in trying to relieve the garrison, and this would further turn the tribesmen away from the government. Instead, not a single government airplane had come. The Groats were even beginning to cheer as the Americans drove off his guerrillas. Bitterly he wished Colonel Can was here to handle the situation himself.

Ding found the Bax rebellion leader, Grak, amid a small knot of Groat survivors. Grak was no longer an aggressive leader. His men complained bitterly at the slaughter being administered by the small garrison that their leaders had promised would be so easy to destroy. Grak, in turn, glared accusingly at Ding as he approached, but the North Vietnamese had made up his mind what he must do now.

He told Grak to muster all his able men and follow the remaining light company of guerrillas into the village. He had ordered the remnants of his company that had attacked the camp from the east to meet him at the gate of Ba To. There he would force the two armed companies of Ba To Groats to help attack the Americans and kill them.

Reluctantly, Grak agreed to commit his surviving insurgents to this new plan of attack. Leaving the mortars to continue periodic barrages against the camp, the column of Groats and Mituyan guerrillas, avoiding the area of illumination, headed for the front gates of Ba To. Altogether, Major Ding realized he would have to make his final assault with fewer than one hundred men unless the Ba To Groats joined the attack. Since the Americans in the camp were as anxious as he had been not to kill villagers, any new surprise weapons they still might have would be aimed east and west. Ding, a veteran of many battles in Vietnam, felt a strong sense of admiration for the American commander and decided not to permit his torture and mutilation if he could prevent it. A man of such intelligence, bravery, and ingenuity deserved a clean execution.

Ding led his ragged column into the village, Grak beside him. The major's command of the Groat dialect was poor, although he had learned to communicate with Grak over the past few months as they planned the Groat rebellion right under the noses of the Americans and Mituyans encamped in the village of Bax. Demanding to see Radam, Ding and Grak were led to what recently had been the American radio shack. Radam was talking over the radio in English.

Radam turned as Ding and Grak entered. Using Grak as an interpreter, Ding requested that Radam, and his father, Chief Beemeer, for the sake of the tribal revolt, join the MFF and the Bax Groats in crushing the Americans, who were dedicated to the principles of the Tuyan City government. Radam stated that Chief Beemeer had gone to his longhouse in silent disapproval of the way the rebellion was being handled. Radam and Grak, the two strongest Groat leaders, discussed the situation.

"The Americans have done much to help Ba To," Radam argued. "It is the Mituyans we hate. They surrendered, and we cut off their captain's head and stuck it on a pole."

Grak approved the Mituyan captain's beheading. "But now we must kill these Americans."

"Why? They do not like the Mituyans either," Radam replied.

Startled, Grak could not answer Radam's question; the Americans also had helped him and his people. He posed the question to Major Ding.

The Communist's answer flowed fluently. "Tell Radam that only the Americans prevent the government of Mituyan from falling. If it were not for the Americans, the Mituyan Freedom Front would govern the country and the Groats would be an independent nation. If we defeat these Americans, no more Mituyans will ever again come into the mountains."

Confident once again, Grak translated Ding's answer. Radam hesitated. Then he raised his voice and decisively declared: "The Americans have helped us. If we have the Americans and no Mituyans, the way it used to be, that is the way I want it. That is the way my father, Chief Beemeer, wants it. We want the Americans to stay and the Mituyans to go. We will not help you kill the Americans."

Radam turned to his radio as Grak translated his words to Major Ding. "Hey, Prescott. You still talk?"

"Talk Radam." Prescott's words cracked out loudly over the powerful radio. Instinctively, Ding knew he was hearing his adversary's voice. He stared at the radio.

"Mitcom boss here. Say Radam must fight you. Radam say no!" His voice rang out in the room. "Ba To Groat no fight American. Mitcom here Ba To. You look out good, Prescott. Mitcom fight you—"

Then Ding panicked and made the mistake that was to cost him his life.

He pulled his prized German P-38 automatic pistol and shot Radam in the back. As the tribal leader collapsed, both hands clawing for the radio, Radam groaned out three beseeching words—"Fight good, Prescott." Then Ding shot him through the back of the head.

"Grak—you tell all Groats to follow me!" Ding cried. "Kill the Americans!" The tribal leader from Bax looked fearfully at his dead counterpart from Ba To. The fierce look of unflinching purpose on Major Ding's small, sharp lowland face instilled the determination the tribal leader needed, and he shouted to his men to kill the Americans.

"Order the Ba To Groats to fight with us too!" Ding shouted triumphantly. Grak shouted that Radam was dead and they must all now follow him as the leader against the Americans.

Ding's men were waiting outside the radio house, and he gave them orders to infiltrate through the village up to the walls of the camp and then blast the Americans with grenades and turn the recoil-less rifle on them.

Back in the radio room, Prescott turned to Panton who was standing beside him. "I think the Mitcom leader shot Radam."

"Sounded that way. The stupidest thing he ever did in his life, whoever he was. That'll cost the Communists any chance they might have had with the Groats."

"OK, we know the attack is going to come through the village. Get ready."

"Shall we turn the rest of the claymore mines into Ba To?"

Prescott shook his head. "The claymores are too lethal. They'll cut down half the village. The Mitcoms just blew their chance of solid support from the Groats—let's not do the same thing. We'll fight them hand-to-hand as long as we can." He gave Panton a triumphant grin. "You know, I think we've won a great victory out here. That Mitcom leader must be hurting badly to have hit the panic button like that and killed Radam. We must have wiped out most of the Mitcom force. While I'm giving a radio report to the lodge, you get everyone posted on the village side of these walls. Tell them not to throw grenades far enough into the village so they can hurt people. I guess all the women and children will go to the opposite end of the village. Get going, Panton! We're damned lucky Radam warned us, or they'd sure as hell have overrun us from the rear."

As Panton left the radio room, Prescott shifted to headquarters frequency and called Captain Jenkins. After reporting everything that had happened to headquarters, he asked about help.

"They've finally cleared it with General Bannort and the province chief to bring in armed choppers at first light. Colonel Gruen will be flying in himself and will land in the village as soon as it's secure. Tell your commo man to expect a call from the colonel's chopper at daybreak. If he can come in without getting shot up, he will."

"Sunrise is almost two hours from now," Prescott replied. "I have about twelve unwounded Groats and ten unwounded Americans to fight off as many as a hundred Mitcoms. Better tell the colonel not to count on us being on our feet to greet him."

The sharp hiss of a rocket followed by a devastating explosion that knocked Prescott off his feet signaled the start of the final attack. He called into the transmitter. "They're hitting us with their fifty-seven. This is it. *Auf wiedersehen, Liebchen. Ich liebe dich.*"

"What?" Jenkins called back.

"Not you, Jenkins. Ba To out."

Prescott turned to Minelli. "Let's go, Sergeant. That radio isn't going to do anything for us now." He pulled a bayonet from his belt and fixed it to the stud under the muzzle of his M-16. Minelli followed his example, both of them loosening the grenades on their combat harnesses.

Outside, flames licked at the center of the wall facing the village where the rocket had hit. Two more dead Groats lay sprawling on the wall, one of them on fire. One of the American defenders was keeping an illuminating round in the air over the village at all times. In spite of the pale light, the stilted buildings cast deep shadows everywhere, and it was impossible to see whether the Mitcoms were crawling toward them or still waiting. Mortar rounds continued to crash into the camp.

Teeter jumped from his observation bunker down to the ground and joined Prescott, pressing himself into the wall for protection from mortar fragments. "Sir," he shouted, "we could hold them off a little longer by firing our mortars into them point-blank."

"We'd kill half the people in the village doing that. Let's try not to lose what we've won."

Suddenly the Mitcoms and Bax Groats charged out from the shadows at the walls. Prescott's tribesmen and Special Forces men hurled grenades and poured their dwindling supply of bullets into the attackers. Although many fell dead and wounded, more kept coming.

"Hold them off, men!" Prescott shouted above the fire. "This is their last one." He switched his automatic rifle to single shot and yelled, "Get your weapons off automatic. We gotta save ammo!"

The Mitcoms were hurling grenades at the walls as they charged, and the flying steel fragments found the defenders one by one as the attackers swarmed through paths blasted in the barbed-wire entanglements by the recoil-less rifles. Now, with the enemy at the edge of the wall, screaming the English words, "Kill Yankees!" Prescott knew the camp would be overrun.

"Over the walls, men!" he yelled. "Let's get 'em!"

Though bleeding both from the shoulder and back, Prescott jumped to the top of the wall and followed by his Green Berets and loyal Groats, he charged down and into the attackers, who were surprised by this sudden tactic. Firing from the hips and stabbing with low upslanted thrusts of their bayonets, the defenders once again halted the wave of Mitcoms and Groats. Prescott somehow noticed, in spite of the intense hand-to-hand fighting, that there were few if any tribesmen now. All the faces in the blur of battle were sharp-featured and yellowish.

The Mitcoms began to fall back at the furious counterassault, and Prescott shouted to his men to regain their positions on the wall. Five Americans and eight tribesmen fell back on the walls, where they lay, exhausted, waiting for another—the last onslaught. Prescott realized both his legs were now torn, and his left arm hung useless and without feeling; but he could still shoot with his right arm.

Miraculously, an unwounded redheaded sergeant appeared beside him. "Not much I can do for you, sir, except stop some of the blood," he said, cutting open Prescott's fatigues and pressing a compress to the rent side.

"Thanks, Cav." Prescott found it a tremendous effort to talk. "Don't waste time with the wounded. We're gonna die. Make 'em kill us fighting. You know what happens when commies get us alive."

Exhausted, Prescott lay on the parapet staring at the enemy, regrouping in the shadows of the longhouses.

Cavanaugh unslung his submachine gun and lay down beside his commander, facing the village.

A rocket shrilled through the air and blew out a section of the wall a few feet from them. Prescott felt sudden jagged pain in his side but remained conscious. Then he heard the chatter of Cavanaugh's submachine gun and turned his own weapon at the oncoming little men in black.

At long last Prescott had a look at their leader, who was yelling at his men to take the fort this time.

"Get 'em Cav!" he rasped. "That's the last platoon they've got."

"I'm afraid it's enough, sir."

In a daze that he forced himself to clear, Prescott watched the forty or more Mitcoms spring through the wire. Their leader had pulled the pin on a grenade, and his arm was back to hurl it into the position Prescott and Cavanaugh were holding when suddenly he collapsed forward, shot from the rear; the grenade fell on top of him. In disbelief, Prescott saw the wounded and struggling Mitcom commander try to push the live grenade away. Then it erupted fire and steel shards, blowing the Mitcom's body into a shredded sack of flesh and bones. Even as Prescott watched, another Mitcom hurled a grenade at him. With all his strength, Prescott pushed himself off the wall toward the enemy. The grenade exploded just behind where he had been lying. Now, almost helpless at the bottom of the wall, he fired at the Mitcoms in front of him, amazed to see how fast they were pitching forward—dead and severely wounded. He couldn't understand what was happening, unless—but another Mitcom bullet ended all conjecture.

With sunrise the survivors of the Ba To battle took stock of themselves. A grim Chief Beemeer accompanied the wounded but mobile Cavanaugh, as the five American survivors laid their dead out to be evacuated by helicopter. Over and over, Sergeant Barton, suffering multiple wounds, had to restrain himself from bitterly reminding the Groat chief that if he had intervened just five minutes earlier Major Prescott would still be alive. The last round in the head had killed him, inflicted even as the Groats were shooting down the Mitcoms from the rear on Beemeer's orders.

Lieutenant Panton, painfully but not mortally wounded, had taken command of the American detachment. Though all five of the surviving Americans were wounded, and though mourning their commander and friends, they were aware of the victory Major Prescott had won. The only casualty in the entire Groat village was the chief's son Radam—killed by the Mitcom leader, who by this act alienated the most powerful of the Groat villages.

Beemeer and Panton talked at length, waiting for the helicopters to come in. Beemeer was no less dedicated to the principles of the tribal rebellion than he had been before and wanted to execute the Mituyan Special Forces prisoners forthwith but Panton prevailed upon him not to shoot them, saying that the last words of Major Prescott were that the prisoners should be spared.

The chuffing of helicopters sounded off in the west, and soon a flight of four choppers appeared in the sky, growing larger as they settled in. Three of the armed helicopters circled the village and the landing area while the fourth settled in and landed. A colonel in sharply creased fatigues and a green baseball cap with his eagle sewed upon it stepped out, followed by a Mituyan colonel and several other officers. They walked from their helicopter unescorted to the front gate of the village and strode toward Panton, who was unable to salute because his right arm and shoulder were bandaged and splinted.

"Good morning, sir," Panton said, "I'm Lieutenant Panton in command of Special Forces Split A Detachment 9, Ba To."

"Good morning, Lieutenant. Colonel Gruen, senior adviser, II Corps. We are proud that you held out."

"Yes, sir. Thanks to Chief Beemeer. The Mitcoms had us when Beemeer and his men gunned them all down."

Gruen frowned. "He is one of the leaders of this tribal rebellion, isn't he?"

"Yes, sir."

"The Mituyan Army wants to send in a battalion of paratroopers and arrest him."

"Don't let them, sir," Panton pleaded. "Major Prescott kept the Groats on the government side against the Mitcoms. It cost him his life. I've been out here four months with Chief Beemeer, and what he asks is reasonable. He's been taking a lot of abuse from the Mituyan Special Forces units."

"Tell Chief Beemeer that we will negotiate with him, but first I plan to take his Mituyan prisoners back to Banthut."

Panton told Beemeer what Gruen had said, but Beemeer shook his head stolidly.

"Sir, the chief says he will keep the prisoners until he receives a treaty that the tribesmen's demands will be granted."

"You tell Chief Beemeer that I am taking the prisoners with me. He has my word that we will negotiate and I will do my best to prevent the Mituyan Army from arresting him."

After a discussion with Beemeer, Panton turned back to Colonel Gruen. "Sir, he refuses. And if the Mituyan Army comes he will lead his people from this village into the hills and join up all the Groat tribes to fight the Mituyans."

"You tell him that I'm taking the prisoners back," Gruen said testily. "He has my word that I will prevent any reprisals against him. You can also tell him that if he interferes with an American officer doing his duty, the Mituyan and American air force will find his people and destroy them to the last man."

Panton relayed this message, vastly softened, to Beemeer.

"Where are the prisoners, Panton?" Gruen asked.

Panton, followed by Gruen and two Americans and two Mituyan

officers, led the way to the prisoners' cage next to Chief Beemeer's longhouse.

The four officers gasped at the sight of Captain Narit's head on the pole. "Why did you let them do that?" Gruen snapped.

"Sir, we didn't even know about it. The Mituyans turned their guns on us and defected to the Groat village."

"The American lies!" the Mituyan colonel cried.

Panton was too exhausted even to react. "What I said is what happened."

"I'm evacuating the rest of the prisoners with me right now," Gruen said sharply. Chief Beemeer and thirty armed tribesmen were standing opposite the prisoner compound, silently watching Colonel Gruen. The two Mituyan officers edged away. "Maybe we come back with paratrooper regiment," one of the Mituyans suggested.

"We'll take them now." Gruen looked the unarmed Chief Beemeer in the eye and said, "Panton, tell him I am giving him my carbine. If he wants to take on the responsibility of shooting an American officer, he and his people will suffer the consequences. Tell him that in spite of the beheading of the Mituyan officer I will prevent the Mituyan Army from taking reprisals if he releases the prisoners."

With that, Gruen unslung his carbine and holding it by the barrel thrust the stock toward Chief Beemeer who took it. Then Gruen turned his back on Beemeer. The two Mituyan officers shrank away as Gruen strode toward the prisoner compound and, pushing two guards aside, swung the gate open. Fearfully, the Mituyan Special Forces troopers crowded out of the small stockade.

Beemeer watched angrily and then raised the colonel's carbine and took careful aim at Gruen's back. The rest of the armed Groats watched their chief intently, ready to massacre the visitors and Mituyans if Beemeer pulled the trigger.

"Beemeer!" Panton cried. "Prescott died to save the Groats. Do not spit upon Prescott's body by killing the colonel. For Prescott, do not shoot!"

Very slowly, Beemeer lowered the carbine and watched as the American colonel led the prisoners out of the village and signaled the circling helicopters to land and pick up the Mituyans.

Never once did Panton stop talking to Beemeer about Prescott and Radam, who had respected each other and who had died at the hands of the same enemy, both wanting the same thing for the Groats. Beemeer watched the helicopters take the Mituyan officers and his prisoners and leap up into the air. Colonel Gruen came back alone to talk to Chief Beemeer. "Now, Panton, tell the chief I am ready to negotiate with him in good faith."

CHAPTER THIRTY-EIGHT

BEN MORRIS, manager of the UPI desk in Tuyan City, looked up from the clattering new Teletype machine sending at the rate of sixty words a minute to the New York offices via Tokyo. The first sight he saw was the striking blonde German writer who was so beautiful no one on the Tuyan City press corps could take her seriously.

"Hi ya, Marlene," he tossed off pleasantly. "What brings you off the diplomatic beat into this den of hard news?"

Marlene walked over to the Teletype machine. "This is what makes me come to you, Ben." He looked up and he saw that her eyes were red-rimmed with fatigue; she seemed to have been crying. "I give you a big story because it must be told. I write it on the airplane from Banthut to Tuyan City. My English need work, but the story is all there." From her purse she pulled five typewritten pages. "You do not need to give me byline even. Just read."

Marlene sank wearily into a chair as the desk manager began to read her copy. As he went through her story, she reviewed in her mind the most unforgettable, exhausting, and tragic days of her life. The awful frustration of hearing Charlie call in from the Ba To battle and not being able to talk to him. She wanted to tell him she loved him; she was convinced she did as she listened to his calm reports from the fight, seasoned with his little endearments to her each time he signed off.

This vital man who had made such vigorous love to her was dead less than twenty-four hours after their last embrace at dawn yesterday. She was thankful she had at least been able to give him that. Marlene had persuaded the American pilot at the lodge to fly her into Ba To the next morning to bring back the bodies of the American dead. Lieutenant Panton had given her many details of the battle that had not been transmitted by radio and expressed the pride they all felt at what they had done under Major Prescott's leadership. Briefly she interviewed Colonel Gruen, whose information officer told her with great embellishment the story of the colonel's heroism. She had flown back with Charlie's body to the lodge, where she found Mr. Cardinez from Tuyan City. He looked as tired as everybody else at the lodge, and had not even suggested that she suppress any of the story. She told him about listening to the radio traffic all night and what she had seen at Ba To. General Macker arrived, and he was clearly shocked that she should have been there even though her story had been officially suggested by Ted Baum. He and Cardinez had left for Ba To, and she was able to get a plane hop into Banthut. In Banthut she had wrangled a short interview with General Bannort and the province chief TrangTi, whose quotes strengthened her story. Then she'd caught the Mituyan Air Service afternoon flight to Tuyan City and headed straight for the UPI office.

Ben Morris shouted for his rewrite man, handing him the story to read page by page. "My God, Marlene, are you sure this is true as you wrote it?"

"I was there," she replied simply. "This is what happens."

"I've got to try and verify it with the MAC-M Information Office," he said. "This stuff is dynamite. It's nuclear!" He looked at his watch. "Fifteen minutes to the five o'clock briefing. I'd like to move this story right away, if I can get someone to verify."

"It's true, Ben."

"I believe you, honey, but—" He pulled a phone over to him and began dialing numbers, trying to get through to the military line. At last he succeeded. "Colonel Wilton, Chief Information Office." His bulky form seemed curled around the instrument. "It's damned important!" he added.

He waited a few minutes and then asked, "How about Major Morton then? He's gone over to the briefing too? Forget it." Morris slammed down the phone. "I believe you. They don't want to talk to the press individually." He thought a moment. "Look, Joe, rewrite that copy in wire-service English. Stick 'by Marlene Straltz' above it, let our operator cut the tape on it, but don't put out the high-speed tape to New York until I get back or send someone back to tell you to go ahead." He took Marlene's arm. "OK, let's go to the briefing."

Every afternoon at five the USIS combined forces with MAC-M Information Office to give a briefing to the newsmen. The briefings were held in a medium-sized auditorium in the USIS building. Either Ted Baum or one of his top assistants briefed the press on the political and diplomatic side of the day's events, and Colonel Wilton gave out such information as General Macker and his staff deemed appropriate.

The reporters crowded into the briefing session and found seats, Marlene as always causing somewhat of a stir when she came in. Most of the bachelor reporters at one time or another had waged a campaign of seduction, but all had given up—especially since the Mituyan girls were so pretty . . . and so attainable.

Vigorously, Ben Morris badgered the military information officers for confirmation on the battle at Ba To. He asked direct questions which caught them by surprise but which they said would be covered at the briefing. Morris kept his Mituyan leg man by his side in the briefing, ready to run back to the office and tell the Teletype operator to send out the story.

Though political briefings usually came first, followed by the military, today Colonel Wilton took the stand immediately. Benignly, he smiled down from the lectern at the reporters seated in front of him.

"Today," he began, "we have a story of real heroism for you. The incident took place this morning at a camp in the northeastern mountains near Banthut." A map of Mituyan stood on an easel beside him and a red arrow pointed at Ba To.

"The highly volatile primitive hill tribesmen staged an abortive and brief revolt against the authority of the central government of Premier

KaritKi. They surrounded a garrison of American and Mituyan Special Forces men at the edge of the village of Ba To. During the night the Mitcoms, taking advantage of the confusion, attacked the American and Mituyan fortifications but were beaten off. The American and Mituyan forces suffered light casualties and, fighting off the Mitcoms, inflicted heavy casualties—over two hundred Communists were killed by body count and double that number wounded. In the early morning the tribesmen called on the Mituyans to give themselves up as prisoners, pending negotiations between tribal leaders and government authorities. The Mituyans complied and were locked in a stockade. The previous day at another tribal village called Bax"—Wilton pointed it out on the map—"the tribesmen are reported to have killed the entire Mituyan contingent camped at the village."

Wilton paused and, seeing that he had the complete attention of all the correspondents, which seldom happened, went on. "General Macker asked the American senior adviser of II Corps to go in and get the Mituyan prisoners out safely and then negotiate the differences of the tribesmen with the central government. Colonel Delbert Gruen went into Ba To. The chief refused to allow the Mituyan prisoners to leave, and Colonel Gruen informed the chief he was going to take them out anyway. The chief and all his armed tribesmen stood against Colonel Gruen."

Wilton again paused, savoring the unaccustomed attention of the reporters, who generally sat sullen, bored and hostile at the briefings. "With great presence of mind Colonel Gruen handed his own carbine to the chief of these tribesmen and announced he was going to release the prisoners. Gruen boldly told the chief that if he wanted to take the responsibility of shooting an American officer he could do it then. Unarmed, Gruen walked to the stockade, released the prisoners himself and led them out of the village to the helicopters—and the Mituyans who had held out against the Mitcoms with our American Special Forces troops were saved. With the Mituyans safely out, Colonel Gruen went back inside the village and negotiated all day with the chief of the tribesmen. By late this afternoon the tribesmen agreed to end the revolt, and meetings between tribal leaders and American and Mituyan officers will be held later to settle Mituyan and tribal differences. I might add that General Macker flew to II corps headquarters at Banthut this afternoon and personally decorated Colonel Gruen with the Bronze Star. He has been put in for a higher award. Gentlemen," Wilton concluded, "we have a real hero in Colonel Gruen. He will be available for photographs and interviews at the MAC-M Information Office all day tomorrow. I ask that you make appointments with me after this briefing session."

Ben Morris stuck up his hand. "Yes, Ben," Wilton said amiably.

"The story I got, Colonel," Ben said, hauling himself to his feet, "is that the Mituyan Special Forces got scared and began shooting at the Americans and deserted the fort, giving themselves up to the Groats.

It was the Americans and a few of their loyal tribesmen that fought off the Mitcoms."

Wilton frowned deeply. "I don't know where such a story could have come from, although I did hear that a certain female reporter happened to be there and talked to some of the Americans who had been in the battle. The young American commander was wounded twice and is suffering severely from battle fatigue after his gallant all-night stand. I believe it is planned to evacuate him to Clark Field in the Philippines, where he will receive psychiatric treatment as well as the best medical attention. I don't have to tell you, Ben, how a story already twisted and exaggerated by a battle-fatigue case can be magnified out of proportion by the female tendency to hyperbole." Wilton laughed good-naturedly.

Once again Ben Morris put up his hand, but Wilton ignored him, asking, "Any more questions?" The journalists had noticed that Ben and Marlene were sitting together, and sensing that the real story—which every reporter in the room knew he would never hear through official channels—might unfold, they kept a stony silence. Finally Wilton could no longer ignore the lone raised hand.

"Colonel Wilton, I understand that General Bannort of II Corps refused to send in reinforcements unless the Americans agreed to let him destroy the entire village of Ba To—men, women, and children."

"Absolute nonsense!" Wilton snapped.

"How do you know that so categorically, Colonel?" Morris shot back. "Also, I understand a famous American officer, one we all know, Major Charles Prescott, was in command and killed in the defense at Ba To."

An excited murmur ran through the room.

"We give out no names until next of kin are notified. The press corps is expected to follow this procedure."

"Why, Colonel," Morris asked, "was Colonel Gruen sent into Ba To instead of some of the experienced officers or civilians whose job it is and has been for the past two years to work with the Groat tribesmen? Does MAC-M feel that the present agency dealing with the mountain tribesmen is no longer competent to handle the job? I notice you said nothing in the briefing regarding the part Major Prescott played in containing the Mitcom attack and the tribesmen's revolt."

"MAC-M has no comment on any of these questions. You can ask them of Mr. Baum when it comes his turn to brief you."

"Thank you, Colonel," Morris said acidly. He turned to Marlene, "I believe every word in that story of yours. We're letting it go." And he gave his leg man a nudge, indicating the door.

Marlene was too overcome with emotion to thank him in words.

Later, when Ted Baum came on, the reporters all bowed to Ben Morris. Before saying anything, Baum looked directly at Morris. "I know, Ben, that the lovely young lady you are fortunate enough to have sitting next to you was practically an eyewitness to all the events that took place at Ba To. It was I, in fact, who suggested she might find an interesting story up in the Groat country." He laughed ruefully. "So as the rest of you can see, I do not deliberately send you off on a paper chase when I suggest story ideas."

Morris raised his hand and was recognized. "Ted, we hear that the tribesmen will not be given a chance to vote in the coming elections. Is that another reason for the revolt?"

Baum looked around the audience of hard-bitten reporters and was received, as always, with a certain warmth, seldom won by the military information officers.

"The truth is that there are serious political implications in this entire tribal rebellion problem. We don't even know all of them, and quite honestly we are proceeding with extreme caution before making any official statements. The motives in high quarters for sending one officer rather than another to try to quell the Ba To uprising have not been made known to me. But the fact remains that Colonel Gruen was successful. If anybody wants to submit to me a list of specific questions, I will try to find out the answers promptly. The truth is, gentlemen, that I do not personally know any more about the tribal revolt than has been released to you officially by Colonel Wilton."

The briefing quickly broke up, and a knot of reporters gathered around Marlene in the back of the auditorium. Even Ted Baum joined them.

"*I'd* like to know the whole story too," he said mildly.

Smilingly, Marlene told the reporters to read her UPI story, which named names and told exactly how the Mituyan Special Forces had deserted and fired on their own allies to ingratiate themselves with the Mitcoms, hoping their lives would be spared.

Tony Ancelli, a celebrated syndicated columnist who had never been known to leave Tuyan City except on VIP junkets, was the most persistent of the reporters questioning her.

"Tony," she said softly as the others trooped out to file their stories, "I can give you an exclusive story I don't use because then General Macker knows who leaks it."

"Meet you any place," Ancelli said eagerly.

"Can you be at my father's house in one hour?"

"I'll be there, Marlene. And congratulations. You're a real reporter now."

From the tough little foreign correspondent this was high praise, and Marlene blushed and basked in her new status with the Tuyan City press corps. She smiled to herself. There would be no one with better readership to damn General Macker. Ancelli would do the job on Macker for secretly ordering experienced soldiers like Charlie not to tell the truth about the Mituyans while the big men from Washington were in the country, she thought with relish. And then the thought of Charlie robbed her of all her elation.

CHAPTER THIRTY-NINE

It was a somber gathering at Jack Cardinez' house in his "bug proof" study. Lawton and Mike Forrester sat around with their boss, gently sipping their drinks and talking about Charlie Prescott, all of them waiting for the Undersecretary of State to make his appearance. The official party would be leaving the following morning to return to Washington and report their findings to the President and the National Security Council. Hartland had requested this one last meeting.

"He said he could skip the ambassador's dinner, but he'd have to stick with the meeting until it broke up," Cardinez said, looking at his watch. "I asked Marlene Straltz to come over and talk to Hartland for a few minutes. She was closer to the situation than any of us. God knows what she's going to write."

"What's the difference?" Mike asked. "By the time those German and Swiss publications print her stuff, it will be old news."

Cardinez smiled crookedly. "You, an old friend of Fraulein Straltz, you of all people underestimate her."

"What do you mean?"

"She told me this was a story that had to be told truthfully and immediately. By now she's given it either to AP or UPI or both. It will be all over the United States tomorrow."

"Good for her," Mike said. "The story *should* be told—and told well. God knows we've all warned the ambassador what was going on up there, and all he'd say was it was 'sensitive' and we should keep away from it."

"What worries me, Mike, is that little note the radio operator made when he intercepted the communications in Vietnamese. Our old friend Can said he had a 'mission' in Tuyan City. What do you think he's got planned?"

"I guess the target he'd like best to hit is me. I sure wish I knew what he looks like."

"I've already sent for Major Song. He knows Can by sight," Lawton said. "Of course, the way things are going, Macker and MAC-M will be trying to take over our special operations too."

"Are MAC-M and MAAG really taking over the entire Groat program?" Mike asked.

"Such as it is, or so it looks now," Cardinez replied caustically. "My superior, Mr. Dickerson, obligingly agreed to get out of all operations that involved military personnel." He walked over to the window; the panes were damp, the hot muggy air outside causing the cool air on the inside to condense on the glass. Cardinez looked toward the street, separated from the yard by a high spiked wall.

"Here's Bob Hartland now, I think." He went to open the front door, and Hartland came in.

"Good evening, gentlemen, I'm sorry to keep you waiting," Hartland said. He sank into the easy chair with a sigh, and cocked up the bad foot. "The ambassador is flapping so hard I expected to see him rise up in the air," he said, unsmiling.

He accepted a drink from Cardinez and after a long pull set down the glass and looked around the room at the others. "Jack, this has been the most eventful, interesting, and potentially tragic week in my career as a foreign-service officer. I don't have to tell any of you what a shock it was to hear about Prescott. He went in precisely the manner he predicted to me—and just one day later. *How* can our top people over here have failed to see what's going on every day in this country?"

The rhetorical question went unanswered. Hartland sipped his whisky thoughtfully. Then he spoke again. "My mind is made up. We will have vast changes here, on both the American and Mituyan side, or I will no longer accept responsibility for helping make policy in Southeast Asia."

"Bob, you can count on us to do everything in our power to help," Cardinez said emphatically. "Even if it means the sacrifice that Prescott had to make."

"All right." Hartland leaned forward intently. "Here's the program. First, get Barkoon ready to make a comeback. Fritz, you can quietly tell Dandig to go ahead and make his plans with the other generals and, God help us all, that mad monk. We need him now to help bring down KaritKi—but I would submit his name as number-one target for Major Song's little group after the coup has been successfully accomplished."

"We had planned to keep Barkoon ready for immediate action at his old lodge," Cardinez said. "Protecting Barkoon there was to have been one of Charlie Prescott's main jobs. But with MAC-M, to say nothing of the Mituyans all over the place, I'm afraid that little hideaway is out now."

"I'm sure you'll think of something, Jack," Hartland replied. He turned to Mike. "You know the country and people better than any American here. What about keeping Barkoon on ice in Mituyan?"

"He is very recognizable," Mike said thoughtfully. A slow smile crossed his face. "I *do* have one idea of where we can keep him safely."

"Where?" Cardinez snapped out.

"I could bring the *Promise* around the peninsula and up to Marashak, which is only a twenty-minute trip by small plane to Tuyan City. In fact"—Mike's eyes gleamed at the thought—"I could bring him right up the Tuyan River and keep him at my company's private dock right here in Tuyan City. They're used to seeing my ship there. Hell, at the palace yesterday, Dhuna even *asked* when we were coming back with *Promise*."

Cardinez nodded thoughtfully. "That sounds like a workable plan. Dangerous—but then the whole concept is dangerous. The only thing worse is to continue with KaritKi's regime."

"When can you put phase one of 'Operation' "—Hartland smiled wryly—" 'switch' into action?"

"We're well under way now," Cardinez answered. "Roger Krakhaur has been a great help. That business with the Mituyan girl he married in Hong Kong seems to have had tremendous propaganda value in showing the world what KaritKi is."

"Yes," Hartland said, "our friend Krakhaur has produced some very thought-provoking articles on the potential statesmanship of Barkoon. They have not gone unnoticed in Washington, let me say. . . . Now, when the Mad Monk gets his Buddhists cranked up against the 'cruel and repressive methods of the religious bigot KaritKi and his brother Tarot,' the obvious solution for restoring order is to bring in a Buddhist leader to hold the country together until the elections can be run off fairly."

"OK, the next step is for someone to go to Hong Kong and get Barkoon ready to move." Cardinez' blue eyes flashed around the room.

"No one official," Hartland said quickly.

"Of course not." His eyes found Forrester. "This is Mike Forrester's job."

"I'm ready . . . of course." The hesitation in Mike's voice made Hartland and Lawton glance at him sharply.

"What's the matter, Mike?" Hartland asked.

"I just mentioned that we were at the palace yesterday seeing Dhuna. My wife has been trying to get an exit visa, but so far they won't give it to her."

"You wouldn't go alone?" Cardinez asked.

"If necessary I will, of course. But frankly I'm afraid for Luna's safety. Both the Mitcoms and certain elements of KaritKi's government would like to get me. Now Can is moving this way too. He knows the part I played in helping wipe out the Mitcom organization in Tiking. But the main thing is, I'm afraid that Tarot and Mayna both feel I've been deliberately thwarting government policy, especially in the matter of getting Krakhaur and Alana out of the country."

He shrugged and took a long drink of his Scotch and soda. "Don't get me wrong, though. Luna and I are committed to this fight just as surely as Charlie Prescott was. If I do have to leave her alone here, she'll understand. I was away from her ten days when I went up to the Groat country."

Mike took another sip and turned to Undersecretary Hartland.

"By the way, what *was* the official reaction to the Groat uprising?"

"A mess," Hartland answered in disgust. "Whittelsie believes the Palace and Macker, who say it was the American Green Berets who caused the whole problem. I'm afraid they're going to make you some sort of a scapegoat, Jack." Hartland smiled sadly. "And, of course, poor Ted Baum is being blamed for every story and information leak. He's even been blamed for sending that German girl up to the Groat country. And then they all remembered that Baum had send Krakhaur to Tiking just in time to file an embarrassing story on that professor's assassination." Hartland raised his glass, sighting through the pale liquid, "Gentlemen, we've got to move fast. Did this German girl really see the entire affair?"

"That's right," Cardinez confirmed. "I've asked her to stand by, in case you'd like to talk to her."

"Why doesn't Mike go and fetch her in my staff car? Would you mind, Mike?"

"Not at all, Bob." He was angry at himself for the quickening excitement he felt.

"There are a few things I didn't want to say in front of him, even though he is unofficially one of us," Hartland said after Mike had left. "First, when I get back to Washington day after tomorrow, I'm going to ask that Whittelsie be relieved immediately. I have one or two ideas for an effective replacement, and I expect the President will also. We need a tough man who will shepherd through this coup in such a way that all of official Washington will be shocked and amazed that such a thing could happen."

Cardinez nodded. "It has to be that way."

"Second, I'll take a little trip over to Langley, Virginia, to see my old friends at Plans and Operations and discuss a change in CIA station chiefs here. I'll suggest they consider moving Cardinez up."

"I'll take it," Cardinez said, unsmiling.

"And I believe that when I have my say at the National Security Council and have presented my personal experiences, it will help them come to a decision that's been pending for a month—to remove Macker gracefully. Then, if the Agency for International Development could find a somewhat more dedicated individual to run its program here, one who isn't afraid to go out to the boondocks, I think Mituyan can survive the Communists and even establish a truly free and representative government."

"Ted Baum is trying to do an honest job as Public Affairs Chief," Cardinez said. "I just hope he can last until these changes can be made. . . ."

Mike returned after twenty minutes with Marlene Straltz. "Thank you for coming, fraulein," said Hartland, taking her hand. "I know you have had a very long and unhappy day. Unfortunately, I am leaving in the morning and this is the only chance I have to hear from you exactly what happened. We all admired Major Prescott greatly."

Marlene sat down beside the undersecretary. "He was the true hero," she said.

Cardinez asked if she had a copy of the story she filed, and Marlene opened a large straw pocketbook and handed him the folded pages. "Here is my story. But I decided to ask Mr. Morris at UPI not to put my name above it. I was afraid it would hurt my father's mission here."

"Very wise," Cardinez approved. "Although the Palace will know you supplied the facts."

Hartland read the story carefully and then handed it to Cardinez. "You may find that certain members of the American ambassador's staff will become hostile to you," he said to Marlene, smiling reassuringly at her. "But the facts should be made known to the American people—and the world, for that matter."

Marlene frowned. "I do not understand why do they try to make a big hero out of this stupid colonel when Charlie was the hero? The colonel does not even help Charlie. So better to let ten brave men die than argue with counterpart. He should be shot, this colonel. . . . But we tell the world who the real hero is."

It was Lawton who explained. "You see, Fraulein Straltz, General Macker and his Military Assistance Command badly needed a hero, one of their own. As long as Special Forces or any other type of military outfit is not under direct command of MAC-M, our conventional-minded generals are suspicious of them. MAC-M feels it must show the world that only *its* men can win the war over here. Therefore, my dear, General Macker is going to be very upset when this story comes out."

"Not half as upset as Premier KaritKi and his crowd," Mike commented.

"Will they do anything to hurt my father?" Marlene asked. "That is only what gives me worry."

"You know, fraulein," Cardinez said thoughtfully, "I think that if you took a week's trip out of the country, say to Tokyo or Hong Kong or Bangkok, by the time you returned everything would be forgotten, particularly since the story does not actually have your name on it."

"Maybe I do that," Marlene agreed. "I think I go to Hong Kong."

Cardinez smiled. "Good. You may have company. Mike may be going to Hong Kong, too."

"Oh?" Marlene looked up questioningly, but Hartland was talking.

"In Washington I will be asked, fraulein, whether our allies really did turn their guns on the Americans and desert. I'm sure that the official reports from the surviving sergeants and the lieutenant will have most of the truth sanitized out of them, so I'd be deeply grateful if you would tell me everything that happened—everything, every detail you can remember. Begin from the moment I said goodbye to you and Prescott the day before yesterday. . . ."

PART VIII

HONG KONG

CHAPTER FORTY

Mike Forrester looked down at Hong Kong from his window seat on the BOAC jet. Hong Kong was the most colorful city of the Orient, and it always excited him, with its bustling commercial life; but this trip promised to be the most exciting of all.

Though he felt guilty that Luna wasn't along, the sense of anticipation at being in Hong Kong with Marlene made him tingle. Only four days earlier he had last seen Hartland and promised to carry out the Hong Kong mission. It seemed longer because the last three days had been spent in a vain attempt to secure the exit visa for Luna. Cardinez had flatly refused to help Mike spirit her out of the country, and both Luna and Mike had agreed with the JRB chief's reasoning: Smuggling Luna out would have been tantamount to declaring war on the Palace, and that would destroy Mike's effectiveness in accomplishing his delicate task.

Mike had not told Luna that he would be seeing Marlene Straltz in Hong Kong. Not that he had anything to hide, he rationalized to himself—but it just didn't seem important. Nor had he told Marlene or Roger Krakhaur on what flight he was arriving, since he was sure he would be watched from the moment he landed, even though the stated purpose of his trip was to negotiate extensions of bank loans and mortgages with the home offices of his banks in Tuyan City.

It was mid-afternoon as he entered the airport. Mike marveled at the ease with which he passed through customs and immigration, in such contrast with almost every other port of debarkation in the world. He had traveled light, and soon a cab was speeding him through Kowloon to the ferry and across the water to Hong Kong.

Returning to the Mandarin Hotel was like coming home. The doorman knew him, the bellboy pounced on his suitcase; and at the desk, where he was handed an envelope, they greeted him enthusiastically. The feminine European handwriting must have been Marlene's—he realized he'd never seen it before. He was starting for the elevators when a jovial, middle-aged Chinese merchant hurried from a lobby clothing shop. "Mike! You back. Good. You need new suit, new sport clothes?"

Mike's pause to talk with his favorite tailor in Hong Kong was briefer than usual, for he was anxious to read the note from Marlene. In his room, looking back across Hong Kong's waterfront toward Kowloon on the mainland, he tore open the envelope. "Dear Mike," the note read, "I love Hong Kong! You made the best suggestion to say I should come. I am at Roger and Alana Krakhaur's apartment. Call the first minute you read this. Love, Marlene."

Mike picked up the telephone at once. Alana answered, thrilled to near that Mike was in Hong Kong. Roger had left word he wanted to see Mike immediately, and she gave him the phone number of the Star Syndicate. Alana expressed sharp disappointment and concern that Luna had been unable to accompany him, and then, almost reluctantly, Mike thought, she put Marlene on the phone. Oriental wives of Caucasians were naturally suspicious of striking blondes, Mike reflected.

"Mike!" Marlene said. "You make it safe?"

"I make it," he replied.

"When do we find time to talk?"

"Meet me for cocktails at five-thirty on the Mandarin roof bar." Now the vague sense of guilt was starting to annoy him.

"That will be all right," she replied noncommittally, perhaps for Alana's sake.

Mike called Krakhaur and arranged to meet him shortly in the roof garden upstairs. He unpacked, leaving the top of his briefcase open in case his effects were searched; he wanted any agents of Tarot's intelligence bureau who might be interested to have a good look at his innocuous papers. For his job he needed no secret documents, no weapons, nothing but his knowledge of the Republic of Mituyan and his power of persuasion in case Barkoon suddenly decided to balk.

"I'm sure glad you're here, Mike," Krakhaur said, as they sat down at an isolated corner table that commanded a sweeping view of the city. "Now maybe I can stop this odious business of playing spook and let *you* take over."

"I'll need your help for a while yet, Roger."

"Well, all right," the journalist said reluctantly. Then he asked where Luna was. Mike told him the story.

Krakhaur frowned. "Aren't you worried about her?"

"Of course. But we both agreed I had to make this trip. She's as committed to the fight as I am."

Krakhaur shook his head. "For the sake of the good Republic of Mituyan, I hope you people can pull this thing off."

"You mean 'Operation Switch.' By the way, how is His Highness?"

"Itching to go back and become King again. You'll see when you meet him. He's been getting restless because nobody official has approached him yet."

"When can I talk to him?"

"Any time. He's got a mansion up on the peak where he lives with his merry little retinue. The first time you go to see him, though, you want to play it strictly social. He likes to look at new women. Since Luna isn't here, maybe you can take Marlene with you. He goes ape for blondes."

"Think you can set up a meeting for tonight?"

"I'll phone his secretary. He's something else, too . . . or should I say *she?* Old roly-poly will go up the wall when he sees Marlene."

Barkoon's Hong Kong exile residence, in an ornate mansion on the Peak, Hong Kong's highest residential area and the most exclusive in the colony was, as Krakhaur had described, overwhelming. An effeminate young Britisher dressed in a white suit and white shoes ushered them into a large foyer, then into an enormous reception room with ceiling-to-floor windows that looked down over the city and the sea. Thick Oriental rugs covered the floor, and though electric lights burned dimly in the ceiling the room was almost entirely illuminated by large, three-inch-in-diameter candles in massive brass candelabras.

At the far end of the room, seated in a thronelike chair framed by two huge, curving elephant tusks, sat a rotund, jolly man of indeterminate age. King Barkoon was in his mid-forties, Mike knew. His bland face belied the sharp gleam in his slightly slanted eyes, and his black hair was brushed straight back from his forehead. To one side of him sat a striking young woman with shimmering copper hair and green eyes; on the other, a suntanned Scandinavian beauty, her blond hair piled high on her head in a coiffure that must have taken the better part of an afternoon to create.

"Ah, my friend Krakhaur, we are indeed happy to see you again," Barkoon said. "And you have brought friends." He stared frankly at Marlene, whose wholesome beauty seemed set off by the King's two mistresses. "Such an *exquisite* friend!"

Krakhaur presented Mike and Marlene to Barkoon, who introduced the two girls. "On my right is Letitia Jones from America." The copper-haired girl smiled at them. "To my left is Miss Brigit Danielssen from Denmark." Brigit also smiled. "We are missing Mademoiselle Francine Tourlon of Paris and Cannes." He winked lasciviously. "An old friend of hers from the Riviera is in Hong Kong and we gave her the night off."

"She would be a brunette, Your Highness?" Mike inquired slyly.

"Precisely, dear fellow. They make a deliciously contrasting threesome." His eyes roved freely over Marlene and he gestured toward an empty chair facing him. Then, in German, he said to Marlene, "Please, Fraulein Straltz, come closer and sit where I can admire your great beauty. Such soul-stirring hair. You must permit me to present you with the services of Henri here."

Then, in English, Barkoon introduced a slim, mustached Frenchman, his hair in a blue-black pompadour. "Henri is perhaps the most skilled and original hairdresser in Paris. I stole him for my girls."

Marlene turned to Mike and explained His Majesty had offered her a hairdo by Henri. "It has been long since my hair is done by a Paris hairdresser."

"His Majesty is known for his generosity to beautiful women," Mike replied.

"I will supervise the entire process," Barkoon went on. "To paraphrase an Americanism, I am the world's finest back-seat hair stylist." His eyes twinkled as he looked Marlene up and down. "I shall also have my dressmaker make a Mituyan-style chongsam for you, my dear. Such legs should be accorded the benefit of our hip-high slitted skirts." Then in German again he said: "Will you come for luncheon with me tomorrow? There will be just the two of us."

Replying in German she said she would love to come, but she had an engagement with Mr. Forrester.

"Then, my dear," said Barkoon, "bring Mr. Forrester for lunch also."

Switching back to English Barkoon coveyed the invitation to Mike, who accepted with pleasure. "Ah, capital, capital. We shall have her measured for the sort of dresses her tantalizing figure so rightly demands."

"And Your Majesty will of course supervise back seat the taking of measurements," Marlene looked at Barkoon directly—giving him an impertinent yet altogether too inviting twist of the mouth, Mike thought uneasily.

Delighted, Barkoon roared out an appreciative laugh and, turning to Mike, said, "A busy American like yourself must be occupied at lunchtime with business matters. We will forgive you if it is impossible for you to accompany Fraulein Straltz."

In the perfect classical Mituyan of the mandarin class, Mike said, as if speaking to an equal: "Your Highness, my entire business in Hong Kong is with you, and I suggest from tomorrow morning onward the converse is also true."

Barkoon straightened in his thronelike chair, his whole bearing suddenly regal. Everyone in the room felt the abrupt conflict between two strong-willed, powerful men.

Finally, after carefully considering his reply, Barkoon spoke in the idiom of the imperial court: "We are aware of your mission. It is only for us to decide whether you are the one to effect it."

"Your Majesty, I am the *only* one to effect it, I assure you." Barkoon's eyes fell from Mike's unflinching stare. Perceiving his point had been unmistakably driven home, Mike added in a more jocular tone; "But all that is for tomorrow." Then in English, "As for tonight, Your Majesty, I do hope you stock Chivas Regal Scotch."

Instantly King Barkoon was transformed back into his mischievously convivial mood, and everyone relaxed, vastly relieved. He beckoned, and two turbaned Chinese houseboys came forward and took everyone's order.

Throughout the evening, Barkoon, always the gracious host, spent most of his time talking to Marlene, frequently in German. But when he offered her a tour of the mansion, Marlene smiled and asked if Mike could come.

Only slightly discomfited, Barkoon not only extended the invitation to Mike but asked Krakhaur if he'd care to join them as well.

"I sure would, Your Majesty. Can I report what I see?"

"About the girls, you may write to your heart's content. But there are some things I would prefer to remain unpublicized."

Barkoon led the way through a green door into a fully equipped hairdresser's salon. "This is Henri's province. The girls like it. The best in Hong Kong."

Marlene looked around enviously. "Those three girls have this all to themselves, complete with Henri?"

"We have other young ladies who do use it from time to time," Barkoon answered, smiling suggestively. "You, my dear, have a standing invitation to use it any time. Perhaps after lunch tomorrow?"

"I'd love to."

Barkoon led them through a downstairs billiard room, where he demonstrated his skill with the cue, and then through his three-room library, divided into several large sections—each devoted to a different language. He showed them the majestic dining room that could seat forty people for dinner parties, and on the second floor the luxurious suites of each of his three mistresses. "It is heartwarming how well the girls get along together," Barkoon commented.

"With such beautiful apartments to themselves, they should," Marlene said. She followed Barkoon down the hall from the girls' rooms, and he flung open the door to his own apartment. Proudly he showed them his own sitting room and library of his current reading, containing the latest magazines and books from all countries of the world; then they walked through an intimate private dining room and through double French doors into his large corner bedroom, with its gold fixtures against cream-colored walls. Marlene gasped at the luxurious canopied giant-size bed, the rich purple draperies at the windows which overlooked Hong Kong and the sea. She couldn't resist falling back into the overstuffed chaise lounge. Laughing, she said to Mike, "That hotel—forget it!"

"There is a vacant apartment fully as comfortable as any you've seen in the house," Barkoon said quickly.

"Be careful, Your Majesty, perhaps you do get another guest. How many nights out do you give your girls?" She winked broadly at Mike, who was frowning in spite of himself.

"I would hope, at least for the first few weeks, you wouldn't even want one night off." And then, looking straight into her large blue eyes, Barkoon said: "I think this room is even more comfortable and conducive to pleasant relationships than the master bedroom at my hunting lodge near Banthut, don't you?"

Startled, Marlene sat bolt upright in the chaise. She caught Mike's eyes and saw that he was surprised also. Before she could reply, Barkoon said smoothly, "Now let me show you the boutique where the girls and their female friends amuse themselves for hours."

They walked back downstairs, and opposite the French hairdresser's salon was a red lacquered door set in black lacquered moldings. He pushed it open, and again Marlene was astonished to find herself in the most delightful and fashionable woman's clothing and notion shop she had ever seen. Beautiful dresses were draped on mannequins or hanging out on clothing trees. Handbags of all sorts were scattered about the shop on tables tastefully laden with scarves, handkerchiefs, jewelry, which, when she examined it, Marlene realized was real, not paste. There were open shelves containing bolts of gold and silver brocaded silks, and on a round ivory inlaid sandalwood table—the aroma of the wood gently touching her nostrils—were the latest editions of the world's most famous fashion magazines.

As Barkoon watched the tall, lithe, blonde wandering about the boutique, he grinned hugely, enjoying her wonderment. When she stopped to admire a double strand of pearls hanging around a black velvet neck, he walked over and, taking them in his hands, said, "Please, let me present them to you."

"Oh, no! Your Majesty. They are more beautiful than I have ever seen. You must not give me anything so valuable."

In German, Barkoon said, "Please, my dear, you would do me an honor to wear these pearls. Each one is perfect, and I have waited for the right young lady to come along so I could place them around her neck." He held them up to her, and Marlene glanced helplessly at Mike, who nodded twice. Marlene stood transfixed as Barkoon placed the pearls around her neck and fastened the clasp; his fingers gently touched the back of her neck, causing a slight spasm that made him chuckle. Then he lifted her right hand and barely brushed it with his lips.

"Look around all you please," Barkoon said. "There is plenty of time. Perhaps you will see a dress you like. My dressmaker comes every day, and she will make whatever pleases you."

Compulsively, Marlene was drawn to the Oriental-style dresses. In Mituyan, Barkoon said to Mike, "A girl like that makes you wish you weren't married, yes? But at least your wife doesn't accompany you on this trip." The understanding smile and twinkle in the King's eyes infuriated Mike, all the more because these had been exactly his thoughts as he'd watched Marlene moving gracefully about the shop, all her femininity revealed in this, Barkoon's woman trap.

"Forrester," Barkoon continued in Mituyan, "she must be absolutely devastatingly beautiful to love." His eyes were fixed hotly on Marlene's every motion as she moved in fascination from one exquisite display of tasteful elegance to the next. "If you have had her, I envy you. If you haven't, I am insanely jealous of what you have in store."

Mike found it impossible to be offended, angry or even revolted with Barkoon any more. He was so openly, candidly a sensualist that Mike could only chuckle. He said in Mituyan, "I have never had her, and I see little likelihood that I will. Of course I would be a liar if I said the thought hadn't occurred to me."

"You will have her," Barkoon said. "She is very attracted to you, even though she knows your wife as a friend. She wants you. And after she has given herself to you and you have tasted what will surely be the most exquisite ambrosia of your life, then you must encourage her to visit *me.* Were she not in your company, I would have persuaded her to move tonight from the hotel to an apartment here."

The suggestion, shocking and repugnant though it was, fitted Barkoon's character so perfectly that once again Mike could only laugh and reply, "You may have a long wait before I sip of this nectar of the gods."

Barkoon smiled enigmatically, "Let us see."

Marlene walked over breathlessly. "Please, Mike, you must take me out of this beautiful place. I want everything." The way she tossed her long blonde hair back, laughing in girlish insouciance, caused Mike to hate himself. For the first time since he had married Luna, he wished he were single.

Two houseboys appeared, one carrying an ice bucket with a bottle of champagne, the other a golden tray with four crystal goblets. "My dear," Barkoon said to Marlene, "may I offer you some champagne?"

Her eyes sparkled, and Barkoon filled a goblet and handed it to her. He poured for Krakhaur and Mike and finally for himself. "To the most beautiful young lady who has ever entered my . . . palace in exile," he said. The three men drank, smiling at Marlene.

"Now it is my turn." Marlene held her glass up to Barkoon, and in German she said: "To the most unbelievable and fantastic man I have ever met!" Barkoon laughed heartily.

"Well," Mike said as they moved out of the boutique, "now that we've had the five-dollar tour, I suppose we should not intrude further on His Majesty tonight."

"Oh, but you haven't seen everything." And now Barkoon's face became serious. "There is one more room that you, Forrester, should be especially interested in." Then in Mituyan he said, "You know, Mr. Forrester, I am something of a mindreader. Right at this moment I can see you saying to yourself, what am I doing to Mituyan bringing this dilettante and decadent man back to rule?"

Mike was no longer surprised at Barkoon's intuition, although he demurred at the implication, saying it was none of his business to think—he just had to get Barkoon back to the palace at Tuyan City. Even so, he was intrigued as Barkoon led them to an elevator door and pressed the button.

"The top floor of this house is closed off and can only be reached by this elevator," he explained, pulling out a key from a chain around his neck and unlocking the elevator door.

The three guests were taken to a room the size of the reception room on the ground floor; it was lined with offices, in some of which, even this late at night, Caucasian and Oriental men and women were still working. The entire far wall of the room consisted of an enormous map of Mituyan, covered with several acetate overlays in multicolored lines, shadings, and markings. A Caucasian and one Oriental, presumably Mituyan, sat in front of an array of radio equipment, earphones on, transcribing onto typewriters the messages they were receiving. Three Teletype machines clattered incessantly. As they watched, another Caucasian came out of an office to examine the continuous sheets of paper spewing from the machines. The length of the room was a Mercator's projection of the world; twenty-four electric clocks, one above each time zone, indicated the time of day or night every place in the world. There was a purposeful air of determination about the people working up here that made Mike think of the war room of a large command. And then he realized: Of course, it was precisely that—King Barkoon's headquarters for following all the developments in the war raging in his country. . . . Mike placed his half-full glass of champagne on a table. It seemed almost dissolute to drink in such an atmosphere.

"As you can see, Mr. Forrester, you will not have to brief me on the affairs of my country," Barkoon said, an air of pride in his tone. "I manage to stay informed hourly on events in Mituyan, and for that matter all over the world, that in any way pertain to my country. We keep a twenty-four-hour-a-day operation going up here."

Barkoon turned to Marlene. "Accept, please, my condolences on the death of your brave and close friend Major Prescott."

"You know I knew him?" Marlene asked. "My name was not on the UPI story."

"You were the only reporter at my old hunting lodge at the time," Barkoon replied. "You and Major Prescott were"—he paused a moment—"close. Particularly during those hours just before he felt it necessary to take command of the Ba To garrison."

Marlene blushed. "How do you know all this?"

"We receive agent reports, sometimes as often as twice a day, from every province in Mituyan. I was most touched to read Major Prescott's final radio transmissions. He never forgot you were listening." The sympathy in King Barkoon's eyes was genuine, she knew, and Marlene found herself actually liking this strange, round, deceptively bland-looking, lecherous and yet, obviously, tremendously intelligent ex-potentate.

He led them past office doors. At the first he said, "In each office there is an expert on one location in Mituyan. This one"—he stopped and let them look in on a bespectacled, studious Mituyan reading a Teletype report"—is devoted entirely to receiving and assessing information on the Palace. DakatLi here is in charge. He has one man who does nothing but follow Tarot's movements. . . . A woman keeps a minute record of everything Mayna says or does and is very successful in piecing together the activities that we are unable to get agent reports on."

DakatLi looked up and smiled, and Barkoon introduced his guests. "Anything new?" he asked. DakatLi grinned and handed Barkoon a sheet of paper. The ex-King read it and laughed uproariously.

"At this moment Mayna has the American ambassador in her villa at Marashak, and in her own effective way she seems to be calming his nerves, after the recent upsetting intrusion of all those highly placed officials from Washington."

They passed on to the next office. "In here I have a man who does nothing but collect and assess agent reports on Poramat and his province chiefs in I Corps." Each corps area in Mituyan, as they learned, came under the surveillance of one of Barkoon's men in his communications center, which controlled and communicated with a cadre of agents. Krakhaur's eyes opened wider and wider as he was shown around the headquarters.

"Your Majesty, you never showed me any of this before, and I've been interviewing you off and on for weeks now."

"I was waiting for the arrival of someone who represented more directly the United States commitment in Mituyan," Barkoon replied. "I understand perfectly, Mr. Forrester, why you were the chosen emissary. However, whether you know it or not, you will soon be joined by Colonel Fritz Lawton. He has just been granted a well-deserved and long overdue rest and recreation leave, and he has chosen Hong Kong as the place to spend it."

"I'll be damned! I'll be damned," Mike repeated. "They were discussing whether or not to send Fritz and had about decided against it until hearing further word from Washington."

"Colonel Lawton left his operations center in Tiking this morning telling everyone how much he was planning to enjoy his vacation. He was taking orders for watches and silk," Barkoon said.

He stopped at another office. "This is where we study the day-to-day economic situation in Mituyan. We can tell a great deal about what goes on there. For instance, today the price of the dollar rose from one hundred and thirty metas on the black market in the Indian tailor shops on Bismarck Avenue to one hundred and fifty. It is obvious that more and more wealthy people are trying to move their money out of Mituyan. Some send it out because they are afraid Premier KaritKi plans to crack down on them—perhaps they tried to seek election as a delegate to the new constitutional assembly without his permission. Others move their money out because they are afraid KaritKi will be overthrown in a coup and they will go with him. In a few days, my contacts at the banks will advise me the names of the actual Mituyans who have sent large cash U.S.-dollar deposits to Hong Kong, and we will be able to evaluate the trends among the merchants and upper classes in Tuyan City."

Barkoon poked his head into the economic-studies office and glanced at a blackboard. "The price of charcoal in Tuyan City has risen by twenty-five percent in the past four days," he commented. "That means there is increasing Communist guerrilla activity in the Tuyan River Delta and that they are raising their tax on the charcoal burners, moving their charcoal along the rivers, canals, and roads for sale in Tuyan City, their prime market."

Barkoon chuckled. "By the way, Forrester, you'll be interested to know that the price of raw opium also is rising in Tuyan City. It would appear that your two little forays into the Groat areas have crippled the traders controlled by Tarot."

Finally Barkoon led them back to the big map of Mituyan. "There *is* one thing that is distressing," he said to Mike. "I think it would be well if you warned Mr. Cardinez that in the past two weeks Peking has sold over ten million dollars worth of gold bullion in Hong Kong. This can only mean that they are planning a major offensive, and I'm afraid it will be aimed at the northern part of Mituyan. Premier KaritKi's unenlightened policies toward the hill tribes, based on his old middle-class prejudices, will lose him all the tribal areas, and the Communists will continue to take advantage of this."

To Marlene he said, "This is not to say that Major Prescott died in vain. He certainly delayed the subversion of the tribesmen, and if we can act fast enough"—he gave Mike a significant look—"we can take advantage of the time won for us by Prescott's death." Again he turned to Marlene. "But, my dear, this must be boring now. Let us go downstairs again."

"I am never so fascinated, so surprised in my life," Marlene said slowly. "This is fabulous. All this time you know everything. I have only one question: How do they get you to go out of your country in the first place?"

Barkoon gave her a sad smile as he led her toward the elevator door. "In those days I spent too much time downstairs and not enough upstairs. Given the opportunity, Mr. Forrester, this is a mistake I will not repeat."

"You have the most remarkable intelligence net I've ever seen," Mike said. "Wait 'til Fritz Lawton sees this place."

"My facilities are at the disposal of your JRB and, when certain changes are made in your Country Team—as they no doubt will be—I will include your CIA station chief in Mituyan."

"It must be an expensive operation," Krakhaur conjectured.

"It is. It requires the entire income of the fortune my father was wise enough to transfer to Switzerland before World War II, and what I was able to get into various Hong Kong banks before the first of that dreary succession of civil-servant premiers successfully deposed me. As a matter of fact, I am compelled frequently to go into capital to support my operation, but it is all I have to live for—except, of course"—he bowed to Marlene—"becoming a close friend of yours."

She tried to smile back noncommittally, but she felt her cheeks and forehead warm. Obviously he had spies right in the lodge who had told him everything.

Mike protested that it was getting late, but Barkoon insisted that they return to his throne room. Barkoon's mistresses were waiting, talking gaily to the effeminate Englishman and the French hairdresser.

Barkoon suggested that Marlene and the men join them in their regular tea ceremony before retiring.

"I *would* like a cup of hot tea," Marlene agreed.

"You will especially like the special aromatic tea I prepare myself. It will give you beautiful dreams and make you sleep well—afterward." Instead of seating himself in his imposing chair set between the elephant horns, Barkoon led them to a semicircle of cushions on the floor facing a tripod brass brazier, behind which the large windows looked out over Hong Kong. A charcoal fire burned in the brazier. Barkoon sat on the center cushion and invited Marlene to sit on his right and his redheaded mistress, Letitia, to his left. He motioned Mike to the other side of Marlene and Krakhaur to Letitia's left. Barkoon's blonde mistress did not join the ceremony.

When they were seated, the candles flickering around them, the red-hot coals reflecting brightly the bronze tones of the brazier, Barkoon very gently clapped his hands. A houseboy knelt beside Barkoon, holding a silver tray on which were the utensils for brewing the tea. He took a silver vessel with a long ebony handle from the tray and from a silver pitcher filled it with water. Leaning forward to place it on the brazier, Barkoon inquired conversationally, "Your wife is in excellent health, Mr. Krakhaur?"

"Yes, Your Highness. Never better. She is completely recovered from her ordeal at the hands of Poramat."

"I am most happy to hear that." One by one, Barkoon took four tiny, graceful ceramic cups and saucers and placed them in front of his guests. "These cups are made of what was known as celestial porcelain from the Tang Dynasty," he explained in low mellifluous tones directed to a fascinated Marlene. "They tried to reproduce the exquisite shade of jade in the glaze of this porcelain, and thus the cups give the tea a more esthetically pleasing appearance than white cups would."

"How interesting," Marlene murmured.

"You are aware of the vexing number of sects within the Buddhist and Confucian population of my country," Barkoon went on. "I actually was brought up as a Taoist, and for us drinking tea is a method of worship in the morning and, as I said, before retiring. I will attempt to translate the Taoist tea doctrine as we proceed, though translation is always a treason and can at its best be only the reverse side of a brocade: all the threads are there, but not the subtlety of color or design."

Marlene felt as though she were indeed participating in a type of prayer which, although she did not completely understand what was going on, seemed to free her mind and allow it to meditate on lofty ideals.

"The Tao literally means Path," Barkoon went on, talking softly to Marlene. "There is a thing which is all-containing, which was born before the existence of heaven and earth. How silent! How solitary! It stands alone and changes not. It revolves without danger to itself and is the mother of the universe. I do not know its name and so call it the Path."

Mike, watching the enthralled Marlene listen to Barkoon's hypnotic sermonizing, clearly realized that the ex-King had her marked for his next conquest. Then he caught Krakhaur's eyes—and silently mouthed the word *bullshit!*

"The Tao is in the Passage rather than the Path," Barkoon continued. "It is the spirit of Cosmic Change, the eternal growth which returns upon itself to produce new forms. We speak of the Tao as the Great Transition. Subjectively, it is the mood of the universe. Its Absolute is the Relative." Barkoon smiled at the blonde girl sitting so attentively beside him, feasting on his every phrase.

"That may be hard for you to understand," he said. "When I say the Taoist Absolute is the Relative I mean that in ethics we Taoists abominate the laws and moral codes of society. To us, right and wrong are but relative terms. Can I make you understand?"

Marlene nodded. "Please go on. I think I understand."

"All right, Marlene. We see that definition is always limitation. The 'fixed' and 'unchangeless' are merely terms expressive of a stoppage of growth. As the American philosopher Emerson wrote, 'Consistency is the hobgoblin of small minds.' So you see, ours is the philosophy of change. We believe the individual must change and resist all moralities forced upon us by society and live the life that allows him to fulfill best his destiny." Barkoon paused and studied his avid listener a moment.

"The observances of communal traditions involves a constant sacrifice of the individual to the state. Do you see? That people are not taught to be really virtuous but to *behave* properly?"

"I do understand, Your Majesty. You make it so clear now why you live the way you do." She stole a furtive look at Letitia, who looked bored. What a dull mistress she must be, Marlene thought.

Barkoon looked into the silver vessel on the brazier. "There are three stages of boiling," he said. "Now we see the first stage, where little bubbles like the eyes of fishes swim on the surface." He reached for a silver salt bowl on the tray held beside him and sprinkled a little salt in the water. "The salt goes in during the first boil," he intoned.

From the tray he took several very small platters containing tea leaves and herbs and placed them on the carpet in front of him. With a small set of tongs he lifted one of the tea leaves up for inspection and then peered at the water. "Now we put in the tea leaves and aromatic herbs as the water reaches the second boil, when the bubbles are like crystal beads rolling in a fountain."

With the tongs he dropped the tea leaves into the now boiling water, and then one by one he placed the contents of the other platters into the silver pan. "The tea must be in before the third boil, when the bubbles billow and surge wildly."

As the tea reached the third boil Barkoon took a silver dipper full of cold water from a bowl on the tray and poured it into the tea. "And so we revive the youth of the water," he intoned. Then he took the long black handle, lifted the silver vessel from the brazier, and filled each cup, placing the pan on a metal stand beside the brazier.

Barkoon lifted the cup to his lips and sipped the tea. The others followed his example. "It is so tasty," Marlene exclaimed, sipping and breathing in the aroma from her cup.

Barkoon filled the tea cups again. "My aromatic herbs give it that pungency," he said. "Let me translate from Lotung, a Tang Dynasty poet, on drinking tea." Barkoon sipped his second cup and recited:

"The first cup moistens my lips and throat, the second cup breaks my loneliness, the third searches my barren entrail, to find therein some five thousand volumes of ideographs. The fourth cup raises a slight perspiration—all the wrong of life passes away through my pores." Barkoon's eyes were looking deeply into Marlene's now. "At the fifth cup I am purified; the sixth cup calls me to the realms of immortals. The seventh cup—ah, but I could take no more! I feel only the breath of cool wind that rises in my sleeves. Let me ride on this sweet breeze and waft away thither. . . ."

Barkoon fell silent. After a moment, Marlene exhaled deeply and reached for her cup.

"I guess I'm like that poet, Your Majesty," Mike said with finality, after they had all consumed several cups of tea. "I can take no more."

"Oh, Mike, it has been so unusual and exciting an experience."

Barkoon gave Mike a solicitous smile. "The tea ceremony will make you sleep happier tonight, I promise you."

The ex-King, in spite of his bulk, rose easily to his feet from the cross-legged position on the floor, and the others followed. Marlene felt as though they had at last been excused by a teacher who had kept them after school.

"Tomorrow I will see you?" Barkoon asked Mike in the reception room.

"First thing in the morning."

Again Barkoon gave him that enigmatic smile. "Luncheon time will be soon enough. You may want to sleep late in the morning."

"I never sleep late," Mike replied.

In Mituyan, Barkoon said, a sly smile on his lips, his eyes twinkling with elfish knowledge: "One of the herbs I brewed in that tea has very powerful properties, good friend. You will notice that Brigit did not partake in the ceremony, since tonight I share with Letitia. Recall, I also asked Mr. Krakhaur if his wife was in quite good health."

As the roguish smile spread across the round face, Mike suddenly understood what Barkoon had done. In Mituyan he asked, "What did you put in the tea? Not—?"

Barkoon nodded. "Yes, dear friend and liberator of my country from the curse of KaritKi—the jiggy jiggy pom pom bark, which you and your beautiful companion will soon feel compeling you, was one of the herbs. It will insure you giving maximum performance and the exquisite blonde girl demanding it from you. So, dear friend, hurry back to your hotel. She will need no nightcap. . . . It won't be long."

Mike's initial fury with this obese reprobate gave way to a sudden burst of laughter. Then, also in Mituyan, he said: "You are an unprincipled rogue of the first magnitude. You give her that dose of your Taoism, poetry, philosophy, religion of tea, and all the while. . . ." Again Mike could not restrain his laughter. "All the while you were giving her Spanish fly. And I'm giving *you* back to the Mituyan people!"

"Just don't forget, dear friend, I'm next. And don't look so jealous. You are, after all, happily married."

Marlene came up to Mike and took his arm, a tentative smile on her lips. "What's so funny?"

"I'll tell you later. King Barkoon just told me a very funny story about a devout Taoist. You've got to understand these Oriental religions to get the point."

"Good night, Your Majesty," Marlene said. "Tonight has been one of the most fascinating and unusual nights of my life."

Barkoon nodded, still smiling, and saw his guests out the door.

CHAPTER FORTY-ONE

"VERY THOUGHTFUL of you to ask the management to put me on your floor," said Mike as he led Marlene down the corridor from the elevator. "In fact not only on your floor but next door."

"I was worried about being alone when I first came here," she replied, digging into her purse for her room key. "Also . . . I thought Luna would be with you." Mike took the key from her, opened the door, and they both entered.

"They gave me a beautiful room," Marlene said, gazing out the window. Mike noticed the large double bed. There were twin beds in his room. Turning, she said: "You are sure my father is not in trouble because of my story?"

"I saw your father at nine o'clock this morning. The West German trade mission is as solid as ever," Mike assured her. "Your father was very happy. The Palace and Grady Rourke of USOM had agreed upon a very large order of West German heavy equipment for the new Tuyan River control project."

"Then really I did not have to leave Mituyan at all?"

"It was probably just as well you did. Your father told me Tarot wanted to ask what you planned to write for your Swiss and German clients. The Palace was curious about how much of the UPI story you had contributed. Yes, I think this trip was a wise move."

Marlene spread her arms wide and looked out the window. "I do love it here." She turned to Mike. "Why are you here? Really, don't tell me about bankers. Why does Barkoon show you everything? He acts toward you as to a superior."

Impulsively, Mike caught her under her outstretched arms. "I'll tell you all about it—later." Her eyes glistened. He nuzzled under the clean-smelling blonde hair and kissed her neck. She started to pull away, but then, just as he felt he would have to let her go, she leaned slightly toward him again.

"This is wrong, Mike," she said softly, though not resisting now. "You have as wife a woman who has become my friend."

"This is Hong Kong. We're together, you and I," he heard himself saying. "If you'll let me I'd like to make this visit the most exciting you have ever had anywhere." He felt her pressing to him. He knew now how much he had needed to make love to her.

"Mike . . . darling," Marlene whispered, "I don't know what is wrong with me. I *know* we shouldn't be doing this. We have no right to each other. But I cannot help myself. I haven't the strength to say no. I want to stop, Mike, but I cannot. I want you. . . . But with a married man I never made love."

Mike kissed her tenderly. Unprotesting, Marlene allowed him to lead her to the double bed. He kissed her ear, and she shuddered uncontrollably. "Marlene, I think it is written that we should become lovers. I've wanted you for so long. I think I love you in a way I have never loved a woman before. Yes, I am married, but I . . . I find I love you. . . . Can you understand?"

Marlene turned her full mouth to his. "Oh, I want you too, Mike." He held her lips until they slowly came apart and his tongue felt the tip of hers. Marlene fell back on the bed. Mike lowered himself beside her; their legs were draped awkwardly over the edge of the bed.

"I don't know what happens to me, Mike," she whispered. "Never have I felt so strong this want to make love. Oh, *Gott!* I hope you will be strong enough to stop for both of us. . . ."

He tried to relax. "I was never jealous before tonight," he murmured.

Marlene chuckled. "You were really jealous?"

Mike replied by caressing her lips with his again. Marlene's arms went around his neck roughly, her lips crushed tight to his, and her breasts moved against him. Mike used the toe of one foot to pry the loafer off the other. In his stockinged feet, still kissing her, he reached back and, taking her legs by the calves, swung them from the floor up onto the bed, then pulled his own legs up so that they were lying close together.

It had been so long since he had made love to a girl for the first time that he felt positively foolish—like some hot youth, trying to get his girlfriend's clothes off. Did one just ask her to undress, or did he do it for her? Whether it was Barkoon's brew, or the prospect of at last realizing an erotic daydream, his inhibitions evaporated. There was nothing in this world now but Marlene and himself.

His hand reached up along the nylon-covered thighs and finding the top of the undergarments gently pulled them downward. Marlene raised herself toward him to make it easier to slide the frail summer panty affair past firm buttocks. Her stockings rolled inside out as he triumphantly pulled a fistful of gossamer apparel toward her feet, the whole ensemble sliding off more readily the further down her legs he maneuvered it. And then he found his progress halted: Marlene's stockings and underwear hung ludicrously from spike-heeled shoes. The thought fleeted through his mind that he was too old to be approaching a young woman in this manner. But then, he told himself, there was nothing superannuated about his passion for Marlene. . . .

She lay on the bed, eyes closed, sighing and breathing heavily. He had to take his lips from hers and awkwardly pull first one and then the other of her shoes off; then, at last, her undergarments and stockings fell in a heap at the end of the bed. Now once again he held her close, one hand caressing inside her thighs.

Her tongue fluttered against his. The fingers of his other hand explored for the zipper at the back of her dress only to find a tiny catch above it that one hand could not manage. Once again he felt helpless and a little ridiculous—wondering what to do, afraid of breaking the spell of his caresses.

She stirred and lifted her body to him. Taking her lips from his she whispered, "I help you, my love." She took her arms from around his neck and quickly coped with the catch and zipper. Then she half sat up and rolled to him so he could pull the dress out from under her and slide it over her head. With another deft gesture she unhooked her brassiere, pulled it over her head and tossed it away.

Never had he been so aroused and excited by so beautiful a sight. Marlene, nude, smiled challengingly at him, her long hair falling nearly to the nipples of her breasts. In their desire to be together neither had turned out the lights, and his eyes delighted at the pure yellow-white tuft of hair above the thighs he had been stroking.

"Darling, you need help with your clothes?" she asked. Her hands reached for his belt buckle and quickly pulled it open, as Mike tugged at his tie and shirt. Then he stood up for a moment to shuck his underclothes. Standing nude above her, taking in the full extent of her loveliness, he thought: Not bad for an old man who hasn't tried this sort of seduction for damn near twenty years. He dropped onto the bed beside Marlene's youthful form, his face impulsively going to the soft blond tuft he had dreamed of loving. Joyously he buried his face deeper into her softness, and her thighs parted.

Marlene moaned. She cried out Mike's name over and over, turning her head first one way and then the other. In all her life she had never felt like this—yet somehow she had known from the start that it would be this way if she and Mike Forrester ever made love. She could feel herself approaching and suddenly breaking through that nameless cold barrier that almost always had prevented her from knowing true ecstacy. Distantly, she heard herself calling urgent words of love to Mike in German. Her thighs undulated against his face as the exquisite sensation built, and then delicious waves of sensuality began sweeping all time and tension from her. She pulled at Mike's shoulders, and quickly he arched up over her, burying his mouth in the hollow of her neck and shoulder. Then she felt his desire pressing to her loins and moved to make the entrance easy. Marlene drew in her breath sharply as she felt his strength deep inside her, and she moaned softly.

"I love you, Marlene, I love you!" Mike cried suddenly with a great shudder. She cried out almost at once, "Oh, Mike! Oh, *Mike!* . . ."

In a moment he lay limply upon her, and she clung to him, every nerve in her body still quivering.

And a whole beautiful week ahead of them in Hong Kong, she mused dreamily after a while. And then? No, she wouldn't allow herself to think beyond then, not right now. She caressed Mike's back and neck with gentle fingers, knowing that this one time with Mike Forrester had been more exquisite than all the love she had ever had. Marlene sighed, smiling to herself, and waited for him to become ready to love her again.

As he awakened, Mike sensed an odd shimmering diffusion of the morning light. He opened his eyes to see Marlene's lovely face above his, her long yellow tresses cascading wispily about him. He and Marlene were protected from the outside world by a golden tent of her hair, the bright sunlight behind softly playing through it.

"Good morning, my beautiful girl," he said.

In reply, he felt her thigh against his groin, her breasts barely touching his chest, her fingers tracing both his cheeks. He felt his desire rising again, and Marlene whispered in wonderment: "Again you make love to me, darling?"

"All day. All night."

Marlene giggled. She lowered her mouth to his and kissed him softly, her tongue running around his lips. Mike could contain himself no longer. Grasping her hips firmly in both hands, he raised her body and then lowered her to him, thrusting upward. Marlene gasped. "My darling, I just can't get enough of you," Mike cried, his hands reaching up to her face, fingers entangling themselves in spun gold. He strained to contain himself until she was ready too. This morning, he thought giddily, Marlene's lovemaking had nothing to do with Barkoon's insidious tea. Suddenly Marlene stiffened and cried, "Mike! Darling! Please. *Now!*" And she fell onto him, her fingers clutching at him, sobbing as he thrust up into her.

The sun was much higher in the sky before Mike and Marlene were ready to consider anything in the world beyond their love and desire. When Mike was finally able to grope with one hand among the scattered clothing beside the bed for his wrist watch, he saw it was a quarter past eleven. He laughed aloud. That wily old Barkoon had predicted it.

"What is funny, Mike?" Marlene asked sleepily.

"Just something King Fatface said."

"You promised to tell me." She rolled over and propped herself up on one elbow, sweeping the hair out of her face with the other hand and then running her fingers through the hair on Mike's chest. "Tell me. There was something funny you and Barkoon were talking about, and I knew it had something to do with me. You were both looking at me funny."

"Do you really want to know?" Mike teased.

"Yes. I want to know everything."

"Well . . ." He hesitated a moment, then asked, "Are you happy about us? You and I together?"

Marlene purred, bending her head to nuzzle his cheek. Then she pulled back and said, "Now tell me, please."

"I'm going to. But first I want to know that you are happy about what's happened."

"I never, in my life, have been made so happy by a man. It makes me worry that almost I did not let it happen. I tell myself yesterday, no, I don't do this with Mike Forrester. He is a married man." She smiled coyly. "But I am glad I do."

"Me too. But I'm afraid we can both thank Barkoon for last night," he said.

"What has he got to do with it?"

"You remember his tea ceremony? All his talk of how the tea should be brewed, and that Taoist business?"

"Yes. It was fantastic. I never know so much about tea."

"Well, just before we left he told me that in the tea he had brewed an aphrodisiac herb that is quite well known in Mituyan and other Asian countries. It makes a man and a woman need each other urgently. I was laughing in disgust, really. All the time he was making that smooth talk he was giving you a sexual stimulant. What worries me," he said mock-plaintively, "it might have been the tea, not me, that did it."

Marlene burst into peals of laughter. "Barkoon," she gasped between laughing spells, "teaching me religion, and sneaks that herb in the tea! He is so naughty, so wicked, so funny. I love him. How *sweet* of him to do that for us. Maybe you are right—maybe I would not give in otherwise last night. I *needed* it. But I tell you, I don't eat or drink anything ever again around that man, without you there."

"He wants you, all right," Mike said grimly. "The idea was that after I had you I would let him have a turn. That's how depraved his thinking is."

"So," Marlene said, recovering, "he helps you to help himself. I hope you don't let him have any of me, darling. I hope you want me all to yourself. You be selfish. I know that king wants something very big from you."

"Yes, he does," Mike said soberly. "Well, I'd better call down and see if there are any messages."

Mike called the main desk, listened for a moment, then laughed loudly. "Barkoon's spy service is pretty good. Half an hour ago Colonel Lawton checked into the hotel. We're going to have one frustrated king on our hands today when you arrive with two escorts."

"You just remember. You are very selfish man. You do not share me with anyone. OK?"

Mike reached up and pulled her against him, kissing her neck. "Right. I *am* selfish. And we don't need any more of Barkoon's jiggy jiggy pom pom tea!"

"What? What you call it?"

"That's the name of the herb. In some of these countries they call sex jiggy jiggy pom pom, too. I don't know whether the name of the herb came from the name of the act or vice versa."

"In my life I never imagine any place in the world could be so strange, so frightening, so funny, so evil, and so much fun. You must show me all of this part of the world."

"I'll surely try, darling."

CHAPTER FORTY-TWO

FOR A WEEK Roger Krakhaur had been trying to find out from Mike the latest plans for the restoration of King Barkoon. Now that he had done his part, he wanted to make sure his syndicate would break the story first. Finally Roger had been able to pin Mike down for a quiet discussion over lunch at the Mandarin Hotel roof.

"You know what the plan is," Mike replied to the reporter's questions. "We're still working out the mechanics."

"It seems to be taking you a long time," Krakhaur observed.

Mike nodded. "We're still waiting word from Tuyan City to go ahead. Meanwhile"—he couldn't contain a smile—"my job is to stay right here in Hong Kong."

"Is Marlene getting a lot of shopping done?" The irony in Krakhaur's tone was unmistakable.

"She seems to be keeping busy. Barkoon's been after her constantly."

"That's the whole damned trouble, Mike. I *want* that story. It's been mine from the beginning, and I don't want some big, beautiful, blue-eyed blonde scoring a news beat on me."

"OK, Roger," Mike said, "I'll see that you know what's going on. Jack Cardinez comes into town this afternoon. I'll call you at home tonight and tell you as much as I can."

Downstairs, Mike found Marlene in her room waiting for him. He glanced at her purchases, and then, once again, they were holding each other.

"Mike, darling. I do not know what it is. I never was like this before. I want you all the time."

All afternoon they lay together—talking, napping, loving. At five o'clock Mike regretfully got up; he had to meet Lawton and Cardinez and go to Barkoon's house.

"Darling," he said to Marlene, "I'll meet you at Barkie's." He chuckled at the name Marlene now called King Barkoon to his royal face. "But take plenty of time dressing, because I don't want you to get there before I do."

"After this week, you think Barkie gets me?" she laughed. "Not a chance."

In the offices of an importing firm that was a cover for CIA operations in Hong Kong, Mike found Jack Cardinez and Fritz Lawton waiting for him. Cardinez seemed excited and on edge as he prowled around the office. "The new ambassador arrived in Tuyan City yesterday," he shot at Mike. "Whittelsie was called to Honolulu for high-level conferences and found himself briefing J. Sheldon Tate to take his place in Mituyan."

Mike whistled. "That fast? Well, Hartland promised us a hard-nosed bastard for the job." He went over in his mind what he knew about the new ambassador. Tate, a most controversial political and diplomatic figure, enjoyed enormous prestige in the United States and the world. Though he had been nominated by his party to run for President of the United States, he had lost by a wide margin. His political speeches had been notably outspoken and frank, to the despair of his campaign managers; yet everything he had predicted in respect to the world situation had come to pass. Even the least informed American voters now understood the need for many of the then controversial and unpopular political, diplomatic, and military surgical operations he had espoused. Mike, along with many Americans around the globe who lived with the daily realities of expanding Communist aggression, had been a great admirer of Tate and was keenly disappointed, though not surprised, when he had failed to win the presidency.

"What about the other members of the Country Team?" Mike asked.

"Tate has been given a mandate to make his own decisions," Cardinez replied.

"What about me, Jack?"

"You just stick with Barkoon. You seem to get along well with him. When we're ready to move we'll let you know."

"But I've been here a week now."

"Don't worry. It won't be long. We should be ready to get him into Mituyan and onto your yacht in a couple of weeks. Yesterday the Mad Monk tore up Tiking and Tuyan City with demonstrations against the government. The demonstrators are suffering harsh reprisals, which were duly reported in the press."

"But my wife, all alone in Tuyan City. What about her?"

"Believe me, she isn't alone. We promised to watch her for you, and we are. She's as safe as KaritKi himself."

"You can't protect her from Tarot or Poramat if they decide to throw her in one of their prisons."

"Ambassador Tate is no Whittelsie. He's the type who would personally cut off the American aid to the Palace if he thought he were being crossed. Wives of American citizens in Mituyan, even if they are Mituyan citizens, like Luna is, will enjoy the full protection of the embassy."

Mike thought of Marlene, whom he knew would love to prolong her stay in Hong Kong, and was ashamed to hear himself say, "OK, Jack, as long as she's safe." He genuinely worried about Luna, and felt guilty about his sudden—and ecstatic—liaison with Marlene.

"Good. We all think it's an outstanding idea to keep Barkoon on your boat. I have already taken the liberty of starting work on a few modifications. The radio room is good, but we're putting in a few extrasophisticated commo devices. Also, we're unobtrusively arming her."

"Anything for the cause," Mike agreed wearily. "*Promise* packed a lot of fire power before I had her converted from a minesweeper."

"I knew you'd feel that way." Cardinez stood. "Well, let's get going to Barkoon's place. We should start drawing up a feasible operational plan."

CHAPTER FORTY-THREE

THERE WAS an ash tray at each man's place at the conference table in Ambassador J. Sheldon Tate's office and two silver boxes of cigarettes in the center of the table. Tate watched in satisfaction as each of the four members of the Country Team eyed these amenities as they took their seats.

"Gentlemen," Tate began, "this, our first meeting since my arrival yesterday, will not be long. And furthermore I plan to call no more meetings of the so-called Country Team. I consider them a waste of time." Tate's eyes roved about the table. "I have informed our IRG and also SIG to expect no more meeting reports because there won't be any.

"From now on no member of my team will contact his agency directly in Washington for any purpose other than routine matters such as budget requirements for furniture, office rent, and the hiring and firing of civilian personnel below the rank of GS-8. All communications will come to my attention, and I will forward them to the agency or department concerned along with my recommendations, or send them back to you disapproved for transmission."

General Macker, who was enjoying the exceptional luxury of lighting a cigarette in the ambassador's office, froze, the match burning in his hand. Dickerson stared unbelievingly at the new ambassador. Grady Rourke shuffled uncomfortably. Ted Baum realized that a new storm had hit the U.S. mission.

The match started to burn Macker's hand, and he vigorously shook it out and dropped it in the ash tray. "These were my terms for coming over and trying to straighten out the mess over here. The President agreed," Tate added.

"But Sheldon," General Macker said, "surely this does not apply to my relations with the Secretary of Defense. I have always worked directly with him through Chief of Staff."

"From now on, Willet, you will work directly with me, and I will talk to the Secretary, the Chairman, and the Chief on your behalf."

"But military communications require a military mind."

"Willet, I am a Major General in the reserves. I think my mind is sufficiently military to cope with the present scale of your activities. We don't have a Vietnam war going here—not yet. Incidentally, they are sending you a new deputy commanding general of MAC-M, Lieutenant General Tom Gordon. I personally recommended his appointment to the Secretary and the President. I know you two will work well together."

Macker's face flushed deeply, and he looked down at the table. This was the way a general officer was fired. A deputy was sent in and a month or two later took command. Macker inhaled deeply on the cigarette.

"Mr. Dickerson, these instructions apply equally to your operations. I know how sensitive they are, but I cannot do the job unless I know everything that is going on in your sphere of influence. I spent a day in Langley with your people. You will receive an advisory on this tomorrow."

"Yes, sir," Dickerson said.

Ambassador Tate fixed the restless USOM man with a cold stare. "We will be making immediate changes in your methods of operating, Mr. Rourke. From now on U.S. personnel will supervise down to the district-chief level, and below if necessary, the distribution of AID imports. That means that you will be spending most of your time in the countryside making sure the new system works."

Rourke shifted irritably in his seat and, looking sidewise at the ambassador, said, "The Minister of the Interior, a fellow named Branot, will never buy that one. And you can be flat sure the Premier and that brother of his, Tarot, won't go along with you."

The look of distaste on the ambassador's sharp features became more pronounced. "The Premier will do it my way or there won't be any more aid. Now, Mr. Rourke, my best advice to you is to start packing a kit bag you can carry over your shoulder, get into the boondocks, and devise a way of accounting for every sack of rice, every radio, every load of fertilizer, every pig, every piece of farm machinery, every item of merchandise, and all the money that the taxpayers back home are sending here. The fact that the province chief signs for it is not sufficient. I want to know *what* peasant, *what* village, *what* hamlet receives the goods that come into this country every day. I guess you know what the tab is reaching each day in your department alone."

"I got a month of work on my desk right now," Rourke protested. "And my wife is afraid to be alone in Tuyan City."

"There is a Pan American jet clipper leaving for the States every day, Mr. Rourke. . . . I'll expect to hear from you several times a week as you travel the Republic of Mituyan from North to South and East to West."

Abruptly, Tate turned to Ted Baum. "Mr. Baum, I will handle the press myself from now on, but of course I'll need your help and advice. It isn't often we get a distinguished journalist to come over to our side of the barrier." Baum didn't know whether he was being patted on the head or pushed aside. He merely replied that he would do his best.

"One thing, Mr. Baum," Tate went on, "I have called an impromptu press conference for eight o'clock tonight at the Public Affairs Office. Will you have the auditorium ready and hot coffee and whatever you do for the correspondents?"

"We never gave them anything like coffee, sir. But I think it's an excellent idea. I'll see to it that coffee is there."

"You'll get nowhere pampering those irresponsible parasites, Sheldon," General Macker grumbled.

Tate stared at the paunchy old general for several moments as he nervously stubbed out his cigarette. Then Tate slowly said, "For parasites they have a surprisingly clear view of what goes on over here. The story of your little letter telling every commanding officer in Mituyan not to give out unfavorable information about our relations with the Mituyans while the Secretary of Defense was here made for a lively discussion in the senate. Upon investigation, the story turned out to be absolutely accurate, including the ludicrous grammatical error."

"I pulled a complete security investigation," Macker said defensively.

"If you'd had something approaching amicable relations with the press, they would have come to you about the memo and perhaps the story could have been softened. As it was, the impression in the United

States is that the top fellows over here are deliberately trying to conceal vital information from concerned officials of the government, to say nothing of the taxpayers who are footing the bill for the mission."

Silently, Ted Baum cheered J. Sheldon Tate, the diplomat famous for his lack of diplomacy as much as for his hard-nosed effectiveness. No wonder he never made the presidency, Baum thought—but what a man for *this* job!

"Now gentlemen, tomorrow I am meeting with Premier KaritKi. I will report to him the changes of policy that I, as the representative of the United States government, expect him to effect immediately. Any comments you may have as to how I can best impress upon him that this time we mean business will be appreciated."

The ambassador looked around the room. Then, as economically as possible, he enumerated the demands he would make. The look of shock on the faces of the members of the team served to convince him that every man, with the possible exception of Baum, would have to be replaced as soon as possible.

"But sir, you can't. We've never asked the Premier to let us inspect his prisons and interview political prisoners." Dickerson's voice rose as he leaned forward. "No American official has *ever* been allowed to visit the Isle of Stones."

"Well, it's about time. If we're going to have elections here, I want a healthy opposition, and if the entire opposition to KaritKi is in his jails—well, we'll just open up those jails and let them out."

Dickerson's voice quavered with emotion. "But sir, it's our job to get along with KaritKi and Tarot. I have enjoyed a close relationship with the Palace for two years. Taking such a tough line with the Premier will jeopardize all the work the Agency has been doing with Counselor Tarot."

"And that's another point," Tate snapped. "I am strongly suggesting that KaritKi send his brother as ambassador to one of the emerging African nations." He softened the impact with a grin. Dickerson looked at the ceiling, raising his hands, then dropped them into his lap.

CHAPTER FORTY-FOUR

NGUYEN VAN CAN felt a deep sense of shame and failure as he approached Tuyan City is one of the Volkswagen buses that plied the roads of Mituyan. His entire Tiking apparatus had been destroyed, his key men killed, and his guerrillas, though once again building up in strength, were without a forceful leader when he was not personally on the scene. Furthermore, as he well knew from his experience in subversion, to be really effective, indigenous guerrillas must be led by one of their own people. A foreigner could advise the leader, but the leader had to be of the same stock and culture as the fighting men.

The defeat of one of his most trusted and experienced aides, Major Ding, at Ba To was another crushing blow to the northern branch of the Mituyan Freedom Front to which he was senior adviser. Two Americans were directly responsible for his defeats in the North—Major Prescott, who was now dead, and, far more important, Mike Forrester, who was alive. Whatever else he did, Can had resolved to assassinate Forrester. Since he was neither at his rubber plantation nor, according to reliable agents, at his tea plantation near Port Raket, he must be in Tuyan City.

There was no excuse, no redemption for his failures in the North, Can knew. He would not forgive a subordinate for failure, and he expected no understanding from Mao Tse-tung's personal emissary in Tuyan City, top adviser and supplier to the MFF, General Quang. But there was one thing he *could* do: get Forrester, before going back north to rebuild his shattered organization. As the bus rolled along, making innumerable stops to pick up and drop off people wearing black pajamas and conical straw hats, and carrying ducks and chickens tied to their backs, Can turned over in his mind many different assassination methods.

He wanted it apparent that Forrester had been singled out for death and deliberately killed. Selective terrorism was always a powerful psychological weapon against government officials and their foreign advisers. It would take a day to locate Forrester, but the MFF intelligence system in Tuyan City should be able to find such a well-known American easily.

Dreading the report of failure he would have to give, Can did not chaff at the slow progress of the bus. It was almost thirty kilometers from the city limits where he had picked up this bus heading toward the heart of Tuyan City. There in the labyrinthine streets of the Chinese quarters the leaders of the MFF were waiting for him. He wished an MFF tax-collecting party would stop the bus and hold them up even longer.

Finally, the bus reached Bismarck Avenue and turned east toward the Chinese section of town, four kilometers from the palace. He was almost there now, and his stomach soured in anticipation of the forthcoming confrontation. He got out in front of the Pagoda to Confucius, according to instructions, and walked two blocks along a narrow, evil-smelling street, thankful that most of his operations were out in open countryside. He watched the numbers on the doors of decrepit buildings and tiny shops, found the door he was looking for, knocked two times, then once, and pushed the door open. The stairs were before him and he walked up two flights and knocked again once, then twice, on the door leading to the back of the house. It swung open, and a young Chinese bowed and led him through a short corridor to another door, which he opened by twisting three different knobs.

Inside, Can recognized General Quang sitting at the head of a conference table in the air-conditioned room that immediately gave him a sense of refreshment. Around the table sat five other men, only one of whom, Can's counterpart in the Tuyan Delta region to the south, he recognized. General Quang had provided a distinguished audience to hear his degrading confession. However, Quang seemed to be in good humor. He smiled at Can and gestured at the empty chair. Can sat down as he was bid and nodded to the others, remaining silent until spoken to.

"Now that we are all here," Quang began briskly, "we can examine the state of our operations in Mituyan and the progress of the Mituyan Freedom Front."

One by one the four corps-area senior advisers to the MFF gave a summary of the subversive activities they were directing, with special emphasis on methods of wrecking the elections by propaganda and terrorism. Can's turn came last. He stood up and, very straightforwardly, with no excuses, told how his Tiking intelligence and operations networks had been destroyed. It was only by an accident, a strange quirk of fate that his own life had been spared: he had impatiently left the Golden Dragon to find Frakit, the owner of the attaché case, thinking he might have stopped off at the camera shop to report to Nowat. Can had found the bodies of Nowat and his mistress and the chilling black cards with the white eye just moments before the explosion at the Golden Dragon had rocked the entire downtown section of Tiking. He held up the card for the other three senior advisers and General Quang to inspect. All nodded grimly. They had seen those cards not only here but during their tours of duty in Vietnam.

"It was the American planter, Forrester, that was responsible for our disaster," Can declared unemotionally. "He is in Tuyan City now, and I will arrange his death."

Then Can told how a battalion of trained guerrillas led by one of his best officers, Major Ding, had been destroyed by a handful of Americans at Ba To. "We would have won the entire hill country if it were not for the Americans," Can said.

"We would have our own government in the palace if it weren't for the Americans," Quang said mockingly. "In spite of all Premier KaritKi and his brothers do to make the people of Mituyan hate the government and come to our side, the Americans still frustrate us. It seems that we are finding our greatest problems in what should be the easiest part of the country for us to control, the northern areas where Colonel Can is in charge."

Quang gave Can a sharp look. "We cannot afford to lose a battalion of our best guerrillas in a defeat. Had Major Ding overrun the Americans, the loss would be worth the victory." He paused as Can bowed his head in humiliation.

"So we institute a new strategy," Quang said, his tone once again hearty. "We must make every effort to destroy the morale of the Americans both in Tuyan City and in the countryside." He reached across the table and picked up the black card with the white eye. "For the first time in my experience our terrorism has become less effective than that of our enemies. This will change." His eyes met those of his senior advisers around the table. Then he went on. "Several days ago Colonel Ping of the School of Subversion in Peking arrived in Tuyan City from a six-month duty assignment in Hanoi. Colonel Ping, will you please stand up?" A wiry, scarred little Chinese stood and smiled bleakly.

"Colonel Ping and his cadre were able to smuggle into Tuyan City the most ingenious and sophisticated device for selective terrorism we have yet been given. Unfortunately we have only one, so we will concentrate on terror against the Americans in Tuyan City. Colonel Ping, will you demonstrate for us?"

Ping clapped his hands, and from another door a shapeless coolie in sackline pajamas and a conical hat walked through the room. A typical yoke across his shoulders held two baskets of vegetables hanging from each end, one balancing the other.

"The most common sight in our countries," Ping commented, speaking Mandarin Chinese, the language of the top-level subversives in Mituyan. "But you are looking at the most useful weapon our electronic scientists in Peking have yet developed for the use of terrorism." He walked to the coolie and ran his finger the length of the yoke. "This is a radio-transmitting antenna," he said. Ping pulled a few vegetables from one of the baskets, revealing a square black metallic box. "This is a radio transmitter," he explained. He walked around the coolie to the other basket. "This is the power source. A regular six-volt automobile battery."

He clapped his hands again, and another of his men wheeled a bicycle into the room, followed by yet another Chinese in tan slacks, rubber shoes, and a white open shirt—a brazier and tin pan of cooking utensils dangling from opposite ends of a pole he carried over his right shoulder. "These are two more common items," Ping explained. "But the hollow tubes out of which the bicycle is constructed are stuffed with C-Four plastic explosive."

He walked to the bicycle. "The long bar between the saddle and steering bar is a receiving antenna." He ran his hands along it. "Under the saddle is a tiny transistorized radio-receiving set and detonator. At a signal from the transmitter," Ping walked to the coolie and pointed at the antenna and the radio in the basket, "the bicycle will detonate and kill everyone within fifteen meters."

Ping placed his hand on the shoulder of his other man. "This sidewalk kitchen is another common sight. The brazier and utensil box are both full of explosives with a transistor receiver in one or the other. The carrying pole is, of course, the receiving antenna. The sidewalk kitchen is superior to the bicycle for two reasons: unattended bicycles cause immediate suspicion in the cities of Vietnam where we have been practicing terror for many years; also, the brazier acts as a large grenade and showers metal fragments over a wide area."

Ping dismissed his three people and sat down. Can had watched the lecture in fascination. He would request permission to make the first use of the device to kill Forrester. But then he remembered what General Quang had said when he introduced Ping: There was only one such device in the country. Did this mean only one assassination? He posed the question and was greatly relieved when Ping replied that, although there was only one transmitter, he had managed to smuggle in more than a dozen of the small transistorized receiver-detonators.

Can made his request, and Quang considered it for some moments. "There is no margin for another failure in your operations," Quang said sternly. "However, I don't see how you could fail with this device. Yes, I will ask Colonel Ping to give you more instruction, and you will be given the first opportunity to use our new method of terror bombing. Have you located the target and learned his habits?"

"I will contact intelligence section, with your permission, and fix the target," Can replied.

"You are excused from this meeting then, Can. When you have fixed the target, Colonel Ping will work with you."

At first Can had been bitterly disappointed to discover that the American Mike Forrester had left some days earlier by plane for a destination outside Mituyan. An agent had reported, however, that Forrester's wife was staying at her parents' home in Tuyan City. The American must have believed both he and his wife were likely targets, because the house of the Englishman Hargraves and his Mituyan wife was closely guarded.

Can borrowed a bicycle and rode to the home of Forrester's parents-in-law. As he passed it, he saw Mituyan plainclothes policemen, obviously armed, walking casually back and forth in front of the house and even across the street. As an experiment he leaned his bicycle against the wall separating the front yard from the street and took a few steps away. Immediately one of the men in white sport shirts came up and began questioning him. After a close inspection of the bicycle, he was permitted to ride it away. He left the bicycle locked in a public rack a few blocks away and came back toward the target's house on foot. Squatting against a wall some distance from the house, Can began a long, patient vigil.

The more he thought about it, the sweeter this form of revenge became. Killing Forrester's wife would inflict far deeper pain on his enemy, until Can decided to kill him also. Furthermore, it would do far more injury to American morale. The Americans, worried about their wives' safety, would not function well as advisers. It was a lucky accident that Forrester was not in Tuyan City after all. Now, he had merely to discover the pattern of the new target's movements.

Late in the afternoon Can was rewarded with a glimpse of Luna Forrester. Two men walked out the gate, looked in both directions, and then signaled for the gate to be fully opened. A small black sedan drove out into the street and turned up toward Can's position. He saw a woman sitting in the back seat with a man on either side of her. An older woman, a Mituyan, sat in the front seat beside the driver. The car proceeded two blocks and turned left into Disraeli Boulevard. He watched the car disappear and then thought about the streets, realizing for the first time that every street was one way. To leave the house for any destination, a car had to follow the same pattern: Two blocks straight ahead and then a left turn on Disraeli. During the left turn, the car had to swing within inches of the sidewalk, and the target would be in direct line of sight and fire through the open window.

It must also be true then that there was only one pattern the car could follow on its return to the target's house. He stood up and walked down the other side of the street from the house. Two blocks further on he came to Bismarck Avenue, one way the opposite direction. Almost certainly the car would return along Bismarck and make a left turn into the street on which the target was living. Therefore he could set up a device on both corners, and if for some reason he couldn't hit his target leaving her home he would get her coming back. In fact, he might even have time to go back to Colonel Ping and get set up on the Bismarck Avenue corner and make the kill tonight. But no, that would be rushing and might cause failure, or worse, get him apprehended. He squatted on the corner where he would set up a street kitchen the next day and waited patiently for the car to return.

He watched for an hour, two hours, more, straining his eyes in the gathering dusk trying to identify the target vehicle. Not many cars turned into this street, but finally a small black sedan whipped around the corner, and, through the open window of the car, Can had a momentary look at Luna Forrester.

CHAPTER FORTY-FIVE

AMBASSADOR TATE fully expected a hostile reception as he was ushered into the oval reception room in the center of the ground floor of the palace. Here, he understood, was where KaritKi conducted his coldest and most formal meetings. Tate had hoped KaritKi might indicate his willingness to cooperate with U.S. aims by receiving the American ambassador in the living room of his apartment, or perhaps the den.

KaritKi without standing when Tate entered, gestured at the chair across the gleaming bare tabletop. Neither KaritKi nor Tate were disposed to waste time in amenities. They had been observed the previous morning when Tate had presented his credentials to the Mituyan Premier.

"You were extremely anxious to have this meeting your third day in our country, Mr. Ambassador," KaritKi began. "I am ready to hear what you apparently believe is so important."

"Thank you for making this time available to me so soon, Your Excellency. My government is indeed interested in presenting to you the measures it feels that you, as Premier, should take in the next few months to win the support of your people in this war against Communist infiltration."

KaritKi listened warily, his hostility growing, his outbursts of protest becoming more frequent, as Ambassador Tate quietly outlined the plan evolved in Washington and Honolulu for a new land-reform program that would give the poor rural population a fair chance to own their own land. Tate explained, unnecessarily of course, he realized, that under the present government system of redistribution of lands the peasants were still unable to meet the mortgage payments on the government loans granted to them for the purpose of acquiring lands. It was surprising, and alarming to those interested in keeping communism out of Mituyan, Tate pointed out, that almost all of the land being redistributed by the government was being used to create large estates owned by Palace intimates.

Only the extreme pressures on KaritKi by those Palace intimates who faced ruin if certain financial cuts in aid to Mituyan businessmen—imposed in the past two weeks directly by Washington—were not lifted, prevented KaritKi from angrily dismissing Tate from his presence.

"We are all concerned," the ambassador continued, "that the spirit of equality and fairness which should prevail in the coming elections is being seriously impaired by the policies of your brother Tarot." Tate was not noted for diplomacy when a hard line was called for, but he thought that here he had used remarkable tactful language in referring to the key issue of Tarot and elections.

"I don't understand you, Mr. Ambassador," KaritKi returned testily. "Counselor Tarot and I together form our policies. He does not act unilaterally."

"Then I suggest the two of you reevaluate your policies. There is a definite feeling among the best-informed Americans on the Mituyan political situation that Counselor Tarot is using his Special Forces troops to terrorize potential political opponents of your regime. You cannot suppress the legitimate opposition, send to your Isle of Stones people who disagree with you, and then claim you are helping to promote free elections in your country."

KaritKi's face reddened. "I know what is best for my country. You Americans come over here and think you can run our country better than we. You don't understand Asia, and you certainly don't understand Mituyan."

"One of the reforms we are requesting is complete inspection of all your political prisons and the right to interview your prisoners."

KaritKi jumped to his feet, slamming his fist on the table. "No!" he shrieked. "You have not the right to meddle in our internal affairs! You are here only to help us contain the Communists."

"That is right," Tate answered calmly, keeping his seat. "And we find that the Communists will take over your country within the year if you do not change your policies and win back the people. In the note that will be formally delivered to you tomorrow, after you and I have had a chance to discuss its contents now, my government calls upon you to make such changes in your government and military personnel as will assure that certain necessary reforms be effected. Although the note does not say so, my government strongly urges you to send your brother Tarot out of Mituyan and keep him out until after the elections."

KaritKi stood apoplectic, speechless with rage, his hands shaking. Tate decided to throw the last demand at him now before the Premier exploded in the torrent of invective boiling up in him. "Mr. Premier, we ask that an impartial commission be appointed by the Southeast Asia Treaty Organization to come to Mituyan within a week to supervise the elections for the constituent assembly."

"I will telephone your President! Now!" KaritKi screamed. "I will ask for your dismissal. Get out! Out of my country!"

"If I go, every scrap of U.S. aid goes with me. Your country will fall in weeks."

KaritKi stared out at the ambassador from under his brow. He was a cornered animal turned irrational with fear and rage. "If your aid means we have to suffer your presence, we don't want it!" he cried.

A door opened behind him, and Ambassador Tate stood up. Tarot, a smirk on his thin face, walked across the room to his brother. "Your Excellency," he said soothingly, "I could hear you outside. What is the problem?"

KaritKi pointed a quivering finger at Tate. "He's trying to blackmail me!"

"Perhaps *negotiate* would be a better term," Tate interjected mildly.

"He threatens to throw us to the Communists if we do not let him run *my* country." KaritKi was still shaking, and Tarot tried gently to lower him into his chair. Tate silently watched Tarot soothing the convulsed Premier, whose mouth was open and working.

"Perhaps it would be better for me to talk to the Premier at a later date," Tate suggested.

"The matter of your recent arbitrary cut in financial aid to our importers should be discussed," Tarot said thoughtfully. "Aside from the personal distress it is causing to many of our most influential families, it will soon start to hurt our war effort against the Communists."

"There is much to discuss from both of our viewpoints," Tate replied. "If Mituyan wants American aid in fighting your Communist insurgency, my government feels that the reforms and policies I've just outlined to His Excellency should be effected now, before the elections."

"The Americans want Communism stopped here as much as we do," Tarot said with self-assurance.

"Not if it means supporting a tyrannical, repressive regime. Not any more. That's why I am here."

Tarot's smile twisted from his face. He looked at his brother, who was slowly regaining his composure. "The press of your country seems to delight in writing derogatory stories about us, accusing us of police brutality, terrorism, arbitrary arrests, and imprisonment. The citizens of your country and your government are given false and misleading impressions of our government. Your first task in our country should be to curb the press, as Ambassador Whittelsie was attempting to do before he was relieved—without any prior knowledge on our part, I might add."

"The press writes what it sees," Tate replied shortly. "If instead of repressive tactics you would show them you *are* making reforms and *are* trying to win the loyalty of the people, the press would write favorable stories about the way you run this country."

KaritKi gestured at the chair. "Sit down, Mr. Ambassador. You do not understand our philosophy. I will try to explain it. Now as to your list of demands upon me—"

"I wouldn't call them demands." Tate sat down. Instinctively he knew that in *twenty* conferences, using diplomacy, tact, or the tough line he had just tried, he would get nowhere with KaritKi and Tarot. "Rather I would say they are principles." He went on talking, although he realized there was only the one possible solution to keeping Mituyan from being taken over by the Communists, and, after Mituyan, all the other countries in this part of Asia.

"If you have alternate suggestions which will bring about honest elections in this country and win the hearts and minds of the Mituyan people to a central government authority," Tate heard himself go on futilely, "I will listen to them with great interest and immediately pass them along to my government."

At a nod from KaritKi, Tarot sat beside the ambassador, and the two brothers settled down for one of their marathon discussion periods that had always overwhelmed American officials like Ambassador Whittelsie who were trying to effect an unwelcome change in Palace policy.

Ambassador Tate, having made up his mind to activate "Operation Switch" as soon as he returned to the embassy, primed himself to endure the next few hours of invective and obfuscations.

CHAPTER FORTY-SIX

It had been another restless day for Luna at her parents' home. Although Mike had asked her not to leave the house, the night before she had gone to the movies with her mother and the men assigned to guard her. Major Song and two of his men were around constantly. The irony struck her frequently. Here was one of KaritKi's top men guarding her life, while her husband was making preparations to overthrow the Premier . . . a fact that made her seriously concerned about not being able to get an exit visa.

As she watched her father sip a highball and Major Song patrol the house and grounds, her restlessness became unbearable. If only she were at Rishram or the tea plantation; there was so much she could do. She stopped Song on one of his perambulations: "Can't I go to the roof bar at the St. George Hotel and have a drink with some of my friends? I feel as if I'm under house arrest."

Song shrugged. "You know what your husband said, and Colonel Lawton too. I am sorry and ashamed that I failed to kill the North Vietnamese, Can, in Tiking, but as long as he is loose I cannot let you go. If I had been here last night, I would not have permitted you to go to the theatre. It was a dangerous thing to do."

"I know," Luna replied apologetically. "It's just that waiting, doing nothing, makes me very uncomfortable and restless." Then to herself she said, Oh, Mike, come back soon.

Feeling angry toward her old friends at the palace who had refused her the exit visa, she decided to try once more to reach Dhuna on the phone. Maybe if she would intervene with KaritKi, he would grant her the visa the next morning and she could catch the afternoon plane to Hong Kong.

Luna succeeded in getting through to the palace, then to Dhuna's secretary, and finally, after much cajoling, the secretary put Dhuna on the line. For ten minutes Luna told the Premier's young wife how miserable she was, not to be allowed to go to Hong Kong with her husband. Finally, perhaps just to get her off the phone, Dhuna promised to try to persuade her husband to issue the visa.

Luna hung by the telephone all evening, but no call came through. She was up with the first light of dawn but it was not until the middle of the morning that Dhuna called. Tarot was very suspicious that Luna was so frantic to get out of the country, Dhuna reported. He didn't believe her sole reason was to be with her husband.

"Can't the Premier do it for me?" Luna asked.

"He has put everything in the hands of Tarot, dear," Dhuna replied. "I've done everything I can. Ever since you and Mike intervened for the girlfriend of that awful American journalist who had been saying such bad things about us at the palace, the Premier and Tarot have been concerned about your loyalty."

"All I want is to be with Mike," Luna pleaded. "I have a terrible feeling that I should be with him."

"Tarot promised to let me know what he decides."

The morning dragged on into the afternoon. At three the phone rang.

"Counselor Tarot wants you to come to the palace," Dhuna said. "He wants to talk to you. I'm afraid, dear, he isn't going to give you the visa. I think you ought to say you can't come. I don't trust my brother-in-law. He gets more suspicious and mean every day. Why don't you just go up to Tiking and wait for Mike there?"

Luna, crushed, knew Dhuna was right. She should not go to the palace if Tarot summoned her. "All right, Dhuna. And I thank you so much for everything."

Less than an hour later the phone rang again. It was Tarot's secretary asking if she would like to come over to the palace and talk to the counselor personally about the exit visa. Mindful of Dhuna's warning, Luna demurred and said she had no transportation and wasn't feeling well anyway. It was possible that Tarot might detain her, even have her jailed. There was a long pause on the phone, and then the secretary said that Counselor Tarot was sending a Palace limousine and an escort to bring her to his office. She hinted that the visa might be forthcoming if Luna could satisfy the counselor as to her intentions. Against her better judgment that told her to wait in this house until Mike came back, even if it took another week, she agreed to accompany the Palace guard captain back to Tarot's office.

She dressed in her most demure dress, pink, with the Mituyan-style slit reaching just above the knee. She was the young dutiful wife being kept from the husband she loved. She knew nothing of politics or business; she only knew she wanted to be in Hong Kong with her husband.

While waiting, she checked the airline schedules. If Tarot did give her the exit visa, she could still get the late-night Air Cathay flight, which would bring her into Hong Kong just before dawn. The last thing she did was pack a suitcase with a few necessities, and she stuffed the plane schedule into her pink handbag. She called for Major Song, who could make no objections when he heard that Tarot had summoned her.

"Please have one of the servants put this suitcase in the car. If I get the exit visa, I'll go directly to the airport."

The sound of a heavy car driving up to the gate brought her to the front door. A brilliantly uniformed guard officer came through the gate.

"You will be all right in the Palace limousine," Song said. "But do not leave the palace to get a cab."

Luna thanked Song. The guard officer introduced himself and led her through the gate. Maybe I'll be in Hong Kong by morning, she thought happily.

At dawn the first sidewalk vendors of hot soup and rice set up their portable kitchens at strategic locations all over Tuyan City. Long before, Nguyen Van Can, with the help of Ping and his cadre, had positioned their two bombs at the two strategic corners and were waiting for the target to enter the pattern.

Can himself carried the yoke on his shoulders; Ping had shown him the little button on the yoke that set off the lethal charge. The transistor detonators were on safety at both locations. The first bomb the target would pass, at the corner of Disraeli, would be unsafetied at a signal from Can and be ready to detonate by radio, and the hot soup purveyor would hastily move away.

All morning Can tensely lurked within sight of the target's house, changing hats frequently to alter his appearance. At midday the gates of the house suddenly swung open and the black car leaped from the driveway. Hastily, Can gave the signal and moved his thumb into position over the button. The lethal sidewalk kitchen was right at the edge of the corner; a slight push would have tumbled it into the street. As the car drove by he saw that the target was not inside. It was another ten minutes before Ping's man cautiously returned to his device and once again safetied the detonator. The target never left the house that day or evening, and at midnight Can and the two members of Ping's terrorist cadre carried their camouflaged lethal device back to Quang's headquarters, where they took a few hours sleep before starting out again before dawn the next morning.

A weary Can, the radio transmitter and battery weighing heavily on his shoulders, took his position for the second day within sight of the target's house. Both devices were in position, attended by Ping's two terrorists. There seemed to be unusual activity about the house, Can noticed. A Mituyan who looked vaguely familiar, although it was impossible for him to recognize the man, walked into and out of the gate several times. Then, late in the afternoon a gray Rolls-Royce rolled up in front of the house, and a gaudily dressed officer, who must have been some sort of Palace guardsman, Can surmised, stepped from the car. The officer was admitted through the gate, and in a few minutes returned to the car with a young woman. Can's heart banged against his chest: the target! The officer opened the rear door, helped the young woman into the limousine, closed the door after her, and walked around to the other side of the Rolls-Royce, climbing in beside her. He had put himself between Luna and the bomb; but, thought Can, there is enough explosive to destroy the whole limousine.

Can made the signal to the terrorist on the corner of Disraeli Boulevard. His head swam with excitement, and he had to fight off a dizzy spell. The target would be killed with a high-ranking KaritKi aide in a Palace car. What a sweet victory! He couldn't have planned it better. The terrorist had fled his sidewalk kitchen. Can's thumb moved over the button as he intently watched the Palace car glide into gear and head toward Disraeli. The car approached the corner. Can held his breath, saw the front wheels start to turn and then, precisely as the limousine made its turn, he pressed the transmitter button.

The explosion shattered the still late afternoon. Metal fell loudly onto the street; the wounded screamed piercingly. Can shuffled toward the bloody corner. To have walked in any other direction could only have drawn attention to himself. Even Can, hardened as he was to battle, was sickened at the scene. The side of the limousine had been blown in. Can forced himself to remember finding the body of Nowat's mistress in the camera shop, and he stared pitilessly at the pink-clad body of the woman who had been his target. It lay crumpled in the bloody street littered with glass and bits of the shattered Rolls-Royce. A pink handbag was clutched in her hand.

The shrieks and moans of the wounded now came from all around the corner. He counted at least ten dead. Severed limbs were strewn about, but the torn bodies of those still living and trying to move was the most horrible sight. Sweating, he pushed the conical straw hat off his head and turned from the carnage he had wrought, feigning shock. It was then he saw the three men running from his victim's house toward him. Can was not worried. He looked like any other peasant carrying home vegetables he had purchased in the market. The men passed him in their rush to reach the tragic scene. He kept shuffling away, shaking his head along with others who could not stomach the horror.

Suddenly his heart jumped and the pit of his stomach went cold. He felt a viselike grip on his arm. His other arm was likewise pinioned, and a chop to the back of his neck felled him to his knees. "Colonel Can," a voice said, "you will beg, slobber, and pray to any deity you know for your death."

Can looked up at the man who had seemed so vaguely familiar the day before. Unsteadily, the North Vietnamese gained a standing position and, in Mituyan, protested he was only a poor peasant who had already endured the greatest fright of his life.

Blood gushed from his face at a second chop across his nose. "Look at me, Can. Do you not recognize me?" Song cried. "The guerrilla who brought you the attaché case at the Golden Dragon?"

Can looked into the face, recognized it—and his dying started.

CHAPTER FORTY-SEVEN

"EVERY NIGHT we go up there it gets harder to break you out of Barkoon's palace," Mike said to Marlene when they were finally in a taxi on the way back to the Mandarin Hotel.

"Tonight he is very insistent I move in with him," Marlene said. "So I tell him I am in love with you, Mike."

"And what happened?"

"He says that you are married and being American can only have one wife at a time. He promises to marry me whenever I am ready."

"Well, you'd have all kinds of other wives and concubines to keep you company."

Marlene huddled close to Mike in the cab. "I am happy with you, Mike."

He put an arm around her shoulders under the spilling golden hair and pulled her to him. The cab reached downtown Hong Kong and wended its way through twisting streets toward the hotel. "Marlene, would you mind if we stayed in my room tonight? I've been asked to be reachable day and night while Jack Cardinez is in town."

"I don't mind." The cab drove up to the Mandarin Hotel, and Mike went to the main desk to see if he had any messages.

"There was an urgent long-distance telephone call for you from Tuyan City, Mr. Forrester," the desk clerk said, handing him a yellow slip. "The Tuyan City trunk lines close at nine o'clock at night, so they'll put the call through in the morning." Mike glanced at the slip, which merely said that Cecil Hargraves would try again to reach him when the trunk lines opened at seven A.M. There were no other messages. His stomach suddenly felt queasy. Why would Luna's father be calling him?

Mike waited in his room for Marlene to come and tried to get the phone call off his mind. Could Luna have obtained an exit visa? No, she would have sent him a cable. He opened the bureau drawer and took out a fifth of Chivas and drank directly from the bottle.

"Mike, you look so desperate. What is wrong?" Marlene, carrying a suit on a hanger and a small vanity case, came into the room, wearing a robe over her nightgown.

He breathed heavily. "I don't know. I had an urgent call from Tuyan City. I'll have to wait till tomorrow to find out what it's all about."

Marlene asked him no more questions, for which he was grateful. He went into the bathroom and brought out a tumbler into which he poured a heavy measure of straight Scotch. "Would you like some?" he asked.

"No, darling. I get all the kick I need from you." She sat on the side of the bed looking at him anxiously. Slowly he took off his clothes; draping them over the back of a chair and then, in his shorts, sat down beside Marlene, holding the tumbler in his hand. Marlene put a hand on his shoulder and the other arm around his neck and leaned toward him. He put his face in her hair and kissed it.

"Why don't you wait until the morning to start worrying, darling?" Mike nodded and slowly forced himself to stop thinking about the Tuyan City call.

He finished his Scotch and turned to Marlene. She smiled up at him and then slipped off her robe and nightgown. "Lie down, Mike," she whispered. He slid off his shorts and lay back beside her, her hands caressing him all over his body, exciting him, diverting his mind, making him want her. Then she bent her head down over his groin, bathing him in the flowing gold she knew stimulated him, and suddenly he began to feel one of the most extravagant raptures a woman can give her man. He plunged his fingers into the bobbing yellow hair and held her tightly, crying out, "Marlene, I love you." He fell back on the bed, emotionally and physically spent. Marlene disengaged herself and whispered, "I love you too, Mike."

It was still dark when he woke from the deep sleep and looked over at Marlene sleeping quietly beside him, a golden fan of hair spread over her pillow. He tried to go back to sleep but could not, and finally he got up, took a long shower, painstakingly shaved himself, and, as the rose-tinted sky outside brightened, he tied a bathrobe around himself and watched the birth of the new day over Hong Kong.

"Mike," Marlene whispered. "What are you doing up so early?"

"Sorry to wake you. I just couldn't sleep."

"Come sit beside me. Maybe we talk, darling."

"What about?"

"Us, of course. Will we still be together after Hong Kong?"

"I wish it could be."

"You are still in love with Luna? More than with me?"

"We have been very close for seven years. I wouldn't want to lose her. We get along well together. *She* does, anyway. I thought I did too, until you and I kept running into each other all over Mituyan. I couldn't help wanting you, and now—" He paused and looked at her miserably. "I love to have you with me, Marlene. I want so much to do new things with you, go strange places."

Marlene chuckled. "When do we leave?"

Mike smiled gently. "That's the romantic kind of dream you awaken in me. Luna and I had our adventures—maybe we'll have more. But we're tied to our properties, and Luna wants to have children. Damn, it's rough to be realistic."

"What will happen to us, Mike? You and I? I'm still young. Why we do not go to some strange place together when you make Barkie the *führer* of Mituyan again. I will write stories for my magazine about travel in the Orient. Then if you still want to stay married to Luna, you do. I have time to find a new life."

"It is strange how you can love two women at once," Mike said quietly. "Because you may have something very deep with one person doesn't make you love the other any less."

"What are you saying, Mike?"

"That I'm going back to Luna, I guess. We've been through too much together to call it quits now. Quite honestly, Marlene, I'd lose all sense of direction in life without her. Can you understand?"

Marlene nodded, staring at him with wide blue eyes. She reached for her robe on the floor beside the bed and pulled it around her. Getting up, she took her vanity case and went into the bathroom.

Mike glanced at his watch. It was six-thirty now, another half an hour before the trunk lines would be open into Tuyan City. Suddenly his phone rang violently. He grabbed at the instrument before the strident sound could fill the room again. He waited a moment and then said cautiously, "Hello?"

"Mike, this is Roger, can I see you now?"

"Now? It's kind of early, isn't it?"

"It's important, Mike. I'm down in the lobby with Alana. May we come up?"

"The room's a mess. Give me a couple of minutes and I'll be down."

Mike quickly finished dressing and called through the bathroom door, "Marlene, Roger Krakhaur is downstairs. He's got something on his mind that can't wait. I'll meet you for breakfast in half an hour. If my call comes through, they'll tell me in the dining room."

"Please call in my room when you are ready," Marlene replied.

In the lobby he saw Krakhaur and Alana waiting for him and wondered at the somber look on their faces. "Be right with you. I'm expecting a call from Tuyan City when the trunk line opens," he called to them. "I'll tell the desk clerk we're having coffee."

Returning, Mike suggested going into the breakfast room, but Roger pointed to a sofa in the corner of the lobby. "Let's sit down over there for a minute first."

He followed and waited until they had seated themselves. "Now, what brings you downtown at six forty-five in the morning?"

"Mike, I had a call from the night man in the Star Syndicate office," Krakhaur began. "A story was moved late last night from Tuyan City, and I thought Alana and I should come tell you personally. It's not confirmed yet, but we felt you should hear it from us."

Dread welled up in him. He tried to control his emotions, fearing what would come.

"The story said a terrorist bomb was exploded on the corner of Bismarck Boulevard and Pangit Road." An image of the corner, less than two blocks from the Hargraves' house, swam before Mike's eyes. "Nine people were reported killed, fifteen wounded. . . . The story said that the wife of an American—Mrs. Michael Forrester—was killed in an automobile that was driving by as the bomb went off."

Somehow since the night before he had known, but he had refused to face the possibility. All he said was, "I made her promise not to go out of the house while I was away." He sat stunned, the reality seeping in slowly. The call from Luna's father. Soon he would hear what had happened. Alana placed her hand on his. "Mike, I feel such a deep personal loss, too. Anything Roger and I can do, please let us know."

"I'll have to go back today," he said dully.

Krakhaur pulled a card from his pocket. "I have the schedule. The best one is BOAC at eleven-thirty."

"I'd better take it." What had he said just thirty minutes ago? Without Luna he would have no sense of direction in life. He felt drained and empty.

"Remember, if there's anything at all I can do, please call me, Mike," Alana said, on the verge of tears. "She was so good to me. She saved my life."

Mike walked to the elevators. At the sixth floor he went down the hall to his room and let himself in. He sat on the bed next to the phone. Mechanically he called to the desk to report he was back in his room. He wondered if he had better call Marlene. She might be expecting his call. He put his hand toward the phone but then, instead, he called Cardinez at the special phone number he had memorized.

"Jack, can you come over to my hotel? I'm leaving. Something happened."

"What?" Cardinez asked. "What happened?"

"Luna is dead."

There was a shocked silence on the other end of the phone. "When, Mike?"

"Yesterday, sometime—probably evening. Star Syndicate has the story."

"I'll pick up Fritz and we'll be right over, Mike. Wait for us. My God, I'm sorry. I was so sure—" He paused. "We'll be there soon."

Never to see her again, to look out over the rubber trees that they had cared for, walk through the tea plantation of which they had been so proud. Never to visit the little dispensaries she had insisted on for the villages where their workers lived. Never to hear her say in wonderment, when she thought she was alone in front of the mirror, "Mrs. Michael Benning Forrester, Jr." She was just thirty years old.

Tears stung his eyes but he held them back, breathing deeply. To keep busy, he put everything in the room that was his in the suitcase and closed it. He decided he *had* better call Marlene in case she was waiting to go down to breakfast.

There was no answer. Either she didn't want to talk to him or she was already downstairs, in which case Roger and Alana would tell her what happened.

It was after seven now; the lines were open. He waited. Finally he walked to the window and stood staring out at Hong Kong. The sudden ring of the telephone shocked him. He whirled and went to pick it up.

He dimly heard Cecil Hargraves' voice. "Are you there?"

"I just heard, Cecil," Mike called out over the poor connection to spare the old man the ordeal. "I'll be back this afternoon," he shouted. "How did it happen?"

All calls from Tuyan City were bad but he managed to pick up most of the words, and repeating his flight time he hung up. The phone rang again, and Cardinez said he and Lawton were in the lobby. Mike wanted to get out of the room. It smelled of Marlene, a scent that had thrilled him until only a few minutes ago. He picked up his suitcase and briefcase and walked out the door.

In the lobby below, Cardinez and Lawton looked troubled as they expressed their sympathies. "Do you know what happened?" Cardinez asked.

"I couldn't hear very well. Luna's father said it was a bomb deliberately planned to get her. He said they caught one of the terrorists involved. That was all I could get."

"Mike, I don't know what we can say. I can't understand what broke down—we had the tightest security measures," said Fritz.

"You can't guard against that kind of terrorism," Mike said wearily. "I know it. Luna knew it. We were fighting a battle together. We both knew what could happen. . . . Just give me a few days and I'll be back in the fight. OK?"

Cardinez and Lawton nodded sadly.

CHAPTER FORTY-EIGHT

FIVE DAYS after the simple Anglican services for Luna Forrester, Mike left the tea property near Port Raket, where he had gone to be alone and ponder the future. Arriving at his apartment in Tuyan City he found a letter bearing the seal of the U.S. Embassy under his door. Tearing it open he found a note dated that morning written to him by Ambassador J. Sheldon Tate.

The note was informal, expressing his deepest sympathy at the death of Mrs. Forrester and requesting Mike to contact him either at the embassy or the residence as soon as possible. It ended with a paragraph passing on to Mike Undersecretary Hartland's heartfelt sympathies and warmest regards.

It was nine o'clock in the evening, but Mike decided to call. The most important thing he could do in memory of Luna, he knew, was to get back into the fight on all fronts as soon as possible. To Mike's surprise, the secretary at the residence connected him with the ambassador immediately. Tate invited him to have lunch at the residence the next day, and Mike accepted.

Going through the mail he had picked up at the Hargraves' house and in his own mail box, he found a note of sympathy from Marlene, postmarked Hong Kong. She said she would be back in her father's house in a few days. There were several official condolences from the Palace. One note in particular was an effusive and emotional confession of inadequacies from Major Song and an invitation to visit him any morning at the offices of the Special Police, where the murderer of his wife was being held.

All right, Forrester, he said to himself, you are in this fight all the way. Let's get with it. No more moping, self-accusations, guilt feelings, no more hiding from reality. The best way to fight back is to know more about the enemy.

At ten A.M. Mike appeared at the headquarters of the Special Police. This was the province of Counselor Tarot and Madame Mayna. He hoped he would run into neither of them. Nobody knew exactly why Tarot had sent the limousine for Luna. Tarot said he wanted to help her procure the exit visa but felt he must discuss certain points with her. It was Mike's personal opinion that Tarot had intended to place her in detainment as a lever against her husband, whose recent actions had aroused his suspicions.

Mike was ushered into an office and asked to wait. Soon Major Song entered and abjectly apologized for not having been able to prevent the tragedy.

"You could not help it," said Mike. "How could you think anything could happen to her in a Palace limousine?"

"That was what defeated me. I could not interfere with orders directly from Counselor Tarot." Motioning Mike to be seated, Song explained exactly how the MFF terrorists had handled the assassination with a new and, for the Mitcoms, highly sophisticated device. Mike tried to remain detached from his personal tragedy as he listened to the detailed explanation.

"Perhaps you would like to confront the man who committed this atrocity," Song suggested. "He has been an old enemy of yours."

"Yes, I would like to see this Nguyen Van Can."

"We will soon get much information from him. He should break today or tomorrow." Song stood up and rang for a jailer, who led them through a back corridor to a long descending flight of stone steps. Finally, far below street level, they came to an iron grill. Another uniformed attendant identified them and pulled the heavy gate back. Mike, following Song's lead, signed his name in a ledger book. Another iron door was opened, and they walked into a brightly illuminated, high-arched tunnel flanked by rows of heavy doors on both sides.

Many of the doors had small grill peepholes, and Mike could not restrain himself from glancing inside. Every cell was well lighted, most filled to overcrowding, and a great deal of moaning and crying could be heard. Peering in, Mike saw many shaved-head monks in brown and saffron robes, as well as teenage youngsters.

Song noticed the revulsion on Mike's face. "You may not be aware of the rioting that has been going on for a week. The Buddhists, led by that cursed monk from Tiking, Li Phang, have been in the streets day and night. Their leaders whip them into anti-government furies, and they roam about breaking into stores, throwing stones, bottles, and even Molotov cocktails at cars. They have killed two policemen so far. Yet when to protect ourselves we shoot back or hit out with our clubs, we are accused of brutality and suppression of religion. I am a Dicut Buddhist myself, and I am ashamed of the way our monks listen to this Phang, who is not of any sect. Confidentially, I am expecting the secret police to receive orders any day to arrest Phang. He does more harm than even the MFF."

"But these children?" Mike asked.

"They will be released to their parents, with stern warnings holding their fathers personally responsible for their conduct. It is disgraceful what total national disorder one shaved-head devil can produce. If we get him in here, I promise you, before he dies he will issue orders to every monk in Mituyan to give the government of Premier KaritKi absolute cooperation."

From the screams that penetrated one solid wood door, Mike had to agree with Song. The major gave Mike a worried look. "Our biggest problem working with the Americans is your inability to understand that in our culture and society our methods work and yours do not. We never had that trouble with the British. They are more sophisticated and adaptable to the realities of foreign countries."

"Have no worries about me, Major," Mike said in fluent Mituyan. "I have been seeing things through your eyes for several years now."

"Yes, I forgot that," Song replied in English. Mituyans of status felt it was a loss of face to be trapped into speaking Mituyan to Caucasians.

At the end of the long corridor they came to another solid door, which the jailer unlocked. They entered a large, square, white room so brightly illuminated with fluorescent lights that both Mike and Song had to close their eyes to let them adjust. The room was agreeably air-conditioned, in contrast with the hot fetid atmosphere they had passed through. Mike had heard of the advanced torture techniques adopted by Tarot's special police and realized he was in the latest thing in torture chambers. It looked more like a dentist's office, with considerable electronic gear; chairs and tables with foot stirrups and arm clamps were placed around the edges of the room.

"I have never seen such a hard case as this North Vietnamese," Song remarked. "He has resisted tortures that I have never seen borne before. Dr. Malakit has had to be careful not to allow Can's mind to become so disarranged that the information he now withholds from us becomes garbled and useless."

"Must require great technique," Mike commented drily.

A door to the bright chamber opened, and a studious, middle-aged Mituyan, wearing thick glasses, walked in. A long white coat covered him from his neck almost to the floor.

Major Song introduced Mike to Dr. Malakit. The doctor nodded. "It was your wife whom the North Vietnamese killed along with eight other people?" Malakit asked.

Mike nodded.

"Well, I expect the complete revelation from him today," Malakit said cheerfully. "The names of all his associates, where we can find them, everything."

"Where is he?" Song asked.

"Number One, still," the doctor replied. "Go right in. Psychologically it may shock him that the husband of the woman he so brutally murdered is here to watch the treatment today."

Major Song started toward room Number One.

"Major, the glasses," Malakit reminded.

Song took two pairs of dark glasses from a shelf and handed a pair to Mike. They both put them on, and then Song knocked. The door was opened by a man in white shorts and T-shirt also wearing dark glasses. The room was shockingly bright, with built-in high-intensity arc lamps burning from the floor, ceiling, and four walls. There was no avoiding the light. Hanging by his chained outstretched arms slumped Can, neither standing nor sitting, his weight on the balls of his toes and his wrists. Can's eyelids had been sewn open to his eyebrows, and his head thrashed and twitched, straining for relief from the glaring lights.

"He is trying to kill himself by not eating or drinking water, so we feed him intravenously. We almost *had* him four days ago, but Dr. Malakit decided we would have to allow him some sleep before he went incurably mad. He has been like this three days now. Today the doctor is using the electric wire inserted through the penis canal, which he assures me delivers the purest pain the human body can know."

In Mituyan, Song said, "Can, the husband of the woman you killed is here to watch today."

Can turned eyes inflamed to scarlet in the direction of the voice. His face was a mask of tight parchment skin. He mumbled in Vietnamese and then, pulling himself together, tried to make a spitting gesture, but a dry whistle was all he could muster. In colloquial Mituyan he said, "I rape your wife's anus and defecate in her mouth."

Song strode to him and chopped him in the throat below the Adam's apple. An arid, racking series of wheezes and shudders shook Can, his head whipping back and forth.

Mike shook his head and walked out of the room. Taking off the dark glasses, he said to Malakit, "I'm afraid, Doctor, you will never get any useful information from Can. I've seen his kind before."

Malakit shook his head. "There is a point, when exhaustion reaches the verge of death, that they talk about the very things they have been concentrating on not telling. We almost had him before. Today I'm sure we will succeed."

"Good luck, Doctor," Mike said wearily.

Major Song came up. "I'll show you out."

In the anteroom now, twenty or thirty frightened, worried men and women were lined up before the official seated behind the ledger. "They have come to identify their children and sign a bill of responsibility for them. If a student is picked up a second time, the father goes to prison. We know that Phang is planning more riots. We expect something this afternoon," were Song's parting words.

Out on the street Mike breathed the humid air deeply. He took a cab to an air-conditioned bar only two blocks from the American Embassy, and sat morosely sipping cognac.

Precisely at twelve noon he presented himself at the embassy. The secretary ushered Mike into Ambassador Tate's sixth-floor office.

Tate walked around his desk and warmly shook hands with Mike. "Thank you for coming, Mr. Forrester. I appreciate it, particularly at this time of such personal sorrow." He was a tall, husky man, handsome, with an iron-gray masculine look.

"I want to do what I can to help, sir."

"Thank you. I thought we'd go back to the residence to talk. By the way, Bob Hartland was mightily impressed with you."

"All of us were impressed with him, too," Mike replied. "It didn't take him long to grasp the situation here."

Mike liked Ambassador Tate. He looked exactly like his pictures, the pronounced high forehead, thinning gray hair, and rimless glasses. His smile was as warm while they drove to the residence as when he had been out trying to marshal votes for what he called "international preventative maintenance."

In the living room of the ambassador's residence, both men took off their coats and loosened their ties. Tate offered Mike a drink. "My predecessor did leave me a fine supply of Scotch," he said.

Mike smiled at the ubiquitous round bottle of Chivas Regal. "I could use one."

"Fix yourself what you like. Personally, during the day I prefer gin." When they'd sat down, Tate said: "From what Bob Hartland says I can talk to you."

"I think that we all agree that changes have to be made damn fast in Mituyan," Mike replied.

"Right. Now, tell me what you think about everything here. American officialdom, KaritKi and Tarot, this Mayna woman, the Buddhist question, your trip to Hong Kong, the works."

"That may take a while, sir."

"Take all afternoon if you want."

For two and a half hours Mike summed up his life in Mituyan, his own problems, his observations, why he believed that the KaritKi regime must be ended if the upcoming elections were to be meaningful. Sandwiches were served but Mike, in his earnest desire to impart all his knowledge of Mituyan to Ambassador Tate, ate little. He finished his recitation with a description of the prison he had visited that morning.

Driving back from the ambassador's residence to the embassy in the air-conditioned Cadillac, Tate said, "I've asked for the loan of a Ford staff car from General Macker. I want to drive around smelling the smells, feeling the heat, and hearing and seeing the people. I guess I'm too inborn a politician not to want to feel close to the people with whom I'm working."

Mike nodded approvingly.

"Time is running short," Tate went on. "We know that we have completely misjudged the scene here. The Communists are making gains everywhere, and we've got to shore up damned fast."

Up ahead there was a cluster of people bulging out into the street, threatening to cut off the limousine's passage. The crowd was listening to a shaved-head monk in saffron robes standing on the roof of a car parked by the curb. As they drew closer Mike said, "By God, sir, that's Han Li Phang! The so-called Mad Monk of Tiking!"

Tate peered through the windshield at the monk haranging the crowd. "Hartland told me about meeting him." He leaned forward and instructed the driver to stop the car. "Let's have a closer look. I'd like to hear what he has to say. I understand you're a number-one translator."

Ambassador Tate stepped out onto the street, followed by Mike. Phang saw them on the outskirts of the crowd, and his tirade increased in intensity.

"By God, Forrester, I can't understand him, but those eyes, that voice! What a powerful man!"

"He plays them like musical instruments, sir. He can make them do anything." They listened a few moments. "Phang tells them that KaritKi has thousands of Buddhists in his prisons. He is telling them that the Buddhists will not be allowed to vote in the coming elections and no Buddhists will be put up for election. That, of course, is a lie." Mike listened further. "He's talking about the land-reform program, saying that all the land promised to the peasants is going into big estates of men close to the Palace. There *is* a lot of truth to *that*."

"Look at all the reporters here," Tate observed. "The whole press corps seems to have turned out, television cameras, photographers. Doesn't the press have anything better to do than cover sidewalk harangues?"

"To answer your question, sir, may I point out that all the protest signs are in English, a language not even Phang himself can read."

"*Staged* for the press, eh?"

"And for you, Mr. Ambassador. Because of the one-way streets, you have to pass this corner to get from your residence to the embassy. They know it."

With his audience at a fever pitch and the Tuyan City police just beginning to arrive in adequate numbers, Phang cried out mightily.

"He's asking who will protest the tyrant KaritKi's crimes against the Buddhists dying and being tortured in the prisons of Mituyan," Mike translated.

A wild-eyed monk ran to the car on which Phang was standing. He grabbed a heavy meat cleaver from another monk, placed his left hand at Phang's feet on top of the car and with his right hand brought the cleaver down in a furious chop, severing the left hand at the wrist.

"Good Jesus Christ!" Tate cried. "What is he doing?"

Before Mike could answer another monk took the heavy knife. As the hemorrhaging monk laid his right wrist on top of the car, it too was also severed. Now the handless monk held both stumps in the air, blood squirting from them all over the crowd, as the television cameras rolled and flash bulbs popped. The crowd shrieked in an orgiastic frenzy as the monk, his face turning white from loss of blood, was held up from collapsing by the crowd and the other monks.

In vain, the police tried to break through the milling throng to the dying monk. The severed hands were brandished above the crowd by other monks, who then concealed them and disappeared with Phang through the crowded sidewalk and into a convenient building.

The police, now considerably reinforced, clubbed their way through the mob of hysterical Buddhist faithful. But by the time they reached the monk, the last of his blood had flowed from the stumps of his wrists as the insatiable photographers snapped the scene, and it was too late to do anything to save him. Monks and rioters alike lay in the street as the crowd ebbed away, bleeding from head wounds. The police tried to take the cameras from some of the press corps, but they fought to save their priceless film.

One policeman brandished his club at a television cameraman just as Ambassador J. Sheldon Tate strode into the melee. He raised his hand at the club-wielding policeman. Tate's picture had been all over the front pages of every paper in Tuyan City, and the officer in charge, recognizing the American diplomat, shouted an order, instantly halting the assault against the newsman. Several photographers caught the picture of the American ambassador standing alone against KaritKi's police—a picture that would speed around the globe within hours.

"Gentlemen," J. Sheldon Tate announced dramatically, "I will personally protest this shameful example of brutality against the American press by the police of Premier KaritKi and Counselor Tarot."

Then, turning to the police officer who had ordered his men to stop, Tate said in Mituyan, "Thank you. The American people are grateful."

The entire press corps cheered their ambassador.

To a startled Mike Forrester, Tate said, "I just learned that phrase this morning. Did it sound right?"

Mike grinned. "Believe me, sir, I never heard it said better!"

"Gentlemen," Tate acknowledged, "and you, young lady," he smiled at Marlene—whom Mike now noticed for the first time—"I will have a report for you at eight o'clock this evening at the Public Affairs Office."

Mike knew he shouldn't have been so surprised to see her. Of course Marlene would have been with the press covering the Mad Monk's demonstration. He felt a gladness spread through him as she advanced toward him, that warm, familiar smile on her lips. And then, as though from a knife, guilt was sharp in the pit of his stomach. . . .

His shoulders sagged, and, for a moment, he felt he would be physically sick. His eyes caught Marlene's smile fade, and the quick anxiety in her eyes and expression jerked him abruptly out of his own morose self-recrimination to the immediate present. It wasn't *Marlene's* fault. She looked so hurt now. He forced himself to smile back at her.

"I'll be with the ambassador this evening, Marlene," he said.

She nodded. "We talk after, maybe?"

"Yes. We'll talk."

CHAPTER FORTY-NINE

ALTHOUGH AMBASSADOR TATE, according to his promise, had virtually abolished Country Team meetings, immediately upon his return to the embassy he called in his top aides and conferred with them about the bloody Buddhist demonstration he had witnessed.

As Macker was about to make a final point, the door to Tate's office opened and his secretary, flustered, handed him a message. He read it and, without looking up, asked, "Where is he?"

"In the chancery, sir. The Marines are guarding the entrance to the embassy, and they're afraid there may be shooting any minute."

"Well then, I suppose I should go down and get this incident straightened out." Consumed with curiosity, the members of the Country Team watched as the ambassador rose.

"Gentlemen, the Mad Monk of Tiking I've just been talking about is down below. Apparently he has asked for asylum in the embassy, and a platoon of Counselor Tarot's Special Forces are demanding that they take him into custody. Our Marines are holding them off." He started toward the door and then turned back; the others were now standing. "We've covered everything, I think. Willet, it might be a good move to reinforce the Marines with some of your men. It shows we mean business."

"Yes, sir," Macker said, hurrying toward the telephone on Tate's desk.

Downstairs, Tate looked outside and saw the platoon of Mituyan Special Forces, dressed in combat camouflage fatigues, rifles held at port arms, ready to drop to firing position. The small contingent of U.S. Marine guards stood in the door, their arms, mostly pistols, at the ready.

"Holster your weapons," Tate commanded. He caught a glimpse of the monk standing in the chancery—a mocking challenge on Han Li Phang's face. Tate knew that he had to make perhaps the most important decision of his career. If he threw the monk to the Mituyans, he would have to take the line that Phang and his Buddhist followers were fanatics and anarchists motivated by political power and that all their demonstrations should be discounted. This would condone the harsh treatment meted out to them by the KaritKi regime and strengthen KaritKi's image. It would also make his dealings with KaritKi far easier and perhaps even help him, as ambassador, to convince KaritKi to adopt the new policies formulated in Washington for the Mituyan government.

On the other hand, if he accepted Phang, gave official recognition to the just grievances of the Buddhists, the bloody demonstration he had witnessed less than two hours ago, coupled with the arrests and beatings, would make KaritKi look to the people at home and throughout the world as a ruthless tyrant suppressing religious freedom in his country. Nothing would crystallize public opinion against the KaritKi regime faster than religious discrimination.

Tate knew perfectly well that Phang was building himself into a demigod and cynically playing on the emotions of the faithful to achieve a high position in his country. But Tate could not only relentlessly make the men who worked for him follow orders and achieve results whatever the means, he could also ruthlessly accomplish the ends demanded of him. His job, quite simply, was either to force

KaritKi to follow the bidding of the United States government within a short time or else effect a change of government.

The party line for dissemination by Ted Baum's Public Affairs Office raced through the ambassador's mind. He would offer the protection of the United States government to this hounded monk who was so desperately attempting to gain better treatment for his impoverished and persecuted people.

Newsmen were gathering around the embassy, and motion-picture cameras on tripods were shooting television footage. Ambassador Tate, the high forehead giving him an intellectual cast, walked alone and dramatically from the front door of the embassy toward the platoon of combat-ready Mituyan troops. The Mituyan commanding officer stepped forward to meet the ambassador, as the cameras recorded the second heroic role of the day played by J. Sheldon Tate.

"What are your orders, Captain?" Tate asked crisply.

"My orders come directly from Counselor Tarot, sir," the Mituyan officer replied in the faultless English of all Palace guards. "I have been ordered to arrest the monk, Han Li Phang. When he heard this, he sought sanctuary in the American Embassy. I must demand that you give him up."

"I can't do that without investigating all the facts," Tate replied.

"Then it is my duty to take him out by force, if necessary."

"You, Captain, would lead a platoon of armed soldiers onto United States soil? You would take upon yourself the responsibility of *invading* the United States?"

The officer looked down at his feet, uncomfortably mumbling something about having his orders. Tate broke in: "Captain, I strongly suggest you take your men away from here until Premier KaritKi and I decide what to do about the monk."

"I have my orders," the Mituyan repeated.

"Your orders won't be much good to you if you are in a jail cell for provoking an incident with the United States!" Tate saw that the captain was weakening, and he pressed his point further. "The monk will be in the embassy, and if Premier KaritKi and I decide that he should be turned over to the Mituyan government, we will deliver him to you peacefully. So go back to the palace now and report this conversation to your superiors."

The Mituyan captain gave orders to his men, who shifted their rifles to right shoulder arms and marched off. When the platoon had rounded a corner and disappeared from sight, Tate turned on his heel and strode back into the embassy, his mind thoroughly made up now that under no circumstances would he turn the monk back to the Mituyan government.

Still, he didn't like anything about the fiery monk, and without talking to him ordered that a room and cot be prepared for Phang until final disposition could be made in the case. The press swarmed into the embassy after Tate, firing questions at him.

"Gentlemen, I realize you all have deadlines for filing your copy, but there is no comment I can make at this time beyond saying that, without a thorough investigation, the United States government will not return a religious leader who has sought sanctuary on American soil to foreign troops who appear to be persecuting him because of his religion."

PART IX

THE COUP

CHAPTER FIFTY

MIKE WAS BREAKFAST host to a tense group of conspirators on the terrace of the Rishram plantation house. General Dandig should be raw-nerved by now, Mike thought. The corps commander had finally and irrevocably declared himself: He could look forward either to success or to execution; there was no middle ground. Jack Cardinez and Fritz Lawton, merely by being at Rishram to meet the plane due in soon from Hong Kong, had exceeded the limit on personal involvement set by Tate. The ambassador had decreed that from the moment Barkoon landed on Mituyan soil until he occupied the palace as acknowledged ruler of the country, no member of the United States Diplomatic and Military Mission to Mituyan—as he now referred to the Country Team—was to see the ex-King or acknowledge his presence in the country.

"I'm still concerned about the German girl being in on this, Mike," Cardinez said in strained tones. "If somehow the thing blows up, she may involve the official U.S. mission in this coup attempt."

Mike shook his head. "She can be trusted. And besides"—he spread his hands and grinned wryly—"Barkie insists."

"You could have talked him out of it, Mike," Lawton said.

Dandig shook his head. "I know the King. When he sets his mind on a girl he pursues her singlemindedly. No mere coup would distract him from the really important things in his life."

Mike put down his coffee cup. "You may be in for a surprise, General. The King has changed greatly. He is more serious about returning to Mituyan than he was about anything in his life. I count Barkoon as a personal if eccentric friend." Mike shrugged. "I hope our friendship survives this boat trip."

"I hope you all survive and prevail," Cardinez said fervently.

"No reason why we shouldn't," Mike replied. "We have General Dandig's protection until we're well under way. The Palace is not in the least bit suspicious. I have official permission and documents signed by Minister Branot. And KaritKi can hardly wait for me to arrive in Tuyan City so he can expropriate *Promise*. The biggest danger we face is from the Mitcoms."

"You're well armed with a 20-mm. cannon and 50-caliber and M-60 machine guns, and you have Captain Jenkins as well as three of my best sergeants, Jennesen, Cavanaugh, and The Animal, Barton."

"After the Ba To battle I would have thought Cav deserved a long rest, and as for The Animal—" Mike looked over at where the big sergeant and his two cohorts in dungarees and T-shirts were breakfasting together. "Is he recovered from his wounds?"

"He's all right. He said he deserved this mission as a *reward* for Ba To."

Mike nodded. "They're all good men."

Above and just beyond the hills came the whine of a jet, rattling the coffee cup in the saucer held by General Dandig.

Cardinez looked skyward. "This is it. No turning back now."

"Jump and die," Lawton said.

Mike stood. "Shall we drive out and give His Majesty the VIP treatment? I'm afraid Rishram is without red carpet, but *Promise* should make up for that."

At the airstrip, the first person to walk off the trim executive jet was Barkoon's personal intelligence officer, DakatLi, who, scanning the area carefully, showed immediate relief at seeing Mike, Cardinez, Lawton, and General Dandig. Next came Henri, the hairdresser. Mike had not long to speculate which of the three mistresses Barkoon would bring. He had been given a limit of two. The French brunette, Francine, deplaned behind the hairdresser, followed by Brigit, the startling blonde. Finally, Barkoon himself stepped down, wearing a white Western-style suit. With surprising agility for one of his bulk, Barkoon pranced across his native soil toward the welcoming group.

"He looks in fine form," Cardinez remarked.

"Speaking of forms!" exclaimed Lawton.

"We'll keep them on deck as diversion," Mike chuckled. He stole a sidewise look at the three sergeants, who had driven up in a jeep, and smiled at their surprised expressions and pursed lips. Then Barkoon was upon him, pumping his hand and looking about expectantly.

"Forrester," he said in low, accusing tones as he glanced about. "I thought you promised me—"

"She's on the boat, Your Majesty."

"Ah, Forrester," Barkoon said sympathetically, "I was deeply saddened to hear of your tragedy. I will erect a memorial to her in Tuyan City when I take over."

Mike nodded but did not reply.

"Your Highness," General Dandig was saying, "I have arranged for an entire battalion to escort you to Mr. Forrester's yacht in Tiking. Not one soldier or officer will know exactly whom the security convoy is for, and the vehicle we have provided for you has concealing sideflaps."

Barkoon nodded. "Let us be on our way." He and the two girls climbed into the draped Land Rover, and the rest of the party followed in two other vehicles. Barkoon was moving out on the first leg of his journey back to the palace in Tuyan City.

Under cover of the battalion escort, Barkoon's party reached Mike's dock without incident where the battalion commander threw a salute at the American and promptly drove off. Mike asked the two girls to get out first and stretch their legs a bit, thus assuring the fact that any casual viewers of the scene would have eyes only for the girls and not spot the fat man in a white suit lightly skip up the gangplank. With Cardinez, Lawton, and General Dandig gone, Mike was now in complete command. Ten minutes after Barkoon had boarded ship, she was chugging out of Tiking Harbor toward the open seas.

When Mike was satisfied that Captain Batki had *Promise* on course, he entered the main salon where Barkoon was holding court and offered to show him his accommodations. Barkoon's party followed Mike down the companionway to the staterooms below and at the rear of the yacht.

"The girls can have one of these staterooms and your intelligence officer, DakatLi, the other," Mike said. "Not the sort of luxury you had in Hong Kong, but certainly there is no boat like this one in the Republic of Mituyan."

Barkoon nodded. "Very satisfactory, Forrester."

"Thank you, Your Majesty. Now I'll show you your stateroom."

He led them to the end of the hall, where there was a luxurious master stateroom. Large portholes commanded a view to the rear, port and starboard. "If you look up, you can see the stars at night and the blue sky by day." He pointed to a generous skylight hatch above the extra-wide double bed across which was thrown a huge Bengal tiger skin.

"A kingly stateroom indeed, Forrester," Barkoon remarked, pleased.

"There is one little inconvenience, Your Majesty. In case we should be attacked, there is a 20-mm. cannon that elevates through the deck you are standing on and swings into position to fire through the rear porthole. *Promise* was outfitted with a stinger just for this voyage."

"Ingenious! And what do we do in case of attack?"

"The engine room forward is armor-plated; if you stand between the engines, nothing can hit you."

"I must congratulate you, Forrester, you have thought of everything," said Barkoon when they had returned to the main salon. Then, turning to Marlene, he said: "I hope your quarters are pleasant, my dear." He smiled. "Perhaps I should inspect them. If they are not adequate, I know that DakatLi will be happy to change with you."

"I thank you for your worry, Your Majesty, "but I have beautiful room at other end of this deck. I will show it to you after lunch," she added coquettishly.

What a voyage this could turn out to be, Mike thought.

It was indeed a luncheon fit for a king. Mike watched Barkoon keep reaching for the giant crab legs on a bed of shaved ice. Ignoring the nutcrackers, the King gustily broke open the legs and noisily sucked the white meat from them, washing it down with chilled champagne. Although Mike hadn't told any of his crew the identity of his corpulent guest, he knew by the air of excitement in all quarters of the ship, from bridge to bilge, that they were aware *Promise* was bringing the former King back to rule once again.

As evening approached, the radio communications were unsettling. There was obvious Palace suspicion that a coup might soon be launched. DakatLi's sources informed him that General Dandig had been summoned that afternoon to a meeting with Counselor Poramat, and that possibly he was being detained. From Tuyan City the JRB intelligence net indicated that General Thannit, the all-important ingredient in the coup, had conferred at length with Tarot and the Premier but had not been in touch with his fellow plotters since leaving the palace. No instructions were relayed to the *Promise*, but the signs were ominous. Mike had planned a strategy session with Barkoon that evening, which, he thought, would prove most illuminating.

The King took the head of the table, insisting that Marlene sit at his right. The exquisitely coiffured Brigit, Mike, Francine, DakatLi, and the hairdresser, Henri, made up the rest of the company. It disturbed Mike to have such a motley group at the dinner table aboard his beloved yacht, yet he knew it was part of his job.

Barkoon was loud in his praise of the turtle steaks and the quality of the wine cellar of the *Promise*. After the dessert of fresh passion fruit, Mike asked Barkoon if he wanted the briefing to be private. The jolly and surfeited king shook his head.

"We're all on this boat together; we might as well all know what's likely to happen to us. Yes, Marlene?" Slyly his hand stole toward Marlene. Mike's lips pressed into a thin line.

"So—bring us up to date," Barkoon requested.

DakatLi produced an easel on which a map of Mituyan, with an acetate overlay covered with notations and symbols, was tacked. "In the first place, Your Majesty, KaritKi and Tarot know there is a coup in the making. A very interesting development has occurred, typical of Counselor Tarot. They called in General Thannit for a long meeting this afternoon. It appears they doubted his loyalty, but he reported to central intelligence for Operation Switch that he convinced them he was wholeheartedly with the Palace. KaritKi and Tarot interrogated him at length as to the loyalty of the other generals, and Thannit replied that he could not see into the hearts and minds of his colleagues.

"That Thannit, he's a good man," Barkoon interposed. "He was a young lieutenant in my guerrilla army. He fought the Japs like a tiger."

"The Palace plan now is for Thannit to stage a mock coup—surround the palace with some of his troops. Then Tarot and KaritKi will call each of the other generals individually and ask for help. Thannit will also call the generals and ask them to join his coup. Those who join Thannit will be executed. Whether it was Thannit or Tarot who came up with this plan we don't know. Probably Thannit planted the seed in Tarot's devious mind, where it grew like a weed in the Tuyan Delta sun."

"Capital, capital!" Barkoon exclaimed. "What an ingenious way to surround the palace with battalions of troops unopposed! Ah, that Thannit! But I should think Tarot would realize that he plays into Thannit's hands if *Thannit* is not loyal in spite of his protestations."

"Thannit reported this afternoon to Operation Switch headquarters that the reason for the complacency at the Palace is that Tarot is convinced that there is no leader in Mituyan around whom all the generals and the people of the country would unite."

Barkoon laughed delightedly. "They are right—there is no such leader *within* Mituyan. The people only know two leaders, KaritKi and that old rogue of an ex-King of theirs, Barkoon the Sixth, who is up in Hong Kong or playing on the Riviera."

"We too have our opportunity for misjudging the situation," DakatLi said gravely. "I talked to General Dandig over the scrambler on my own band. Dandig was called into a conference with Poramat this afternoon, and although he swore his loyalty to the Palace, Dandig is afraid Poramat does not believe him."

"So what is our problem?" Barkoon asked.

"Dandig is afraid that if the anti-KaritKi forces begin to weaken, Thannit will switch sides and turn in all the generals who fought with him against the Palace. In other words, Thannit will win no matter which side prevails."

"Thannit would not betray me at the last minute, not after all we have gone through to make this coup a success," Barkoon declared.

"Perhaps you are right, Your Majesty," DakatLi said doubtfully. "But when Mr. Forrester asked for protection from the navy and air force for tomorrow—we'll come to that in a moment—Operation Switch headquarters reported that Thannit was unwilling to protect or even recognize the mission of the *Promise*."

"Does he give any reason?" Barkoon asked.

"He claims he does not want to call attention to us at so vulnerable a time," DakatLi replied.

Barkoon thought about that statement, a somber expression on his face. "Ah, my cunning countrymen, self-interest above all else," he said sadly. "Already we have mistrust between the two principal elements of my coup d'état."

DakatLi nodded. "It is possible, sir, that one or both of them have betrayed you. . . . At any rate, Mr. Forrester has ordered a complete blackout aboard the ship tonight in case government aircraft should be dispatched to find us."

"If we have been betrayed, they'll find us in the morning," Barkoon said matter-of-factly.

"We could change course and run all night at flank speed and reach the waters of neutral Yanna by mid-morning tomorrow," Mike suggested.

"But if General Thannit and General Dandig did *not* betray us, we upset their coup plans completely if I am not available," Barkoon pointed out. "It is my wish that we proceed on course."

"I was merely thinking of your safety, Your Majesty," Mike said.

"You may not believe it, Mr. Forrester, but my personal safety is the last thing on my mind. Somehow we must arrive at Tuyan City. If one plan fails to work, I am confident that another one will. I will go back and rule my country or fight for my throne as long as I am alive on Mituyan soil. The people will support me. I know it!"

DakatLi pointed to the mouth of the Tuyan River in the center of the two-hundred-mile-wide delta. "We have reports that there is a Mitcom fleet of perhaps two hundred boats ranging from two-man sampans to armed junks. They have been engaged in smuggling arms and trained guerrillas from the North into this, our country's most fertile region and main source of our food supply."

"Did you know this when we left this morning?" Barkoon asked.

"As I reported to you in Hong Kong we knew such a fleet was trying to make up, but only this afternoon two government patrol boats were attacked. They both got away up the river suffering light casualties. Neither my net nor Premier KaritKi's intelligence organizations have realized how much progress the Mitcoms have made with armed junks. This is why we worry about tomorrow. With no protection we fight our way up the Tuyan River before dark. The appearance of this boat signals the changeover from the false coup to the real attack on the Palace."

"We will do it!" Barkoon declared. "What other reports do we have?"

"There has been further unrest among the tribesmen. Everything that rash American colonel, Gruen, promised them has been withheld. The chief of the Ba To Groats was taken into detention when he ventured into Banthut for treaty talks."

"The Palace promised the tribesmen immunity from reprisal!" Captain Jenkins, who had been assigned to the ship's radio room by Fritz Lawton, exploded. He looked around the table and subsided, chagrined. "Sorry, sir," he said to Mike.

"Not at all," Barkoon said. "My sentiments entirely. Any flank speed we are laying on should be in the direction of Tuyan City before there is no Republic of Mituyan for us to regain."

For the next twenty minutes DakatLi gave him a complete summary of the day's events as reported by agents all over the country and relayed from Barkoon's intelligence headquarters in Mituyan to the *Promise* via their special frequency band. Once again, marveling at Barkoon's dedication to regaining his throne, Mike found himself rationalizing the King's blatant sensuality as the whims of a typical Oriental strongman.

With the briefing completed, Mike said: "Because we will be running without lights, I want everyone in their cabins right after dinner. It will be dangerous walking an unlighted deck. Nobody should go on deck under any circumstances. Understood?" He looked at Barkoon pointedly. In reply, Barkoon dismissed his party, leaving Mike, himself, and Marlene alone in the main salon.

"I say, Forrester, aren't you exaggerating the danger? I always like to take a constitutional before turning in. Also I like to have company—I was hoping to see our charming journalist safely . . ."

"It's you I'm most worried about, Your Majesty," Mike broke in. "I will see that Marlene reaches her cabin safely."

"Now dammit, Forrester—" Barkoon lapsed into Mituyan: "We had an agreement about the girl. After you—me. You can have either one of my girls."

"Your Majesty, I am not interested in having any girl. I am in command of this mission to get you to Tuyan City. You do not seem worried about the next few days. Believe me, I am! Good night, Your Majesty."

Moments later Marlene joined Mike on the deck, slipping her hand into his. "Do you really think maybe the government sends airplanes to find us, Mike?"

"No. But it *is* possible. Dandig probably wouldn't betray us, and Thannit doesn't know how Barkoon is being delivered to Tuyan City. But if Tarot believed Dandig *was* plotting seriously against him, he would torture the general until he talked."

They reached her stateroom, and he looked down at her. He really couldn't blame Barkoon for wanting her. "It's been a long day. Get some sleep, dear," he said at last.

Then he went up to the wheelhouse. With only the red instrument lights on, he talked with Captain Batki, who finally dredged up the courage to say that he and the crew knew they were taking King Barkoon to Tuyan City, where he planned to overthrow Premier KaritKi.

"Will you be happy with King Barkoon ruling the country?" Mike asked.

"We will be most happy. We all love the Barkoon dynasty. Mituyan will be great again with Barkoon back. It is what we have hoped for. Premier KaritKi does not care what happens to the people. All the Barkoon kings loved the people."

"Does the whole crew feel this way?"

"Even the ones who do not know or remember King Barkoon agree that any leader would be better than KaritKi."

Relieved, Mike placed an affectionate hand on his captain's shoulder. He turned away to poke his head into the communications room. "Anything happening?" he asked Jenkins, who was sitting in front of the radio console.

"No contacts, sir."

Sergeant Barton was seated next to Jenkins, his wide face pressed into the black rubber mask around the radar scope. "See anything unusual, Barton?"

The Animal looked up at Mike. "No sir, the usual air traffic over the coast. Patrol planes trying to spot Mitcom arms smugglers."

Mike nodded. "I'll be on the aft deck below for a while. Call down if anything looks threatening." He walked back through the wheelhouse and out onto the bridge, where he stood a few moments breathing the sea air and looking down at the bow plowing through the phosphorescent sea. He and Luna used to stand out here frequently on the long trip across the Pacific. With the automatic pilot keeping the ship on course and the compass he had mounted outside to show that the delicate mechanism was steering the ship straight, he and Luna would talk for hours, planning their future in the peaceful country of Mituyan, kissing occasionally, until their desire for each other became too strong and they went back into the wheelhouse and made love on the bunk. He and Luna alone had crewed the ship over long stretches of the South Pacific when they had been unable to pick up a captain or a mate—*Promise* was that sort of a ship. And now all that planning and nurturing, fighting nature, the banks, and finally the Communists—what had it all come to? He and Marlene had been having a passionate affair in Hong Kong while Luna was marked for death. Guilt tortured him, but he knew he could not give into it. At least not until he delivered one King, two mistresses, one hairdresser, and one intelligence officer to Tuyan City.

He heard someone coming up the circular staircase to the wheelhouse and whirled, angrily, as Marlene's head, shoulders, and body appeared behind Captain Batki, who was staring at her in surprise. Mike strode from the bridge into the wheelhouse.

"Damn it, Marlene, I gave orders that no one would walk around deck tonight! Do you think you're someone special, some privileged character . . . just because you happen to be a beautiful woman?"

Marlene shrank back at his fury, her lips parted, eyes wide. "I'm sorry, Mike," she whispered. "It was the light. I thought you would want to know."

"What light? What the hell light are you talking about?" He hated himself for being so harsh with her, and wondered why he was.

"The King's, Mike. His skylight." Her voice was hardly audible. "I'm sorry. But you want blackout, you say. I don't know what to do." She buried her face in her hands and her shoulders shook. Captain Batki concentrated hard on the binnacle in front of him.

Mike walked to her and put one arm around her. "I'm sorry, Marlene. Of course you did the right thing. I don't know what's the matter with me. I'll walk you back to your cabin."

He climbed down the iron staircase and then helped her, holding her tightly to him as she stepped down to the galley floor. "Please, darling. Forgive me for snapping at you. You did what was right." With his arm still around her he led her back to her cabin, and as they came around to the afterdeck he saw the bright light shining up through the skylight from the master stateroom.

"Thanks for telling me, baby," Mike said soothingly. "An airplane would spot that ten miles away."

Marlene cuddled against him, grateful that his anger was spent. "Well, let's knock on the hatch," he said. "There's a black shade that can be pulled across from the inside."

Marlene's quavers took on a different tempo.

"Please don't cry, Marlene," he said softly, kissing the top of her head.

Still shaking, Marlene said in a choked voice, "I don't cry, darling. Not now." She lifted her face, and he saw in the soft reflected light of the moon that she was laughing.

He was relieved but puzzled. "What's so funny?"

"You soon see. I start to take my shoe and hit that window with the heel and call down and say, Barkie, you dumkopf idiot of a never-make-it King, kill the *Gott* damn light. Yes, I am about to say it—but I look first. Then I decide I must get Mike."

Mike crept across the deck and looked down on a brilliantly illuminated scene. Marlene came up beside him. "So tell me, Mike. *You* will knock on the hatch?"

Mike was too absorbed to answer. For at last he understood the full fascination of Barkoon for women's hair—blonde or red hair in particular. Barkoon, his hideous paunch hanging far out, was standing over a nude Brigit, whose dimensions, Mike had to admit, were superb. At least Barkoon hadn't been offering to trade anything but first-class merchandise, Mike admitted to himself.

The blonde Swedish girl's hairdo was still intact, and Barkoon was caressing it, apparently, with that part of him that remained hidden from directly overhead.

"My God! How long has this been going on?" Mike asked.

Marlene giggled. "I was afraid if I say something he come up on deck after me."

"You did just the right thing," Mike repeated, continuing to stare down through the transparent hatch as Barkoon inserted himself deeper and deeper into Brigit's hair. As Mike watched in fascinated disgust, Barkoon redoubled his plunges into the silky golden tresses and then fell on top of her, forcing her back on the bed, his jelly-like thighs capturing her head, his hands tightly holding masses of the upswept hair.

"You know, Marlene," Mike whispered. "Tonight Barkoon wanted to trade both his girls for you!"

"*Gott in Himmel!* And you don't make the deal?"

Systematically, Barkoon destroyed the tower of gold until finally, with a vicious lunge, he lay quivering. Brigit, after permitting him to pay full honor to Henri's sophisticated skill at coiffure, wriggled out from under his pinioning form and, leaving him pitched on his face, removed herself and her now disorderly cataract of golden locks from sight.

"We'll *have* to black it out from above," Mike said. He got a tarpaulin, and draped the heavy covering double over the skylight, completing blacking out the rear deck of the boat.

Marlene was waiting at the door to her cabin.

"Mike, why don't you sleep here tonight? With so many people aboard you say you will stay up in the pilot house. But you can never sleep there."

"Yet that's where I feel I should be, dear," Mike said.

She looked up at him, brushing her hair back from her face. He bent and kissed her, and Marlene's arms went around him tightly. She leaned to him, her knees bending slightly, increasing the intensity of their contact. Mike felt an overpowering urge to make love to this beautiful woman whom he was truly beginning to love. It was curious, he thought, how watching Barkoon's depraved performance a few minutes earlier, trading facetious remarks with Marlene, had relieved so much of the tension he had felt about their own relationship. Perhaps his bitter self-castigation for Luna's death would come to an end some day.

But he still needed time. . . .

CHAPTER FIFTY-ONE

STANDING ON THE BRIDGE of *Promise* with Jennesen, Barton, and Cavanaugh, Mike could make out off the starboard bow the distant mangrove jungles and open water of the Tuyan River Delta in the faint light of dawn. "We'll be laying off the main stream in less than two hours," he said. "Then, with the sun behind us, we'll charge into the river and make it full speed all the way up to Tuyan City."

"Well, Mr. Forrester, you'd better get His Highness out of the sack, because we just may need to use his quarters," Jennesen said.

"Right. All other positions ready to fight?"

"I've set up the dispensary in the forward crew quarters," Cavanaugh reported. "I got me two M-60 machine guns pointing out through the slits over my port and starboard operating shelves, so I can shoot and dress wounds at the same time."

"Let's hope we can avoid a confrontation," Mike said. "All that extra armor plating has cut twenty percent off our speed."

"If we get into a Mitcom fighting junk fleet, speed wouldn't help us anyway," Jennesen said. "I remember down in the Mekong River when I was on my third tour in Vietnam, the Communists had the river so jammed with sampans you couldn't outrun anything, just had to blast through."

Mike nodded soberly. "OK, I'll rout out our King so you can swing the weapon into place. Get everyone in position."

He went to Marlene's cabin and found her just finishing dressing. "I just wanted to make sure you were up. Wouldn't want you to miss anything."

"Can I help, Mike?" she asked smiling at him brightly.

"As a matter of fact you can. You can go below and make sure Barkie and his girls are up. Tell them if they want anything to eat they'd better get it now, because in an hour the galley will be closed for the duration."

"If I go down to the master stateroom, Barkie will be *up* all right!"

Mike grinned. "Better get some breakfast yourself. We've got an hour before battle stations."

Back on the bridge, Jenkins advised him: "Sir, good news. Agent reports indicate that most of the Mitcom armed junks have left the main stream and are in one of the Tuyan River tributaries hiding from the government patrol boats."

"Good. Have you heard anything from Operation Switch central?"

"No, sir. But DakatLi has been making radio contacts with agents all night to find out what's going on."

"I guess we're on our own." Captain Batki changed course, and Mike checked the compass and the land mass, cut by hundreds of streams and rivers ahead, washing silt down from a thousand miles of fertile crop lands, staining the blue tropical sea a yellowish brown. Mike did not interfere with Batki's handling of the boat; he had been a Tuyan River pilot for many years, guiding foreign shipping through the frequently treacherous currents and twists in the river up to the capital city.

"How soon do we get in main stream?" Mike asked.

"Maybe half hour," Batki answered.

Silently, tensely, Mike watched them approach the mile-and-a-half-wide mouth of the Tuyan River, passing the lesser tributaries that irrigated the thousands of square miles of the country's rice bowl.

After a while Marlene appeared on the bridge wearing slacks and a bright blouse; she had a mug of coffee in her hand, which she handed to Mike. "I'm glad you let me up here, darling. Barkie tried to follow me, but he doesn't get his big belly up the little steps."

"He's out of his stateroom?"

"Yes, and now Sergeant Jennesen is down there. He opens the rear porthole and has that big gun ready."

"I hope to hell we don't need it."

"In main stream now!" Batki sang out.

"When will we be in Tuyan City?" Marlene asked.

Mike glanced at his wrist watch. "It should take about five hours from here, because we have to slow down on some of the curves where the river bottom is always changing depth. This is one time we *can't* take a chance on running aground."

When *Promise* was well up the stream on her way to Tuyan City,

Mike took Marlene on an inspection of his ship; Captain Jenkins left the radio room in DakatLi's care to accompany them. "I can't figure why we don't hear anything from Operation Switch," he complained. "Maybe they think that Tuyan City radio monitoring will pick up their transmissions; but Colonel Lawton said JRB had two advisers in government radio security whose job was to make sure our band was never monitored."

"We have our orders, Jenkins. We're following them. No need to keep up a constant chatter with Operation Switch HQ."

"I guess you're right, sir. But boats make me nervous. I like to do my fighting on land."

"Maybe we don't have no fighting," Marlene said hopefully. With the possibility of a real battle looming, the girl was suddenly subdued.

Barkoon and his two mistresses were in the main salon with Henri, his black suitcase brimming with hair curlers and his portable hair-dryer. "Ah, Forrester," Barkoon hailed him cheerfully. "And Marlene. Well, we are almost there, what? My dear girl"—he fixed Marlene with a lascivious stare—"I want you to walk into the palace on my arm tonight. Should make great pictures for the local photographers and television people, what? Why don't you let Henri here give you one of his very finest coiffures for the occasion? I will watch closely to make sure he lavishes all his true artistry on your glory in gold." Barkoon bounced from his chair and went over to her, running his hands in Marlene's loose locks. "Henri, for tonight, may I suggest for this delightful beauty your Andalusian swirl?"

Henri, who had been nervously surveying the near river bank, obediently studied Marlene and forced enthusiasm. "How right you are, Your Majesty."

"Barkie," Marlene scolded, "how can you think of a hairdo when we may all be killed in an hour?" At her words Henri's hands began to shake violently. His mouth opened and closed but no sound came. Both Francine and Brigit were clearly terrified.

"A king must not think negatively, my dear, nor should those who surround him. Henri, if you don't get over your damned palsy you will be unfit to perform the most important coiffure of your career. My consort tonight, when we take over the palace, must be ravishing."

Recognizing the fear in all of them, although he had to admit that Barkoon concealed it in true kingly fashion, Mike said, "Why not, Marlene? You've been up and down the Tuyan River before. If anything happens I'll call you."

"You kidding!" Marlene exclaimed.

"But no, my dear," Barkoon took her arm and started leading her to the bar stool in the center of the salon. "It's hours to Tuyan City yet. What better way to spend the time?"

Marlene looked helplessly at Mike, who nodded approval, eyes twinkling. Then she shrugged and laughed, breaking the tension. "An Andalusian swirl? Yes, I think for the palace tonight it would be good."

"Ah, capital, dear girl," Barkoon exulted. "Now if you will just sit on this stool for Henri—"

"Now *Gott* damn, Barkie!" Marlene exclaimed, "you watch, OK. But you don't touch!"

Two hours later Mike and Captain Batki were back in the wheelhouse, worriedly studying the chart of the river. Occasionally, government patrol boats cruised by, and there was a constant stream of sampans and small junks plying the river close to its stream. One large cluster of houses after another, making up hamlets on stilts built out over the river, punctuated the shoreline. The hamlets increased in size as *Promise* moved closer to the capital.

On the chart Batki pointed with the inch-long nail of his right little finger at one of the larger tributaries of the Tuyan River. They would reach this point in less than an hour, he said. "Many Mitcoms use that river to hide boats." He shook his head in worry. Mike nodded and left the wheelhouse to look in on DakatLi and Jenkins.

"Have you given our latest position report?"

"Right, sir. DakatLi is talking to central now." They watched as the Mituyan intelligence officer, bobbing his head in excitement, almost lost his earphones. "The sham coup has just started!" he cried. "Both Thannit and Dandig know we are on the way, yet Thannit still refuses to send air force or patrol boats to escort us." DakatLi frowned darkly. "I never have trusted that Thannit. Right up to the end he can go on either side. All the other generals are committed and have moved troops in around Tuyan City to help crush any resistance."

"What excuse does Thannit give now for not helping us?" Mike asked.

"Again he says that this will point us out and perhaps give us away to the commanders still loyal to the Palace."

"No good asking JRB for help," Mike muttered. "They refuse to know about this coup until it's successful."

"At least the commanders of Operation Switch know we're getting close," DakatLi said. "As soon as we are actually in sight, the real attack starts on the palace, the radio station, the post office, the police stations. I must go now and tell the King. He will be happy."

Mike watched the excited DakatLi descend the stairs to the galley. The next hour was the most critical. If they could just get a mile past the tributary they would be safe.

"Next bend, eh, Batki?" Mike said.

"Next bend. I have to go close to left bank. Sand bars all around here," he muttered.

Tensely, Mike watched the left bank of the river as they edged toward it. He called to Jenkins, who left the radio room. "I don't want to get everyone aboard upset, but this is about the likeliest place for them to hit us. As fire-control officer I thought you'd better be ready."

"Right, sir." Jenkins reached for the modified field telephone and checked out Barton, Jennesen, and Cavanaugh.

"We're as set as we'll ever be, sir," Barton reported back.

Promise rounded the bend close to shore. Beyond it they would soon reach the tributary. "At least no one is throwing rocks at us from shore," Jenkins observed.

"If the Mitcoms hit us it will be above the tributary. That way if patrol boats come whipping down river from Tuyan City the Mitcoms can disappear into that shallow tributary, and if the government boats follow them in, the guerrillas can blow them up with electrically detonated mines under the water. Government boats rarely go in there. . . . Well, here we are, coming up on it."

"Oh, Jesus Christ!" Jenkins cried out.

As *Promise* passed the tributary, forking off to the left and approximately paralleling the main stream the heavy foliage along the bank seemed to burst out with boats of all sizes and shapes. There were two-and-three passenger sampans with outboard engines, the propellers on shafts two feet long so the whirling blades could be easily dipped into and out of shallow water. Large cargo barges slipped from the banks, raising gun ports as they came. Junks, small boats of all kinds, possibly a hundred or more, moved out from the dense foliage of the river bank to intercept them.

"Christ, there must be half a mile of 'em we've got to get through," Mike said. "Take over, Jenkins. I'll be back as soon as I get the royal party settled."

Marlene's coiffure had been finished, and Barkoon and the two girls were praising Henri's efforts when Mike entered the main salon. "I'm afraid our trip up river will not be entirely uneventful," he said. "Your Majesty, I would appreciate it if your party would take battle positions in the engine room. I know it's hot and uncomfortable down there, but it's safe."

"What's happening, Forrester?" Barkoon asked calmly.

"Just look out front." Mike pointed out the window and over the bow of the ship. Barkoon stared, and for the first time real concern showed on his face. The half-mile gamut of hostile sampans and junks splashed from camouflaged positions along the river bank, moving to block *Promise*. Both Francine and Brigit gasped. Henri's immaculate hands began shaking.

"We're going to have a hard fight on our hands." Mike stared ahead grimly. "We'll radio for help, but I don't think we can expect it."

"Do you think we can fight our way through alone?" Barkoon asked.

"That's what we'll have to do. It's going to be rough."

Barkoon went out the forward door and stood on the deck, peering at the Communist fleet for a few moments. Then he reentered, saying, "They don't know how well armed we are. They probably think we're exactly what we look, a pleasure yacht. We'll break through. . . . But Forrester, it would be a mistake to radio Operation Switch headquarters and tell them what we're up against and ask for help. If Thannit thinks King Barkoon will not be in Tuyan City at the head of the coup, he'll almost surely sell out the other generals and take credit for discovering who is plotting against the KaritKi regime."

"You're right," Mike said. He was constantly surprised at Barkoon's logic and calm in the face of potentially disastrous situations. "We're going to run straight up the river at flank speed and rip our way through them. Now, will everyone unessential go below, please? Marlene, tell them in the bridge that Barkoon says do *not*, repeat do not, radio central." Marlene nodded and made for the companionway.

"Now please, Your Majesty, they'll be upon us in minutes. Get down between the diesels."

"Forrester, you forget I am an old guerrilla fighter and I have kept up with weaponry. I'm still proficient with a machine gun, rifle, grenade launcher—whatever you have aboard ship."

"I'm sure you are. But every man on this ship is fighting for only one purpose, to get you to Tuyan City alive and healthy. Otherwise we could always turn around and run away from them."

"Very well, Forrester." Barkoon sounded resigned. "Come girls, Henri, to our *battle* stations."

Mike regained the bridge and found Marlene staring at the ragged line of Mitcom boats. Her eyes were wide.

"Can we really fight through all of them? There must be over a hundred."

"We have to," Mike replied. "Now get back in the wheelhouse. It's steel-plated. And don't come back out on the bridge again, understand?" She nodded and went inside as Jenkins came back out again. He was carrying a bulky weapon that Mike only partially recognized.

"It's the latest blessing from Colt," he said, "the newest thing in over-and-under arms. An AR-15 automatic rifle on top and an automatic five-shell grenade launcher below. The ideal weapon for this fight." He leaned it against the railing and went back into the wheelhouse. In a minute he struggled back onto the bridge with a heavy wooden case. "Here's a box of grenades. From the bridge we're in fine position to lob them into any boat that gets close."

"Are all your people ready?" Mike asked Jenkins.

"They are, sir. And your own gun crew is ready to set up on the foredeck when we give the orders." Mike grunted and turned into the wheelhouse. Captain Batki was sweating, glaring at the incredible masses of small and medium-sized river boats beyond the windshield. *Promise* was rapidly closing on them now. Mike opened his personal-weapons locker and pulled out a .45-caliber machine gun and a canvas bag, containing twenty magazines of thirty rounds each, which he slung around his shoulder. The weapon had a maximum effective range under one hundred yards, but it was the action at twenty and thirty yards that he was thinking about.

Promise was about two hundred yards from the dense mass of Mitcom boats when a bull-horn-amplified voice roared down the river, speaking in English: "Forrester, we have been waiting for you. The

Mituyan Freedom Front, in the name of the People of Mituyan, who have made you and the other capitalists in this country rich, demand the use of your ship until our war with your corrupt friends, the tyrants of the KaritKi regime, has been won. The boat will be returned to you then. We ask you to surrender your ship to us. The Mituyan Freedom Front guarantees you and every person aboard your boat a safe passage to Tuyan City if you surrender now."

Mike went back into the wheelhouse and brought his own bull horn out onto the bridge. All the while he was thinking hard, wondering if there was some way he could avoid this battle and still get Barkoon into Tuyan City. Raising the bull horn he answered the Communists in Mituyan.

"If you need my boat so badly, you need it in good repair," he began. "I am willing to turn it over to the MFF—but only if I am permitted to take my guests to Tuyan City safely aboard this ship. Once everyone now aboard the ship has been landed in the capital, I will turn her over to you."

Mocking laughter blasted across the fast narrowing gap of water between the Communist fleet and *Promise,* now drawing all the power the straining, overworked diesels would give. "We know how little to trust you, Forrester. We know how you betrayed the Front at Rishram and Tiking. Even so, we will still give you safe conduct if you turn the boat over now."

"I keep my word—even to Communists," Mike called back. "I will give you the boat, or make it possible for you to take it. But only after my guests are safely in Tuyan City."

"Then you force us to kill all of you," was the harsh reply.

Promise plowed sturdily up the river, heading into the gathering boats. "They would like to take us with as little damage as possible," Mike said over his shoulder. "They have no idea how heavily armed we are. They'll try and take us by overwhelming the ship with guerrillas."

"Let 'em try," Jenkins said happily. "Old Charging Charlie Prescott kept me out of that Ba To fight, but I'll make up for it this time." He surveyed the pending river battle and laughed. "My first sea fight!"

As many as thirty sampans, some holding up to twenty guerrillas, were converging on the left bow of *Promise*. In each sampan Mike could see two or three black-clad men holding grappling hooks; now, with less than fifty yards between the strange armada and the oncoming yacht, the men were beginning to swing their hooks, ready to let them fly as soon as *Promise* slid into range.

"Let's wait as long as we can before we show them our heavy stuff," Mike ordered. "If they've got fifties, they could have blown us out of the water as we came around the bend. They want the boat all right, but they're not about to let us get away either."

Jenkins nodded. He picked up the field telephone and gave orders to his three sergeants. Then, just before the guerrillas startd to heave their hooks, Jenkins sighted on the closest boat and fired a 40-mm. grenade.

Even as the first sampan full of guerrillas blew into splinters, Jenkins pumped another grenade into the second boat. It disintegrated in a blast of sound and fire and water. Mike, beside him, poured machine-gun rounds into the other sampans within range. The guerrillas began firing back at the bridge from the mass of boats pressing in on the port bow. *Promise* kept going. Now the sampans were directly off her beam.

"They still figure they can take us without destroying the boat," Mike cried. "Jenkins, I'll take them on the beam, you hit 'em off the bow!" He crouched below the steel plates around the bridge, firing through the slits that had been cut for this purpose. "Christ, Jenkins," Mike yelled, "there's a hell of a lot of them out there. They'll shoot out the wheelhouse. We'd better escalate!"

Jenkins pressed a signal button, and down below Cavanaugh opened a gun port that had been cut in the side of the ship. Out poked his heavy-duty M-60 machine gun, which immediately began firing 7.62 NATO rounds into the fray. With a 250-round belt he sprayed the first wave of fighting sampans from a withering foot-and-a-half above the waterline. Before their eyes, the hulls of the boats nearest *Promise* came apart, filling the river with dead and wounded guerrillas. The M-60 rounds, with an effective range of one thousand yards, were passing through two and three boats at these close quarters. Within moments, about thirty boats of the first-attack flotilla had been obliterated, but the huge Mitcom fleet was still massed in front of them. In minutes they would be fighting off armed boats on all sides.

"So far, no damage," Mike said, looking around the bridge.

"Just let's pray they still want to take this boat in usable shape," Jenkins said. "Those goddammed junks up ahead could have *anything* aboard them."

"Right. But now they're wondering what else *we've* got. Thank God we have a perfectly straight stretch of river ahead." Mike, still crouching behind the protective plate around the bridge, pushed open the door to the wheelhouse. Batki was grimly holding course. "Put her on automatic pilot, Captain," Mike ordered. "I'll take the right and left switch on deck."

DakatLi beckoned to Mike from the radio room. "I have followed orders, and I do not mention this little problem. The Palace is surrounded by the false coup, but no shots fired, of course."

A stinging hail of machine-gun bullets reached for the bridge and clanked against the plates. Mike ran from the radio room.

"They're all around us now!" Jenkins shouted needlessly. "Let's give 'em everything we've got. Maybe we can destroy the big boys that might have fifties, before they decide to sink this ship they want so much."

"Go to it," Mike agreed. He ran from slit to slit, pouring out bursts from his grease gun, as sampans with their grappling hooks kept trying to edge alongside. Then he heard the splintering of wood and saw first one and then several grapples dig into the deck below. He reached into the box of grenades and began lobbing one after another at the boarding sampans. The boats splintered; men screamed and pitched into the river as *Promise,* on autopilot, pulled the splintered crafts, still attached by their hooks, inexorably up river with it.

Suddenly the welcome deep-throated roar of the .50-caliber machine guns could be heard in the bow of the ship. Barton had gone forward and opened the two gun ports cut into the starboard and port sides of the prow of *Promise,* and the heavy-caliber machine guns were pulverizing all in front of them. Aft, Jennesen was blasting with the 20-mm. cannon at one of the big, armed junks, which managed to return only one short burst before the heavy automatic cannon tore it apart. The water was taking on a pinkish tint now.

All at once Mike spotted what had to be the Communist commander's flagship. A junk far larger than *Promise,* it had signal flags hanging along the halyards and two big staring eyes painted on either side of the prow. The war junk was directly on *Promise*'s port beam, four to five hundred yards off. It must have been lying back in the foliage, awaiting the propitious moment to close in for the kill. But now the Communist fleet commander must have decided that his own flagship was needed to finish off *Promise.* Mike yelled to Jenkins, who popped his head up for a look just in time to hear the distant staccato and see the winking flashes of a dreaded .50-caliber machine gun. One shell slammed high into the side of the deckhouse, another caught the aft corner of the bridge, riping it off. Jenkins grabbed the telephone. "A big one with a fifty direct off the left side of us!" Jenkins called to Barton. Forward, Barton looked behind him and saw that Cavanaugh had picked up the enemy and was sighting and firing at the junk with the M-60.

As they watched, cautiously peering over the steel plate, the .50-caliber gun on the deck of the junk swung slightly and opened up again. *Promise* shuddered and pitched, and the M-60 suddenly was silent. Jenkins held the phone to his ear waiting for a report. "Sir," he heard Barton shout finally, "they zapped us bad. The M-60 is out. Cavanaugh's hit."

"Can you give the forward guns a crack?" Jenkins asked Forrester.

"Tell him to get ready," Mike cried. He pressed the left button on the automatic pilot control, and *Promise* responded instantly, swinging over into a head-on course at the junk. The enemy .50 caliber now concentrated on the bridge and wheelhouse. In a deafening clanging of bullets against steel, the entire glass front of the wheelhouse shattered, as Mike and Jenkins dropped and pressed themselves to the deck behind the heavy steel plates of the bridge. Mike prayed that Marlene was down too. He never should have let her stay in the wheelhouse—never! Looking through a slit, Mike saw that *Promise* was now headed straight at the Communist junk, presenting the smallest possible target to the enemy .50-caliber gun. As she turned, other junks began to attack her from the rear. But the pounding of Jennesen's 20-mm. cannon resumed.

Now it became a duel of the .50-caliber machine guns. The .50 on the junk continued to rake the bridge and wheelhouse. The entire top half of the wheelhouse was torn jaggedly off the ship, pieces of it dancing into the air. And then, as they looked through the slits, Mike and Jenkins let out a cheer. Down below, Barton, firing his twin .50's, began savagely blasting apart the hull of the huge war junk a foot above the waterline. Before their eyes the once solid ship began to crumble; chunks flew into the air. And then the enemy .50-caliber machine gun was silenced once and for all.

Immediately Mike pressed the right button; *Promise,* in spite of the lacerating fire she had taken, responded easily.

"I bet they think we're some kind of headless horseman," Jenkins yelled, as Barton continued the destruction of every Mitcom junk and sampan that came into his sights. The bow of the ship swung upriver, settling back on course for Tuyan City. Several other war junks that had been waiting along the course swung in behind *Promise* and continued firing at her. Bullets whined around the bridge and wheelhouse from down river. *Promise* plowed ahead. Suddenly, the aft 20-mm. cannon was quiet. Emboldened, the junks, avoiding the machine-gun fire from the front of *Promise,* fell upon her rear. Mike and Jenkins moved around behind the destruction of the radio room and began firing at the junks with their machine guns. Looking down at the aft deck, Mike groaned at the wreckage. *Promise* had taken many hits. With the 20-mm. cannon still silent the junks moved in, raking the boat with thirty caliber machine-gun bullets.

"I've got to get back to that cannon," Mike yelled. "We're almost out of here—but those bastards will knock us off without our stinger. They must have got old Jennesen too." Crouching, Mike started around to the front of the bridge and got to the iron steps when, with a furious *pom pom pom,* the cannon came back to life. The closest junk exploded, showering its sister ships with its wreckage. Systematically, as the remaining junks tried to turn away and run down river, the cannon lashed out its lethal spray, one by one obliterating the last of the Mitcom capital war junks.

And all at once the river was silent again, clear of all boats ahead, strewn with the devastation of the Communist fleet behind. Mike picked his way through the debris and jagged steel to which the bridge had been reduced. He kicked open the door to the wheelhouse and, the pit of his stomach convulsing with dread, went inside. Captain Batki and Marlene were stretched out on the floor against the steel bulkheads. Marlene's face, dead white, was pressed one cheek to the deck, her long hair filled with the debris strewn over her whole body.

In a choked exclamation of grief, Mike uttered her name. Slowly one lid fluttered open; a blue eye stared up at him. "Is it over?" she asked in a hoarse whisper.

"Marlene!" There was elation in the cry as he fell to his knees beside her, gently running his hands over her body, hoping they would not encounter wounds or broken bones. "Are you all right?" he asked anxiously.

"I think so." With Mike's help she stood up and began slapping the debris from her dress and fluffing it out of her hair as he held her firmly around the waist.

"I was so worried. Every minute I wondered. . . ." He caught himself short and stared at her in relief, reassured now that she was not hurt. Then, "Damn it, Marlene," he snapped, "you never should have stayed up here during the fight. Risking your life. And for what? One lousy story the newspaper readers will forget the next day. While I worried myself sick. Is that all you care about? Getting the story?" His hands shook with the tension he had been under.

"No, that is not all what I care about," she replied. A slightly saucy smile replaced the lines of strain in her face. "Were you that much worried about me, Mike?" She paused a moment. "I did not really know you cared so much?"

"Care?" he cried. "I'd worry about any woman up in this wheelhouse during that fire fight. And when that woman is you . . ."

Mike failed to see her face suddenly radiate joy. Out the corner of an eye he suddenly noticed the sand bank looming up in the river ahead. With an alarmed grunt he threw himself at the spokes of the badly chewed wheel, wrestling it to port, overriding the automatic pilot. The boat twisted violently, throwing Marlene against the dazed Captain Batki who had slowly managed to stand up and was brushing himself off with great dignity. A moment later, Mike began to bring *Promise* back on course. Marlene and Batki regained their equilibrium and then made their way through the battle wreckage to the wheel.

"We damned near went aground," Mike rasped.

"Oh, no!" Marlene groaned. "After all what we been through?"

Still staring straight ahead, Mike reached his arm out and caught Marlene around the waist and steadied her against him.

They were dimly aware that outside there was cheering among the crew. "Let's see what the situation is, darling," Mike said turning the wheel over to Batki. With difficulty, Marlene followed him down the torn steps through the shattered galley and into the companionway from the main salon to the staterooms below deck. The main stateroom was a shambles, all the bulkheads torn by bullets. The steel plates around the gun port were frayed. Barkoon and Cavanaugh, his head and arms crudely bandaged, were there. Lying on the bed and bleeding from wounds in the head and both shoulders, his arms almost useless, was Sergeant Jennesen. Barkoon was anxiously talking to him in gentle tones. Cavanaugh looked up at Mike. "They cut me up a little with fragments, but I can still work."

"He will be all right, Sergeant?" Barkoon asked.

"This tough bastard?" Cavanaugh asked. "Christ, nothing can hurt *him* too bad. This is the second time in a month I've patched him up."

"I'll be around," Jennesen said weakly. "Sorry I let you down."

"Let us down!" exclaimed Jenkins who had joined them. "You saved us just when I thought we'd had it!"

"Christ, yes," said Mike. "When your gun stopped . . . But you did the job."

"No, sir," Jennesen barely rasped. "The King did it."

Everybody looked in amazement at Barkoon. Finally, Mike asked, "Is this true, Your Majesty?"

"You may recall I mentioned that I am experienced in most weapons. When I was young and before I developed this," he patted his paunch, "I was a guerrilla leader fighting the Japanese. It was nothing, really. I could hear the 20-mm. cannon going, and then suddenly—the girls and Henri will tell you—the whole rear of the ship shook, and we heard bullets ricochet. Then, no more twenty. I knew it was all we had to protect our rear, always a very important position." He smiled.

"So I crawled down the hall to the sergeant's position and saw him on the floor wounded. I helped him onto the bed and took over his weapon. There was plenty of ammo in the belt, the cannon was charged, the mounting superb—all I had to do was press the trigger. It was like old times."

Mike and Jenkins looked at each other and shook their heads, grinning. Then Barkoon caught sight of Marlene's disheveled hair. "What a pity. Maybe Henri will have time to do something about it before we get to Tuyan City."

Mike stared at her a moment. He began to laugh. Then they were all laughing together.

CHAPTER FIFTY-TWO

ORDINARILY AT this hour in the midafternoon, a large crowd would have gathered to view the battle damage inflicted on the beautiful yacht sailing through Tuyan City. But only General Dandig with an aide and two armed escorts were on the dock as *Promise* tied up. Dandig switched his swagger stick in agitation as he surveyed the bullet-frayed boat. Mike and a crewman slid down the gangplank, and Dandig walked aboard.

He silently inspected the scarred deck and bulkheads and finally, as though afraid to pose the question, asked, "Is King Barkoon all right?"

In answer, Barkoon appeared on deck. He was attired in the resplendent dress uniform of Chief Marshal of the Mituyan Armed Forces.

"Your Majesty!"

"Dandig," Barkoon put an arm on his loyal soldier's shoulder, "have you managed to keep control of the coup?"

"Now that you are here, success is assured. We badly need Thannit, but I was never certain when he would change sides."

"I should have flown into Tuyan City rather than cause Forrester to nearly lose his boat bringing me here."

Dandig shook his head. "Tarot suspects you are in the country. This was the only way, Your Majesty. Whether it's a guess, or his agents in Hong Kong somehow found you had left, but every airport in Mituyan has been taken by his Special Forces and every plane inspected. He even has his own agents in the control towers and supervising the Americans closely at central radio monitoring. That's why we were afraid to radio you unless it was absolutely necessary.

"Well, now that we are here, what do we do?"

"KaritKi and Tarot are still under the impression that this is a false coup, but they are restless because none of the generals has answered their calls for help either in a negative or positive way—we have merely been unavailable. However, we have surrounded the radio and television station, the post and cable office, the Joint Chiefs of Staff headquarters, the palace, the police stations, and the Tuyan City International Airport. Everything is waiting for your appearance, Your Majesty."

"The plan?" Barkoon persisted.

"You will accompany me in the armored car to the radio and television station, where you will report to the Mituyan people that with the backing of the army you have returned to resume ruling the country. You will call upon KaritKi to surrender, and you will promise him a fair trial. You will guarantee free elections."

Francine and Brigit appeared on deck with Henri. "How many people have you room for in the car?" Barkoon asked.

Discomfited, Dandig looked at the girls. "Your Majesty, I think it would be advisable if you made this appearance, uh, solo, so to speak."

"I quite agree. But I have had a correspondent with me all the way on this trip, and I would like her to see the resolution of this affair."

"I'd like to see this thing through too, Your Majesty," Mike said—"if you don't mind."

Barkoon sighed sadly. "Forrester, are you never going to give me a chance to be alone with Fraulein Straltz?"

Marlene sliped her arm through Mike's. Barkoon chuckled ruefully. "I see you are not."

Barkoon, Dandig, DakatLi, Marlene, Mike, and the two armed guards climbed into the rear of the armored car. Through the small slit windows they could see the wild turbulence in the streets. Tanks, troops, milling crowds were everywhere.

"It's been like this all day," Dandig said. "Nobody knows what's happening. The American Embassy has been constantly in touch with General Thannit and myself. There are two regiments from II Corps surrounding the city, and I have a regiment of paratroopers, combat ready, beside their planes at Tiking Airport." Dandig laughed. "Tarot's Special Forces officers in Tiking think they are loyal troops ready to go to the aid of the Palace when KaritKi calls for them!"

A ten-minute ride through the hot, teeming streets of Tuyan City brought them to the television station, housed in a large government building. "General Thannit's troops control the station," Dandig explained. "However, there is a Mituyan Special Forces company across the street still loyal to the Palace. If the commander recognizes you, Your Majesty, there may be shooting. Our troops will keep you covered."

The armored car pulled to a halt. Dandig peered out. "Here we are, Your Majesty. Please get into the building as quickly as possible."

Dandig's aide opened the rear doors, and Dandig and DakatLi exited first. Then, with one of his surprising demonstrations of agility, Barkoon leaped from the back of the car and bounded up the steps. Mike and Marlene followed, the soldiers making a path for them, staring admiringly at the blonde Caucasian girl. In the large marble-hall government building a cordon of guards formed around Barkoon and Marlene, and Mike followed the King's bulky form to the second-floor studios.

When a full colonel blocked Mike and Marlene at the door, Marlene cried out: "Barkie, tell them let us in!" The King, turning, gave a crisp command; the colonel bowed, apologized, and escorted Mike and Marlene inside.

The excitement in the studio was contagious. Marlene squeezed Mike's arm as she took in the scene. "There is General Thannit," she whispered.

"They're all here," Mike said. "Except for the admirals. Maybe the navy doesn't go along with this coup."

A disembodied voice filled the studio, ordering quiet, and instantly the generals and Barkoon and the rest obeyed the compelling command of some obscure technician. A red light winked on one of the cameras.

The floor manager pointed to Barkoon, who looked into the camera and said, "People of Mituyan: This is your King, Barkoon the Sixth. I have come back to you, my people, because I am needed to free you from the oppressive tyrant KaritKi and his family and circle, who suck the life blood of the people of Mituyan like the leeches of the Tuyan River Delta.

"I call upon KaritKi to leave the palace and the country. I will open the political prisons and free those brave people who have dared raise their voices against this cruel regime that has enslaved the people of Mituyan. I will dispatch ships to the Isle of Stones immediately. The ships will take the men of KaritKi's regime who have enslaved the people of Mituyan and place *them* in this infamous prison, and then bring back the patriots who seek a freely elected government of our country.

"It will be my first mission as your King to insure the coming elections are honest and that men and women truly representative of the people of this country can campaign for election to the constituent assembly, without fear of reprisal from dishonest and repressive government officials."

The floor manager, kneeling under the camera, pointed at a telephone that had been placed before Barkoon.

"Those of you who are hearing me on radio but cannot see me on television, I am reaching for a telephone. On the other end is Counselor Tarot, the brother of Premier KaritKi. You will hear what I say to him." Barkoon held the phone to his mouth and in commanding tones said, "Counselor Tarot, what you thought was a false coup is a real one. I call on you and your brother to surrender. I will guarantee your safety—"

Tarot's voice, amplified in the studio, snapped back, "You will be executed within the hour for violating your exile. Premier KaritKi has the army under his control."

The red light winked off on one camera and glowed on the wide-angle camera. "If you are watching your television, Counselor Tarot, you will see that you are *not* in control of the army." Thannit and Dandig walked on camera, flanking Barkoon.

"In the name of the Army of Mituyan, we welcome King Barkoon back to govern our country!" General Dandig cried out in ringing tones.

"The Army of Mituyan will no longer permit the people to suffer the abuses heaped upon them by the evil regime of former Premier KaritKi," echoed Thannit.

"If you wish to save lives and bloodshed, you will immediately surrender," Barkoon demanded. "But if your palace guard puts up a fight, it will be crushed in the name of the People." The King glared into the camera. "What is your answer, Tarot?" A loud click cut off further communication from the palace.

"The regime of KaritKi defies your King, my people," Barkoon said in a tone of regret. "The army will now, on my orders, move to take the palace and make every official of the KaritKi regime a prisoner."

He looked into the cameras, which had zoomed in close. "People of Mituyan, I will stay here on radio and television to bring you news of our attack on the palace, until KaritKi and every one of his bloodthirsty minions has been imprisoned. As we wait, I will tell you my plans for a better life for every man, woman, and child in Mituyan."

"He really knows how to give a political speech," Mike whispered to Marlene, for whom he had been translating the King's words. Marlene's eyes were shining with excitement.

General Thannit and General Dandig saluted the King. Barkoon returned their salutes smartly, and the two generals walked off camera. Barkoon then began what was to be a marathon political speech.

Mike and Marlene followed the generals into the hall, where Mike caught up with Dandig and asked his battle plan.

"We will now go out and take the palace. I'm afraid it will be a hard, bloody battle. A battalion of Special Forces is quartered on palace grounds. And worse—Mayna has two full companies of her female paramilitary unit quartered around her wing of the palace. I hope they realize they cannot hope to save the family, and will surrender. The tanks should make them think twice before engaging us."

But before they could reach the ground floor, staccato bursts of machine-gun fire echoed through the marble halls. "The Special Forces must have already been ordered to take the radio and television station," Thannit said. "Fools!"

The sounds of an intense fire fight increased, and bullets whined into the government building. The two generals, along with their aides and armed bodyguards, flattened themselves against the stone walls; Mike and Marlene followed their example.

"Are you getting tired of being shot at yet?" Mike asked. "We could go back to *Promise* and wait the thing out."

"I don't miss this. Not for anything!" Marlene cried.

The fight was a short one. After several minutes' silence, the generals ventured out the front door, where a bloody scene awaited them. Across the street, Mituyan Special Forces men lay dead or dying. Several of Thannit's men also lay crumpled on the stone steps; others, bleeding from wounds, awaited medical attention. All the surviving Mituyan Special Forces men had discarded their weapons and were standing hands upraised.

"The first fight won!" Thannit said. "Now, the palace! My troops have orders to shoot to kill, but I do not believe the police will be as foolish as Tarot's men were."

Mike and Marlene piled into the armored personnel carrier with Dandig, as Thannit went on ahead in his own staff car. As the armored car raced down Bismarck Avenue toward the palace, a desultory fire fight was taking place around the iron-spiked pickets surrounding the twenty acres of the palace grounds. One block away, they detrucked at a tall office building.

"This is our command post," Dandig said. "On the fifth floor we will have a perfect view of the palace. The telephone line to the palace switchboard should be open. I will negotiate with KaritKi and Tarot while General Thannit supervises the attack."

They climbed to the roof, where, behind a two-foot-high parapet, a group of officers and men had set up a complete command post. The long late-afternoon shadows dappled the bright green, close-clipped lawns of the palace. From this strategic rooftop, Mike and Marlene had a detailed view of the impending battle.

General Thannit's regular troops surrounded the palace, keeping up a constant harassing light-arms fire that was returned by the palace guards and Tarot's Special Forces troops from behind the bunkers surrounding the palace. Along the street running parallel to the palace, four tanks squatted malevolently, the long muzzles of their cannons pointed at the ornate building.

"We can attack at any time," Dandig said. "But if we can negotiate a surrender, we will save a great deal of blood. Also there is the matter of the children of Mayna and Tarot. It would set world opinion against us if they were killed."

He turned to an aide and asked if he had the Palace on the phone. The man nodded. Dandig asked the palace switchboard operator, who was holding the line open, to connect him with Premier KaritKi.

In the parlor of the Premier's quarters in the west wing of the palace the entire family had eyes glued on the television set, on which King Barkoon was keeping up an unceasing flow of comment.

Tarot read a communiqué and turned to his brother. "Poramat has a full regiment of Rangers on the way by road," he reported.

"They could not be flown in?" KaritKi asked sharply.

"Dandig has control of the Tiking Airport with a regiment of paratroopers. Poramat felt that rather than waste time fighting in Tiking, it was better to take a chance on the roads." Tarot paced the living room shuffling communiqués. "Our brother is negotiating with General Kit, whose Eighth Division was ordered by Dandig some days ago into the border area. Kit was never invited to join this coup attempt by Dandig. Of course his loyalty to us is unquestionable."

Tarot smiled sadly at Dhuna. "Your cousin is trying to regroup his division back in Tiking. Then they'll capture the airport from Dandig's paratroopers and fly the airborne regiments of Eighth Division over the palace and drop them on us."

"What about the Twelfth Division in Banthut? General Bakalit was an obscure captain until Mayna recognized his ability," KaritKi fumed. "Surely his loyalty is unshaken."

Tarot's lips were a thin line. "I should have recognized the significance of the orders sending his division out into the mountains last week to 'pacify the mountain tribesmen.' It will be two days before he can come to our aid."

"What *can* we count on, husband?" Mayna asked irritably.

"There are two regiments on the way by truck, one from the North sent by Poramat, the other from the Tuyan Delta. Neither can reach us until late tonight or early in the morning. General Kit's paratroopers might be able to make a drop by noon tomorrow if they can capture Tiking Airport."

"Then we must hold out tonight."

"We only have three hundred and fifty half-trained Special Forces men in the compound," Tarot replied.

"There are two hundred of my girls," Mayna said fiercely—"well trained and well armed."

"And General Thannit's entire First Division controls the city," Tarot said dourly. "No doubt his Second Division is in reserve."

"If we can just hold out tonight—" Mayna insisted. "Our support will build up. It always has. Oh, if only Whit was still ambassador. He could threaten the generals with no more American support."

As if on cue, an aide came in to announce: "Ambassador Tate is on the phone. He wants to speak to the Premier."

KaritKi nodded. "Put the call on the amplifier. We all shall hear what he has to say."

"It is all Tate's doing, this coup." Tarot frowned darkly. "I should have made you refuse his credentials, brother. I knew he was the executioner."

"I will insist that he be removed when this is over," KaritKi replied. He gestured at the amplifier, and the aide pressed the transparent button. It glowed orange, and Ambassador Tate was in communication with the family.

"You wished to talk to me, Mr. Ambassador?"

"I want to offer you the protection and sanctuary of the American Embassy, Mr. Premier," Tate said. "I fear you are in an untenable situation. My advisers tell me that the soldiers and the mobs are becoming uncontrollable. I will arrange safe transportation for you and your entire family to the embassy."

"So that your puppet, King Barkoon, can illegally take the country away from its rightful Premier?" Tarot cried hysterically.

"I am concerned about the personal safety of all of you," the voice of the American ambassador continued, unruffled. "Once you are all safe in the embassy, we can negotiate a settlement with the dissident generals and King Barkoon, who seems to be rapidly gaining the support of the people."

"If we leave the palace, we give up all our power!" Mayna shrieked. "We will stay! Our loyal officers are even now coming to the aid of the rightful Premier."

"I hope, for your sakes, you are right," Ambassador Tate answered. "But my offer stands. Whenever you need the sanctuary of the embassy, it will be granted you."

"It was *you* who made this coup!" Mayna stood and walked toward the amplifier. "*You* betrayed us. The Americans who pretend to be our friends, our allies, all the time plotting against us. We don't need help from the Americans. You are the cause of all our trouble!"

Tarot quickly pressed the button, cutting off the amplifier. Then he looked at the television set, cursed loudly, and switched it off as well. "How did that fat fool get into Tuyan City?" he growled. "I knew he had left Hong Kong. But how did he get here? We had the airports under close surveillance. He couldn't have come by road. . . . How?"

"The point is, he's here," KaritKi said mildly. "I suggest you have one of your Special Forces squads do something about him as soon as possible."

Tarot stared at his brother, who was looking dreamily at Dhuna. Tarot knew that KaritKi had a tendency to drift into an unreal world whenever crisis threatened. But now? With everything at stake? Tarot, too, had a terrible desire to go to his quarters and smoke several pipes. But he knew he could not give in now.

An aide again entered the room. "General Dandig wants to talk to the Premier or to Counselor Tarot. Shall I put him on?" KaritKi waved at Tarot to push the button. It glowed.

"We are listening to what you have to say before deciding our disposition of your case," Premier KaritKi said in clear, firm tones.

"Listen to me, KaritKi," Dandig came back, uncompromisingly. "We offer you safety. We will guarantee the safety of the entire family if you surrender now. But if you force us to fight, we can guarantee nothing. We do not want to see the children of Counselor Tarot and Mayna die. But we will fight if you force us to."

Unconsciously, Mayna looked at her three children. They were all badly frightened. Her instinct to protect them clashed with a savage determination not to allow her husband and brother-in-law to surrender forever the power and prestige of the Ki family.

"General Dandig!" Mayna's voice was a lash. "We made you from nothing. And now you betray our trust. We will *not* surrender. The loyal generals are on their way to help us. If you do not lift this siege, you will pay dearly for the traitorous attack on the legal government of Mituyan."

"Time is short," Dandig replied. "But because of the reasons you have just given, I will grant you five minutes to surrender while I can still guarantee your safety. By the time help can reach you, there will be no KaritKi in the palace to accept it. The five minutes begins now. If you do not walk out of the west wing of the palace in five minutes —four minutes and fifty seconds—the tanks will blast you out."

Before Mayna could scream out a reply, Tarot pushed the button again breaking the connection.

"We must stay and fight!" Mayna cried. "As long as we are here, our Special Forces and my girls will resist."

"But the children?" Dhuna said, speaking up for the first time. "Must *they* be killed?"

Mayna hesitated. "No, they must be spared. Someday they will take over the rule of Mituyan."

"Then you must take them out through one of the tunnels now," Dhuna urged. "Before the cannons open fire."

"No! I will stay and fight with my girls. We will hold the palace until help comes. From all over the country our loyal officers will be mustering their forces to relieve us. Are we to give up our power now?" Mayna's children stared at her wide-eyed and silent. "Dhuna, take them from the palace. We have friends. In the Chinese section—the powerful merchant Yen, whose family has become rich through us. He will provide a safe hiding place. When our loyal officers relieve the palace, you can bring them back."

Dhuna looked to her husband, who once more seemed to have lost comprehension of what was happening. She knew he could not stand bad news; already he had fled reality. Dhuna also knew that if she left the palace now she would never again be First Lady if the coup failed. Mayna, who stayed and fought, would be the most powerful woman in the land.

Again an aide came into the room. "There is a phone call for Madam Dhuna," he announced. "It is the American, Mike Forrester, calling."

Just hearing his name gave her an odd sense of security. "Let me talk to him," she said. "Mike! Where are you?"

"Nearby, Dhuna." His strong, confident voice gave her strength. "Dhuna," he sounded urgent, "you must leave the palace. They've got military superiority. They'll demolish the palace and everyone in it."

"But I can't leave, Mike. My husband needs me!"

"Listen to me, Dhuna, I just arrived in Tuyan City. My boat, *Promise,* is at my dock. You know where it is. I can promise you safety on board. But get out of the palace. Use whatever escape routes are open to you, but get out. I will make your safety my personal business."

Tarot suddenly whirled toward the amplifier.

"Forrester, this is Counselor Tarot. So it was *you* who betrayed us. *You* brought Barkoon into Tuyan City aboard your boat with a safe-conduct pass issued by me."

"Counselor, I don't know what you're talking about," Mike's voice cracked out. "I am only interested in the safety of my dead wife's dear friend."

"You lie, Forrester!" Tarot cried. "There was no other way he could have arrived in Tuyan City. No other way!"

"Dhuna"—Mike's tones were comforting—"you and anyone with you will be safe aboard the *Promise.*"

"Betrayer!" Tarot screamed. "We made you rich, and this is how you repay us!"

"Dhuna, remember—" Tarot hit the switch and cut off Mike's voice.

"You don't *know* that he did it!" Dhuna cried. Then to Mayna: "I'll take the children to safety."

"Not to that Judas!" Tarot exclaimed.

From outside the palace the voice of Dandig, amplified through a giant bull horn, roared into the air-conditioned room through the closed windows. "Exactly one minute! Then we attack!"

The children cried out in fright and jumped from the sofa and ran to their mother. Mayna took them in her arms, kissed them, and then turned to Dhuna. "Take them to safety. When the palace is relieved, you can bring them back."

KaritKi smiled at his wife. "Yes, take the children away for a while. When you come back, this will be over."

The voice of Dandig again blared: "Thirty seconds, twenty-nine seconds . . ."

Dhuna gathered the three children under her arms and led them out of the Premier's quarters and down to the escape tunnel.

"Five seconds, four seconds, three . . . two . . . one . . . Fire!" Dandig's voice boomed across the palace grounds, and the sudden sharp concussion of the tanks' cannon tore the atmosphere.

Looking down on the palace, Mike and Marlene could watch every detail of the battle. The four tanks kept up a slow fire of shells that crunched into the palace walls, splattering masonry as they methodically destroyed the stately edifice. On the lawns, palace guards and Mituyan Special Forces men appeared, firing machine guns and rifles, launching grenades at the attacking troops, who were detonating charges that blew out and twisted the iron picket fence.

"I wish there was some way of keeping Dhuna safe at least," Mike said.

"They could all be safe if they surrendered," Dandig said. "But if we have to go in after them, the soldiers, even the officers, will vie for the opportunity of killing members of the family. Most of our soldiers are Buddhists; they believe that Mayna has had Buddhists turtured for her personal enjoyment. That's what Han Li Phang told them, and they believe him."

"Maybe the family are out of the palace by now," Mike suggested. "Dhuna once told Luna and me that there were many tunnels from the palace that led out as far as half a mile."

"Well, Mayna must still be there. Look at that," Dandig said bitterly.

Over one hundred Mituyan girls in tightly cut camouflage fatigues, carrying light machine guns and carbines, suddenly charged out of the west wing of the palace at the walls being breached by the troops. Screaming, the girls closed on the walls, their long black hair streaming from under visored cloth caps. The surprised soldiers watched them coming, too stunned to shoot back—until one, another, then several of the soldiers dropped, killed or wounded. The regular troops, shouting curses, finally opened up on them. The line of girls broke as grenades began to explode, blowing steel shards through their bodies, while those who could continued firing at the soldiers.

"That woman, she is a monster to send the girls out!" Marlene cried. "How horrible. Oh, *Gott, I* cannot look! Why do they do it?"

"Mituyan women are tigresses," Dandig said. "What a terrible waste of pretty young women."

More and more girls fell before the fire of the well-disciplined troops, until the survivors turned back toward the bunkers manned by the Mituyan Special Forces and palace guards. A few made it, but most pitched violently to the grass, staining it red. As those in the command post watched, the attack began again. Most of the fighting was concentrated in the southern half of the palace grounds, where the tanks continued their bombardment, covering the slowly advancing regulars with heavy machine-gun fire.

"It won't be long now!" Dandig called out triumphantly. Two of the tanks depressed their cannons and began blasting at the bunkers from which light-arms fire poured into the ranks of the attacking troops. First one, then a second bunker erupted in grisly showers of dirt and flesh. Seeing the lethal destruction, the remaining Special Forces and palace guards and the few surviving paramilitary girls abandoned their bunker and ran for the palace. The regulars stepped up their pursuit.

"That's the end of the palace," Mike said to Marlene. Suddenly, to their horror, a second company of paramilitary girls, who had been held in reserve on the north side of the palace, swept around the west wing, screaming shrill cries as they charged directly into General Thannit's oncoming regulars. Leading them, firing a light machine gun from her hip, was a woman in a red Mituyan dress. Her legs flashing through the slit skirt, she ran at the head of her combat-garbed girls.

The sight of Mayna, shrieking defiance and exhorting her female troops to keep fighting, galvanized the retreating palace guards; they turned and joined the paramilitary girls' assault. The regulars were shocked to a halt at the sight of the fiercely screaming woman, followed by a company of fighting girls and backed by the revitalized Special Forces men. Machine guns and rifles crackled, and the troopers began to fall, their momentum broken. Then the palace defenders were upon them, shooting, stabbing with fixed bayonets. Mayna herself gunned down men before her.

In confusion and fear, the troops backed toward the fence, finally turning and running for the pickets and line of reserve troops covering them. The girls and newly inspired palace guards followed, ripping thc retreating regulars with fire, littering the palace lawns with wounded and dying. "It's not possible!" muttered Dandig as he watched from his command post. "That woman is a banshee straight from the depths of hell!"

As the troops dove for cover outside the palace grounds, the tanks opened up with their heavy machine guns, zeroing their fire on the pursuing, battle-intoxicated palace defenders. Once their own men were behind them, the reserves also opened up with machine guns, and the momentarily triumphant palace troops were mercilessly cut down.

Then a heavy round from one of the .50-caliber tank machine guns caught Mayna. Her broken body was hurled through the air. Instantly, demoralization swept through her girls, who turned and ran back toward the palace, many throwing down their weapons. The Special Forces and palace guards followed their example, dropping their weapons and running, hands held high, in aimless patterns around the palace grounds. They were sliced down as they ran.

"Cease fire! *Stop shooting!*" General Dandig bellowed through his bull horn, but his commands were of no avail. The regulars wreaked vengeance on the remnants of the defenders until at last, slowly, the officers gained command and at last stopped the slaughter. But with the cessation of firing, a mob of civilians, screaming for the death of KaritKi, stormed onto the palace grounds behind the troopers. They yelled in thunderous approval as members of the mob, finding the torn body of Mayna, tied a rope around one of her legs and began dragging her corpse out toward the street.

"If only they had surrendered," Dandig said, sadly surveying the carnage below.

Mike, sickened, led Marlene from the roof of the building. By the time they made it to the ground floor, the screams of the mob had reached a chilling crescendo.

Mike spotted a small cab, its driver nowhere to be seen; all taxis in the street were empty. In his excitement, the driver had left the key in the ignition. Mike pushed Marlene into the back seat and drove through the streets, swirling with crowds, toward the U.S. Embassy. It took him half an hour to reach the chancery entrance.

Ambassador Tate greeted them warmly in his office. The telephone jangled incessantly. On TV, King Barkoon was well into his third hour of broadcasting. Mike told Tate about the death of Mayna and asked what the ambassador wanted him to do.

"Find KaritKi and Tarot," Tate said. "They apparently escaped from the palace. But don't worry," he said when he saw the dismayed look on Mike's face, "no one is going to remain in hiding." Already Barkoon himself was exhorting the people of Mituyan to be on the lookout for their former Premier and his brother.

Then the King, staring directly into the camera, said: "KaritKi, Tarot, know this: Mayna died to give you two *men* time to escape. How does that make you feel? If you want to be beaten to death by the indignant people of Tuyan City, and your bodies dragged through the streets, you need only once show your faces. *But,* if you want to be treated with dignity and receive a fair trial, you will surrender yourselves by telephoning me here at this station, or by calling the Joint Chiefs of Staff headquarters. We will provide safe conduct."

"Mike, do you think they'll give themselves up?" Tate asked.

"It's hard to tell, sir. I think if they truly realized their situation was hopeless they might do so."

"And what would make them realize that?"

"When the United States officially recognizes the new government of King Barkoon."

Tate looked at him in amazement. "Are you suggesting I go over to that station and tell the people of Mituyan to recognize King Barkoon as their lawful leader?"

When Mike said nothing, Tate protested, "But I have no such advice from Washington."

"Mr. Ambassador," Mike said quietly, "as soon as you declare the U.S. is behind Barkoon, there will be no chance of KaritKi getting back in power."

"I've sent a cable to Washington asking for instruction. But it's only six in the morning there. It'll be hours before the Security Council can meet and get off a cable back to me."

"Meanwhile, the troops still loyal to KaritKi are apt to arrive in Tuyan City, and we'll be in for a real blood bath." Mike regarded the ambassador sympathetically. "I'm glad I don't have to make this decision, sir."

"You really think a pitched battle could occur?"

"It's possible. Dandig and Thannit were able to shunt off the division commanding generals known to be loyal to KaritKi. But for how long? And there's the navy. The admirals, every one of them, are staunch KaritKi men. They don't have much military power—but they could certainly destroy the dock areas, keep a civil war going."

"So you *are* suggesting I should jeopardize my government, to say nothing of my own career, by prematurely recognizing Barkoon?"

"You could get the Country Team in on the decision," Mike suggested craftily. The hoped-for explosion occurred.

"Forrester," Tate exclaimed, "we no longer use that term 'country team' in Mituyan. We now are the United States Diplomatic and Military Mission. Furthermore, any decision of this magnitude is *my* responsibility entirely."

"Yes, sir," Mike replied, winking at Marlene.

The ambassador caught the wink. "You're as bad as all the other plotters. Well . . . if you'd like to accompany me to the studio, I'll *give* Barkoon our support."

"May I suggest, sir, that you release the monk Han Li Phang and get him on television? Barkoon probably will have to do something drastic about him later, but he's a demigod and at this moment could be useful."

"Good suggestion."

It was after dark when the ambassador arrived at the television station. Barkoon and the generals greeted him as a savior. The coup seemed a success, temporarily at least, though an entire division was reported trying to reach Tuyan City and rally around KaritKi.

Mike overheard Han Li Phang bargaining with DakatLi. Phang was insisting that his price for supporting Barkoon now was the early trial and execution of Poramat. DakatLi looked about, nervously, but Barkoon could not be disturbed, so, as the King's chief aide, he pledged his word that the execution would take place. Phang nodded and made ready to go before the cameras and radio microphone.

Dandig sidled over to Mike. "We are thankful for your part in the ambassador's early declaration of American support for King Barkoon. Now if only we could take KaritKi, dead or alive. With him in our hands, and the United States behind us, Thannit and I could quickly reunite the army."

"Maybe, just maybe, I can help you," Mike said thoughtfully.

"It could mean the overnight reunification of the country," Dandig said.

Mike approached Ambassador Tate, who was standing by to go on the air, and told him there was a chance he might be able to direct the army to KaritKi.

"Do it, Mike, for God's sake!"

"Of course they might kill him, and it would be my fault."

"Yes, I hadn't thought of that. We certainly want to spare his life if he's still alive now. Just a minute." He and King Barkoon went into a private conference, and a few minutes later Tate told Mike the King had repeated his assurances that if KaritKi gave himself up he would receive a fair trial. "Go ahead, Mike, and good luck."

The *Promise,* even after dark, looked forlorn. But the worst of the wreckage appeared to have been cleared away, and Captain Batki was waiting at the gangplank in a state of high excitement. "Your friend and the children are here."

"Good," Mike breathed with relief. "Where are they?"

"We repaired the master stateroom. I was afraid in the main salon they could be seen too easily from the dock."

In the master stateroom, Mayna's two youngest children were stretched out asleep on the big bed. Dhuna was seated in an easy chair. She rose with a smile when Mike and Marlene came in. He went over and put an arm around her shoulders. "I'm glad you came. It is the safest place in Tuyan City."

"Is my husband safe? What happened to Mayna? I begged her not to stay. . . ." Dhuna asked the questions breathlessly.

Softly Mike told her Mayna was dead but that her husband and Tarot were not in the palace when the troops broke in.

"Thank God. I left before the battle, but Tarot and my husband were resolved to stay. They thought help was coming."

"But where would they stay until help arrives?" Mike asked.

"With the Chinese merchant Yen, who Tarot made so rich; I was supposed to go there too, but—"

Suddenly she clamped a hand over her mouth, looking at Mike fearfully. "Tarot said you betrayed us. I don't believe it . . . but I mustn't say where my husband is. He will give himself up if he must. But we know that loyal troops are coming toward Tuyan City from all directions. Perhaps he will take power again tomorrow."

Mike knew there was no sense in explaining that Tuyan City would be awash in blood if the two factions of the army battled each other. He could only think it was a fantastic stroke of luck that Dhuna had gone to his boat for safety and had so thoughtlessly told him where her husband could be found. There was no time to lose.

"Marlene, you stay with Dhuna and the children."

"But I've got to go to the UPI office and file my story," Marlene protested.

"Just let me check the communications room to see if there are any messages."

He picked his way up to what was left of the wheelhouse and communications room. Captain Jenkins was still on duty.

"I have most of the radio equipment working, and the shore telephone is installed," Jenkins reported.

"Just what I want." Mike grabbed the phone and called the TV studio. A studio technician answered and brought Ambassador Tate to the line.

"Mr. Ambassador," Mike said in excitement. "I know where KaritKi and Tarot very likely are. But remember, the generals would rather kill KaritKi than keep him alive and chance a countercoup."

"The King and the generals have given their word," Tate snapped. "Where is he?"

Mike told Tate about the Chinese merchant named Yen. He was sure the generals or DakatLi would know the exact address.

"Good work, Mike!" Tate cried jubilantly. But Mike was already on his way to the stateroom to pick up Marlene and let her see for herself the climax of her story.

The driver of the staff car Dandig had put at their disposal was well acquainted with the location of the residence of Yen. "He is very rich and has one of the biggest houses in the Chinese city," the man said as they drove off.

It was a ten-minute drive through crowd-choked streets. All the citizens were out to see what was happening, their transistor radios blaring forth King Barkoon's words.

"This is the house of Yen," the driver said finally.

"Park right here, in front." Mike leaned forward and looked out at a solid two-story house with an iron gate around it. Lights were on inside, and nothing unusual seemed to be occurring.

Then, from all sides, army vehicles began to surround the area, and high-intensity searchlights played on the merchant's house. General Dandig pulled up in an armored car and stepped out onto the sidewalk with his bull horn and began talking in Mituyan: "KaritKi, Tarot—we know you are in the House of Yen. The coup is over. Ambassador Tate has recognized the new government. You will be treated with humanity if you come out now. Otherwise, we will drag you out."

Dandig nodded to a young officer by his side, who marched up to the gate and pulled the bell rope sharply. A servant, shaking with fright, appeared at the gate and opened it. Two smartly uniformed sergeants with automatic carbines slung over their shoulders followed the officer into the grounds of the house.

"KaritKi," the bull horn boomed, "you will come out with the escort that has gone in for you—or we attack. If you do come out, we will negotiate peacefully the conclusion to this entire affair."

Dandig grinned at Mike, now standing beside him. "The ex-Premier loved nothing more than negotiating, when he held the whip hand."

All eyes were on the gate. Then, almost anticlimactically, the two brothers walked slowly out of the gate. They looked haggard, white suits rumpled and dirty, their black hair, usually plastered to their heads, fluffed out untidily. Dandig marched forth to meet them.

Dandig silently pointed at his armored car, and KaritKi and Tarot entered through the back, followed by the officer and two sergeants. The back door was closed from within, and Dandig watched as the vehicle rolled away.

"Forrester, if you don't mind, I will ride back to the television station with you and the beautiful girl journalist."

"Could you let me off at the United Press office?" Marlene requested.

"Darling, if you'll take the advice of an old Mituyan hand, the story isn't quite over yet," Mike said, his expression grim. "Do you agree, General?"

"I wouldn't know, Forrester," Dandig replied blandly. He said a few words to the driver, and off they sped through the streets back to the radio and television station.

Ambassador Tate was anxiously waiting to hear what had happened.

"They picked up KaritKi and Tarot, sir," Mike reported.

"Good! That ends the possibility of a bloody civil war, then."

"It would seem so, sir," Mike replied. "There's nothing left to fight about. I guess that's why the brothers finally gave up."

"Where are KaritKi and Tarot now?" Tate asked Dandig.

"The armored car was taking them to the Joint Chiefs of Staff headquarters, where they'll be held for trials."

Mike noticed a fleeting but significant glance pass between Barkoon and Dandig. He understood perfectly what they were communicating to each other.

"Your Majesty," Mike said, "I know you are a student of political philosophers. Have you ever read Machiavelli?"

"But of course. For a Westerner he was very sound."

"What was it he said about political killings? Get them over with immediately after a coup d'état and people will forget? But the long drawn-out imprisonment and trial of a living deposed prince is the most dangerous political risk his conquerors can take?"

"What are you getting at, Mike?" Tate asked irritably.

"Very interesting, Mr. Forrester," Barkoon said with a twisted smile of admiration. "But now I must tell the people that KaritKi is our prisoner." And he walked out in front of the camera again.

"What was all that about, Mike?" Tate asked.

"By now the armored car should have arrived at headquarters. Why don't *you* ask to speak to KaritKi?"

"I think I will!" Tate said "General Dandig, can you call the headquarters and let me talk to KaritKi? I would like him to know that I have recognized King Barkoon on behalf of my government and that it would be disastrous for him not to encourage the generals still loyal to him to unite under King Barkoon's leadership . . . and that if the people of Mituyan should truly want him back in power, they will have an opportunity to vote for his supporters to the constituent assembly."

"I will attempt to make the call, Mr. Ambassador," Dandig agreed. "It may be difficult, however." The expression on the general's face now worried Tate. "Only Thannit can allow us to speak to KaritKi," Dandig explained.

Finally, after ten minutes, Thannit came on the phone. Several times Dandig had turned to the ambassador to say that there seemed to be a state of unusual confusion at the headquarters. Mike watched the whole performance with unconcealed skepticism.

Considerable talk in Mituyan followed, and Tate looked from Dandig to Mike and back, noticing the hardening lines in Mike's face. Then, still holding the phone, Dandig said to Ambassador Tate, "Would you like to speak to General Thannit yourself, Ambassador? A dreadful thing has happened."

Mike looked at the ambassador significantly. Fearful of what he was about to hear, Tate took the phone from Dandig. "Yes, General. Yes—"

He listened a few moments, disbelief, then anger, mirrored in his face. He glared first at Dandig; then his gaze fell on Barkoon, still indefatigably talking to the Mituyan people. Without saying a word he passed the phone back to Dandig.

Mike studied the shock on Tate's face. "You aren't really surprised, are you, Mr. Ambassador?"

"But they all gave me their word." The tough-talking Tate sounded bewildered.

"What has happened, Mike?" Marlene asked, her voice quavering.

"I didn't hear Thannit's part of the conversation, but I didn't have to. The brothers apparently tried to escape from the armored car—and both were shot."

Tate nodded. He turned toward the TV camera, thought better of it, and stepped back into the shadows. He snapped at Dandig. "Get Barkoon off the air. I want to talk to him right now!"

As Dandig walked to the camera, Tate coldly said to Mike, "I want you present for a little chat. I don't want those two jabbering in Mituyan so I can't understand what they're saying to each other."

"My advice, for what it's worth, sir, is to try to understand their way of thinking and not get too upset."

"Your sole worth at the moment is as an interpreter," Tate snapped.

Barkoon came over, a smile on his round face, Dandig beside him. Tate led them into a sound-proof studio next door and shut the door.

"Yes, Mr. Ambassador?" General Dandig said with more than a touch of patronization. "What did you want to say to His Majesty? We all deeply appreciate your recognizing the new regime. You have saved many lives."

"But not the lives of KaritKi and Tarot," Tate replied harshly. "You, King Barkoon, have not kept faith with me!"

"What is all this?" Barkoon asked. He looked truly perplexed.

Dandig said tersely, "KaritKi and Tarot both tried to escape. They were shot by trigger-happy guards when they swung open the door of the armored car on its way to JCS headquarters."

"But this is a terrible tragedy!" Barkoon managed a shocked expression. "This is very bad. I gave my word to Ambassador Tate." Barkoon started to say something in Mituyan to Dandig, remembered Mike could understand him, and shifted to English. "We will make a thorough investigation of this affair."

"General Thannit is conducting an inquiry now, Your Majesty," Dandig said with assurance. "He will get all the facts. Apparently the brothers first insulted and threatened the officer of the guard and then, when the door somehow came open, Tarot attacked while KaritKi tried to bolt."

"Enough of this," Ambassador Tate roared. "You two do not fool me for one minute. This was deliberately planned. The death of these two men, monstrous though they were, will be blamed on the United States. My government will be embarrassed before the world."

"The investigation will prove it was an accident. The excitable guards will be punished and—"

"Your regime is dependent upon my government!" Tate snapped. "I will not have the United States government deceived in this way. I will recommend we cut off aid completely and disassociate ourselves from the government of King Barkoon."

"Mr. Ambassador!" Barkoon's voice cut across the silent studio. "I am the King and the Chief of State of Mituyan now. You are the American ambassador. It is possible I may want to review your credentials if you refuse to understand the manner in which we operate in Mituyan. Over the past years, with a great deal of time to think, I have, independently of American advisers, planned almost identical reforms to those which you propose. In a matter of months the people of Mituyan will begin to feel they have a government interested in their welfare. It was my idea two years ago to have an election of delegates to a constituent assembly which would draft a new constitution and rules for a congress representative of the people and a chief of state elected either by the people or by the congress. It was also my idea to request that SEATO police these elections, so that the world and the people of my country would know they are fair. Already I have given orders that all political prisoners be freed. I meant what I said about my own role. I will be more a focal point than an active politician once the first chief of state and congress have been elected. Do you begin to understand me?"

For the first time in his life, Ambassador Tate was speechless.

Barkoon pressed his advantage. "I will accept, in fact I will solicit, your advice in every aspect of running this country for the benefit of its citizens. But I am not a puppet ruler attached arms and legs to the American Embassy. And never forget that, Mr. Ambassador! I intend to rule this country until I can turn it over to the people to govern for themselves as they see fit. If I happen to countenance something you don't like, well"—Barkoon smiled gently—"I *am* the King now."

"But political murder?" Tate finally managed to protest.

"It was an accident, obviously, Mr. Ambassador," Barkoon said—"an accident, however, which I feel history will count as a fortunate one. With KaritKi alive there was always the possibility that those elements in the military and government who personally had benefited so handsomely would overthrow my new regime or, later, even the duly elected government. History *has* shown that true despots never give up as long as they're alive. Now, Mr. Ambassador, once and for all, do we understand one another? I am not afraid, because I know how to unify my people—without your aid if necessary."

There was a long pause, and finally Ambassador Tate said, "I think, Your Majesty, that you and I *can* work well together . . . as long as you are sincere in what you have told me."

"It won't take long for you to see my words in the form of works, Mr. Ambassador. And now, I must go back to the people and announce this distressing *accident* to their former Premier."

Ambassador Tate walked from the studio.

Barkoon grinned at Mike. "Tonight the people should not be too dismayed. By tomorrow we shall all be working together for the new government and fair elections, and soon the death of the KaritKi family will be quite unimportant."

"True, Your Majesty," Mike said softly, "though perhaps not to his widow and Tarot's three children, who at the moment are occupying your stateroom on board the *Promise*."

"So that's how you found out where KaritKi was hiding?"

"Yes, I betrayed her husband. I was responsible for his death tonight. Now I must go back and see what can be done to make life possible for her."

"From what I hear," Barkoon said gently, "KaritKi and Tarot were responsible for the death of your own wife. If they had let her have an exit visa, she would have come to Hong Kong with you, still been alive, and"—the old lecherous Barkoon grin returned—"*I* would have been free to pursue my acquaintance with one young blonde German journalist."

"It is strange the way things work out, Your Majesty."

Barkoon pushed open the door to the hall and walked outside. "Forrester, old companion in battle, let me tell you one thing: Until the day that this blonde who so disrupts my dreams and thoughts, the exquisite Marlene, is married, I will put out maximum effort toward possessing her."

"You give *me* a daring idea, Your Majesty."

Barkoon laughed uproariously; then, just as suddenly, his mirth subsided. "Now I *must* go to the people. No more lewd and lascivious behavior for King Barkoon, I fear, until an upstanding, utterly dedicated chief of state can be elected. I wonder if I couldn't move the elections up a bit? . . . Well, let us keep in touch, eh, Forrester?" The King strode smartly back into the television studio, and Mike headed out to find Marlene.

CHAPTER FIFTY-THREE

THE SUN BEAT DOWN on the press corps and spectators invited to the execution. Marlene clutched Mike's hand. "Thank you for coming with me, darling," she said. "After all I see that long day of the coup, you think I get used to it. But this little execution I don't like."

"I wish they'd get the damned thing over with," Mike said. "One thing about Mituyan, everything is late. They can't even shoot a criminal on time."

"They can't shoot him until the people from the Tiking execution arrive," Roger Krakhaur, standing alongside with Alana, pointed out. They were supposed to execute Yunakit at one P.M. in Tiking. Then the government promised to fly those who suffered under Poramat down here to Tuyan City to see *him* get it at four. Damn it, it's almost five now."

The entire Tuyan City press corps was gathered in the enclosure around a small Buddhist pagoda located at one end of the soccer field inside the city prison. The somewhat festive mood was rapidly deteriorating as the journalists sweated in the hot sun. Many had been there since long before the scheduled time of the execution.

Ted Baum came up to Krakhaur. "How do you like being back to Tuyan City, Roger?"

"Great. And I'm glad to see you're still on the team."

"I'm the oldest in tenure!" The public affairs chief looked at the post that had been implanted in the middle of the field and shook his head. "Just because Barkoon's new information minister made this scene I have to be here too. I wish they'd get it over with."

"*Gott*, yes!" said Marlene.

To Mike, Baum said, "Hey, what's this I hear about you coming over on our side?"

"You're the information man. What did you hear?"

"Someone said you're getting the rank of Ambassador-at-Large out here, reporting directly to Robert Hartland."

"I heard that too, Mike," Krakhaur said. "I've been trying to find you for two days to confirm."

Mike laughed. "You meet just everyone at the better executions."

"Seriously, Mike, is it true?"

"It's a possibility," Mike conceded. He squeezed Marlene's hand and smiled down at her. "Of course Mr. Hartland has to get a special ruling that I can take the job with a wife who's not a U.S. citizen."

Ted Baum grinned. "Well, to quote someone, I'll sleep a little better at night knowing Mike Forrester is on the prowl in this part of the world."

At the far end of the soccer field, a procession of Volkswagen buses drove onto the execution grounds, proceeded up the length of the field, and stopped abreast of the post. Mituyan men and women began to climb out slowly.

"There they are," Krakhaur said. "Families of Poramat's victims, and the few, like Alana, who survived his prisons." Alana said nothing, but took his arm and held it tightly. "We shouldn't have to wait long now."

Ambassador Tate lounged in an easy chair in his office. Across the desk were Jack Cardinez and Lieutenant General Thomas Gordon. "So you feel, General, there's no way of containing this insurgency without bringing in more U.S. troops?"

"Correct, sir." Gordon was a lean, hard-looking officer of fifty years with close-cropped, iron-gray hair and a self-confident bearing.

"For two years General Macker said we didn't need more American troops," Tate pointed out.

"Perhaps that's why you suggested me for the job here," Gordon replied with a smile. "The Mitcoms are attacking everywhere. They plan an all-out terrorist campaign during the elections, and the army is still divided into dissident elements. Today's execution wipes out the last hope of the old KaritKi generals to put a member of the Ki family back in power, but the bitterness in the armed forces will persist for some time to come. And meanwhile the Mitcoms will take advantage of all this to gain more and more real estate."

Tate sighed. "The direct line from Washington is going to buzz in about ten minutes. Protest groups all over America are raising hell about the executions, as though they're something *I* can control. And that woman, Dhuna, who we allowed to keep some of the KaritKi money, has the whole Anglican Church establishment in Britain protesting—to the President of the United States no less."

Looking at his watch, Tate picked up the phone, a direct wire to Barkoon's desk. "One last time I have to go through this charade."

The King answered at the other end: "Yes, Mr. Ambassador?"

"Has Your Majesty reconsidered the matter of this execution?"

"Yunakit was shot two hours after the appointed time, after all last-minute appeals were carefully considered."

"And Poramat?"

"His execution *will* take place. My information officer even now is telling the newsmen that because of the earnest and strong appeals of the American Embassy, the King and his ministers are conferring on an eleventh-hour stay of execution. Thus I hope to take the onus from *you* somewhat. But really Tate old boy, I *must* execute the bugger, you know—and we did promise the Mad Monk that night when we needed his support. Can't have another Buddhist riot, can we, old boy! Not before the elections."

Tate made a last effort at taking a tough line. "My government is gravely concerned with the unfavorable opinion that has been generated around the world over this execution. The United States mission in Mituyan is being severely criticized for condoning . . . this *murder*."

"Now look here, Tate," Barkoon's voice raised in irritation, "I am running this country until we can elect a government—which can't come soon enough to suit me. I am the boss, and I'll damn well call the shots the way I see them. This whole business of your meddling—"

"It's not a case of meddling, Your Majesty, merely pointing out—"

"Well, do your pointing out somewhere else. I'm executing the bastard—and let me tell you, it'll be in a way to really give you people something to dream about. Sorry you're going to miss it."

"Please, Your Majesty"—Tate's heart sank in despair and frustration—"don't make it harder for me to help you fight the Communists."

"Then don't you keep putting the tusk to me. I know my people. They want Poramat dead, and he will be—damned quick."

"Then I suppose there is nothing more I can say to you."

The King's tone abruptly changed to one of friendly concern. "Tate, I worry about you, old boy. You aren't getting enough recreation and relaxation. Come around some evening—unofficially I mean. Confidentially, I have just brought in some new talent from Sweden. You'll think more clearly, get rid of those tensions . . . what?" And King Barkoon the Sixth clicked off.

Tate turned to Gordon and Cardinez, his face somber. "I'll have to tell the Secretary when he calls that despite careful review of all circumstances, the Mituyan government has decided to go ahead with the execution."

Cardinez nodded and said, "Well, it's the end of a regime. We did *our* job. . . ."

Ambassador Tate shook his head slowly. "No, our job—our problems and frustrations—all lie ahead of us, I'm afraid. May God, and the White House, give us the strength to carry on."

EPILOGUE

The government's guests at the execution of Poramat were becoming irritable. Standing in the hot sun, chafing at the delay, some sifted through copies of the latest international edition of *Time* magazine, which had just gone on sale. Newsboys had wisely hustled from the news distributor to the gates of the prison to hawk their magazines. The face on the cover was that of Mituyan's King Barkoon VI.

The families of Poramat's victims, having viewed the execution of the infamous province chief, Colonel Yunakit, in Tiking, patiently awaited the second act of the double bill. Finally, one hour and three-quarters after the hour fixed for the execution, the iron gates of the forbidding, fortress-like cell block clanged open. From the blackness, four prison guards appeared struggling with a large, square cement block. Laboriously, they carried it out to the middle of the field and placed it on the ground near the post. The members of the press corps began buzzing to one another, and the spectators from Tiking stared wide-eyed at the block.

A few moments later, cries rose from the Mituyans as an elephant, draped in a silver-trimmed black robe that covered its head except for large round holes through which the beast's eyes shone, plodded onto the field. Sitting just behind the head of the elephant was a man, also dressed in black, in a black hood with eye slits. Behind the elephant marched an honor guard of spear-carrying warriors dressed in the ancient red and yellow silk ceremonial robes of the early Barkoon dynasty; they were led by a flagbearer holding a tall staff from which waved the red and yellow flag of Mituyan—with two huge facing elephant tusks symbolic of the great victory of King Barkoon the First with his war elephants over invading hordes from the North.

The startling procession moved up the middle of the field and stopped next to the concrete block. The officer in charge of the ceremonial display, gaudy in bright silks and plumage, strode toward the cell block. He paused and waited while Poramat was led out, a guard on either side holding his arms firmly. Poramat flinched and blinked in the sudden brilliance. Then he saw the elephant, and with a loud gasp collapsed.

At a signal from the officer, the guards hauled Poramat, the tops of his toes dragging, toward the concrete block. When they reached it, Poramat was slapped back to consciousness. Looking up in terror at the gleaming white tusks of the elephant, he began to struggle violently; fearful screams broke from deep in his throat. At a signal from their commander, two of the costumed warriors jammed the shafts of their spears into the ground and began to prepare the execution.

Two thin nooses were forced around the wildly struggling Poramat's neck, and then he was thrown to his knees, his head held down on the block. On either side of the victim a ceremonial guard held one end of a noose, forcing Poramat's neck down against the block, his head forward. His eyes bulged as, in his struggles, the two nooses slowly and painfully threatened to strangle him. He stopped writhing and knelt more quietly.

In the press section, the Caucasian journalists were horror-stricken. A woman turned away, burying her face in the shoulder of the man beside her.

At a signal, the great beast lifted one huge foot and placed it almost gently above Poramat's head, balancing its weight on the forward foot on the ground. A long sustained moan came from the Mituyan witnesses as the elephant stood poised for what seemed minutes. Poramat knelt perfectly still.

The brilliantly garbed officer finally raised his spear. A slight movement of the trainer's prod, and the elephant shifted his weight from the foot on the ground to the one above Poramat's head.

The mesmerized spectators sensed, more than heard, the soft clop, like a horse's hoof on a cobblestone street. And then the elephant shifted its weight again.

The commander inspected the remains on the block of the last Ki brother, nodded, and, with military precision, turned and mustered the ceremonial procession into ranks. They marched smartly from the field, the imperial elephant lumbering slowly behind.

• MITUYAN •

KEY TO MAP

Mountains

Borders

Corps Area Boundaries

2¾" = 100 Miles